THE RAVEN
Returns

Drew James was born and raised in South-East London, and studied at The BRIT School for Performing Arts & Technology.

With over fifteen years experience in the world of luxury fashion—working as a personal shopper for some of the most famous designer brands—he was inspired to write a series that gave a true insight to the industry.

It is with experience of both boutique and online fashion, that he invites you to step into the glamorous world—behind the smoke and mirror—of an industry you may *think* you already know...

For more information and contact, please visit www.drewjamesauthor.com.

BOOKS BY DREW JAMES

A Farce On Fifth Avenue

The Raven Returns

THE RAVEN Returns

Drew James

Print edition, Great Britain 2020

(ISBN: 978-0-9926021-3-0)

Also available as e-book:

Version 1.0, Great Britain 2020

(ISBN: 978-0-9926021-4-7)

First published, Great Britain 2020
By C A P O C C I Publishing UK

Artwork by Tess Tolmatcheva © 2020
@tess.laf

If you're stuck on the bottom rung of the ladder for too long, then I'm afraid you don't have a career—you have a job.

1

Stepping off the plane at Heathrow airport was a new start for Dom. The smell, the feel—the *accent!* He wanted to forget everything that had happened in New York (where dreams were made as well as crushed), an attempt at erasing the past. Still rushing from the excitement of New York Fashion Week had made him feel even more positive about his future, even if he had suffered some setbacks.

He was also excited to see his mother again, as well as the friends he had left behind when he first moved to New York a decade ago. He had given so much to other people, it was now time to prioritise himself; no more bad choices in men, no more dead-end jobs. With his experience in the fashion industry, what better time to start looking for new opportunities other than London Fashion Week?

After collecting his luggage from the carousel, he struggled his way through customs to find his mother, who was eagerly awaiting his arrival. The flight from New York to London had seemed longer than usual, his skin was sticky, his eyes were tired and his legs ached from being cramped for more than six hours in a passenger seat. But he was relieved to have finally touched down in his *real* hometown.

"Oh my goodness... Look—there he is!" That familiar voice confirmed he *was* indeed home. Dom looked down the line of people to see where this unmistakable cry came from, and once spotted, he picked up his pace.

"I'm so happy you're here!" his mother said, grabbing him for a close hug; forcing him to let go of his cases. As she held on tight to her son, who she hadn't seen for a while, tears of joy inevitably followed.

"Mum—*Stop!* You're embarrassing me."

"Welcome back," his step-father said. Michael was in his late fifties, already retired, and now spent most of his days with Dom's mother. Mainly going on European weekends away and devoting afternoons to watercolour painting in their conservatory.

"Come on, let's get to the car and get you home—I bet you're starving." His mother led the way, grabbing his arm and leaving Michael to deal with the cases. Home was south west London and although it was now late evening, the King's Road looked just how he had last seen it. Lit up and alive, and of course, rammed with traffic. All the way home in the back of the car, Dom dodged the endless barrage of questions from his mum with short 'yes' and 'no' answers—until she realised that he was just too tired for this right now.

"I'm so happy you're home... You can stay for as long as you want!" she said, finally pulling up outside the house (leaving poor Michael with the luggage yet again). "Your room's exactly how you left it, although I did have your bedding refreshed and I dusted…You must be shattered *and* hungry. Shall I make you a quick bite to eat before we settle for the night?"

"Gwen—*Dominic!* Can I get some *bloody* help out here with these cases, or what?" Michael called through heavy puffs, clearly struggling with Dom's transatlantic haul.

"That'll be great. I'm starving, and yes, tired... I need a good night's sleep. London Fashion Week is in full swing and I plan on catching up with Pandora from college... Remember her?"

"*Really?* Straight away? Don't feel like you have to jump straight into work, love... It would be great to finally spend time together… See the sights, lunch dates—that sort of thing... Can't work wait until the good weather has gone at least?"

His mother was excited to have Dom back and was hoping they would spend some time shopping, lunching and getting out of the house, away from Michael for a change. He would only get annoyed and impatient with her by the time they left Harvey Nichols, and that was only the first leg of the spree. Dom, on the other hand, would pick out dresses and spot age-appropriate shoes for her, and she loved to splash out on him too.

Although all of that sounded fabulous, Dom was here for professional reasons—not to folly with his mum around town. New York Fashion Week had been as much of a journey for him as it had been for his best friend, Chloe. A journey that questioned love, friendships, and where exactly his life was heading—culminating in this move back to London.

The unforgettable experience of attending the Palazzo retrospective fashion show with Chloe and her newfound fashion gang had opened his eyes—and he wanted a piece of the glory for himself. His arrival in London had been perfectly timed and he wasn't going to waste time getting back in touch with his old girl-friend from his London College of Fashion days.

"There'll be plenty of time for all of that," he said, wanting to get her off his back—he had only been home five minutes. "It's just, this is the perfect opportunity to let everyone know I'm back and to see what's going on... You know—network."

"Well, in that case... I'll fix you a boiled egg and some toast." Gwen knew him well, and accepting her adult son's freedom was going to be easier than trying to make him do otherwise. Dom was too determined to let someone change his mind (mother included); he was too focused on his ambitions to let a shopping trip and a free lunch sway him (although, tempting).

"Thanks, mum," he said, smiling. Just like how he used to, growing up. "I'd better go help Michael with the cases."

*

A hot shower and a soft boiled egg with warm buttered toast were just what Dom needed. After dumping his suitcases in the corner of the room, he set up his laptop on the desk—finally, he had WiFi. His phone was switched off, and for now, it would stay that way. Sorting out a U.K phone line was another task on his list of 'things-to-do.'

Opening up his email inbox, he saw a message from Chloe already sitting in his inbox, but that too could wait. He was too tired to start a conversation with her right now, and what he really needed to do, was to get on with *his* life—not constantly hearing about hers.

From: Dominic Fraser
To: Pandora Simmons

Subject: Guess Who's Back

Hi Pandy,

Guess who's back in London? Are you showing at LFW? I'd love to come and see you. Email me, I don't have a UK number until tomo but I'll be around... So get in touch!

Dom x

Now nearing midnight, his eyelids felt heavy as he stared at the computer screen hit 'send,' but with the seed now planted it was time for bed. There was much to do tomorrow and he could no longer fight his itching eyes that were begging for sleep. As he lay in bed, waiting to drift off, Dom wondered what Chloe was up to back in New York. Even though he had fled the Big Apple, he couldn't help but wonder what was happening without him there—especially as Chloe was achieving all that he wanted for himself.

She too was thinking of him, and more importantly if he had heard from Jason yet? She wanted him to be just as happy and excited as she was, and she knew how much Jason meant to him. All summer he had been longing for him to get back in touch and typically he had turned up at Dom's door after he had already left for London—only to find Chloe now living there. But that was fate for you, as Jason was also heading to London and had come to ask Dom to join him. Jason tried everything to contact him with no luck, but he hoped that was because he was busy travelling and not 'ghosting' him (although he wouldn't blame him if he was). He too had landed in London, staying at the Conrad Hotel in St James

Park. He had been invited to show at The Southbank Gallery after they had snapped up his portrait of the nineties supermodel, Kate, at his New York exhibition—the same week he met Dom.

The gallery loved his contemporary pop-art style and asked him to showcase more work at their 'London Calling' exhibition, which he couldn't turn down. This was his big break, his first taste of European exposure. Jason worked tirelessly on new pieces, which meant little time for everything else, including his long-distance relationship with Dom back in New York. He was an artist and, like most creatives, he worked alone.

Openings at art galleries (especially ones in London) were rare, even rarer than finding love and Jason assumed Dom would understand that. Cutting everyone off, Jason focused on his work—just as focused as Chloe was on her career at the same time—which is why Dom now needed to focus and make something of himself. Something that no one could let him down on, because it was his and no one else's.

Resting in his hotel room on the super king-size bed, Jason checked his smartphone for the hundredth time. No messages, no missed calls, and no replies from the tirade of emails he had sent to Dom, begging for him to simply reply and simply let him know he was still breathing at the very least. He called Dom's number once more, but it was still switched off. With no other way of contacting him, all he could do was wait and hope that he would reach out while he was still in town.

Giving up once more, he realised he also needed to rest. He had a big day ahead of him installing the pieces that had just shipped over from his studio back in L.A. Laying in bed, a mix of emotions came over him. He was frustrated that his plan to get back with Dom hadn't been as easy as he had thought, but he was also excited at the prospect of finding him in London and impressing him with his art once more. And if this exhibition was a success, it may not be the last time he visited London. So, with this positive thought in mind, he took in a deep breath and melted into his soft luxurious pillows, telling himself that everything was going to work out just fine.

**

Dom's first day back was turning out to be rather hectic. His mother had let him oversleep, which was not the plan. Despite that, Dom managed to get up and out to go shopping for some much-needed skincare products and that important U.K SIM card. With his phone back online, he checked to see if Pandora had replied to his email. Ignoring the adverts and junk mail that had accumulated, he scrolled past to see that Pandora had indeed written back.

From: Pandora Simmons
To: Dominic Fraser

Subject: RE: Guess Who's Back

O.M.G! Dominic-Fucking-Fraser!

What are you doing back in London? How long for? Of course I'm showing at LFW! I'd love to see you... Come out tonight, we are going for drinks, about 7-ish, at Shoreditch House.

Meet us there—can't wait to see you!

P x

So far things were working out well and catching up with his old partner in crime was a huge box already ticked. Especially as he had a plan to get back in with her circle of friends and find work again. The rest of the afternoon was a rush around town getting all the necessities out of the way (and a nap was very much needed before going out), but after a quick dinner and a refresh, Dom squeezed himself into his black skinny jeans and put on his favourite pair of Saint Laurent boots—ready to set out for the evening. He sifted through his suitcases, looking for a jacket to wear. Something not too heavy and not too light at the same time, as the evening air was starting to turn cold. Looking at the time, he started to panic. "Tomorrow, I am unpacking this shit!" he told himself, it would certainly make getting ready much easier.

Tossing underpants, T-shirts and endless odd socks on the floor, he stopped in his tracks as he revealed exactly what he was looking for—Jason's leather jacket. The worn-in, tan leather bomber was more than that—it was a reminder of the man who had broken his heart, as well as his dreams of moving to L.A. An emotional blast from the not-so-distant past wasn't what he was looking for right now, but it did serve the purpose—so he slipped it on and left the house. Pandora had sent the location of this evening's festivities by text, helping him forget and focus on the here and now. It was on the other side of town, but Dom didn't care. This was a chance worth travelling for so he headed out to Knightsbridge tube station.

West London was the perfect area to live in, but east was where it was all happening, and getting there would be quickest via the London Underground. Unlike New York, where taxies were the mode of transport, the tube network was the only way to get about quickly (efficient, but far from glamorous). East London was also where Fashion Week-er's naturally flocked to. Although he was eager to get back into the swing of social life, his main aim was to see if up-and-coming Pandora was about to hit the big time, just like Chloe Ravens had.

If he was going to stay in London for long, he promised himself he wasn't going to get another boring shop job and simply swap cities. No, he was better than that and he had learnt his self worth from the events of the past few weeks. His crazy romance with Jason Hart also taught him that true love came from the self and it was important to not rely on others for happiness.

This move wasn't about men or dwelling over exes; this was not a vacation to mend a broken heart. In fact, Dom had set an archive to divert all emails from Jason into a junk folder, and with a new U.K number, he could keep his old line switched off and stay distraction-free from his old life. What he really needed was a project of his own, something he could sink his teeth in to and apply all the knowledge and experience he had learnt from his time spent in the fashion industry. He had guided Chloe to success, surely he could do it for himself? Plus, if he were to ever see Jason Hart again, it would be as a 'somebody' and not the sales assistant he once knew.

Dom was fired up, and Pandora was the perfect target. She was his best friend back in college and if he hadn't moved to New York, you could bet they would still be best of friends. Pandora was the daughter of eighties pop star, Rod Simmons, and had somewhat of a success on the London fashion scene due to her father's fame. She had graduated from Central St Martins and thanks to her family's wealth had walked straight into her own fashion label: Pandora Simmons London, or P.S.L for short.

It was, however, yet to produce a collection that made her a hit with buyers and editors or to create a style that the masses would go crazy for. She was very much still a young talent finding her creative direction. Some critics said that her designs were 'too busy,' or that she needed to 'refine her style,' which made her want to go even more heavy-handed with colours and print in retaliation. She was a rebel and what was 'cool' now, wasn't cool to her.

***

Dom arrived at Shoreditch House and walked through the discreet side entrance (if you didn't know where it was, you never would find it). Its swish yet laid back sixties Danish style decor had Dom feeling right back at home in New York. He was used to this sort of place and he was glad he still knew people in London to get him back into the right scene. There was a small gathering of people signing in (or trying to weasel their way), with Fashion Week just starting, the place was full of blaggers.

"Hey... I'm on Pandora Simmons guest-list," Dom said to the model-like guy behind the front desk, certain that this name drop would work whether she was indeed a member or not. Pandora was a face on the scene, always out and about and establishments instantly recognised her for being the offspring of one of the country's most celebrated singer/songwriter's. They loved to have her frolicking around their clubs, if not just for the publicity, but for the fact she would have her dad call himself and settle her boozy bar tab the morning after.

"Oh yes... Your party is up on the rooftop," he confirmed with a smile, although he probably would have let him in any way with his good looks.

Dom headed towards the moodily lit elevators where he crammed himself inside with other guests, all vying to get up onto the rooftop. The rooftop pool area was one of the few trendy outside places to be seen at, as Londoner's squeezed every last drop of Sunshine and warmth they could before the season changed instantly back to winter—seemingly skipping autumn altogether. Dom noticed a sign stating 'no more than six passengers,' but he counted there to be about twelve, with nowhere to even turn his face.

Finally arriving on the roof level, everyone poured out of the lift car. Steam flowed breezily out of the pool and into the air as a giant glitter ball turned slowly above it in the dusky sky. The decking was under-lit, with candy-striped sun loungers lined all around. The surrounding patio was packed; trying to find Pandora here was going to take some time and skill—walking around the crowded pool without getting pushed in by some drunken hipster.

He walked past groups of friends all chatting loudly (as if they were extremely important people), casually dressed in ripped jeans, checked shirts and vintage floral dresses (purchased just down the road for a hefty sum on Brick Lane no doubt). But it didn't take too long until he heard Pandora's undeniable accent billowing out from the other end of the pool.

"Dominic-*fucking*-Fraser... Oi—Over here!" a semi-posh, cockney voice called out over the disco beat.

Almost everyone in earshot turned around to see who *the* Pandora Simmons was shouting at, allowing Dom to pass through and escaping his fear of getting dunked in his designer outfit. Pandora was petite with flame-red hair that was coiffed into a fifties style up-do, with a bandana and a perfect curl at the front. Her image and vocal cords made up for her height and she certainly wasn't lacking in personality. She only wore her own creations, which were sometimes risqué and this evening's choice was a leopard mini-dress from her latest collection with a corset-style top half that gave her a cleavage she could rest drinks on.

"I can't believe you're here," she said with a back kick of her leg as she forced him to lift her. "I thought you were gone for good!"

"You know me, Pandy... Full of surprises!" he said, slightly struggling to put her unsteady feet back down. She was tipsy, that was for sure.

"Gosh... You sound right Yankee now!" she said, pulling a passing waiter by his arm, merrily downing the last few drops of her drink. "Bring us another round of G&T's, plus one extra... We got another gang member back! Guys... This is my old partner in crime, Dominic. We met at LCF and were best mates... Until he buggered off to New York that is."

With Pandora's introduction, Dominic quickly scanned her crew, who seemed to be slightly put out at having to entertain a newcomer as they puffed on their electronic cigarettes and roll-up's. Her entourage consisted of her studio workers: Jonty, Heather and JoJo. Jonty, was a pattern cutter, while JoJo and Heather helped with producing her collections (and anything else for that matter). They all welcomed Dom, except Jonty, who gave a weak handshake and a suspicious look. He was the only gay in their circle as far as he was concerned and he didn't like the sudden competition (even though Dom's style was totally different from his).

He was tall and skinny—very skinny in fact. With a wet shaved head that had a rash on the back of his neck where he had been scratching it, and a thick dark brown moustache. He wore stonewashed jeans that were held up by red elastic braces (that served no real purpose other than aesthetic) over a white T-shirt with rolled-up sleeves. Around his waist was a grey fleece hoodie that looked like it could do with a wash. Dom, however, had already assessed that Jonty was no competitor to him and greeted everyone warmly—including Jonty.

Heather was a pretty girl dressed in a flowing tribal-print jumpsuit teamed up with cork wedge sandals, while JoJo wore a crop top with blue cut-off denim shorts and a pair of black Dr. Martens. Her brown braids were wrapped up in a coiled bun, and her septum piercing told Dom that she was the 'rocker' out of the group. They greeted him with air kisses, not seeming to be that bothered at all, assuming he was just some fashion-gay Pandy knew and that they probably wouldn't ever see him again anyway.

"The last time I saw you was when I came to New York… You said you would come and visit me in London, but you didn't… Twat." Pandy said, grabbing Dom's arm to follow her over to sit on a nearby lounger.

"I'm here now aren't I? Anyway… Shouldn't you be working on your collection right now?"

"Well, we wanted to escape the studio and celebrate early. The show isn't until Wednesday; I have until Wednesday to complete the collection and it's kinda nearly there," she said taking a huge gulp, before taking out a Marlboro and sparking it in one flick of a Clipper.

What she actually meant was that they needed to get a move on—and fast! This year she was given a slot to show at the London Fashion Week show space in Soho by The British Fashion Council, and all eyes would be on her. This was her time to break into the mainstream and she was under pressure to produce a hit runway show that insiders would rave over. The trouble was, the pressure was starting to get to her. Hence the big night out on the opening night of London Fashion Week, when she should be knuckling down to work in the studio; pulling an all-nighter with her team.

"Look, it'll all be fine," Dom reassured her. "It's always a scramble on the run-up to a show—you know that. One thing I've learnt lately is that life is full of good surprises, but you need to put in the work first. I've just helped my friend back in New York launch her website and directed her social media, as well as help seal her first online capsule collection."

Of course, that wasn't entirely true, but he had to ham it up a bit if he was going to stand a chance landing a role with some importance at her label (which was the whole point of this evening's excursion). "In fact, you may have seen her draped on Gianni Palazzo's arm last week?" he shamelessly dropped. "Chloe and I used to work together at Palazzo before she launched StacksOfStyle.com, we left to work on that full-time... Now she's up and running, I've decided to move back here and try to get something going myself."

"You're not gonna launch your own label here, are you?" Pandy snapped with a sharp neck turn—blowing smoke in his face.

Pandora knew Dom was talented, he had an eye for style and a knack of making things work to his advantage. He was a force to be reckoned with if she recalled back to their college days, and she could see that with his good looks, he could wrap anyone in this industry around his little finger.

"No—not quite… I've had a few offers here and there, to work with designers and for brands, but I was thinking maybe you needed someone—a style consultant maybe?"

Pandy was rather taken by surprise, she wasn't currently looking to expand her team. She already had trouble justifying to daddy why Jonty, Heather, and JoJo were worth putting on payroll, and with minor finances coming in, it wasn't a position she had considered hiring for—she *was* the style consultant. However, Dom was like an angel sent to her at exactly the right time; if anyone could tell her how to make this collection a success it was him, and it was better to have him on her side than anyone else's at this crucial moment in her career.

"Actually… I could do with another queer eye around the studio. A sexy, charismatic one if ya know what I mean?" she said, leaning in far from Jonty's direction. "Why don't you come down to the studio tomorrow and look at the collection? Tuesday I'm casting and right now I don't know what to cut, what is missing… My arse from my elbow basically."

"You mean to tell me that the show is on Wednesday, and you're only casting models the day before? What about fittings?"

"Ah, *fitting-schmitting!* Minor details," Pandy dismissed, taking a long and stressed drag on her cigarette. "The B.F.C are supplying models for us and it's the only day we have free."

'Well, yeah... 'Cause you're out drinking when you should be working,' Dom thought, trying not to show panic on his face, which he knew he wasn't doing very successfully (he could feel one eyebrow raised high on his forehead). This was exactly the attitude she had back in their college days, and she knew exactly what he was thinking.

"Look, if this collection goes down well, we can see about making it a permanent thing—and paid... Deal?"

"*Deal!*" Dom said, kissing her cheek. "Just like old times in college when I would improve your work."

"Improve? You used to lean over and scribble on my sketches, you wanker."

They both laughed with nostalgia and the excitement of being reunited, back working together. Dom breathed a sigh of relief as they both raised their glasses to celebrate. Even though it wasn't a paid job now, he at least had a purpose and a ticket to London Fashion Week where he could continue riding the wave he had caught back in New York with Chloe—this time with her English counterpart.

Rapidly growing more and more jet-lagged, and not wanting to sleep-in again and miss his chance working with Pandy, Dom said his goodbyes and left his new friends. It was still early enough to catch the tube back west, and once again, it was the fastest way across town without sitting in traffic on the night bus for hours.

Dom set off for Liverpool Street station, breathing in the London air and taking in the atmosphere of the bustling streets around him. It felt different to New York but in a good way. Brick arches were strewn with graffiti, 'pop-up' restaurants had opened up in disused petrol stations, with crowds of people only just making their way out fro the night, and life felt great again. He walked on with a spring in his step knowing exactly where he was going, he knew these streets like the back of his hand. Stopping at a pedestrian crossing, waiting for the lights to change, something from across the street caught his eye. Looking up and over, he spotted a billboard on the side of a building that made him look twice and his heart drop to his stomach before his brain could even process what it was he was looking at.

There was no mistaking the iconic image of a screen-printed Kate on a Union Jack background staring back at him. Jason Hart, the man he had been trying to escape from had followed him to London. The fourteen-foot high poster advertised the 'London Calling' exhibition at The Southbank Gallery where Jason's work was being shown and due to open during Fashion Week.

Dom's heart sank even further at this sudden reminder, it appeared that even though he had run away to another country, his feelings were still the same and he couldn't escape the heartache he tried so hard to cover up. The beeping of the pedestrian crossing threw him out of this uninvited memory, and he dashed across to the other side before he missed his chance. Robbed of his newfound excitement, he briskly walked to the station, desperate to just get home.

His pace grew faster and faster as he realised what this meant, whilst trying to rationalise the stomach-lurching feeling that had pounced on him out of the blue. Looking down at himself, realising he was wearing Jason's leather jacket, he felt sick. He could smell him, feel him all over his body even and it was again all too real. The visual reminder alone that Jason still existed was enough to handle. He paused outside the station, trying to recalibrate and gain control of his emotions before riding the stale and rickety loud underground all the way home.

Standing outside Liverpool Street station, feeling alone despite the masses of people rushing around him, his mind swirled with questions that he thought were already answered. Was he ever going to get away from this feeling? Was moving back to London not enough? He had left New York behind, but it seemed Dom had brought along all the old baggage and his feelings were something he was going to have to deal with—no matter where he escaped to.

2

Standing in a half-empty apartment, having boxed-up her most needed belongings in a flurry, it finally hit Chloe that she was on the precipice of something spectacular—as well as a new apartment conveniently situated in Greenwich Village. Originally, Dom said she could house sit and just pay the bills while he was away (which was for the foreseeable future), but his father knew its true value and made her pay a subsidised rent on top.

Nevertheless, it was a bargain considering the area and the money was sure to roll in from her first capsule collection that had just been commissioned off the back of her recent notoriety. Compared to her first-floor apartment in Williamsburg, it was a palace at paupers prices. She was sad to leave Williamsburg, trendy, vibrant and creative Williamsburg, but this move was vital in making her success last. She needed to be nearer to inner-city New York, and now she was working freelance in fashion, status and image was everything.

She couldn't be seen riding the night train home from a swanky event now that she had garnered attention from the world's fashion media; she now had the city at her fingertips but her plan was to have it eating out of her hands. All of the memories, the nights staying up late chatting and drinking with Dom, consoling him over his ill-fated relationship with Jason, the early mornings waking up late with throbbing hangovers and running out the door late for work with wet hair and half a face of make-up.

It all seemed like it was being left behind. The days where she dreamed of doing something big with her life, and the nights where she would stay up late on her laptop, trying to make a name for herself—it all happened here. This over-priced one-bed apartment was where she had lived so many moments in her life. It definitely had a vibe, electricity that she was to leave behind for whoever got conned into renting it next. It was also where she had founded her fashion blog: StacksOfStyle.com. She had worked night after night uploading pictures of her posing in second-hand designer clobber given to her by her client, Mrs Ruthenstock out of charity—a charity Chloe was only too pleased to be the face of.

It was also where she had begun to build her future, unknowingly of just how successful she was to become, and where she had dreamed of this exact moment. Now it had finally arrived, it was almost surreal. What was this new chapter going to bring? What was going to happen after she closed the door on this apartment, and would she be able to do it all again without her friend Dom by her side?

One thing was certain, and that was she had learnt her lesson about being held back by fear, and she couldn't wait to see what the other door would reveal once this one closed. "Time to say goodbye Williamsburg and hello Greenwich Village!" she said, switching off the lights and heading out the door for the last time.

*

Chloe planned on spending the coming week unpacking and making her new place feel like home, but that would have to wait. Just a few months ago she was worried about being the eternal child, with no real career. The boredom of life on the shop floor at Palazzo and the frustration of being held back by the store director, Regina Hall, had somehow transformed into an exciting new life working for herself in lower Manhattan.

The whirlwind that had been New York Fashion Week had created much hype and drama in the world of Chloe Ravens, and she needed to make the most of it—there was no time to stall now. Not only was her Instagram account on fire with new followers and hundreds of 'likes' every minute, but visitors and clicks on StacksOfStyle.com had skyrocketed like never before. Everyone wanted to know who this new girl on the scene was, even the likes of Vanguard Fashion magazine wanted to uncover Chloe Ravens. The trouble was, Chloe was only just finding that out for herself.

This summer certainly had her questioning some of her own morals and beliefs.

Panicked by the thought of turning thirty without a career had led her on a journey of success that involved letting down good friends on the way, but she was putting all those mistakes down to experience and was determined to go forward with a positive outlook and a new set of rules—her rules. Not even Regina Hall could tell her what to do now, she was free.

Having said that, Chloe wasn't exactly free from naivety (and neither would you be if Gianni Palazzo invited you to Milan, first-class). Gianni Palazzo, the most sought after man in fashion wanted Chloe Ravens to attend *his* show, and that was big news. Chloe had experienced being big news herself, having been pictured on the front page of the tabloids hanging off Gianni's arm at the Palazzo retrospective after-party. That very event had put her name on everybody's lips, including her old boss's.

Regina Hall imagined she would never see Chloe ever again after driving her out of Palazzo. Unfortunately, it wasn't going to be that easy and she now knew it, the moment she witnessed the sizzling chemistry that was between them on the red carpet. The very man who owned the store, the brand (and Regina for that matter) was clearly falling for Chloe and there was no way she could compete with her in that department. Regina knew that if Chloe dated Gianni, she would try to poison him against her, and in the worst-case have him fire her.

But instead of feeling bitterness, she was empowered now—not by the likes of Regina—but by her friends and a newfound ambition which was stronger than ever. She had discovered that keeping friends close was the only way to a successful future and only fear of change had led her to a stagnant life before and that some friends came from the unlikeliest of places. She had Kim to thank for that lesson—and for her invitation to Milan.

There was once a time she had considered Kim to be an enemy, pipping her to the post in the press office of Palazzo, but it was Kim that secretly delivered Gianni's invitation to Milan—knowing the importance of it and that Regina would simply tear it up. Kim also wanted to see Chloe succeed, fed up of the unwritten rules set by Regina Hall and her puppet-like management team beneath her. Now, there was no going back—an exciting future lay ahead in the form of a trip to Milan Fashion Week—and in a new position at rival brand Maison Marais for Kim.

Before all that could happen there was much work to be done and that had prompted Chloe to wake up early on a Sunday morning to get straight to work, for she only had a week to settle the business of her upcoming interview with Vanguard and submit the designs for her capsule collection with DivaFeet. She had evolved from sales assistant to blogger, to fashion stylist and now designer. All of this she would have never achieved without her mentor, Carmen by her side—whom she depended on. "Hey, where are you?" Chloe said, her phone nestled between her ear and her shoulder as she dashed from her bedroom to her make-shift office on the kitchen counter.

"Darling, calm down… I'm getting coffee and then I'll be right over; don't you worry your little head. I'm bringing you a latte… Just the way you like it!" she snapped in her Italian hinted accent before hopping into a taxi.

Carmen Visconti was an experienced stylist and consultant, and she knew exactly how to handle Chloe's newfound success. She had seen the potential in her from day one and knew that she was worth investing time in, and she understood how to handle the overwhelming excitement Chloe was feeling right now.

She had struck an unexpected friend in Chloe, but not such unexpected employment; she was achieving the things Carmen desired and through sharing her contacts and experience, she made herself a part of Chloe's success. She could see that Chloe had vision, passion, and most importantly, like-ability. If only you could bottle this combination—one would be very rich indeed!

Carmen had also helped Chloe to seal the deal with fashion mogul Veronica Meyer, the owner of DivaFeet—a fashion website that churned out the latest fashions recreated from the catwalk at affordable prices. The first deadline for the 'Raven, by Chloe Ravens' collection, was imminent. Veronica was just as savvy as

Carmen when it came down to investing in Chloe, and now that she was front-page fashion news, she wanted to capitalise on that and get this collection to market pronto.

Desperate to get to work Chloe rang Carmen's phone again.

"Okay, okay… I'm outside your posh new apartment… Now open the door, Mrs Palazzo!"

Carmen enjoyed teasing Chloe, even though she could have done with a much-needed lie-in herself, having been out partying for most of Fashion Week. The baton had now been passed to London, but there was still much work to be done in New York and no time for rest. Chloe was equally as tired, like had never before, but she was energised by the excitement of being catapulted into her new career, so she raced to the door to let Carmen in.

"Okay, let's get started," she ordered, barely stepping through the doorway. She handed Chloe her cup of coffee and took her designer shades off as she entered the hall. "Well, this is a nice pad, darling… Dominic did very well!" Carmen said, overlooking the masses of boxes and Chloe's half-hearted attempt at unpacking.

"Yes, speaking of… I haven't heard from him yet; I wonder if he's made contact with Jason? I was expecting to hear from him by now."

"Yes, well… I'm sure he is busy with his family, and of course Jason… Just as busy as you, darling… Let's get down to business shall we?" Carmen said, clapping her hands for attention and pulling her laptop out from her new Palazzo bag, making sure Chloe noticed it.

"Erm… Is that a new bag I see you have there?"

"We finally get discount at Palazzo after all these years, thanks to your new 'friendship' with Gianni… Did you think I was going to waste time in getting what I want out of this too?"

Chloe giggled, of course, Carmen would make sure she was the first to rub Regina's nose in the fact that she now had store discount. All thanks to Chloe Ravens, the dumb little shop-girl that used to work beneath her.

"So, this interview with Vanguard… Let's hold back on it for this week."

"What?" Chloe said, hardly believing she was suggesting they said 'no' to Vanguard. This was the coup of a lifetime and now Carmen was suggesting to put a freeze on it?

"Darling, we are under contract to come up your capsule collection, by tomorrow might I add… We cannot get sidetracked now by glamour and fame. Plus, the setting is better in Milano and everyone will be in town then, so I have requested an interview while you are there… And we will still meet their deadline for the December issue—which will coincide with the collection's launch… See, it's perfect! Now—designs!"

Chloe was lucky to have Carmen as her mentor cum manager. It was true, it did make sense that Vanguard interviewed her in Milan. After all, they only wanted to interview her because of her connection with Gianni and what better fodder it made for gossip than her being interviewed where she was going to be his guest at the latest Palazzo spring/summer fashion show.

"Right, well I was thinking we knuckle this ten-piece capsule collection down to two bags, five pairs of shoes, and three smaller accessories—so that everyone has a chance to buy something," Chloe began without further argument, trusting in Carmen's master plan.

"Great… I also have the sketches from our mood-board we presented to Veronica, but I want you to think about the core value of what you want this collection to be."

Now, that was easy… Chloe was all about looking and feeling empowered through fashion. Fashion of all price tags, from thrift stores to high-end boutiques; it was all about style and elegance than it was about the label inside. She believed that if it made you feel great, then you would look great—which was why this collaboration with DivaFeet was perfect. She wanted to present a luxurious looking collection with an affordable price range that also came with a name brand—her very own label.

Chloe flicked through reference after reference found from books, fashion magazines, and hashtags on Instagram. What were people wearing, what were people *not* wearing that they should be? All these questions came up, but one thing stuck in Chloe's mind. Being at the Palazzo retrospective show had inspired her to think about the heritage, the history of such a strong fashion house and its iconic designs which made it all the more desirable.

Her collection needed to pack a punch and that meant power-dressing pieces with *oomph!* This was not going to be any old 'everyday lifestyle' collection that every rapper who thought themselves as fashion designers were all now churning out. This collection would incite glamour, high-fashion, and the good old inspiration of sex. If there was one thing that Chloe had learnt from her time working at Palazzo, it was that sex sold.

Chloe wanted high heels fit for the runway, not just for a night out on the town. Bags that were striking and detailed, but also interesting and practical. Just like the pieces you would find on Fifth Avenue, like the ones she had been surrounded by for the past five years on the shop floor of Palazzo. And thanks to that experience, Chloe was well equipped with a backlog of Palazzo collections to now come up with her very own, using all of that product knowledge which was stored in her server-like head. She didn't know it back then, but now it would all come to some *real* use that she would truly benefit from.

**

Sunday wasn't a day of rest for Dominic either. Having just about adjusted to the time difference, he was up early and ready to meet Pandora at her studio. After being reminded by a gigantic billboard that his ex-lover was in town, his mind and heart were all over the place. What he needed right now was a distraction and seeing Jason's name in lights gave him the kick he needed to get out of bed, rather than sinking into depression in his well softened and warmed pillow. Dom stored Jason's leather jacket away in his closet (the only thing he had managed to hang up right now), out of sight.

His mother was hoping they would stroll down to the King's Road for Sunday lunch and afterwards maybe a trip to Harrods, leaving Michael to his watercolours. He was currently painting a portrait of their white Yorkshire Terrier, Bertie, but it was starting to look more like a polar bear which had frustrated him since the initial sketch was perfect. It was best to keep out of his hair and shop for shoes instead, which is exactly what she was going to do—with or without her personal stylist.

Pandy's studio in Shoreditch was situated in an old bread factory that had been converted into modern, new office space. Dom's instant reaction was that it must be costing daddy a fair bit of money, not that Rod Simmons was short of cash—but that was the issue. Pandy never had to work a day in her life, so the worth of money never really resonated with her. It was all just mathematics, an endless pit of numbers that she didn't have to worry about. The only thing on the line was her name and credibility, and that she *was* bothered about.

"Great set up you have here," Dom said, walking straight over to the rails to see what he was working with. He noticed Heather and JoJo in the background and gave them a wave, they were surprised to see him and didn't make an effort to move from the kitchen, where they were leisurely eating bagels.

"Thanks… These are the samples we have so far, but we are still working on some looks as you can see," Pandy said, shooting the girls a look to let them know break was over. "I just don't know if I should keep the blazers or ditch them?"

Dom could see exactly where she was going wrong with the collection already, and it wasn't the blazers (well, not the particular one she was holding up anyway). "Listen, why don't you guys just get on with it and imagine I'm not here?" Dom said as the studio door swung open.

It was Jonty, he had only just turned up for work—in the same clothes as the night before Dom noticed. "Oh—you," he said, rather surprised to see Dom again—and so soon.

"Yes—me!" Dom said, taking off his leather biker jacket before sitting on a wooden stool to watch them work.

"Right, okay—break's over now guys… We have a lot to do and I've asked Dom to help us pull all this together in time… Which we don't really have on our side right now," Pandy said, sifting through remnants of fabric on the work table, trying to clear workspace.

Instead of giving his brutal opinion on the collection right away (which had been roughened even more somewhat by the Big Apple), Dom wanted to see them in action, and that was the real issue. Looking around the studio he noticed no planner board on the walls, no sketches, no swatches, no look-layouts hanging up. This whole label was a complete vanity project—a hot mess powered by her name and her father's money. Pandy was talented, but anyone with a bit of cash to blow could call themselves a designer if they wanted to. But it was another thing to understand what a designer actually did, and playing dress-up from scraps of fabric on a dress form was something that little girls did with their dolls—not fashion designers with an international audience.

Dom sat with an intense stare as he thought about how he was going to be able to offer any kind of help, and if he could at all this late in the game. How was he going to tell Pandy that the whole operation was a complete madness without coming across like a know-it-all superior bitch… And just days away from her show? The last thing he needed was a highly emotional Pandora, which was like a hurricane at the best of times if he remembered rightly.

He watched Jonty faff around smoking roll-ups and drinking espresso's made from a rather expensive looking coffee machine in the kitchenette, more so than making any effort to problem solve patterns or garment fit—which supposedly was his speciality. And as for Heather, Dom quickly assessed that she was a complete waste of space; she was more interested in her phone more than anything else.

JoJo was the only one who seemed to have any motivation, the fact she was stood up next to Pandy at the mannequin trying to help was a good sign. "I think the blazers are cool," JoJo said, cocking her head to one side. "We're just not making them *look* cool."

"What do *you* think? I mean, you've been sat there all morning!" Pandy snapped. After all, he was here to solve this problem for her, wasn't he?

Dom slowly got up off the stool and walked over to the bust which had a semi-fitted blazer on it, still with chalk and basting intact. He grabbed some pins out of Pandy's pincushion on her wrist, and placed them between his teeth with a sarcastic look as if to say: 'Watch this *bitch!'*

Walking around the back of the mannequin, he grabbed the centre seam and pin by pin he adjusted the fit. "See… The reason why this boring jacket looks like a boring jacket—is because it *is* a boring jacket!"

Pandy and JoJo looked at each other as if the whole world had changed before their eyes. Heather hadn't even noticed what had happened, only that she had got fifty more likes on her vegan breakfast bowl that she posted that morning on Instagram. Jonty, however, looked rather pissed off, Dom was essentially questioning his pattern cutting technique.

"Look, guys, it is so late in the day to be getting this collection together, so tweaking instead of cutting is the way forward here… This blazer for example… Great fabric, a nice pinstripe, but such a sad fit. No offence, I know quirky and boxy is your 'thing' but only butch lesbians want to wear a bust eliminating smock," he said, before realising that Heather could quite possibly be a lesbian, so quickly moved on. "I mean, the pants you've teamed it with are stunning, feminine, high-waisted—almost a sailor-style culotte… And you styled them with this baggy blazer? Let's fold the lapel right down to create a sexier, lower opening front… Why not remove one side so we only have one wide lapel, and a collar stand on the other—that's very punk and very *you* Pandy… Then, taper in the back seams a little, re-align the breast darts so they are higher and show this suit with just a bra underneath."

Dom stepped away and sat back down, waiting to see what kind of reaction his honest assessment would receive.

Silence.

Everyone was miffed and he couldn't sense whether it was a good or a bad thing. There was only one way to eliminate the uncertainty, and that was to take direction of the situation by putting the team to work.

"Okay, I thought so… Jonty, I want to see all the exits you have," Dom ordered.

"They're on the rail over there," he said, cross-armed and puffing out harsh tobacco smoke in his direction, suggesting he was not going to be told what to do by some other queer.

"No, I mean on the wall… Laid out in order… You know, as if we are about to put on a fashion show or something? I want to see the line drawing or sketch for each look. Start with casual then day wear, leading into formal and evening last… We can re-arrange the final order later, but I need to see the show in its entirety."

Pandy suddenly realised what was going on. Dom was here to organise her mess and with that, she woke up from her dazed state of confusion. She quickly rifled through a drawer and chucked a pack of Blu-Tack at Jonty without looking to see where it was aimed, almost smacking him bang in the face. He awkwardly caught it with flapping hands, making him drop his roll-up. Dom acknowledged this as permission to act from Pandora, so he carried on.

"Hev, take this blazer off the bust and start working on refitting the back panel and lapel construction as I just said," he directed, fast-tracking his way onto a shortened name basis with her whether she liked it or not.

Heather did exactly that as if she had been told off by a school teacher and put down her phone for the first time that morning to take the jacket over to her work station.

"Right, us girls… Let's start by talking about the inspiration here," Dom said, moving over to the kitchenette to make himself a well-earned coffee from the posh coffee machine that everyone except him had taken advantage of already.

Pulling up a stool, Pandy started with her 'arty-farty' vision for a modern summer collection for today's woman.

"Imagine Sofia Loren in her twenties, moving to London with nothing but her mother's clothes but managing to make each piece look sexy and current," she began, her eyes drifting off into the ether. "But mixed with today's colour palette and forward-thinking mentality."

JoJo nodded in agreement like she had just heard something really new and fresh. At this point Dom could literally hear his eyes rolling; this was typical Pandy, whimsical nonsense which only she believed. She had never lived (or needed to) in the real world, and by having him around, that was exactly what she was about to get—reality.

"So, basically a timeless edit of clothes appealing to women of all ages from a current viewpoint?" he said in one effortless long breath, stirring his coffee with a chime of the spoon against the cup when he was done.

"That's exactly it!"

"Look, that's all great and everything, but if it isn't unique then no one will give a *fuck*… The one thing you have—that everyone knows you to have—is personality. And that's what we need to inject here—just like I did with the lapel on that jacket just now… That wasn't me, that was you! Don't you remember back in college? We'd all be wearing cheap knock-off's while you would stroll in dressed in real Gucci—only to tear it up and adjust it on the sewing machine?"

Pandora laughed, he knew her well. She always did think she knew better than the established fashion designers, and she saw where he was going with this. She needed to make each piece individual, pretend she was just remaking someone else's clothes rather than making her own from scratch.

"We have one more day to get this collection together and you don't have any running order yet… So how are you going to cast models on Tuesday, I don't know? You don't even have your line drawings up on the wall," Dom reminded. He tried not to sound too judgmental, but it had to be said; it was time to get real.

If he had this opportunity, he would never squander it by producing clothes for the sake of reeling off a collection to put his name onto something. Besides, you could simply do that for much cheaper than running a whole company into the ground. Fashion to him was all about the unique style a designer could bring to a brand because let's face it, almost everything has been churned out already. Making a bold new statement was the way forward, and Dom had to redefine Pandy's signature style if this collection was ever going to be a success.

***

After finishing their lunch hour in a nearby pub, they returned to the studio which was now glowing amber in the afternoon Sun. Dom wasted no time in snapping them back into work; he could see Heather about to perch on a stool in the kitchenette, phone already in hand.

"Right… Let's take a look at the collection shall we?" he said, walking over to Jonty's morning project, prompting the others to follow.

Jonty, reluctantly at first, had done exactly what Dom asked for—and some. He had made a perfect wall display of every exit they had produced for the show. Even though Jonty didn't like being told what to do by some newly appointed 'consultant,' he could see the point of the exercise—and not wanting to be outshone by Dominic—he had even included fabric swatches.

In total there were thirty–four looks, and looking at it all set out in front of him, Dom had come to realise that it wasn't as bad as he had initially thought—it was just badly organised. "So, these are all the looks we have in the collection and the colour palette… As you can see, we need to make more sense of the colours and fabrics… This neon colour clashes with the floral, and the floral doesn't go with the pinstripe," Jonty said, talking them through his layout—and he was right.

Dominic finally saw some spark in him that showed that he did have a curated eye after all. The acid neon yellow was too bright to start the show with and it did indeed look jarring next to the fuchsia floral section, while the pinstripe business wear in the middle seemed to slow the showdown, only to pick up again with bold evening wear at the end.

"Yes, it's too disconnected," Dom agreed. "Why don't we start with the pinstripe tailoring? The wide-leg pantsuit is the perfect first look: confident and strong with a neon bra underneath to hint at what's to come… Then we can introduce the daytime floral, then the neon in the evening section—end on something a bit punchy."

Dom and Jonty started to peel off the sketches from the wall to rearrange them before stepping back to reassess the situation. "What do you think?" Dom said, attempting to show some respect by asking for Jonty's opinion.

"Well, I think it's perfect!" Pandy said, excited at finally being able to see where this was all heading.

Heather, Jonty and JoJo all nodded in agreement, squinting at the wall—Dom did know what he was doing after all.

"Okay, great stuff… Well, let's leave it like this for now," Dom said. There was still much work to be done if they were to cast models in a day and a half and then show the collection the day after. Time was tight and Dom still hadn't inspected all the garments for their cut and fit. If the pinstripe blazer was out of line then he suspected the rest of the collection would be too. "Hey, how's that jacket coming along?"

"Nearly there… Although I have to reconstruct the lapel completely."

"Great… You crack on with that while the rest of us hang the looks on the rails in the new order… Then we can review how it really all looks together," Dom said, wanting to capitalise on this burst of productivity.

The studio was buzzing with the entire team working at full steam, and with Dom's direction, they were working the most efficiently they had ever done. Once all the garments were sorted in their order of exit, it started to look like a presentable collection—which Pandora looked rather pleased with. Looking through the garments, Dom noticed one dress in particular which was sexy and had commercial appeal. What Pandy needed was a seasonal hit, something that would be instantly recognised from the collection and wanted by editors, buyers, and shoppers alike. This dress was just that.

A simple bustier style that had a figure-hugging, ruched skirt, made from an acid neon yellow crepe. The bustier had black lace sprouting from inside, while the skirt had a thigh-high slit. Dom thought it needed some tweaking, but more to the point, it should be a piece that was reiterated throughout the entire collection in all fabric swatches.

"Pandy, this dress is sublime! The standout piece from the collection I'd say. I'm thinking… The slit needs to be a touch higher to make it daring and visually exciting on the runway… You can always close it back up for the commercial pattern."

He walked over to a shelf where the fabric was stored, running his hand over different materials and checking out what else she had in stock—a leopard print roll of fabric seemed to call him. It had been over-ordered from her previous collection (which hadn't garnered the sales from buyers that they had anticipated). In fact, this year's autumn/winter collection was dubbed 'out of season safari on a budget' by the harshest fashion critic on the London scene, Lou Banks.

"Let's make it in every fabric swatch," he said. "Not just neon, but in pinstripe, fuchsia, floral, plain black crepe to contrast with the lace in neon yellow—and also in a longer gown length for the evening section… We also need this leopard print in the collection… What do you think, Pandy?"

"I'm thinking that this all sounds brilliant and everything… But these samples were made by a factory up in Manchester weeks ago—we'd have to do it all ourselves this late in the day!"

"Wait… Your production is in Manchester?" Dom snorted. He wasn't exactly expecting her to say they were made by Italian artisans—Portugal at least, like most small scale designer brands. "Let's just say they're made in England from now on."

"Manchester, Paris, Pluto—who cares? How the hell are we going to make all of that in time? That's at least six more pieces, and we only have one more day left before the model casting on Tuesday—*and* we haven't properly styled the final looks yet."

Pandy's mind was now spinning out of control; it had just dawned on her the extent of work that was still needed to be done to bring this collection up to scratch. Dom looked at her as if to say: 'It's your call.' Did she want this show to be the best it could be? After all, this is exactly why she had taken him on.

Until now, she had been in a creative flap, letting her team get away with murder while she took all the burden of an upcoming failure of a fashion show. Now it was getting pulled together, she could slowly see her vision becoming reality, and she was impressed with Dom's impact in just one day—and she wanted more of that stuff. This needed to be the show to finally put Pandora Simmons London on the map, even it did mean hard work and a bit of risk-taking.

"*Fuck it*—let's do it!" she said before clapping her hands for attention. "Right, listen up guys... Dom's had an idea and we are staying here until it is done. If you guys aren't up to it, then fine—but I *really* need your help."

Jonty, Heather, and JoJo all stopped what they were doing to listen to the plan.

"Hev, we need to run up this dress in all of the fabric swatches—plus leopard," Dom said, to which she looked panicked.

"*Leopard?* We got savaged for leopard last season... How can we even think about showing it again so soon?"

Heather had a point. They all looked to Dominic, including Pandy as she recalled the panning she received last season. But Dom, being Dom, had it all figured out.

"You make them like it! You shove it down their necks and make them eat it... Leopard print is a Pandora Simmons staple—it's *you* babe. Visually strong and a house signature that will never go away! Every collection from now on will have some leopard pieces; you can't expect a trend to catch on right away, you need to insist on it and stand firm... Let's cover the cups of a black bra in leopard to be worn under the tailoring, the blazers can have leopard underneath the collar stands so that lapels that can be popped up with a sexy attitude... The Devil is in the details, and the detail is leopard in our case."

Listening to Dom made it all sound so easy, but it was already four in the afternoon and they were all hoping they would be back in Shoreditch House swigging G&T's by now. This meant staying up around the clock and sleeping over at the studio if they had a chance of even getting started on all this extra work. But there was a sense of excitement in the air which hadn't been felt in the workroom for a very long time. They all looked to one another, trying to gauge reactions before eventually committing to taking on the last-minute change in direction.

"Perfect!" Dom clapped. "Jonty, get the pattern for this dress and cut the pieces for it in each fabric, including a longer length gown with a daringly high front slit in both black and leopard," he said, pointing to how high the slit should go on himself. "JoJo— you help him cut and baste the lining, I want contrasting colours, please. Think punk, daring, jarring almost… Heather and Pandy, you guys run up the dresses—they don't need to be perfect. I'll make a start with hand sewing leopard onto the jacket collars."

And just like, that the studio was in pandemonium once again with everyone getting stuck into their designated jobs. This was going to be one long night, so before setting up her machine, Pandy dug out some Pizza menus that were stuffed in the drawer of the kitchenette and ordered a selection (including a cauliflower base vegan option for Heather, of course).

****

Pizza boxes could be found in every corner of the room, some with slices still leftover and one which was full of crusts that Jonty had perfectly nibbled around and discarded (it wasn't like he needed the carbs or anything). Now approaching midnight, productivity was naturally waning and eyes were starting to droop, but progress had been made. Jonty had drafted the pattern for the longer version of the dress and cut all the pieces out, both in black and leopard, ready for the samples to be made.

Dom had very neatly sewn leopard fabric onto the collar stands of all of the tailored jackets, as well as to the cuffs so they could be turned up and styled. Heather had finally finished making adjustments to the blazer and matched all the new dresses with their alternating lining. Pandy was also sat at her sewing station, stitching the short dress in leopard with a neon green lining and black lace accents. While all of this was going on, JoJo was taking a nap in the armchair with her legs over one of the arms, curled up into the back of the seat in a foetal position. Having done his part, Jonty was also taking a rest outside on the balcony tucked up on the recliner using an old blanket for cover.

Dom was also feeling the strain, but he was not going to sleep on the job, especially as he was the one who had led them all into this. But it was going to be worth it in the end, so he continued by prepping the floral and leopard dresses for sewing, even though his eyes began to sting. He watched Pandy sew her dress so he could follow the pattern, and once he was confident enough to, he took the spare machine out of the cupboard and set up his own make-shift station on top of the cutting table. It wasn't ideal to stand up and sew, but at least it would keep him awake he had gathered.

The sound of sewing machines going full pelt was the soundtrack of the night, sending them into the early hours. There was only one more full day of work left to be had, and in his mind, Dom had racked up even more bullet points for their 'to-do' list. It had dawned on him that he had no idea of the space where Pandora was showing, what music had been selected (if any), and more importantly—where was the showroom going to be set up afterwards? He started to feel like he had taken on more than he could handle; if the design process was a mess, then he could bank on there being no internal systems to handle taking orders.

The truth was, P.S.L had only ever taken small orders from a few of the trendy department stores and independent boutiques, but Dom was certain this show would be her best yet and he hoped orders would flood in, after the show. Then there was the model casting, and with that thought, he suddenly realised that one vital element was missing from the collection entirely... *Shoes!*

3

Chloe and Carmen sketched and scrapped paper until they were finally happy with ten designs to present to Veronica. Time was something they too were short of right now, but it was exciting. For both of their career's combined, Chloe and Carmen had dreamed of designing their own collection that would be produced and sold.

Plus, they had all the ideas and knowledge from the years of experience they both had dressing and styling people, understanding what customers really wanted and being surrounded by the best designer pieces day in, day out. Exhausted, they sat back on the couch reviewing their work, feasting on a Chinese take-out banquet for four.

"I'm just not sure about this heel?" Chloe said, picking at the prawn crackers (which she never normally touched).

"I mean... Does it really matter? Veronica's team will tell us tomorrow what is possible and what is not from their supplier; I'm sure they will edit our designs anyway... What's important here is that the detail is not missed, and by detail, I mean your name on the sole!" Carmen said, picking up the last spring roll and taking a bite.

'She's probably right,' Chloe thought to herself. She was too concerned with the small insignificant things that would inevitably be changed without her knowing anyway. What was vital was that they had a clear vision for the collection and that it was *shit hot*! Both of which Chloe was confident in.

"Right, tomorrow is going to be huge and you need your beauty sleep Mrs Palazzo," Carmen teased.

"Will *you* stop calling me that? I mean, he's only invited me to the fashion show, I'm sure we are just getting over-excited about all this; I may not even get to see him again."

"Okay, Sure," Carmen snorted as she got up to gather her things. "No, no—you're right… I mean, he only just got his assistant to track you down like some psycho stalker and invite to you to *the* Palazzo fashion show in MILAN! Like… Hello? Wake up, bitch!"

Yes, it did sound a bit more than just a casual invite when it was put like that. Plus, recalling the sizzling chemistry that she felt between them at the retrospective after-party was something that Chloe could not shake off. Ever since then she had relived that moment, the burning tension and thrilling sensation that Gianni made her feel with very little effort. And *this* was the real reason she was going to Milan.

Of course, she was excited to be invited to Milan Fashion Week and to have a front-row ticket to the most sought after show in the calendar. It was also going to be her first time in Europe which was exciting enough on its own, but she was desperate to know where this random connection with Gianni was heading. In her mind, Chloe Palazzo did have a ring to it which she secretly enjoyed.

"We have to be at DivaFeet at ten–thirty in the morning, so I'll come by at nine in the car and we'll grab coffee before, okay? Ciao, darling," Carmen said, kissing Chloe and heading out the door to the Uber she had only just ordered.

Left alone in Dom's apartment, Chloe started to think about him once more. She was desperate to know how he was getting on in London and whether Jason had managed to reach him. By now, she fully expected him to have called her and be gushing over the phone about how Jason had swept him off his feet, but she hadn't even received a simple text message so far. So, before shutting down her laptop and getting to bed, Chloe composed an email in the hope that it would reach him, and she could hear all the gossip—as if he had never left the city.

*

The studio was silent as the morning crept in through the skylight, which had woken Dom up. That and the stabbing pain in the arch of his back, which had caused him to have the strangest dream ever. One-eyed, he peeped around the room, unsure of his surroundings. He could see JoJo still in her curled up position on the armchair, but shifted the other way; Jonty was still outside with more blankets heaped over him as the cold air settled in overnight. Already distressed, Dom closed his open eye and swapped it for the other.

Pandy and Heather were 'topping and tailing' on the three-seat sofa bed, while he was on the floor on a makeshift mattress made from cushions and fabrics for covers (No wonder he had crippling back pain). His mouth tasted stale and his teeth felt furry as he ran his tongue across them before giving the top set a rub with his finger. 'Is this what success tastes like?' he wondered.

Dom searched for his phone in the pocket of his jacket to check the time, he could see an email in his inbox—but more importantly—it was only six a.m. He decided that if he was going to survive the day ahead he would need at least one more hour of sleep. But laid there on the floor of the studio, he suddenly remembered his dream—and he was brought back to reality with a lonely shudder.

He had dreamt that Jason was looking for him all over London, but instead of running into his arms, Dom hid from him in the strangest of places. It was so weird to think that Jason was also in London right now and that he wasn't rushing with excitement to see him. Seeing him again was the last thing he wanted to do right now. Although, if he was really honest with himself, he missed him and very much wanted to see him again. Alas, this was not the time to be having such thoughts and distractions, so he closed his eyes...

**

"Morning!" Pandy chirped from the kitchen.

Dom opened an eye to see who was rudely awakening him with accidental chimes against mugs. *'Really?'* he thought to himself, checking his phone once more—it was now eight a.m. The past two hours felt more like five minutes, but he couldn't sleep on this bed of bumpy cushions any longer, so he sat up and accepted the cup of coffee from her.

"Why don't I go out and get us bacon rolls, then we can crack on? We've got shit loads to do today before the casting," Pandy said, loud enough to stir the others.

Dom's head swirled, recalling the mental list he had made the night before, there was a whole lot more to be done other than just the collection itself—but *real* coffee and bacon rolls were a good start. "Don't forget hash browns... And Heather's gluten-free porridge," JoJo mumbled from the armchair with her back to them, still curled up in a ball.

"Guys, last night I realised we don't have shoes..." Dom said, stifling a yawn.

"London Sole is lending us some press samples from their archive," Heather answered with a stretch as she attempted to wake up.

"Oh right, well that's one thing sorted... Can you email whoever it is and tell them we need the samples by tomorrow morning, the latest?"

"Sure... After Pandy's back with breakfast though," she said, closing her eyes again.

Now his eyes had finally adjusted to daylight, Dom picked up his phone expecting there to be endless calls from his mother, wondering where he was (which there was, with voicemails to match). He quickly sent her a text message to let her know he was indeed okay and had crashed with Pandora, before opening the email that was waiting for him in his inbox and replying straight away—before Pandy returned with breakfast.

From: Chloe Ravens
To: Dominic Fraser

Subject: Answer Me, You Fucking Bitch!

Dom,

How are you and why the hell are you ignoring my messages? Have you forgotten me already??? Anyway, I hope you are having a fab time in London!

Write, text, call me when you can. I have so much to tell you and I'm sure you do too. In fact, I am surprised you haven't called me already... Any news at all?

Tomorrow, Carmen and I are presenting our ideas for the capsule collection at DivaFeet! So watch this space!

Love u lots—RING ME!!!

Chloe
X

From: Dominic Fraser
To: Chloe Ravens

Subject: RE: Answer Me, You Fucking Bitch!

I know, I know! I've been super busy here as well!

Wow! I am so excited for you... You're going to rock it! Can't wait to see the collection... I am so proud of you.

All is well here. I'm working with my friend on her collection for fashion week. Sorry, I haven't called, but it sounds like you're going to be busy as well! Have you heard from Gianni yet LOL?

Also... You will never guess who is in London too!

Miss you xxx

After hitting send, Dom scrolled through Chloe's previous emails which were all pleas for him to call her as soon as he could. He made a mental note to video call her later if he made it back home at a reasonable time. That way he could properly catch up and hear all about what had happened in New York after his departure.

Right now he needed to get the gang up and running again, so he switched on the radio and washed his face in the kitchen sink. Meanwhile, Pandy had made it back with breakfast, which they all devoured in record timing. As they ate, Pandy ran through the day's to-do list, making sure everyone knew what needed to be completed by the end of the day.

The new dresses they had stayed up all night to make needed finishing, while the longer evening gowns *still* needed to be made—then they had to style the looks and finalise the run of the show. Dom rubbed his face, fearing he had led them down a path they were unable to finish; they were down to the wire on time, but for once it was Pandy whipping them into shape.

Heather and JoJo continued with finishing the new dresses while Pandy, Jonty and Dom reviewed the calico sample for the long gown. The silhouette was perfect: a bustier style with a long and flowing skirt slashed to the thigh in the front. "I think the black version of this should be fitted and sexy," Dom said. "Just a longer length version of the original, while the leopard fabric can be made in this floaty pattern—very 'beachy' and light."

"Love it!" Pandy said, trusting Dom's judgement. "Jonty, you get on with cutting those pieces then pass them to me and I will start making them up."

"Oh, one more thing, Pandy… What about the music?" Dom said. The list of things needing to be finalise seemed to be growing by the minute, and his obsessive need to know that everything was covered was starting to trigger him.

"Well, I have a DJ friend who has been working on some cuts; I should have the files by this afternoon and we can pick what we want to use… Heather's chasing London Sole and tomorrow we have models coming from ten through to lunchtime—don't worry! We've got this!" she said, sensing he was the one that was starting to lose it.

"Okay, guys—I've got some bad news!" Heather said, stopping to check the studio laptop for emails. "London Sole isn't going to be able to send us shoe samples in time for tomorrow's casting!"

"FUCK!" Pandy shouted. "What are we going to do now?"

"It's fine… How much cash do you have in your purse?" Dom said. Pandy scrambled for her handbag and emptied the contents of it on the worktop; she had three screwed up £20 notes, which she handed to Dom. "Jonty, go down to the charity shops… Buy as many shoes as possible, and if worst comes to worst, the models can wear their own."

Jonty rolled his eyes but didn't question Dom, instead, he grabbed his bag and took the cash to begin his mission. "Right, we don't want any more mishaps, so I suggest you message your friend and remind him we need the music right away," Dom ordered Pandy, which she did without question.

The rest of the afternoon was a mad rush to complete the dresses as best possible, leaving detailed finishes out as they wouldn't be seen on the runway anyway. By now, Jonty had been gone for at least two hours, but they continued to pick up the workplace of his absence. Heather and JoJo had now finished the dress samples which they were now inspecting, and the addition of the longer gowns which had been pieced together excited them very much. But they still needed to rearrange the running order, so they had an idea of how many looks they needed to cast models for—as well as having another look at the entire collection.

Dom gathered the girls over by the rails so they could decide on which pieces would make a complete look, even with the shoes missing. Looking through the collection, Dom had an idea. *"Berets!* The models should all be wearing them… That way we won't have to care about hair, *and* we'll have an accessory to add which will be the symbol of the entire show."

Pandy shot him a furious look. 'More stuff to make?' she thought to herself. "And just how are we going to make thirty-four berets in under twelve hours? Assuming we'll have a break of course!" Pandy said, deciding that berets were not going to happen.

"Duh, we buy them of course!" Dom quipped back at her. "Get Jonty on the phone… Tell him to pop down Brick Lane and get us five navy, five black, five bright pink and ten white ones…

We can colour some of the white ones with acid yellow spray paint and add leopard trims to them in no time!"

Heather, called Jonty with the new brief but he was already struggling with bags of second-hand shoes, so JoJo set out to meet him. With or without the addition of berets (which she thought weren't necessary), Pandy could now see the light at the end of the tunnel, even with so much still to do.

Dom, on the other hand, had set up his own office over by the laptop and began making a spreadsheet of all the individual pieces—trying to decipher some sort of cost price—not fully understanding how much it all exactly would cost to make (since Pandora kept no record of costing and invoices). In this case, Dom's strategy was to set a retail value price and then work backwards, by deducting fifty percent to have a rough idea.

If the showroom was to run smoothly and professionally, then he needed to organise that side of the business too (because no one else was). At the casting, he would make sure that they photographed each look on the model, making a simple look-book to present buyers and editors with after the show. This was by far the most organised P.S.L had ever been and Pandy knew that with Dom onboard, her brand was about to turn a major corner.

***

Monday morning had come around very quickly, but Chloe woke up with much excitement for the day ahead. She got up early to shower and make sure she looked her very best with a full face of make-up and had enough time to decide on what she was going to wear. But as the morning went on, her feelings surged from excitement to nervousness—feeling underprepared all at the same time. She shrugged it off—it was nonsense. Carmen had her back covered and everything had been considered, she told herself. And at eight–thirty sharp, Carmen arrived at the apartment with a driver waiting outside—just as she said.

"Grab your things, darling!… Do you have the mood-board and plan?"

"Yep," Chloe said, before double checking she actually did have everything in hand before leaving the apartment.

With Chloe now in the back of the car, Carmen began her pep talk. "Okay, so we'll grab coffee and quickly run through the collection once more so we are totally confident in our concept—which we are of course! Then, we'll make our way over to DivaFeet for ten."

"But our meeting's at ten–thirty, we have plenty of time," Chloe said, wondering what the rush was about.

"Darling, always be early! Surprise these people… You want to turn up and say: 'I'm here bitches!' And the way to do that is to always be early!"

In a diner, nearby to the DivaFeet headquarters, Chloe wasted no time in ordering one latte and one triple shot cappuccino for Carmen before going over their presentation once more. Everything seemed fine and in place, but Carmen could sense Chloe's nerves building up—watching her squirm in her seat. "Darling, we've got this… Besides, we've done the hard part and negotiated the deal—now we just have to sell it. Either way, it's up to them to make this look fabulous—we are simply handing over the blueprint, remember?"

Chloe smiled. Once again, Carmen had all the advice she needed to hear, which helped her to relax a little—taking a sip of her coffee.

This was what she had been waiting for her entire life and now the time was finally here; she knew she had to enjoy the moment and take it all in, rather than worry about it and make a mess of it. But with Carmen by her side, Chloe was ready more than ever and she was confident that her collection would get the go-ahead. With the caffeine now starting to hit, psyched up and ready to go, Chloe couldn't wait to get into the boardroom.

"Come on you, let's take a slow walk over to DivaFeet—nice and early!" Carmen said, downing her cappuccino.

****

"You're slightly early, but I'll call Ms Meyer and let her know you're here—take a seat," the receptionist said, picking up the phone.

Chloe and Carmen sat on the sofa in the waiting area of Diva-Feet's reception; Chloe knew they should have just been on time instead of being early—but here they were, waiting. After some time, they were met by Veronica herself, emerging from one of the elevators. "Ladies!" Veronica boomed in her loud, brash voice. "I'm impressed… I thought we said half-past? Bethany, would you mind to call the others to the boardroom for me?"

"Certainly, I'll bring refreshments through shortly," Bethany smiled, pleasing her boss.

Veronica was a very savvy businesswoman, she had founded DivaFeet back in the early noughts (back when everyone said online retail would never work, except for people wanting to buy books as those were easily received in the mail). But, she had, in fact, spotted a gap in the market to produce and sell fast-fashion online to consumers all over the world, who wanted to shop celebrity looks on a budget.

She also knew that Chloe would be a savvy prospect to snap up before anyone else in did. She could see that Chloe had personality and was pretty enough for her online followers to look up, but also relate to. She was a real person, giving real fashion advice through her blog, StacksOfStyle, and her link to Gianni Palazzo had sent her social media alight with new followers—and Veronica knew that social influencers meant serious money!

That and the fact that Chloe was receiving press from the fashion world—thanks to her being photographed with Gianni at New York Fashion Week—which she would be mad not to cash in on. Veronica led them into her boardroom, which overlooked the entire office floor on a mezzanine floor. Her design team scurried along to the meeting not long after, followed by another woman who didn't attend their previous meeting—along with a gentleman dressed smartly in a blazer and chinos combo.

Chloe had assumed DivaFeet to be a female-dominated company, and was rather surprised to see a male employee, dressed conservatively. But DivaFeet was different. With Veronica at the helm, she employed mostly women, women who loved shoes and bags and throw-away fashion. But she also employed fairly, and that meant if you were good at your job then you were good enough for DivaFeet—man, woman or goat.

"Ladies, you already know Sam and Lily, and this is Morgana—our marketing manager—who'll be able to offer advice on how we can get the most out of this partnership... Bill here is our head buyer... Now, before I begin, I apologise for not getting the contract over to you sooner, but as you can imagine these things take time," she said, handing them white envelopes. "You'll both need to countersign each other's, and there's a copy for yourselves too—read those over in your own time... Today we're here to discover what you have in mind for the collection, but I will need the contracts signed before I can put this project into production... So with that all aside, I can't wait to hear your ideas!"

Carmen and Chloe stood up, taking out the sketches and mood-board to present the 'Raven, by Chloe Ravens' collection to the team. "Okay, well good morning everyone," Chloe started, clearing her throat with a gulp of water. "As you know, Carmen and I have over a decade of experience working for some of the most luxurious brands—and celebrities—in fashion. I worked at Palazzo for several years; I'm sure you're well aware by now that we were present at the retrospective show last week," she said, getting the obvious reason as to why she was here out of the way.

"We want to capture the same essence of luxury and heritage, but with something affordable and wearable for the fashion-savvy consumer," Carmen continued, bringing the conversation back to the collection and not the gossip columns of the New York News.

"Right—exactly," Chloe picked up. "'Raven, by Chloe Ravens' is a reflection of me... It's chic, super sexy, but it's wearable and affordable at the same time... These pieces will inject style into your existing wardrobe, enabling you to dress up your casual clothes or sit alongside your designer pieces."

"We have come up with a ten-piece collection which includes an evening purse, a day bag, five pairs of shoes, and three entry-level accessories, so that everyone can enjoy this collection—whatever your budget," Carmen added in, ensuring that they too knew the market well.

Chloe handed out copies of their rough sketches for the collection, to which Sam and Lily nodded as they flicked through them, appearing to like first impressions. "As you can see, the shoe line consists of an evening sandal, a classic heeled pump in two colour variations, a knee-high leather boot, and a comfortable flat ballet shoe for the city," Chloe said, now standing back at the top of the table with Carmen, waiting for a reaction.

"Well, this looks fantastic… I love the style, it's very… Palazzo!" Veronica said.

"Yes, it's simple enough to produce but glam and effective at the same time," Lily agreed.

"Morgana, what're your initial thoughts?" Veronica said, turning to her and relaxing back in her chair.

"I have to agree, it has that glam 'Palazzo' feel, which makes it easy for us to tie into a story on our website, and for our editorial team to sell *you* and your past with Palazzo… As well as being able to capitalise on your connection with Gianni, of course."

Morgana was the typical marketing guru, quick to pick up on anything that could help push sales. She appeared to very perky and almost too much to swallow, even for mid-morning. It was like she had sucked a canister of helium before entering the meeting and was now deflating all around the room, buzzing with ideas. Chloe sighed inside, of course, they wanted to drag this 'Gianni thing' up at every opportunity. She felt like she was exploiting him, even though she didn't know him that well; it seemed everyone had pigeon-holed her as 'Gianni's new girl' already.

"That's perfect because Chloe is jetting to Milan next week as his guest at the Palazzo show… She has an interview with Vanguard lined up too while she is there, so we'll make sure to mention we have partnered on a capsule collection with DivaFeet… That should make print for their December issue, which is when you're planning to launch the collection?" Carmen said, talking as if it was all signed and sealed.

"Well, that's the idea, but Sam and Lily will need to supply our factory with patterns and fabrics and such at the earliest to meet that deadline—which is why I need those contracts signed," Veronica reminded them, turning to her designers for clarification.

"We'll need to finalise these designs into patterns first… We can do that effectively by tweaking existing styles in our archive so that our factory can push them through as quickly as possible. We can plan to have samples in about three weeks at the earliest for you to see, and once we've all agreed, we can approve the collection for production," Sam said, explaining how they were able to turn it all around so quickly.

"So, this collection will be *your* designs but with *our* style and *my* name?"

"Correct," Lily said. "If we want to get this collection to market as soon as possible, and gain on your current status, then this is the easiest and quickest way possible… All we need to do is come up with your logo graphic to put on each piece."

That was the easy part, Chloe had that thought out already and whipped out her business card. "It's a gold raven… Get it? 'Raven, by Chloe Ravens'?" she said, rather stupidly—of course they got it—it was hardly the riddle of the century. "Gold lettering on the insole and I want the soles of the shoes to be gold—so you see a flash of gold and instantly know it's from the 'Raven' line."

Veronica had a huge smile on her face, chewing her bottom lip, she was impressed with the pitch so far. An interview with Vanguard to advertise the collection, a brand name and logo already thought of, as well as a clear vision for the brand image. All that was left to decide on was the math—which was where she came in. "Bill?" Veronica handed over. "Thoughts?"

"I think this is very well thought out and something our customers will love—trendy pieces with a story… They also like something that is linked to relevant fashion influencers, such as yourself, so if we can get some hype and press around the collection beforehand then I think we'll have a hit on our hands."

"Wonderful work ladies… So, Bill and I will crunch the numbers on how much to order… Sam and Lily, if I can get the final designs as soon as possible, we can work on unit prices once we know the cost price—but it needs to be low cost/high margin of course! In terms of units, I want to create demand so we won't go too deep in stock… I'm predicting this to be a huge success, so the quicker we sell out, the better! I want customers calling our phone lines complaining that they can't buy the 'Raven' collection… But of course, you will have a hand in the marketing and creating that hype. Once the demand is there, then we can re-stock and go even bigger with the next collection," Veronica said with her calculating business mind.

Chloe's heart was pumping with excitement as she listened to Veronica and her team hammer out the details.

"Also, I have this idea of putting the collection on your website for purchase too… That way we can divert traffic from StackOfStyle back to our site to purchase—funnelling both of our audiences into one place. I'm sure we can get the digital team to produce those pages for us, clicking through to DivaFeet for checkout… We would need access to the back end of your site though," Morgana said, looking at Veronica for approval.

"That's all do-able, I'm sure… Get the tech team in on the project ASAP! Amazing work here gang," Veronica said clapping her hands together. "So, when will you be in Milan?" Veronica said, getting up.

"Next week… I fly this weekend and Monday is the Palazzo show," Chloe said, realising she had survived the meeting.

"Perfect… Just make sure you get snapped again hanging off Gianni's arm looking stunning as always, kid."

Chloe understood that the reason this had all come about was due to her newfound connection with Gianni, but the expectation was starting to overwhelm her. What if this 'thing' with him wasn't anything at all? What if it were to go nowhere except for a pleasant meet and greet at the show? Chloe was feeling the pressure to make an even bigger impression on Gianni, almost as if it were an arranged marriage.

"Okay, well I think that we can take this project on from here… Just get me those contracts signed and sent over as soon as you can, and when we have more information— samples and such—my people will be in touch with your people as they say," Veronica said, holding out her hand to them both.

Chloe was excited but also surprised at how quick the meeting went, but she felt confident that it was all going nicely to plan. She was also relieved that she wouldn't have to stress about the details of the designs as Sam and Lily would be taking charge of everything in that department. This was simply a branding exercise that would have her name on it, and the more she came to realise that, the better she felt about the upcoming workload.

The last thing she needed right now was to have to work a nine-to-five at DivaFeet trying to come up with all this by herself. At least this way the responsibility was with DivaFeet and not entirely all on her, which meant she could focus on creating content for StacksOfStyle and on her trip to Milan. Especially because now she had a whole lot more riding on it being a successful trip—in more ways than one.

*****

Back in London, the P.S.L Studio was winding down for the evening with all the extra samples knocked up just in time. Jonty and JoJo had successfully returned with bags full of charity shop shoes and berets from the market—they had even begun the task of spraying acid yellow paint on the white hats. Everything was coming together now, but before Dom suggested they all go home for the evening, he wanted to make sure everyone knew their role for the model casting.

"Okay, guys… So let's make sure we are clear on what needs to happen tomorrow. We need a minimum of twelve models—that's about three looks per model. We need each model to try on their looks so we can photograph them for a look-book against that white wall over there," he said pointing to a blank space in the studio. "Let's clear the tables to one side of the room now, so that we have a runway-ready for the girls to walk down in the morning… Heather and JoJo, you can help the models get dressed once Pandy and I have chosen who's wearing what—Jonty can then take a picture of each look... Is that a plan?"

"*Yes!*" they all shouted in unison.

"Perfect, let's move these tables to one side and get the hell out of here, and back in at eight a.m. tomorrow morning."

Jonty and JoJo started to make space for the tables to be pushed into, while Heather fetched a broom to sweep the room free of fabric remnants, loose threads and lint.

"I'm so happy you're here... I can't thank you enough!" Pandora said, pulling Dom to one side while the others moved the room around.

"Just one more thing," Dom said with a smile. "I've marked up each piece with cost and a retail price for the showroom... We need to be ready for taking orders as soon as possible after the show," he said, stern and clear.

"Like I said, I'm glad you're back." Pandora was relieved that he was already thinking of the aftermath of the show; he was fast proving his worth and she knew that if this collection was indeed a success, she would need him permanently on her team.

By now everyone was shattered and desperate for a hot bath—Dom included. He didn't realise the mammoth task he had taken on, but his aching muscles did. Completely knackered, the journey home seemed like another huge marathon to overcome, and passing the exhibition poster once more reminded him that somewhere in London, Jason Hart was walking about—breathing the same air.

But right now, in this moment, he was too tired to even care; he was now committed to making the P.S.L fashion show a hit. He had his sights set on becoming the CEO of Pandora Simmons London and to take over the operations of the brand globally, while she focused on designing and being the face of the brand. There was no room to be feeling regret now, or for men who had missed their chance.

This was *his* chance now, and this new start in London looked as though it was coming together. He could finally see the possibility of making a name for himself in fashion. No more shop jobs, no more answering to bosses who knew far less than he did; he *was* the boss in his eyes and people were finally listening to him and respecting his opinion—and it felt rather nice to be needed once more.

4

Dom was pleased to be home at last. He could hear Michael in the living room with the BBC news on full blast. "Dominic? Where have you been?" His mother called, coming out of the living room to the hallway to greet him.

"Long story mum… Been at Pandora's studio working on her collection—didn't you get my message? The show's on Wednesday and Pandora being Pandora, was nowhere near ready… She is now, of course—thanks to your talented son!" he said, quickly pecking his mother on the cheek before heading up the stairs.

"You've been home five minutes and already you're working too hard… I thought you needed to relax and step back a bit?"

She felt like Dom was pushing himself too hard and that he felt obliged to find work, now he was living rent-free under her roof—which wasn't the case. She knew Dom was ambitious but she didn't want him to feel pressured into finding work straight away. She finally had her son back home after all these years, and she wanted him for lunch dates in Knightsbridge more than anything.

"I'm gonna take a long hot shower… And then I'm gonna brush my teeth, they feel like death," Dom said, carrying on up the stairs—now was not the time to get into it with her.

"Well, come down afterwards… I'll reheat some dinner for you," she said, letting him do what he needed to do while she did what she did best—being a mum.

A hot shower was exactly what Dom needed. His body felt relaxed, his muscles all soft and doughy, and his hair smelt fresh again. With his teeth now brushed and flossed, it breathed new life into him (as did a home-cooked dinner) but he was still exhausted. He could just crawl into bed and sleep for a thousand years right now, but he was desperate to speak to Chloe.

He was eager to know how her meeting with DivaFeet went, and he did miss her. Plus, he had some rather exciting news of his own to share now. Pandora didn't know Dom like Chloe did, and he couldn't exactly tell Pandy everything and seem like an emotional wreck too soon. He was the strong one, the one who had his shit together—Pandy was the scatterbrain.

What he needed right now was a familiar friend, someone who was going to tell him he was doing the right thing—that person was Chloe. Back in his bedroom, he switched the desk lamp on along with his laptop so he could video call her.

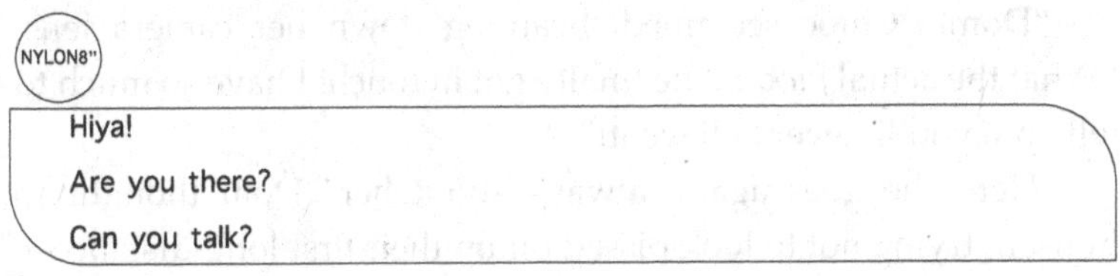

Dom waited for a reply, reclining back in the office chair, stretching his arms behind his neck. It was starting to get late and he desperately needed to sleep if he was going to make tomorrow's start time of eight a.m, back in East London. Tomorrow was an important day and he knew he would once again have to call the shots, because if he left it to anyone else, then they would probably end up having to model the collection themselves.

The laptop pinged...

Dom sniggered whilst typing a quick reply; he hadn't used Skype in a long time and he didn't think she would notice his online moniker.

NYLON8"

Awkward :/

We never web cam'd before and I didn't think to change my handle

lol...

Oops...

Oh, well! Can you speak?

Within seconds, his laptop starting ringing and he hit the 'accept call' button. He quickly ran his fingers through his quiff, using the camera as a mirror, whilst they were still connecting.

"Dom!" Chloe screamed, beaming down her camera lens. "What the actual *fuck!* So he finally got in touch! I have so much to tell you, you'll never believe it!"

'Here she goes again, always about her,' Dom thought to himself, trying not to look pissed off on their first long-distance— things will stay the same—call.

"After you left New York, who do I get a visit from?" Chloe said, excited to finally tell him everything that had happened. The Internet was a wonderful thing.

"Erm... Brian?" Dom said, assuming her ex-boyfriend would be back on the scene. But he didn't really care, he just wanted to tell her all about life in London so far.

"Wrong!" Chloe laughed. She hadn't even thought about Brian in the slightest. "Regina-*Fucking*-Hall—that's who!"

"*What?* At your apartment?" Dom said flabbergasted, not expecting the direction this conversation had suddenly taken.

"Yes... You *are* hearing me correctly," Chloe said, realising that he had missed so much already—and that wasn't half of it.

At this point, Carmen camera-bombed Chloe in the background—entering the room from the kitchen with a champagne bottle in hand.

"Hi, Carmen!" Dom said, waving to the camera. His apartment was now Chloe's HQ and he was pleased that she and Carmen had already gotten comfortable, with Carmen making the most of the facilities it appeared.

Chloe looked behind her to find Carmen goofing around dancing before inviting her over to join in on the conversation. Carmen sat down and started to peel the foil off the cork while she continued. "So anyway… Regina turns up to basically threaten me, demanding that I stay away from Gianni—otherwise she'll ruin my career in fashion forever! I mean, who does she think she is? Naturally, I told her to get out and that she couldn't tell me what to do any more—"

"Fuck off… She told her to *fuck off!*" Carmen interjected.

"Yeah, that—but that's not all… After that incident, I needed to get out of my place—what with Kim also dropping by unannounced—but that's another story… I'll get onto that in a second… So, I immediately packed up some things to stay here for a few nights, and who do ya think knocked on *this* door?"

Dom felt his stomach lurch suddenly, he tried his best to not look freaked out—aware that he was on camera. But this came as no surprise; he knew exactly who knocked on his door, or at least who he wanted it to be. It was all starting to make sense now. He was a big believer in fate and he had already received a pretty big sign that things with Jason weren't quite over yet. A billboard-sized sign, no less. He took in a deep breath before reacting. "Typical… Of course, he came back for me after I had left!"

"So, you've spoken to him? What's he said?" Chloe pressed, eager to know if their romance was back on.

"Oh, no—I haven't spoken to him."

"Wait… Back up. How do you know he came looking for you then?"

"The other night, I was making my way home from seeing a friend, and I saw a poster for the exhibition he was commissioned for… I realised he must be in town. So, when you said guess who came knocking, well it's him—isn't it?"

"So, has he been in touch at all? He was begging me to tell him where he could find you… I just gave him your email and said to keep trying your phone, but it would probably be switched off," Chloe said, still trying to figure out why Dom wasn't over the Moon about Jason wanting to see him again.

Jason was Dom's world for the past two months, so to hear him speak so blasé about him now was strange. What was all that misery and moping all about? What was the point of their one and only argument? All of that didn't matter now, what did was why the hell was Dom not falling madly back in love with Jason in London? The way he would have wanted to just a matter of weeks ago.

"Well, I wouldn't know if he has tried to get in touch, to be honest… Before leaving New York, I junked all of his emails and blocked his address. You know, I just wanted London to be a fresh start without being reminded of him… And what happens? I walk straight into a giant billboard with his name in lights!"

"Dom, he was desperate to see you… And you know you are desperate to see him too. Cheek your email at least, and then make a decision. This is too freaky to ignore… He's in London now and so are you—don't you think that's fate trying to play its hand?"

Surely this was text-book romance? She couldn't bear it; why wasn't he seeing this too? This was rom-com, chick-flick gold!

"Anyway, sounds like you've been out on the *razzle* already," Chloe said, seeing he wasn't keen on discussing this any further.

"Kinda… Remember I told you I was friends with Pandora Simmons back in college? Well, I met up with her and she's taken me on as a consultant. Her collection needed tweaking lets say, and the show's in one day… I'm telling you, she has no clue what she is doing! She needed someone like me to steer the ship, bring some structure… Tomorrow we're model casting, so lots to do as you can imagine… How did things go with DivaFeet?"

There was simply too much to discuss in one sitting, but Chloe got him up to speed on the success of the meeting.

"We should have samples when I come back from Milan… I can't wait!" she said, clinking glasses with Carmen and taking a sip of champagne.

"MILAN?" Dom shouted, surprised at this flippant piece of information.

'Gosh,' Chloe thought, so much *really* had happened. He hadn't even heard all about her visit from Kim and about the ticket to the Palazzo fashion show. Carmen helped her out, pushing Chloe out of the way so she could dominate the camera space.

"Darling, Gianni Palazzo has invited her to Milan, first-class—all expenses paid… And we have an interview with Vanguard while she's out there!"

"*What!* Are you shitting me? Why haven't you told me this sooner?"

"I've been trying to get in touch! What's even crazier is that Kim came to tell me face to face… Fancy that, we were once enemies and now we are besties; she hand-delivered the invite because his assistant contacted the Palazzo PR office, and if it reached Myra and Regina then I never would've got the message—can you believe that? Anyway, she has a new job at Maison Marais now—as the assistant to Dionne. You've probably heard that Palazzo has acquired them? Let's see how this one goes down… You can bet Regina has her eye on becoming group director! Anyway, can you come to Milan? I leave at the end of the week; I'll be there for two days," Chloe said, excited at the possibility of seeing Dom so soon after his departure.

"Ah! I'd love to, but I can't… I'm too busy with this collection and we need to prepare the showroom for buying season straight after the show."

Dom was faced with making this collection a financial success and he needed to get the showroom ready for buyers instead of gallivanting around Europe already. He envisioned this season to be major with his input, and Pandora had no internal structure for taking orders, which he would have to organise. He had already started on making an inventory of the collection, noting down the individual pieces, and giving them a numbered code, all in readiness for orders to come flooding in.

"Sure, I understand… I probably won't have time myself," Chloe realised. Carmen was relieved to hear it too. She had no time for frolicking around Milan with Dom.

Her schedule was just as tight, what with the Vanguard interview, attending the Palazzo show, and being Gianni's guest of honour and making him fall for her. Any extra time she had needed to be spent in Gianni's circle of friends. Carmen decided to save this pep-talk for the end of the week, just before she left for Milan—so it would be fresh in her mind.

Over an hour had passed and it was getting late. As much as he was enjoying catching up with Chloe and Carmen, Dom needed to get to bed. Tomorrow was a big day, a lot had to be done, and sleep was very much needed. "Well, it was great catching up… Let me know what happens in Milan, okay?" Dom said, wrapping up the call.

"Totally!" Chloe said with excitement. "Good luck with the show… I'm *so* happy things are happening for you over there already. I'm sure it's going to be fabulous, Pandora's a lucky girl to have you!"

Hearing this vote of confidence from his best friend made him smile. She was right, Pandora was lucky to have him. He had helped make things happen for Chloe back in New York, and he was sure he could repeat the success for Pandora in London.

"Oh, one more thing," Chloe added before he could end the call. "Think about giving Jason another chance… I know in your head you've moved on, but he was pretty desperate to find you. Maybe it would be good to see him again… On your turf? That's all I'm saying."

He understood perfectly what she was saying, and on that note, they said their goodbye's, promising to be in touch again sooner rather than later. Dom got up from the computer to make a start on packing his holdall. Tomorrow was surely going to be another long day and another late night, so it would be wiser for him to stay at Pandora's rather than trekking all the way back to West London—especially as the following day was show day.

He needed a casual look for the model casting, ready to change into in the morning, and a look suitable for the show itself—nothing too fancy mind as he would be running about getting sweaty backstage. Going through his clothes, searching for appropriate items of clothing that he had brought to London, Chloe's plea rang through his mind. It *was* rude to ignore the fact that Jason was in town, and he clearly still had feelings for him no matter how hard he tried to distract himself with work. Seeing the gigantic poster of Jason's artwork had sent a pang of sadness through his heart; he was very much still in Dom's thoughts and from what Chloe was saying, it was apparent Jason still had feelings for him too.

With his bag now successfully packed, Dom began shutting down his laptop to get ready for bed. But before he clicked to shut down, curiosity caught him at the right moment and he opened up his email inbox instead. This time it wasn't the inbox he was interested in—it was the junk folder.

Now, all of a sudden he had the urge to check it, but he stopped himself. 'What if I see something that's going to change my mind and make me want to see him again? What if I don't and I feel even more disappointed?' he wondered, hovering the cursor over the junk folder. It was far easier to just ignore all of this and carry on submerged in work and creating the P.S.L brand. Now was not the time to start having all these feelings for Jason again, whether it be love, depression or hate. He was in two minds, but with his heart pounding, before he knew it… *CLICK*.

His breath got shorter and his stomach started to tighten with anticipation. He knew this was the wrong thing to do, but if what Chloe was saying was true about Jason coming back for him, then he had to know. Only then could he make a decision to bury his feelings for good. But just as Chloe had said there would be, a string of emails—all from Jason—sat in the junk box. Un-opened.

Dom flicked through them, skimming the contents before scrolling to the next—all begging for him to get in touch or explaining himself. Dom was shocked, yet pleased. His heart pounded with joy, finally knowing that his feelings for Jason were mutual and that they weren't all completely in his head. There were days when he thought he was crazy—he shook his head before reading the latest email. It was sent just yesterday.

From: Jason Hart
To: Dominic Fraser

Subject: <u>One Last Shot…</u>

Attached: SouthBank Gallery Presents 'London Calling'

Dom,

I know you don't want to see me again, but I need to see you!

Please consider coming to this, I've put you down on the guest-list. This work wouldn't have been possible without you! Plus, it's my last day here in London already and I can't go without seeing you...

JH x

Dom's eyes started to well. How could he ignore this? His heart was full of love and sadness all at the same time, while his head was full of confusion. Not a great cocktail to be making decisions on, so he quickly shut the laptop lid down before he could reply and regret it in the morning. He stood up sharp and forced himself to brush his teeth, but standing at the sink with the tap running, Dom stared at his reflection in the bathroom mirror. 'What is the point of all this?' he asked himself.

He thought he understood what he wanted in life; back in New York, he had decided to love himself and live the life of his dreams, not someones else's. But now he was torn between love and his career, and just like that, he was questioning his life all over again. His brain was pushing him to make a decision on what to do about Jason as he rinsed his mouth—or was it his heart?

One thing was for sure, he was racked with indecision. From sticking to the original plan in one moment to telling himself that he would reply to Jason's email in the morning. He was having a conversation with himself in his head that was making him anxious, which wasn't the ideal state for sleep.

His heart pounded, his armpits were wet with nervous sweat, and his head was spinning. 'I can handle a career and a relation-ship,' he told himself, but with the next heartbeat, he also knew that his dreams were far too big for both. He had made a huge step towards them already, it would be foolish to abandon his dream for love again—and there was no way he was leaving London now.

His eyes, puffy and full of tears were becoming harder to suppress. Rather than tell himself he was being silly and to 'pull himself together,' he just let them come. He couldn't bear to see himself cry in the mirror, so he covered his face with his hands and sat on the bathroom floor by the sink, with the tap still running to drown out intermittent sobs—the sound of running water was rather comforting.

After a while, he just stopped crying—it was like he was all dried up. He got up off the floor and quickly washed his face with the now warm, running tap water, before finally heading to bed and setting the aslarm for six. With the lights turned out, he lay down and took a deep breath. In the warmth of his bed, curled up in his familiar but lonely bed, he could feel the tears trying to make a return.

He wished he was with Jason now, feeling the comfort and security of his warm body, like he once did in New York. Shutting his eyes tight and burying the side of his face into his pillow, he wondered how he had got himself into this mess. Would he ever be able to move on from Jason, or would he be tortured eternally between love and work, even if he did meet someone new?

A question his body was not allowing him to answer right now. With all the fatigue of the busy week (and the fresh emotions of discovering Jason's emails), his body went into automatic shut down and sent him off into a deep sleep... Something his computer should have done much earlier.

5

His phone caused a racket as it vibrated on the side table. Dom reached to turn it off, so it wouldn't wake up the rest of the house; just because he needed to be up early, it didn't mean his mother and Michael also had to—even though they most likely were. He thought it funny that they woke up so early each morning, rather than lay in bed a little, wasn't that what retirement was for?

His eyes were sore, having not gotten to bed early enough, and so he allowed himself to snooze for just five more minutes. Last night's revelations seemed like a mad dream, but he knew it had all happened for real. His heart told him so, it felt heavy. He also knew that today was casting day and needed to be there in two hours, so everything else—heavy hearts included—would have to wait.

He started mentally going through the tasks that needed to be completed by the end of the day, ensuring it would be as successful and smooth as possible. If he allowed it, he would fall right back to sleep, but that wasn't an option. Swinging his legs off the mattress so his feet could touch the carpeted floor, he told himself that he was practically up now—so he might as well get his ass in gear. Dragging himself to the shower through half-opened eyes, he turned on the water whilst stepping out of his boxers and into the tub where the shower head hung above. The not-quite-warm water startled him, forcing his eyes open wide.

Now he was awake.

He quickly washed and got dressed, spraying ample cologne on before making his way downstairs to the kitchen for a quick breakfast. Dumping his holdall by the door, he could hear his mother and Michael already at the table with the news on the TV; he could smell the toast had already been made, and as he walked in he saw his mug of tea already poured out for him. "Morning! You're up early again, have some breakfast... What's happening today?" mother asked, trying to show interest.

"Another big day at the studio! We're casting models for the show tomorrow, so there's a lot to be done."

"I can imagine," she said, fetching him a slice of toast and all the jams and spreads she could find in the cupboard.

He still couldn't believe that Pandy hadn't scheduled in the proper time for casting and fitting—what designer did that? He wasted no more time in thinking about it, this was happening—so he gulped down his tea and practically inhaled a slice of toast (simply with a thin scraping of butter on top) before getting up to chuck his mug and plate in the sink.

"Right, gotta be off! Need to be there in an hour... Oh, and I'm probably gonna stay at Pandy's tonight as it will be another late one, and we'll need to be in town super early for the show—so don't freak out if I don't come home for a few days."

"But what abou—" she started, stopping herself from commenting further. She knew by now not to argue and just go with the flow. He *was* an adult after all and not her little boy anymore. On the other hand, she was happy to see he had drive and wasn't moping around the house all day with nothing to do; at least he seemed to be enjoying himself.

*

The studio was already hectic by the time he had arrived; entering the studio bang on eight, he was pleasantly surprised to see everyone there ready to work. JoJo and Heather were printing off the model profiles the agency had emailed over, while Jonty was setting up a camera to capture the looks on models. Pandy was sat at her sewing station adding leopard trims to the hats that Dom had ordered under his last-minute direction. 'Wow. I really have made a difference,' he said to himself with a smile.

"Morning gang!" he shouted as he dumped his bag and jacket down. "Right, how long have we got before these models arrive?"

"The agency's sending girls from ten until one, but they are prepared to hang around if needed—although some have to dash off to other bookings," JoJo answered, looking through the list.

The room had already been re-arranged for models to walk down the centre, and the collection hung on the rails in readiness. Everything was going to plan so far, but Dom took the chance to go through the daily schedule once more, while he still had everyone's attention.

"Heather, I want you to send in the girls and answer the buzzer for those arriving. If it's not busy, you can help JoJo dress them… Pandy and I will watch the girls walk and decide who we like. When picked, we'll send them back over to you… Just give the first girl look one, and so forth—unless we ask for a specific look on a girl… Sound good?"

The guys nodded in agreement, they were pleased that someone who knew what they were doing was finally onboard. In previous years it had been a matter of screaming and arguing in front of models, with some getting involved in tittle-tattle and threatening never to walk for Pandora ever again. This year was going to be different, model casting had been made much easier thanks to The British Fashion Council who had funded the costs by partnering with an agency who were sending up-and-coming models to be tried out for future bookings.

"Jonty, once a girl is dressed and has walked, take a picture against the wall for our look-book… We'll continue to cast the other girls, depending on how many we have at one time… We just need to nail this as quickly as possible so we can do a full walk-through with everyone," Dom finished, heading over to the bags of shoes Jonty had found the day before.

Pandy realised there was a lot to be done in a day, but instead of panicking she focused her energy. For the next hour, they went through the collection together and matched shoes to outfits, as well as deciding which look got which colour beret. That task made the morning whizz by and ten o'clock soon came around as the studio buzzer rang—forcing them to stop what they were doing and get in position.

Pandy rushed over to the window to see if she could catch sight of their first arrival. *"Fuck!"* she shouted. "There's about twelve girls outside already!"

"Okay people… Places please," Dom called as he took his seat behind a table at the end of the makeshift runway.

Heather raced downstairs to guide them up, while Jonty took the last puff on his roll-up before stubbing it out in a nearby plant pot. JoJo handed Dom the list of models as Pandy clapped her hands in excitement, taking her seat next to him. Heather had now lined the girls up outside the studio on the stairwell, before popping back in with a huge grin. "Okay—there's fifteen girls outside."

"Perfect! Send the first one in and thank the others for their patience… Tell them we'll zooming through everyone as quickly as possible," Dom ordered, not wanting anyone to give up and run to their next appointment.

The first girl entered the room, she looked about sixteen, five-foot-nine tall and her face didn't have a single blemish. She seemed very confident for such a young girl new to modelling and walked straight up to Dom and Pandy to hand her portfolio over. Pandy took a quick flick while Dom asked her to walk the length of the room and back. As she did, he marked her Z-card with a red tick before sliding it over to Pandora. She looked at Dom and nodded; it was a 'yes' from her too.

"Okay, thank you… Please see JoJo by the rail who will dress you, we'll ask you to walk again shortly," he said, before signalling to Heather for the next girl to come in and do the same.

The momentum of the next two hours went on very much the same; some girls got sent away, while even more turned up. Jonty had managed to take a few photographs of the girls in their looks that JoJo had assigned to them, but during a short break, he took the initiative to check the studio's email. "The music file is here!" he called out.

"Thank God for that! Stick it on, we need to create the atmosphere of the *real* show," Dom said. Jonty plugged the laptop into the speaker and tapped the volume button rapidly on the keyboard until it reached its max. It started with a propulsive drum beat that got faster before electronic keys trickled in, followed by a catchy riff that repeated itself with strings flying lightly on top of it all—blending into a 'Studio 54' style disco track that was simply infectious.

A smile spread across Pandy's face as she bopped her head to the sound—adding a few finger points in Dominic's face in jest. She was clearly pleased with how things were coming along, and for the first time, she was enjoying the process of putting together a show. Something she had never experienced before, which gave her the sudden gut feeling that this show was going to be the *one* to show the industry that P.S.L was the label to take note of.

"Okay, okay," Dom laughed, flapping Pandy's hands away. "Let's go—next girl please."

JoJo prompted the next girl to walk down the centre of the room and back. She took the bait and lifted her head high as she flicked out her leg to take her first stride, one hand on her hip, while the other swung down by her side as she walked. Her flawless skin made her glisten with youth as she strutted down to the desk where Pandy and Dom awaited, hypnotised.

They only noticed her fresh, freckled face once she came closer, which they both found very intriguing. Pandy gave Dom a look, a look that said: 'She's in,' and Dom couldn't agree more. They didn't take their eyes off of her as she walked back towards JoJo, and she even had a superstar name to go with her aura—Carly Wattmore.

It was now approaching lunchtime and they had managed to get through most of the girls that had come to be cast. So far, they had kept ten models; more than what they expected—but since they were already paid for—it was a case of the more-the-merrier. It seemed crazy to limit themselves and make these inexperienced girls change looks two or three times during a hectic show. The less stress backstage the better, and the more girls dressed and ready to walk in their looks, meant less room for error.

Dom and Pandy sped through the last few models, keeping sixteen models in the final cut. After the last model had walked, they agreed to break for a quick lunch. "Good work team!" Dom called, signalling to Jonty to cut the music. "Girls, let's take a quick break… I know some of you may have another casting to get to but we want to do one more walk in your looks, so please stay dressed."

"How exciting is this?" Pandy said, tugging his arm. "Right we need to eat… Guys, take my credit card and go to the sandwich shop. Get platters, fruit, bottles of water and things that models eat."

"Models don't eat!" Jonty said, licking the seal on his roll-up.

Heather and JoJo accepted the mission, they were having fun taking part in the casting and could see how smooth and organised the operation was under Dom's new direction—they too were excited about P.S.L's comeback.

"Okay, Jonty… Let's see the snaps you got so far," Dom said.

Puffing on his roll-up, Jonty brought over the laptop so they could sit down and see how the girls looked on camera. Pandy was impressed, she never had a look-book before or had images of her collections—and while these were just 'reference worthy' snaps—to her they looked fantastic. The white painted brick background made them look somewhat professional, and Dom agreed that they had turned out much better than he had imagined.

Scrolling through the images, they discussed how the garments looked and had already noted some changes to be made and looks to be switched with other girls. The random mix of shoe styles Jonty had gathered from various charity shops looked rather good too, while on other looks it simply didn't matter since the hemline disguised them fully.

By the time they had gone through the entire shoot, Heather and JoJo had returned from their lunch run with bags of food. They laid it all out on the kitchen worktop, which the models surprisingly attacked. Mostly ditching anything that contained bread; hammering the fruit platters and reaching for the cereal bars, like seagulls swooping down on a bag of chips.

"Okay, attention everyone," Dom shouted as he dipped in to nab two chicken salad sandwiches in one pinch. "We've made some edits, so let's switch those looks quickly." He handed Heather and JoJo the notes taken during the walk-through's before returning to Pandora, who was scoffing her way through the sandwich platter with handfuls of crisps.

"Yeah, that one's good—I get it all the time," she said, trying to convince one of the models that carbs during Fashion Week was fine.

"Pandy," Dom said, pulling her back to the desk, away from the food table. "We need to be on-it this afternoon, so if you don't like a look on a certain girl—or even the girl herself—just say… Go with your gut is all I'm saying, after today, we have to stick with our decisions—because tomorrow is D-day bitch… No last-minute decisions backstage at the show—no room for error—agreed?"

Pandy was on board, one hundred percent. She would be a fool not to be; for the first time she could be assured that she would enjoy her own show and experience the atmosphere of being a British Fashion Council backed designer (and all the hype that went along with it), thanks to Dom.

"Right girls… Listen up! Heather and JoJo will put you in order of exit and we will ask you to walk one after the other for us—so we can see a full run… Here's what you're gonna do," he said racing to the top end of the room. "You're gonna walk down the middle, all the way to the end desk, pivot once, then return back up on your right side—clearing the centre for the girl after you," he said, walking through the steps to show them exactly how he wanted them to walk.

"Let's rock on guys!" Pandy air punched, which received a few laughs from the models—Jonty included.

She was the daughter of a rockstar all right.

"Jonty, play the music from the start… Heather, when I raise my hand, send the first girl. When she's just about approaching us, send the next," Dom commanded.

Model after model, they walked up and down the room as he had choreographed, followed by all the models walking down two-by-two for the finale. Although there was no time for a proper fitting session (what with the show being tomorrow and all), Dom had scribbled down some notes for Heather and JoJo with minor alterations that needed to be pinned so they could work on them overnight.

"Girls, take a look at the alterations needed on these looks and quickly pin them up… Pandy, what time can we be at the venue for a dressed walk-through?"

"Well, the show is at midday… We can be in there from early morning, but we have to clear when people are set to arrive… I'd say up to eleven?"

"Right then… Jonty, print out some slips with the venue address and call time for eight a.m tomorrow… Okay ladies," Dom said turning to the models. "If you need to dash, then let us know and we'll pin you first, otherwise we'll appreciate you sticking around for a little while longer… Jonty will provide you with the call time and venue address, but we'll email your agency the details later this afternoon too."

Dom and Pandy assessed the first girl that Heather had pinned up, before passing her to JoJo, who helped them undress and hung up their look with their name on the hanger. Looking at the pinning, Dom felt even more frustrated that they didn't have enough time for a proper fitting. He had to overlook some errors, that he knew wouldn't be visible on the runway, but he still knew some pieces weren't up to his high standard.

Being surrounded by luxurious clothing in Palazzo for years, he had a well-honed eye for detail—but he shrugged it off and tried his best to keep the alterations to a minimum. He had already created enough work for them as it was.

**

With the models finally gone, the team were spent. Sat on the floor next to heaped rails with clothes slumped over, and shoes scattered all around. Even though they were exhausted from the day's antics, there was still so much to be done. The collection had to be rehung and placed in garment bags with a corresponding model's name on the front, not to mention the alterations that had to be completed. All they could do was sit there picking at the left-over platters to help restore their energy, while Pandy handed out freshly made tea in mismatched mugs. Hot tea was just what they needed right now, way better than any alcoholic drink. As they drank the last dregs, they knew it was time to get back into action but they savoured the last few drops. As the afternoon went on, they grew more tired, but they had a sudden burst of excitement to stoke their enthusiasm.

"This time tomorrow, the show would have been a success and we'll be celebrating!" Pandora predicted.

"This time tomorrow, we'll be doing the exact same thing and getting these samples back here," Jonty said through puffs of smoke, pessimistic as ever.

"Right, come on guys… Let's get these looks back on hangers and in garment bags, ready for tomorrow," Pandora said, leading by example; getting up off the floor. "And stop smoking around my collection—I don't want them reeking of smoke down the runway! Make yourself useful and print out the images for the look-book or something…"

Jonty did as he was told and they all worked late into the night, tidying up and making sure all the samples were in order, bagged, and correctly named. There were a few hems that needed to be finished, which Heather and Pandy had made a start on, while Dom looked back through the images with Jonty.

Dom was impressed with how smoothly the day had gone, considering the mountain of work they had achieved. Utterly shattered, with aching shoulders from being hunched over sewing machines and tables all day, he did his best to keep the momentum going by working with Jonty on making a file of all the images in exit order, ready to print for the showroom.

He printed a few copies for the team as a reference for show day, checking to see what the time was simultaneous, he looked around the room to see the team in full flow. Pandy and JoJo were making sure all the garment bags had the correct model's name on once more, Heather was hand sewing blind hems, and Jonty paired up the left and right's of shoes—ready to be boxed up.

Dom could see they were all starting to flag as simple tasks took longer to complete and the room got even more silent by the minute (he wasn't the only one who ached all over). The room was now starting to turn into nervous energy, he could sense it in the air.

"Did you definitely pack the shoes Jonty?" Pandora asked for the third time.

"*Yes*, woman! Go check for yourself if you don't trust me!"

"What about the rest of the alterations? I don't think I'll be able to complete them in time," Heather panicked.

"Okay, guys… Let's call it a day—Urgggh!" Dom moaned, stretching his arms out behind his head. "We've done everything we can do for now, and we still have time tomorrow to all chip in with alterations and finishing touches if we get enough rest tonight. Hev, pack up your machine and your sewing box so we can work on the alterations from the location. Let's all meet here again at six a.m… We can help pack the van and Jonty can drive us to Soho for eight."

Things were starting to get serious now. Pandora realised that tomorrow was show day; this was it, make or break time. But one thing she was sure of, she was grateful that Dom had turned up when she needed him the most. Things could have been so different if he hadn't come back to London; he was her fashion angel and he had arrived at the perfect timing. She completely trusted him and with that thought fresh in her mind, she wiped all the doubt away from her mind and started to close down the studio.

"Come on guys, let's all go home… Dom, you're staying with me, right?" she said with a look that told him he had no other choice—even though he had no intentions of schlepping all the way back to West London anyway.

***

Pandora lived nearby, in Old Street. Her apartment building was very plush and way overpriced for such a built-up area, and it was virtually situated on a heavily trafficked roundabout. But it was convenient to get to the studio, and of course, financed by dad. Dom expected nothing less as he looked around; he could see it was very much indeed the party palace. It was situated high up on the twentieth floor and the main living space was dominated by a large white leather sofa and an impressive glass coffee table with a large disco ball hanging above (he could only imagine the parties that went down in here). Pandy dumped her handbag and headed to the kitchen, pulling a bottle of wine from the fridge. "Nightcap?" she offered, already pouring two glasses; it was an order more than an offer.

Dom perched himself at the bar in her open-plan kitchen and accepted the glass, filled well past the normal measure. 'One glass to de-stress won't hurt,' he told himself.

"What a day!" Pandy said, before raising her glass to clink Dom's. "Thanks for everything… I just don't know where all your knowledge comes from! I've been doing this for a while; you would think that I would've learnt all this by now! God only knows I've made enough mistakes to learn from… I'm just used to people telling me: 'You're Rod Simmons' daughter! Of course, you'll be successful.' Then, not *really* wanting to help me, because they assume my success is a given and they're just looking for an easy ride… In some ways, it's a fucking burden! Every season I see new talent coming out of these art schools and doing better than me—I'm not saying I'm not grateful that I can afford to do what I want—I just want to be successful too… Do you know what I mean?"

Dom *did* know what she meant. In a way, they were quite similar; he also just wanted to be successful and recognised. And she was right, he was knowledgable, talented, and worthy of being respected in the industry also, and he felt that to be true more than ever. Part of that was down to Pandy, without her failing brand he wouldn't have a role to step in and step up to.

"Did you know, before you came along, I told myself that this would be my last shot?" she continued through sips of wine. "There's only so much rejection one can take at the end of the day, but this time it feels different… Organised, edited, slick!"

'That's because it is,' Dom thought to himself. However it wasn't only about proving a point to himself, it was about helping an old friend realise a dream—and helping friends with their dreams was something he did well. Plus, if Pandy's show did well, it would ultimately seal his future with her at P.S.L and giving his life meaning—and a reason to stay in London.

Sat there in the kitchen, drinking their last drops of wine, this moment reminded him of how he and Chloe would sit and drink together, reassuring each other about the future and dreaming about where it will take them.

"Shall we have another glass?" Pandy said, hopping off her stool; already half-way to the fridge.

She looked back and saw Dom wince as he checked his phone, it was now Midnight and waking up with a hangover was not an option. "Actually, let's go to bed… There'll be plenty to celebrate tomorrow," she said, reading his expression.

"Talking of… Where is the after-party?" he said, realising that there hadn't been any mention of one, and that was strange coming from the party Queen of London.

"*Bitch*, three days ago I was struggling to put a fucking collection together… Do you really think I was capable of planning a party as well?"

And with that said, they called it a night. After brushing their teeth and cleansing their faces in tandem by the bathroom sink, they both tucked up in Pandora's—as comfortable as a hotel's—bed. Praying for perfect skin when he woke, he was happy to settle down for a good night's sleep after a long day, knowing that tomorrow would be just as much hard work—but much fun too.

As his mind slowed down and his breathing deepened, he closed his eyes and tried to shut down, still running through everything he needed to do for the show in his mind. His thoughts whirled and whirled with the endless list of things to complete, with no time left at all, until it felt like the room was spinning—and that was with only one glass of wine.

He reassured himself that he was just excited, and knew exactly what he needed to do to get through it all—everything was under control. 'If this was how I feel, then how must Pandy be feeling?' he asked himself. And then, out of nowhere, he remembered that tomorrow wasn't just Pandy's show day—it was also Jason's exhibition opening!

Dom had been so frantically busy that this important piece of information had completely escaped him. The conversation with Chloe came flooding back, the emails all came back into his mental inbox, the apologies and the pleading to see him again—the invitation! Dom could feel tears coming to his eyes as he lay there, trying not to make any movements that would stir Pandy. He sniffled back tears in one snort, which made her turn over to face him.

"*Are you sleeping?* What if tomorrow doesn't go so well?" she whispered.

He didn't answer; he just laid there, pretending to be asleep and took the opportunity to shift position. He could feel Pandy roll back over to sleep on her side of the bed, while he tightened his eyes shut, forcing himself to sleep. But all he could do was think about Jason and feel sorry for himself.

Why was it that his friends seemed to be able to have it all, but not him? Was he a victim of his own actions, or was it simply down to luck? If the latter was the case then he couldn't help but feel cursed, like everything he did would only be for the benefit others.

6

"*F*uck, *Fuck, Fuck!*" Pandy shouted, reaching for the alarm; waking Dom up in the process. It was half-past five in the morning already; they had to be back at the studio in half an hour, load the van and get to the venue for eight. Not a massive problem, since she had the luxury of living just minutes away, but she still had to shower and plan her outfit for the show.

Scrambling out of bed, she stripped off and stepped into her en-suite shower. Dom took his cue and reluctantly got out of bed too (not having had the best night's sleep himself), but they had a rather exciting day ahead, and with that he skipped his way to the apartment's main bathroom, sliding across the shiny wooden floors.

Naturally, he managed to get washed, dressed, and cologned before Pandora (she had only just pulled up her knickers and starting to fasten her bra by then). And she still had the task of choosing an outfit for her appearance at the show, by which time it was already well past their call time. "Right, Dom… Help me! What the *fuck* am *I* going to wear?"

"Calm down," he said, taking charge yet again. If he allowed her to, she would spiral into a panicked stupor—and outfit trauma wasn't a scratch on what the rest of day was sure to serve up. "Chuck on something comfortable and let's just get to the studio… We'll do what we have to do and then you can come back here and get ready… I'll order a cab."

That sounded like the best plan right now, so she bungled her hair into her classic up-do with a bandana, and applied a quick red lip. 'That will have to do,' she told herself and grabbed her handbag of useless things, ready to leave the apartment. As they pulled up outside the studio, the rest of the gang were punctually sat waiting outside for them on the curb. "Oh, here she comes!"

Jonty teased through final puffs of his cigarette, before chucking the butt into the gutter.

"Sorry guys!" Pandy said, climbing out of the Toyota Prius, embarrassed by her own lateness as she clambered to find the studio keys in the depths of her handbag.

Once inside, the studio was a tip! Leftover sandwich platters were scattered about the place, the floor was covered with fluff and loose thread ends, and discarded garment bags lay there like unused body bags—waiting for someone's corpse to fill them. Dom didn't recall it looking this bad when they left, but it didn't matter now, they needed to crack on (otherwise it would be his corpse in the bag).

"Right, let's go through the rails and make sure we have every look in each of garment bags just to be safe! Then, we'll load the van—don't forget the box of shoes and beret's!" Dom reminded them; the last thing they needed was to leave something behind in the panic.

"I've packed a sewing machine for alterations… Somewhere," Heather confirmed, looking for it in the wall of packed boxes.

"Bring the steamer!" Pandy randomly shouted.

Jonty separated himself from the madness and made sure that copies of the look-book were in his bag, ready to hand out when they got there so they all knew the running order. It was always the tiny details that were usually forgotten, not huge dresses or equipment like steamers. More importantly, he saved the show's music to a USB stick and placed it inside his tobacco tin, which was sure to be with him at all times.

Meanwhile, Dominic was once again taking control of the situation, making sure everybody had a job. Heather was assigned to checking inside each of the garment bags to make sure every piece was present, while Dom ticked it off on one of Jonty's print-outs. It was then handed to Pandora, who placed it on the spare rail in the running order of the show—ready to be taken down to the van by JoJo.

"Right Pandy, get your self back home and dressed for the show… Full make-up please!" Dom ordered. Pandy looked at him, grateful and trusting that he would take care of everything once they got to the venue. "Be quick and get yourself in a cab and into Soho by nine, the latest!" he said, sending her on her way while he locked up the studio. Besides, it was probably best to have her out the way for as long as possible, so he could organise everything the way he had envisioned it. Then she could turn up and enjoy experiencing her show as much as possible and with little to worry about. "Us lot—in the back of the van—now!"

It was coming up to half-past seven, and with the show due to start at midday, they were really starting to push for time if they were to get a rehearsal in. Dresses still needed to be steamed, hems needed to be taken up—and that wasn't including the unknown. There was bound to be a popped button or a jammed zip, or some other kind of fashion show failure. Luckily, Dom had considered everything and packed spare buttons and safety pins in the event of a catastrophe.

Jonty was like a demon behind the wheel, taking every corner sharply and scraping through amber lights in precision timing— he even cursed at other drivers. "I've got right of way you *wanker!* Are you blind?" he boomed out of the wound down window.

It was a side Dom hadn't seen of him, this builder-like white-van driving man. Something Jonty had instilled in his DNA, being born and bred a Northerner. They even passed Pandora running back to her apartment as they went around the Old Street round-about, clutching her breasts and handbag in a flurry (which Dom and Jonty laughed at). But the traffic into Holborn was as stubborn as ever, and there wasn't much they could do about it except sit and wait—which was frustrating.

Heather and JoJo were smuggled in the back of the van with the collection, gasping for air. "Are we nearly there yet?" Heather annoyingly asked. With no windows in the back, they had no idea of where they were, or how far they still had to drive.

"Not long now guys," Dom said through the cage back panel.

"The second I am out of this van, I am getting a skinny cap-puccino!" Heather said, in a mood. "With full-fat milk!" That was quite a statement for a supposed vegan, causing JoJo to gasp. With that said, it was clear that things *really* were starting to raise hairs now; nerves were running high and stress levels were reaching, but not quite to the maximum (that was still on the menu for brunch).

"The minute *you* get out of this van, I am sending you to get us *all* cappuccino's with full-fat milk—triple shot!" Dom joked (although, he wasn't joking).

Finally out of traffic, Jonty was back to mastering the gear stick and sped down Oxford Street as fast as lawfully allowed, before turning off into Soho—which was equally as unbearable with morning deliveries and cut-through traffic all trying to make a short cut. Manoeuvring a van down busy a narrow street was quite a skill, and Dom was relieved that Jonty knew what he was doing—relieved to be pulling up outside the NCP car park on Brewer Street.

"Right—we're finally here gang!" Dom announced.

In fact, they all sighed a breath of relief, but not for long—the day was only just beginning.

*

The British Fashion Council had completely transformed the multi-storey car park into London's fashion destination. They had selected a group of young designers to sponsor and show their collection at the official LFW show —pandora was one of them. It was rather a big deal for an emerging designer, not only did they have the most central venue, but models, tech crew and all the backstage things—like hair and make-up—were all taken care of.

The other thing it guaranteed was press! Anyone who was someone in fashion would be present from around the world as they made their way through the Fashion Week calendar; New York, London, Milan, and Paris. That's if they even bothered stopping at London and not bypassing it for the more commercial brands in Milan and Paris. London Fashion Week had waned somewhat, losing its most talked-about designers to Paris and desperately needing someone new on the scene to rave about.

Security guards were situated at the gates outside, allowing early entry for special deliveries only, with eager fashionistas hanging around for the morning shows. In the meantime, they made use of the postered walls and overdressed outfits to capture content for their social media (some even came with their own photographers). Dom wound down the passenger window as they approached the barrier. "Hi, We're Pandora Simmons London—showing at noon."

"Yep, got you down… Park in one of the empty bays on the ground floor and see my colleagues at the security desk… They will give you your passes for the day."

Once they were parked up, they signed in and received an official backstage lanyard which had the Fashion Week logo and their brand name. Dom made sure to take Pandora's so he could give it to her later (not that she needed it). They would most likely let her in anyway and photographers would surely stop her to take her photograph, which would warrant instant entry—pass or no pass. "Right, everyone… Lets unpack and get all our stuff up to the backstage area. Then you are on the hunt for coffee!" Dom said, talking to Heather.

Jonty and JoJo carted in the rails while Dom went back and forth to the van for the boxes of accessories. Once Heather had finished setting up her sewing station and plugged the steamer into the first outlet she could find, she took on the mission of getting everyone a well-earned cup of coffee. The others wasted no time in steaming the collection, ready for showtime.

Dom introduced himself to the hair and make-up stylists, making sure they had received Pandora's brief and were well prepared. They nodded as they listened to his simple request for a bold red lip and edgy eighties blusher, on a blank skin of foundation with a smokey eye á la 'Addicted To Love.' Having only just explained the vision to them, Dom's phone buzzed—it was Pandy. "I'm here… Where am I going?" she said, pulling up outside in her cab.

"Stay there! I have your pass… I'm coming to get you!" Dom shrieked, hanging up instantaneously.

Running through the backstage car park area and down ramps, he got back outside by the security barrier as quickly ah he could—dodging lighting technicians and backstage crew. Looking down Brewer Street in search of her, she was, of course, being snapped by photographers. She was wearing a navy blue shirt dress that was belted at the waist and showed plenty of cleavage. Her flame-red hair was neatly back into her classic up-do and bandana style, finished off with her red lipstick, of course. Her signature style was easy to spot in a crowd, even without a gathering of paparazzi buzzing around her.

"Pandy! You made it—and you look fantastic!" Dom said, handing her a lanyard. "Come on… We've set everything up and have started prep, and I have had a chat with the hair and make-up team." Pandora started to make her way through the main guest entrance before Dom stopped her. "No babe, we're going through the security entrance… You're not here to see your mates and drink Prosecco!"

Which reminded him, with all the last-minute antics this week, he hadn't been able to give her *the* pep talk. Flashing their passes at the barrier and briskly walking through the car park, he started to give her a breakdown of exactly how things were going to run.

"After the show, press will be wanting to speak to you back-stage… Give as many interviews as possible, then we'll go out to the front and put you in a car, in case we can get you papped some more. Remember these things: 'I feel this show is my best collec-tion yet and the true start of P.S.L… It's taken me a few collections to really define the P.S.L style, which is what you saw today, and will see more of in the future… This collection is for the modern woman; any age, any background, personality or belief,' got it?" Dom reeled off, mimicking her perfectly.

"Modern woman… The P.S.L style defined… The start of things to come," she muttered back to him; trying to remember it all, feeling somewhat ambushed.

Running up to level one and making their way through fake walls and set flats, they reached the backstage area where they had set up camp. Heather had returned with coffee and the team were pleased to see Pandora had made it. It was now half-past eight and only a handful of models and arrived for hair and make-up.

"Where the *fuck* are they?" Dom yelled.

"It's okay babe, some are modelling for the other designers, remember? I'm sure the rest have probably been stopped at the security barrier… I mean, that's the line for every fashionista to try and get in, isn't it? Hi, I'm one of the models," Pandy joked. For once it was her that was calm and Dom who was on edge.

"I'm going down to look… You guys carry on without me," Dom said before leaving in a rush, grabbing his coffee from the cardboard tray, still in Heather's hands.

"Didn't get me one by any chance?" Pandy said, taking a cup anyway. She had been right, most of the models had been stopped at security as no one had thought to give them a register of who they were expecting. Thank goodness Dom had gone down to get them, otherwise, they would be walking out with lank hair and not an inch of foundation. Once he got them in and backstage, he lined them up with hair and make-up to get ready for rehearsal.

Pandora was checking in with the team on how she wanted simple flat-back ponytails—as every girl was wearing a beret—making sure they emulated her red lipstick. Dom was impressed with how calm and together she was, it seemed like this part of the process was where she was the most relaxed, which gave him room to fluster. Backstage was now starting to heat up, what with the steamer on full blow and all the extra body heat.

Models sat around not knowing what to do with themselves except look at their phones while they waited for their hair and make-up to be done. Dom handed out bottles of water, while Heather ploughed on with alterations. Pandy and JoJo started to match up each model with their runway look but hadn't started to dress them yet. With just over an hour before the show, they didn't want the looks getting creased and sweaty.

"Can I have Pandora Simmons please?" a young girl with a headset called out.

Dom looked up and rushed over to her, eager and nervous to know what she needed from them. "Hi, I'm from P.S.L."

"Perfect—the guys at sound desk need your music please."

His face suddenly sank and fell white in a flash. How could he forget the music? Dominic Fraser, the man who apparently knew it all (and was so well organised), had forgotten the *fucking* music! Jonty could see the panic on Dom's face and went over to see what the problem was.

"Music? We need your track for the show?" the crew girl impatiently pressed.

Reaching for his shirt pocket, Jonty took out his tobacco tin—this time not for a roll-up. He opened it up and to Dom's surprise pulled out a black USB stick. "It's the only file on there, it shouldn't be too hard for your sound guys to find," Jonty quipped before proceeding to roll his first cigarette since they had got there.

Dom had never felt so relieved and gave him a smile. A smile which confirmed he had indeed earned a smoke.

"The stage will be clear in ten minutes, so you have time for a quick walk-through… After that, guests will be allowed to enter the show space," she said before rushing off with the music, now in hand.

"Play it nice and loud… The louder the better, okay?" Dom ordered. "Jonty! Wait up!"

He chased after him and grabbed Jonty's shoulder to halt him. "Roll one of those for me would you?"

******

Back inside, things had escalated very quickly. Models had been painted with strong red lips, their hair brushed and scraped back into ponytails (for those that had long enough hair), while others had sleek gelled bobs. "Right, I think it's time we started the run-through," Dom said to Pandy, who was busy inspecting each girl's face.

Jonty started to hand out the shoes to the models and got them lined up backstage while Pandy made her way to the end of the front row. Heather and JoJo made sure all the models were accounted for and in line, in their order of exit.

"Okay, listen up!" Dom said, his voice raised. "It's time for a walk-through so you girls know where and how you are walking… Remember, the music is energetic so we want nineties power walking—think strong supermodel—give it some shoulder on your final pose, if you want… You're exiting on your right-hand side, walking down the centre of the runway and back up on your left side to exit. A few of you have outfit changes, so see Heather and JoJo who will assist you… Once the last look has come back, you will all walk again in pairs—like we practiced yesterday—simple."

Dom grabbed the backstage crew girl and asked her to signal to the tech desk that they were now ready to go. The lighting engineer faded the lights down on the runway as she spoke quietly into her headset. "Tell them two bars of eight on the music, then lights up on the first model," he further requested.

Sat outside in the front row alone, Pandy was starting to feel nervous. Although she knew Dom would be whipping them into shape, it dawned on her that they really were underprepared—half an hour wasn't enough time to rehearse. Even though her shows were usually 'organic,' this time she was showing on a Fashion Council funded runway, which meant it had to look polished. People had known her to be arty and wacky, but now was the time to show P.S.L in a new light—a professional and serious one.

With the first few bars of music played, Dom tapped the shoulder of the debut girl to walk out down the runway. It was a simple set up: two flats at the front hid the backstage happenings with a white wall in-between them, which had 'Pandora Simmons London' projected on to it. The runway itself was also a simple affair: a light grey sheath of linoleum flooring evened out the tarmac surface, with a scaffold light rig above it all.

Dom watched closely on the small monitor for her to reach the half-way point, before sending the next out, then repeating it until one-by-one, they had returned backstage like homing pigeons. With all the girls back in line and now in pairs, he asked the crew girl to dip the lights for a moment, and then back up for the final walk-out.

"Okay, go-go-go! Everyone, one more time, and clapping please," he ordered.

Once the last two girls were about to turn off the catwalk and back home, he burst out onto the runway. "And this is where you take your bow, Pandy!" he shouted, pretending to be her.

Pandy stood up and clapped, turning back to the sound desk with both thumbs up. The rehearsal ran slightly over time, but it was always the case in fashion to be late, and no one ever questioned it. No doubt the show wouldn't start on time either, but it was crucial to not keep the big fashion names waiting and risk a bad review, setting their schedules back for the next show (most likely for a designer far more important and showing half-way across town).

Knowing that time was tight, Pandy sprinted up the runway to get backstage again. "Guys, you looked so fierce out there! Do exactly that again for the actual show please!"

"Come on, let's get these girls dressed and ready," Dom said, reminding her that there was still a lot off work to be done before they celebrated.

Jonty and JoJo began the task of assigning each girl to her look and helping them get dressed, while Heather was on hand with her pincushion—ready to hand sew and pin last-minute adjustments. Pandy and Dom also helped with dressing models, making sure each one had accessories and a beret that matched their look. Hair and make-up also returned with cans of hairspray as they were getting dressed, making sure they were coiffed to perfection blotted.

Outside the venue, guests had started to turn up and take their seats already. Time was edging nearer to the crucial moment and everyone knew it—things started to get even more manic. Heather was stressing out at her sewing machine, trying to reinforce seams and fix alterations in place. JoJo made sure each model had all the pieces to their look, while Jonty got them ready for a final line-up—ready to be assessed by Dom and Pandy. As Pandora re-arranged the first look on the model, Dom could see her hands were shaking.

"Relax, this is it… There's nothing we can change now, so even if it does all go tits-up, there's nothing we can do about it except enjoy the moment and learn from it for next season."

She took a deep breath and nodded; she knew he was right but she wanted this to work out so much. And with that advice, she carried on perfecting the looks on each model, pulling out shirts and tying belts over the top; pulling blouses off one shoulder and lifting trouser waists higher. Dresses got the same treatment, with some needing more temporary pinning to nip in the waistline. These dresses were the highlight of the show and they needed to fit perfectly. The air backstage was thick as the hair stylist's blow dryers had been on full blast, with the lack of air conditioning. Through the smog of hairspray, the crew girl came over to give the final call.

Fifteen minutes to go.

"Okay ladies, let's get you in exit order, please!" Dom shouted.

Pandy double-checked each model in line while make-up artists touched up lipsticks and blotted foreheads once more. But the quarter flew by and from the side wings, Pandy could see the front row was starting to fill up. The 'frow' was always the last to be seated, and no show started until the fashion critic Lou Banks and the editor of British Vanguard were in place. They were the best of friends and Lou's opinion was very important, he pretty much influenced what Vanguard printed and shot—they had just made it to their seats.

"Pandy!" Dom called, snapping his fingers to get her attention. "Come on… Let's go; we've got five minutes until lights down."

The feeling backstage had now suddenly calmed, with nothing else to do except show the collection, for real. They walked the line of girls once more as they made their way to the monitor where the crew member was waiting for them to start the show. "Okay, everyone is seated now so we are ready for lights down when you are," she said.

"Right girls, have fun, plenty of attitude, feel your looks, feel the runway!" Dom instructed one last time; just in case they needed reminding.

Pandy was on edge with excitement and proudly looked on at her models, dressed in her latest collection which very nearly didn't see the light of day. This was it!

"Are we ready now?" The crew girl said.

Pandora gave her the nod. Dom walked the first model to the edge of the exit wing, as he waited for the lights to go down. The crew member counted down into her headset: "Cue music in five, four, three, two, one."

And with that order, the lights dipped and Dom tapped the back of the first model to step out into darkness. The music started, the lights came up, and off she went down the runway in the first look of the show: a pinstripe blazer with matching long wide-leg trousers, shown with a neon yellow bra underneath. A black beret with a spattering of neon yellow paint and clashing leopard gloves finished the look with a touch of edgy London style.

Dom waited by the monitor—ready to cue the next girl—and model after model they were sent down the runway in precision timing (which was an achievement given the lack of rehearsal). Pandy watched the show on the small screen, witnessing how the show was looking from the front of house.

It seemed unreal to her that this was her collection, her show. It was as if she was completely in a daze, not realising that it was actually all happening. And just like Dom had said, there was nothing else they could have done, the verdict of the show was already being decided by the critics.

7

The models had returned from their final group walk to applause from the audience; the show had gone down well and without a hitch. Each girl had modelled her look with sex and style, showing everyone that P.S.L's spring/summer collection was a turning point for the brand.

"Well, go on then!" Dom said, pushing Pandy out onto the runway.

She clasped her hands to her face in shyness as she stepped out and gave a quick bow, before leaving with a single wave to the audience. "We did it! We actually did it!" she said to Dom, grabbing him for a hug.

"Okay, remember what I told you?" Dom said, noticing that journalists had already begun to seep backstage.

Lou Banks was one of them, with British Vanguard's editor on his arm, which warranted everyone else to wait until they were finished speaking to her. "Darling, that was fabulous! Everybody is talking about that *gorgeous* bright yellow dress on that *amazing* model—what's her name?" he said, grabbing her shoulders for a double-sided fashion kiss.

"Oh, thanks—that's erm…" Pandy looked to Dom for help, she didn't know any of the models' names, let alone what they were wearing; adrenaline was running high and she didn't even know her own name at this very moment.

"Carly Wattmore," Dom said.

"Well, Carly Wattmore is a *star*, darling!" Lou said, eyeing Dom, who he had never encountered before at a Pandora Simmons show.

Lou was in his fifties, a cuddly-looking man with a friendly face (but a cutting opinion when it came to critiquing a collection), and had both discovered and destroyed careers with his blunt—and sometimes scathing—reviews. He also had the power to make a designer (or a model) an international name with just a few words in his column. He had seen decades of fashion and could spot exactly what it was that made a designer special, and the industry hung on to every word he printed.

They all relied on him to tell them what was 'hot' next season, even the high street stores who reincarnated designer originals into mass-produced knock-off's, just moments after his Fashion Week reviews were out. And hearing good feedback coming from him was the seal of approval Pandy was hoping for, which prompted the editor of British Vanguard to echo his thoughts with a nod and a smile, and an air kiss on either cheek to match.

"We love, love, loved the dresses! As well as the pop of colour and the leopard print," he continued.

"Well, thank you!" Pandora said, hardly believing he was complimenting the same leopard fabric he had trashed just months before. "This season we really wanted to capture the true essence of P.S.L, and after the past few collections, I feel like we've finally discovered the DNA of the brand… I wanted to create an instantly recognisable signature style, something very true to myself—as well all the women out there looking for daring clothes to empower them. I want them to feel like P.S.L is their new armour, they can conquer anything they want to in my clothes. Whether she's sexy, smart, casual, elegant—this collection has all of that with a little bit of rebellious attitude thrown in."

"And what was it that made you finally find your direction?" Lou pressed.

"Well, I Just…" Pandy started, before taking a moment to think about it.

What was it that had led her to create this collection? The truth was, that while she had indeed designed it, she hadn't wrapped it up into a finished product on her own—that was Dom's doing. He had come along and made sense of it all, helping her see how her clothes could be understood by the industry.

"Well, to be honest with you, I couldn't have done all of this without my friend, Dominic Fraser."

"And who is this Dominic Fraser?" Lou said, eager to know more.

Pandora looked behind her, catching Dom's eye with a wink. He had given her a successful show and she was about to give him the moment of recognition he deserved in return. "This is Dom, we met at the London College of Fashion… He's been working in New York for Palazzo, and more recently for his friend, Chloe Ravens."

Lou held out his smartphone to record this nugget of information (it would be a great titbit to include in his review), and of course, being the primo fashion critic in the industry and fresh from NY Fashion Week, he had witnessed Chloe's dalliance with Gianni Palazzo on the red carpet for himself. "So, what exactly is your role with Pandora Simmons London, Dominic?"

'Good point, what is my role at P.S.L?' he wondered.

"Dom is our new brand director… He's collaborated with me on this collection and helped me edit down all my ideas into a collection that I'm very proud to present. Sometimes, I have a lot going on in my head and it needs someone who knows me well to tie everything up and tell me when to stop… He's the perfect person to do that because we've been friends for many years, but also we have had that distance where he has been working in New York, so it feels like I have a friend who I can trust, but also someone with a fresh set of eyes and who isn't going to bullshit me at the same time."

Dom was just as surprised as Lou was to hear of his new appointment, but he was extremely pleased at the same time—he had done it! Finally, he had landed a role that would make people stand up and take notice of him.

"Congratulations, Dominic! We can't wait to see how you propel the brand forward in the future—and congratulations both of you on a fantastic collection," Lou said, before kissing them once again and escorting Vanguard's editor to the next show in town.

Dominic was astounded and grabbed Pandora by her shoulders.

"Are you sure?"

"Of course! Anyway, bit late to go back on it now… You can count on Lou to stick that in his review."

But it was only what he deserved; she couldn't have done this without him, and now she had felt what success felt like, she didn't ever want to do it without him from here on—she needed him. Pandora was being called for more interviews, to which Dom urged her to give and say exactly the same as what she had just said. In the meantime, he helped the rest of the gang to undress the models and hang all the pieces back in their garment bags, ready to drive back to the studio.

Some model's had other shows that they were walking in and needed to leave for, so quickly undressed and left their looks slung over chairs and rails—some on the floor even. Heather and JoJo did their best to gather everything up, while Jonty unplugged the sewing machine and steamer from the mains. On top of the clear up, another designer was coming in to set up for their show later that afternoon, which wasn't helpful. Dom instructed everyone to get everything packed up and out to the van so they could escape immediately. The after-show glory was a cause for celebration, not a major clean up operation.

Typically, once the packing up had been more or less completed, Pandy returned from giving her interviews. "Right, what's the plan?" she said, buzzing with excitement—now ready to party.

"Drive all of this back to the studio, and then celebrate I guess?" Dom said.

"Sounds like a plan! Let's get all this stuff back home, then we can quickly refresh at my flat and get ready to go out."

Clearing up the last few bits (shoes, berets, and gloves), Dom couldn't help but feel he was forgetting something important. The day had gone well, even better than he could have planned it, but in the back of his mind, something important was still being neglected. He pulled out his phone to check his messages, knowing that he had covered everything and he hadn't forgotten anything important, but the first saved email in his inbox said otherwise. Of course, today wasn't only P.S.L's fashion show, it was the opening for Jason's exhibition at the South Bank Gallery.

He had been so rushed, excited and busy with the show, that he hadn't a second to even think of Jason. But now everything was over, his stomach flipped from excitement to confusion. His heart told him he should go and see Jason while he was still in London, but his head told him to leave it. Jason was the past and Pandora was the future, a future that Jason couldn't offer and something that he had worked hard to get for himself.

Heather and JoJo loaded themselves into the back of the van with the collection as Jonty shut them into darkness with a slam of the doors. "Come on Dom, get in… There's room up front," Pandora called, her head stuck out of the passenger window.

Jonty walked around the van and got into the driver's seat, wasting no time to start up the engine to make a quick escape out of the car park.

"You know what… There's something I've gotta take care of while I'm in town," Dom said.

"Like what? Can't it wait another day? Come on—*get in!*" Pandy said, brushing him off. "We've got some drinking to do!"

It was difficult to explain to her what was so important that he had to dash off for, having not mentioned a single word about Jason, he couldn't exactly tell her he was popping by to see an art show—not on her big day. But it seemed right that he at least showed up to see Jason in person. Maybe then he would get some closure on this whole doomed romance; maybe then he would see him in a different light and not feel the same, but more to the point—Dom wasn't sure if he could live with himself afterwards if he didn't.

"I need to go back home and change into something for going out in… It would be silly of me to come all this way into town and not pop home for a quick change… I mean, I can't go out in the same clothes I've been slogging around in all day!" he said, which was also very true.

Pandora couldn't argue with that, she would never have shown up looking a hot mess for her show, and it was only fair that she let him have a moment after he had let her have a costume change.

"Okay then," Pandy said rolling her eyes. "Meet back at mine... And don't be long!"

*

Jason had been working all day at the gallery, finalising the display of pieces he had created especially for the 'London Calling' exhibition—proudly framing the featured painting of supermodel Kate in the centre. He too was having an exciting day, but something was missing that would make it even more special. That something was a someone—Dominic.

Jason knew he hadn't exactly left things how he had hoped, after all, he had expected Dom to be waiting for him to return back in New York. That, however, was not the case and Jason kicked himself for it; he should have known that Dom wasn't the kind of guy to sit around and wait for a man to rescue him.

Dominic was not only handsome, but he was also intelligent, driven, and just as talented as Jason—which was what was so special about him. When Jason had discsovered that he had left for London, it all seemed rather serendipitous. But of course, it was, they had met in New York and now they were to meet again in another big city—this time to make up.

Not wanting to smell like body odour in front of this evening's guests, Jason headed back to his hotel—he also wanted to look his best in case Dom showed up. Even though this was his last day in London, and Dom hadn't replied to any of his messages, Jason still had hope of seeing him once more. Checking his email one last time for a reply, he threw his phone back down on the bed, unsurprised that there was nothing but junk mail, before heading to the shower.

**

After filling his mother in with how well the show went (and more importantly that he was now the brand director), Dom showered and got dressed—ready to head back out. He looked in the mirror, happy with how he had brushed up; he was glad he came back home to freshen up. His outfit was perfect for meeting Pandy and the gang for celebrations later—as well as for 'bumping' into Jason. It was smart but casual enough to seem like he hadn't over thought it. Just a slim pair of black jeans with a white shirt that was unbuttoned at the collar—topped off with a sexy cologne—did the trick. It was all about the finishing touches and a scent trail left more than an impression—it left a memory.

Speaking of memories, as Dom looked in the closet for a jacket to throw over it, Jason's tan leather bomber stuck out, like it was calling him to choose it. He hadn't even looked at it since he wore it last (which nearly made him throw up), but he didn't hesitate to yank the jacket off its hanger in one swoop—it was time to get rid of the elephant in the room.

Heading back into the centre of London on the tube, Dom second-guessed whether he should get off at Southwark or just head straight to Pandora's place. But it was like his body had overridden his mind, as Dom found himself making his way to the Southbank on autopilot—knowing exactly where to get off and which turnings to take once outside the station. His thoughts had moved on and were now occupied with what was he going to say to Jason when he saw him, and how he was going to act. Was he going to fling his arms around him like nothing had happened, or should he act cool and wait for Jason to make the first move?

The Southbank Gallery had the gigantic image of Kate's portrait blown up outside, just like the billboard in Liverpool Street. Although Dom was expecting it this time, it didn't have the same impact, but knowing that Jason would be inside made him apprehensive. The art scene wasn't his crowd and the only person Dom would know was Jason—which made him feel out of place. But he came to the brave decision that he would take a look round inside and leave if he felt uncomfortable and if he happened to 'bump' into Jason, then so be it.

Making his way inside, Dom grabbed a glass of champagne from the waiter at the entrance, quickly taking a large gulp. Alcohol was needed and the sharp, fizzy taste hitting the back of his throat gave him the kick he required. The exhibition was rather large, consisting of a few rooms which were crowded with critics, journalists, trustees of the gallery, the artists themselves and their friends.

Not having anyone there to chat to (other than Jason), Dom stuck to his plan and walked around the exhibition, looking at the pieces on display while nervously checking the corners of his vision for Jason. By now, Dom was on his second glass of champagne, which wasn't helping. 'I thought booze was supposed to loosen you up?' Dom said to himself, still wondering why on Earth he was here, walking around the display from room to room.

As he turned another corner, a familiar face stared back at him. Kate's silk-screened face on top of the Union Jack covered an entire wall—she looked magnificent—and stood alone in front of her was Jason! Dom stopped and immediately stepped back around the corner and into the previous room.

His heart flipped with excitement and pain, in what seemed like a twist of a dagger. Even from just behind, Jason looked as handsome as Dom could remember. He was tall and broad, with shoulder-length blonde, sun-kissed hair that made him stand out from the rest—you could tell he was from California. Wearing a white linen shirt and a black blazer, which he had casually pushed the sleeves up to his elbows, with saggy blue jeans and white grubby sneakers. He dressed typically 'American' but also like an artist, which made Dom smile—but he wasn't ready to confront him just yet.

Instead, he waited and watched from the entrance of the room before it, watching Jason being approached by a group of people. Some looked like they were important gallery or collector folk, pointing to the portrait as they introduced themselves. Was this a good time to walk up and say hi, or had Dom missed his chance?

Minutes passed and Jason hadn't moved an inch. In fact, more and more people gathered around him, making it impossible to see Dom lurking in the background even if he did happen to turn around. One thing was clear, Jason had moved on. He too had made a success of himself, and even though he had bombarded

Dom with messages to see him again, he was just as happy without him. Dom watched on as Jason's admirers all clambered to meet the hot and gorgeous new talent, all the way from L.A. Feeling rather lonely in a room full of people, Dom drained the last drops of his now warm champagne (that tasted more like Prosecco now he had two glasses to decide on it). He had the sudden urge to be surrounded by the people he did know and cared about him—team P.S.L.

Besides, seeing Jason wouldn't change anything that had happened between them, and it certainly wasn't going to change Dominic's mind about anything else. He had something to stay in London for now, and it was far greater than the benefits of any relationship. He had purpose, he had a title in fashion for the very first time in his career, and he wasn't going to give that up for someone who had given up him so he could focus on his own dream of being an international artist. 'I shouldn't be here,' he whispered to himself, turning around to excuse himself, through the party guests that were now starting to fill the rooms.

Jason was too busy talking to some of the gallery trustees, the most important people there to notice anyone else around him. They were excited to add the painting of Kate to the gallery and had big plans for advertising and merchandise, such as postcards and tote bags, which would see Jason's work become even more popular and notable around the world.

"Well, all of that sounds exciting and I'm thrilled my work has a home, here in London," Jason said, with the sudden urge to look around—it was as though he could feel eyes burning into him.

Casually brushing a strand of hair behind his ear in his typical cool fashion, Jason politely changed his footing to change position without rudely cutting off the conversation by turning his back completely. And for a split second, he swore he had just seen the back of Dominic wearing his leather jacket—a ghost. Just like an apparition from their first date back in New York, when Jason took him to see the Kate portrait as it hung on display for sale.

Jason didn't know what to do—was it possible that Dom *was* here? The gallery was now dense with guests, and he didn't catch where this ghostly figure had disappeared to—it was as if he had vanished into the walls. But there was a possibility that Dom was here, a niggling feeling in his mind, and he needed to get out of this bubble of people that had surrounded and was holding him hostage.

"Sorry… Do excuse me—I'll be right back," Jason said, taking his chance for a breather and to investigate if he was right, or whether it was just wishful thinking.

But by now, Dom had already reached the foyer—but before he left the gallery for good, he paused. He remembered why he had worn Jason's jacket. It was time to give it back to him, just as he promised he would, back in New York in their last moments together. Jason's leather jacket was sort of on loan, both having made a pact to meet up and reunite with both himself and his jacket. Whilst he couldn't honour one side of the promise, he could at least keep the other.

Dom took the jacket off and placed it on the bench in the foyer before taking a deep breath. As he breathed out slowly, he started to feel lighter—like he had shed a heavy burden—and that feeling told him that he was doing the right thing. And so, he left the gallery, briskly, before anyone could stop him to hand the jacket back, walking out onto the Southbank and heading back towards the tube station.

The evening was burning orange with a warm sunset in the sky, and as he made his way along the river Thames with his black sunglasses on, he couldn't deny that he had his power back. Although he wanted to fall in love again, he also knew that everything between Jason and him was done, and right now he had another party to go to—his own!

Jason scanned the place, looking for who he could have sworn was Dominic. He checked the face of every guy that had his back to him, staring at a painting, in case it was him—until it led him back outside to the foyer. With still no sign of him, Jason dipped his head down in frustration and scraped his hair back off his face, and as he looked back up he spotted the tan leather jacket draped over a wire bench in the ticket hall.

Jason was gutted; Dom had come after all. He rested his hands on his head in disbelief before sitting down next to the jacket, touching it to feel the residue of Dom's body warmth. Realising he couldn't stay outside in the foyer all evening, he hung the jacket over his arm and made his way out to the smoking area. "Hey man, can I borrow a smoke?" Jason said to the first person he saw smoking.

He was wearing a white polo that showed off his arms, with a sweater draped over his shoulders. He had wonderful wavy brown hair, but none of this was obvious to Jason right now—he just wanted a smoke. "Borrow? You can have a cigarette, but I certainly don't want it back when you're done," he answered, passing Jason a single Marlboro Light.

"Thank's—appreciate it."

"No problem… So, you're American," the guy said.

"Ha! Yes, am I that obvious?"

"Well, the tan and sun-bleached hair—not to mention the accent—kinda gave it away… I'm Chris."

"Nice to meet you, I'm—"

"You're Jason Hart… Your work is really cool, I have to say; I was looking at your stuff earlier."

"Well, thank you… I wasn't expecting to be recognised already. This is my first European gig, so I wasn't expecting people to know who I am, or even give a shit ya know?" Jason said, blowing out smoke, away from Chris's face and cocking his leg up on a nearby railing to lean on.

"Oh, I *know* who you are," Chris said, looking him up and down before returning his eyes back on Jason's. "Well, I do now anyway… How long are you here for?"

"Oh, only until tomorrow, then I fly back to L.A."

"Right then," Chris said with a smirk as he stubbed out his cigarette. "Let's make your last night in London one to remember!"

Jason looked at Chris and smiled—now realising he was being hit on. 'What is it with me and English guys?' he asked himself. But he couldn't deny it, Chris was handsome and it was now obvious that he was flirting with him.

"So, what's with the double jacket thing," Chris said, nodding towards the jacket that hung over his arm rather cumbersomely. "Thought it was already freezing in London? We're having a late summer I guess, blame climate change... I mean, I came out just like this! I'm sure I'll regret it later..."

"Oh, this—a friend came by to drop it off for me... Long story. Here, maybe you should have this, ya know—in case it gets cold later... Listen, I gotta hang around a bit longer since I'm headlining this show, but stick around and I'm sure we can escape in an hour or so... And don't leave without giving me that jacket back—it's already been around the block!"

8

Pandy's living room had been transformed into a disco—which wasn't difficult to achieve—with music blaring and the mirror ball spinning above the glass coffee table. 'So *this* is what goes down in here,' Dom said to himself as he entered her apartment.

Pandy was sat in the kitchen with a full glass of Prosecco, while she did her eye make-up in one of those light-up mirrors. The ones that were meant to help you apply your make-up naturally, but actually made you cake on *way* more than what was needed. "Dom, you're here! And looking sexy might I add!" she said, happy to see him finally; she jumped up off the kitchen stool and poured him a glass of fizz. "Here, get that down ya!"

Dom took a large gulp—almost half the flute—which hadn't gone unnoticed by Pandy. She thought it strange of him to do so, but she didn't question it—he had some catching up to do after all. JoJo and Heather were queuing up the tunes in the living room, making the most out of the free drink and disco ball before they headed out. "So, what's the plan?" he said.

Pandy dropped her jaw as she stared into the mirror, edging slippery black liquid liner on her eyelid to create a flick. "Well, I called Shoreditch House and we have a table booked for us to eat in the restaurant, dinner's on me!" she said, fanning her eye so the liner dried faster.

'How predictable,' Dom thought. This lot *lived* in Shoreditch House, it was like there was nowhere else to go. It was, of course, the most convenient for them as they all lived east, and Pandora especially was only a stone's throw away. It was her local and it was a safe bet for a good night out, she was bound to bump into someone she knew there and get free drinks off the back of her successful show. Dom finished his drink and went to pour himself another, but the bottle was empty—so he reached into the wine cooler and popped open a new bottle.

Pandora was just happy to see him willing to loosen up after all of the hard work, but she had the feeling that something else was motivating him. This wasn't happy drinking, this was 'drowning your sorrows' type of drinking, and she knew from experience what that looked like. Usually, it was *her* caning the wine fridge after a bad date or a stressful day at the studio.

She looked around for the others; JoJo and Heather were spinning each other under the mirrorball to Madonna, and Jonty was leaning over the balcony flicking ash onto her neighbour's decking, so this was the perfect opportunity to quiz him privately. "Everything okay?"

"Yup… Why wouldn't it be?" Dom said, pouring fizz into his glass. He wondered how he could explain where he had been all this time, and what had happened in New York with Jason, without dragging up too much of the past. Although he had decided to leave the gallery without even speaking to Jason, it still affected him. He knew it was for the best, but it seemed so final. That part of his heart was now buried, no going back to the way he used to feel, and no more Jason Hart.

This new direction in his life was good. He knew it was right to choose a career over a relationship—a brittle relationship where one was succeeding while the other was still finding his way. 'Surely it would only end in jealousy or someone cheating anyway,' he had told himself.

Either way, he didn't want to find out because both of those options didn't make him feel good, and it would only mess up his emotional equilibrium all over again. What did satisfy him was the prospect of running a fashion label with Pandy, and that had won Dom's heart over Jason's.

"Everything's fine… I'm just feeling tired, that's all… You know how it is, the anti-climax of the show—I keep thinking there was more I could've done. I'm sure the bubbly will perk me up," Dom said, taking a sip to stop himself from saying more. It was better to cement over the crack in his heart than to crank it open even more. Besides, after today Jason would be out of London and out of the picture for good, and Dom would be back to work getting the label ready for the buying season.

This was all going to be a memory—just a blip. And there were better memories to create now he had a job that would take up a lot of his time. A job that elevated him away from the shop floor and into the spotlight with a new level of respect. This was going to open doors for him, and after years of slogging it out at Palazzo as a sales assistant, this was a leg up the ladder.

He had done it. Chloe would be proud of him! She believed in him as much as he believed in her, and after all, without his help, she wouldn't be where she was today. He had spurred her on to get StacksOfStyle back online, helping her create content, taking pictures of her dressed in hand-me-down couture in the hallways of her Williamsburg apartment block—attempting to recreate scenes from the pages of Vanguard. Even though the veil of smoke was thin, it had still worked out and now it was his time in the limelight.

*

Back in New York, Chloe was now the one starting to feel the nerves getting the better of her. 'What do I pack?' she thought, rifling through her closet. She had emptied most of it her onto the bed, but still, nothing seemed right for her trip to Milan. 'What does one wear on the front row of an international designer's fashion show?'

Then, her phone pinged—an email had dropped into her inbox. The perfect distraction from packing her case.

From: Bill Green
To: Chloe Ravens; Carmen Visconti
CC: Veronica Meyer; Morgana White; Samantha Stiller; Lily Cooper

Subject: Line Drawing Proofs

Dear Chloe and Carmen,

Further to our meeting, Sam and Lily have completed the line drawings and production notes for the shoe range. Please see attached the existing shoe lasts/fabrics in our inventory that best match your designs. Also attached is an idea for the line's branding from Morgana's team. I can also confirm that gold soles are possible within our budget.

@Veronica: these styles are all within the cost price budget and we have spoken with the supplier, who have confirmed they can start production as soon as sign off is given.

Samples can be delivered within two weeks, and once they have been approved, production can commence. Delivery estimated for early December, which just about meets our deadline for the Holiday season. Obviously, the sooner we can approve the samples, the quicker production can begin.

We are still finalising the accessories, but given the short time frame for this project, buying need us to proceed with the bulk of the collection—which are the SKU's for the footwear range.

Please review the attached and reply with any questions at the soonest possible, otherwise I shall assume production on samples is fine with everyone.

Thanks,

Bill Green
Head Buyer
DivaFeet.Com. United States.

Veronica sent a reply straight back, which had only Carmen and Chloe in copy—it simply read: 'Get me those contracts, ladies!'. Ignoring it, Chloe excitedly opened the attachments in Bill's email. A ten-page presentation opened up on her phone, which she couldn't wait to scroll through. She flicked through each page once in a rush of excitement, before going back to the first to take it all in properly. Her heart was beating fast from the elation of seeing her collection for the first time. The line drawings showed the silhouette of each style with a colour swatch beside it, along with a fabric code.

The leather knee-high boots stated they were '100% Nero Calf Leather,' while the evening sandals had another code for both 'Argento' and 'Oro.' A size table ran along the bottom of each style's page, with proposed numbers for units to be produced. Chloe moved onto the next attachment which filled her heart with joy and pride even more (if that was even possible). A design for a gold stud, in the shape of a raven that would be nailed into the arch of the sole, stared back at her. Underneath that was a logo in gold lettering for the collection's branding.

R A V E N
X
CHLOE RAVENS

On the next page, a line drawing showed how the raven shaped stud would look on a gold leather sole, with the logo stamped beneath it. Chloe couldn't believe her eyes. Her vision was coming together and she hadn't done anything, except present her ideas and then sit back and wait for them to make it a reality—with a dash of luck of course. There really was such a thing as being in the right place at the right time!

This collection was going to be a major success. She could just feel it! The madness of the past week had now been worth it, and a sense of addiction brewed inside of her. She wanted more, she wanted to be busy as ever with her own projects—and more importantly—she wanted to be in charge of how she worked.

Chloe made herself a cup of coffee and allowed herself to sit on the couch to have a moment to look over it all once again. The sun radiated on her through the window, and as she basked in the sunlight, she couldn't help but envision what would happen next, sipping her coffee and allowing the caffeine to run through her veins and power her positive thinking even more.

She thought about what her ex-colleagues would say when they saw the collection. 'I used to work with her at Palazzo!' she could hear Sarah say (the loudmouth, who was sure to be the main source to spread the news). And furthermore, how would

Regina react? The psycho who tried to stop her from chasing her dreams would see that she was unstoppable and more than just a silly shop girl. She would even be able to spot people on the street wearing *her* designs! And flick through magazines and read style columns raving about the collection—not to mention witness the collection sell out in minutes. Her eyes filled with tears of both joy and relief, and as a smile started to break out, she asked herself: 'Is this really happening?'

Chloe's phone rang and woke her from her dream-like state. She flipped onto her legs in one sudden motion (that a pro gymnast would be proud of) to grab the phone on the kitchen side and save the call.

"Have you seen?" Carmen said on the other end. "How amazing does it look—I'm so happy!"

"Well, all thanks to you!" Chloe said, wanting to make it known that she knew all of this wasn't down to her alone.

"Honey, it's *all* you! Take some credit for your hard work and savvy attitude for once... Anyway, listen, I've called my lawyer to see where she's at with the contract—she's going to get back to me by the end of the day... But, the sooner we get that signed and delivered the better... And then it sounds like we'll have samples by the time you get back from Milano baby!"

Things were happening and it felt great, but they couldn't afford to get ahead of themselves. Chloe's trip to Milan was just as important as the collection, and Carmen wanted to make sure she was ready for it. "Speaking of that, darling, I've got some pieces for your trip... I'll swing by later so we can choose what you're going to take, okay?"

"Oh my gosh... You have no idea how grateful I am; I'm tearing my hair out, and the entire contents of my wardrobe!"

And this was why Chloe couldn't have managed to do all of this without Carmen. Here she was, scrabbling through her closet, while Carmen had coolly—and without fuss—been gathering the latest pieces for her to wear behind the scenes. Of course, Chloe couldn't turn up to Milan fashion Week wearing seasons old Palazzo, or whatever else she had accumulated from photo-shoots and sample sales. She needed to be seen in the latest trends and Carmen knew just the people who would happily chuck clothes at her for free. Especially now that she could say she was dressing Chloe Ravens—Gianni Palazzo's new girlfriend! Even though that wasn't official, that's the line she was using—and it was working.

Hilary Van Furstein, celebrated New York designer, was delighted to offer up her latest collection, which Chloe thought was crazy. It wasn't too long ago that she had worked backstage as a dresser on that show, and now thanks to Carmen she was going to be one of the first women to actually wear it.

Having met her personally—and now that she had been thrust onto the fashion main-stage—Hilary thought it made perfect sense for her to be seen in her dresses. Of course, Chloe would *have* to wear Palazzo at the fashion show (she couldn't turn up wearing another designer's creations), but once again, Carmen had already negotiated that as well.

From: Carmen Visconti
To: Joli Andrade

Subject: Fashion Week, Chloe Ravens

Hi Joli,

I hope you are well? I'm Chloe's stylist and creative partner and we wondered if we could kindly ask you about the dress code for her attendance at the show in Milan next week?

Would it be acceptable for her to wear past collection pieces by Palazzo?

Any advice would be very helpful,

Carmen

It was a polite yet tactical move (and one of the oldest tricks in the book that stylists pulled on the regular), and Joli responded asking for Chloe's dress and shoe sizes. Although this was a secret that Carmen wanted to keep from Chloe—she wanted everything to be a surprise. She wanted Chloe to enjoy the fairytale moment that she was about to live for *real*. Plus, she enjoyed watching Chloe fret about the small stuff, it was endearing and entertaining.

Like Dominic, Chloe had entered a new era. Long gone were her days on the shop floor, gone were the trivial problems, like the whereabouts of a client's alteration or whether the next shift was an early or a late one. Now she had other things to look forward to, and a capsule collection to promote at Fashion Week—and *that* interview with Vanguard. Then there was the small matter of actually seeing Gianni Palazzo all over again.

Carmen was certain that this invitation to Milan was just an extravagant date to impress her with, but to Chloe, it was just him being polite after they had met at Palazzo's retrospective party. By posing with her on the red carpet, he had unknowingly pushed her into the deep end of the media pool. The very least he could do was invite her to his fashion show—or that's what she kept telling herself. It was best to keep her feet on the ground as much as possible, especially as everything else was beginning to lift off.

******

"Come on guys!" Pandy yelled, turning off the blaring music.

"Wait... I need a jacket," Dom said, realising that he had left his first choice at the gallery. He dashed to the bedroom and pulled out a black hoodie from his holdall to wrap around his waist, before joining the others to cram into an Uber.

Shoreditch House was in high spirits, as Fashion Week-ers flooded the top floors after a day of shows. After work friendship groups met mid-week for a drink, while regular members left the gym to go home; it was always a popular spot and tonight was no exception. Sat at the dinner table in the restaurant on the fifth floor, Pandy ordered two bottles of champagne straight away without looking at the menu. "Right guys, get whatever you want," she said with a flourish of her hands, signalling this one was on her (even though so was every other night).

"Let's not get too drunk!" Dom said, to which he received several raised eyebrows and unimpressed looks. He didn't want to sound like a killjoy, but they had plenty to do back at the studio in the morning. Boxes of dresses, shoes, equipment, and other things that they hadn't even brought along (but was now somehow theirs) awaited them dumped—and needed to be unpacked.

Dom wanted them to have fun, but when you had a success on your hands, it was too easy to sit back and let the opportunity slip through your fingers, and before you knew it the momentum was gone. He knew that hard work created more hard work, he saw that with Chloe. She wasn't resting on her laurels and Pandy needed to take that on board too.

"All I'm saying is that tomorrow we need to be back at the studio to unpack the collection... We need to restore normality as soon as we can and set up for our showroom appointments. The whole industry is in town and will most likely want to drop in to see the pieces, in their own hands... We must present it to them straight away because this is how we're gonna secure press, buyers, interest!"

He could see them all take a breath, deflated from hearing about more work that needed to be done. Couldn't they just enjoy their achievements for one-second? Even Pandora looked down at him as if to say: '*Really* mate?'

Couldn't they have just one day off at least? No, was the answer. He hadn't worked this hard for nothing. Now he was the brand director, he was going to make sure he did just that—direct! This was the first time that P.S.L had received such a great reaction from the front row of the industry, and it was his responsibility to ensure that Pandora didn't allow her team to squander it. That and the fact that he needed to sink himself into work—more than ever.

'If they want a day off, then fine,' he thought to himself, he would still be hard at work in the studio.

"Okay, okay... Enough of that," Pandy said, clinking her knife against her glass. It made the other diners look up to see what the upstart socialite, was now up to. "I just want to say, a massive thank you to you all for pulling this out of the bag for me... I couldn't have done it with you, and I think it's fair to say that we were struggling... Until you came along! Thank *fuck* you came back to London in time, and with that said, I want to let you guys know that Dom is staying on board with us as brand director!"

Heather and JoJo drunkenly whooped and cheered, while Jonty wasn't particularly surprised by the news and gave no new expression (other than the blank one he always wore), although he *was* pleased. For the first time, P.S.L had made a collection he was proud of and he was hopeful that many more were to come with Dom now on hand to dampen Pandy's whimsical ways.

He finally felt like he was working for a designer that was going to make a mark on British fashion, and he was contributing to that just as much. He secretly hoped that one day, when the brand was a stabilised fashion icon, that he would be interviewed for a documentary and he would recall these early days on camera. After all, everybody just wants to be a somebody to someone.

"A toast," Pandy said, standing up and leading the raising of glasses. "To Dominic, and to P.S.L!"

***

Waiters began clearing up their plates as the party stayed sat around the table drinking. Probably an attempt to politely usher them to the lower, and much louder, levels of the members club—having managed to take over the entire restaurant with their raucous chatter. But Jonty was rolling up a cigarette, which prompted them to move outside onto the terrace anyway, where they sat poolside. Dom joined him in having a smoke, this was the second time today that they had shared the social ritual of smoking together. The respect for each other was now mutual it seemed.

Pandy had ordered round after round of G&T's. There was no way that they would be back in the studio in the morning at this rate. She handed out the drinks as Heather and JoJo were rolled up on the sun lounger in a giggling fit, managing to contain themselves and sit up now the free drinks had arrived. When she got to Dom, she noticed his disapproving glare. "I know what you're thinking… But listen, it's been a hard few weeks; I think they deserve a day off at least… We can pick up where we left off on Friday and get everything ready before the weekend—ready for a new week selling!"

"Fine… Let's take the day off and reconvene on Friday," Dom said taking his drink from her.

Anyway, would anyone really expect a small brand such as them to have their presentation open for buyers the very next day after their show? Dom also wanted to relax and enjoy the moment, he wanted to drink his troubles away and celebrate his new future at the same time. Pandy watched him ditch the straw and practically neck his G&T, and she was loving this new version of him. She was sure he was going to be a great asset, someone she could rely on as well as have fun building the brand of her dreams together.

As the night went on, Dom drank more than usual (he also smoked more than usual) and he grew desperate for the bathroom. He could have simply used the toilets nearby the pool but being holed up around the pool chain-smoking all night gave him the feeling he was 'missing out' on something. So he left the group to go take a stroll downstairs to the third floor instead—where it was 'happening.'

He wanted to see people, be amongst the crowd and be seen, now that he finally felt good about himself thanks to the booze— and he wanted to have a little fun too since they were taking the day off. He strutted his way through the moodily low-lit third floor en route to the bathroom, passing the packed out bar area and booths of people all shouting to converse with each other over the music.

Almost dancing into the men's room, ready to burst any second, he was relieved to find a cubicle free. He hated urinals, the fact there was no tissue to wipe with after freaked him out, and he didn't want unfortunate drips (or other people's 'splash-back') on his Saint Laurent boots. He flushed and came out of the toilet to head over to the sink and rinse his hands, running the excess dampness through his hair to perk it up a little. Stepping back to adjust his shirt in the mirror, he quickly assessed himself. 'God, I'm drunk,' he summarised, before heading back out and through the third floor to rejoin the gang upstairs once more.

The third floor was pumping; the DJ was spinning some great tunes and although Shoreditch House wasn't really a venue for dancing, Dom wanted music and thought that it was about time they changed the scenery. He spotted a table over in the corner that was starting to clear. They had spent too long upstairs and being outside was encouraging him to smoke, so he bound up the stairwell to the pool terrace to tell the others before they lost out. "Guys, there's a huge corner table that's clearing now… I'll go down and grab it!"

"Amazing! Come on guys, grab your shit," Pandy shouted, rounding up the troops.

The lift had a queue of people, all waiting to get down to the ground floor, so they took the cement stairwell down to the third floor instead—even though Pandy was in platform heels. But then again, when wasn't she in platform heels at Shoreditch House? She had handled these stairs many times before, and in worse states too.

Dom flung the double fire doors open onto the third floor, allowing them to all to go though before him—kindly holding the doors open for two guys to pass before he did. And as he looked up at them, he nearly dropped down dead as they carried on walking through. Dom quickly ducked his head to escape through the doors, but he did it so abruptly that it brought attention to him.

"Dominic!" Jason said, catching the door before it swung shut in his face

The waft of burnt oud wood confirmed that it was indeed Jason, way before Dom looked back to see for sure—but Dom was even more shocked to see the guy he was with wearing Jason's leather jacket. It was another sign that Jason had moved on, even though he had told himself that he had moved on from Jason. But still, Dom's stomach flipped as his evening meal and alcohol were about to come back up and hit the floor. Not a good look for Shoreditch House, and if he was going to stay at P.S.L then he would have to hold his guts—this *was* their local hang out.

"I—" Dom started, not knowing what to say.

He had run away from this exact moment, only to be confronted with it off-guard. This wasn't on his terms—this wasn't how he had imagined it—this was *not* supposed to be happening right now!

"I have to go," Dom said, quickly making his way to the elevator to hit the call button.

Jason let the door swing close for a moment—he had some explaining of his own to do. As Dom waited for the lift, he looked back around to see Jason filling in his new 'friend' on what had just happened through the round glass of the fire doors.

"We'll have another round of G&T's please!" Pandy ordered, now sat at their table with a waiter at hand. "Where's Dom?" She walked back through the bar to find him, only to see him jamming the lift button several times. "Dom? Where you going?"

"I gotta go—I need to get outta here."

"Why… What's happened?"

"*NOTHING!*"

All this time he had hidden his feelings about Jason from her because he didn't want to seem weak, yet here he was feeling weaker than ever in front of everyone. Finally, the elevator door opened and Dom pushed his way in before letting people out, which caused them to moan at him, but he didn't care. He just wanted them out of the way so he could close the door before Jason could come in. He pressed the close button without a word to Pandy, but she stopped the doors from closing—she deserved an explanation.

"Wait! I'll get my bag and come with you."

"*NO!* I mean, we'll talk later… Please Pandy!"

Hearing the real panic in his voice, she backed off and let the doors close—just in time for Jason to miss it. He turned back to bound down the stairwell to catch Dom on the ground floor. Pandy was confused, something had clearly happened with this guy, but she didn't follow them, she was too drunk and in platforms to give chase (she wasn't going to break her neck on the night of her successful show) and returned to the others instead.

Dom took in a deep breath. A weight was released from his mind not having to confront Jason, but his felt body tense—like it wanted him to turn back. 'Why can't I just speak to him? Why am I running away like this?' he asked himself. The truth was, it was easier this way. Dom had made a decision and he was sticking to it. Jason would be gone by tomorrow and this dilemma would simply disappear.

Finally reaching ground floor level, Dom made a quick exit out of the reception that led back out onto the side street. The narrow road was full of cars waiting for their pick-up's to come down, which Dom couldn't wait for—by then Jason would have made it down and he just wanted to get out of the area. Even though it was starting to rain, he started to make a run for it.

Jason didn't know exactly where he was going, giving Dom the upper hand on making an exit, but he had made it to the reception. It was full of people arriving for the evening and waiting for the lifts—cluttering the entrance. He headed straight for the door and looked up and down the street. There was no sign of Dom, and with Shoreditch High Street as busy as always, there was no hope of finding him in the crowd—not knowing he had fled the other way up the street. All he could do was head back upstairs and drink the night away. He did have Chris waiting for him, and he was sure as hell going to get that leather jacket back off him!

Without thought, Dom continued running towards the studio without stopping—even in his boots. His feet pounded the wet, shiny cement floor and his heart pounded against his wet shirt—his hoodie swinging around his waist. The studio was the nearest place of solace, and now he had a set of keys, it was a safe place to hide—at least until it stopped raining. As he ran through the streets on autopilot, he caught a glimpse of himself in a shop window which forced him to stop from this moment of craziness. He was literally running away, which seemed rather pathetic for a grown man.

"What the *fuck* am I doing?" he said to his reflection, now starting to get drenched. This wasn't the person he was trying to be, the strong and determined version of himself that he told himself he could be.

****

Switching on the workroom lights, a total shit-tip awaited him. The sight of the chaos, mixed together with his own mess in his mind, started to give him a headache. He took off his soaked boots and damp socks before heading to the kitchen to find a towel and dry his hair off. He reached for the cupboard for a pint glass (stolen from a nearby pub) and drafted himself a cold glass of water, which he instantly downed in one.

'What's this all about?' he wondered. 'What if Jason speaks to Pandora and asks her about me?' She would tell him everything for sure: where he lived, worked—and with this in mind, Dom quickly switched his phone off. He had already received several missed calls from Pandy, and he didn't want her to come to the studio to talk over it—or worse—bring Jason. Instead, he made himself a strong coffee from the machine, the last thing he wanted to be was hungover, on top of all this.

A coffee turned into two strong coffees, and as he lay on the sofa staring at the boxes, he decided that now was the time to roll up his sleeves and get to work. He found a blade and ran it along the top of a box, opening it to find sewing equipment—which he put to the side for later—and continued to open the rest. He set up rails and started to hang the heavy, filled garment bags until finally all of the boxes were empty and flattened.

The night was now running into the early hours of the morning, but that didn't stop him—his mind was too active and he didn't want to slip back into thinking about Jason again. Instead, he began to envision how he wanted the collection merchandised and set up for the showroom appointments, and started to rearrange the rails around the edge of the room, with the tables dragged into two rows for taking down orders. Dom began to unzip and remove every garment bag—neatly folding them up into an empty box—so he could make a start on organising the rails with each look in order of appearance from the show.

By the time that was all done, he had six fully merchandised rails—three rails on each side of the room—that ran the length of it. The boxes were all taped up, ready for the bins, and he returned Heather's sewing machine and sewing box to her workstation. All that was left to do now was to sweep the room and steam the clothes, which could wait until tomorrow.

He finally sat back down on the sofa, now physically tired as well as mentally drained, looking at all the work he had managed to get done by himself. He knew it would be better for him to do the showroom set-up himself anyway, without any of the other guys questioning his decisions or reasoning. Before settling down to sleep on the sofa, Dom got back up to lock the door and switch off the lights.

The darkness of the room, with the light of dawn-break starting to seep in from the skylight, gave Dom the calm he needed. Curling up into a ball to keep himself warm, the stillness eased him into trying to sleep, trying to forget that for at least one night, he could have been in the warmth of Jason's arms instead.

9

The studio was great for working, as it filled the room with natural light and you could see every stitch, every woven thread of fabric and its true colour—but it wasn't so great for a good night's sleep. Dom rubbed his eyes and stretched as the daylight forced him to wake up. His head ached and his mouth felt stale and dehydrated (a feeling he was starting to get used to since being back in London).

Even though he had gulped pints of water the night before, he also had a few coffees and the concoction was now starting to take effect (he felt as though his head was being clamped in a vice). The slew of G&T's and Prosecco he had necked, was also not helping. He slowly planted his feet on the floor, remembering he had taken his socks off to dry and felt the cold floor on the bottom of his soles as he walked to the kitchen. He poured himself another pint of water before rummaging through the cupboards to find a packet of green tea.

He didn't bother to check how long they had been there and emptied the kettle so he could fill it up again with fresh water. Limescale chunks fell out as he drained it down the sink (he made a mental note to buy some de-scale solution); he couldn't have press and buyers coming here for appointments, serving them tea from this rotten kettle! However, it would have to do, for now, so he ignored the rancidness and continued to boil some water as the tea bag awaited inside a mug that read 'Fashionista At Work.'

It was the kind of mug that someone (not related to the fashion world) bought for your birthday from a cheap card shop, or more likely, Pandora had found in Poundland and purposefully bought it for its tackiness and irony. Dom sat back down on the sofa and sipped the piping hot tea cautiously while he switched his phone back on.

He was aware of the missed calls and voicemails from Pandy after he had left the party without an explanation—but that was fine—he was mentally prepared for that. What he wasn't prepared for was the missed calls and messages from Jason. He didn't want to confront any of that right now, but he knew it was better to get it over with, rather than procrastinate and have all of this resurface yet again in a week.

Slowly, yesterday's events started to resurface: the fashion show, seeing Jason at the gallery, leaving the gallery empowered, running into Jason at Shoreditch House—running out of Shoreditch House! He cringed as he replayed it all like a movie in his mind, imagining how he must have looked to his crew, as well as to Jason and his new admirer. 'Why did I run like that?' he asked himself.

After all, he wasn't the same person Jason had met back in New York, he was the brand director for a cutting edge fashion label now. And what was he going to tell Pandy? How was he ever going to show his face around here again? Not that she would care, she was just pissed that he had taken off like that when they were all having such a good time. If he had barfed his guts up, then she would have understood (she had been in that position many times herself), but to leave without explanation was simply odd.

The studio phone rang, waking him from his shameful memoirs of the night before. 'That'll be Pandy… What am I gonna say to her?' he moaned with his sorry, fuzzy head. He cleared his throat before picking up. "Hello, Pandora Simmons London."

"Oh, hello there," a female voice said—not Pandora. "I'm the womenswear buyer for Selfridges… I wondered if we could book a showroom appointment for the spring/summer collection?"

Dom was astounded—and grateful. Grateful that it *wasn't* Pandora, than it was a major new client. But he was still surprised that Selfridges—London's most famous department store—was calling to book an appointment.

"Oh—right… Well, we're open right away… Whenever's good for you."

"Perfect, we'll drop by tomorrow afternoon before we shoot off to Milan if that's okay?"

'It's more than okay,' Dom thought to himself. "Certainly, I'll be here and so will Pandora herself."

"Wonderful! And I am speaking to?"

"Oh, I'm so sorry… I'm Dominic Fraser—Brand director."

"Okay, well we'll see you around three," she said and hung up.

No one as big as Selfridges had ever ordered from Pandora before, and even though Dom thought he had covered the internal processes for market season, he hadn't prepared for such a big account like them to walk through the doors. He thought he had at least a few days left to finalise such things, and that he would have to do a huge outreach to buyers to remind them of the collection before anyone would get back to them—especially as everyone was getting ready to head to Milan. Selfridges had the potential to put in a huge order, and not only that but put P.S.L on the map of international designers in their stores.

And just like that, Dom had taken their first buying appointment for the season. He immediately sent Pandy a text telling her he had exciting news, although he doubted she'd even be awake. This sudden wake-up call had been the perfect hangover cure, as Dom felt the urgency to get back to work on sending out showroom invitations. If there was interest from Selfridges already, then surely there would be others?

He switched on the studio computer and got working on an invitation, using the P.S.L logo and the studio address, along with opening times. Most buyers preferred to do their orders after they had been to all the Fashion Week shows and knew where to put their money, other's liked to do it while they were in town—especially the smaller boutiques—as it cut their travel costs. Dom calculated that from now until mid-October should be enough time for them to secure orders and give them enough time to get the production underway. The earlier the delivery the better, as that gave retailers maximum time to sell their stock, and Dom wanted them to sell out quickly so they could place re-orders before the season ended. The studio phone rang once more, which Dom grabbed quickly—in case it was another enquiring buyer.

"What the *actual* fuck?" quizzed a croaky voiced Pandora. "Why the hell are you at the studio and at this time? I thought we agreed to take the day off?"

"I know, but after last night, I just couldn't go home."

"You mean to tell me, that you have been there all night long? Why didn't you come sleep here, you idiot?"

"I know, but I needed to be on my own after what happened."

"Well, that's the thing… I don't know *what* happened!"

Dom rubbed his oily face out of awkwardness, realising he had some explaining to do, and now was the time to come clean; he couldn't keep on running emotionally as well as physically.

"Some guy asked me about you—he was really hot… Tall, blonde, American fella."

"You didn't give him my number or tell him where we worked did you?" Dom said, panicked by the thought. She wasn't to know who he was, but this was the sort of dumb shit she would do to try and impress someone.

"Why, should I have? I mean he didn't ask for it… He just asked if I knew you; I said you had just left and then he fled—just as quick as you did."

Dom blew out a deep breath down the phone, he was relieved. Relieved that her intro to Jason was a brief one, but he still owed her an explanation. It was time he confided in her as a friend once more. Until now, he had used her as a stepping stone, because going up a level in the industry was all he was focused on, but he had forgotten a vital ingredient as to why he even had this chance—Pandora *was* once a friend. And she deserved to be treated like one too.

If this working relationship was going to work, then he had to make their friendship function too. No more secrets—no more hiding. She had invested so much trust in him, that she allowed him to step in just days before her fashion show and completely change its vision. Of course, it was the best solution as she was up shit creek—but that wasn't the point. She believed in him after all these years, she allowed him to step back into her life as though they had never left college. It was now time he trusted her in the same way. "Look, when you're up and ready, let's go grab coffee and something to eat… I'm sure you need a hangover cure anyway… I have something I need to tell you."

*

Lying in bed, Jason also couldn't get what had happened out of his mind. It kept playing out over and over again in his head like a bad dream. He raised his hands to his head and ran his hands through his tangled bed-hair in frustration. It was time he got up, he still needed to pack. Today was the day he was due to fly back home unless he stayed for another week to track Dom down and sort this out. All kinds of thoughts came to mind, but one thing was clear: Dom didn't want to see him, no matter how much he wanted to see Dom.

Besides, there was no point now; next to him laid Chris, still fast asleep with a smile on his face. He had never felt like such a man-whore in his life than he did at this moment. How could he pine over Dom when he had no qualms about picking up some other random English guy and sleeping with him? No, today was time to go back to L.A and start over again. The Southbank Gallery had asked Jason to present more pieces to them, so he had work to take his mind off it all back home. Men and dramatic love trysts had no place in his life right now and just like Dom, he had chosen his career over love—and what better than to channel this emotion into his art?

"Dude," Jason said, nudging Chris. "Dude, get up… I gotta leave this hotel in like, an hour," which was a lie. He didn't need to vacate until midday, he just wanted him gone; just looking at him made him feel dirty.

Chris woke with a yawn, reluctantly opening his eyes until he saw Jason. 'What a vision to wake up to,' he thought. This handsome Californian stud, with broad shoulders and a body that looked like it was naturally ripped from surfing all day. 'I bet he doesn't even need to work out,' Chris pondered, before stretching his arms out to pull him next to him—but Jason's body stiffened as he resisted and swiftly got out of bed instead. He was miffed, morning sex with this hunk was clearly out of the question!

But he got the message. What happened, was to only *just* happen for one night, and that was that. He sighed in annoyance and flipped himself up off the bed, wasting no time to pull on his jeans and T-shirt, which were now a bit baggy compared to how snug they had fit him the night before. "Well, I'll be seeing you… If you do want to get in touch, then that's my card," he said, placing it on the bedside table. With a kiss goodbye out of the question, he saw himself out—looking back once more in case Jason changed his mind.

He didn't.

With Chris finally gone, Jason laid back in bed, burying his head into the pillow feeling like a complete piece of shit. He didn't know it, but not so long ago it was Dom feeling this way back in New York when Jason had left him to go back to Los Angeles. Of course, he didn't know how Dom had sobbed that day into the pillows of The Plaza Hotel as he departed, and ironically Dom would never know how the tables had turned, as Jason lay crushed and defeated in his hotel room in London.

He stayed there for a while until he pulled himself together… He had done everything he could and it wasn't good enough. Plus, he had commitments back in L.A, he had work and friends—a life—to which he wanted to get back to like never before. Leaving these empty feelings behind in London for good. With this sudden urge, Jason got up and headed to the shower to wash the night's mistakes away. If he felt clean, then his mind would 'think' clean, and he would be able to move on.

In some ways, it had worked, but stepping out of the shower and seeing the bed where he and Chris had laid together the night before brought it all back to him. He needed to get out of this room entirely—and out of London in fact. Jason yanked the clothes off the metal hangers in his open-plan hotel closet, causing them to rattle and chime next to each other, before tossing them into his aluminium Rimowa suitcase. He quickly dressed into his tracksuit that he wore for flying with his white sneakers, and a hairband to keep his damp hair away from his face (with no care to blow dry it). A baseball cap would complete the 'do not disturb' look, as well as dark sunglasses for when he landed back in the Sunshine State. He cleared his toiletries in the bathroom into his wash bag with one clean swoop, feeling more upset and angry with himself as he gathered more of his belongings together—and his momentum reflected that.

Double-checking for his passport and wallet, he zipped up his suitcase and lifted it off the bed so its wheels thumped on the carpeted floor. He lifted the top handle and grabbed the room key to leave right away (even though he had hours before he needed to get to Heathrow Airport), he just wanted to get there as fast as he could. This trip to London had been a huge success for him work-wise, but there was another reason why he was here and that was a massive failure. And for the first time in a long time, Jason was dealing with rejection—and it felt like crap.

He wasn't used to this feeling, a cold empty feeling of not being wanted; he was used to everyone throwing themselves at him. Men, women (even dogs in the street when he went jogging along Venice beach), everyone jumped at the talented and creative hunk that was Jason Hart. Every part of Jason's life was an instant recipe for success. All except for his love life it seemed.

Looking out onto the row of aeroplanes sat waiting to be boarded, Jason figured that he was destined to be that eternal bachelor. The one that always got what he wanted but never felt happy with his lot… Or maybe he was just feeling sorry for himself because things didn't go his way for once? Whatever it was, one thing was for certain: they were nothing but a whirlwind romance in New York, and that's where he should have left it.

**

"Why didn't you tell me all this before?" Pandy said. They had just polished off a full English breakfast in a greasy spoon on

Shoreditch high street, but Dom had managed to tell her everything about Jason and how he had come to London in search of a new start in between mouthfuls.

"Well, I couldn't exactly turn up and say: 'Hi-ya, I'm back with loadsa baggage—but please employ me.' Plus, I didn't know Jason was gonna come looking for me in London!"

Dom took a sip of his coffee (it was his second that morning), desperate to be caffeinated once more—coffee was life!

"Anyway, I was just determined to get back into work, you know? After seeing Chloe make such huge leaps in a short space of time, I just felt like it was my time too… I was so fed up of watching other people achieve things—while I sit back and watch!"

Pandora knew exactly how he felt. She yearned to be successful in her own right and not just known as the daughter of a rockstar, and it wasn't until now that she was starting to see that it was a possibility—thanks to Dom. "Well, here's one thing you've achieved… Have you seen the reviews for the show?" she said, scrolling on her phone for the online article she had saved. "This proves you *are* making progress!"

<u>A NEW DAWN AT PANDORA SIMMONS</u>
<u>*Lou Banks, Reporting from London Fashion Week*</u>

Pandora Simmons strikes back with sexy silhouettes, and for the first time, a coherent direction for the brand, more commonly known as P.S.L.

Thanks to the new appointment of Dominic Fraser, brand director, this collection gives us a glimpse of what Simmons has been trying to show us for the past four years. A vibrant new collection with all the eccentricity of a cool and fresh London based designer, to rival that of Vivienne Westwood and Zandra Rhodes—something we haven't seen for quite a while. Colours and fabrics have finally come together to make a collection worth your wardrobe space, sexy pantsuits and edgy cuts finally makes sense. Leopard prints, neons, pinstripes and paint splashes with plenty of attitude make for a sexy statement in an exciting new era for British Fashion.

Pandora didn't usually agree with Lou Banks (having been on the sharp end of his tongue for as long as she could remember), but he was already proven to be right with Selfridges already on their case.

"See, I told you!" Dom said, grabbing her phone from her to read it himself; he couldn't believe his name was right there, in print.

"Listen, I understand that seeing Jason yesterday was a big deal, but don't feel like you need to sleep in the cold studio... Certainly, go there when you want peace and quiet, but come back to mine next time and sleep in my spare room... Just say: 'Pandy—not now,' and I'll get the message... Anyway, what's this other news *you* have for me?"

"Well, it's a good job I did stay here because early this morning we received a phone call ... From Selfridges! Their buyer wants to come and view the collection tomorrow."

"*What!*" Pandy said, slamming her hands on the table, causing a table of builders to look over (they, of course, recognised who she was).

"I know... We need to get ready for market season... Let's open up right away and send the email invite out to all of your past buyers and more! We need to let them know we're open for appointments and ride this wave of good press while everyone is still in town."

"Right then... We better get back to the studio, write this email and get it sent out," she said, drinking the last drops of her tea.

***

Chloe couldn't sleep, the excitement of flying to Milan was too much to ignore and had woken her up at four a.m. The first-class ticket had been wedged into the frame of her bedroom mirror, ever since Kim came rushing over to hand-deliver it a week ago. Every morning, when she brushed her hair in the mirror, the ticket reminded her that this *really* was happening. Sometimes she couldn't quite believe it, but then she would catch a glimpse of the ticket out of the corner of her eye while pottering around her room—picking up panties and clothes for the laundry—suddenly to be hit with the fact that it *was* indeed happening. It would stop and make her think: 'Wow, Gianni wants *me* at the Palazzo show!'

Sitting up in bed, she turned the bedside light on, checking that the ticket was still there and not in her imagination once again. And there it was—that flicker of wonder as she spotted it in the early morning light. A crack in the curtains had set the room a cool shade of blue. This hour of the morning, the day untouched and virginal, there was something very honest about it. And looking at the ticket, stuck there in the frame made it feel more real than ever. It was finally sinking in that she going to Milan, and satisfied to know that, her head hit the pillow once more…

The corners of her eyes were sore as she tried to open them wider, regretting not taking a sleeping pill and passing out. Looking around her bedroom, she knew she had so much to do before she was ready for her trip. On a rail next to the wardrobe was a selection of dresses and clothes that Carmen had picked out for her. In true 'Chloe' fashion, she still had to pack them. That was a task for today, she didn't want to be rushing to the airport last minute because she had been packing her case at the very last hour.

Chloe looked at her phone, it was now approaching six and it was better to get up rather than allow herself to sleep in all day. She had also planned to upload her latest article on StacksOfStyle (a review of New York Fashion Week, the parties and shows she had been at, accompanied by pictures and selfies of herself and Carmen in the looks they wore), which was already late to be posted since everyone was now talking about London Fashion Week. But to keep up with the times, she had another article roughly written covering London. She wanted to support Dom and feature a write-up of Pandora's show—that was also on today's list of things-to-do.

Chloe shuffled her way to the kitchen, where she had left her laptop on the breakfast bar and booted it up, ready to work. She made some coffee while it was starting up, before taking a trip to the bathroom as the machine brewed. Sat on the toilet, she could hear the alarm on her phone ringing in the kitchen. 'Typical,' she thought, as she sat on the toilet peeing. But she couldn't remember setting an alarm for this time in the morning. She hadn't done that since she quit Palazzo and had to shower and dress for the subway commute to Fifth Avenue. The ringing was going on for much longer than usual until she realised it wasn't an alarm at all—it was a phone call. She quickly finished up and rinsed her hands, before dashing back to the kitchen to answer it, stubbing her foot on the doorway as she did. "Ouch, damn it!" she cursed, missing the call as she had only just reached it.

The pain searing through her big toe seemed to get worse, now having no good reason for it to happen in the first place. She checked to see who the missed caller was; it was only Carmen. 'What does she want this early in the morning?' she thought, calling her straight back—which she answered pronto.

"Bongiorno, darling... Sorry for calling you so early, but I have news about the contracts and we need to talk."

A sudden pang rang through Chloe's entire body and worry started to brew inside of her. What was wrong with the contract?

"I'll get myself ready and come over to talk about it... It's nothing, darling."

"Well, it must be something... What is it? You're worrying me!"

"It's nothing *too* serious... Just a few points that my lawyer pointed out that we should consider before signing—that's all."

"A few 'points'? Like what exactly?"

"Look, it's just business things... Calm yourself down. I'll get dressed and grab a taxi to yours... Have you packed yet?"

"Not yet, but I will by the end of the day—I promise!"

"Okay, I'll see you in an hour and we can go over this contract... Ciao for now."

Carmen ended the call so she could get herself ready to come over. Even though there were important things to be discussed, there was no way she would ever step out not looking her best. Chloe knew this would be the case, giving her time to get washed and dressed. No longer needing the coffee to wake her up, she went back into the bathroom and turned the shower on to warm up the water. As she scrubbed her body furiously with a soap bar, she couldn't help but fill with panic. She knew from the start that all of this was too good to be true, and here it was—the deal-breaker. She was so anxious about it, she only spent five minutes under the water before stepping back out to brush her teeth and towel dry her dampened hair. Throwing on a T-shirt and a pair of boyfriend jeans, Chloe decided that she now needed that cup of coffee. Purely because it was too early for vodka, and she needed something to steady her nerves.

Sat on a stool in the kitchen, she finally looked at her laptop and set her mind to use this energy into working on the new posts instead. She pushed the New York Fashion Week party article live and started the research for her review of the P.S.L show. After a Google search, she too stumbled across Lou Bank's review, and the mention of Dom's new appointment made Chloe forget her issues for now.

She was delighted to see that Dom had landed an important role at the fashion house and thought about emailing him with her congratulations, with a note to say she was writing an article about the show and that it was bound to reach a new army of fashion followers. But before she could act on her sudden burst of enthusiasm, the buzzer forced her to stop what she was doing and get the door—it was Carmen bearing latte as per.

"Morning," she said, kissing Chloe on the cheek before passing her the coffees, carrying on through to the kitchen as if it was her own place.

Chloe noticed the white A4 envelope sticking out of her Palazzo handbag. "So, what's the story?" she eagerly asked, sitting back at the breakfast bar and grabbing a coffee out of the grey cardboard carry tray.

"Okay, first of all, do not freak out! There are just a few parts that my lawyer wanted to point out, but he's assured me it's all very normal for such a deal." Carmen pulled the contract out of the envelope and flicked a few pages to a highlighted section in neon yellow. "This part here in particular states that DivaFeet will be the sole owner of the brand name: 'Raven, by Chloe Ravens' and any other variables such as—but not exhaustive: 'Chloe Ravens,' 'C.Ravens,' 'C.R,' 'The Raven,' 'Raven,' 'Chloe, by Chloe Ravens.'"

"*What!*"

"Wait… There's more—don't freak out, remember! This part says that DivaFeet has the right to carry the brand name, with or without the co-signees of this contract—meaning us… Then it goes on to say: 'DivaFeet reserves the right to produce under the brand name for as long as they wish.' Basically meaning they can drop the label whenever they want or carry it on for eternity without us."

"*NO!* No *fucking* way!" Chloe shouted, raising her hands up to her head.

How could Veronica do this to her? This wasn't a contract, this was a deal with the Devil, and it sounded like she expected her to sign her soul away.

"I know, but this is such a good opportunity! Veronica just wants to cover her back, that's all… You know, in case the first collection doesn't work out—which it will! That way she's not bound to putting money into something that's not making a profit," Carmen said, trying to cool her temper. "And, she's upped your advance back up to the $10,000 we originally asked for at least."

"Oh, I bet she has! And stealing my name in the process… It's not just a brand, that's my name! Say if I want to make my own independent line in the future, I won't be able to because Veronica would own my name, right? What price would you put on your name?"

Carmen shrugged, that's what the contract stated, but for her, it was a small price to pay to have a capsule collection backed by a major investor.

"And then this whole, 'we reserve the right to produce with or without you,' says to me: 'Thanks for the idea ladies, now see ya later!'"

Chloe was now in a rage and pacing the kitchen (which wasn't exactly the largest room in the apartment), throwing her hands all over the place. Carmen could only watch and wait for her anger to simmer, but seeing Chloe in such a flap made her giggle. Her Italian gestures had rubbed off on her somewhat, but this was not a time for humour. "So, now what?" she said, sitting back on the stool, taking a sip of her latte.

The trouble was, that Carmen didn't really know; all she knew was that if she were in Chloe's shoes, she would just sign the darn contract and hope for the best. But it was true, it would be daft to sign away the rights to the brand name. Even though Veronica was on Chloe's side today, Carmen had seen how business relationships in fashion could suddenly sour. Usually over money or control of a brand, which was when clauses such as these either made or destroyed you. The long pause gave Chloe time to think, and under pressure and with a quick temper, it forced her to come to a decision.

"Okay… Let's just not sign it—for now anyway. I'm off to Milan tomorrow and Veronica isn't going to wait until I get back to start sample production… She's eager to make a quick buck and will plough on—even without our signatures."

"But what do I say—she *will* call to find out why we haven't returned the contract, signed." Carmen seemed more worried than Chloe about it now, the tables had turned. Chloe suddenly appeared to be calculative and controlled, as she sat there holding her coffee cup to warm her hands, going through the plan in her head—staring out of the window before answering.

"Let her call… I will ignore all of her emails and if she calls you, just pick up and say that all is fine, we're both busy as I'm in Milan and we will be in touch as soon as I'm back."

The plan was to stall her, but no matter how long they ignored Veronica, there would still be a problem with the contract.

"But you're forgetting one important thing… She holds sixty percent of this partnership and she's paid us an advance on the collection, which we would have to pay back."

"Exactly! She's already invested cash—a drop in the ocean to her all the same—but she's not gonna pull the plug! All she has right now is the rights to *one* capsule collection."

Carmen smiled. Chloe had changed from shop girl to stylist, from stylist to blogger—and right now she was changing again in front of her. Chloe was evolving from a little website owner to a savvy PR and businesswoman. It was almost as if Carmen had watched her brain grow an additional chamber of knowledge right there and then, proud to be on this journey with her. This was what Veronica instinctively saw in her in the first place. Surely Veronica would understand how Chloe felt about the contract if they talked it over?

Chloe was no longer naive like she was when she worked at Palazzo, being pushed around and told what to do by Regina. She had escaped her controlling ways to be set free, not to be chained up again by other people's rules and expectations of her. Now she was working for herself and past learnings meant more to her than ever before. No one was going to screw her over again, not Regina Hall and certainly not Veronica.

Carmen had always wanted her own label, she had the ambition but not the determination. She was happy being a successful stylist to the rich and famous and enjoying a glamorous lifestyle, but she didn't have the motivation that Chloe had—which made her special. She had the talent, the personality, but also the nerve to carry out her dreams.

"Okay," Carmen agreed. "Let's just carry on as normal… I'm sure she'll still press ahead with the samples as you say, and when you're back we'll sort this out. By then, you and Gianni will have made it *official* and she'd be crazy to say no to whatever you want!"

Chloe smirked, here was Carmen going on about her getting together with Gianni once again, she just wouldn't let it drop. "Let's just wait and see, shall we? Anyway, let's talk about Milan—what's going on with the Vanguard interview?"

Carmen pulled out her phone and scrolled to an email she had received from their office. "They want to interview you on Saturday morning at nine a.m, just before the Palazzo show at The Four Seasons, where you're staying… So that's easy! I've told Joli that you have a commitment in the morning and she's arranged a chauffeur to drive you straight to the show afterwards."

Chloe was glad Carmen had it all planned out for her, it was one less thing she had to worry about amongst everything else, but she couldn't hide the fact that she was nervous about the interview—especially with the additional news of the contract no on her mind. How could she promote the collection when there was a possibility that it might not even happen?

"Have they said what they want to interview me about, or sent any questions over at least?"

"Nope… It's just going to be like a casual chat—try not to get worked up about it. But remember, you need to look amazing! A photographer wants to take a few snaps—just something small to piece together with the article," Carmen said, not wanting to panic her further now she had managed to calm herself down. Although, she could see her forehead had created lines—that weren't usually there—from frowning.

"Don't worry! This is going to be fun! Trust me… What do you prefer: working at Palazzo bored all day, or flying to Milan all expenses paid to stay at The Four Seasons? Oh, and while you're there, Vanguard—*Vanguard magazine*—want to interview you about being the next big thing in fashion."

Chloe clapped her hands over her mouth, stifling a giggle. She was right, this *was* fun. Who wouldn't what that to happen to them? Her old shop floor colleagues would kill to be in her position, that's for sure.

"Okay, okay… I got it. So, will you be okay to look after S.O.S while I'm away?"

Carmen already acted like her PA, but she had agreed to push the rest of the website's content live for her, all Chloe had to do was take lots of pictures and post on Instagram at every moment possible. If she could get a few snaps of her with Gianni too, then that would make the perfect post to gain more followers and space in the gossip columns.

For the rest of the morning, they continued to strategise content and Carmen even helped come up with a few possible one-liners for her Vanguard interview to try and squeeze in. But lunchtime soon beckoned and they were desperate to leave the apartment (since the day was cool, crisp and sunny). What was the point of living in Greenwich Village if they weren't going to be ladies who lunched?

****

It had been a productive day at the studio (given that it was meant to be their day off) and Pandora was surprised to see that Dom had been working during the night, setting up the studio ready for viewings. Her showroom appointments had never been this organised before. In fact, she didn't really have formal appointments, she just took orders ad-hoc as they were never guaranteed to come.

Together, they created and sent out an invite email to fashion buyers, writers and bloggers, letting them know that their presentation space was ready for viewing and to take orders. Attached to the email was their makeshift look-book—to remind people of the hottest collection to come out of London Fashion Week—along with a link to the video of the runway show, which Dom had already posted onto P.S.L's website.

By late afternoon, a few more replies had come back requesting appointments, which had surprised Pandy even more than the Selfridges appointment. Never before did she have such interest after a show, she wasn't entirely sure she would be able to cope with everything if all of them placed orders.

Together, they set out a calendar with two-hour windows for each booking and responded to emails with available time slots. Three smaller boutiques had confirmed, while another big department store said they would be in touch. Pandora was thrilled beyond her wildest imagination, this meant that her collection would be in two major department stores and potentially in boutiques dotted around the world. The logistics of it all did make her mind boggle, but she knew that Dom would know exactly how to figure this all out. "Okay, now we have potential buyers, we need to code the collection," Dom said. "For now, let's just keep things simple and give everything a three-digit code starting from 001."

Every piece had to be numbered, that way it would be a lot easier for them to know which item the buyer wanted to order, rather than 'that neon dress'—which would just be confusing (as there were many neon dresses in the collection). And to outsiders that were used to a slick operation from their own businesses or high-end brands that they dealt with, they needed to at least appear to have their shit together—and looks were everything to Dom.

After going through the rails and sticking each item with a code, it was time to print off order sheets. Again, Dom had to show Pandy exactly what information would be needed for them to fulfil orders and not make a mess of the deliveries. This was where his experience working at Palazzo came to good use. All those years working for a luxury brand, dodging bullets from in-store politics and putting up with various nonsensical bullshit didn't entirely go to waste. But now it was time to get down to the real business of money.

"I've been going through the books," Dom said, gesturing quotation marks with his fingers (because there was no bookkeeping to go by). "It looks like your profit margin in the past has been way too small... Some orders were obviously rushed through to get made last minute, and you ended up losing money doing that it seems. So, I've gone through the collection and drafted up retail prices which should cover fabric and production costs, as well as make a small profit to keep us going into the next collection... Without needing to dip into your own money, hopefully."

"That would be a first!" Pandy huffed, both happy and sarcastic.

"Right, well I think that's everything then," Dom said. "Tomorrow we'll briefly the guys on who's coming and how to take down orders.... Oh, and we also need to run to the supermarket and stock up on tea, coffee, and Prosecco. One way to get people ordering more than usual is to get them *pissed!*"

10

"Time to wake up!" Carmen said softly, through the crack in the doorway. She had slept over to ensure Chloe was up early and on time for her flight.

They had stayed up quite late drinking wine, while Carmen briefed her on what to do and where to go once she had landed, as well as helping her pack all of the essentials (outfits and accessories, most importantly).

"Huh?" Chloe moaned, reaching to take off her eye mask.

"It's seven… Time to get up. The day has finally arrived!"

'*Damn!*' Chloe thought, sitting up in bed. Drinking two bottles of wine wasn't a good idea—would she ever learn this? Probably not, this lesson would have to be retaken later… Right now, she needed to get up and get it together.

Carmen left the bedroom and returned with an espresso, placing it on the bedside table. Chloe took a sip before downing the rest; what she really needed was a pint of ice-cold water. The need for hydration urged her to reluctantly get out of bed, and as she did, she caught sight of the ticket wedged in her mirror for the very last time. Today was the day that she would finally take it out from its safe place and start her adventure.

Before all those thoughts could simultaneously excite and panic her once more, she poured herself a glass of water from the filter jug in the fridge and gulped it down. 'God, that feels so good.' By the time she had showered and came out in her robe (with a hairdryer and a round brush in hand), Carmen had miraculously managed to look her normal self, with her long brown hair neatly plaited into a side pony.

"Feeling better?" she said. "I've booked a car to take you to the airport, it'll be here in a couple of hours, so you can check-in and have plenty of time to enjoy the members' lounge."

Chloe had forgotten all about the perks of flying first-class (not that she had experienced them before), and couldn't wait to pick up new lipstick colours and perfume from the beauty counters, as well as sample the free food and drink. Carmen had laid out a simple white T-shirt and a comfy track top with matching fitted sweatpants, printed with a palm tree design and completed with sneakers (all courtesy of Hilary Von Furstein).

"But let's start the first-class experience now," she said, guiding her to the kitchen stool, taking the hairdryer and brush from her. "Remember what I said last night? When you get to Milano a car will be waiting for you, just lookout for a driver with your name on a piece of card."

Carmen ruffled her hair gently, blowing it softly to take the dampness out.

"He'll drive you to The Four Seasons, where you're booked in until Monday morning... Your return ticket is included with your outbound—which you have," she continued, turning the heat setting up and taking the brush to her hair, raising her voice so that Chloe didn't miss a word over the blast of hot air. "You should reach the hotel around nine—maybe ten p.m... I suggest you stay in the hotel, eat, and go straight to bed. Your interview with Vangaurd is at ten a.m, so wake up nice and early so you can prepare—and by that I mean a full face of make-up!"

Listening to Carmen give her pep-talk as she coiffed her hair made her feel like she had made it. It wasn't so long ago that she was assisting Carmen style the Latin-American pop sensation, Gabriela Gracia before her movie premiere. She had helped her hairdresser style her hair by passing grips, clips, and hair extensions... Now, she was the star!

"Then a car will come to collect you to take you to the Palazzo show... Remember, Gianni may ask you to dinner after the show—so don't be nervous. Just be yourself and go with the flow.... And most importantly, say yes!"

She knew Chloe didn't want to hear it, but Gianni wanted to see Chloe again after their encounter in New York. That was the whole premise of her going to Milan, not for work or blogging—

Palazzo didn't need social influencers to promote their collection. They had all the press they could want or buy; this was obviously a very extravagant date.

"Okay, all done... Now you don't have to worry about your hair tomorrow," Carmen said, admiring her own handy work now that Chloe's hair was softly blow-dried into bouncy curls.

Chloe got up and admired her reflection in the kitchen window, grateful that Carmen had stayed over. She would have made a total mess of it if she was left on her own to do it, probably ending up bunging into a top-knot (and overslept, of course). "Thanks, Carmen, what would I do without you?"

"Well, that's easy... Miss your flight, of course," Carmen laughed, unplugging the hairdryer. "Right, go get dressed—the car will be here soon."

Chloe didn't argue, she was too excited to start wearing her new clothes as much as fly to Italy. Carmen had wheeled Chloe's suitcase out by the door, ready to go and just as she had, a black car pulled up outside and sounded its horn. "Car's here!" she yelled.

Chloe was now in the bathroom, packing toiletries into a clear bag, ready for security check-in. "Coming!" she called back, checking her make-up in the mirror before she left.

"Don't forget your laptop... Have you got your phone?"

Chloe diverted into the kitchen to grab her laptop and phone, which were still on the kitchen worktop. She shut it down and wedged into her already stuffed handbag, keeping her phone in hand. Carmen had the suitcase handle extended, ready to help carry it down to the car for her.

"Passport—ticket..." Carmen continued to list.

"Shit—*Tickets!*" Chloe still had them wedged in her bedroom mirror.

Carmen rolled her eyes at her scattiness. "Go get them! I'll carry this down to the car and let the driver know you'll be down in five."

Chloe darted back into her room, flinging the door back so it hit the wall. She hated it when she did that because it had made a dent in the wall already, and this was not her property to be wrecking. Racing over to the mirror, she quickly grabbed the tickets, and as she did, she felt a tingle down her back that made her shudder with a thrill.

Shit had just got real.

She placed them into the internal pocket of her handbag, so there was no way they would be lost, along with her passport. Grabbing the door keys from the dish in the hall, she left the apartment and made her way down to the car. The driver was waiting with the passenger door open for her to appear, luggage already loaded.

"Right, here's the apartment keys in case you need to get in," Chloe said, handing them over to Carmen. "I'll see you on Monday night... Meet me at the airport?"

"Sure, we'll keep in touch... Let me know everything that happens, and I'll keep you posted on the Veronica situ."

Chloe kissed Carmen on the cheek and gave her a hug. Carmen held her close and tight, she was excited for her and knew that this trip was just the start of her life journey.

"Take lots of pictures too, remember!" Carmen squeezed in as Chloe got into the car.

"I will—I will, I promise... I'll send everything over to you, so you can post them on the site," Chloe also reminded, as the driver shut the door and walked around the car to get back behind the wheel, ready to set off.

"Ciao, darling!"

The driver started to pull out and drove off with Carmen still watching, waving in the distance as it gathered speed. Sat in the back of it, Chloe's eyes started to feel heavy again, the journey to the airport would be the perfect time for a quick power nap... If the driver hadn't insisted on talking!

"Good morning... Off to anywhere nice?" he started.

Chloe sank deeper into her seat and put on her sunglasses; there was nothing worse than a chatty taxi driver.

*

Thanks to Carmen's precision planning, Chloe had arrived in perfect timing at JFK airport. Having already checked-in online, all she had to do was hand her suitcase over at the desk and get through security, before she could breeze through to the members' lounge. But before that, she excitedly browsed the beauty counters and ended up choosing a new lip colour from Chanel. It was called 'Lover,' which she thought was quite appropriate—given what Carmen had drummed into her head about the reason for this trip. But now was a good time to head to the lounge and relax, before she blew too much on make-up and fragrances she didn't need.

The members' lounge entrance was similar to that of a hotel, with a front desk and super-smiley staff, smartly dressed in pressed uniforms, welcoming members. The main lounge was fully furnished with rich fabric sofas and leather armchairs, even the walls were velvet. Chloe looked around lost, not sure where to go or what to do now she was finally here.

"Good morning, M'am," a young steward said.

"Good morning, erm… Where do I go?" Chloe said, feeling her cheeks warm with embarrassment. "Sorry, this is my first time… I'm usually downstairs with the peasants."

"Oh really, in that case, come right this way—I'll give you a quick tour and get you settled… Where are you flying to?"

"Milan, it's Fashion Week there… *Mark*," Chloe said, reading his name badge as she walked alongside him through to the first lounge.

"Welcome to the members' lounge… There's departure screens visible in each room and we'll announce flights too. You can sit and relax anywhere you wish, but over here we have our bar serving brunch, any beverage you wish and of course, champagne—which is coming right up!" Mark said, heading over to the ice bucket on the bar to pour her a glass.

Alcohol wasn't exactly on Chloe's mind (considering last night's consumption), but maybe it was what she needed to perk up.

"Okay, well sit yourself down and I'll be right back… Miss?"

"Oh, I'm just Chloe."

As she sat by the bar on a leather stool with a soft back, Chloe was rather impressed by the service and stylish decor, overlooking the terminal below through the glass window that spanned the whole side of the wall. Sat there in her designer tracksuit, waiting to fly first-class to Italy, she *really* did feel like a star. 'I could get used to this,' she said to herself.

"Here we go," Mark said, placing down a fresh glass of fizz. "Just sit, relax, and I'll look out for you when your flight's boarding."

Even though she was now sat in the members' lounge sipping champagne, Chloe still had to pinch herself. She shook her head, knowing that she needed to learn how to live in the moment. Her life had been such a madness lately, it was hard to take everything in all at once. She began to list all the events leading up to this point in her mind, trying to de-clutter her head and make sense of it all whilst drinking champagne (the perfect mind-loosener).

How *did* this all come about? Well, she had gotten herself fired from Palazzo after using her discount for a client, but before that, she had met Carmen on the shop floor. And then she had received boxes of old designer clobber from one of her top clients—Mrs Ruthenstock—who was desperate to get rid to make room in her wardrobe for the new season collections.

Then there was Brian. Oh, how she felt bad about how she had treated him, but the timing just wasn't right for a relationship. She couldn't focus on turning her life and career around, as well as engage in a romance. Brian was the tech-guy at Dollars4U (Karen Saunders' online loan company) and was drafted in to help rebuild her website—which he did whilst falling for her. But at the time, it was a small price to pay to get S.O.S back online; Karen had offered Chloe the help of her tech-guy in exchange for a discount on a Palazzo clutch—which ultimately ended up getting Chloe fired.

New York Fashion Week and Gabriella Gracia's movie premiere was where things really started to get crazy. Not to mention the Palazzo retrospective show and after-party where she had met Gianni Palazzo and connected with him on the red carpet—that was *really* crazy! That was the very moment that had catapulted her into the public eye, with the media questioning who this new girl on the fashion supremo's arm was.

Even though the press had been somewhat unexpected, it had helped her to secure her collaboration with DivaFeet. But then there was that weird visit from her old boss, Regina Hall, at her apartment in Williamsburg. She had invited herself over to give Chloe a threatening monologue about how she would never work in fashion again if she pursued Gianni. Little did she know, that it was he who was pursuing her, and would eventually invite her to Milan. And that was just a brief history of the past few months.

'What if Carmen's right,' she started to wonder. 'What if this is his way of wooing me?' That thought soon started to make her feel nervous again and it threw up all kinds of questions like: what would she say, what would she wear, where would they go—what would she do if he tried to kiss her? And then she remembered Carmen's advice once again: 'Just say yes!'

Not realising she had stared into space—recalling her recent past for quite some time—Mark had now returned. "M'am, your flight is now boarding and as a premium traveller, you can go straight through."

"Oh, right…. Thanks," Chloe said, picking up her handbag and grabbing her track top off the back of her chair.

He escorted her to the terminal, handing her over to the stewardess who checked her boarding pass and guided her to her seat. The front section of the plane was laid out with rows of separate cabins, complete with a personal TV screen and tabletop—the kind that Chloe had only seen in the movies (but never thought she would experience in real life). So, she was thrilled when the stewardess presented her hand to one of them, this was where she would be sitting for the next ten hours. There was even a bar area at the back of the section. Not exactly what she was used to, being cramped and sat next to some screaming child in economy.

As take-off time grew nearer, Chloe got accustomed to her private seat and checked out all the gadgets and inflight menu, which was posher than the regular plane food she had expected.

The chairs reclined like beds and were extremely comfy, which she was over the Moon about. It meant she could relax and leisurely work on completing the London Fashion Week article, just in time to post when she arrived at the hotel. But first, she was going to sit back and relax for taking off.

'This is definitely something I could get used to,' she smiled as she reclined back, reminding herself she had better enjoy every second of it. This was most likely just a lucky one-time experience; she'd be back in economy in no time, no doubt.

**

"Thank you for flying with us, please fasten your seat belts as we prepare to land," a hostess said over the plane's tannoy, followed by the perfect translation in Italian.

Chloe peeled off the eye mask that had been in the passenger pack and returned her reclined bed seat into upright position, lifting the window shutter to look outside—tiny yellow and orange lights shone brightly back at her. She had arrived and looked on in amazement at what was the city of Milan at night. It was early evening and Chloe had slept well on the plane, but she was looking forward to a fresh bed and a beautiful hotel room—and not just any hotel either.

Another fantastic thing about flying first-class was that the baggage reclaim had been much quicker, now all she had to do was find her driver. She pulled her case out towards the airport exit (which was heavier than what she remembered it to be), along with her handbag that was also heavy, with the weight of her laptop. But thankfully, Linate was a small airport and she didn't have to walk far before she found the exit.

Many drivers awaited, all with name placards or holding up iPads with passenger names onscreen, welcoming international fashionistas to Milan Fashion Week. 'Where's my name, where's my name?' she murmured to herself. Looking along the line, she eventually found her driver—looking for the best dressed to identify him. This was a Palazzo car after all, and she had been right for once. He wore a fitted black suit with a white shirt and a slim black tie, holding a card up with her name and the gold Palazzo logo underneath.

"Ciao, I'm Chloe Ravens," she said with caution.

The driver spoke little to no English, but he understood that she was his pick-up. Plus, Joli had supplied him with an image beforehand—so he knew who to look out for. She was very professional like that, and when you were the assistant to the hottest designer in the world, you needed to be on top of everything.

The driver took her case and led her outside onto the concourse and through the top floor car park, where a black Mercedes awaited. It was shiny and clean like it had just been freshly waxed and the interior had cream leather seats complete with Palazzo's italic 'P,' logo embroidered onto the headrest. This car wasn't just any car, this was one of the official Palazzo fleet—probably used by Gianni himself.

Sat in the back, Chloe couldn't believe her luck. A private escort in a Palazzo Mercedes. 'If only Regina could see me now!' she thought to herself. That bitch would be furious, especially because Chloe had gone against her advice to stay away from Gianni and Palazzo, for good. In the moment, she reached into her bag for her phone to take a selfie but stopped herself.

She felt greasy and horrible, having just stepped off a long flight and if she felt like crap, then she probably looked like crap. And that wasn't something she wanted to post on social media now she had a following—including Gianni. No doubt this would be her car for the whole weekend anyway, so there would be plenty of opportunities to take that shot later.

Instead, she just looked outside the window, catching a glimpse of her smiling reflection in the glass. Inside she felt alive, excited, and the happiest she had been in a long time. She took in as much as she could, driving in the darkness of the night until they eventually reached the centre of Milan. Driving down the narrow street of Via Montenapoleone, she sat up—taking notice of the designer stores that lined it. Versace, Gucci, Dolce & Gabbana and of course, Palazzo!

The store shone brightly in the evening light, reflecting off the car lights as they drove past which seemed to make it sparkle even more. Now she was being chauffeur driven in one of their cars, which made her feel special. Something that she never thought would happen after being forced to leave her job at their Fifth Avenue store.

Now she was going to be Palazzo royalty, sat on the front row—something that even Regina hadn't accomplished. The driver slowed down, pulling into an even narrower side road that Cartier flanked on the corner. This was going to be easy to remember if she ever got lost—just find Cartier! They carefully drove down a bit further until they stopped outside an arched entrance with Italian flags regally hanging above it—this was her home for the weekend.

"Good evening, welcome to The Four Seasons, Miss Ravens," the doorman said, opening the car door for her to step out.

Chloe was impressed, they were clearly expecting Palazzo's guest of honour. "Oh, I'll just grab my—"

"Please don't worry, we will take care of your luggage," he said, opening the doors for her to enter.

She stepped inside the foyer which was beautifully decorated, with slippery cream marble floors and wooden textures. The doorman walked her to the front desk, where she was greeted once again by name. Behind the desk, a beautiful woman sporting a bold red lip and with neatly tied back glossy, dark brown hair took Chloe's passport to check her in. Chloe looked around the lobby as the woman did her thing on the computer, it looked better than how she had imagined it, although what she had imagined would have never compared. "*Perfetta!* We will show you up to the penthouse suite on the other side of the courtyard. Signor Palazzo would like to wish you a very pleasant stay… This is his personal favourite room at The Four Seasons."

"Oh, there must be a mistake," Chloe said, hearing the word 'penthouse' and the inevitable price-tag that came along with it.

"It's all taken care of," she smiled reassuringly. "You must be hungry after your journey, so please order whatever you wish from the menu… Giancarlo will be your personal room assistant while you stay with us, and I'm here on the other end of the phone if you need anything else."

Chloe double blinked at her, hardly believing what she had just said. Yes, she heard correctly, she had the penthouse all to herself and her own butler. A young gentleman dressed in a white double-breasted blazer with a black tie and matching pants introduced himself and escorted her out through the courtyard and over to the building where the penthouse nestled on top. The hotel's interior was simple yet luxurious, and the courtyard was neatly kept with outdoor seating—lit up with lanterns along the patio. But the most breathtaking part—apart from the fact she had her own private elevator—was when the elevator doors opened.

A white and wooden walled suite, stylishly furnished with designer furniture and fittings awaited her. Chloe's eyes widened as she stepped in and immediately walked over to the tall windows in the living room, giving views over the traditional red-tiled rooftops of Milan city centre. She could just about make out the marble spires of the Duomo in the near distance.

"Through here is the master bedroom, walk-in closet and bathroom," Giancarlo said with his hand held out. "And this way we have the kitchen, and a reading room which leads out to the terrace."

Chloe followed him, looking around the stunning suite with her phone in her hand, filming it all for Carmen. The terrace was dazzling and romantic, illuminated by candle-light lanterns around an outdoor sofa and a dining table set. 'I could move in tomorrow, quite easily,' she thought to herself.

"This is the menu… Let me know if you would like to order anything, the kitchen is stocked with drinks and snacks also," Giancarlo said, offering her a white leather-bound menu.

"Pizza! I'd like a cheese and tomato pizza please," Chloe said, eager to sample what *real* pizza tasted like—not the sloppy New York slices she was used to.

She opened the doors and stepped out onto the terrace overlooking the courtyard below. She wanted to scream with joy, but she also didn't want Giancarlo to hear her as he left the room to fetch pizza. Although he was probably used to the many women Gianni brought here for his pleasure anyway—and their reactions. Shattered from travelling, she slumped on the sofa outside and took in a deep breath before texting Carmen to let her know she had made it—quite literally!

Remembering she was yet to see the other rooms, Chloe sprung to her feet and skipped back through to the living room to discover another smaller lounge on the other side that was an ante-room, complete with a green velvet chaise, leading to the master suite.

The Kingsize bed, dressed in cream and white bed linens dominated the room—but so did the large gold Palazzo box sat on top of it. She gasped before picking up the notecard, which was laid on the lid of the box underneath the light champagne ribbon which held it all together. She opened it and noticed the feminine handwriting, most likely to be Joli's.

Chloe,

Welcome to Milan! I hope you enjoy your stay and I am very much looking forward to seeing you again at the show, wearing this dress exclusively created just for you. In the closet, you will find a selection of looks for the weekend, hand-selected by me as a thank you for coming to Fashion Week.

Gianni x

Excited by what she had just read, Chloe sat on the bed and instantly whipped off the ribbon in a flash. Lifting the lid, featuring the gold Palazzo logo, she unwrapped layers and layers of tissue to reveal what lay beneath—eager to see this dress he had designed just for her!

Until finally, she revealed a white, lace dress which she carefully lifted out. Her jaw dropped as the dress unfolded in front of her eyes. It had thin satin straps with a corset style bust, beautifully made with the most delicate lace she had ever touched—light and net-like with a floral and italic 'P,' monogram pattern.

Then she remembered what the note said: there was more in the closet! She carefully placed the dress back down and hopped off the bed to find it. She peeped into the next room, but that was the en-suite bathroom which looked just as wonderful (that could wait a moment). It was the opposing room that she was looking for—the walk-in wardrobe—which was fully stocked with clothes on gold Palazzo hangers, merchandised just like one of their boutiques. "*Whoah!*" she cried out, her hands automatically slapping her cheeks in amazement.

Running her hands through the clothes, she found jeans, T-shirts, blouses, skirts, and a selection of shoes laid out beneath it all. There was even a white leather biker jacket that she knew was worth thousands of dollars in stores. Chloe counted twelve pieces in total and wondered how on Earth she was going to bring them back home in her already full suitcase. She snapped more pictures and sent them to Carmen, but of course, she already knew what was waiting for her. She had arranged it all with Joli, after all.

Chloe heard Giancarlo return with a trolley and headed back out to the living room. He had set up the table with a green salad, pasta, and her Margherita pizza as requested—topped with fresh basil that filled the room with its light fragrance. After seeing the dress she was expected to wear at the show, there was no way she would be able to finish all this food *and* fit into it. Cutting a slice of pizza with a slicing wheel, Chloe folded it up and took a bite. "Oh my gosh, this is the best," she said, unable to stop herself with her mouth full.

"Italian pizza is the original *and* the best!" Giancarlo said proudly, gesturing with his hands, before finally leaving the room to give her some privacy.

She waited for him to turn his back before sitting down to devour the spread he had laid out for her, trying not to overeat, but it was impossible no to—she was starving. After she had scoffed all of the pizza and most of the pasta (leaving the green salad untouched), she took herself back through the bedroom to use the bathroom. It was wall to wall white marble, even the floor tiles were marble (which she could feel were heated). This was pure luxury! A large bathtub, a spacious shower cubicle, and a toilet and bidet completed the look—as did the beautiful vanity mirror and sink.

Chloe carefully washed her hands, all she needed was to get pizza fingers on her fabulous white custom made dress (that would be impossible to replace should anything happen to it). The dress lay discarded on the bed where she had left it, like a bride awaiting her groom on her wedding night. Picking up the box the dress came in, she heard a rattle from inside it and finished removing all of the tissue paper to see what else was hidden in there.

A small gold jewellery box was left inside, and when she flipped the lid, she was amazed to find a set of large pearl cabochon stud earrings, bearing the gold '*P*,' logo set in the middle. "*Holy shit!*" she said, recognising them to be from the fine jewellery range that used to grace the ground floor of her old store on Fifth Avenue.

She closed the padded box with a soft thump of the lid and carried them carefully with the dress to the closet. She placed the earrings down on the side table and hung up the dress so it wouldn't get creased overnight. She quickly scanned the shoes to see what she could wear with the dress to the show, but it was clear to see that the white stilettos covered in the same fine lace were intended to be worn with the dress. After looking through her new wardrobe one more time, she sat on the floor of the dressing room to try on the shoes, finally admitting to herself that maybe Gianni was interested in her? He certainly wanted to impress her, and it had worked.

Now nearing Midnight, there was only one thing left to do, and that was to shower and get some sleep—tomorrow was going to be a big day and she needed to look her very best for Gianni and the cameras of the front row. But not only for that, the Vanguard interview was arranged to take place in the suite in the morning, and beauty sleep was essential.

***

For once, Chloe was up early and showered. It was hard not to be, she could hardly sleep with all the excitement of the Palazzo fashion show and seeing Gianni again—not mention all of the goodies she had received. All that excitement (and nerves for the interview) mixed together, meant that she had a very shallow sleep and a very prompt wake up call.

Sat at the vanity table, she did her make-up perfectly—taking her time—and ran a brush through her hair to plump up the curls, before pumping mousse into it to give it new life. She wanted her hair to be free and bouncing down her back, given how exposed her décolletage would be in the dress.

Knowing that she had to leave for the fashion show straight after the interview, she decided to get dressed in her custom dress. It was perfect for looking her very best for the interview and photo-shoot, just as Carmen had urged. There was no point going through her case for a crumpled outfit when the *only* thing to be seen in the pages of Vanguard was right there, hanging in front of her.

She headed to the closet, where she had left it to hang, and slipped the dress off the hanger. Unzipping the back carefully, she stepped into it and pulled it up over her thighs and waist. So far, she was surprised to see how snug it fitted her without any fitting taking place. The dress was of short length, with a long piece of lace that hung down the front—disappearing down to the ankle like a wisp. The waist was nipped and the bodice was fitted with a bustier inside, which meant no need for a bra.

Chloe slipped her arms through the thin satin straps before pulling the dress up to cup her bust, readjusting the straps on her shoulders. She smoothed the dress out with her hands before turning her back to the mirror to close the zip as far as she could (she would ask Giancarlo to help her with the rest).

Catching her reflection in the mirror, the dress was gorgeous and almost ghostly in appearance—she could imagine a fashion shoot in a spooky graveyard. The lace was soft and the dress felt svelte, lined in a silky white satin next to her skin. Taking the matching shoes out from underneath the rail, Chloe stepped into each one, afraid to sit down in case she clean split the back of the dress—all the way up. "Why did I eat so much?" she moaned, only now counting the carbs.

Then, there was a knock on the bedroom door.

"Madam, there's a phone call for you from front desk," Giancarlo said on the other side.

As she emerged from the room, his face quickly swapped to one of amazement—this was not the woman he had seen the night before.

"Madam, if I may say... You look sublime!"

"Thank you… Oh, could you just get the zip for me?" Chloe said, sweeping her hair off her back so he could pull the zip all the way up, and finish the hook and eye at the top. Afterwards, she slowly walked to the lounge to take the call, being careful not to slip in her unworn leather-soled, high heels.

"Good morning, Madam, your guests from Vanguard Fashion magazine have arrived," the receptionist said.

"Oh, could you please send them up—we'll have coffee and pastries in the suite."

"Certo."

Placing the phone back down, Chloe looked around to order breakfast but didn't need to ask—Giancarlo nodded and left the room to prepare a continental breakfast. Chloe quickly darted back to the bathroom to check her face in the mirror one more time, spritzing herself generously in the Palazzo 'Gold' fragrance that was already laid out on the vanity.

"Earrings!" she gasped, before heading back into the wardrobe room to grab the box.

Fumbling an earring through her lobe, she closed the bedroom door and headed back out to the lounge to fix the other. As she was doing so, a hotel porter exited the elevator with a woman and a photographer.

"Hi," Chloe said, standing up and walking over to shake her hand. "I'm Chloe, you must be from Vanguard?"

"Ciao," the woman said, taking her hand and kissing both cheeks as fashionistas do. "I'm Dina and this is Marius."

"Welcome... I've already ordered some croissants and coffee," Chloe said.

Dina smiled a smile that said she didn't do breakfast, which Chloe instantly understood. She could kick herself for thinking a journalist from Vanguard magazine would dare eat breakfast during Fashion Week (if at all), but her heels were too high and pointy to commit such self-punishment.

"It's a beautiful morning, shall we sit out?" Chloe said, leading them through the suite to the private terrace.

"Your dress is wonderful—just stunning! It's Palazzo?" Dina said while Marius snapped away, catching Chloe by surprise.

"Erm... Yes, it is," Chloe said, before realising that this was her chance to ham up her profile and not act coy. Carmen's words suddenly rung through her head, forcing her to perk up with confidence—shoulders back. "It's a custom dress Gianni designed for me to wear to the show—you get a sneak peek!"

"Of course... Could you just sit on the sofa over there," Dina said.

Chloe carefully sat on the edge of the cushion so she wouldn't pop the back seam, and readjusted her hair to trickle over one side of her shoulder. Marius quickly clicked away, which Chloe reacted to—changing her position—trying not to pout too much. There was nothing worse than having duck-lips in a Vanguard spread!

"Okay, let's start with how you met Gianni," Dina started, sitting down next to her.

"Oh, well it was purely by chance, at the retrospective after-party in New York... We happened to both arrive at the same time, and he recognised me from a prior event."

"Oh yes, that's right... Didn't you dress Gabriela Gracia for that? How did that come about?"

"That's right, I did... I simply featured the dress on my website, StacksOfStyle, and she reached out to say she loved it," Chloe said, directing Dina back to the reason why they were here—her capsule collection.

"It *certainly* was the talk of the red-carpet... Did Palazzo, or even, Gianni, help you with that?"

"Err… No, I just happened to start working with her stylist at the time—that's how that came about," Chloe said, not letting Dina put words in her mouth.

"And you also *just* happened to meet Gianni Palazzo that night too? *Wow*, now that is a coincidence."

Paranoid already, Chloe forced a smile. 'What does this bitch *really* know about me?'

"Can you describe what StacksOfStyle is, and why you launched your own online platform?"

"Sure… StacksOfStyle is an online fashion destination for women who want to look good on any budget. We don't just cover designer fashion, we include accessible and affordable pieces to recreate seasonal looks and trends… Fashion, for me, is about looking and feeling your best and if you don't know how to do that on your budget, then we'll show you how. Which is why we're collaborating with the perfect partner on this collection."

"Tell me about the collection and what we can expect."

"'Raven, by Chloe Ravens' is a twelve-piece capsule that's an easy way to upscale your wardrobe with high-end looking shoes and accessories. Maybe with a pair of heels or flat shoes, or a handbag—or simply just a stylish fob for your door keys! There's definitely something for everyone and all budgets… I want to make every woman feel like they can own something special. And you don't have long to wait, it will be available online at DivaFeet.com this winter."

"Amazing, I can't wait to see it—can we have access to samples?"

"Of course! I'll have them sent over to you as soon as we can," Chloe said, slightly worried since they hadn't even signed the contract yet.

"And let's talk about Milan Fashion Week… Will you be spending time with Gianni after the show?"

And here it was again, the question that managed to crop up no matter how she deflected it. Everyone knew that this was something else other than an innocent invite to the fashion show. Carmen and Regina knew it, and now even Dina knew it, or so it seemed. Luckily, Giancarlo reappeared with a tray of coffee and a plate of fresh melon and pastries, which he set out on the terrace dining table. "Oh look, coffee's here," Chloe said, getting up and leading Dina over to the table. She could sense that this article was going to be about her and Gianni and her plush, romantic weekend in the penthouse suite of The Four Seasons (Marius was now snapping away at the interior).

"I mean, you hardly know him... But here you are in Milan, attending one of the Week's highlights... Surely, that's every girl's dream?"

Chloe took a sip of her coffee, allowing her extra time to think about how she was going to answer. With no Carmen by her side, she was going to have to think quick and clever. Placing her cup back down on the china plate, she still didn't have an answer, but her lips started to part—she hoped for the best.

"No, you're completely right... We haven't known each other long, but Gianni is a creative pioneer and when we first met, I think our creative souls instantly understood each other. I mean, Palazzo is now a fashion group—having secured Maison Marais—and he needs creative people around him."

"Are you suggesting that you are working with him on the new brand vision for Maison Marais?" Dina pressed.

'Is this bitch gonna twist everything I say?' Chloe cursed, trying not to wear the matching expression on her face.

"No, not at all," Chloe politely laughed. "I simply meant that Gianni is a man who can spot creativity, and I like to think he is behind what I'm trying to achieve with StackOfStyle... But of course, I wouldn't turn down such an offer if he wanted to hear my ideas."

Waiting in the background, Giancarlo could see that Chloe was uncomfortably taking a grilling so he left the terrace, taking her empty coffee cup and giving her a subtle nod as he did.

"And what does the future hold for StacksOfStyle?"

Finally, a question Chloe could answer.

"I want to grow it into an e-commerce site—not just fashion editorial. I want my followers to read an article and then click and shop the items… I see StacksOfStyle as the future of online shopping for both designer and affordable fashion… Like I said earlier—something for everyone… But of course, I have a lot of work before then, but the 'Raven, by Chloe Ravens' collection is the first step on that journey," Chloe said, coming back to the collection once more.

"Miss Ravens," Giancarlo said, returning to the terrace. "Your car is waiting outside for you."

"Oh, right—thank you, Giancarlo."

"Of course, you'll need to be leaving very soon—it's a good hour to get to the Palazzo showroom," Dina said. "In fact, we better get going too—we'll see you there."

Chloe stood up and firmly shook Dina's hand—no air-kissing this time—while Marius continued to take her picture. Giancarlo showed them out to the elevator as Chloe sat back down at the table—her face in her hands. "God, that was not good!" she said to herself.

But she didn't have time to wallow now. She quickly got up and dashed inside to the lounge, where she had left her phone and laptop—damage control was needed. She quickly typed an email to Carmen, explaining how the interview had gone down, attaching her London Fashion Week article for her to upload as well. "Giancarlo… Thanks so much for that," she said, noticing his return to the suite.

"What? I did nothing," he said, palms out.

"You saved me and you know it!" Chloe said, giving him a smile.

"Okay, but seriously… Your driver is waiting for you."

"*What?* You're serious! What time is it?" Chloe said, checking her phone to see it was half-past ten already.

If what Dina had said was true and the showroom was an hour away, that meant she would reach there by half eleven—just thirty minutes before the show was due to start. Closing the lid on her laptop, she skipped back to the bedroom to grab her clutch—quickly stuffing it with the essentials. She was about to leave, but she realised that it was September in Milan and if she were suddenly asked to stay out for the afternoon, then she should bring a jacket of some sort. She rifled through the rail of clothes in the closet, but nothing quite matched the exquisite dress she was wearing. There was only one thing she could do, and that was to make this look into a 'Chloe Ravens look' by going for the complete opposite style. She grabbed the white leather biker off the hanger and ripped the Palazzo tags off with her teeth.

"Okay, Giancarlo... I'm off—thanks for everything. I'll see you later this afternoon; not sure what time I'll be back, but don't worry about me... Take the rest of the morning off or something."

He smiled, appreciating her kind offer in return for his chivalrous assistance, but unfortunately for him, taking the rest of the morning off was out of the question. He called the elevator and walked her down to the car, which was now starting to back up traffic down the narrow side street. As they made their way through the courtyard, passing other guests sat having brunch out on the patio, Chloe could feel their eyes on her as she wiggled by in her dress.

You didn't have to know about fashion to see that this was not the kind of dress one picked up off the rack, and the fact she was being watched made her feel fantastic! If this was the reaction she was getting from the general Joe's, then how she was going to be received when she stepped out of the car at the Palazzo fashion show?

11

The traffic had been terrible, what with every Fashion Week-er trying to get out of the city centre, all at the same time. Sat upright and alert in the back of her private Mercedes—still fearing she would rip the back out of her dress if she slouched—Chloe's phone buzzed with messages from Carmen.

> Ciao Bella! Sounds like U did a great job... Don't worry about the interview. I've just uploaded the LFW article on S.O.S.

> The room looks amazing BTW!
> & Check out all those new clothes...

> Can't wait to try them on when U get back... Send more pix of your outfit & remember 2 Instagram lots @ the show! C X

She smiled. She knew Carmen would help her see the lighter side of things, and as she had already experience—there was no such thing as bad press. With the car standing still in traffic, now was the perfect time to take that selfie in the Palazzo decorated Mercedes—especially as she was all dressed and ready for that close-up now. Turning the camera onto herself, she made sure she captured the '*P*,' logo headrest in the background. Just as she managed to take a few snaps in succession to review for her approval, the car jolted out to make a U-turn—forcing her to reach for the passenger handle above the window.

"Very busy— I take a-new way," the driver said. The car whizzed down a side street, another Via that seemed way too narrow to be going down in such speed, but Chloe trusted her official Palazzo driver to know where he was going—and what he was doing. Most of the Milanese streets seemed narrow to her compared to New York. Managing to now let go of the handle, she quickly looked back on the pictures and cropped her favourite so she could post it on Instagram (with the Paris filter, which was becoming her favourite), along with the caption: 'On my way to Palazzo S/S fashion show!'

Looking out of the window, it now felt like they were driving out of the city at last. The buildings got smaller and more residential until they finally reached a freeway, which the driver sped up to the maximum limit. In the distance, she could see what looked like an air-field with a large white structural building, which she could instantly tell was the Palazzo showroom. As they got closer, she could make out that it was covered in large, white, shiny tiles with 'P-A-L-A-Z-Z-O' in large golden letters spaced out across the side.

Palazzo had built their very own showroom and auditorium, becoming the official address for all of their Fashion Week shows. Having a permanent space allowed them to produce the visions that Gianni had for their collections, no matter what the scale. It was also the international showroom for their wholesale team, where official retailers from all around the globe flocked to, some six times a year to place their orders.

The car slowed down and pulled off the freeway, driving up a road leading to the white building, which looked rather imposing in the middle of nowhere. The road turned to smooth tarmac and as it drew closer, Chloe felt a burst of excitement and nerves start to build up within her. Driving closer towards the entrance, Chloe looked out of the window as they passed photographers, journalists, and plenty of fashion folk, all dressed up in their Palazzo outfits as they made their way to the entrance.

There were plenty of try-hard guests sporting their signature gold and beige 'P,' monogram jackets, trousers, track-tops, overcoats and hats—even at Fashion Week you couldn't escape the famous logo. The car stopped outside the main entrance, which had been roped off and also carpeted in gold and beige monogram. As the driver came to a halt, a young woman dressed in a black suit stepped forward to open the door for her with a clear plastic umbrella in hand—it was typical that it had now started to drizzle.

"Welcome to Palazzo," the assistant said, offering her hand to help Chloe step out.

Chloe put her phone away in her clutch and wrapped the leather jacket over her shoulders as she accepted the hand. The last thing she needed was to be photographed face-planting in high heels outside the venue as she made her entrance. That was one way to make the headlines, but Chloe was hoping to be the talk of the show for a different reason.

The assistant, complete with an iPad and a headset, guided her to the row of photographers who were line dup behind the velvet ropes and waiting to snap the stars as they arrived. They had already started clicking away at her with full flash on—even in daylight. The assistant briefly took the umbrella away from Chloe so they could get a clear picture of her. And just like that, she had to recall how to pose. What was it she did at the retrospective after-party? One hand on hip, right knee bevelled and chin up—mouth slightly parted.

As more photographers edged closer to get the best picture— now realising who she was—it sparked the attention seeker inside of her. She removed her white leather biker jacket and passed it to the assistant who was patiently waiting nearby and quickly flipped her hair over one shoulder, before resuming her pose in the opposite direction. She could feel cold drops of rain sporadically drip on her shoulders, but she didn't care.

"Miss Ravens—turn this way please," a photographer said. "Chloe—*Chloe!* You look amazing!" egged another. "Chloe Ravens, who are you wearing," one journalist called, reaching out over the aluminium barrier with her microphone.

Chloe laughed as she flipped her hair once more. "Palazzo, of course!"

"Follow me, Miss Ravens," the assistant said, returning the clear plastic umbrella over her head. "The show will start soon, I'll take you to your seat."

As they walked past dozens of guests and security, Chloe dipped her head shyly—not wanting to appear like she was swanning in with superiority. She *was* a newcomer to all this after all. Walking down a long white-walled corridor, Chloe could have sworn the entrance was back towards the front—it seemed like they were walking *away* from the auditorium. Finally, they reached the other end of the building, which began looking a lot like a loading bay with a breeze-blocked back wall, full of rails, crates and boxes—and chaos!

"Please watch your step," the assistant said, leading her towards what looked like a set of fire escape doors flanked by two burly security guards with earpieces, sporting blacked-out shades. She flashed her security pass and they let Chloe through.

'Holy fuck!' Chloe cursed in her head. This was the backstage area—was she taking her to see Gianni already?

"Ah, Joli—Joli!" she called. "Questo é, Miss Chloe Ravens."

Joli looked like she was about to run off, rushing around and being pulled in every direction, but stopped in her tracks once she heard Chloe's name. "Ciao, welcome… I've heard so much about you! I'm so glad you made it," Joli said, giving her a quick air kiss on both cheeks.

Joli was a petite, cherub-faced girl—no older than Chloe—wearing a black blazer with an embroidered '*P*,' patch on the breast pocket. Her dark skin was flawless and her cheeks were bronzed and glowing—either that or she was perspiring. "Here… This is your pass," she said, taking one of the multiple lanyards that hung around her neck, passing it to Chloe. "Follow me—I'll take over from here."

Chloe carefully stepped over cables and dodged crew runners, rushing to get to the other side of the stage. Excitement was definitely in the air, it tingled like live electricity. She looked over in the opposite direction of where they were heading and saw models being pulled and prodded with hair and make-up brushes, getting fumigated with hairspray like they were in some sort of quarantine. Chloe tried to see if she could spot Gianni somewhere in all this madness, but Joli was walking too fast to be slowed down by celeb spotting.

They reached a bumpy carpeted area covering more cables, which was far easier to stabilise her footing on in high heels, until

Joli pulled back a huge black-out curtain revealing rows of seats and a long runway. It was a long strip of what looked like shiny white plastic, stretched out for a hundred meters or so.

"That's her!" Chloe overheard one man say to the woman next to him, elbowing her not so discreetly.

One recognition ignited a domino effect of heads, all looking in her direction as Joli guided her to her chair—some even whipped out their phones to take her picture.

"This is you," Joli said, stopping half-way down the runway. "Enjoy the show—I'll see you after!"

But before Chloe could get a word in, Joli had run off backstage again. Here she was, left alone with hundreds of faces all starting to look in her direction. She was dressed in custom Palazzo after all, and she was labelled with being Gianni's new girlfriend—what did she expect? With no other choice but to accept the spotlight she was under, Chloe slowly took her seat. She couldn't quite believe that she was sat centre runway—these seats were usually reserved for big fashion names and editors.

Awkwardly smiling at the people around her as she sat on her own, she was aware that they were all talking about her—having recognised her from the gossip columns. But then again, she didn't expect anything less; here she was, wearing a revealing couture dress that no one had ever seen before. Carmen had been right yet again and Chloe hated her for it; everyone knew that she was 'Gianni's new girl' except her, but she was pulled out of the surrounding whispers by a man shouting loudly to his companion as he approached her.

"Oh—I just hated the collection darling! Laziness, that's what it was—*Lay-Zi-Ness!*"

It was none other than Lou Banks.

Chloe brushed a strand of hair behind her ear, resting her clutch in the groove between her seat and the next—trying to look like she wasn't awkwardly sitting on her own while everyone talked about her.

"Hello darling, you must be Chloe Ravens!" Lou beamed, stopping at the seat next to her.

'How does everyone know my name?' Chloe asked herself, not realising that her headline with Gianni had made it global. She stood up to kiss him on the cheek and delicately shook his hand.

"And you're Lou Banks of course, so nice to meet you," she said.

Lou was hard *not* to recognise; he was a lively man with a bubbly character who always wore loud Prada print shirts (or some sort of print that made him distinguishable in the front rows). Today was no different, he was wearing a black Hawaiian shirt featuring a gold brocade of gold chains intertwined with thorny roses and of course, the famous interlocking '*P*,' monogram.

"I think I met one of your friends in London—Dominic Fraser? He mentioned he knew you… He's a handsome chap that one!"

"Oh yes, he is… We are old friends from New York, but he left to work for Pandora Simmons in London."

"Now, that was a great show! Don't you think Paulina? Do you know Paulina, darling?" Lou said, touching Chloe's arm with a camp pat.

Chloe knew Paulina all right, but Paulina didn't necessarily know her. Paulina was the supremo model booker and Founder of Thunder Models, she was responsible for most of the supermodels walking high-fashion shows. Lou invited them to sit back down in their seats as he carried on chatting. "Paulina actually just signed the most gorgeous model from Pandora's show, didn't you dear?"

"I certainly did… In fact, I booked her onto this show last minute—she's going to be BIG!" Paulina said, exploding her hands out in front of her.

While they chatted, a photographer had dashed over to them, prompting Lou to cosy up to Paulina and Chloe to take a picture. Chloe had a sudden moment of disbelief—everything was happening so fast. It only felt like a few hours ago that she was back in her room in New York, staring at the plane tickets in her mirror—and now she was sat next to Lou and Paulina on the front row.

As Chloe's eyes regained focus from the camera's flash, she could see on the opposite side of the runway, Vanguard's editor had been seated next to the English rapper, Shockzy, who was fully decked out in Palazzo monogram from head to toe. Next to him was Gianni's sister, Graziana—she was unmistakably recognisable with her long, platinum hair shining like a beacon in the darkness of the auditorium. They had barely touched their seats when the lights went down and the drumbeat of the show track had kicked in.

Chloe suddenly sat up as everyone looked towards the front of the runway, holding out their phones to capture every look. It seemed like no one watched shows anymore, only via their phones. Chloe hated that, what was the point of being at a show if you were going to focus on making sure you had the recording on your phone? Surely that's what the Internet was for? Alas, Chloe blended in with everyone else and had her phone on standby—as per Carmen's strict instructions to take lots of pictures.

*

The first model, was none other than the legendary supermodel Naomi, stepping out wearing a full white suit that juxtaposed her dark skin, holding an over-sized white envelope clutch with the iconic '*P*,' Logo in gold hardware on the front. The whole look was completely white, right down to leather biker gloves and ankle boots, and as she pounded down the white runway, each tile she stepped on lit up like a disco dance-floor—which delighted the audience. That was a snap to take right there!

As Naomi came down the runway, Chloe made sure she stopped tapping her phone to grab the best picture, looking attentive—following her with her eyes—before looking back for the next model who had already stepped out. It was a similar suit, this time with a skirt in full pastel pink monotone featuring a large belt with the logo—again over-sized. The next model wore lavender, then pistachio, followed by a soft coral and then a light camel tone—this time in a full trench overcoat.

The theme of the show so far, seemed to be full block colours, until the next model came out wearing a long camel cardigan with a white pencil skirt, carrying a pastel pink quilted shoulder bag jangling with gold letters, spelling out 'P-A-L-A-Z-Z-O.' It was Paulina's new signing from London—Carly Wattmore—resembling a soft scoop of Neapolitan ice cream.

The next series of models all wore combinations of the soft tones, until the music changed, introducing the next section of the collection which went back to all-white looks—including a high waisted swimsuit that was sent down the runway with just a wide-brimmed sun hat and a pair of wedge platforms. Chloe remained hypnotised by the new look Palazzo, this was much different from what they had ever done before. The palette was neutral and feminine; usually, they were known for loud prints and bold pop colours. Look after look offered something different, yet still in the same theme tones until the lights faded down once more and the music quickened—making way for the evening dresses.

The first look was a soft pink tuxedo pantsuit with silk lapels and a low V-neck lace cami underneath it, with a pastel pink fedora. As she passed Chloe, the next model was already storming her way down towards her wearing a flared pantsuit in camel, this time carrying a gold clutch bag very similar to the Palazzo Gold Rush bag that Chloe risked her job getting for Karen Saunders with her discount—it made her chuckle.

How far she had come since the days of working in the Fifth Avenue boutique under the fearful reign of Regina Hall—if only she could see her now. But that was the thing, she certainly would see her once the show coverage got out, and this made Chloe smile even more and reminded her to sit tall and upright. She had made it further than Regina had estimated of her.

Snapping out of her thoughts, her attention drew back to the clothes coming down the runway, and it was now time for some stunning evening dresses—starting off with the sexy cuts that Palazzo was known for. Yes, Gianni had opted for the soft tones in the main part of the collection, but here came the signature pieces that oozed sex appeal. Drawing on from their successful retrospective show back at New York Fashion Week, Chloe noted a few nods to their archive. Most notably, a sexy long white silk gown, with large gold letters down the side connecting the front to the back panel—again spelling out the brand name.

Long evening gowns in pistachio, pink, yellow and white all came floating down the runway like phantoms. Some flowed with the stride of the model, with beautiful light silk streamers wafting behind them, while others were fitted and revealing with high slits that flashed a lot thigh. On closer inspection, Chloe could make out that some were in fact made from the same lace as the dress she was wearing. She was wearing a piece from the collection, before anyone else!

The show came to a close with a romantic white wedding dress (a long pencil-shaped gown in white lace with a bustier top), with at least twenty metres of train trawling behind her with her face covered in fine 'P,' monogrammed lace. She was swinging a bag in the shape of a bouquet of flowers, made from folded up lace and satin, oozing gold letters that jingled from gold chains as the model walked the length of the runway. Two more models walked behind her (the bridesmaids) in shorter versions of the bustier lace dress.

As they reached the point where Chloe was sitting, heads began to turn to her direction once more. Chloe looked down at her own ensemble, which was now obviously made in the same style and fabric. Was she really sat in the frow, wearing some sort of pre-wedding dress? Chloe felt awkwardly strange, but she re-mained poised to watch the models reach the end of the catwalk. She wasn't going to hide—and it wasn't like she could do that anyway—sat bang front and centre of it all.

As the wedding dress finally made the exit, the full line-up of models came flowing out from the left side of the stage to the audi-ence, clapping. The army of models did the rounds before heading back to exit stage right—and as soon as they were out of sight—the spotlight that following them faded with a beat of darkness before the designer himself took a bow. Dressed in a full white suit with flared pants, and an open white shirt that revealed a gold Palazzo medallion, Gianni made a brief appearance to applause. Chloe's heart skipped a beat at the sight of him (this was the first time she had seen him since their encounter), she had to catch her breath to regain control. Lou nudged her with his elbow as he clapped as if to say: 'There's your man!'

**

With Gianni stepping back, the music dimmed and the auditorium lights came up to reveal the glare of the white show set. It was only now that Chloe realised just how many spectators there had been, and most importantly, who. She noted many a familiar face, including legendary supermodels, socialites, and famous faces from the fashion and music industry. The whole day had been such a crazy series of events that she hadn't had the chance to take it all in—and now it was all over.

"Are you coming to the Versace show, darling?" Lou said as he got up to leave.

"Yes, grab a ride with us… You'll need to leave right away to get back to the city on time," Paulina added.

"The Palazzo show is always fabulous, but this location is a pain in the tits, isn't it?" Lou complained.

But Chloe had no complaints, she was just thrilled to be here in person and not back at home watching the show on the live feed of the Palazzo website. "Sadly not… No Versace for me I'm afraid."

"Well, it was fabulous to meet you, darling," Lou said, going in for another kiss on the cheek.

"And you too… Oh, be sure to look out for my interview in Vanguard. They're covering my capsule collection with DivaFeet," Chloe squeezed in.

"Will do, darling—Ciao for now," Lou said, making an escape back to his waiting car with Paulina in arm.

The auditorium was now thinning out, some guests had lingered to photograph the set and take selfies, but being a lone guest, Chloe felt too embarrassed to do all that (even though she knew Carmen would give her a telling off for not doing so later). 'Well, I suppose I'd better get myself back the hotel,' she thought, picking up her clutch and draping her jacket over her shoulders, getting ready to leave. As she slowly began to walk towards the exit, she felt a hand on her shoulder.

"Chloe, did you like the show?" Joli said, taking her by surprise.

"Yes, it was amazing!"

"Come, he's waiting for you." Once again, Joli was already marching towards the exit where the models had come out from moments before. But Chloe didn't argue or try to stop her, this was the moment she had been waiting for. Joli was a woman who had very little time on her hands, and a lot of things to get done (she wasn't interested in unnecessary chat with Gianni's flings).

Chloe's stomach started to flip with excitement, not only was she about to witness what went on behind the curtains at a Palazzo fashion show, but she was clearly about to be reunited with Gianni again. 'This is it!' she squealed to herself, with an exciting sort of panic.

Backstage, models were hugging and kissing each other, some had already stripped down to their bras and panties while others were being photographed in their looks. Chloe continued to follow Joli through the haze of it all, watching her footing in her high heels that were now pinching her toes. Joli started to slow down as they reached a huddle of people, and as they got closer, Chloe could hear Gianni voice somewhere in the middle of it all.

"Pastels are going to be everywhere... You can expect similar tones to appear in the menswear collection too. Some of the pieces, like belts and jackets, are in fact unisex—gender-fluid fashion is going to be another huge thing for luxury brands in the near future."

Joli muscled her way in through the crowd, leaving a space that gave Chloe a clear view of Gianni in his white suit. Although he was wearing gold-framed aviator sunglasses now, so she couldn't quite see his eyes. Joli whispered into his ear, letting him know he had a visitor, which made him look through the gap and lift them up onto his head—locking his vision onto Chloe in the dress he had designed for her.

And there it was again, that sensation she felt deep inside for him like she had been winded with just his stare. For a moment, Gianni stopped talking to the press and took in her vision. Journalists and fashion writers continued to bombard him about the collection, but he was focused on Chloe now.

He smiled at her which made her laugh and dip her head, looking away at her feet to break his gaze. The pain of her shoes had miraculously disappeared as her veins coursed with excitement and pure lust. She could feel the attraction rising up in her body—it made her feel alive.

"Excuse me guys, can you let my friend through?" Gianni said, reaching his hand out to her.

The crowd looked behind them to see who he was talking about, and was pleased to see it was the mysterious girl from New York. Photographers started clicking once more as Chloe stepped forward and took his hand. Her palm was damp with sweat and the touch of his manly hand on hers made her pulse even more and now she was right next to him, she could smell his cologne which made her take a deep breath to breathe him in.

Gianni pulled her close and kissed her cheek in a friendly manner, before encouraging her to pose for the cameras once more. "Did you like the show?" he asked, taking her by the waist as she stood next to him.

Another shock of electricity fired off inside her whole body, she felt like she could collapse into his arms quite easily in front of everyone. "I loved it—congratulations!" she said, managing to keep it together.

"How long have you been seeing each other?" one reporter courageously asked.

Gianni dipped his head and puffed out a laugh, putting his sunglasses back on to hide his eyes. He waited before answering that one, hoping Chloe would step in with an answer—but she too was blushing.

"Well, we have only recently become friends… And it was finally wonderful to meet the stylist behind Gabriela Gracia's most recent looks wearing vintage Palazzo—which was so well-timed with our show there—and I wanted her to see the collection. In-novative stylists, like Chloe, are crucial for Palazzo's commercial visibility—which I am always extremely grateful for... I hope that this is the start of a creative and collaborative future," he said, with his hand still around her waist.

Chloe could feel that the question was about to come back to her and she had nothing to add, and she didn't want to say something dumb or stutter on the spot. Luckily she didn't have the chance to do so.

"Giiiaaannni! Amore mio! La collezione è bellissima!" a wom-an called out, pushing her way through.

It was none other than Graziana with her assistant, Marco, not far behind her. She was petite with dark, tanned skin, and long blonde hair that swept across her buttocks as she sashayed over to him. Marco, on the other hand, was model-like, tall—gorgeous some would say. He wore black fitted leather jeans held up with a gold buckle *'P,'* logo belt, showing off his physique in a black and gold Palazzo brocade print shirt that was open from his navel up.

"Graziana!" Gianni said as she grabbed his face to kiss him—forcing Chloe to step aside.

"Isn't my wonderful brother talented?" she said to the report-ers in her thick Italian accent.

Now the photographers were really going wild, making sure they got the perfect shot of the famous duo. Although Gianni was the man behind the creative side of the brand, Graziana was re-sponsible for the business side of things as chief executive officer. Gianni looked around to find Joli, who hadn't moved far from his side and gave her the nod—the nod to call an end to the press conference.

"And who is this?" Graziana said, taking off her black wrap-around sunglasses to reveal a surgically enhanced face—it was almost as if she had a bulldog clip holding back layers of sagging skin.

"This is my friend, Chloe, remember?" Gianni said, looking around for her, taking Chloe's hand to bring her back into his circle.

"Oh… Of course, nice to meet you," she said in a deadpan tone, handing her shades to Marco who was stood behind her, staring at Chloe in support of his boss. "I've heard so much about you."

"Lovely to meet you too," Chloe said, not quite believing that Graziana Palazzo had heard of her—of course, she had not. Graziana was a style icon herself, famous for her blonde skin, black leather body-con ensembles and for exuding the luxurious glamour of Palazzo—Chloe was a nobody.

"So… How do you two know each other," she said, sweeping her pin-straight hair off her shoulders.

"We met at the retrospective show in New York," Gianni said, taking Chloe by her waist to reassure her (he knew that a grilling from Graziana was inevitable).

"Ah! Of course, I leave my brother alone for one minute…" Graziana said, scanning Chloe with her small eyes that were made even smaller with black, smokey eyeshadow. "Unfortunately I had to be in Paris during New York Fashion Week, finalising the Maison Marais deal."

Graziana cut her a side-eyed look. If she *had* been in New York for the event, she would have made sure that Chloe wouldn't have had the chance to get near her brother; she knew Gianni well, and he couldn't keep his dick in his pants at the best of times. Graziana's assessment of Chloe had already been made. She was nothing more than the other girls before her, here today—gone tomorrow. She didn't need some young upstart—some ten years younger than Gianni—stepping in and getting involved with her brother now. But seeing Chloe dressed head to toe in Palazzo, it seemed she already had.

"So, are we doing dinner?" Graziana said, pulling Gianni's arm to walk off with him alone.

Chloe just stood there, not sure what to do next amongst the backstage bustle as they walked ahead.

"Of course, I'll see you there… Are you coming to dinner, Chloe?" Gianni said, looking back around to see her stood in the same spot.

"I'm sorry?" Chloe said, confused by what was happening and unsure whether Graziana would even allow her to.

"Dinner... You're coming to dinner, right?"

"Oh, she doesn't want to waste her weekend in Milan with us," Graziana said with piercing eyes.

"Oh, I wouldn't wanna—" Chloe started, but then realised this was exactly what Graziana wanted her to say.

She was here to see Gianni again and she wasn't going to pass up another opportunity to spend more time with him; this brief moment backstage was not enough for her to discover the potential between them. Graziana was right, she *didn't* want to waste her weekend in Milan! Carmen's words of advice started to ring through her mind once again: 'If he invites you to dinner—say yes!'

"Sure... I'd love to come to dinner," Chloe said with a smirk, making eye contact with Graziana. It was a bold move to go up against his sister, but if she cowered to her now then it would only tell Gianni that she wasn't strong enough to stick around and cope with the egos around him—and it had worked. She had stared in the face of Medusa and survived.

"Great!" he said, smiling back at her. "Head back to the hotel and get changed, be ready in two hours... Joli will send the location to your driver."

And before she could ask any more questions, Gianni blew her a kiss and headed off with Graziana to congratulate the models and styling team. Again, Chloe felt like a spare part in all of this as she stood there watching Graziana introduce Gianni to the latest modelling sensation, Carly Wattmore. Was she now simply meant to slink off back to her car? Whatever it was, she needed to do something quick; she wasn't sure how much longer Marco was going to stand there, staring her down with his arms folded.

Luckily Joli had come back just in time to her rescue. "Hey... What have I missed?" she asked, always needing to be up to date on the latest going's on.

"Well, apparently I'm going to dinner with Gianni and Graziana."

"*Really?* Well, then we need to get you back to the city pronto! Pack up your cases and be ready to leave by four, sharp!"

"*What?* Why do I have to pack my case for dinner?" Chloe said, even more, confused than she was already.

"Because the dinner, Chloe, is in Paris!"

"Holy *fuck*—sorry!" Chloe said, realising she had said it out loud, rather than in her head.

"Exactly… I couldn't agree more. Now, let's get you out of here." Joli swiftly escorted her away from Marco (who had noted every word between them to relay back to Graziana) and back to the car out front. Chloe's driver was perched against the car smoking a cigarette, but he quickly stamped it out on the floor when he saw Joli and Chloe approaching—he opened the passenger door for her to climb in. "Ciao, Franco… Chloe will be flying to Paris with us, so please drive her to the jet which is leaving at five."

Franco, her driver, simply nodded and wasted no time getting into the driver's seat to start up the engine, ready to speed back to the city. Joli didn't wait to wave them off, instead, she ran back inside to keep control of matters… With Graziana around, anything could happen, and so far, enough had already happened for her liking!

***

The suite doors flew back, causing a loud crash as Chloe blundered her way through to the bedroom. "Miss Ravens?" Giancarlo said, quickly getting up from the sofa, not wanting to get caught taking a break, making use of the suite for himself. Chloe was in too much of a rush to notice, or even care. She had to get her things together quickly as it had taken them an hour to get back to the hotel. She lifted her case and threw it down on the bed with a swoop that a powerlifter would have been proud of, before heading into the closet to grab what she could with overarm.

"*ARGGGGHHHHH!*"

Looking around, there was too much to pack, what with her suitcase almost already full to capacity. She looked around, at a complete loss of what to do. She could feel that she was about to cry in desperation—but there was a knock on the door.

"Miss Ravens, can I help with anything?" Giancarlo said, waiting in the doorway for permission before he entered.

"Actually, yes! Yes, there is… I've just found out I'm going to Paris and I need to leave in an hour!"

Giancarlo could hear the panic in her voice, but he was used to this sort of thing happening. It wasn't the first time he was in this situation with one of Gianni's 'guests' and knew exactly what to do. "Okay, no problem… Just let me know what you want to bring, I will pack it for you while you freshen up, take a shower—whatever you need to do."

But that was the trouble, she needed to fit the impossible inside her case. Realising that she was to be in the company of the Palazzo's, she figured it made sense to at least stay on brand and pack the clothes he had given her. The rest she could leave behind and have Giancarlo ship back to Carmen in New York for her.

"Thank you! I'll be fifteen minutes!" Chloe said, darting off into the bathroom, leaving Giancarlo to it. Slipping off the dress, she picked it up off the floor and hung it on the bathrobe hook behind the door—wincing as she did. It was almost criminal for her to treat a couture dress in such a way, but she didn't have time to think of an alternative right now. She quickly turned on the hot water and stepped inside to wash her face and body without getting her hair wet, which was quite a skill.

When she had emerged from the bathroom, Giancarlo had almost packed everything, leaving her D.V.F clothes laid out in neat piles on the bed. "Okay, are you sure you don't want any of these things?" he asked.

"No… I think?" she said, not entirely sure how long they would be in Paris for (but then again, she was travelling with Gianni Palazzo and clothes were not something she needed to worry about).

Paris was home to one of their flagship boutiques on Avenue Montaigne, and no doubt Chloe could have whatever she wanted from there should she need it.

"Perfect, we are all done then," Giancarlo said, zipping up her case. "I left some clothes in the closet for you to wear to the airport."

Chloe sighed with relief, she hadn't thought about that and was glad he had; it was obvious to her also that this was not his first time in this situation.

With her plush bathrobe snuggly wrapped around her, she walked into the closet to see what he had picked out and was rather surprised to find he had kept out the pair of jeans and the white T-shirt (with 'P-A-L-A-Z-Z-O' emblazoned on it in a gold decal). He had hung up her white biker jacket (that she had thrown on the floor upon arrival) and placed the sneakers underneath the rail. 'Giancarlo is wasted, he should be a stylist,' Chloe smiled to herself.

"I'll leave you to get dressed," he said, happy that she was satisfied with his service.

After getting changed and running a brush through her hair, she quickly reapplied her makeup, ready for the flight with Gianni in his private jet. The thought excited her, but it also gave her the jitters. This was going to be the first time they would be alone for a good few hours, and anything could happen—unprepared. She shook her head, this was not the time to entertain thoughts that would throw her off—she was up against the clock to look shit hot before the car was ready to whisk her to the airport.

Finishing her fresh face with her Chanel lipstick once more, she packed her makeup bag and threw it in her handbag, rushing over to the notepad on the bedside table. She scribbled down her address back in New York, with the attention to Carmen. Doing so had reminded her that she needed to let her know what was going on—she would freak out! But then again, now was not the time to bring on a tirade of questions via text—she would handle that matter in the back of the car en-route.

"Giancarlo," Chloe called, walking out into the living area to find him on the phone.

"That was reception… Your driver's outside, ready when you are."

"Oh my God!" she started to freak, before taking a breath to compose herself. "Okay, this is my address back in New York… Please can you forward my clothes here?"

"Do not worry, I will take care of everything," Giancarlo said, taking the piece of hotel notepaper and folding it into four—putting it into his jacket pocket.

"Well, I guess I better go down… Thank you for everything!" Chloe said, grabbing her handbag, which still weighed like a brick with her laptop wedged inside.

It was a becoming a bit of an inconvenience to lug around since she had no time to write articles for StacksOfStyle as she had imagined—and now she was jetting off to Paris—it seemed Gianni had other ideas about what she would be getting up to.

12

Back in the car on the way to the airport, Chloe finally had a moment to check the dozens of unread messages left on her phone—all from Carmen. Mainly asking where her Instagram posts were and more importantly, what was going on! She hadn't heard from her since this morning and was fully expecting Chloe to be posting live from the show (as they had discussed), which didn't really happen.

Realising it couldn't be all play and no work, Chloe took her laptop from her handbag and loaded it up to write a quick review on the Palazzo show. Considering how things had gone so far on this trip, she definitely wouldn't have time to write once they got to Paris, and this short car ride was her best chance of getting anything done.

Palazzo's next move in fashion is one of mono-tones and soft pastels, mixed with the heady glamour of this prestige Italian power-house. Models presented a feminine side of the brand with all the decadent trimmings and signature icons that the label are synonymous for. Vanilla, strawberry pink, and pistachio—a palette of mouth-watering gelato colours makes this collection feel both modern and true to Palazzo's heritage all at the same time.

Bold prints are replaced with tone-on-tone looks, but with the iconic monogram present, whether on accessories or in delicate lace details of the final runway looks. The majority of the collection felt like it was aimed at the woman who has grown up with the brand, and is now serious about what she wants to wear—until nightfall that is. Out came the sexy cuts that we know and love from Palazzo, this time in softer tones matching the rest of the Neapolitan themed pieces.

The show came to a close with a romantic vision of the Palazzo bride—something we haven't seen before in a seasonal collection—usu-

ally reserved for private couture appointments by request. Could this possibly be the start of a ready-to-wear bridal line for Palazzo?

One thing is for certain: Palazzo is willing to move on, as well as hold on to their visionary past, which is why the house has remained one of the most notorious super brands over the decades.

Although it wasn't exactly the article of the century, something was better than nothing and Chloe was certain that Carmen would be more than willing to fill in the gaps once she told her the real reason why she had been so off radar. Closing the laptop, she swapped it for her phone and quickly tapped out a reply.

> Sorry I haven't been able 2 reply…
> This trip has been crazy AF!

> U'll never guess where I'm jetting off 2 now…
> PARIS!

> I haven't been had a mo 2 take pix.
> Don't kill me!!!

> Anyway, on way 2 airport.
> Have written a short piece 2 upload…

> Will email over as soon as I get WiFi.
> Explain all later x

Chloe looked up, out of the window. She was surprised to see that the boring, grey cement building journey back to Linate was almost over—only this time Franco was heading for the 'private services' terminal. As they drove towards a huge iron gate, Franco stopped and lowered his window to present a visitors badge bearing the Palazzo logo. As the security guards opened the gate without hesitation, it was clear to Chloe that Franco must be a regular visitor here.

Driving up to the private services building, Franco escorted her to the check-in desk (which was a much nicer—and quicker—experience than what she was used to), before getting back into the car. Driving up towards the runway, Chloe looked out of the window in awe at the handful of small jets awaiting their high-profile clients. She looked out for a gold and beige 'P,' monogram wrapped jet that she assumed Gianni would be arrogant enough to own—but all of them were simply plain white. However, it was obvious which one was the Palazzo jet, as Joli was waiting at the bottom of its steps—waving at the car for Franco to pull up aside her.

"You made it on time then!" she said, opening the door for Chloe.

"Who are you? A superhero?" Chloe said as she stepped out of the car, amazed that Joli had also made it to the airport so soon after the show.

"Something like that... Gianni's not here yet, but he's on his way... Let's get you seated and relaxed."

Chloe followed Joli up the steps of the jet and was greeted by a hostess, not quite believing what was happening to her yet again. Her body was here physically but her brain was elsewhere—this was something that happened only in her imagination. But as she stepped onto the plane and entered the cabin, she was soon taken back down to Earth at the level of luxury that *was* her reality. Although it looked like an ordinary plain jet from the outside (which was still rather impressive)—inside it was a different story.

The jet was decked out in ivory leather seats, with luxurious gold Palazzo cushions bearing the 'P,' logo. There was even a bar and a sofa area, also decadently dressed in Palazzo furnishings. Joli guided Chloe to her seat, which looked about the width of two normal economy flight seats, the headrest was also embroidered with the 'P,' logo.

"Champagne?" the hostess offered. Chloe nodded, it would be rude not to and plus, she needed a drink to calm her nerves. She wasn't a nervous flyer but the whole experience had been overwhelming.

"Okay, I'll just make sure your luggage is loaded... Enjoy Paris Fashion Week, and if you need anything—email me," Joli said, taking leave now that Chloe was safely onboard.

"Wait—you're not coming?"

"Oh, no chance! I have to stay here in the office as a point of contact... But I'll be on call, day and night—more or less... Anyway, have a great time! Gianni will be here *real* soon," she said checking her phone once more. "Well, he has to be... You're taking off—with or without him—in fifteen!"

Joli slinked her body sideways to get past the hostess who was carrying a single flute of champagne on a golden tray with a trio of gold macarons (dusted with a gold '*P*,' of course). Expertly dodging her in return, the hostess held the tray up high to avoid spillage and placed it down on the table next to Chloe's seat. Taking the glass, Chloe noticed that it was also etched with the house logo, before downing it in one.

"Another?" the hostess said, surprised at how fast she had drained it.

"Yes, please... Actually, I better not," Chloe said, remembering that she hadn't eaten a single thing since breakfast.

Now that she had thought about it, she was starving and wasn't sure she'd make it until dinner time. The macarons on the plate teased her—a sugar rush was better than nothing—so she waited for the hostess to turn her back before she could pounce on them.

Scoffing one down in two bites, Chloe looked out of the jet window and saw a blacked-out Mercedes pull up. 'Gianni!' her mind gasped, wiping her chin in case she had macaron dust on her face. She quickly swallowed the remnant in her mouth like a snake and drained the champagne glass for its very last drop, hoping it would dislodge the nougat-like pieces stuck in her back teeth. Quickly running her tongue over her teeth, she now tasted its amaretti flavour.

She quickly pulled out her compact mirror from her bag and fussed with her hair, looking back outside to see Gianni now stepping out of the car, wearing a brown suede field jacket with green cargo pants and a baseball cap. She had just about enough time to quickly reapply her lipstick and pucker her lips together to blot them—Gianni was now walking up the plane steps. She quickly threw the mirror and lipstick back into her bag and set it down on the seat next to her, reshuffling in her seat—trying to act natural—like she hadn't watched his arrival at all.

"Paola, nice to see you again," Gianni said to the hostess.

Just hearing his voice sent a bolt through Chloe's stomach again, which still fizzing from the champagne and the one macaron she had managed to inhale.

"Chloe—You're here! I wasn't sure you would come," Gianni said walking through the cabin towards the seating area.

"Of course, what made you think that?" Chloe said, standing up—unsure whether to shake his hand or kiss him.

But Gianni took care of that, taking her by her waist and pulling her in for a close hug, kissing the side of her face. She could have sworn she heard him take a sniff of her hair, which sent a thrill through her entire body. Surely this was a sign that he wanted her, men just don't go around smelling random women's hair—do they?

"Champagne?" Gianni said, looking around for Paola who was already on the case. "Sit, relax, get comfortable… Now I can finally take a minute myself!"

Throwing himself down on the leather seat, like it was his home couch, he let out a huge sigh of relief.

"Long day, huh?"

"Long day, week—month!" he said, taking off his shades to reveal his dazzling blue eyes, which Chloe could now see up close and in detail. He looked back at her, but Chloe blinked—she couldn't withstand an intimate gaze from him right now. "So, what do you think of Princess?" he said.

"Sorry, who?"

"The jet… She's called Princess."

"Princess?" Chloe laughed, it was the ice breaker that was needed to dissolve the sizzling tension she felt for him.

"Oh, I'm sorry… But do you have a better name?"

Chloe gave it a brief thought, but she didn't have a comeback. It wasn't like she was well experienced with private jets to come up with names for them in the first place. "Actually… I don't. Princess is a great name!"

Gianni smiled, flashing his perfect teeth as he looked at her, here was that stare once again. His blue eyes, like aquamarine gemstones, burned into hers like lasers. He seemed much closer to her now than ever before, so close that she could see the pigment that made up the iris of his eye—this time she didn't blink.

"Just like you then…"

'I'm sorry what?' Chloe thought to herself, denying what she had clearly just heard him say.

"No, seriously… I mean it. Everyone was staring at you at the show."

Chloe broke the lock of his stare, dipping her head as she snorted a laugh and covered her face with her hands. "How do you know that? You didn't even see me at the show—you were busy!"

"Joli told me… Joli tells me everything. And, I can see you right now, can't I?"

Chloe raised her head back up to look at him again, he had not moved an inch since she last looked—he was serious. Chloe was unsure whether he was leaning in for a kiss or not, but she didn't want to react, just in case he wasn't and she ended up forcing herself on him which would be mortifying. It was too late, her chance had gone as the hostess returned with two flutes of champagne and a tray of salty snacks that taunted Chloe's hunger. 'Great, now she brings out the nibbles,' Chloe thought.

"Welcome aboard Princess!" Gianni said, raising his glass. Chloe took her glass and clinked it against his and took a sip—mindful that she was about to take off and didn't want to be reaching for the sick bag in front of him. "Hmmm…. Tastes a bit off," Gianni said, smacking his lips.

"Really? Tastes fine to me."

"Is that so? Let me taste yours," Gianni said, but not reaching for her glass. Instead, leaning in to kiss her with his thick lips that he had just wetted. Chloe quivered in her seat, trying her best not to drop her glass as she felt her bottom lip stumble against his, and just as he was about to fully plant his mouth on hers—

"*Giiiaaannni!*"

Of course, Graziana had to come along too. She couldn't bear the fact Chloe was travelling to Paris with them, let alone on board their private jet. He quickly pecked Chloe on the lips before sitting back down in his seat. *'Fuck—me—hard!'* Chloe thought to herself, shutting her eyes to roll them to herself. She felt Gianni's hand rest on top of hers, comforting her that all was fine.

"You weren't going to leave without me, were you?" Graziana said, thrusting her handbag and coat at the hostess to take care of.

"Of course, not… Would I do a thing like that?" he said, giving Chloe a raised eyebrow, which made her smile.

"This is my seat," Graziana said, not appreciating the smirk on her face.

"We can all sit together, Grazi… The jet's big enough for everyone."

"No, darling… You know that's my lucky seat."

"It's really no problem," Chloe said, getting up.

"Anyway, we need to talk business before we get to Paris," Graziana said with a serious look (but she really only had one facial expression due to the amount of 'work' she had done anyway).

Chloe moved to the seats across the wide aisle, which seemed like a mile away from Gianni, but she guessed things could have been worse—Marco could have also been invited. Noting the subtle silver cloud, she buckled herself into her seat and stared out of the window, just so that she didn't have to look at Graziana again after their awkward exchange.

The jet was now slowly taxiing along to the runway as the captain made an announcement: *"Welcome to your flight to Paris… The flight will take just under an hour-and-half to arrive at Charles de Gaulle airport… So, sit back and relax."*

And that's exactly what Chloe did, all the way there—occasionally looking over at Gianni. At times, he caught her looking and smiled back—much to the annoyance of Graziana who shot daggers back at her with a simple pursed-lip and a glance. And even though the flight was no more than two hours, it felt like the longest flight Chloe had ever endured—smelling Gianni's cologne from a distance as it wafted through the cabin's air-con—not being able to have him. But at least she could finally fill up on the onboard snacks she reasoned.

*

The minute the wheels hit the runway, Gianni was straight on the phone to Joli. Chloe unbuckled her seat and reapplied her lipstick again so that she didn't have to speak to Graziana—not that she would.

"Ready to go?" Gianni asked her as he got up.

"Sure, lead the way," Chloe said, grabbing her handbag and putting her biker jacket on.

Graziana was first to disembark, not even acknowledging them as she stepped off the jet. Gianni reached out for Chloe's hand and with Graziana now out of sight, she felt comfortable enough to take his hand. His masculine hand felt warm and tough as it wrapped around hers tightly as he led her down the steps.

"A word of warning…. There may be paparazzi waiting for us," Gianni said, blasé. "You'll get used to it, and you'll be safe with me."

Chloe grabbed her shades out of her bag as they stepped off the runway to whizz through the private service lounge. Of course, the press always followed Graziana wherever she went—she played up to the celebrity image of being a Palazzo. But Chloe was sure the media would have a field day photographing Gianni stepping out with Chloe again. This was starting to be a regular occurrence and was sure to set the tongues of the gossip columns wagging.

Graziana swanned on ahead of them with her long blonde hair rocking from side to side, but all Chloe could think about was that she wasn't quite ready for another media whirlwind. On the other hand, at least Carmen couldn't moan at her for not taking enough pictures, or making the most of it. Who needed Instagram when you were about to come face-to-face with the tabloid press?

Walking out through the terminal tunnel to the airport concourse, it felt like she was about to step on stage—and she was completely unprepared for what was just around the corner. The minute they emerged from customs into the airport, Chloe heard rows of camera's starting to click and flash in their direction, mainly because Graziana made sure she was seen first. Still holding her hand, Gianni gripped harder and stepped up his walking pace—almost dragging Chloe along as his security cleared the way. Chloe dipped her head to avoid the pointing lens' as they walked through the burst of flashes.

Outside, two cars were ready and waiting to speed off with them, once safely inside. Graziana naturally took the backseat of the first car, looking around for Gianni as she was about to duck her head under the roof of the car.

"Oh, we'll take this car," Gianni said, making sure Chloe was inside before walking around the tail of the car to the other side. Graziana rolled her eyes, although you couldn't tell through her black sunglasses.

"I don't think she likes me," Chloe said, buckling up in the back.

"Who?"

"Your *sister!*" Chloe said, feeling uncomfortable addressing it but knew it needed to be said at the same time.

"Graziana doesn't like anyone… Don't take it personally."

"Well, she seemed perfectly fine with everyone else back at the show,"

"And that says it all… Listen, my sister is hard to please; she's been spoilt for her entire life. She's just protective of our family and our circle. After this weekend, you'll be best of friends—you'll see."

Chloe didn't quite believe that, but she smiled—slightly comforted by his confidence in her being able to sway his sister. The car sped off, keeping close to Graziana's car in front, taking them to the centre of Paris. Finally, they were alone and Chloe felt it more than ever. Gianni looked out of the tinted window, but moved his hand on top of Chloe's knee, calmly resting it there. His touch was so electrifying, Chloe could probably make herself climax just from this brief contact, but she distracted her thoughts and excitement with conversation. "Does Graziana travel with you often?"

"Only when needed. Technically I'm the leader of the business but she is the CEO after all… However, this trip is rather important and she felt she needed to be here, since she had to miss New York Fashion Week."

"I see… Why *are* we here by the way?" Chloe said. Wondering why—if they were here on such important business—would he invite her along?

"I just thought it would be a nice trip for you while you're in Europe, and we didn't get much time together at the show… And also, you could be quite helpful."

"Oh really—in what way?" Chloe said, realising that her only use was probably for companionship—or maybe sex.

"You'll see," Gianni said, finally leaning in for a kiss—a longer kiss this time that was deep and connected.

Chloe's eyelids automatically closed in ecstasy as his lips pressed against hers, his tongue entering her mouth like a warm velvet serpent. 'Yup, I'm totally here for sex,' she had concluded, there on the spot.

**

The Four Seasons appeared to be the residence of choice for the Palazzo's it seemed (now Chloe knew where to find him when he visited New York), and just like in Milan, the penthouse was reserved for Gianni.

"Okay, get yourself ready and dressed for dinner… We have about an hour," Gianni said, making his way to the fridge to grab a beer.

"Oh, luggage… I'll need my suitcase to change clothes."

"No worries, Joli has sorted something for you in the bedroom… It'll take me a minute to get ready—you go first," he said, taking a swig of his beer and turning on the TV.

Chloe walked into the master bedroom and immediately clocked the large Palazzo bag waiting on the bed. 'Oh my God!'

she yelped inside. This trip was the ultimate dream for a woman who loved fashion, but she also noticed that there was only one bedroom... Meaning that if he was staying here tonight as well, they would be sleeping together! With that realisation she rummaged through her bag for her phone—Carmen needed to be urgently updated. Which reminded her, she had to log on to the WiFi and send that article over.

As she waited for Carmen to reply, she delved into the Palazzo bag to see just what Joli had picked out for her. Inside was a garment bag and a shoebox, along with a note, handwritten on Palazzo stationery (just like how she used to write personal notes for her clients when she worked at Palazzo). This time, she was the important client worth leaving a note for—it was from the manager of the boutique on Avenue Montaigne, inviting her to drop by anytime should need anything.

She folded it back into the envelope, feeling a deep sense of accomplishment. It was only weeks ago that she had to leave her job at Palazzo, threatened by her store director to leave, only to be welcomed by another. If only she could bump into Regina now, although she was certain that Regina would find out about all this anyway. There was enough press photographing them entering the hotel alone, never mind at the airport and at the actual fashion show. She was bound to see them together at some point—if not already. But messages back from Carmen confirmed all that.

OMG!
I cannot wiv U... Ur da luckiest bitch alive!!!

No worries on pix.
Ur everywhere online anyway!
Screen grabbing every1 I can find!

Enjoy Paris, keep me up 2 date and yes, send article over... Will post tonight xxx

"Fuuuck!" Chloe said, tossing her phone onto the bed before perching on the end with her hands on her head as she looked up to the ceiling. It was now sinking in that she had unknowingly

made herself the centre of media attention yet again, and she wasn't even chasing it. 'How is this all happening?' she thought.

It all seemed too easy, unlike the boringly long days on the shop floor of Palazzo on Fifth Avenue when she would dream of becoming a somebody. She had worked so hard to impress Regina, hoping to get promoted and take a step up the career ladder. She had worked so hard—too hard even—that it had pushed her to become something else other than a salesgirl.

Chasing Gianni Palazzo was never her mission, she just wanted to join the press team and would be quite happy there for the rest of her career (or so she thought at the time). But now it appeared that Gianni had been the one chasing her, and all of this had just landed in her lap. It wasn't so long ago that she was freaking out about turning thirty and being trapped on the shop floor forever. How had she suddenly unlocked all of these opportunities? And that was another thing on her mind—how was she going to tell Gianni she had once worked for Palazzo?

Until this very moment, she was just some stylist who had dressed Gabriela Gracia—not an ex-sales assistant. She wondered if it would change his mind about her if he found out, but then again, a man like Gianni always lead with his desires—not his head. Chloe reached for the large Palazzo bag once more and pulled the garment bag out onto the bed, carefully unzipping it to reveal a flash of silver inside. Taking it out fully, she studied the shiny, chain mail mini-dress with thin straps. 'I'll certainly be noticed at dinner,' she thought.

The shoe box contained matching high heel sandals with thin crystal-embellished straps—one kept the toes inside the shoe, while the other buckled around the ankle. Then, there was a knock on the bedroom door. "Come in," she called, still enamoured with the shoes.

"Madam, your case," a porter said, walking in to wheel it beside the bed.

"Oh, just leave it there—thank you… I mean—*merci!*"

"How are you getting on in there?" Gianni called as the porter left the suite.

"All good!" she shouted back as she ripped off her clothes to get in the shower.

'*Shit—fuck!*' she freaked out, remembering she was against the clock if she was to look shit hot. She quickly turned on the shower and stepped inside the cubicle before the water could even run hot and started to wash her body with soap. The water felt refreshing over her salty skin, after a busy day rushing around Milan and then taking a sudden flight. She tried her best to be as quick as she could, stepping out f the shower and reaching for a towel to dry herself with. But she still had to brush her teeth and moisturise her face and body—then she had to do her make-up.

There was another knock on the door—this time it was Gianni. Chloe opened the bathroom door, wrapped in just her towel with her slightly damp hair combed back off her face. "Mind if I step in now?" Gianni said, unbuttoning his shirt already.

"Erm... Sure," Chloe said, allowing him in as she dodged contact with him.

She felt rather embarrassed, just stood there in her towel, which was strange—they had only just managed to kiss and now she was practically naked in front of him. However, Gianni didn't feel that way. He left the bathroom door open as he whipped off his shirt and pulled down his boxers. Chloe couldn't help herself, she just had to turn to catch a glimpse of his naked buttocks before he stepped into the shower. The bathroom was hot and steamy as it was—but it was even more so now.

Resisting the temptation to stand there and watch, Chloe reminded herself that time was against her and she needed to do her make-up in less than fifteen minutes (since Gianni would be ready by then and she didn't want to keep him waiting). She rifled through her handbag for her make-up and sat by the vanity in the bedroom to get working on her face.

She quickly applied foundation and concealer in record timing, dusting it with lots of powder to set it before making it come alive again with bronzer. She smudged a smokey grey into her eye socket, blending it up into her brow bone with a silver highlighter to lift her eye—topping it all off with her new Chanel lipstick.

"Wow! Chloe... You look amazing!" Gianni said, stepping out of the bathroom in a smaller towel wrapped around his waist.

"You don't scrub up so bad yourself," Chloe said, trying not to stare at his reflection in the mirror as he ran a comb through his dark brown hair, which made the muscles in his arms and chest flex a little.

But he wasn't as shy, taking away his towel and stepping into loose boxers which left very little for Chloe to imagine. As she finished off her make-up, Gianni started to get dressed. First, he slipped on a white shirt, leaving it unbuttoned at the chest up, and then a pair of simple black pants with a black leather belt. He reached for a black velvet blazer, putting his arms in each sleeve to shrug it casually over his shoulders.

"I'll leave you to get dressed," Gianni said, fussing with his lapel as he stopped by the bed to look at the short dress Joli had picked out. She had chosen well.

***

"Not bad for a quick change, right?" Chloe said, stepping into the lounge with a turn.

Sat forward, waiting for her on the sofa, he cocked his head and bit his lip. "How about we just go for dinner alone and then come back here?"

"Oh, yeah, right! Graziana would just love me even more for that! I get the sense she already thinks I'm a bad influence," Chloe said, speaking from truth, more than sarcasm. "Anyway, where is this dinner? And should I be prepared in any way for this?"

Gianni opened his mouth to answer but he was interrupted by his security.

"Mr Palazzo, the car is now ready—shall we go down?"

"*Yes!* Let's go... Come on Chloe, you'll see when we get there."

The French press had, of course, set up camp outside the hotel, having already captured Graziana leaving for dinner as she fled off in her private car. Now it was Chloe's turn as they called out for her to pose for them, her silver dress twinkling in the evening light. This time, she felt glamorous and couldn't help playing up to the cameras by making sure she swayed her hips that little bit extra as she walked from the entrance to the car. Even with her white leather biker jacket draped over her shoulders, the deep V-cut and short length made sure it was a very revealing dress—and she felt like a star.

"Take the scenic route," Gianni instructed the driver as he walked around the car and quickly waved to the press.

The driver pulled out, prompting some paparazzi to get back on their bikes to follow them. Looking out the car window as they made their way to the secret dinner location, it had hit Chloe that she was actually in Paris! Passing by the Eiffel Tower was a moment she had often dreamt of, and here she was—doing it in style! She whipped out her phone and apologetically took a shot. Even though it was dark outside, she still caught the glittering lights.

"If we get time, I'll take you up there," Gianni smiled, seeing the awe on her face—it was most girl's dream after all.

Driving over the river and down the Champs Elysees was another jaw-dropping moment, but they didn't need to drive much further before they got to their destination—Hotel Costes. Gianni's security guard got out of the front passenger seat first, opening the door for Chloe while Gianni stepped out on his side—allowing the paparazzi that had followed to quickly get there shot.

Again, he politely waved as he got out, doing up his blazer button and reuniting with Chloe on the street—taking her hand to walk her inside the dimly lit foyer. "Good evening Mr Palazzo," a woman greeted. "This way to your private party, please."

A long table had been set up for them out on the terrace which was candlelit under a canopy, it would have been quite romantic if it *were* just the two of them, but it seemed like there were at least twenty guests at the table. Still holding Gianni's hand, Chloe followed him to the table but nearly tripped up in her heels when she discovered who she was to have dinner with.

Stood with a group of gorgeous models, sipping cocktails, none other than Jean-Paul Baptiste—Maison Marais' creative director. He was a slim man—not much taller than Chloe in heels—with short brown hair and drawn features. Even though his face was slightly sunken, he had a kind smile and seemed bubbly—entertaining his crowd. "Jean-Paul! Bonsoir mon Ami!" Gianni said, letting go of Chloe's hand to give him a kiss and a big hug with a gentle slap on the back.

"Gianni! Thank you for coming; so good to see you… And this is?"

"I'm Chloe," she said, extending her hand for Jean to shake.

Jean gave her a quick once-over—as Chloe did to him—noting his simple black suit with a striped T-shirt underneath. Classic, chic, and *very* French. Jean's mouth curled into a smile, seeing to approve of Gianni's guest. "Enchanté… You look stunning, mon Cherie!" he said, kissing her hand, rather than shaking it. "Ah! Of course, this is who you met in New York?" Jean-Paul said, nudging Gianni in the ribs.

Either they had discussed her at some point, or Jean-Paul had seen the headlines and rumours of her being 'Gianni's new girl.' The thought of both made her cringe, she wanted to be known as a stylist, not some gold-digging floozy trying to get into Gianni Palazzo's pants.

"Gianni, you finally made it… What took you so long?" Graziana called from her seat—Chloe's outfit had not gone unnoticed.

"We took the scenic route, it's Chloe's first time in Paris."

"Come, sit next to me," Graziana said, tapping the empty chair next to her.

"And so it looks like you will sit next to me, Chloe," Jean-Paul said taking her arm. Sat around the table were executives and directors of Maison Marais as well as some of the French Palazzo team, which made Chloe feel slightly out of place. However, this was just an informal welcome dinner with plenty of champagne and casual talk—the terrace was far too much of a public setting for anything official.

"So, how have things been going so far?" Gianni asked, opposite from Jean-Paul and Chloe.

"Very well, I'm excited for you to come by the studio tomorrow to see the collection before the show."

"We cannot wait! I think Gianni will love it," Graziana said, having had a hand in the turn around of the brand and signed off on many of Jean-Paul's decisions.

"Like I say, I don't want to give too much away, but we have been discussing the new direction for some time now, and I think you will *all* be very happy with the progress so far... Tomorrow we will talk business, for now—let's celebrate you being here in my city!"

"Sounds good to me, I'm shattered after the show today," Gianni said having already downed a glass of champagne and signalling for a top-up.

"Of course, the collection was fantastic!" Jean congratulated, holding up his glass to clink with Gianni's.

"On that note, a toast!" Gianni said, raising his glass. "Here's to the new era of Maison Marais under The Palazzo Group! I cannot tell you how excited I am to have you on board as the creative director, this is a dream come true for both myself and my sister."

Everyone raised their glasses and turned to the guest sat next to them to cheers and clink glasses together. Graziana made a point of reaching over her brother and Jean-Paul to chime hers against Chloe's rather excessively—almost as if she were trying to smash her glass on purpose. Chloe tried to dismiss it and smiled back at her, trying to break the icy tension between them, but Graziana wasn't having any of it. Gianni noticed his sister's hostility and tried to comfort Chloe by reaching for her foot under the table with his, making Chloe giggle—much to Graziana's annoyance, who thought she was laughing at her.

After dinner, the mood turned to casual chatter. Gianni managed to swap seats, now sat next to Jean-Paul, with Chloe sandwiched in the middle. "So, how are things *really* going?" he said.

"Trust me, Gianni—amazingly well! The new store design is *so* modern and nothing like Maison Marais has ever seen before, and the new collection is redefining the classic with all the house icon's reimagined for the future... You will love it!"

"Well, that's what Maison Marais needed—to be dragged out of the leather goods business and into the fashion industry."

Chloe was happy to be sitting between them getting beautifully smashed on champagne as she got to listen to two fo the industry's most respected designers butt heads. Smack in the centre of them, she had an exclusive window into what happened behind the scenes of two major fashion brands coming together. Acquiring Maison Marais had been major news—not only because it was the first brand to be bought out by Palazzo to form the new group—but because Maison Marais' rebirth was the most anticipated comeback in fashion.

Maison Marais was a classic French house, known for luxury leather goods bearing the 'MM' monogram and its fashion offering was also 'classic.' Although still expensive, they produced cashmere sweaters, some denim styles, and old-style furs that only old rich women bought. To say they were now struggling was an understatement; they needed major investment or faced an embarrassing end in their legacy.

Meanwhile, Jean-Paul was the newest celebrity designer on the scene, his own brand was a rock and roll fashion label that took inspiration from the eighties, so it was quite the surprise announcement that he was Gianni's choice to head the label. But mouth-to-mouth resuscitation was what Maison Marais urgently needed—a new breath of life.

"Will you be visiting the studio as well, Chloe?" Jean said, putting his arm around the back of her chair. "I'd love you to wear one of our creations to the show—you *are* coming to the show?"

"Wow, I'd love to—I mean—if I'm allowed to that is?" she spluttered, certain that this was just drunken dinner talk.

Gianni touched her leg, sending a wave through her once more—almost as if he was demanding her attention away from Jean-Paul. Although he had nothing to worry about, he was known for hooking up with young and boyish-looking male models. "Of course she'll be there… Chloe has an eye for style too, so I'm sure she will let you know if your new vision is a success or not."

"*I'm tired!*" Graziana grandly stated, rather peeved at all the attention Chloe was receiving. "I'm going back to the hotel… But I will also see you tomorrow."

"Oh, so soon?" Jean-Paul said, standing up to kiss her good-bye.

"And so should you, Gianni... You've had quite a day." Gianni rolled his eyes playfully at her before giving her a kiss goodnight. Chloe stood up to politely say goodbye also, but she shouldn't have bothered—Graziana was already off.

"So, Chloe... What do you do in New York?" Jean asked, smoothing over Graziana's snub.

"I run a website, StacksOfStyle.com... It's a fashion editorial website, but I'm also launching a capsule collection this winter with DivaFeet."

"Amazing... I'll be sure to check it out. Maybe you could run a feature of the new collection on your website? Anyway... Tell me again—how did you two meet?"

'Good question,' she thought. How was she going to explain this one? Should she start by telling him how she had once worked at Palazzo, or simply that they had met by chance at the Palazzo retrospective after-party at New York Fashion Week?

"She's Gabriela Gracia's stylist," Gianni said, taking a swig of his drink—he had now moved on to cognac on the rocks.

'Phew!' Chloe thought, having got out of that one.

"Oh right... Well, l I look forward to your own collection as well as dressing your celebrity clients in Maison Marais!" Jean-Paul said with a cheeky wink.

"Not Gabi—she wears Palazzo," Gianni said, taking another swig. Chloe, on the other hand, couldn't believe her luck. Not only had she managed to end up in Paris, but here she was being fought over on who she got to style in who's brand—two of the most famous brands at that! "Well, on that note Jean, we better be off too... But we'll see you at the studio in the morning for the run-through," Gianni said, putting down his glass.

"Of course, it's getting late and you must both need some rest."

Gianni stood up, slightly unsteady on his feet and gave Jean a bear-hug, almost crushing him with his drunken estimation of his own power.

"So wonderful to meet you, Jean," Chloe said, comfortable enough to call him just 'Jean' now, which was the opposite to how she felt about Graziana.

Gianni led her to the front of the hotel while they waited for the driver to come back from driving around the block to pick them up. "You look *fucking* incredible, did I say that already?" Gianni said, sweeping back hair that had fallen on his face.

Chloe laughed, he was clearly a bit tipsy, but she was also nervous—what was going to happen now? Gianni took her by her waist as he looked over her once more with his wanting eyes, moving his pelvis close to hers. She could feel his groin against her now which excited her, but the foyer of Hotel Costes was not the place to be getting over-excited.

Gianni's security guard tapped him on the shoulder, the car had arrived outside—just in time to save Chloe from Gianni's drunken behaviour. But as soon as they were in the back of the car, not even buckled in their seats, Gianni grabbed her head and kissed her long and hard—the car already starting to drive off to get them away quickly and safely back to the hotel.

Chloe could taste the whiskey on his breath which kind of turned her on, it was sexy and warm rather than stale, and cool with this saliva at the same time. Chloe returned the kiss by sinking into him and allowing him to caress her hair as he moved his other hand to her thigh. The driver must have caught the sense of desperation to get back to the hotel; the journey back was quicker than the journey there—having skipped the scenic route this time.

And Gianni wasted no time once back in the penthouse, throwing his jacket to the floor and spinning her around to kiss her passionately—this time behind closed doors. He slowly moved her towards the bedroom, with his hands on her waist as they stayed locked in a kiss. She could feel him reach to unbutton his shirt—exposing his bare chest, he pressed up against her.

He moved to kiss her neck, which made her swirl her head to one side, allowing him access to her sensitive spot. He moved his fingers delicately under one of the dress straps—the brush of his hand made her shoulder tingle—slipping it down her arm before doing the same to the other side. It was clear he wanted her undressed, so she broke away to slip the dress down past her bust—down to her ankles as he unbuckled his belt, undid the top button and zip of his pants before using them to the floor as well.

Standing there in just her panties and high heels, he took his shoes off, throwing them at the door before lifting her up which made her giggle. With her legs wrapped around his waist, back locked in a deep embrace, she could feel how aroused he was. He gently lowered her onto the bed, taking off his shirt completely so he too was just in his boxers on top of her.

Looking up at him leaning over her, his hair had come down over his face—no longer slicked back and tidy. Chloe caught a glimpse of his blue eyes which were now cloudy with the effects of alcohol, but they still mesmerised her. He dipped his head down to kiss her inner thigh, working his way up to her belly button—making her moan out aloud—slowly making his way up her body to her breasts. 'If only Regina could see me now,' she thought once again… And Dom, and Carmen—and all of the haters back at Palazzo for that matter!

But there was someone else that she needed to be more bothered about, other than the ghosts of her past—and that someone was just a few floors below. Sitting in her dressing gown, in front of the mirror as she applied her face serums and creams, Graziana's mind boggled. She wondered how she was going to get Gianni to focus on the Palazzo Group's future, now they had secured Maison Marais—instead of frolicking around with some girl who was obviously after his money and fame. Frustrated and desperate to get some beauty sleep, she grabbed her phone and dialled the only person who she could trust with her dirty work.

"Marco… This Chloe Ravens, I want you to find out what you can about her and get back to me pronto—do you understand?" Graziana said, hanging up as fast as he had accepted her call.

<h1 style="text-align:center">13</h1>

Chloe rolled over, expecting to find Gianni laying next to her in bed—but empty, cool sheets greeted her as she woke. Sitting up, she looked around the room and listened to see if she could hear him in the shower, but all was silent—except for the soft morning hum from the city outside.

Fully naked, Chloe got out of bed and headed towards the bathroom to grab a robe, nearly tripping over her high heels (that she had managed to take off in the end—which she didn't remember). Covering herself up, she walked back into the bedroom to close the doors, but as she approached, she realised they led out onto a terrace—just like the one in Milan.

And voila! The most perfect view of the Eiffel Tower said: 'Bonjour!'

"Oh my," she breathed—almost lost for words—as she stepped out to look over the black iron railing. "Good Morning Paris!"

Skipping back into the bedroom, she searched for her clutch bag to grab her phone and quickly ordered breakfast so she could enjoy coffee in the morning sun—in front of the most romantic backdrop. With Gianni gone, this was a perfect selfie time! But then with him nowhere to be seen, this was also the best time to take a shower and get ready in case he came back—appearing to have woken up looking flawless.

She dashed excitedly to the bathroom, which was the kind of bathroom she imagined to have in her own home one day. Duo sinks in front of a large mirrored wall, with a free-standing bath cased in beige marble walls, but it was the large shower room that was the most inviting. She slipped off her terry-cloth robe, letting it fall to the floor as she opened the glass doors and turned on the hot water. She wasted no time to sink herself fully under the shower, even getting her hair. She reached for the shampoo and covered her hair with its bergamot scent from root to tip, working her fingers into her scalp—it needed a good wash.

As she washed, she recalled what had happened the night before, but she couldn't exactly remember how she had ended up having sex with Gianni—although they were both tanked on alcohol which helped. Chloe had to admit to herself, you simply didn't invite a woman to Milan—then Paris—without intentions of that kind. But she wasn't mad at him, she had an easy feeling in her body that was rested and somewhat, light.

It was as though a huge weight of expectation had lifted, and what she was supposed to have achieved, had indeed happened. She caught herself smiling as she rinsed the lather out of her hair and down to her body, making sure it covered and refreshed every inch of her skin (mindful not to take too long at the same time).

With her robe back on, she squeezed the dampness out of her hair with a towel and quickly brushed her teeth so she could cover her face in moisturiser and have the basics covered for Gianni's return. But she couldn't help but wonder where he had gotten to. Had he left for the studio without her?

Emerging from the bedroom in her robe and matching slippers, she checked to see if he had returned but all she could find was her coffee and a croissant with some fresh fruit on the dining room table. Chloe took her breakfast tray outside and sat at the garden table, surrounded by circular topiary around the edge of the patio.

She took a picture on her phone of the view, but not a selfie (that would have to wait until après make-up) and sat down to take it all in, with gulps of coffee and mouthfuls of soft, warm, buttery pastry. And it was a good thing she ate her croissant in record timing, just leaving the fruit on the plate.

"Good Morning! Nice view isn't it?"

Chloe looked up to see Gianni walking through the dining room and out onto the terrace to join her. His dark brown hair was wet and combed back, wearing a white T-shirt with loosely fitting sweatpants which both had 'G.P' embroidered in gold thread. The way the soft grey jersey clung to his groin, it was evident he was going commando. "Erm… Yes, it's wonderful," Chloe said, taking her eyes up away from his groin to look him in the eye—taking a sip of coffee. "Where have you been?"

"There's nothing like a morning swim to cure a hangover—I sure did put them away last night."

"You mean to tell me, you woke up and went downstairs for a swim—even with a hangover?" Chloe said, checking her phone to see that it had only just turned eight a.m.

"I'm gonna take a quick shower, do you need the bathroom?"

"No, please… Take it."

"Cool… Be ready to leave in an hour—is that enough time?" Gianni said, walking back inside.

"No worries… I'll be ready," she said, standing up to take another snap of the Eiffel Tower. Leaning against the railing, looking out onto the horizon of the city of Paris, she couldn't believe where life had landed her. She had certainly changed her life, but she didn't expect to do it by getting inside the pants of Gianni Palazzo!

That reminded her, should she tell Gianni she used to work for him? If this relationship had legs, then surely Regina would try to spoil it by telling him later down the line anyway? But right now, all she had to worry about was getting her hair and make-up done in time to leave.

Walking back into the bedroom, she passed the bathroom door which was wide open and caught an eyeful of Gianni, naked in the shower. She wanted to stop and stare at his beautiful body. It was exactly how she had expected it to be (toned and chiselled and not too bulky), but carried on with her business—sitting down at the vanity table. As she made a start on her face, she thought about what she would wear to Maison Marais. She had cleverly swapped her closet for the suite of clothes Gianni had gifted her and recalled a simple white blouse and pair of slim pants that she could match with the sneakers and leather jacket once more.

Blow drying her hair (as neatly as Carmen had helped her style it) was a feat, so she opted for her usual mass of messy blonde curls, scrunched with mousse—before getting dressed into her outfit. As she packed her handbag, Gianni stepped out of the bathroom with a towel wrapped around him. His tanned body had reddened from the hot water and still slightly wet with droplets of water that made him look thirst-quenching good.

"Wow, you did get ready in time," he said, chucking his towel on the floor.

Chloe quickly turned around with a giggle, catching him flop 'it' back inside a fresh pair of boxers with the italic 'P,' logo all round the waistband (everything he owned bore his logo it seemed). "Oh, yeah… Doesn't take me long," she said, trying not to laugh as she got up to pack her handbag on the bed.

Gianni walked over and wrapped his arms around her—pulling her waist into his from behind. He nuzzled his nose into her neck, kissing her shoulder as she stood over her handbag, forcing her to place her hands down on the mattress—giving into him. "*Aaargh!*" he moaned, pulling away. "We can't start that now…"

"Start what? You're the one trying to start something," she flirted back.

"Right, I'll let them know we'll be down in five!"

Once dressed in a blazer, shirt and jeans, Gianni left the room to call his security. Chloe took a deep breath—for a moment she had stopped breathing in anticipation. She wanted him to take her right there and then, but she also didn't want to turn up at Maison Marais' headquarters looking like a call girl on twenty–four hours duty—which is exactly how Graziana had estimated her.

*

Maison Marais' studio was situated on Avenue George V in a privately owned townhouse, where the atelier and offices had been based since the sixties. The morning sunshine made the white stone seem whiter, and the windows looked particularly Parisienne, with black iron Juliette balconies covering them. The only thing on the outside to alert a by-passer, that this was where the famous French fashion house resided, was an engraved plague (although anyone who lived in Paris and knew about fashion, knew that this was the legendary fashion house's HQ).

Gianni's security guard stepped out of the car and opened the door for Chloe to step out while Gianni opened his side himself—buttoning up his blazer as he joined her on the pavement.

"Good morning Mr Palazzo, it's wonderful to have you back in Paris," Jean-Paul's assistant said, with her French accent that tinkled like piano ivories; greeting Gianni at the door with the usual 'kissy-kissy' fashion thing. "Jean's excited to finally show you the collection, the team have been working so hard ahead of the show."

"As am I, Claudette," Gianni said, guiding Chloe through the front entrance which was secured by two guards. The foyer was a lot different to how Chloe had imagined it to look like. The old store on Fifth Avenue was very classic in style, with teak wood furniture and shelves, and glass vitrines that held their world-famous leather goods. This time, a white marble-floored entrance greeted her, with a long reception desk made from a black marble slab, marled with swirls of white.

Behind the desk sat a receptionist in a classic black suit with a black and white polka dot shirt underneath her jacket. Behind her, 'MAISON MARAIS' was displayed on a white wall in silver, mirrored letters. The smell of fresh paint led Chloe's nose over to a workman painting the skirting board in the corner. Claudette showed them to the main studio where Jean's team had been working furiously, day and night on the new collection. Rows of large cutting tables, mannequins, fabric swatches, and a wall covered with clippings awaited them. Already the drone of sewing machines and chatter between atelier premières, wearing white lab coats, filled the air. Chloe was in awe—once again she had first-hand access to behind the scenes of a fashion house.

"Gianni—Chloe! Welcome!" Jean beamed, getting up from his office chair in the corner of the atelier.

"Nice job on the entrance… How much did that cost me?" Gianni said, shaking his hand.

"Oh, not much…"

"Only joking! This is why I employed you—to shake things up!"

"Claudette, coffee please... Or would you like champagne?" Jean offered.

"Oh, coffee please," Chloe said, waving her hands at the suggestion of more champagne.

"Sparkling water for me, Claudette... Let's take a quick tour of the studio, and then I'd like to see the collection," Gianni said, wanting to get down to business so he could attend to more important matters back at the hotel which involved Chloe.

"Of course... So this is our main studio, and upstairs we have two more floors where the petite mains work on our precious fabrics, and above them is our fabric technicians and digital studio. This is also my office," Jean said to Chloe, as Gianni had already viewed the space before deciding to take over the fledgeling brand.

The seamstresses all nodded as they walked around the floor, getting straight back to work after they had politely acknowledged them. Jean led them over to the huge wall covered with images and cut-outs that had inspired him.

"So this is my inspiration for the first collection... I have completely changed the look of Maison Marais, keeping only the best aspects from the archive of course. The classic French mariniere T-shirts, the 'MM' monogram, the fine quality fabrics all remain—I assure you—but this new direction is younger and sexier."

Jean-Paul stood rather proud before his wall of influence, before turning to them for a reaction. Gianni nodded in agreement like he knew and trusted where Jean was going with the brand, but Chloe, on the other hand, was miffed. It was completely different from the Maison Marais she had known all her life. Maison Marais was one of the most aspirational brands around, with their brown and beige monogram luggage being the epitome of luxury. What Chloe had seen so far was a million miles away from all that.

"Here, the team are finalising some of the dresses which will be core looks of the show—we are using this sequin fabric created in-house by the petite mains," Jean continued excitedly, pointing to a black and white polka dot dress having its label sewn by hand by a seamstress with a single white glove on. Chloe noticed that even the label itself had had a complete overhaul: a large white ribbon embroidered with 'MAISON MARAIS' in black, with simple tack stitches at each corner holding it onto the lining.

"All the basics will be redefined and covered in the cruise collection—while the show is going to be the 'big reveal,' with all the stand-out dresses and also a few men's looks ahead of the main show next year. By then, we would have covered the groundwork on the new style for menswear and ready to show a full collection."

Claudette returned to join them—standing by Jean's side—whispering into his ear that refreshments were ready and waiting in the salon for the run-through.

"*Bon!* Let's go upstairs and we can have fun watching the fashion show—just for you! Ladies—all the looks upstairs in fifteen!" he called out with a clap of his hands.

Claudette immediately disappeared to ensure all the premières and assistants rallied to gather the collection, as Jean led Gianni and Chloe upstairs. The elevator to the fourth floor opened into a room that was flooded with natural light from the glass ceiling above, along with white light that beamed down from hanging lights—ensuring every minor detail could be seen in the garments before they were sent down the runway (and more importantly before they were sent to production in Italy).

Walking through the salon, tables of bags and accessories caught Chloe's eye—like sweets to a child. New renditions of classic shoulder bags, holdalls, and clutches were all laid out, making her want to grab them. Instead, she walked through the room to the other end, where a desk and three white chairs were set out in a row behind it. Her coffee was waiting, along with Gianni's sparkling water which he started to pour out for everyone.

"D'accord?" Claudette said, slightly out of breath as she sped her way up from the floor below via a black spiral staircase.

"*Oui!*" Jean clapped. "Let's go… Okay, please take your seats and we will begin our preview."

The elevator pinged and the doors parted open to which Chloe expected to see their first look step out on a model. What she wasn't expecting was Graziana to step out.

"NOT without me!" she boomed, extending her arms out to greet Jean. She was followed in by a beautiful, girl—clearly a model. But not just any model—it was Carly Wattmore of course. Model of the moment. "I hope you don't mind, but I invited Carly to model for us—I think she would be a great face for the new brand."

"Thank you, Graziana," Gianni said, almost through gritted teeth—taking a sip of water before nodding at Carly to acknowledge her.

"Absolutely… This is the new, fresh face on the scene! She looked stunning in your show Gianni—I must simply have her too!" Jean said with a sparkle of playful competitiveness in his eye. "Claudette, show Miss Carly to the premières so she can get changed… We have our in-house fit model ready to walk for us too, so this really will be like a mini fashion show!"

Graziana immediately took seat in between Jean and Gianni—forcing Chloe to take a seat on the cushioned window sill, discarded almost on the side. But she didn't care, she was growing accustomed to Graziana's bitchy ways and if she were honest, she preferred to be as far away as possible from her, sipping her coffee in the Paris sunlight. Even the smell of her rich floral perfume made her feel putrid.

Plus, she had a glorious view of the streets of Paris below, which she snapped a picture of with her 'MAISON MARAIS' banded coffee cup in the foreground to send to Dominic. It was times like this that she missed her supportive friends and allies, but then again, did she really need to be bothered by Graziana's attitude when it was Gianni's affection that mattered?

> Guess where I am???
>
> PARIS BABY!!!
>
> Can't U get a train here & meet me 4 a day?
> Not sure how long I will be here…

"Claudette, put some music on for the models to walk to," Jean shouted across the long room, with its centre cleared to allow the models to walk up to the table and then back again. As the music started to fill the high ceiling room, Chloe felt eyes one her watching as she quietly sat perched on the window seat. She was determined not to turn her head and show Gianni that she couldn't take her eyes off him—but she couldn't help it. Although, it wasn't Gianni gazing her way—it was Graziana. Giving an unimpressed expression as she lit up a slim Vogue cigarette.

Luckily, one of the models had walked up the spiral staircase from the floor below and began walking towards them, diverting everyone's attention in a black puffball party dress. Carly followed her wearing a navy and white striped, long jersey dress that clung to her slender frame, cut across the shoulder in a boat neck style with long sleeves—very French in style. The next look was a black tuxedo suit made entirely out of black matte sequins with a wide silk lapel and shoulder pads that the eighties would have been jealous of. Carly made her second turn in a leather biker jacket and black leather jeans that were 'spray-on' with stretch lycra. Underneath the leather jacket, she wore a navy and white striped sequinned boob-tube with black patent high-heeled pumps.

Look after look, it was like the greatest hits of the eighties reimagined with plenty of attitude. It had a sense of 'rock and roll' about it, a feeling of rebellion and power dressing. Chloe sat patiently and attentive as Gianni suggested edits to pieces and minor tweaks on —the première listened while Jean translated back to her in French. Even Graziana gave her opinion which caused Chloe to huff, almost too loudly—she could have sworn it was audible to everyone in the room. 'Does she think she's a designer now too?' she laughed to herself, checking her phone to see if she had a reply from Dom.

OMG! What?

Sadly I can't leave Ldn... Too busy with showroom appointments :(

Even though she was disappointed, it was probably for the best and for all she knew Gianni could be jetting her off to somewhere else. Which led her to wonder exactly how long she would be staying in Paris with him? She had to get back to New York to iron out the agreement with Veronica (which rather worryingly, she hadn't heard anything about from Carmen). But it *was* Paris Fashion Week after all, and maybe Gianni had more shows lined up to take her to—and then there was the trip to the Eiffel which he had promised her.

"Chloe," Gianni said, breaking her thoughts as she gazed out of the window. "What do think of the collection? Brilliant, huh? With the men's looks added in, this will be one hell of a relaunch!"

"Er… Yeah. I mean, it's completely different to what the brand has become known for… And as you said, a complete shake-up—just like you wanted," she said, trying to not sound negative. After all, she did like the overall feel of the collection.

"Why don't you take the car and go shopping? I'm sure you're dying to see Paris and have lunch somewhere *authentic*… We gotta have a quick meeting here—boring stuff," Gianni said.

"Before you go… I saw you looking at the bags," Jean said, walking over to her. "Claudette, help Chloe choose one—my gift!"

"Really? Oh, my… You mean I would be one of the very first to carry a new Maison Marais bag?" Chloe said, clutching her neck—almost choked at the idea of more designer gifts being checked at her.

"And while you're at it, why don't you pick a dress from the pre-collection to wear at the show? Gianni can't be the only one to dress the hottest girl on the scene now, can he?" Jean said, giving Chloe a kiss on the cheek, before leading Gianni and Graziana down to his office to discuss profit projections and his new store concept—leaving Claudette and Chloe alone together.

"So… What do you *really* think of the collection?" Claudette said.

"Well, it's certainly different… It's very…"

"*Fresh?* I know what you're thinking," Claudette said, walking Chloe over to the display of handbags. "You're thinking, this isn't

Maison Marais… That Jean will ruin the house… But do you know the origins of the Maison?"

Of course, Chloe knew about Madame Marais—the Founder of the brand who had started the house in the 1920s—but she could sense that she was about to hear all about it from Claudette.

"Madame Cecile Marais was a seamstress for a prestigious French cloth-house by day, but by night, she was a singer in one of the underground clubs—a showgirl with many influential lovers, that she had to keep a secret... She wanted to be loved, she wanted to live in luxury, but all her lovers ended up deserting her for marriage with more 'suitable' women, or for war. And so she started to depend more and more on herself, selling straw hats and simple dresses. She would make costumes for the other showgirls and it was these designs that got her noticed by an English gentleman who frequented the clubs when he was in Paris on business... He believed in her strange and unique style, and it was he who bought her a tiny store in the Marais—Maison Marais."

Chloe listened as she picked up bag after bag, admiring the butter-soft leather of one, and the sequin embellishment of another, as Claudette continued with her ramblings—leaning against the mirrored shelving with her arms folded as she watched Chloe—wondering if she was truly listening.

"You see, Madame Marais herself was a rebel and it is with this attitude that Jean-Paul will reinvent the brand... With Palazzo's backing, we can be a fashion label once again and not just some luxury luggage brand for the super-rich... Madame Marais created this brand for the artists, the gays, the performers—les créatifs!"

"Sounds like he has it all planned out," Chloe said, not really caring about any of what Claudette had just said. "I'll be sure to include all that in my article."

"What *is it* that you do, Chloe?"

"I run a fashion and style website—I'm a stylist."

"A woman of many talents... And how long have you been dating Gianni?" There it was, the question that everyone seemed comfortable to ask her, despite just being introduced. But she wasn't going to brush it off, she wanted to put Claudette in her place after she had received a lecture on Maison Marais like she was some idiot.

"A month or so… It's still fresh and I live in New York, so we are keeping it casual."

"And which bag is your favourite?" Claudette asked, satisfied that her question had been answered, now wanting her out of the way so she could get on with the mountain of work she had to do before the upcoming show.

"Definitely this one," Chloe said, wearing a black quilted leather handbag on her shoulder that had silver chain straps and an overlapping silver 'MM' buckle on the front closure.

"Funny… This is Jean's very first design for accessories; it's his favourite too. I will tell him… He will probably end up naming it after you."

"Really?" Chloe said, as if getting a free bag wasn't enough—he didn't have to name it after her too.

"All the bags are named after models, I'm sure he will love the fact you just picked out his first baby… Come, let's go downstairs and pick a dress for you to wear to the show."

**

After picking out her favourite dress from the pre-collection (a black and white polka dot dress with a side ruffle, billowing out of the left-hand hip), Chloe sat and ate lunch in the window of a bistro—asking herself how on Earth did her life change this much in such little space? Of course, she knew what had happened up until this point (she *had* lived it), but she just couldn't fathom why it was happening to her?

Although one mystery was solved. Now that Jean-Paul had invited her to the Maison Marais show tomorrow night, that meant she would be staying in Paris until at least Tuesday morning. Which got her thinking—she needed more clothes if she was to keep up with Gianni (and he did say to go shopping after all). After sitting for a while, people watching and drinking coffee, she asked Franco to take her to the Palazzo boutique on Avenue Montaigne. The boutique manager had welcomed her (after Franco had escorted her inside and explained that it was 'on the house') and his eager staff helped her choose an elegant black velvet cocktail dress, with a matching pair of shoes and a velvet pearl clasped clutch. With her Gold Palazzo shopping bags on her arm—and her outfit problems now solved—Franco drove her back to the hotel so she could rest and replenish her energy for when Gianni returned.

But it was the bathtub back at the penthouse that she was most looking forward to, ordering a glass of champagne to enjoy with a nice soak. Relaxing back in the tub, she wondered what was happening back in New York and if Carmen had heard any news from Veronica. It was strange that nothing had been said or emailed over to her yet, which made her want to end her relaxation to find out. With her mind now fixated on it, Chloe got out, wrapped herself in her robe and fetched her laptop to set it up on the coffee table by the sofa in the living area.

After logging onto the WiFi, she quickly jumped online to view S.O.S, and as Carmen had promised, she had posted her latest article complete with an image of her and Gianni at the show. 'If she's managed to find this image online, what else is there?' Chloe wondered. She couldn't help but to do a Google search of herself, and was surprised to see the amount of coverage on her and Gianni together—almost every article covering the Palazzo show dismissed the collection and speculated on their relationship. "*Wow!* They're really focusing on this shit," she said, not believing it was any of this was relevant to the fashion industry.

But her alone time was suddenly over—the penthouse doors crashed open, nearly making her heart stop. "*Pack your bags!*" Graziana said, storming in with her back shades covering her eyes.

"W-*what?*" Chloe started, making sure her robe was covering her completely.

"You heard me… I want you out—*gone!* Pack your bags and leave!"

"Excuse me, but you can't just barge in and—"

"When it concerns my brother and our company, I can do what I like!" Graziana said, whipping off her shades, pointing them at her.

"I'm sorry but I can't just… What will I say to Gianni?"

"Leave him to me," Graziana said, walking over to her, slamming the lid on Chloe's laptop shut.

"Okay," Chloe said, standing up to meet Graziana in the middle. There was no way she was going to let this five-foot-two prima-donna tower over and dominate her. "What exactly is going on here?"

"You know exactly what's going on… It's Gianni that's being played a fool! Do you really think I will say nothing and let you ruin my brother's reputation? I know about you—I know everything!"

"Oh really now?" Chloe snorted. "And just what is it that you know about me? You haven't even given a chance to know me!"

"Oh… You've had your chance! I know enough to ask you to leave, so just please get out! Don't make me call security, there's paparazzi all over the streets outside and I don't want to embarrass you further."

"Embarrass *me?* You're the one embarrassing yourself here." Chloe said, all the while her mind was trying to figure out what she had found out—and who from.

"If you go now, I won't tell Gianni about how you are an ex-employee of ours," Graziana said, blinking at her with a pursed lip.

Chloe's heart sank to her stomach—she had been rumbled. But how? Well, that was obvious. There was only one person she knew that would be willing to dig up dirt on her. One person who *really* wanted to ruin her, and probably even more so now that her picture with Gianni was splashed all over the Internet. Unknown to Chloe, her suspicions were correct.

Marco had done a stellar job, eager to keep his job and impress Graziana even more. But unfortunately for Chloe, Kim wasn't there this time to take the call when he requested a bio on Chloe Ravens from the New York press office. Of course, his call had been diverted straight to Regina (who had simply just waited for this moment to finally arrive), to give her a very revealing character reference.

"How do you think this will make my brother look if this got out? That he's having a fling with an employee? He will be destroyed… They will make him out like some sort of predator!" Graziana flapped.

'Well, he kinda is,' Chloe thought. It *was* Gianni that had tracked her down, not the other way around. But to Graziana, that's exactly how it had looked; Chloe looked like the desperate star-fucker (exactly the portrayal she had wanted to avoid on this trip but was nonetheless branded with).

"Just pack your bags and go, and I won't mention any of this to Gianni," Graziana said, lighting up another Vogue cigarette in desperation.

Chloe was stunned, here she was once again—being bullied by a forceful female in power. It reminded her of the night Regina had barged into her apartment and demanded her to leave Gianni alone—now she was being threatened by his sister! 'What is it with these bitches?' Chloe wondered. They all wanted his attention, or to protect his attention on them diverting onto someone else—they all wanted to be seen by him. But she hadn't come all this way, simply to be diminished and walk away with her tail between her legs. She hadn't put up with Regina's crap all this time to now swap it for Graziana's. "And what if I don't? I have no issue with telling him myself who I am, where I come from," Chloe said, now staring back at Graziana with her arms folded.

Graziana walked back up to her and exhaled a thin slew of smoke in Chloe's face. "He doesn't want you, my dear… I know my brother and trust me, you will be long gone out of his mind after this week is over… So, do yourself a favour, save yourself from humiliation and just leave quietly with the good memories you have of this once in a lifetime experience… Because believe me, this won't be happening again."

"What are you trying to say? That I'm not good enough to be here, not good enough for Gianni?"

"I'm not *trying* to say anything—I am *telling* you that you are not good enough!" Graziana snapped, bobbing her head side-to-side. "You know just as much as I do that Gianni can have any woman he wants, and he will want more than you… Do you really think he will be happy with a simple shop assistant with a blog? He deserves more, and he will have more… So on that note, why don't you book whatever flight you want, back to where you came from—or anywhere else for that matter! I've told reception that you can put any flight booking on the penthouse… Just don't come back and don't contact Gianni ever again!"

Graziana stubbed out her cigarette in Chloe's half-filled Champagne glass and left without looking back—slamming the doors. But with her now gone, Chloe slumped back down on the sofa in total disbelief. 'What just happened?' she asked herself. With the rush of conflict still flowing through her veins, not coming up with all sorts of sassy lines she should have come out with.

'How *fucking* dare she,' she cursed, now raging. She shuddered with a cold feeling tingling down her spine, still sat in just her bathrobe. Sitting there, she could feel tears starting to well in her eyes. 'Why does everyone want to destroy me?' she wondered, now sobbing into her hands.

Even though she desperately wanted and had tried so hard to change her life, she knew Graziana was right—she wasn't enough for Gianni. Maybe Graziana was right, maybe she should just leave? Chloe got up, wiping her face, forcing herself to stop crying which made her feel so weak and defeated. What she needed to do was to get her things together and leave fast, before Gianni returned. Even if she stayed to explain what had happened to him, Graziana would only twist the truth and besides, what she said was true—Gianni would feel misled if Chloe told him now who she truly was.

She darted into the bedroom and quickly got dressed into a T-shirt and a pair of jeans before stuffing her suitcase (which wasn't hard since she never really unpacked), throwing all her belongings into it without care—forcing it to shut by leaning over it with her weight and running the zipper around to close it. But where was she going to go? Back to New York? Back to Milan to try and catch her returning flight?

She had an idea—she knew exactly where she was going to go next. She bunged her hair up in a messy bun and slipped her leather biker jacket on, looking around for anything she had left behind. As she was about to leave the bedroom, she spotted a hotel notepad on the dresser and quickly scribbled a parting message.

Sorry, I can't make the MM show, I have to return to NY.
Thank you for a lovely weekend.

Chloe
x

With her goodbye left on the side for him, she wheeled her suitcase to the door, dashing to the sofa to grab her laptop, stashing it inside her handbag (which seemed to weigh heavier each time she packed it). Making her way down to reception in the private elevator, Chloe couldn't believe she was escaping like this—that it had ended this way. But it was probably for the best, she didn't want to end up broken once Gianni was done with her and Graziana had ridiculed her. Making her way over to the front desk, Chloe wiped her eyes again, making sure there was no evidence of tears.

"Good afternoon Madam, how can I help you?" the receptionist said.

"Hi, yes... I'd like to book a ticket for the Eurostar to London, please... You can charge it to the account on the penthouse," Chloe said, handing over her passport.

"Of course, give me a moment and I'll see what's available—take a seat," the receptionist said, having had prior word from Graziana to do so.

"Thanks, I'll wait in the bar," Chloe said, leaving her suitcase behind.

Sat in the bar, she dug around her handbag for her phone—she needed to speak to Carmen right away. There was much more pressing issues to discuss with her now, other than her deal with DivaFeet. "Chloe! How are you? Where are you now?" Carmen said, picking up within two rings—the bustling noise of New York traffic in the background.

"Hey Listen… I'm kinda on my way to London."

"*What!* Milan, Paris, and now he's taking you to London!"

"Not exactly," Chloe said, unsure how she was going to admit she was being driven away.

"What's going on?" Carmen said, hearing that there was a hint of trouble her tone.

"It's Graziana… She's demanded that I leave, that I leave Gianni alone otherwise she's going to tell him I used to work at Palazzo and I'm nothing but a gold-digging shop girl."

"*Whoah*, wait a minute! And you're just going to leave—just like that? At least try to explain it to him," Carmen shouted into her phone as she crossed the sidewalk, her coffee steadied in her other hand.

"What use it that? I mean, she's right… After this weekend he'll forget all about me anyway. This is for the best, I never truly believed he wanted me in the first place… It was everyone else that put that idea into my head!"

"Chloe, listen to me… You haven't come this far to be bullied by his fucking sister! What matters is what he thinks, and it was Gianni that invited you to Milan and Paris… You must stay! You owe him an explanation at least."

"Madam?" the receptionist said, returning with her passport and an envelope.

"Carmen, I gotta go… I'll call you later," Chloe said, ending the call sharply.

"I've booked a Eurostar to London that's leaving in an hour… If you leave now you will make it in time to check-in and board."

"Thank you so much," Chloe said, taking her passport back with the envelope. "Can you take my case out to the car? I'll be out in a moment."

The last thing she needed was to be photographed dragging her suitcase to the car looking sorry for herself. She reached into her handbag for her sunglasses, even though it wasn't bright outside, she needed to hide her eyes. She stood up and grabbed her handbag, her phone vibrating relentlessly inside (it was most likely Carmen calling her back to talk her out of leaving), but she didn't stop to answer.

Luckily there weren't many photographers' outside as most had left to follow Graziana, and the ones that were left didn't seem to recognise Chloe without Gianni by her side—and with a scruffy top knot. Sat in the back of the car on her way to Gare Du Nord, she finally took out her phone.

Ignoring Carmen's missed calls and texts, she scrolled for Dom's new phone number—she had to let him know she was coming to London. After multiple rings, he still didn't pick up (he was too busy working in the showroom to take calls right now). Chloe started to panic, she had nowhere to stay and needed him to meet her at the other end. What if she got to London and had nowhere to go? But it was too late now—Franco was pulling in as close as he could to the train station.

"Thank you for everything," she said to Franco, checking the time, realising she had to run if she was going to make it through customs in time. He helped her with her case and gave her a departing smile, a smile that said he wished her the best of luck. Just like Giancarlo back at The Four Seasons in Milan, Franco must have seen this many times with countless girls. Extending the top handle, Chloe rolled her case over the uneven cobblestones, towards the entrance of the station.

Gare Du Nord was incredibly busy, with a surge of extra people only just arriving for Fashion Week shows. She weaved her way through the station, dodge the crowds with her case in tow, but luckily the escalator to the Eurostar check-in wasn't hard to find—or far away. Rushing to catch her train, Chloe was surprised by the security measures in place to simply board a train. First through passport control, then having to empty her pockets and take off anything that would set the scanner alarms off—just like at the airport. Gathering her things back from the tray, she waited for her case to come through on the conveyor belt.

"Excuse me... Where do I go for this train?" she said, stopping a passing attendant, holding up her printed out ticket.

"Gate B, just straight ahead—it's leaving in twenty minutes."

"Thank you," she said, already on the move—walking past the shops and waiting travellers. She had to swerve kids sitting on the floor while their parents did nothing at all to move them out of her way, tired tourists with bags of shopping all heading back to London, and step over the stretched out legs of backpackers.

Finally reaching gate B, she joined the line of people having their tickets checked. Looking at her ticket, Chloe was pleased to see that the receptionist had at least booked her a business premier ticket and with no time to grab anything to eat, she was hopeful of a cup of coffee at least once seated. She dragged her case, with her handbag resting on top onto the moving walkway down to the train platform, where she was guided in the direction of her carriage by an assistant. Shattered, and now finally on board, she left her case on the shelf by the doors and walked down the carriage to find her seat. She was pleased to find the train wasn't that busy and she had a four-seat section with a tabletop completely to herself—ideal for catching up on work.

Taking her phone and her laptop out of her handbag, she placed it on the table in front of her (with no intention to start writing really), relaxing back with a deep breath in—and exhaled. Looking at her phone once more, she had several missed call from a withheld number, which was sure to be Gianni finding out where the hell she had gotten to.

Chloe dismissed them (it wasn't like she could call it back) and started to tap a message, she had to get hold of Dom to let him know she was just two hours away from reaching Kings Cross.

Hey Mr... Current sitch:

I'm on a Eurostar coming to London...
Can you meet me? Please? x

With the message sent, all she could do was sit back and get some rest—that's if her whirling mind would allow it. She had come up with at least five alternate scenarios to how she should have dealt with Graziana, as well as contemplated turning back around in the space since then and now. But she was emotionally and physically drained.

She had gone from first-class to high-class, back down to—well business premier class at least—in a matter of a weekend. As she closed her eyes and tried her best to wipe her mind blank for just a moment, she felt the train pull out of the station, leaving Paris for London—praying that a familiar face would be waiting for her on the other end. 'So much for staying in Paris until at least Tuesday,' she thought to herself.

14

"Chloe! What are you doing here?" Dom laughed, holding out his arms. He was more than surprised when her text message came through—but she was pleased that he finally messaged back to say he would, of course, be there to meet her at St. Pancras. Unable to speak with the relief she was now in safe hands, Chloe ran into his arms and held him tightly. She could feel tears beginning to fill her eyes, seeing him in person was better than how she had imagined.

"What's the matter? Why are you here?" Dom said, cradling her. He could hear she was upset.

"I know. I'm so sorry, but it was a last-minute decision and I just wanted to see you," she said, sniffling back her emotions.

"Come on you, let's get a car and go back to mine… Mother's excited you're here! She has the spare room all done up and every-thing—she's preparing dinner as we speak!" Dom said, extending her case handle to take it back outside to the taxi rank.

'Ah, thank God!' Chloe thought, just the mention of food made her stomach roll. The train food had consisted of cold quiche, mushy quinoa salad, and an apple tarte tatin that was clearly out of a packet. Obviously, she ate it, but a hot home-made meal was what she really needed. "Thank you so much for this, you always come to my rescue," she said, walking with him through the brick arches of the station's mall.

"So, tell me… Why exactly were you in Paris and why are you here now—not that I'm *not* pleased to see you… I'm just confused."

"Where to start… So, Gianni invited me to the Palazzo show, right? Well, I went and met him there and he invited me to Paris with him, but Graziana came barging in the suite this afternoon, demanding me to leave—so I came here," she abbreviated.

Chloe did have to admit, it was a lot to keep up with and she wasn't entirely sure herself why she had taken herself to London—especially when she had business matters to attend to in New York. All she knew was that she had to see Dom—only he would understand the predicament she faced with Gianni Palazzo. Sure, Carmen would be supportive, but in an abrasive, straight-up, 'tell it to your face' kind of way—which Chloe wasn't in the mood for right now.

"Wait a minute... You've been hanging out with Gianni and Graziana all weekend, and now you've come to see me?"

"It's a long story, but yes... Graziana hated me from the start and obviously done some digging around about my past, and standing there arguing with her, it hit me—she blatantly spoke to Regina and she's told her everything! She said that if the press found out I was an employee, it would ruin Gianni—make him look like a sexual predator."

"Well, he is—isn't he?" Dom said with a chuckle, confirming what she had thought. "And how can you be so sure she found out from Regina—she's a just an employee to them too, you know?" he said, raising an eyebrow at her paranoia.

"You know when you *just* know? The shit she was saying about me not being good enough, it was like Regina had schooled her... When she said about me being just a shop-girl and how I wasn't good enough for him—it just clicked.... It took me back to Regina invading my apartment to tell me what a nobody I am... Anyway, she told me I could book any plane or train I wanted to get out of Gianni's way—she wanted me gone *baaad*! And that's when I thought I'd come here; I should have just got a flight back to New York, but I wasn't thinking straight."

"Of course you weren't, and I'm glad you're here... You did the right thing! You got a free trip to London!" Dom said, trying his best to make her feel lighter as he opened Uber on his phone.

"She just threw me off... I mean, it was clear we were never going to be best friends, but I didn't expect her to be so... Nasty!"

"*Really* girlfriend? It's Graz-ian-na Pa-laz-zo, we're talking about here—everyone knows she's a fierce bitch!"

"Yeah—I get that—but it was like Regina had made her way back into my life all over again... I should have listened to her. I should have stayed away from Gianni—she did warn me she'd find a way to ruin me no matter what... And it looks like she has—again!"

"Oh, pur-lease!" Dom said, now getting sick of the 'poor me' act—like everything was always about her. "Look, let's get back home and have a cup of tea, that always makes things better—a good old English brew!"

"I'm doing it again aren't I?" Chloe said, wincing at his sharp tongue, smoothed over with the suggestion of tea.

"Doing what?" Dom said, double-taking her; pretending to be coy.

"Talking about myself like the world revolves around my dramas... How are you, how have you been doing? What happened with Jason!"

"Well, there's a story," Dom said as they walked out of the station. It was now dark and drizzling outside. "I took your advice and I went to the opening night of his exhibition, but I couldn't face him."

"Why?" Chloe said, being greeted by the cold English weather as Dom checked his phone for their car's number plate on his phone.

"Well, technically I saw him—the back of him—and then I left."

"You left... Without speaking to him?"

Dom didn't need to answer that one—his face said it all as he walked ahead to locate their driver. He opened the car door for Chloe to get inside, away from the drizzle which was getting heavier, as he collapsed her suitcase handle to chuck in the back—before coming up with the perfect comeback. "Anyway bitch, look who's talking... Didn't you just flee Gianni?" he said playfully, climbing into the car after her.

"Touché... I'm in no place to talk, but he wanted to see you."

"Yes, but I didn't want to see him... I realised I have to move on, and it was the day of the fashion show, so I was feeling all empowered and independent and shit—yep that's it," Dom said, confirming his address with the driver.

Chloe nodded, she understood where he was coming from—she just hoped she could feel the same way too. Instead, she felt downtrodden and exactly the type of person Graziana said she was—not on their level.

"Anyway, I did see him again," Dom said, which made Chloe's head turn sharp—there was more to this story. "Pandora arranged a little after-show dinner at Shoreditch House and I happened to bump into him there."

"No way!" Chloe said, enjoying the unexpected twist. All of a sudden, it was like Dom had never left New York and they were back gossiping together like old times.

"Yeah, but he was with some other guy—he clearly had moved on as well! *Aaand*, he was wearing the leather jacket he gave *me*—the audacity!"

"Wait, back up—how did this other guy have the leather jacket?" Chloe said, completely lost.

"I left it at the gallery on a bench for Jason to find… I didn't want any reminder of him, so I just left it there."

"And what did you say when you saw them together?" Chloe urged, gripping Dom's arm in the backseat.

"I ran," Dom said, smirking at her.

And with a quick, comedic look, they both fell on each other's shoulders—laughing uncontrollably at the tragic situation they were both in.

"What a pair, we are!" Chloe said through laughter, it had brought tears of irony to her eyes.

"Looks like we are both runners, kiddo… Whatever, to hell with men! You and me—we do what we can to survive," Dom said, quite seriously.

Chloe caught the truth in his voice and she was glad that he was surviving. It was a much better state than what she had left in him, she just wondered if she had it in her to survive also. "So, tell me about the label," she said, changing the subject—it *was* indeed time to move on.

"It's going great… Well, it wasn't when I turned up, but I soon saw to that. You saw the show right?"

"I did, in fact, I've written a piece on it… But now I'm here, maybe you can take me to the studio and I can try some things on… Get you to take pictures of me like old times?" Chloe said, thinking about how he would shoot and style her for her very first blog posts.

"Sure, we can go there tomorrow—this week we have our last showroom appointments. It's been busier than ever because of the good reviews we had."

"Ah yes, I sat next to Lou Banks at the Palazzo show and he told me he had met you!"

"He did?" Dom said, rather pleased to hear it. "Also, Carly modelled for them, right?"

"Uh! Carly *frickin'* Wattmore? Yeah she was there… In fact, Graziana flew her out to Paris to model for Jean-Paul."

"Are you serious?" Dom squealed, raising his voice a pitch higher.

"At Maison Marais, that's when I messaged you," Chloe said flippantly, forgetting that she hadn't mentioned any of that yet.

"Okay, so let's rewind… You're at Maison Marais with Gianni, Graziana and Carly Wattmore…"

"Well, we had dinner the night before with the Maison Marais crew—that's where I first met Jean-Paul—then he invited us to come by the studio to see the collection… Jean has that team working around the clock before the show tomorrow night, it's all changed!"

"What was it like?" Dom said, eager to know more about the newly invested fashion house.

"It's all… Eighties… Shoulder pads, sequins, tuxedo suits, camouflage, and safari jackets," Chloe said wafting her hands in the air, passing it off as nonsense. "The atelier has had a complete refurb too it seems…. I was expecting the old, classic wood panelling thing."

She looked at Dom for agreement, to see that he also had the same classic vision of the brand, but he nodded at her to hurry along with the details. "Well, now it's all white walls, black and white marble, mirrored tabletops and shelves… I bet that's what the new stores are going to look like too, no doubt."

"Wow, a big turn around then?"

"Yeah, Jean's assistant—this stuck up chick called Claudette—gave me some monologue about how they're restoring the house back to its origins… They're going all '*fash*' and rock and roll… For the artists and the gays, so she said," Chloe said with a huff.

"It was obvious Palazzo was gonna do something like that though," Dom said, sounding like a know-it-all.

"Bullshit, you didn't know that!" she said, calling him out.

"Of course it was… Think about it, Palazzo is all about sex, showing off—that's why they bought Maison Marais… To create disruption and completely flip it over."

"Anyway, you can see the show yourself tomorrow night—they're showing the first men's looks too ahead of Men's Fashion Week," she said, now feeling disappointed that she wasn't attending the show herself and would have to resort to watching it online instead.

They had chatted constantly the whole drive home, that it made the journey back to South West London go by quickly. By now it was early evening and Chloe was just glad to reach a comfortable home where she could relax. Walking up to the house, Chloe could feel her phone still vibrating in her bag but she wasn't interested in taking anyone's calls—Gianni's or Carmen's. Right now she was here, home. "*Muuum*, we're home!" Dom called, after turning the key and stepping through the door.

"Chloe! Oh my!" his mother said, stepping out from the kitchen into the hallway, rubbing her hands with a tea towel. "So great to see you! We haven't seen each other for years!"

"Mrs Fraser, thank you so much for allowing me to stay at such short notice," Chloe said, stepping forward to kiss her cheek.

"Oh, anytime… We had no idea you would be in London," she said, giving her a hug.

"Neither did she!" Dom said, taking off his jacket and hanging it on the bannister.

"Dinner's nearly ready… Dom, why don't you show Chloe to the guest room and I'll call you down when it's on the table?"

"Thank you," Chloe said making an appreciative face, folding into herself like she was a burden on them.

"Gwen! You can call me Gwen—you have enough time to take a shower before dinner, if you like."

"Come on, I'll take your case up, you just bring yourself," Dom said, lifting the case and making his way up the stairs.

Chloe followed him to the guest room, which was next door to his. It was decorated with white walls and soft pink curtains which were tied back with bows. The window overlooked the garden which was always neatly kept by Michael. Dom dumped her case in the corner of the room as Chloe rested her weighty handbag down on the bed—overloaded with pillows. "Yeah, you might need to take some of those off… My mother has an obsession with cushions!" Dom said, chucking a few on the floor.

"It's wonderful and homely… So, this is what a good old English home looks like?"

"I guess, it's a bit creaky—and the bathroom's always freezing by the way—but it's home."

"Hmmm, well…" Chloe said, sitting on the end of the bed.

"What's that mean?"

"*Home* is New York."

Dom rolled his eyes, he knew where this conversation was going and he didn't want to entertain it, there was no way he would return to New York—not now anyway.

"Okay, I get that you're here for the foreseeable future… But I know you'll return one day."

"Maybe… Tomorrow you'll see for yourself why I'm here— and you'll meet Pandora and the team and understand exactly why I want to stay here! They're a cool bunch, but I'm sure Pandora would love to meet you—I've told her lots about you… Not that it's an issue, but how long are you staying for?"

'Good question,' Chloe thought. For the past few days she had been coasting from city to city with not a clue, and now she had to look after herself and find her own way back to New York.

"I should probably check flights tomorrow… But let's just enjoy hanging out for at least one day?" she said, just wanting to forget about everything else for a moment.

"Sure," Dom said with a smile, getting up to leave the room. "I mean, you can't come all this way and not stay for at least a day or two… Anyway, the bathroom is down the hall—come down when you're ready."

Chloe lifted herself off the bed and searched her phone in her handbag. The screen was already alight with missed calls and voicemails, all of which were from an unknown number —bound to be Gianni. But she couldn't face them right now, she was in a safe place free from the fashion circus and that's where she wanted to stay… For now at least.

*

"So what brings you to London, Chloe?" Gwen asked, passing the greens around the table.

"I was in Milan and Paris for Fashion Week and I asked Dom to join me, but since he is so busy being the brand director for Pandora Simmons, I decided to come here to see him instead." Dom dished out some roast potatoes on his plate, before passing them to Chloe with a look that playfully said: 'How sweet of you!'

"Milan and Paris? Wow, it sounds like you get around quite a bit these days," Gwen continued.

"*She certainly does!*" Dom cheekily said under his breath.

"You could say that…" Chloe said, burning her eyes into him. "Thanks to Dom, he helped me set up my website again and this time it's taken off—which was unexpected, to say the least. Our old boss, the designer of Palazzo, he noticed me at a party we were both at back in New York and he invited me to Milan and Paris Fashion Week."

"And, Chloe here, has a collection coming out too," Dom added, starting to dig into his pan-fried sea bass.

"How exciting! I'm so happy to see you two finally flourish! No time for a boyfriend then?"

"*Mum!*" Dom scolded, it was fine for her to pry into his private life but quite another to give Chloe the inquisition too.

"What? What did I say?"

"It's fine," Chloe chuckled, through a mouthful of fish and potatoes. "I mean, there is *someone*, but I'm not sure exactly where that's going, to be honest, and as Dom says—I'm probably too busy for all that."

"Oh, well… Don't leave it too late!" Gwen said in a tone that was true but harsh. And on that note, the dinner table fell silent as they ate. Chloe pursed her lips and nodded her head, she knew Gwen had a point. In just a few months she would turn thirty and although she had managed to change the direction of her career, she was still nowhere where she thought she would be at this point in her life.

She had imagined that she would have amassed a fortune by now, got married and possibly had a kid or two. But when she thought about it, none of her friends was really doing that either; only her sister had managed to do that (the get married and have children part at least), but it was easier for her. She never had dreams of having a career—or leaving Boston for that matter.

Even though she had imposed these targets on herself, she secretly knew it was what everyone else expected from an attractive, young woman—so the ticking time clock wasn't entirely in her own head. And maybe Graziana was right—maybe Gianni wasn't the *one?* Although she fantasised about the possibility of being with him, she knew it was an impossible dream and Gianni would only get bored of her 'normality' after he had had his fun.

"So, what are you two up to tomorrow?" Gwen said, noticing the table had got awkwardly quiet. "Maybe we can go shopping, show Chloe some sights and have a fun day out in town?"

"Sorry mum, we're meeting Pandora at the studio tomorrow."

"And this is the problem with you young people!" Gwen huffed, cutting a chunk of fish to mash it against her fork with a side of potato. "You never just take a day off to experience things, meet people… It's all work, work, work!"

"Welcome to modern life," Chloe said with a grimace.

"You know when I was your age—"

"When *you* were our age, things were much easier and women weren't expected to have it all!" Dom quipped.

"Well, I'm just saying… You should be having fun as well as working hard—that's all."

"And I think that's been my issue… I've been having too much fun when I should have been working hard… Or smarter, at least," Chloe said, bringing the table talk back to silence once more.

Having gotten the message that talk of relationships and dating was off the cards, Gwen didn't bother making further conversation—instead, she just let them eat. Chloe was happy to have a decent meal in her stomach and much looking forward to dessert, which she had presumed would be just as delicious—and she wasn't wrong. After their main, Gwen brought out a homemade tiramisu cheesecake from the fridge, served with vanilla ice cream. Chloe had to stop herself from eating it in one go, reminding herself she wasn't at home on her own, but Gwen was simply pleased to see her cooking had gone down well. It was rather nice to have another mouth to feed and take care of.

"Wow, your mom's a really good cook!" Chloe said, in between restrained mouthfuls. "Now I understand why you came back to London!"

"This is the first time he's sat still! It's my pleasure to cook for you guys… You must be tired, feel free to relax in the lounge… Maybe we can have a game of scrabble?"

"Thanks, mum, but I think we're gonna go upstairs and catch up before bed… We have an early start tomorrow," Dom said, getting up.

"Fine," Gwen said, collecting the bowls off the table—accepting the only entertainment she was going to get this evening was by filling the dishwasher. "Chloe, bring down anything you want me to wash for you, I don't mind."

"That would be amazing! But only if you insist it wouldn't be any trouble?"

"I wouldn't have offered if it was!"

"Don't worry mother… Most of it's probably dry clean only anyway," Dom teased. Chloe smacked him in the ribs, it was the gesture that mattered. "Thank you, I'll take a look and bring down the essentials," she said following back upstairs. "Sorry about all the questions," Dom said, now on the landing and out of earshot.

"Oh, it's fine… She's just concerned, that's all… My mom is the same!"

Which got Chloe thinking, she hadn't seen her mother since Christmas last and would most likely not see her to this year's Holiday. Having worked in retail for the past six years, Chloe usually skipped going home for Thanksgiving (spending it with Dom curing a hangover) and took the train to Boston on Christmas Eve—returning to work before the New Year. But this year Chloe didn't have to rush back to the city to drag her tired ass back onto the shop floor of Palazzo.

In fact, for the first time in ages, she could go home for Thanksgiving and the Holidays—and New Year! Back in her guest room, Chloe's thoughts of her family were interrupted by the illuminations of her phone screen. "Uh!" she huffed, throwing her phone back down on the bed.

"What is it now?" Dom said, sprawling across the bed sideways.

"Gianni… Wondering where I am most likely."

"Well, aren't you going to answer and let him know you're okay at least?"

"No… I mean, what's the point? Graziana's probably made up some excuse… Anyway, I left a note saying I had to leave for business back in New York… It's been fun—don't get me wrong— but I need to focus on *me!*" she said, propping up the pillows to rest her head.

"Yeah, I get all that… But don't you think he could help you? It's one hell of a contact, especially in this industry."

"I just feel that I need to fully close this chapter on Palazzo and move on with my own thing… Anyway, I don't have his direct number and he's probably expecting me to chase him like all the others before me… Sometimes, you have to play hardball."

"Oh, so that's what you're doing now?" Dom laughed, vaguely remembering it was Chloe who urged him to get back in touch with Jason not so long ago.

She could sense from his tone where he was going to go next and immediately sat up to defend herself with a pointed finger in his face. "No! It's not the same! Jason was *into* you, he came back to New York for you! You *had* to see him again."

"Okay, hold up," Dom said sitting up to face her with a finger snap. "So having one of the most famous designers in the world track you down, fly you to Milan—then fly you to Paris—means he *wasn't* into you?"

Chloe laughed, he was right—it was exactly the same. But she wasn't ready to speak to him either way and she didn't really want to speak about it anymore. Like she had said herself, there was much more to take care of back in New York that needed attention—but Dom needed more details before he was going to let her drop it.

"So, what *really* happened in Paris?" Dom said, hitting her with one of the many pillows still on her bed. "Did you sleep with him?" Chloe raised an eyebrow—as if that was actually a question! "I knew it! See, that's why he's ringing your phone down! He's had a bite of the apple and he wants more! Chloe, you would be daft not to speak to him again—*fuck* Graziana! Well, fuck Gianni, not her—you know what I mean."

"And that's what's so dumb about this," Chloe laughed. "Oh, I dunno… I'll sleep on it and see how I feel in the morning I guess?"

"All I'm saying is that it's fine to finish a chapter and all that—but you have to finish the story before you can close the book… On that note, I'll leave you to get some rest," he said, getting up to leave the room. "Set your alarm for seven-ish, I have to be at the studio for nine."

"Night, see you in the morning—I can't wait to finally meet Pandora," Chloe said, giving him a hug before he got up.

But as Dom reached the door to leave, he looked back around with a smile. There was one more burning question that he simply had to ask—otherwise he would be lying awake all night wondering. "So… How big was it?" he said, gesturing length with his hands. "This big… Or *this* big?" making the distance in-between ridiculously large, which made Chloe howl.

"Let's just say it's above average," she winked.

**

"Morning, Chloe," Gwen said as she entered the kitchen. "Would you like tea or coffee?"

"When in London… Tea, I guess?" she smiled back, taking a seat at the dining table.

"Who are *you* kidding?" Dom said, catching the latter as he entered the kitchen. "She lives on coffee."

Chloe smirked at Gwen, who turned around in confusion—was it tea or coffee?

"You know me too well," Chloe said, confirming it was indeed coffee that she wanted/needed.

"You look nice," Dom said, pouring himself cold orange juice from the fridge door.

"It's all I have with me," Chloe said, detecting a hint of sarcasm from him at her head to toe Palazzo look. "Oh, I've separated some laundry in the basket in the bathroom… If you still don't mind?"

"Of course not, I'll have it washed and dried for you for when you get back," Gwen said, handing Chloe her coffee.

They only had enough time to quickly eat a slice of toast and down their hot drinks before they had to set off for the tube station, escaping Dom's mother who would only want to set them back and have an entire coffee morning meeting. Chloe had to borrow a jacket from Dom's closet, noticing that the weather was getting chilly now.

"Bye mum!" Dom said, slamming the door shut and waiting until they were down the street a bit before asking for an update. "So, have you had more calls overnight?"

"No, he's stopped… Finally!"

"And how do you feel about him now?"

"The same… I know I have to speak to him at some point, but I can't bring myself to right now—and I'm more worried about how I'm gonna get back to New York!"

"Trust me, I know that feeling—I couldn't face Jason in the end… And I know you have to get back to oversee your collection, but you can stay here for as long as you want—you know that. But we can take a look at flights later if that will help ease your mind… Have you spoken to Carmen yet?"

"Not since leaving Paris—I should really call her," Chloe said, walking along briskly to match Dom's pace.

"Sure, let's just get to the studio and enjoy at least one day in London! We'll worry about everything else this evening when we get home."

The tube ride and interchange to get to Liverpool Street was quite an ordeal for Chloe, she had almost forgotten what riding the subway was like during rush hour, which made her second guess her decision to forget all about Gianni. How she missed his private jet and fleet of cars right now. Dom's march-like walking pace led Chloe through herds of commuters and bankers, all the way towards Shoreditch High Street up to the studio—pointing out places of interest on the way (namely Shoreditch House where he had spent most of his time socially).

Pandora and the team were already at work, having had a busy week of showroom appointments and were now equally as busy finalising quantities for production. They had had a very successful season, like no other before, which made Pandora feel slightly panicked about how they were going to fulfil all of the orders on time.

"Where's Dom when you need him?" she yelled, just in time for him to enter and hear her outburst.

"Did someone say my name?" he said with sass.

"*Dom!*" Pandy said, relieved to see him. "I've just tallied up the orders for the zero–one–five dress and there's no way my the factory can handle that amount in time for November delivery," she said before noticing he had a friend with him.

"Pandy, this is Chloe—Chloe, this is Pandora."

"Oh my God! Chloe? As in, your 'mate' from New York? I'm so sorry, you've caught me during a stress attack," she said, reaching out to shake her hand.

"Which is often," Dom added, walking over to say good morning to the rest of the gang.

"No worries… I hear you guys have had a storming season!" Chloe said, placing her handbag down on the table.

"It's been the best ever! Too good almost—I just dunno how we're gonna make all the shit people have ordered!"

"Pandora… Have I let you down since I got here?" Dom said, rather cocky. "Guys, this is my friend, Chloe Ravens… Remember I told you all about her?"

Jonty, JoJo, and Heather all stopped what they were doing to wave and say hi to her—but just as they were with him on his first arrival—they dismissed her just as quickly to get back to work. Jonty had to re-cut all of the patterns so the factory had fresh templates to produce the orders from, while JoJo and Heather were desperately calling fabric suppliers to secure extra rolls to be able to make everything they had orders for. Chloe was like a filing to a magnet, already looking through the rails of clothes still set up in their makeshift showroom, pulling out pieces that caught her eye for closer inspection.

"What did you think of the show?" Pandora said, joining her at one of the rails.

"I loved it! It was exciting and new, a bit punk, a bit raw… Fashion's missing that right now, so I'm not surprised buyers snapped it up."

"Well, I wouldn't say they snapped it *all* up… Most just wanted this one dress," Pandy said, taking it off the rail to hold it up in front of her.

The short bustier dress had been the key look of the entire show, thanks to Dom's brainwave to run it up last minute in every fabric swatch. It had been so popular that they had now named it after its three-digit code: the zero–one–five dress.

"This, I love!" Chloe said, taking the dress to hold it up in front of her in the mirror.

"You should try it on," Pandy said, excitedly. "In fact, we could send it to you to wear back in New York... Help us get exposure over there too!"

"Really?" Chloe said, flabbergasted. "I haven't had so many free clothes thrown at me like this!"

"I saw the pictures of you at the Palazzo show—that dress you wore was amazing!" Pandy said while Dom watched them gush over fashion. He was rather pleased that they were getting on well rather than there be any rivalry between them—that would not be a good threesome to be a part of.

"So, what's going on with you and Gianni then?" Pandy said.

Dom rolled his eyes, knowing that this was the last question Chloe wanted to hear right now, but she had to expect it at the same time. In a way, she had become used to it. It was all anyone wanted to talk to her about, and she understood why it was such a hot topic, she just didn't know for herself exactly what *was* going on. "It's cool," Chloe said, waving off Dom's expression. "To be honest, nothing... I mean, we both like each other, but it is was it is—nothing more."

"Darling, it doesn't look or sound like nothing to me," Pandy said, adjusting garments on the rail so they were spaced equally.

"We're just friends... For now at least," Chloe said, hoping this would satisfy Pandy's thirst for knowledge.

"Well, maybe he can help us produce all the orders for the zero–one–five dress... Seriously, Dom, if we can't get enough of the fabrics in time we're gonna have to let people down and that would be a PR disaster! Could you imagine? People would be saying we are bankrupt after one successful collection!"

"Calm down... I have a plan—as always!"

"What's the problem exactly?" Chloe chipped in, not quite understanding why it was such a problem having a successful dress on their hands.

"Well, we're trying to run this business off some kind of profit and not Pandora's father's bank account," Dom said, again with sass. "Which means we need cash... But I have a plan! I say we offer a ten percent discount to stores that can pay for their orders upfront, rather than on delivery—that way we will have some money to put into production."

"Ah, I see," Chloe said, catching up. "What you really need is an investor!"

"Maybe…" Dom shrugged. "Just *not* her dad!"

"Hmmm, but that would mean I would have to give up shares—and creative licence no doubt," Pandy said, which was partly why she relied on her dad in the first place.

"Sure, but it would also mean you wouldn't have to worry about cash—or discount your collections before they hit the stores… And if you went with someone that was in alignment with your brand, then you would be both on the same page—the real question is who!" Chloe said, stepping into the bustier dressed, having got undressed in front of them.

"Could have been Gianni, if you weren't ignoring him," he whispered in her ear, as he zipped up the back. Chloe gave him a look in the reflection of the mirror that said: 'Very funny indeed!'

"That's all good, but we don't have time to find someone and fulfil these orders—they need to go to production, like yesterday," Pandy said, now seeing at how well the dress fit Chloe.

She grabbed her pincushion and prompted Chloe to get up on tip-toes—as if she were wearing heels—so she could adjust the hemline. Staring back at her reflection in the mirror, Chloe liked what she saw, this was the dress she wanted to see Gianni again in. It was powerful, sexy, and gave her an oomph of confidence. Wearing free Palazzo clothes also felt good, but it also felt like she was being kept like some sort of pet. This dress, however, gave her personality, her own voice. She immediately envisioned how she could style it, with black heels and her curly long blonde hair worn down. And once again, she had another brainwave. "Have you got any U.S retailers yet?"

"Why else do you think I'm gifting this dress to you?" Pandy said through gritted teeth, holding pins in between. She knew Chloe was the latest fashion influencer on the scene in New York and by wearing her dress, she hoped it would get some attention Stateside.

"And you don't have a website either?" Chloe said.

"Hun, I'm not sure if you noticed but we are struggling to design and produce the collections as it is… We're a very small team and now you want us to run an e-commerce business on the side?" Dom said, with flouncing arms.

"I really do need to get back to New York," Chloe said, smirking at him.

"Why? What are you thinking?" Dom said suspiciously.

"I'm thinking I need to sort out this contract with Veronica once and for all and get paid! She's giving me a small advance on the pre-sale of the capsule… And I'd like to invest it in P.S.L. Of course, you'll pay me back once you get your payment's from your vendors, but at least you won't lose money by discounting stock upfront, right?"

Pandy and Dom looked at each other in shock. 'Just how much *is* she getting paid?' Dom had wondered. But he liked the idea of it. Chloe was someone they could trust, someone who wouldn't want a ridiculous return for her investment—she was someone who understood the industry and simply wanted to help her friends succeed. Plus, Pandora's shares would be safe and so would Chloe's money—it was a no-brainer!

"Are you sure?" Dom said, making sure she understood what she was offering them.

"Of course I am… I mean, I'm no millionaire, but I can give you $10,000 towards your production."

"We'll have to set out proper repayment terms, of course," Pandy said standing up, having completed her adjustments.

Although they really needed an investment of hundreds of thousands to secure the future of the brand, $10,000 would at least see them through producing the orders they had here and now.

"Just one thing," Chloe said, admiring herself in the mirror. "While I'm not asking for a return on my money, what I do want in return is the U.S exclusive rights to sell P.S.L online—just for *one* year!"

"*What!* Are you gonna be selling clothes on StacksOfStyle now or something?" Dom teased.

Chloe spun around, still on her tip-toes and pinched Dom on the chin. "You know something? You just read my mind!" she said with a cunning smile.

"In that case, we better get you back to New York," Dom winked.

<h1 style="text-align:center">15</h1>

Having travelled to three major cities in less than a week, Chloe was beyond shattered on touch down at JFK airport. Her luggage had somewhat accumulated, now having grown to a case full of Palazzo clothes and two garments bags—one with her custom Palazzo and the other with the altered P.S.L dress—plus that laptop laden handbag which had been a burden.

As she waited for her case to come around on the carousel, Chloe messaged Carmen to let her know she had finally landed. And as promised, when she first set off for Milan, Carmen was waiting for her to arrive. Plus she was eager to find out what had happened since she went MIA. It was about time Chloe came back home, Carmen also had news to share—urgent news.

"Chloe!" Carmen shouted, waving her hands as she spotted Chloe emerge from arrivals.

Yet again, Chloe was relieved to see a familiar face waiting for her—and to be finally home.

"It's so good to see you," Carmen said, kissing her head. "How are you?"

"Tired, like *fucking* tired—but let's just get home," Chloe said, letting Carmen take her case for her.

"Of course, let's get a taxi… I'm dying to hear everything!"

"Likewise… Have you heard from Veronica?" Chloe said as they walked out to the taxi rank, a line of waiting travellers all wanting yellow cabs to take them back into the city.

Carmen took a deep breath, but there was no dressing up the situation—she had to just come clean with the news. "She's pissed… Like, really pissed! I explained your reservations around ownership of the brand name and she understands, but she thinks you're overreacting—she wants a meeting, ASAP! I told her we would be in touch the moment you get back."

"Well, we knew she wasn't going to be thrilled… But none of that matters now Carmen. I have a new idea, a new proposal for her that will require her to take my name in some ways."

"What do you mean?" Carmen said, amazed that Chloe had returned from her trip with a change of heart.

"While I was in London, I secured the rights to stock P.S.L exclusively in the U.S!" Chloe said, perking up from her tired state to reveal her latest idea.

Carmen didn't understand, looking at her blank—shaking her head slowly to encourage her for a more detailed explanation.

"Don't you see it? Instead of just owning the 'Raven' label, I want her to invest in S.O.S!"

"Wait a minute… You had an issue with her owing your name as a label, and now you want her to own your website?" Carmen couldn't believe she was willing to give up even more control considering she had felt so strongly about the original stipulations, but the subject certainly passed the time, edging closer in line for a cab.

"Well, not completely… I haven't gone totally insane! Remember our last meeting? Veronica's team suggested turning S.O.S into a shop-able site for the capsule… But what if StacksOfStyle *was* an online store, even past this collection? Think about it, we could be the online destination—not just for a quick article or pretty picture—but for shopping too! And who knows more about online shopping more than Veronica?"

Carmen was impressed, she could now see where Chloe was coming from, but it was a bigger dream than simply having a capsule collection with DivaFeet. This was a business proposition, something that required proper planning and neither of them had experience in that. But Chloe was right if anyone could help pull this off it was Veronica, with her well-oiled retail team, dispatch centres, and years of experience in the e-commerce market.

"We'll start off small, launch with the 'Raven' line and then introduce smaller international designers, like P.S.L—and keep adding more once we have made those a success," Chloe continued, now filling back up with energy as she set out her vision.

"I better call Veronica then," Carmen said, reaching for her phone, unable to argue with Chloe's plans.

"No, I'll call her when we get back to the apartment... She'll want to speak to me anyway," Chloe said, grabbing her arm to stop her. "I'll explain everything... It's time I took responsibility for this—you've done more than enough already."

This wasn't the return Carmen had expected. She had imagined she would be consoling a broken heart, left in tatters by Graziana. All of a sudden, she was in the presence of a fashion mogul in the making, which was quite a relief as she had started to feel rather guilty about filling her head with notions of romance—but she still wanted the gossip. "So, changing the subject... Can I ask how Milan and Paris were yet?"

"Let's get in the car first," Chloe said, now at the front of the line. "I'll fill you in on the way home..."

*

"So, just to recap—Graziana asked you to leave and you did?" Carmen said, hauling the case out the back of the taxi.

"*Yes!*" Chloe shouted, walking up to the apartment entrance— she had gone over it twice already. "Listen, you would have done the same... That woman is something else!"

"Well, we knew that," Carmen puffed out, wheeling her case through the entrance towards the elevator.

"Dom said the same thing... I just didn't expect her to be so controlling."

"Well, I suppose it's in her interest as well... She doesn't want him distracted from work I guess?" Carmen said, pressing the button to close the doors, hitting the button for the third floor. "But you have to speak to him!"

"One thing at a time... Veronica first, then Gianni," Chloe said as the elevator doors opened. "Besides, he's been calling from a held number—I'll email Joli an apology or something."

"Well, just keep your options open, that's all I'm saying." Carmen fumbled for the keys in her purse and opened the front door—hitting against two boxes of clothes that were lined up in the hallway behind it. "Oh, these are your things that The Four Seasons sent… I'm dying to see what you have in this case," Carmen said, knowing it was full of Palazzo goodies.

"Knock yourself out… I'm gonna take a shower," Chloe said, leaving her handbag in the hall, walking through to the bathroom—stripping off as she did.

Carmen took the case into the living room and lifted it up onto the sofa to unzip it like an excited kid. Dom's mother had washed and neatly folded almost every piece of clothing that Gianni had gifted her—except for the dry clean garments which Chloe had left out. Carmen held up piece after piece before checking out the custom gown in the Palazzo garment bag—holding it up against herself to see if it would fit her too. "I can't believe you got a whole new wardrobe from Palazzo!" she shouted, so her voice carried through to the bathroom and over the buzz of the shower.

Chloe didn't answer, she was too immersed under the hot water, replenishing herself after seven hours on a plane—economy too. Carmen placed the dress back down and picked up the other, non-branded garment bag to check what was inside it. Unzipping the bag, a flash of neon green surprised her. She pulled out the dress, unhooking the hanger from the hole at the top and releasing the dress as she fully slipped the cover off.

'Wow,' she thought, her mouth parting slightly at the look of the dress. Its black lace bra underneath peeping out of the ruched bustier—it was like a dress from the early nineties that one of the supermodels would have worn down a Versace catwalk. But it was edgier, less glam and more rebellious—something Amy Winehouse would have worn. "Now I see why you wanted the rights to Pandora Simmons!" she called out even louder.

"Right?" Chloe said, walking into the living room with her hair wrapped up in a towel as she cleaned her ears with a Q-tip.

"You really cleaned up on this trip… The Palazzo dress is amazing!"

"Yeah, but it's not like I can wear it ever again… Everyone knows it's the dress I wore to the show," Chloe said, perched on the end of the sofa holding onto her towel, thinking what a shame it was she never did manage to get the Maison Marais dress in the end. Or the bag!

"Well, that won't stop me!" Carmen said, pleased to hear Chloe was over it already.

"Knock yourself out… I'm gonna get changed—be right back." Chloe slipped on a pair of jersey shorts and a vest top and dried her damp hair before scrunching mousse into it to set her curls. It felt good to be home with all her comforts close, but staring into the mirror, something felt missing. Of course, the plane ticket to Milan was no longer wedged into the frame. She couldn't believe it was all over already, and she couldn't believe how it had panned out. Milan, Paris, London—Graziana!

It all felt like a crazy dream, but she had returned with another in its place. A dream to create a new business, a dream to take StacksOfStyle to new heights—one that would make money and not rely on her being some influencer relying on partnerships and one-off payments. And just like when she had split from Brian, now was the time to lose herself in work—hard work. It wasn't the time to get upset, thinking about what could have been if she stayed in Paris. Now was the time for action, the time to prove to everyone (Graziana and Regina included) that she was more than just a shop-girl who got lucky. She had brains, she was creative, she was going to make a difference and take herself up to their level—make them see that their efforts hadn't dragged her down.

"Okay… I suppose I better call Veronica," Chloe said, walking into the kitchen to make coffee. "Are you hungry?"

"You bet I am… I'll head out and get us some high-protein sushi or something," Carmen said, still rummaging through her suitcase.

"Okay, well you get yourself that and you can grab me pancakes, eggs, and bacon from the diner on the corner of the street," Chloe said, with an attitude that could have only have been passed on from hanging around Dom.

"You got it… Looks like I'll be wearing *all* of these clothes for you!" Carmen said, grabbing her bag and jacket.

Taking a sip of her coffee, Chloe went to get her laptop out of her handbag and stick it on charge—setting it up on the breakfast bar. She had so much to catch up on, emails, articles to finish and upload, and more importantly she had to review the order for the P.S.L collection she had selected in the showroom—that was something else she was yet to tell Carmen.

After briefly discussing her plans with Pandora and Dom, she selected some pieces to order—just in case Veronica backed her idea. That way, she was certain to have stock coming in to execute her plans for S.O.S right away. But before all of that exciting stuff could get the 'go-ahead,' Chloe needed to make that dreaded phone call to Veronica.

Picking up her phone, she went to dial the DivaFeet office, but the red notifications leftover from the dozens of voicemails were still waiting for her to clear them. It was time she confronted what she had been putting off... Then she would deal with Veronica.

**

The front door slammed, prompting Chloe to hang up from listening to her voicemails, pleased that her soul food had finally arrived.

"Did you get syrup as well?" she said, snatching the brown bag from Carmen.

"Down boy! Yes, I got you your pancakes, eggs, extra bacon, and a side cup of syrup," Carmen said, only just through the door.

Chloe didn't bother plating it up, instead, she ate it out of the cardboard tray and even used the plastic cutlery it came with.

"So... Did you call her?" Carmen said, getting a plate out of the cupboard for her tuna salad and tray of sashimi.

There was a moment of silence as Chloe chomped down two mouthfuls of golden pancakes drenched in sweet syrup, picking up a deep-fried rasher of bacon to eat it like a potato chip. "Yeah, I called her... She wants to see us tomorrow morning, can you make it?"

"Of course... Was she mad?"

"Mad as hell! But I explained that there had been some crossed wires—I threw you under the bus a little… Hope you don't mind," Chloe said with a wink as she carried on eating.

Carmen sat next to her at the breakfast bar, opting for proper cutlery and chopsticks for her sushi. "What did you say?"

"Well, I told her that it wasn't the issue with owning the brand name as such… Just that I had a rethink about what was on the table and I needed some time to think about what I wanted to propose to her while I was away… I explained that I had a better proposition for her and that if she wasn't on board, then I'll happily sign the existing contract—but best to let me explain it all in person… And I was right too, she pressed ahead with the samples production—I knew she would."

"I just hope she shares your vision for S.O.S," Carmen said, hoping this wasn't going to backfire and completely turn Veronica off—but at least Veronica had ordered the sample production. That meant she was still serious about going ahead with the collection at least.

"I listened to my voicemails too," Chloe said, wiping her mouth with a napkin.

"Really? What did they say?"

"One of them went like this: Chloe, where the *fuck* are you? You're worrying me, do you need me to come and meet you—I can catch a flight to Paris."

"Yeah… That was me," Carmen said, with her head cocked to one side. "You know what messages I mean!"

"All the rest were from Gianni, of course—same thing. I'm worried about you, where are you, I thought we were having fun together, blah, blah, blah," Chloe said, wafting her plastic workaround nonchalantly.

"What are you going to do?"

"Like I said… I'll email Joli—let her know I'm back home safe—thank her for the wonderful trip… Ask her to pass on my thanks to Gianni—since I don't have his number… A diplomatic response some would call it." Carmen left it there, she knew as much as Chloe did that this wasn't going to be the last she heard from him. If anything, she was making him want her even more by being so elusive. He was used to women doing crazy things for him, stalking him when he cooled things off, pestering his office for him to call them.

If she knew Gianni in the slightest—from the little she had to go by—then it sounded like Chloe was setting herself up for an even bigger date. But maybe that was her plan, maybe she wanted to drive him wild, so wild that not even his own sister could put him off? Either way, Carmen was happy to have her back in one piece and not an emotional wreck—she had come a long way. "So, what're your plans for the rest of the day?"

"Oh, you know… Chill out, watch some crap TV and sleep! I have some unfinished articles and pictures I'd like to upload at some point too," Chloe said, eating the last bite of pancake left in her tray.

"That's another thing… I thought I told you to take lots of pictures?"

'Here we go,' Chloe said to herself, she knew she was going to get a telling off about this. "You try taking editorial worthy pictures when you're in the moment! I was too busy wearing Palazzo couture in the front row with Lou Banks, and then flying to Paris and getting cut down by Graziana… Oh, and sleeping with Gianni at some point in between it all—did I forget to tell you that?" Chloe listed, as she cleared the sofa of clothes so she could stretch out on it.

Carmen was fully aware of her hectic itinerary—sex included—having got the low down in the back of the taxi, which had been an earful for their driver to listen to. "Fine… Point taken! Anyway, there's some fab pictures of you online," Carmen said, unplugging Chloe's laptop from its charger, bringing it over to the sofa.

Chloe shifted her legs so she could join her, sitting up to see what Carmen had found online. Google alone came up with many images of her at the Palazzo show—even Vangaurd had uploaded pictures of her in their coverage of the show. Chloe took the laptop from Carmen to look closer, eager to see what else there was from her Fashion Week escapades. And she didn't have to look far, the very first headline caught her attention: 'Gianni Palazzo Gives His Date An Eiffel.' She clicked on it right away and was shocked at the news link that popped up in front of her. Instead of seeing the paparazzi pictures outside Hotel Costes, or leaving The Four Seasons in her sparkly dress, Carly Wattmore appeared hand in hand with Gianni on a night out.

"What the actual *fuck*!" Chloe shouted. "He took Carly on a dinner date to the Eiffel Tower?"

Carmen took the laptop back from her to read the article. It hinted that he was now dating the latest model to hit the scene. "I mean, this is just gossip… You know this sort of news follows him wherever he goes; you've received similar headlines don't forget… Besides, I thought you weren't that bothered by him anymore?" Carmen said, giving her a nudge with her elbow.

"This is all Graziana! She set this up, she invited Carly to model at Maison Marais and wanted me to leave so this story could break… I suppose Carly is more on his 'level' compared to me, but she's also like—a child!"

Carmen slammed the laptop shut. "Listen, none of this matters… Your plans for StacksOfStyle is what matters now and you should relax—you need to be on top form tomorrow," Carmen said, getting up to get her things together.

"Take all this shit with you too while you're at it," Chloe said, flipping her hand towards the bundle of Palazzo clothes on the floor.

"Whatever, you'll feel differently in the morning… Get some rest," Carmen said, putting on her jacket, noticing a letter on the kitchen side. "Oh, this came for you by the way." Carmen threw it over to Chloe like a frisbee, careful not to throw it too hard to paper cut her in the face.

Chloe caught it clumsily with both hands and ripped open the white envelope. It felt sturdy and rigid like there was a card inside.

"Anything important?"

"It's an invite to Melinda's leaving party," Chloe said.

Melinda Rogers was finally leaving Palazzo after thirty-plus years of service in personal shopping. She had helped Chloe and Dom get out of Palazzo, helped them to see how to use their time wisely and network for their own good—not just make the company money.

"It's tomorrow night… Uh! You know who's gonna be there!" Chloe said, flipping her head back on the sofa.

"Regina?" Carmen said, now with her jacket on and handbag on arm, ready to leave.

"Exactly! And she'll just love rubbing my nose in the fact that she told Graziana everything! Ruined me, just like she said she would… Will you come with me?"

Carmen rolled her eyes, this was the Chloe she knew too well. The version that would flip out at any little thing and get herself in a twist (which was rather hilarious to watch at times). It was the complete opposite to the creative business mind that she was displaying just an hour ago—it was amazing how someone like Regina could rile up her so much.

"You want my advice?" Carmen said, walking to the hall and turning back with a flick of her long brown hair. "Wear one of those fabulous dresses, turn up and turn it out! Revenge is best served dressed up!"

Chloe smiled, she was right. Seeing Regina this time would be different compared to the last when she had threatened her as a downtrodden jobless nobody. Now she was making it happen for herself, and she was going to make sure she embodied that persona. Plus, she simply had to be there for Melinda after all she had done for her, and it would be empowering to see all her ex-colleagues who would swarm around her like a superstar, especially after everything that had been written about her and Gianni in the press.

"Now rest! I'll see you tomorrow at Veronica's office," Carmen said, satisfied that her work here was done—for now.

***

"Sorry, I'm late!" Chloe said, walking into DivaFeet's reception with a P.S.L garment bag in hand. "I overslept—jet lag."

"Can you please let Veronica know we're here now?" Carmen said to Bethany, behind the front desk. She wasn't surprised by her late arrival, she just hoped she had her shit together and had rehearsed her proposal. This could go either way and this time Carmen wouldn't be able to dig her out of a hole, should she bury herself one—this was unknown territory.

"You can go up to the boardroom now—I'll take you up," Bethany said, leaving her station with her stack of bangles jangling as she walked around the desk to call an elevator.

"Are you ready for this?" Carmen muttered as she stood up.

"We're about to find out," Chloe said, with feigned confidence. If she faked it, then she could make it—or so she told herself.

"She'll be through in a moment, she's just ending a call," Bethany said, holding the glass door open for them to enter the boardroom, complete with white leather chairs and jugs of water already set out on the large glass table.

Chloe hung up the garment bag on the back of her chair and sat down, tugging on her blazer to straighten it out, as she shifted nervously in her seat. 'Hold it together girl,' Carmen thought, just as nervous for her.

"Good morning Ladies," Veronica said, marching into the boardroom. "Good to see you're back in town, Chloe."

Veronica gave her a sarcastic look, but she was also impressed with Chloe's escapades in Europe (she had kept herself up to date on her latest signing's online headlines). She was soon followed in by her team, Sam, Lily, Bill, and Morgana. After they had all exchanged greetings, Veronica wasted no time to start the agenda. She had already been waiting for the signed contracts to come back and was keen to learn more about what the deal was after her phone call with Chloe. "So, I understand you have an idea you want to lay on the table—which is why you haven't signed the contract?"

Chloe took a gulp of water, she could feel her mouth drying out already and she hadn't said a word yet. She cleared her throat.

"As you all know, I've been travelling, attending Fashion Week in Milan and Paris—which is why it's taken us some time to go over and return the contract," Chloe said, trying to dress up her excuse. "And I know we're on a tight deadline to deliver the 'Raven' capsule, but I believe I have an exciting idea that is much more of a unique proposition for DivaFeet—and you may just want to combine that with the current offer."

Veronica sat forward and folded her arms. 'This better be good,' she thought to herself.

"Well, I had this idea… And Morgana, it's your genius that sparked this," Chloe said, looking at her with adoration.

If there was one way to seduce a marketeer, it was by making them believe they were really great at their job.

"You said about making StacksOfStyle transact-able—a 'pop-up' site that feeds back to DivaFeet to capture the sale… But what if StacksOfStyle could do all of that? What if it *was* a fully functioning e-commerce site on its own?"

"Well, first of all, what Morgana had suggested was actually viable, given our deadline," Veronica said, checking her phone, seeming disinterested already.

Carmen gritted her teeth, smiling on the outside to the others to hide her inner anxiety.

"Yes, and I am still on board with that… But while I was in London, I happened to secure the U.S rights to sell Pandora Simmons online—for one year… My good friend is their brand director," Chloe said, throwing her connections in there to make her sound even more credible. "Now, they have had a great reaction to their spring/summer collection and I want to be the first to introduce this exciting brand to America… Just imagine if S.O.S was not only a fashion blog, but one you could read, click, and then buy from! A one-stop-shop for niche designers."

"Like I said, this will take months, even years to develop—it will require a whole new website and back-end stacks to be built," Veronica said, looking up from her second phone, in what seemed to be frustration. Just because she ran a blog, it didn't mean she understood what it took to run an online business.

"And with this team, I believe we can make that happen… You want to own the rights to 'Raven, by Chloe Ravens,' but what I'm suggesting is that you buy a portion of StacksOfStyle instead. Think about it… With a small investment, Carmen and I can slowly grow the site season by season, sourcing fresh new talent in the fashion industry. And we all know what happens once something becomes trendy and cool—the rest of the industry follows!"

Veronica sat up a little, beginning to like where this was going—she flipped her hands to encourage Chloe to divulge more—giving nothing else away other than she wanted to hear more.

"Let's build the 'pop-up' page for the collection as planned, in the meantime, we'll prove to you that we can sell on our own platform."

Carmen shot Chloe a surprised look. How on Earth would they be able to fulfil this promise? All they had, was a basic website (that they couldn't exactly upgrade, as Chloe had dumped its developer), there was no way they could build product pages on their own. Chloe saw the panic on Carmen's face, but she was determined to prove her point.

"I've just come back from Fashion Week with a suitcase full of clothes from Palazzo… So to prove to you that we can do this, we will list the collection online in a chic way that is in style with our brand. Including the custom gown made especially for me—which I'm sure will attract attention on its own… However, I can see that this will seem a little tacky to some… So, all the proceeds will go to a charity of your choice—which we'll clearly state and write about in an article on our homepage."

'Are you *fucking* nuts?' Carmen wanted to say—and bang went the idea of her borrowing any of it.

"And how will you photograph the items, ship them, take payment? Who will take care of all your customer service responsibilities?" Morgana asked, in a way that suggested her idea was flawed from the start.

"Well, Morgana—just like your idea—we will redirect the click-throughs to good old eBay listings… That way we can take payment and ship it all ourselves… I have over thirty items, so it will look like a full Palazzo collection on StacksOfStyle—and *we* will do everything! Photographing the items, list them, ship them—everything to show you that we can sell on our own."

"But isn't all this just going to divert your attention from the 'Raven' collection?" Veronica said, throwing another hardball at her.

"On the contrary, with S.O.S set up for future e-commerce, I'll be even more invested in the capsule... After all, we will be needing a brand to re-stock each season, and what better else than to have our own in-house brand? We can also start by selling some of the high-end brands that you currently sell on DivaFeet—further adding to your revenue stream."

"Hmmm," Veronica sighed, mulling over all this information that Chloe had spewed out in one long breath. "And what has this deal with Pandora Simmons cost you? You have to consider all the overheads if you're going to run your own business, and rights to exclusivity don't come cheap—I should know," she laughed, here she was haggling with Chloe over her rights.

"Well, between us, they're struggling with production costs... This season has been their most pre-ordered yet, with huge orders from boutiques and department stores. They need a small injection to be able to fulfil the production... And I have suggested that I invest my advance from the 'Raven' collection," Chloe said, the latter in a lower tone—taking another sip of water.

"Ten grand?" Carmen blurted out, unable to hide her alarm any longer. "You'll have to go back to work to cover your own living costs!"

"Yes, I have to agree... Big ideas, Chloe, come with bigger risks... And I like your ideas, but can *you* execute them? Are *you* the one to bring this into the world?" Veronica said, looking like she was ready to get up and leave the meeting already.

Chloe needed to pull out all her aces now if she was going to come up trumps, so she got up and whacked the garment bag on the glass table. Taking her time—almost seductively to create anticipation for her audience—she unzipped it. As she pulled down the zipper, they all leant forward to see the flash of green that lay on the inside, like Frankenstein on the table about to come alive. Now she had set the scene, Chloe whipped out the dress, holding it up for them to see it in its full glory. "This is the zero–one–five dress… Do you know how many units they have sold already?" Chloe said, looking around for estimates.

They all shrugged—Veronica included—but her reaction was one of intrigue rather than dismissal.

"Five–hundred! And that's just in this one colour-way, which was featured on the runway at London Fashion Week—modelled by Carly Wattmore—only the hottest and latest face in fashion," Chloe said, looking around for a reaction as she passed the dress around the table. "This is next season's must-have dress and I am the very first person to own one—and I plan to be the very first person to sell them to the many women of America who want the latest fashions from London!"

"Okay," Veronica said, now interested. "And what will I get from all this?"

"Wait!" Carmen said, leaning across the table having had a thought. "What if *you* were to put in the investment into P.S.L instead? That way you would own stakes in both StackOfStyle and Pandora Simmons?"

This was the only way to protect Chloe's earnings from the 'Raven' capsule—saving Chloe from heading back to the shop floor. Knowing Veronica was a sucker for financial gains, Carmen clasped her hands together as she waited for her verdict. Veronica leant back in her chair, which was slightly nicer than the others around the table. Not a word was spoken, by Chloe or her team— the ball was now in Veronica's court.

"Investing in a brand is a big financial commitment, Chloe. One you're not quite ready for… Carmen is right, it would be wiser for someone in my position to invest… But what can *you* offer *me*, Chloe? You have had reservations about my existing proposal over ownership, what's changed?"

This was the part that Chloe hadn't fully thought through— the part where she was now going to get shafted. She sat back down, trying to buy herself some time to think.

"Let me just add, this would be a huge financial burden on my part, and therefore I would be looking for at least seventy percent in Stacks… I can negotiate with P.S.L separately... But if you're the exclusive retailer—and can possibly extend those terms—then that's where the money will be. An investment like this would set me back at least $200,000 to set up in its primary stage—and we haven't even purchased any stock yet."

Veronica had pushed all her chips on the table, now it was up to Chloe to meet her somewhere more on her side, than in the middle. She looked to Carmen, but she had a perplexed expression that said: 'Not my call.'

"What if I was to say this," Chloe said, almost hearing Carmen scream 'what now?' in her head. "What if you were to own sixty–five percent, but five goes to Carmen? That way, collectively, you will have the majority share of S.O.S—and in return, Carmen will act as the president of StacksOfStyle."

Carmen kicked Chloe under the table with a knee jerk reaction at what she was laying on the table—this was too much of a gamble.

"So, let's get this straight… That includes both the 'Raven' line and Stacks? Sixty–five percent—five to Carmen?" Veronica said, amazed that Chloe was willing to give up this much control. "And then the P.S.L shares would be mine to negotiate, but exclusively to sell on Stacks?"

Now Veronica was interested, she was getting three brands for the price of one: Pandora Simmons London, StacksOfStyle, and 'Raven, by Chloe Ravens.' And she was sure that in time—after they had grafted hard and got tired—running such a competitive business in the fashion industry, that she would be able to cash Carmen out and get her hands on that full seventy percent.

Chloe nodded, smiling—she was certain that what she was now offering had bagged Veronica's attention. 'Who's just a shop girl with a blog now, bitch?' Chloe thought to herself, remembering Graziana's venomous words.

"Okay… Prove yourselves with this charity sale, Palazzo idea thing. Show me the money and the sell-through in two weeks—

then I'll make a final decision... As you can imagine, I have my own investors to assure—so I need to see numbers! In the meantime we'll carry on with production of the capsule in readiness for the Holiday launch—when are the samples due, Bill?"

"They should arrive next week," he said, the first thing he had added to the meeting.

"Fine... You should be well into your sale by then and Morgana will go ahead with creating the 'pop-up' page for Stacks with our tech team," Veronica said, getting up from her chair, scooping her phones off the tabletop. "All the best ladies, you have a lot of work to do... We'll see you next week—with results I hope!"

Veronica and her team left the boardroom, this time with no pleasant goodbyes—the tone had clearly shifted into one of rivalry rather than support.

"Have you gone mad?" Carmen whispered.

"Mad, crazy, insane... All of it! But we're onto something here, I just know it!"

"Chloe, what you're offering is too much—we can't sell your Palazzo collection and do all of that stuff you promised just now... And don't even get me started on giving me a percentage of the company!"

Chloe took a deep breath, finally restoring her energy to get up and zip the dress away in the garment bag. "Look, you've helped me on this journey and I want you to stick around for the rest of it," Chloe said, folding the garment bag in half to carry it by the handles. "I want you to get something back; I want you to have a major part in my success, both financially and in your career! Just think what this could lead to—we could run our own company! We could be the one's brands flock to, the people that everyone wants to be associated with, to be seen with at fashion shows... And I know we can do it because we have the experience, we know what people want, and we have *it!*"

"Yes but—"

"No buts! It's our time now... We need to step our pussies up and stop flying around styling people, running about the city, waiting for clients to cough up money... Now we're the bosses and we'll show them what we can do," Chloe said, heading out the boardroom, looking back. "Are you coming along, or what?"

Carmen stood stunned to the spot, weighing up everything Chloe had just said—it did sound rather good. Finally, she would be part of a brand that she would have influence over—and shares to boot. This was an invitation, not just to leave the DivaFeet offices side by side, but to walk through the door with Chloe on an entirely new chapter in their lives.

"Fuck it… I'm in!" Carmen said, picking up her handbag with gusto with a devilish smile—a look that said to Chloe that *this* was going to be a success with both of them on board.

Together they walked through the offices of DivaFeet, looking around like they would one day own the place until they reached the elevator. As soon as the doors shut, Carmen grabbed Chloe by her shoulders and pulled her close. "I can't believe you sometimes! Let's celebrate—let's have dinner and plan how the fuck we are going to pull this off—I still can't believe you are willing to sell your new clothes!"

"For this? I'm willing to sell my own mother! Anyway, we can celebrate at Melinda's party… Are you coming with?" Seeing all the old Palazzo crowd wasn't exactly what she had in mind in terms of celebrating, and they now had a lot of work to do—and as president of StacksOfStyle, she felt like she needed to set an example.

"No… You go. I'm gonna go home and set out a plan of action—don't get too drunk! Tomorrow we need to get this all in motion, we only have two weeks to get this deal signed off remember?" Carmen said as they reached the ground floor of DivaFeet.

"You really are taking this seriously?" Chloe said, pushing the doors open onto the street.

"And so should you be… StacksOfStyle is in your hands now."

16

Melinda's leaving party was quite the deal, she was a Palazzo veteran and just as much an icon at their Fifth Avenue store as the '*P*,' logo was. After all, she had helped rescue the brand and turn it into what it had become today (even revived the monogram from their archive)—but that was another story. In the end, she became the pillar of the personal shopping team; she was such an integral part of Palazzo, it was impossible for her to simply slink out the back door—a leaving party simply must be had.

And it was just as much an important event for Chloe. This would be the first time she saw all of her ex-colleagues, since her explosive departure, which had left them all guessing and gossiping. Wondering not only what had happened that made her leave, but what was she doing now—and is she dating Gianni?

Leaving Carmen after their meeting at DivaFeet, she dashed back home to have lunch and quickly shower once more. The intense meeting had caused her to nervously sweat, and she couldn't wait to feel fresh again. Then there was the small issue that was her apartment—it was a total mess. Boxes were stacked up in her hallway, bundles of clothes lay all over the sofa from her trip, and now she had created a whole lot more work for herself—which meant little time to sort all this chaos out. Just looking at the dumped case, spewing out Palazzo clothes, made her want to get started on her project. She was rather pleased to be getting rid of it all now.

She sat down on the floor and flipped the case open, going through it piece by piece and folding the garments, neatly into piles. T-shirts, blouses, jeans, dresses, and shoes were separated and sorted around her. Then she had the custom runway gown, matching shoes, and jewellery to add to this lot. Just a few weeks ago, she would have been devastated to let go of a complete Palazzo wardrobe gifted to her by the man himself—now she couldn't wait to flog it. In fact, just looking through them made her want everything to do with Gianni and his label out of her life.

But not just yet… She still had to look good for Melinda's leaving party at least. Turning up looking average was not an option; she had to look, feel, and be on top form. She wanted to make them gag—in a good way! Setting up the counter in the bathroom, Chloe laid out all of her brushes, foundation, concealer, and powder compacts to start getting ready. If she was going to look good, then she needed to take her time.

She brushed the liquid base all over her face and neck, before dabbing it with a sponge to seamlessly even it out. Next, she had to tackle the dark rings around her eyes that had formed (thanks to her travels, late nights, and early mornings). She patted light concealer around her eyes, making sure her lid and brow bone was covered for a quick 'lifting' effect. Stepping back from the mirror, she inspected her progress so far before setting it with powder, moving on to eye make-up, then bronzer and blush. Finishing it all off with another light dusting of her brush, her attention turned to what to wear. It had to be something that said she had 'made it,' despite what her old workmates may (or may not) have heard.

Going through several outfits in her mind, nothing seemed to be the perfect look (which was ironic since she had accumulated more clothes than ever). But there was one dress still yet to be worn (thanks to Graziana). Skipping to the bedroom, thrilled to have the perfect solution, Chloe unzipped the Palazzo garment bag, where she had hung the black velvet dress so it wouldn't get creased in transit.

Slipping it over her body, she hobbled over to the mirror to zip it up, turning sideways to model it for herself on tip-toes. The black mini-dress had a halter-style neckline with silver crystal strips that dangled down the back—long past the hemline—while the waist was nipped, hugging her tightly. 'Is it a bit much for a leaving do?' she asked herself. Smiling back at her reflection, the answer, was no.

Walking back into the lounge, snaking her hips like a supermodel (even though she had no audience, not even the builders across the street), she found the matching shoes from her case and slipped her feet inside before teetering back to her room to dig out a black tuxedo blazer to drape over her shoulders. She then loaded the black Palazzo velvet clutch (also unused from her Paris trip) with lipstick, keys, and cards, before locking the apartment door to meet her Uber driver outside.

Sat in the back on her way to the bar where the party was at, nerves started to creep in. Apart from Melinda—who would be swamped for attention—there wasn't anyone she could really hang out with; she feared being lumbered with dull colleagues that she had nothing in common with. She wished she had Dom by her side, he was the only person she had truly made friends with at Palazzo, and he disliked everyone else as much as she did—bar Melinda. Even Carmen had bailed on her, but then again, it was a much more powerful thing to do alone—turning up confident *and* stunning, not giving a fuck.

Getting out of the car, she took a deep breath outside, holding her head up and shoulders back to poise herself before entering. The minute she had walked into the bar and saw the backs of familiar faces, her attitude instantly changed to one of authority. She had left Palazzo as a trouble-maker, but now she was returning as CEO of StacksOfStyle—and this time she really believed it. She really *was* living by the motto: 'Fake it until you make it.'

And compared to this lot, she had *made* it!

"Is that Chloe?" Sarah said to the rest of the womenswear team as they stood around, drinking free Prosecco.

"No, it's not… Is it?" petite Soraya said, craning her neck to see over people taller than her.

"Yeah that's Chloe all right," Tristan confirmed, taking in an eyeful.

Her old team members were both surprised and pleased to see her, having never heard the full story about her leaving (other than Sarah's account, which was undoubtedly an embellished version of true events). This was their opportunity to hear it from the horse's mouth. Not wanting to look around awkwardly, waiting to spot someone she knew, Chloe headed straight to the bar to grab one of the glasses that were poured out and lined up. "Chloe?" Sarah said from behind, placing her hand softly on her shoulder.

Chloe turned around, recognising that squawky voice anywhere, but for the first time, she was actually pleased to see her. "Sarah! So good to see you again!" she said, giving her a kiss on the cheek. "Champagne?"

"Oh, that's not champagne—this *is* a Palazzo party remember?" Sarah laughed, swapping her warm glass (smeared with greasy fingerprints) for a fresh, cool glass.

"How have you been?" Chloe said, clinking her glass before practically necking the entire flute in one go.

"Same old really... But great, now I've seen you! You have no idea what has been happening since you have gone... Everyone's been wondering what's going on between you and Gianni—people are saying you're an item now... Although, I told them that Gianni and Carly are a *thing* now, so..." Sarah said, proud to have the latest scoop on something that she really had no clue about.

'If only you knew,' Chloe thought to herself, doing her best to not smile and hint that she knew differently—she knew more about Gianni's 'particulars' than Sarah could ever possibly imagine.

"Francesca has practically banned your name from being spoken on the shop floor—she says we're all too distracted by gossiping about you," Sarah carried on rather loudly over the music as she looked over in Francesca's direction, who immediately felt eyes lock onto her and looked back.

Francesca was the womenswear department manager at Palazzo, and partly the reason why Chloe got fired from her position. To say they were enemies was putting it politely; Chloe had no interest in saying hello to that bitch whatsoever. Instead, she smirked back to acknowledge her, with no intention of speaking to her for the remainder of the evening. Subtlety was never one of Sarah's good traits, but gossip was, and she had given so much away already.

There was nothing more satisfying than haunting her old colleagues with unanswered questions that had made her a Palazzo legend, which was clearly annoying Francesca. And if it annoyed her ex-manager, then it certainly meant it was annoying Regina too. Chloe scouted the room, listening to Sarah rattle on, looking to see if she could spot her in the crowd, but she couldn't—which was a relief for now.

"Come and say hi to the gang, we have so much to catch up on," Sarah said, pulling at her arm. As she followed Sarah, Chloe realised she had now caught the attention of the entire room—everyone was gawking at her, whispering into each other's ears. Taking off the blazer from around her shoulders, Chloe showed off the fact she had turned up dressed in the latest Palazzo creation worth thousands of dollars, to the very people that sold it every day—secretly enjoying the attention.

"Oh my God, it *is* you," Soraya said, going in for an air kiss

"Yep, it's me!" Chloe said, sipping the last drop in her glass and catching sight of a passing waiter serving top-up's—holding out her glass for an emergency refill.

"You look smoking!" Tristan said, looking her up and down.

'Yep… And I'm still not gonna sleep with you,' Chloe thought to herself. Tristan hadn't changed a bit and Chloe was probably the one girl in that store he hadn't had the pleasure of seducing at a staff party.

"So, what's going on?" Soraya started. "We've all seen you in the press with Gianni at the retrospective fashion show—how the hell did you get an invite to that after you got fired?"

"Well, first of all, guys… I left! Secondly, I dress Gabriela Gracia—which I'm sure you know by now—so we were invited as her guests… That's how I met Gianni and he invited me to Milan Fashion Week," she simply abbreviated.

"We've been searching for you online every day… But what we wanna know is, what are ya doing now?" Sarah said, eager to know how she was able to survive life beyond Palazzo. Because if Chloe could do it, then maybe she could too? Chloe, on the other hand, was surprised they were so enthused with her next move.

Then again, she *was* romantically linked to Palazzo's owner and she recognised that it would have been a massive scandal on the shop floor if it had happened to someone else when she and Dom were working there. "Well, it's all in the pipeline still, but I'm working on my website and at the end of the year you'll be able to buy 'Raven, by Chloe Ravens,' my first line on DivaFeet," Chloe said, watching their faces drop in awe.

"And what about Dom?" Sarah added.

"He's doing well, I visited him in London just a few days ago on my way back from Paris."

"*Paris!*" Soraya shouted, almost spitting out drink all over her dress.

"And London? Wow, maybe I should leave too?" Tristan sarcastically laughed, taking a sip of his drink to hide his jealousy.

"Chloe!" a voice called out from behind her, which made her turn to find another recently departed Palazzo employee.

"Kim!" Chloe sang, relieved at the chance to escape this lot's questions for now.

"Hi guys," Kim beamed, although they didn't seem as impressed to see her as they had with Chloe.

After all, it had only been a week that she had left Palazzo for her new role at Maison Marais, and she hadn't left in a blaze of glory quite like Chloe had.

"Oh my gosh, we have so much to talk about… Let's grab a seat—sorry guys but Chloe and I have business to attend to," she said, equally as unimpressed to see them again so soon.

Chloe looked up to the ceiling to thank the Gods for this welcome distraction, and it was true—they did have a lot to talk about.

"How was Milan?" Kim said, walking away from them. "I saw you were photographed with Gianni at the show… Everyone's been talking about it—seriously! The amount of questions I got from these bitches asking me if I knew what was happening."

"Milan was… Interesting," Chloe said, sitting next to her, perched on the cushioned window seats. "Let's just say it was an experience I will *never* forget! But tell me, how is the new job? Have you started yet?"

"Just this week actually... Dionne is already freaking out about the Palazzo take over."

"Oh really?" Chloe said this wasn't like the Dionne she knew who was always so serene and collected.

"I guess you know by now the news?"

"What news?" Chloe said, taking a sip of her Prosecco.

What else had happened that she had managed to miss during her own escapades? Not being in the Palazzo loop anymore, she had forgotten how quickly things changed there. It only took a day or two for a drama to unfold—like her very own departure, for example.

"You haven't heard? Regina has been appointed as the director of the Palazzo Group... That means she's now overseeing the whole operation—both Palazzo and Maison Marais!"

"Wow!" Chloe said, touching Kim's knee. Although she could have guessed it would happen eventually, it had now been confirmed.

"Dionne is *pissed*, I can tell... To be honest, I've walked in on another shit show," Kim said, taking another huge gulp. Kim had hoped she was leaving Palazzo's politics behind, swapping them for the newly reformed Maison Marais, but the drama was only to follow her.

"*Shit!* I'm so sorry!"

"What for? It's not your fault!" Kim said, shrugging it off.

"I guess we could all see it coming anyway... But now I know for sure it was her!" Chloe said, as if she had solved a mystery.

"What's that?" Kim said, now it was Chloe who had the gossip.

"Well, when I was in Paris—"

"Milan... You mean, Milan," Kim corrected.

"No—Paris... Long story, but I went to Paris with Gianni to visit the Maison Marais studio."

"*Are you kidding?*" Kim gasped, trying to keep her voice down.

"I know!" Chloe giggled, shaking her head. "Anyway, in Paris, Graziana basically told me to leave Gianni and leave Paris altogether... She suddenly knew all about my past working at Palazzo—and I just knew she had spoken to *someone* about me. Now I know that *someone* was Regina—for sure!"

"No way… You really think?"

"Well, who else would it be? Joli is far too busy with Gianni's affairs to act as a private detective, and she's loyal to him—it must have been Regina… I mean, she did warn me that she would ruin me if I didn't stay away—and here we are."

"But why would Graziana care?"

"Well, she is the CEO of the business side of Palazzo… She must have appointed Regina ages ago, all of this was in their expansion plan… And Graziana must have contacted her to find dirt on me… She's another one that hates me, by the way—in case you didn't get that."

"Oh, right," Kim said, amazed that Chloe had been to Paris and Milan with Gianni, as well as rub shoulders (and argue) with Graziana.

"So, what's happening at Maison?" Chloe said, wanting to hear all about the shit show Kim was now faced with.

"Well, the store on Fifth Avenue has been closed down for refurbishment."

"Have you seen the plans? It's a huge difference to what we know," Chloe said, enjoying the fact that she was in the 'know' for once.

"Not yet, Dionne has of course… Why—have you?"

"I haven't seen the store concept, but you can be sure it's going to be modern and streamlined like Palazzo. The offices are all black, white, and silver."

Lost deep in conversation, a sudden round of applause had erupted and distracted them as Melinda finally made her entrance. She was wearing her vintage Palazzo gold skirt suit that she usually reserved for the staff Holiday party. She was amazed to see all of the people she had worked with over the years, and that they had even bothered to turn up in the first place. Chloe and Kim both stood up and joined in with the applause of Melinda's arrival, and standing next to her was Regina, with her side-kick in tow—Myra from the press office. Myra was Kim's boss at Palazzo (after she had beaten Chloe to the promotion of press office assistant) and also the reason why she had left Palazzo. Chloe turned to Kim with a dry smile, here they were presented with the people they least wanted to see right now in the same room.

But as the room started to settle down and people dispersed, Regina scanned the room—only to set eyes on Chloe who had clearly made the effort this evening—wearing current season Palazzo! She cocked her head to acknowledge her, with a smirk that looked down on her somewhat—like she had had the last laugh. "Do you think she will use this moment to announce her new role?" Chloe muttered to Kim through gritted teeth like a ventriloquist, so that Regina couldn't lip read.

"Nah… She'll want her own crowning party."

*

Having successfully dodged Regina for most of the evening (apart from the odd glance at each other), Chloe had managed to get Melinda on her own for a few moments, allowing everyone else to push themselves on her first. "I'm so proud of you!" Melinda said, giving her a motherly hug. "Didn't I tell you there was life outside Palazzo?"

"Yes, you did," Chloe agreed, shrugging her shoulders.

"You look amazing too," Melinda said, grabbing her hand for a twirl which made the silver crystal strands that draped down her back, whip around behind her—attracting more unwanted attention from the room (including Regina's).

"And so do you, but that's nothing new! So, any plans for your new life?" Chloe said, sitting down at a booth nearby to cosy up to her—so they could *really* talk.

"Ah, well a holiday to Mexico first of all… And then I'm thinking to write a book about my years dressing New York's elite—you know—warts an' all kinda thing! But what's the latest you with you?" Melinda said, she too was left on tenterhooks by Chloe's disappearance and sudden rebirth, photographed with Gianni Palazzo in almost every Fashion Week round-up she read.

"Well, Gianni invited me to Milan—as you know by now—and I've just been so busy since leaving Palazzo… I literally just had a meeting this morning with Veronica Meyer—you know my investor? And she's agreed to help me turn StacksOfStyle into a retail site—but it hasn't been signed off yet," Chloe excitedly shared.

"*Really?* Oh my—girl, you are flying! I just knew you could do better than working at Palazzo."

"Please don't say anything to anyone, I haven't even told Dom yet… I wouldn't want anything getting spoiled," Chloe said, looking over at Regina.

"Oh, I totally know what you mean… Or should I say *who*," Melinda agreed, spying who she was looking at.

"So, I heard the wicked witch is now group director," Chloe said, knowing that Melinda would know much more than Kim.

"Oh, you know already?"

"Only because I spent time with Gianni and Jean-Paul in Paris at Maison Marais," Chloe said, making sure she name-dropped and kept Kim out of it.

"I can't with you—*actually*—I can… Why am I so surprised?" Melinda giggled, taking a mouthful of Prosecco. "Yes, it's true… But is it really a surprise? You know what Regina's like."

Everyone who worked under Regina's regime knew what she was like, she was more than determined—she was relentless. And it seemed that Regina's ears were now burning from their conversation—Chloe saw her walking over to join them. 'Oh no,' she said to herself, sinking the contents of her glass before she had even made it over to their table—she needed it if she was going to make polite chat with her.

"Chloe, how *wonderful* to see you," Regina said, as insincere as she possibly could.

Just the sight of her made Chloe's skin crawl and now fully believing it was Regina who had dished the dirt on her, she wanted to punch the battle-axe (not that she actually would). But even a verbal bruising wouldn't get her very far, not with Regina's new powerful title under her belt. And no matter how satisfying it would be to let her know, that she knew it was her that had talked to Graziana, this was Melinda's leaving party. It was not the time for another showdown.

"And great to see you too," Chloe equally feigned.

"Well, I'm not stopping… I just wanted to say bye to Melinda before I shoot off."

"Of course!" Chloe said, getting up from the booth—grateful for an exit from this awkward scenario. After excusing herself, she made her way to the bathroom—reapplying her lipstick at the sink, before looking back at her appearance in the large wall mirror. 'Thank *fuck* I did get dressed up!' she thought to herself, admiring her own reflection as the bathroom door swung back with a crash. For a heartbeat, Chloe held her breath—expecting Regina to barge her way in to say what she really wanted to outside.

"There you are! I've been looking for you," Kim said, to which Chloe let out her pent up breath of air.

"Oh, it's *you*… I just needed a quick escape from Regina," Chloe said, adjusting her dress.

"What did she say? I saw you talking to her,"

"What didn't she say? Her face said it all… She still has a problem with me of course."

"Of course she does, Chloe… You left Palazzo by calling her out on her bullshit, then you went to Milan to hang on her bosses arm—which was flaunted all over the Net, might I add."

Chloe laughed, Kim had a point, but did the director of The Palazzo Group really have time for this pettiness? The truth was, Regina made time for anyone who had crossed her and she wouldn't stop until they were fully squashed and out of her sight. And even though Chloe had walked away from Palazzo, Regina knew that she had walked straight into the arms of her boss—and Gianni's interest in Chloe meant that she was still a threat to her. But Graziana's assistant had provided her with a way to make sure Chloe kept well away for the foreseeable future.

And that was exactly what she *was* going to do, for now at least. She had bigger plans to see through and pursuing Gianni wasn't a part of it. Her mind was fully focused on StacksOfStyle, and Carmen's words of wisdom about not getting too drunk ran through her head—providing the perfect excuse to leave. "I better go... I have a big day tomorrow," she said, putting her lipstick back into her purse.

"But Regina's just saying bye to Melinda... Now we can really have some fun!"

"No, I really gotta go... But call me, we'll do lunch or something once you've settled at Maison Marais," Chloe said, really meaning: 'When you have more news to share.'

Walking back into the party, Chloe headed back to the table where she had left Melinda and her jacket. Expertly dodging people on the way who tried to stop her (she had learnt from Gianni how to walk through a room confidently and not stop for pleasantries).

"Melinda, I'm off... I have a big day tomorrow," Chloe said, giving her a hug.

"Really? Okay, thank you for coming out to see me... Remember what I told you! Always stay one step ahead, but by the sounds of it, you are!" Melinda said, hugging her back.

"Let's do lunch, I wanna be the first to read your book too, by the way!" Chloe smiled, draping her jacket back over her shoulders. Satisfied that she had done what she had come to do, now was the perfect time to leave without saying bye to everyone else—otherwise, she wouldn't get out of there for some time. Out on the street, Chloe stepped to the curb to hail a cab, and as she did she caught a glimpse of Regina stepping into her car on the other side.

Chloe's hand, held up in the air, had equally attracted Regina's eye, making her pause for a beat as she got into the backseat. She gave her a look that Chloe had become immune to by now, but knew too well. Not lingering for too long, Regina ducked her head and slammed the car door shut, allowing her driver to escort her home—a Palazzo driver, of course—she was group director now.

Chloe watched as Regina's car drove off, still with her hand up trying to hail a cab—realising that she wasn't going to stop one here. She wasn't exactly wearing walking shoes, but she had to get out of the area—not wanting to be seen struggling by her colleagues still inside the bar. On the other hand, a few blocks of New York air could be what she needed after seeing Regina again. She started to walk, but her feet started to hurt in her never worn before shoes just after a hundred metres. Passing a pizza place just around the corner, she thought about grabbing a slice—having had no dinner and plenty to drink. But as she was about to enter, she saw the back of a familiar man and backed out to make another brisk escape.

'*Fuck!*' she cursed to herself. 'Why is this evening turning out to be a total blast from the past!'

But it was too late.

The man had already turned around, having paid and stuffed the corner of his folded pizza in his mouth, before pecking the woman behind him on the lips.

"Brian!" Chloe said, realising that she couldn't run from this one—as well as being horrified that he had kissed this woman with his mouth full at the same time.

Chloe discreetly scanned the girl he was with, and although she was pretty, she was no match for her. She was dressed down in one of his sweaters, a pair of jeans and grubby converse. 'Clearly out to grab an after-fuck bite to eat,' Chloe assumed. Once again, she thanked the Heavens for her outfit choice—seeing Brian at her very best was the most she could have wished for right now.

"*Chloe?*" he answered back, startled.

He quickly swallowing the chunk of pizza he had bitten off, not expecting to bump into an ex-girlfriend. But that was the trouble, he had considered Chloe as a girlfriend, but to her, he was just a stepping stone. Someone who could help her design her website and have sex with on the side. A friend with benefits, and extra benefits—but no commitments.

"How have you been?" she awkwardly asked, not really caring.

"Erm, great!" he said, shocked to see her dressed to kill in his favourite pizza slice shop. "This is Laura—Laura, this is Chloe."

"Oh, hi… *That* Chloe?" Laura said, holding on to his arm, with her pizza slice in her other hand—stage whispering the latter.

'*That* Chloe?' Chloe repeated in her head. He had obviously filled her in on what a total bitch she had been to him, used him for his body and computer skills!

"Great… So nice to see you," Chloe lied once more. She had faked so many greetings in one evening, she was expecting her nose to grow past her very own eyes.

"Likewise… See you around?" Brian said, holding the door for his new girlfriend to walk through, cheekily having a second look at Chloe behind her back.

'Not if it's up to me you won't,' Chloe said to herself—waving them off with a patronising flap of her fingers. There was no denying it, Chloe was sexy and like no other girl Brian had had before—but she was also unattainable. Chloe was too ambitious to settle down and Brian knew his limits, he was more suited to a 'Laura' sort of girl.

Someone who *wanted* to be in a relationship, someone who didn't care what she looked like in public, someone who would want to get married and have kids. Chloe, that was not—she had rocked up to a pizza joint wearing Palazzo! And considering what she was wearing, a dirty slice of pizza down the front of it was not the look she was going for.

After waiting for them to have walked a few hundred yards at least, Chloe grabbed the door and left, before the stench of Pizza could cling to her velvet dress. Walking further down the street, Laura's remark stayed with her. She wondered how much Brian had told her, and *what* he had told her—more to the point. But did any of that really matter now? Laura was right about one thing— she was '*that*' Chloe!

She *was* good enough to be in Graziana's league and she *was* good enough for Gianni. But it wasn't enough to simply want to get back in touch with him and apologise for her French exit. She needed to prove herself first, and this evening served as a much-needed reminder. A reminder to her ex-colleagues, to Regina—and now to Brian—that Chloe Ravens *was* still, that bitch!

<h1 style="text-align:center">17</h1>

Suffering from a hangover today was not an option; she was glad to have taken Carmen's advice and had left early. Melinda's party wasn't exactly the occasion to be getting messy anyway… Maybe if Dom was with her?

Then they would have happily stood by and watched, critiqued outfit choices and binned bad make-up—having a giggle together like the pair of untouchables they thought they once were. But then again, Chloe was grateful that they had both moved on since then, not stuck in the rut of Palazzo life. Now she had something to wake up for—something to truly work towards—and seeing all of her old colleagues (and ex-boyfriend) had motivated her to get started on the things that were actually going to propel her life forwards. She quickly gave the apartment a spritz (nothing too major, just a vacuum), ready for Carmen to come over and help with the sales listings.

She had already cleared a space in front of the only area in the apartment that had a blank white wall—ready to photograph against it. The roller-rail from her bedroom had also been cleared (and emptied onto her bed), so she could hang garments and take clean pictures for the product images, and while she waited for Carmen to arrive, she had set up the eBay account for StacksOf-Style. It was the only way she could see possible to make her website 'transact-able,' without the help of Brian, who *would* know the right way to go about it.

That was definitely out of the question!

By adding images and links that clicked through to the listings, Chloe could easily put up the clothes for sale on S.O.S and prove to Veronica that traffic from her website could lead to sales. Checking her phone for messages from Carmen, wondering where she was, she saw an unread email from Veronica—stating that she would like the proceeds of the sale to be donated to the New York Women's Shelter. Right on time, as Chloe put down her phone, the apartment door buzzed.

"Did you bring coffee?" Chloe said, as soon as she opened the door.

"What's the matter with your machine? Of course, I brought coffee... Who do you think I am?"

"An amazing human," Chloe said, grabbing the cup with 'L' for latte scribbled on the side, noticing a medium brown bag in her other hand. "Ooh, what else did you get?"

"Just some pastries for us... I guessed you would need breakfast after last night, but you seem surprisingly sober."

"Oh, it wasn't that kind of affair... Plus, I had the ultimate hangover prevention experience on the way home," Chloe said, perching on a stool in the kitchen to catch up before they got down to work.

"Regina?"

"Oh, she was there... She didn't say much—but then again—she didn't have to... But, I found out from Kim she's just been promoted to group director of both Palazzo and Maison Marais."

"And... Are we surprised?" Carmen said, biting off a piece of croissant, covering her mouth with her hand.

"That's not the point... Don't you see? That means she was definitely the one who told Graziana about me, it just confirms everything—obviously, those two have been in touch about work matters—"

Carmen rolled her eyes. 'This old nugget again?'

"Think about it... Gianni and Graziana have probably been speaking to her about the new role, and she knew I was in Paris with them—thanks to all the press coverage. All it took was one quick-fire email to Graziana to warn her about me... Anyway, that's not all—guess who I bumped into last night!"

Carmen mulled it over for a few moments as she ate her croissant, followed by gulps of coffee. "I give up," she said, not really trying.

"*Brian!* I saw Brian with his new girlfriend!"

"No way! Where did you see him?" Carmen perked up, interested to hear something else other than about Gianni, Regina or Graziana for once.

"Don't judge me, but I stopped by to grab a slice of pizza."

Chloe could see Carmen's face drop, to say: '*Really?*'

"I hadn't eaten a thing and I had a few drinks… Anyway, I saw him in line—so I turned around to leave—but it was too late… And then he introduced me to this 'Laura' chick—who then turns to him and says: 'Oh *that* Chloe?' THAT Chloe! Can you imagine?"

"I would have died!" Carmen said, loving the gossip. "So, what did you do?"

"Well, after a while, I waited for them to leave and make some distance before getting the hell out of there myself."

"Well, you could have asked him to come round and fix all this stuff for us," Carmen said, flicking her wrist at the pile of clothes Chloe had made a start on.

"No chance! We don't need him to help us! Anyway, I have it all planned out and I've already made a start—oh and Veronica says we are to donate to the women's shelter."

"Right, well I suppose we better get to work then," Carmen said, walking over to the sofa. "Where do we start?"

"Well, this is our studio over here," Chloe said, with a flourish of her hand towards the rail in front of the blank wall, like a game show hostess. "We'll photograph everything here and then create the listing for each one… I've made a quick template for descriptions that will make it easy for us to write each piece up and make sure we have all the details. Once that's done, we'll write a quick article for the homepage and post the links to each product—simple!"

It did sound rather simple, but it also sounded like a full day's work. Knowing that there was a lot to do (and a lot at stake), Carmen took off her sneakers and rolled up her sweater sleeves. All morning they snapped, measured, and posted each piece online, complete with a description of the item—right up until lunchtime—working non-stop like a factory chain.

__PALAZZO, WHITE LEATHER BIKER JACKET__

Hardly worn by Chloe Ravens at Milan Fashion Week, this beautiful jacket from the current F/W collection has been crafted from the finest Italian calf leather and completed with gold-brass zips, signature 'P,' button fastenings, and monogram lining.

Italian size: 38
$2,000 + shipping
(All proceeds will go to the New York Women's Shelter)

Considering there was a selection of items to list, it turned out to be more time consuming than they had originally thought. Especially when Carmen suggested that Chloe should model everything herself to add to the images. Getting in and out of each piece—making sure not to get make-up on it—and then approving it, slowed things down majorly. Carmen then searched her laptop for the images she had saved from online articles during Fashion Week—especially the ones of Chloe wearing the custom gown (which was the 'star' item at $3,500).

"My back is killing me," Chloe moaned, being bent over measuring clothes all day and hunched over her laptop filling out the listing pages.

"Same, but we're nearly done," Carmen said, arranging the roller-rail with all the sale items.

"What are you doing now?" Chloe whined, just wanting to slump on the sofa (which she couldn't, because it was covered with clothes, hangers, and garment bags).

"Come… Stand here," Carmen said, showing her what to do, making sure she could get a good angle. "Right, explain what the sale is about, where it can be purchased, and all of that stuff! We'll post it on Instagram and on the S.O.S homepage to go alongside the announcement."

Chloe reluctantly got up off the floor, rubbing her lower back as she fussed with her hair, but she knew it made sense—she had to plug it somehow.

"Come on!" Carmen egged, if she couldn't handle this much work then she sure as hell wouldn't be able to cope running a full-on website. Veronica had set them a test, and Carmen was going to make sure they passed it. Her role as president was on the line as well. Standing in front of the packed-out rail, Chloe gave it her best shot—managing to nail it after a few attempts.

"Hi, guys! I have an exciting new project to announce... I'm selling all of these beautiful Palazzo goodies behind me—which were gifted to me by the brand—and now I'm selling them for a very good cause: The New York Women's Shelter! You can find the listings by heading over to StacksOfStyle.com where they will be available to purchase at a great price until stock lasts! No waiting for auctions to end, just buy it now for the price you see and we will ship it straight to your door... Happy shopping, and thanks for your support!"

"Got it! Great job," Carmen said, stopping the recording on her phone.

"Now all we have to do is write the homepage article and then we can push all this live... But first, I think we deserve pizza and wine!" Chloe said, getting her appetite for pizza back again.

This time Carmen couldn't argue with her, they hadn't eaten lunch and she could definitely do with a drink to loosen up her stiff joints. They swapped the apartment floor and sofa area for the more civilised breakfast bar in the kitchen, sat upon the stools with their cold wine glasses nearby to hammer out the homepage article. "You write the copy while I'll crop some images together and make a photo-block," Carmen said, stretching out her knuckles, effecting a soft 'click.'

They sat there tapping away at their laptops until the pizza eventually came—even then they propped the box open on the kitchen side and ate as they worked. The evening had now crept upon them, time seemed to speed by them, but they had plenty to show for it. After an empty bottle and a few slices left in the pizza box, they finally had the homepage article drafted up and inserted into S.O.S—ready to publish. Together, they made sure the text was perfect and that all of their links clicked through to the correct listing, ready to be snapped up. "Well, I guess we'll just have to wait and see," Carmen said, posting the video of Chloe onto the S.O.S Instagram account—making sure she had tagged both Gianni and Palazzo in the post to grab the attention of their followers. "Who knew eBay selling was such a full-time job?"

"I just have a feeling this is going to work! These pieces go for double the amount in-store and they are practically brand new," Chloe said, finally laid out on her sofa, now that most of the pieces were hung up on the rail.

"Listen, I'm gonna head off—I'm done!" Carmen said, putting her sneakers back on.

"Thanks for helping, I couldn't have done all this without you," Chloe said, getting up to walk her to the door.

"Well, I am the president now," Carmen winked.

"Not yet… We still have to get Veronica to back us first," she winked back.

*

Waking up to ringing from her phone alarm, she squinted at the screen to silence it before putting it back down on the bedside table. Then she remembered… She should really get up and check her emails. Sitting up in bed (still squinting through half-opened eyes as she refreshed her inbox on her phone), she waited for new messages to download and come through. As she waited, she swapped her inbox for Instagram—opening it up to a flash of red notifications—a huge number of 'likes,' comments and private messages had surged her account. Not to mention a whole list of new followers to boost her numbers even more.

A bolt of energy excitedly told her to wake up—shit was happening! She scrolled through some of the comments, trying to make out names of accounts she may recognise, before swiping back to her emails. A flurry of new messages had suddenly pinged through, mostly confirmation emails from orders and payments received overnight from around the world. Wiping her eyes, she flicked through each email, noting what items had sold, amazed to see that someone had even purchased the 'star' item—her custom gown! "Holy shit!" she said, flinging back her duvet. "This really *has* worked!" She got up and skipped into the living room to turn on her laptop, before making herself a strong coffee to help wake up.

While she waited for her laptop to fire up and connect, she opened Instagram on her phone once more to take a better look at the activity her video post had received. But scrolling through the list, one notification stuck out amongst the rest—he eye was immediately drawn to his name—and the 'blue tick' against his name helped. Gianni had reposted her video on his official account, urging his millions of followers to help out a good cause with the sale of his clothes. Chloe was now in a state of shock—not only because Gianni had added and reposted her on Instagram—but because it was all going to plan with little effort.

She stopped what she was doing and called Carmen. "You will never guess what has happened?"

"Have we sold something?" Carmen said on speakerphone, already up and stretching in the gym after yoga class.

"Have we sold something? It's nearly all gone!"

"Are you serious?" Carmen said, putting her leg down from around her neck to take the call properly.

By now, Chloe had logged into eBay and was checking the dashboard to see exactly what and how much they had sold. "You won't believe this... We've made over $9,000! The gown, shoes, earrings, dresses—all of it has sold—only a few tops are left."

"Wow! You did it—you actually did it!" Carmen said, surprised at how quickly it had all shifted.

"No, *we* did it! But that's not all, check Gianni's Instagram... He reposted our video—that's why it's blown up like this!"

"Of course... I tagged him in the post to get his followers attention," Carmen said, this time not so surprised. "You should message him back to say thanks.... Listen, I'm gonna finish up here and I'll head straight over!"

Still in surprise, Chloe hung up and sat staring at her laptop with her morning coffee in hand, mesmerised by how much she had made (for charity, of course). She opened up Instagram again and thought about what Carmen had just said; maybe she should say thanks to him at least. She simply typed 'Thanks' with a red heart emoji and sent it via DM. But as she placed her phone down on the breakfast bar, the reality hit her.

"How the *fuck* am I going to ship all this?"

She hadn't even thought about shipping cartons, wrapping paper, or actually taking it all to the depot to be sent out. With a busy day ahead, she dashed her mug in the sink and got dressed so she could head out to buy much-needed supplies. Small and Medium boxes, plastic mail bags, tissue paper, packing tape and labels were all needed—as well as breakfast! Grabbing all her supplies from her local stores (which had cost her much more than expected), she struggled to bring it all back home on her own. Stopping every now and then to swap hands, with the flat-packed boxes tied up with string cumbersomely carried under her armpit.

Finally reaching her apartment, she was relieved to see Carmen sat outside waiting. "Where have you been? I've been calling you," she said, taking the boxes from under Chloe's arm.

"I know… Not sure if you can see, but I didn't have a spare hand to answer; where does it look like I've been?"

"Let's get this stuff boxed up and shipped out—the last thing we need is people kicking off!" Carmen said, following her inside.

Chloe dumped her shopping in the apartment hallway, while Carmen carried the flat-packed boxes through to the living room, where they would set up their temporary warehouse for the rest of the morning. "Urgh! Who's calling now?" Chloe said, feeling her phone buzz inside her jacket pocket—knowing it couldn't be Carmen this time. However, after seeing who it was, she quickly answered. "Veronica! You will never guess—"

"Congratulations kiddo! I've already seen!"

"You have? How?"

"Have *you* seen the NY Post this morning?"

"What? No, I've been busy getting ready to ship all the orders—did you pick up the NY Post by any chance?" Chloe said to Carmen.

Carmen shook her head.

"Ah! The early days of an online business," Veronica said taking in a deep breath. She knew what hard work awaited them, because she had been there herself—turning DivaFeet into the machine it was. "Well, on page three there's a small article about your charity sale—and how it has been endorsed by Gianni! I don't know how you do it girl… Do you realise how many years people work to even get a sniff at the success you seem to get overnight? Then again, I guess that's what happens when your boyfriend is the most powerful man in fashion!"

Chloe could hear Veronica had changed her tone—sounding upbeat and positive—which was a contrast, compared to their last meeting. But Veronica could smell the aroma of money rolling in, and that was when she was at her happiest. "Listen, your samples are on the way over here this afternoon… Why don't you ladies drop in tomorrow and take a look? Then we can talk about the collection's launch and some more about this investment you want me to take out on you and P.S.L… I have news."

"Okay, sure… Just let me know what time and we'll be there!" Chloe said hanging up, excited to hear that her samples were ready and that she would be able to actually hold her vision in her hands.

"Who was that?" Carmen said, already taping up a box to get started on packing.

"Veronica… Apparently, the NY Post featured our sale in the paper this morning, and the 'Raven' samples are being delivered this afternoon—she wants us to drop by tomorrow."

"*Already?* Wow, she is not messing about!" Carmen said, ripping packing tape off the roll with her teeth.

"And something tells me she is not going to mess us about either!" Chloe said, looking at her disapprovingly, holding up a tape gun. "This is what *this* is for, you savage!"

Packing up the orders had been hard and long work, mainly because Chloe was being precious about how they were packed and wrapped with black tissue—even writing a personal 'thank you' note to slip into each box. But having spent all afternoon, making sure everything was wrapped up perfectly and addressed to the correct buyer, they sat exhausted on the sofa—surrounded by twenty-something packages—all taped up and ready to go. The living room now looked like a postal depot.

"How the hell are we going to get all this shipped out?" Carmen said, not thrilled with the possibility of carting it all down to the postal office. It would take them several trips, and days, to ship them all out.

"No idea," Chloe said, staring back at the wall of boxes, just as perplexed. If StacksOfStyle was going to become a fully fledged e-commerce site, then she hoped Veronica was going to supply budget for the packing staff.

"It can wait until tomorrow… Veronica will know a shipping company," Carmen cleverly thought.

**

Veronica was excited to see the girls again, as excited as they were to see the samples in person—they had arrived early at the DivaFeet offices. Leading them into the meeting room, with her team waiting inside, all of the pieces from the 'Raven, by Chloe Ravens' line had been laid out on the table in front of them. "So, what do you think… First impressions?" Veronica said, leaning on the sideboard cupboards with pride.

Chloe held her hands up to her face, this was unreal—the moment she had been waiting for was finally here! She looked to Carmen, who was equally as impressed that their ideas had become actual designs that they could now hold in their hands—and wear! Chloe picked up one of the high-heels—a strappy sandal in a champagne leather, complete with a gold sole bottom and a raven gold-shaped stud embedded in the arch of the sole. "These look incredible," she said, passing the shoe to Carmen, exchanging it for a black leather knee-high boot.

"Don't they just?" Veronica said rather cockily, propelling herself off the sideboard with her hip. "So, we need to go into production with this collection ASAP if we're going to receive delivery by December… This week, we're sending these samples to the studio to be shot—that way our product team can build the website pages, ready for uploading onsite once the stock does eventually arrive… In the meantime, we have the small issue of contracts to iron out."

Carmen looked to Chloe this time; this was going to be very telling. Either she was going to stick to her original offer, or she had considered Chloe's business plan and wanted in on it.

"I've been doing some thinking and your charity sale has done better than expected—you've even managed to get press out of it! I just wonder how far we can take it?" Veronica said, sitting down at the table. Chloe put down the boot and sat opposite her, as did Carmen—the final decision was about to come.

"You'll be pleased to know, that I can see StacksOfStyle as its own platform… I just think it should be slightly more high-end in terms of brand offering. I still stand by my advice *not* to invest in Pandora Simmons London at this time—and here's why… It would be foolish for you to sink your own cash into an already set-up business—it's not your fault they haven't managed their cash flow," Veronica said, putting her finger to her lips for hush, sensing Chloe had a comeback. "Especially when you're looking for investment yourself… You see what I'm saying here? Why would you give away cash, and ask for more from someone else, when you could simply use that money to fund yourself? Do you know *exactly* how much you would need to turn Stacks into the website you want it to be?"

Chloe shook her head, she had very little idea of what was needed to start up a business, but now she realised that it was more than $10,000—which made her feel stupid for even suggesting she could invest in P.S.L.

"Here's what I suggest we do… And if you don't like it, then the original contract is still on the table… As we discussed last time, I'd like to accept your offer of a stake in StacksOfStyle.com in return for an initial first round of investment worth $250,000."

Chloe blinked rapidly, was she hearing correctly? A grab of her arm from Carmen next to her confirmed it was indeed true.

Catching the moment of excitement, Veronica continued with her stipulations, before they jumped for joy too soon.

"But here's the thing—first we launch with the 'Raven' capsule on DivaFeet and with the 'pop-up' micro-site on Stacks, just as planned… That means we'll need to move your operations here to the DivaFeet offices, where you will have access to our network of teams. We'll focus on this launch first and set the style for the new look S.O.S site at the same time—before I commission our tech team to fully rebuild it with a functioning back-end system. This would have taken up most of your investment back in the day, but the good news is ladies, I have done all the hard work for you already! By replicating DivaFeet's in-house ordering system, all you need to do is work on the branding and design for the site. Then I will send you to market to hunt for the latest designers to stock—which is what you will mainly use this money for… Of course, you can pay yourselves a small sum for living costs, but I don't want you thinking you got rich quick! This money is for setting up the business… Am I clear?"

Chloe stared back at Veronica—she was speechless. Everything had just been handed to her on a plate, just like she had always wanted, but never thought she could achieve.

"Well? How does that sound?"

"It sounds perfect!" Chloe said before Veronica could change her mind, shaking with excitement. She wanted to jump out of her seat and hug her, but she knew this probably wasn't the correct way of doing things—not with her team present anyway. Instead, she stayed sat down to listen to the rest of Veronica's demands.

"Just so we're on the same page, this means I will own sixty percent of both StacksOfStyle and the 'Raven' brand—I will honour the five percent to Carmen… Providing that you *are* willing to step up as president?"

"Of course," Carmen laughed, hardly believing she was about to own more than what she had ever dreamt of—but what she had always hoped for.

"Good… Which leads me back onto Pandora Simmons. Put me in touch with them, let me take control of this from here…

I will ensure you have exclusivity for the U.S market on Stacks. That way, you get everything you want and I get a little something extra… Since I'm losing a ten percent stake in Stacks, I guess I'll just have to gain it elsewhere."

Once again, Chloe was surprised, but nicely so. This meant she could hold on to her cash as well as her promise to Dom—and reap the benefits of having the first major brand stocked on her website. She looked at Carmen once more who nodded back at her, as if to say: 'Go for it!'

"Deal!" Chloe blurted out, without further hesitation.

"Perfect… So this means I will need to redraft the contract entirely and write you in properly," Veronica said, looking at Carmen. "But I don't want any delays in getting it back to me this time, we need to strike while our ideas are hot and we have a lot of work to do… I'll arrange desk space for you to relocate here and I expect you both to put the hours in with my team… If I ever feel that you are not doing enough, I will be sure to tell you, and I won't hesitate to pull the plug if I think you're losing direction… Also, any profits made from the 'Raven' collection is going back into the brand for a second line. Agreed?"

"*Yes!*" Chloe and Carmen agreed in unison, hugging each other with hysterical laughter—unable to control their emotions any longer.

"Excellent, welcome to the team ladies!" Veronica said, firmly putting her hand out to shake on it.

"Oh… One more thing," Carmen sheepishly said, taking the opportunity to establish herself as president, right away. "I don't suppose we can use your warehouse team to ship our charity sale orders?"

***

It had been a long day in the studio, calling all of the buyers that had placed orders in hopes of drumming up some cash upfront to finance production. Jonty, JoJo, and Heather had all packed up and finished for the day, after clearing up the makeshift showroom from an intense week of appointments and returning it back to the studio setting—ready to design the next collection.

"I've managed to source extra fabrics for the dresses," Pandy said, coming off the phone to her supplier. "At this rate, we're gonna have to go to China to produce the next collection!"

Dom didn't look up from his laptop screen, where he had set up an office in the corner of the room for the past two weeks; he carried on tapping away on his keyboard. "Right, so far I have agreed a ten percent discount with six distributors in return for their order to be paid upfront," he said, finally looking up at her.

"Will that be enough?"

"It will do for now," he said, closing the laptop lid, stretching his arms behind his head.

"Have you heard from Chloe?"

"Nothing," Dom sighed, knowing that her big plans were too big to pull out of the hat in the first place (even for her).

Pandora could see how hard he had worked, as well as how tired he looked. She sat down on a chair in front of his desk, perching her chin on the backrest. "Look, I can always just get a 'loan' from my dad? It's not a big issue and I'm sure he will understand... He's always wanted me to do well and with your help, I am!"

"No!" Dom said forcefully, standing up to get his jacket and bag. He hadn't come this far to rest on daddy's bank account, he was going to make this brand float on its own accord, and that was that. He was too stubborn to let this all come easy for him, and he wanted Pandy to learn how to run a business properly—even though he was discovering it all for himself at the same time. This was as much of a life lesson as it was an ego trip. Pandora could see he was getting irate at the suggestion of getting financial help, and the last thing she wanted to do was piss him off.

"Fine... So, what's the plan for next week?" she said, changing the subject.

"Well, the girls and I will make sure all of the orders are calculated and submitted for production... We need as much of the collection ready for the first delivery drop, and the dresses to be ready for early delivery next year—that way our buyers won't drop the rest of the order once we've supplied them with what they really came for," Dom said, slipping on his jacket; not taking off his business hat.

"And what will I do?" Pandy said, starting to feel like a spare part in her own company.

"You, my dear, have the biggest task of all!" Dom said, walking back over to her.

"Oh yeah? What's that then?"

Dom rolled his eyes, she really didn't have a clue about what she needed to next. "Oh, you know... Like, finish designing the next collection, for example.... That's if you've even started?"

Pandy sat up, her face almost turning white with panic. It was true, she did need to make a start designing if she was going to make another collection good enough for the next London Fashion Week—in just under five months! Usually, she would have already made a start, but after having her first successful collection and an actual showroom for buyers, this year it had completely escaped her mind.

"Sit down with Jonty, he's the best person to start brainstorming with and get some ideas down—although I suggest you use the success of the zero–one–five dress to build upon," Dom said with a gentle smile of encouragement. "Then you can present your ideas to the rest of us and we can start working on tweaking and producing the samples... I—of course—will edit the collection and make sure it's even better than this one."

Pandy smiled at him, instantly she was reminded of her role in this operation—she was the designer. Without her vision, none of this would be possible and instead of feeling like Dom was trying to take control, she was reminded that he was here to make her work to the best of her abilities—the business and financial side of the brand, it was not.

Locking up the studio, they both parted ways with a hug and Dom began his walk back down to Liverpool Street station. Walking into Shoreditch, he stopped once more at the crossing where Jason's billboard had once dominated—although this time it was replaced with an underwear advert for Calvin Klein. The past had well and truly evaded him it seemed, and the only way forward from here on was, forwards.

Crossing the road, his phone vibrated in his jacket pocket. He reached into it to take the call, expecting it to be Pandora calling him with her next big idea already—but it was Chloe. 'And in the eleventh hour she arrives,' he thought to himself after he had spent the past two days ripping his hair out, trying to find the money they desperately needed.

"Chloe, what's the latest?" he said, continuing to walk briskly to the train station. "Have you heard from Gianni?" This was, after all, why she was calling him he had assumed.

"Dom... I need you to stop what you're doing and come to New York!" she screamed down the phone.

'Not this again,' he thought at first, but the excitement in her voice was too upbeat for her to be calling him to say she simply missed him again. "What? I can't, we start designing the next collection next week... And the orders—"

"I know, I know—you're busy! I get it, but I told you I would get you your money and I have... And some!"

'What the?' Dom said to himself, stopping outside the station so he could concentrate, sat down on a stone bench carved into the walls of the luxurious offices lining the street. "I don't understand?" he started.

"You don't need to understand... You need to come to New York—you and Pandy! Listen, I know this is going to sound crazy, but I did it! Veronica has invested in our website and now she wants to invest in you! I know I said I would give you guys some cash, but Veronica has an even better offer for you—for both of us! You gotta come back to New York—just for a few days at least!"

It was a good job he was sitting down. His whole body turned to jelly, shaking with total disbelief. 'Is this really happening?' he thought, leaving Chloe hanging on the other end of the line. He had worked tirelessly for the past few days (at times it seemed hopeless, doubting his abilities), and suddenly a golden hand was being held out to him.

It seemed almost impossible, but it *was* happening. And even though there was indeed a lot of work to be done back in the studio, visiting New York to see a potential investor was exactly what they needed right now. This wasn't some silly jaunt to The Big Apple for a long weekend of shopping (although he was sure Pandora would want to squeeze that in too), this was their very first business trip and for once, Dom welcomed the bank of Pandora's father to make it happen.

"Okay, you better roll out the sofa bed—we're coming… And my apartment better be spotless!"

18

Signing the contract was a huge moment in their lives. Chloe never really believed she would actually get this far (although she had always imagined). She had become accustomed to the 'Regina's and Graziana's,' always telling her she was no good—always letting others take centre stage. Now it was her turn, and with Carmen now stepping up from mentor to partner, she felt good about what was yet to come.

Setting up their desks, and overtaking one of the glass-walled meeting rooms up on the mezzanine at DivaFeet's head office, meant that StacksOfStyle had officially become a 'thing.' Eight a.m starts were a regular thing now, as were endless meetings about the launch of the capsule collection.

Both Chloe and Carmen had forgotten what working full days shifts felt like (leaving after nine p.m. most evenings). Although it wasn't like a tedious office job, they were building their future career together. And creating the new, shop-able, StacksOfStyle website had begun behind the scenes. For week's they had designed the layout, stylised the house fonts, and redesigned the logo—which was printed out over several sheets of copier paper and sticky taped to their office wall.

Details, like packaging, had also been decided on: white boxes with 'StacksOfStyle.com' printed on the lid in black lettering, with a simple black ribbon and *plenty* of black tissue paper on the inside. They wanted every customer to experience a 'feel good' factor each time they —like they had purchased a luxurious gift for themselves—even if the item was worth the lowest amount possible.

To get things started, Veronica had tasked them with coming up with another capsule collection, as well as ear-marking potential brands to approach that was already under the DivaFeet umbrella. But before she could sign all these exciting things off, the capsule collection had to be a success first. "When are the samples due to arrive back from Vanguard?" Carmen said, getting off the phone with another publication wanting access.

"Sometime this week… I'll email them again," Chloe said, glued to her email inbox.

"Right, well once they're back, I'll send them out to the next on our list—I can't believe all of these people *actually* want to shoot them!" Carmen said, looking at the list of stylists sent over from the press team.

"Girls," Veronica said with a light rap on the glass window. "You have a visitor!"

Carmen didn't recognise who was standing next to her, causing Chloe to finally look up after a lengthy pause. "Karen! Oh my… I haven't seen you for ages!" She bolted out of her chair and flung her arms around her. Chloe couldn't believe that one of her best clients, Karen Saunders—the person who had helped her make S.O.S a reality—had turned up out of the blue. Chloe owed her everything. Without Karen, she would never have got her blog back up online, not to mention introduce her to Veronica in the first place.

Karen was also the reason why she had to leave Palazzo, after she returned the Gold Rush clutch bag—originally bought on Chloe's staff discount—in return for expert help, building Stack-sOfStyle's website (introducing her to Brian in the process too). But Chloe's pitfalls weren't Karen's fault, she was just providing the catalyst—it was Regina who had been gunning for Chloe's blood, but that was all in the past now. Well, some of it…

"I've been meaning to contact you… Veronica's been keeping me informed and I have to say… I'm very impressed… I hope I'm getting a cut?" Karen said with a wink, elbowing Veronica in jest.

"Oh, I'm sure we can stretch to a few cocktails and dinner," Chloe said, kicking herself at the very suggestion. These long days and early morning starts were getting to her, and going out for drinks was the last thing she wanted to do with her evenings (although a drink is what they probably both needed).

"I'm so happy for you… I can't help but feel responsible for what happened to you at Palazzo with returning the bag and—"

"Don't mention it!" Chloe stepped in.

"I can't wait to be your first customer… Veronica showed me the product shots, it looks amazing! Didn't I tell you this woman was a fashion genius?"

"You did—and she certainly is!" Chloe said, making sure she puffed up her new investor's ego, in case she hadn't enough already. "Oh, this is Carmen, my partner—*NOT* like that—business partner! She's the president of StacksOfStyle and she's helped me immensely with the collection… I can't take all of the credit."

"Nice to meet you, Carmen… Well, I can see you ladies are very busy, but give me a call for those drinks—you got my number."

"Yes, you guys have a meeting with Morgana and marketing in five—don't forget!" Veronica said, leaving with Karen to go for lunch.

Although it was strange seeing Karen again, she *was* happy to see her. It reminded her how far she had come and how quickly her life was changing, all down to taking a few risks and some silly decisions that all had a weird way of working out in the end.

"Come on, Morgana will be waiting… You know how she always starts without us," Carmen said, grabbing her notebook and pen, while Chloe undocked her laptop from her desk monitor to studiously bring along.

"True… She also likes to book meeting rooms at the other end of the office!"

Morgana had indeed made a start without them. On the presentation screen, was the layout for the overlay that had already been built and was ready to be plugged into the existing S.O.S website.

"So, on the screen is the homepage for the 'Raven' capsule, which will be pushed live on launch day," Morgana said as they finally made it, trying their best not to rattle the metal legs of the chairs together as they pulled them out and sat down—as if they had always been there—but they had failed miserably. "I was just saying, the tech team have now completed the overlay for the 'Raven' capsule, which I'm about to present to you all," Morgana said, thumbing her clicker to the next page, now that the two most important stakeholders had arrived.

Chloe was rather excited to see how it was all going to look, sat upright and attentive. It was times like this that she wore spectacles so she could rest them on the end of her nose. The screen quick-flashed onto a tiled page, featuring every item from the capsule.

"So, when you click through to the 'Raven' collection on StacksOfStyle, you will be greeted by the collection overview—which you can then click on to navigate to their individual product page... What do you think so far?"

"I love it—it's exactly how we discussed!" Chloe said, happy with how it would appear onsite so far. Finally, this was all about to happen. Weeks of meetings and endless talk about how it was going to look had now come into fruition; she was now actually able to see it with her own eyes. It suddenly dawned on her that soon enough, launch day would come and the expectation of selling-out was growing inside of her. What if no one wanted her designs? Although, the endless requests for samples from editors told her otherwise—it was just nervous excitement.

"It's fantastic!" Carmen echoed. "Better than we could have imagined!"

"I think so too... When you click on the individual products, you will be taken directly to DivaFeet's website—where the customer will be able to click 'purchase' and checkout." Morgana clicked again, bringing up the product page for the leather knee-high boots. All the images, description and 'buy now' buttons appeared, which made Chloe clap with delight. "Of course, we still have some work to do... Chloe, we were thinking it would be great if you could feature in a press shoot, modelling the collection for editorial features on both Stacks and DivaFeet."

"*Me?*" Chloe gasped.

"Well, yes... It *is* your collection?" Morgana said, surprised that she would even question it.

"Err, sure… Okay, I'm up for it," she said, looking around the table to see if she had missed a joke. It wasn't that she didn't want to appear in her own campaign, she just assumed they would hire a professional model for that stuff—who would want to see *her*?

"We just think that with your status and newfound notoriety in the fashion industry, that you should really be the face of the brand—as well as the ambassador." Chloe knew exactly what Morgana meant by 'notoriety' but was unsure whether that would be enough to capture the attention of fashion-savvy buyers. It had been weeks since she had last heard from Gianni, and that connection to fame was now starting to fizzle, it seemed. "Can I leave you guys to call in samples for the campaign shoot? Veronica said you can borrow clothes from DivaFeet's stock to help push sales cross-site," Morgana said, looking at not one—but two—super-star stylists that were in the room. Surely this was a walk in the park for them?

"Great!" Carmen said, putting her hand up. "I can do that… That's what I do!"

"Perfect, so we just need to arrange some time for the shoot and brainstorm the creative direction."

"Why don't we just shoot it out on the streets? I mean, let's make it look real… At the end of the day, I want to walk down the street and see *real* women wearing the collection."

"Okay… But we were thinking more of a studio shot campaign," Morgana said, clearly not understanding where Chloe was coming from. But then again, Chloe didn't expect her to—she wore the same thing to work every day. "Put together a moodboard and we'll take a look in the next meeting."

"Will do, Morgana—leave the fashion to us and we'll leave the details down to you," Chloe said, getting up from her seat.

"You know what would be good?" Carmen said, gathering her notebook, which was *so* not needed in the end. "We could shoot around iconic parts of the city: the steps at Times Square, on the bonnet of a cab, down Fifth Avenue."

"You know where else we could shoot?" Chloe said with a cheeky grin. "At a peep show, downtown."

"*YES!* Do you think Veronica would let us?" Carmen said, wide-eyed.

"*NO!* I was being sarcastic… But maybe the lights of downtown would be a cool backdrop?"

Walking back to their office cubicle, Chloe flicked through her phone—reading the emails she had missed during the meeting. "Vangaurd are couriering the samples back to us tomorrow afternoon."

"Great, I can send them out to the next stylist," Carmen said.

"Cool—but let's make sure we get them back in time for this campaign shoot… Can you believe how great the collection will look onsite?"

"I know, I can't wait for launch day—we should gift a pair of heels to Gabi… You know she will wear them for us!"

Everything was now slotting into place, all except the actual delivery of the collection, which was still being rush produced by several factories and suppliers to meet the deadline. But waiting on the stock was the last thing on their 'to-do' list, which now included a photo-shoot. "What time are Dom and Pandora landing tomorrow?" Carmen said.

"Morning sometime… *Shit!* That reminds me, I gotta drag the sofa bed out… I hope this meeting with Veronica goes well."

Carmen could see Chloe was starting to stress, but they had come this far already and she was certain there was nothing to worry about. After all, Veronica knew what she was doing when it came down to business. But there was so much still to do, and with every meeting they attended, more work seemed to land on their laps. Now they had to approve every product image, every product description, and organise the campaign shoot. Carmen could see why she was getting herself in a twist, but she also wanted Chloe to enjoy the work—they had worked so hard to get here.

The rest of the afternoon consisted of a desk lunch and discussions about potential locations for the shoot, which Carmen wasted no time in printing off several images for their moodboard—making use of the office's laser printer. She even looked on DivaFeet for clothes to call in as samples to dress Chloe in, inspired by a New York 'street' theme. Mesh tops, mini-skirts, feather boleros, sequin dresses, and tulle skirts were all on her samples list. Meanwhile, Chloe was consumed with going through the product pages for the collection, adding in her tweaks, which took up the rest of the working day.

"What you up to tonight?" Carmen said, gathering her things.

"Well, I hired a cleaner to drop by today—so hopefully it's perfect and the fridge is fully stocked. Dom would have lost his shit if he saw the state I let it get in lately."

"Don't be so hard on yourself, you've been working hard and travelling… He'll understand that, surely?"

"You clearly don't understand Dom's high standard of hygiene!" Chloe joked, but serious all the same.

"Right… Well, I'm off home… Enjoy your sterile apartment— see you tomorrow."

Chloe didn't even look up from her computer screen, too busy emailing the copy revisions back to the editorial team. Her neck ached. She dipped her head forwards and massaged herself, she knew it would be best for her to leave and get some rest too. Tomorrow was set to be a big day—and stressful—with both Dom and Pandy in the office. They would most likely want them to go out in the evenings too, which wasn't the most thrilling idea when sleep was becoming a luxury, but she tried to stay upbeat and energised. She was finally getting what she had always wanted: her best friend back in New York.

Back at the apartment, Chloe sighed with relief, but as she stepped out of the elevator she was rather miffed to see yet another large box outside her door. She had hoped that no more boxes would turn up after the cleaner had been and gone—leaving the place spotless. Nevertheless, she opened the door and kicked the box in the hallway without a care for its contents.

However, she suddenly remembered that she wasn't expecting anything to arrive; her clothes from The Four Seasons had been shipped immediately and were hanging back in her wardrobe; she had been making full use of her Hilary Van Furstein collection every day at work—so what could this be? Kicking off

her shoes she walked into the kitchen to grab and knife to score
the top open, and as she did she noticed the shipping label said:
'MAISON MARAIS, PARIS.'

Excited, she ripped open the box flaps and was immediately
faced with sheets of crisp, black tissue paper, with a white envelope on top bearing the new house logo in a black sans-serif font.
Opening the envelope she took out the card, handwritten by Jean-
Paul himself on personalised stationery—printed on considerably
thick stock. Even his compliment slips felt expensive.

Cherie,

*Gianni and I missed you at the show! I was looking forward to seeing
you wear this dress, and as promised, your new bag—which I have
decided to name after you! See you in Paris next year!*

J.P x

Although the note alone was interesting, the contents were far
more alluring, so she continued to lift the layers of tissue to reveal
a black box—embossed with the logo in white—and a garment
bag folded in half. Chloe whipped the lid off the box first, and
cushioned with even more black tissue paper—safely inside a
black dust bag—was the 'Chloe' bag she had picked out at the
Maison. As she picked it up, the soft black leather glistened with
buttery newness and the silver 'MM' buckle was shiny, without a
single hairline scratch.

Putting it to one side, her heart beating with joy, she unzipped
the garment bag—now knowing what was inside it. Chloe smiled,
pulling out the polka-dot cocktail dress she had chosen to wear at
the very first Maison Marais fashion show—but never got to. Alas,
Jean had wanted to keep his word and sent them to her regardless,
along with a rather interesting message which she picked up to
read once again. It was short and simple, yet very telling.

*

The phone alarm sounded at five–thirty in the morning these days—weekends included. The crack of dawn was now the only time she had for working out, as the weekdays were filled with office-life that seeped into the evenings. But today was different, Chloe had an excitement about her that got her up and out of bed, without the wish to hit the snooze button—Dom and Pandora were due to land.

After getting dressed, she made sure that the sofa bed was made-up, ready for her guests to stay for the rest of the week, before grabbing her new Maison Marais handbag to head out the door in time. When she arrived at the office, she was surprised to be greeted by Carmen glueing images to a massive mood-board, which she had stuck to the wall.

"What's all this?" Chloe said, throwing her coat over her chair, carefully placing her new Maison Marais bag on her desk—on show

"Ta-da! It's your photo-shoot… I worked on it all evening… What do you think?"

Carmen passed Chloe her latte (which she had got for her every day from the cafe downstairs), watching as she assessed her project. The board was filled with locations, outfits, and shots of New York fashion shoots which she had gathered together, in one bite of the Big Apple. Tilting her head, she noticed a 'Girls! Girls! Girls!' pink neon sign was included, which made her raise an eyebrow, but she had to admit it—she did rather like the idea.

"You know, I was thinking we could do some shots on the roof—get the skyline in and the breeze in your hair!" Carmen said, swishing her head.

'Where does she get her energy from?' Chloe wondered, taking a sip of her coffee. She was absolutely shattered from it all and caffeine was her fuel. Carmen continued, rattling off ideas in the background while Chloe switched on her computer and zoned out—checking her phone for messages from Dom. Nothing had come through yet, which made her feel even more nervous.

"Have you heard from Dom yet?" Carmen said, catching her checking her phone every five minutes.

"No—nothing… What if the flight's delayed? I'm gonna check online."

"Relax! They'll be here… Besides, you need to get the samples back so I can send them out, and get them back again in time for *our* shoot… Anyway, don't think I haven't noticed that *thing*," Carmen said, pointing her coffee cup at the Maison Marais bag, quietly sitting on her desk.

"Oh, gosh—how could I forget! I came home last night to a delivery, all the way from Paris! Jean sent me the bag and dress that I was supposed to wear at the show—before Graziana sent me packing."

Carmen put her cup—far away from the bag to avoid any mishaps—and picked it up with both hands, like a newborn baby. "Wow, it's *sooo* soft… And so chic!" Carmen said, noticing the new style, far from the 'MM' monogram bags that had been the house staple for decades.

"I told you, the new image is very 'rock n roll,' nothing like before… What's more, there was a card from Jean… It said: 'Gianni and I missed you,'… What does that mean?" Chloe said, sipping her coffee, still without a clue—even after an entire evening trying to decipher the hidden message.

"Duh! Can't you see?" Carmen said, looking at Chloe as though she was a complete idiot. "Gianni has obviously asked him to say something… I mean, you have totally ignored the guy since. I'm surprised he's even bothering, even indirectly, if I'm honest with you." And just like a cold, hard slap across the face, Chloe realised this was indeed another attempt to reach out to her. It was easier for an outsider to assess the situation, and she was grateful for Carmen's honesty—but she wasn't ready to entertain this all again. Although, she could do with industry contacts such as Gianni and Jean right now.

"Morning Ladies," Veronica said, poking her head around the glass door; checking in on them, as usual. "All set for the meeting later?"

"We sure are—they have landed and are on their way as we speak!" Chloe chipped in, woke from her thoughts about Gianni.

"Great! Well, I have some good news… Very good news! Bill's just got an email from the shoe factory and they will be ready to ship by the end of this month! Which means we'll be on course to launch at the end of November when the other pieces arrive—ready for the Holiday's as planned." This *was* good news, it meant that all these discussions and talks about 'the launch' were all for good reason, and the launch date was now in sight. But it also meant that things would start to ramp up pretty quickly (which would no doubt mean more late nights at the office). "I'll get Bill to confirm when the rest can be delivered, which means you girls need to speak to tech about the micro-site going live—I want everything finalised and presented to me at the end of next week… What's all this?" Veronica said, eyeing up the mood-board.

"This is the art direction for the campaign," Carmen proudly presented, like a car show hostess.

"Well, just keep it on the cheap side… Which I can see you have done," Veronica said with a raised brow. "I have to make some sort of a profit don't forget… Is that a new bag?"

"It's the new Maison Marais bag—gifted to Chloe from Jean-Paul Baptiste and Gianni!" Carmen said with it draped over her shoulder.

"Oh, fantastic! So, you guys are talking again? Good move," Veronica said, pleased that Chloe hadn't completely sacked Gianni off. She too knew the importance of their relationship, even if just for commercial reasons.

"I haven't spoken to him as such, but I guess we're still friends… It's named after me too; what you're looking at is the 'Chloe' bag," she said, making sure Veronica knew that she was *still* that savvy, business hungry woman she had invested in.

"What are you like?" Veronica raucously chirped almost in disbelief—but totally believing that this was something she would pull off.

"*What!* You didn't mention that!" Carmen added.

"Yeah, apparently Jean likes to name bags after his models and his assistant told me that I had chosen his personal favourite, which has obviously pleased him."

"Well, make sure we get editorial on StacksOfStyle with that story," Veronica said, leaving to get on with her hectic schedule—running DivaFeet and now StacksOfStyle. "I'll see you guys—with Dominic and Pandora—in my office at twelve sharp for the meeting."

With Veronica now gone, Carmen punched the air with her fist, looking at Chloe wide-eyed. "Oh, come on! You have to be excited by this… First, the deliveries are on schedule, the site is on course to go live, and we're about to run a real fashion business! Aaand, on top of all that, you forget to mention that you are now an official Maison Marais muse! Chloe, this is fantastic—can't you see things are starting to get exciting? I mean like, *really* exciting!"

Put like that, Chloe couldn't help but raise a rueful smile. All this hard work *was* starting to pay off and maybe Gianni wasn't a terrible contact to have after all (in whatever capacity), and if that meant putting up with Graziana as a token for that relationship—then so be it. She made a mental note to write back to Jean-Paul, equally being as covert as him in her response—which would surely get back to Gianni. But what she really needed right now was for Dom and Pandora to arrive on time.

Instead of fretting about it, she decided to use this wave of excitement for something productive and arranged to have the samples collected from the stylist who was working on the Vangaurd shoot, but the state they were received back in was questionable. "What the hell did they do to them?" Chloe shouted, emptying the box of samples and checking them, one-by-one.

The soles of the shoes were scuffed and dirty (like they had been on a night out in a club) and the knee-high boots were splashed with what appeared to be muddy rainwater. The hand-bags were creased from having been stuffed back into the box without their dust-bags and paper filling, and the accessories were rattling around loose at the bottom of it all. "Jeez, well at least we'll get a good spread to go along with your article, I guess?" Carmen tried to compensate.

Chloe wiped her brow, feeling anger brewing inside of her—these were the only set of samples they had—but a loud ping on her phone made her drop the boot in hand and dash back to her desk. "It's Dom, they've landed!"

"See, I told you everything will be fine… I'll clean these up and get them out to the next publication on the list while you go through this," Carmen said, handing her a printed email. It was a list of brands that Veronica wanted them to consider for stocking onsite.

All of them were niche, independent designers that DivaFeet supported and could be a great fit for the all-new-and-shop-able StacksOfStyle.com. None of them were recognisable, but she needed more tasks to take her mind off the impending meeting, and researching brands to buy was rather exciting. It meant that Veronica was one step closer to releasing their budget for buy-ing—which meant Fashion Week! This time, they wouldn't be trawling around the city looking for work or trying to muscle in on parties—they would be official attendees with a purpose.

Another thing—to keep her mind off matters—she owed Jean an email to thank him for his generous gifts. Taking out the note-card from her Maison Marais bag, Chloe began typing his email into the address bar of a new message—another influential name added her contacts.

From: Chloe Ravens
To: Jean-Paul Baptiste

Subject: Thank you!

Dear Jean-Paul,

Thank you for the lovely gift you sent. I cannot thank you enough, and I cannot apologise more for having to return to New York so soon.

Congratulations on a beautiful collection! I am excited for the future of Maison Marais, which I hope to be a proud ambassador of.

I would love nothing more than to be able to wear your beautiful dress in Paris next time around, which I hope won't be too long.

Chloe x

StacksOfStyle.com
New York, NY

**

"Where are they?" Chloe fretted, slipping on her black blazer, prompt for the meeting in Veronica's office. It was a quarter to twelve and there was no sign, or word, from Dom and Pandora. Even after Chloe had called him several times, leaving message after message.

"They'll be here… They just got a flight all the way from London—cut them some slack," Carmen snapped, now starting to get worked up herself for no good reason. She was the one that held it all together; there was no use in her losing it as well.

Then, Chloe's desk phone rang—cutting through the tension in the room. "Yep… Okay, I'm coming!" she said, slamming the handset back down. "They're here! Go to the meeting and tell Veronica we're on our way—I'll run down and get them."

Carmen did exactly that, she was eager to please her if that meant she would calm the fuck down! Chloe dashed off in the opposite direction and jammed the elevator button to call it up. DivaFeet employees slowly emptied the elevator car, not really wanting to get back to their stations so quickly, as Chloe barged her way in simultaneously.

Impatiently waiting for everyone to get out, she held her finger ready on the button to close the doors. Finally reaching the ground floor, Chloe's heart rate plateaued as the doors parted to reveal Dom and Pandora, waiting calmly (but also nervously) on the sofas in reception.

"You made it!" Chloe said, skipping over to hug Dom as they both stood up. "What's all this?" Chloe said, noticing they had brought a suitcase with them which cramped their style—she was eager for them to make their very best, first impression. "Let's just leave this behind the front desk."

"This isn't our luggage babe… Did you really think we were gonna come all this way and not bring examples of our work? We quickly went back to the flat to drop off our cases—which I am pleased to see you've been keeping tidy, by the way—then jumped in a taxi to come here… Can't you tell?" Dom said, pointing at his pristine face.

Chloe smiled, of course, he had come equipped and fully prepared—why did she ever doubt him? "Come on you two—we better get upstairs—Veronica's waiting!"

Everyone was now waiting for their arrival in the boardroom. Bill from buying, Morgana from marketing, and Veronica—along with two of her investors—were sat around the table. Carmen kept an eye on the outside and was pleased to see Chloe, Dom, and Pandora marching along, pulling a suitcase behind them.

"Sorry to keep you all waiting," Chloe said as she slid open the doors. "This is my best friend Dom, and of course, Pandora Simmons."

"Hi-ya guys!" Pandora said in her cockney accent, which sounded like the dull ring of a dented bell—but its novelty seemed to charm. They all stood up to greet and shake her hand, already impressed with her sense of style, with her red hair swept up in a silk bandana, sporting her classic red lip and winged eyeliner.

"Thanks for coming all this way to see us," Veronica said, shaking her hand.

"My pleasure, I haven't been to New York for a long time, so it's great to be back… This is Dominic, he's an old school friend—and also a friend of Chloe's, which is how we both met too," Pandora explained, presenting him.

"Dominic, I have heard so much about you—welcome!"

After everyone had exchanged greetings, Veronica sat down, leading the rest to follow so she could commence and get down to business. Chloe looked nervously at Carmen, and then to Dom, with her legs, fingers (and toes) crossed beneath the table.

"So, now we have introduced ourselves, let me begin… Chloe has told me that you are having a fantastic season—I love the collection, by the way—but you need some help with production?"

"Well, it's not production as such," Dom said, eager to squash any doubt that they were unable to manufacture the line on their own. "We have our factories and supply chain in place—what we don't have, is the money to fulfil demand… As a small business, we have scaled up quickly in one collection—and that is what we need help with."

"So, you need a cash injection to help you tick along?" Veronica said, making sure she understood the situation; jotting down notes as she spoke.

"Exactly! As the brand director of Pandora Simmons London, I want to make it a profitable business on its own and no longer rely on Pandora's own resources—which is how we've been surviving so far… But this season, our orders are up by seventy percent, and we need the money to produce higher quantities and a wider selection. Because of this, we haven't been able to think about designing handbags and shoes—that's something we wish to expand on in the near future." Now he was talking Veronica's language, she wanted to know about figures and what was in it for her—and Dom knew money was the way to swing the conversation to their favour. "To combat this, we have offered trade discounts to vendors who can pay for their orders up front to meet the demand and make the collection… But of course, if we had the finance in place, we wouldn't need to do that…"

"Handbags and shoes are what *we* do well," Veronica said, looking up from her note-taking with a grin. "In fact, Chloe's very own line is due to launch very soon as I'm sure you are aware… We have suppliers who can help with that, but as a luxury label, I'm sure you will want to produce in Italy? But to do just that, you will need investment to grow the business further… What are your plans?"

Pandora looked clueless as Veronica directed this question to her, which hadn't gone unnoticed by Chloe—who in turn looked at Dom for saviour. So far, the meeting was going rather well, but she knew that one slip could make Veronica feel as though this wasn't going to be worth her bucks—and the whole deal would collapse.

"Well, like you say… Shoes and handbags are an area I'm yet to go into—and we know they make big bucks! But at the moment, I need to focus on the ready-to-wear collections, which we have some samples with us to show you," Pandy said, looking around the table.

"*Yes!* Let us show you some of the pieces from the latest collection, which is the real reason why we're here," Dom said. "In fact, we bought a selection of Chloe's order that she would like to have on S.O.S."

Veronica nodded discreetly to Bill, with a raised eyebrow—a sign for him to take note and to make subtle expressions to guide her on his thoughts. Dom and Pandy both stood up and started to unzip their suitcase and garments bags on the floor, which looked slightly unprofessional, but the fact they had brought samples with them showed that they were somewhat prepared.

"Let's waste no time, shall we?" Dom said, holding up the zero–one–five dress in a bold leopard print, with a black lace buster underneath. This is the dress which has lit up our orders this season, the reviews were all about this dress and this is the exclusive we really want to give you for the U.S market… Most of our buyers are from Europe—except for StacksOfStyle, of course," Dom smirked.

He passed the dress around the table before it reached Bill who inspected it, right down to the seams inside.

"Do keep in mind that this is just a show sample," Dom chipped in defensively; he didn't want them to think this was the finished quality.

Pandora continued to pass other pieces from the collection around the table with shaky hands, which initiated a discussion about the collection—and more importantly—what the inspiration would be for the upcoming season.

"We've just begun with storyboarding the next collection… We want to include all the things that are our brand signature: female empowerment, London eccentricity, and garments which are modern in construction and style," Dom said, touching Pandy's shoulder to let her know she was doing well.

But as Bill passed Veronica the leopard dress, Dom saw him give her a wink—which he hoped was a sign that he liked what he saw.

"Pandora will be back to work on the upcoming fall/winter collection once we are back in London… I, on the other hand, am working tirelessly on meeting the demand for our zero–one–five dress and making sure orders are fulfilled on time… As you can imagine, for a small brand this is quite a task, but it is imperative to capitalise on the success on this show with a good reputation to our buyers—and also getting our designs out there, into the world."

"And how will you do that? What exposure do you have other than a great show?" Veronica pressed, pressing her lips together tightly as she handed the dress onto Carmen.

"Well, this is where we need you," Dom said brazenly with pointed fingers, like two hand-guns. "With your experience and backing, our time will be spent on creating—not manufacturing… We'll leave that up to the suppliers, and if you can help with finding more cost-effective factories, then great! But with that burden lifted, Pandora and the team can focus on design whilst giving me room to work on press opportunities—until we're in a position to outsource PR."

"Actually, I can see Gabi in this," Carmen said, standing up to wrap the dress around her. "Do you have a longer version of this?"

"In fact, we do," Pandora said, smiling at Dom. In hindsight, his idea of making more styles in this pattern was a stroke of genius.

"Can I See? I'm thinking… Awards season will be upon us in no time; I usually gather ideas for the Golden Globes around this time of year… That would be an excellent press opportunity for you."

Suddenly, Veronica sat straight—she liked what she was hearing. Not only could Carmen censure that the world-famous singer and actress, Gabriela Gracia, would be snapped in their creation, but at a major global event too—and that equalled dollar signs!

"And for your next collection, we can supply you with accessories and shoes from the 'Raven' line!" Chloe added, also seeing more potential in their working relationship. "I'm sure if you let us know what colours/fabrics you need in time, that we could make the samples for you?"

"Now, that's a very good idea! We could sell it as a collaboration line on Stacks," Veronica said, seeing the bigger picture on where this could actually lead to. "Okay, well there is certainly a lot of possibilities here that we can work with, so let's talk money."

Chloe drew a deep breath of relief, now that Veronica was convinced this could be a fruitful investment for her, Dom and Pandy just needed to show her where the money was—which wasn't too difficult. All they had to do was show her the orders for the zero–one–five dress alone for her to see where they were making heady financial gains so early on. Not to mention the rest of the collection that they had sold, which Dom had forced buyers to take, to access the dresses in the first place (a salesroom tactic that had impressed Veronica).

It was clear to her that Dom was leading this whole operation, and that he had excellent experience on how to run a brand. And knowing he once worked with Chloe at Palazzo, if he was just as switched on as she was, then he too would be a good bet to put money on. "So, what you need is cash to take the heat off a bit," Veronica said, waiting for their agreement—to which they nodded. "We can help with press and exposure Stateside, but you will need to ramp that up on your end for the European market."

"Carmen, if you *can* get Gabi to wear Pandora Simmons London to The Golden Globes, then I'd say you are on course to make a very strong, global brand presence," Morgana said, looking at Veronica as a way to give her blessing.

The nods from around the table were almost in a domino effect. Chloe now had a huge smile on her face, now that the worst was over and Veronica was talking strategy and money. Veronica made them wait in silence while she jotted down a few more notes and worked out calculations—passing her pad to her two investors on either side of her to take a look. No one said a word, leaving them to have a brief discussion before Veronica finally put her pen down—commanding the entire room's attention.

"I would like to be included in your brand's success, however, for me to do that, I need a few things back in return… I would like to offer you $250,000 for fifty percent of the brand—with a buy-back scheme for you to regain equity over the next five years—leaving me with a minimum of thirty percent at the end if you choose to do so. As a brand partner, Stacks will also need to have U.S exclusivity to sell your next season online too… And I also like the idea of you working with Chloe and Carmen on a capsule collection of bags and shoes—so that *has* to be a part of the deal. I will review the situation every six months… How does that sound?"

Pandora looked like a deer caught in headlights, not only was she not expecting such a large investment, but she also wasn't expecting to hand over that much of a share-hold. Fifty percent sounded like a lot, even though the clause was there to buy back shares, but what if she couldn't? What if for some reason, the brand took a nosedive and she couldn't pay Veronica back? Plus, for the first time in her life, she would be working for someone and making *them* money—this was a big decision that she hadn't really thought about.

"Look, I can see this will have to be discussed between your-selves, so let's call a break and meet back here in fifteen?" Veronica said, standing up for her team to follow, just leaving Chloe and Carmen with Dom and Pandy to work this one out on their own.

"What are you guys thinking?" Carmen said, breaking the silence, once everyone had left.

Pandora looked stunned, glued to the spot and totally out of her depth, and so did Dom—which wasn't like him.

"Guys, I know this is scary, but think about it," Chloe began, now versed in negotiating big deals herself lately. "With this investment, you can do so much—and we can work together! Plus, she is offering the chance to buy back shares… Not many investors do that. If Carmen can get Gabi to wear one of your dresses, then that's instant global media on your brand right here!

You will make $250,000 in no time—then you're square and level with Veronica… I know it sounds like a lot of money at first, but with what we're trying to do, this is just a drop in the ocean that's necessary."

"I'm in," Dom said, looking at Pandy for a reaction.

"I know I can get Gabi to wear your dress! And the collaboration with us on shoes and handbags—that will absolutely catapult your brand!" Carmen added, pushing her that little bit further to come to a decision.

"Okay," Pandy said, pushing out a bellyful of air. "Let's do this… My dad's accountant will be relieved at long last."

19

Agreeing to Veronica's deal naturally came with celebration, going out to the bars that Chloe and Dom used to get smashed in after a bad day at Palazzo. For once, it was a night out that Chloe was happy to stay up for—she too had something to celebrate about the P.S.L deal.

Now that Veronica had bought shares, it had secured Chloe's exclusivity rights, meaning that Veronica had given them the go-ahead to buy stock for StacksOfStyle without needing to say so—ready to launch as an online retailer. But before they could celebrate that feat, they had to first launch 'Raven'—and get Gabi to wear Pandora Simmons to the Golden Globes.

A late start at the office was called for, thanks to too much drinking at Mission (one of Chloe's favourite gay bars). Chloe, Dom, and Carmen all sat drinking instant coffee in the living room, while Pandy sketched away—sat on a barstool at the breakfast bar. "There... I think I'm done," she said, cocking her head as she put her pen in her mouth to assess her drawing.

Carmen propelled herself off the sofa, almost spilling her coffee—it was the most energetic she had been all morning. "It looks fantastic!" she said, looking down at the sketch, taking it from Pandy.

Pandora had drawn a longer, gown version of the leopard print zero–one–five dress. Only it was more spectacular than the longer runway design, with a corseted top and black lace bustier underneath, and a fishtail skirt that trawled out at the back into a small train. It was definitely fit for the red carpet—and for a superstar like Gabriela Gracia.

"Do you think she will wear it?" Pandy said, still doubting the deal and whether she'd be able to take her label to the next level at all.

"Are you kidding? Leave it to me… Say nothing more—this is strictly between us! Gabi will be in touch to contact designers, ahead of award season—it's the same every year. But this time, I will be ready to strike with this sketch… In the meantime, start drafting the pattern and be ready to make the dress at the drop of a hat!" Carmen warned, passing the sketch to Chloe.

"She'll love it, but we *do* have a lot of work to get on with, on top of all this exciting stuff," Chloe reminded, not wanting them to forget their contractual agreements with DivaFeet, which were yet to be signed and sealed—but she didn't want them to get too giddy, too fast.

Between now and Christmas, Pandora had to design and produce a stellar fall/winter collection for London Fashion Week, make this dress for Gabi, and also design a range of shoes and accessories in time for Chloe to work with Bill and the buying team on making the samples—as well order the stock to sell on S.O.S.

"Don't worry… I have an idea for the next collection already," Dom said, struggling to sit up. He had forgotten just how much Chloe and Carmen could drink. "We'll get to work on it as soon as we get back to London, and we'll send you ideas for shoes and bags—we'll keep it simple."

Chloe gave him a raised eyebrow, with a pressed-lipped look. She knew from experience that he was incapable of keeping it simple, which was exactly why they had to get to work on it right away—time was short.

"But these *are* exciting times, guys! Don't forget to have fun… Do you realise how far we've come?" Carmen said, the most excited by it all.

"Okay, we better get to the office," Chloe said, eyeballing Carmen as she downed the last dregs of coffee. "What are you guys doing with your last day in New York?"

"A bit of sightseeing and shopping," Pandy said with glee—she had earned herself a treat.

"Wish I could come along too, but let's meet back here for dinner at seven? I'll be back about six-ish," Chloe said, putting on the tweed Chanel jacket she had rescued from Mrs Ruthenstock.

Carmen slipped on her heels, not quite ready to get back to work, having not made it home from the night before. She borrowed a pair of jeans and a hoodie from Chloe to make the day more comfortable, but it was still going to be a long day. They hadn't even reached their office before they were accosted by Morgana, walking along the office walk-ways past banks of DivaFeet workers at their desks.

"Morning guys! Congratulations for yesterday... Veronica's really excited for us all to start working together... Anyway, on that note, we need to meet—in about half an hour—to go over the campaign ideas?" she said, walking beside them, making them slow their pace.

'*Really?*' Chloe thought to herself, couldn't she give it a rest—just for one day? "Sure thing, let us settle in and we'll be there," she managed to politely say.

"Perfect, because Veronica wants us to shoot tomorrow."

"*Tomorrow!*" Carmen and Chloe both screamed at her.

"I know it's short notice, but she wants to strike while the iron is hot and get all our assets together... I've spoken to the production department and they're holding on all their other projects to get this done and dusted—see you in the boardroom!"

Chloe wiped her brow, feeling both the pressure and the alcohol seep from her pores. But she couldn't let all this get on top of her; like Carmen said, she needed to start enjoying the process.

"*Fuck*—that means I have to get the samples back, pronto... I'll grab the mood-board," Carmen huffed (her sore head wasn't ready for a boardroom meeting either), looking behind her to find Chloe heading back out of the office. "Where are you going?"

"If we're going to survive a Morgana meeting today, then we need more coffee—*real* coffee!"

*

Chloe took Carmen's coffee out of the cardboard holder and placed it on the table in front of her, just making it to the boardroom in time for the start of the meeting. "So, as I have explained to you all separately," Morgana began, perky as ever. "Veronica wants us to start shooting the campaign from tomorrow… I can see you've been busy gathering ideas, can you talk us through them?"

Carmen reluctantly got up out of her seat to present the mood-board inspirations to the room, which was packed with almost every department from buying, art and production and of course, Morgana's team—marketing. "To simplify things, we want the city to be the backdrop of the shoot—as little production necessary," Carmen said, directing her point at the production team members (who appeared to sigh with relief). At least they didn't have to quickly source props and set, which would have been impossible. "I still need to get the samples back from the magazine who has them currently, as well as the looks I have selected from DivaFeet's website, but if we all agree on locations then we can start shooting as soon as those are all delivered."

"We'll request the 'Raven' samples back today, and the looks to be sent over from the warehouse… They could get here late to-morrow, I guess?" Chloe said, trying to make everyone aware that shooting with no warning was both impossible and ridiculous.

"Well, I see some of the shots are at night—we can shoot those tomorrow evening if that buys us time in the day to get everything ready?" Derek said. He was the in-house art director and responsi-ble for all of DivaFeet's campaigns and advertising. He was used to Veronica's last-minute calls and knew how to get the results she wanted in little time.

"Perfect, so we can shoot downtown tomorrow night, and day shots the following day… I especially like the rooftop scenes you have there—we can just use the office rooftop for that," Morgana said, regaining control of the meeting. "Make sure we capture enough product shots... Close-up images of Chloe and the collec-tion, and also fashion shots for the website and the StacksOfStyle editorial… That way we should have enough assets to push the collection on all channels and platforms."

"Got it, Morgana," Derek snapped, apparently she rubbed everyone up the wrong way with her eagerness. "We'll make this as easy as possible with a small crew… Carmen, we'll need you on hand to dress and style Chloe, but we can just drive down-town and shoot some of the neon sign and street scenes you have there—that's easily done. I'm thinking it's best to style the shoot like an Insta story, easy content that looks good and that people can recreate themselves… I think that will resonate most with our target audience."

"Amazing idea!" Morgana chipped in. "We can even run a competition for customers to photograph themselves in the collection around New York, and repost on their social!"

Suddenly, shooting the campaign around the city seemed like a clever idea after all, and Chloe began to feel excited again; she had to learn to trust Carmen's instincts more (and her own). The meeting went on for another hour before they could escape and actually do the work necessary to meet the tight deadline. Carmen urgently called the publication who had the 'Raven' samples, while Chloe called in the clothes from the DivaFeet distribution centre in New Jersey.

"I'm gonna have to call Dom and tell him we can't make their last night in town," Chloe stressed, hitting her keyboard furiously as she typed out the sample request in an email.

"It'll be fine… We won't have to work *that* late," Carmen tried to soothe, having successfully arranged a courier for the samples. "We have everything under control, and tomorrow evening will be fun!"

"Oh no!" Chloe moaned, putting her face in her hands. "I've just had a thought: what about hair and make-up? Morgana hasn't thought about that, has she? There is literally *zero* budget for this campaign!"

Carmen's faced dropped, she was right—who was going to take care of hair and make-up? This shoot had to look professional *and* billboard worthy. "I've got an idea," she said, quickly tapping away on her phone. "Gray and Zoe will help… If they're not in L.A that is."

Gray and Zoe were Gabriela Gracia's hair and make-up duo, whom Chloe had already worked with (having styled Gabi with Carmen for her movie premiere). And Carmen was certain they would want to help Chloe, now that she was a rising star in fashion. Plus, she needed to get back in touch with them anyway to discuss the upcoming awards season. If she could also persuade them that Pandy's design was the perfect dress for her, then Gabi would be sold on it too.

"Morning!" Veronica said with a knock on their glass door.

Chloe sat up and tried her best not to look angered by her impromptu demands of the impossible.

"All ready to shoot the campaign?"

"In fact we are," Carmen said with a huge grin before Chloe could open her mouth and say something she regretted. "I'm just securing Gabriela Gracia's very own hair and make-up team as we speak—free of charge you'll be pleased to hear!"

"*Fabulous!* Can't wait to see the proofs... Will you be seeing Dominic and Pandora this evening?"

'If we ever get out of here!' Chloe thought, before actually saying: "We sure are, they leave tomorrow so we're having a farewell dinner."

"Tell them the contract will be with them by the end of the week, I want it back ASAP! Oh and on that note, you guys need to meet with Bill and decide on who you want to work with from the list of designers I gave you."

'Oh right—yeah that,' Chloe said to herself like she hadn't enough to do already.

"He'll approach them and ask if they can produce exclusive pieces for the site relaunch, early next year—just select five or six brands... Now we have the P.S.L deal in the bag, we need to start working on your website—fast! The 'Raven' line is being looked after by the wider team, for now, so you can focus on Stacks," Veronica said, turning to leave. "Oh, and don't forget the next 'Raven' line is in collaboration with Pandora—we need to get cracking on that too!"

"We need an intern," Chloe said, with Veronica just out of earshot.

"One day we will each have an assistant, and a team behind us even bigger than DivaFeet!" Carmen smiled.

"Either you've been drinking this morning, or you're getting paid way more than me," Chloe said, getting back to her email.

"I'm just high on life," Carmen grinned sarcastically. "Look at me, I'm hungover and just as tired as you… But guess what? We're working for ourselves! What we say goes—no more Regina's!"

And that was all it took for Chloe to snap out of her funk. Carmen had hit her with the truth; Chloe was now wide awake with reality which made her sit up and get on with it. Yes, there was a lot of work to be done for the shoot, and for the website, and for the collection launch, and the collaboration with Pandora—but it was all for her own legacy.

**

Leaving slightly later than planned, Carmen took a taxi home to shower and get ready for dinner at The Grill in The Seagram Building (which called for much dressier attire than jeans and a hoodie), while Chloe rushed home to meet Dom and Pandora back at the apartment. "*Eurgh!* So sorry guys!" Chloe said, slamming door shut—just on seven. "It's been quite a day."

They were sat in his kitchen drinking wine, already dressed to leave for dinner. Dom looked handsome as ever, wearing slim black pants, a black shirt and his signature Saint Laurent boots. Pandora had her hair down for a change, swept behind one ear in a fifties style finger wave, and wearing one her own dresses with clompy platform heels to make up for her lack of height.

"Wow, you guys look amazing! Ready for your last night in New York?" Chloe said, dumping her bag down with the last ounce of energy she had.

"We don't have to go out," Dom said, knowing how hard she was working.

"No, no! Give me half an hour… I'll be ready!"

Chloe quickly showered off the sweat from a hungover day at work, which made her feel like just getting into bed. But at least finding an outfit was easy, she had dozens of looks from Hilary Van Furstein that she was yet to wear out—choosing a leafy green jumpsuit that was wide-legged with a plunging neckline. Being a busy businesswoman had taught her to slap on make-up to an acceptable standard, in what she liked to call a 'fifteen-minute-contour.'

Midweek at The Seagram Building was packed with after office diners, trendy groups of friends who wanted to be seen, and those that didn't have to get up in the morning (which didn't include any of them). But Carmen had contacts everywhere that could get last-minute bookings and it was perfect for a chic evening to see Dom and Pandora off back to London.

Carmen had somehow made it to the bar before them, as though the night before had never happened. She also looked like the night before (or the day at work) had never happened. She just had that sense of style which made her effortlessly glam—no matter what state she was in. Wearing a simple shimmery black dress, with her hair neatly scraped back into a long pay tail which glistened down her back, she perched on a bar stool with a martini in hand—waiting for them to finally arrive. "Back on the drink?" Chloe teased, sneaking up on her from behind.

"When was I ever off it? I see you've managed to scrub up," she said, eyeing up the green jumpsuit she had picked out for her from the H.V.F showroom, before noticing Pandora's outfit. "Oh, now… This is glamour, darling!" Carmen held out her hands and stepped down from her stool to kiss Dom and Pandy.

"I used to get that too, just so you know," Chloe said with sass.

"You look amazing as well!" Carmen said, as though she were talking to a puppy. "You'll look incredible tomorrow night too!"

"Why? What's happening tomorrow?" Dom said, feeling a case of FOMO coming on.

"Didn't she tell you? We're shooting the campaign for the 'Raven' line… Zoe and Gray have just confirmed this evening—they will meet us at the office around six."

"Shame we're going back to London, we could have helped," Pandora said, wanting to stay in New York a little longer.

"It was a surprise for us too… Veronica's ramping up the calendar in preparation for launch—"

"Which *is* next month," Carmen reminded her, checking her Cartier wristwatch. "Come, our table should be ready by now."

Leading the way into the restaurant area, Carmen attracted a few looks from guys out with their girlfriends, while a few seemed to recognise the daughter of a rock legend in her entourage. The restaurant was cased in tall glass windows and wood panel walls, with white clothed tables set out around—a little candle lantern in the middle of each. A host dressed in a smart black suit and bow tie showed them to their table. It was a cosy round tabled booth, ideal for them to talk in private as well as watch the other diners come and go. Chloe, Dom, and Pandora all opted for steak, while Carmen ordered minted black bass and a bottle of white wine for the table.

"So, tell us more about the shoot," Dom said, resuming the conversation as they sat.

"We're gonna start shooting in the evening, downtown against neon lights—we want to capture the essence of the New York fashion scene, rather than a studio set," Chloe said, taking a sip of wine.

"That reminds me, wash your hair in the morning—but just tie it back or something... Gray wants a blank canvas to work with," Carmen said before she forgot. "It's going to look organic, not manufactured—we want people to go out and take their own city shots with the collection and post onto Instagram."

"Sounds like it's going to be a lot of fun!" Pandy said, really wishing she didn't have to leave so soon.

Now she was relaxed with friends (and drinking again), and the more she thought about it, Chloe realised it *was* exciting. Carmen had hit it home to her earlier when she said about how they had broken free of the managerial regime and were now in control of their own futures.

Yes, Veronica was calling the shots in some ways, but she was supporting them rather than dictating. And with her experience, she really did know best; if at times it seemed she was pummelling them with work, it was because she knew they were about to create something special.

"That reminds me, Veronica wants us to get cracking with designing the shoes and accessories for your next collection," Chloe said, rather upbeat about it this time. "I say we keep it to just a handful of styles—we can make several colour variations to suit the looks. But we'll need to hand over the designs for production in a matter of weeks."

"We've been talking about the collection today actually… We have some great ideas so far. Send us over the line drawings of the shoes in your current line, we're happy to work with them and simply tweak," Dom said, agreeing that any extra work at this point was a death warrant—they too had a lot on their plate.

"And don't forget to work on Gabi's dress too! We have plenty of time to execute this if we plan ahead," Carmen added.

"I just can't believe we are leaving New York with $250,000 behind us!" Pandora squealed, hunching her shoulders in delight.

"I told you she would come through, didn't I?" Dom said, giving Chloe a wink (meaning her, not Veronica).

Chloe smiled back at him. Although she felt as though she had lost him to London, they had been through too much together to completely lose their friendship—and now they were bound in business. The future looked stronger than ever, and with her friends around her, Chloe couldn't help but feel excited about what it was going to bring. And with this sentiment, it made her think about Gianni, without whom she wouldn't be where she was now. Her phone pinged, jolting her away from thinking of him for much longer.

She didn't want to seem rude by looking at her phone at the dinner table, but curiosity got the better of her. Fetching her phone from her Maison Marais bag, she had received a new email, which she continued to open. She read the email once—and then once again—to make sure she had read it correctly.

"Can't you put your phone away for one minute?" Carmen said with a duck-faced pout. "Veronica can wait until tomorrow!"

"No… It's not Veronica—it's Jean-Paul!"

"Jean-Paul? As in, Jean-Paul Baptiste?" Pandy shouted across the table, which got her a few dirty looks from nearby tables.

"Well, what's he saying?" Carmen urged.

"I emailed him yesterday to say thanks for sending me the goodies," Chloe said, catching Dom and Pandy up to speed with the drama. "And now he's asking me if I would design a limited edition version of the 'Chloe' bag for the grand opening of the new Fifth Avenue boutique next year!"

"*What!* That's amazing!" Pandy shouted once more, not giving a fuck about who stared over at her this time—this news called for raised voices.

"A limited-edition 'Chloe' bag!" Carmen reiterated.

"He's named the bag after you?" Dom asked, even more surprised by that than the news of Jean-Paul asking her to collaborate with him.

"What's the email say exactly?" Carmen pressed.

"Dear Chloe," she began, squinting to read it off the bright screen which hurt her eyes in the moodily lit booth. "It was my absolute pleasure to meet and dress you. It was fate that you chose my very first bag design for Maison Marais, and I have just had a crazy thought... Would you be interested in helping me design a limited edition version of the 'Chloe' bag to celebrate the opening of our Fifth Avenue store? We will make a small edition, only available to attendees of the grand opening next year. There is no one else as sexy and fresh as you on the New York scene right now, and I do hope you will consider it. I look forward to seeing what you come up with—Jean-Paul."

Placing her phone back down on the table, Chloe blew out a deep breath before taking a large gulp of wine to take the news in. Thinking back on her interview with Dina from Vanguard, maybe she was right to predict that Gianni would ask her to work creatively with him on Maison Marais after all? It was certainly a coincidence that Jean-Paul had asked her to collaborate after she had snubbed Gianni somewhat. Those two *were* great friends and had obviously been talking about getting Chloe involved with the re-opening of the Fifth Avenue store.

Carmen, Pandora, and Dom all stared back at her with wide-eyed smiles as Chloe thought it all over, equally finding what they had just heard hard to believe. This was another amazing opportunity under Chloe's belt, and proof that things were only just beginning. But to Chloe it meant so much more, it meant that things with Gianni hadn't come to close just yet—and that thought excited her more than she would care to admit.

Just thinking about Gianni made her quiver, let alone the thought of them sleeping together in Paris. After all, she had nothing really to be mad at him about—and whether Graziana liked it or not—Chloe Ravens was not done with her brother yet.

***

Even though there was much to celebrate, they had responsibilities far bigger than their alcohol limits, calling it a night at a reasonable hour. Dom and Pandy had woken up early to pack and prepare for their flight, while Chloe had to shower and get ready for a full day's work in the office—before being the star of the 'Raven' shoot.

Leaving them at the apartment she said goodbye, knowing that this time she would be seeing Dom sooner rather than later at the next Pandora Simmons London fashion in London. Carmen had also got up early and was at the office before Chloe, as per usual. "Morning!" Carmen beamed, already caffeinated and sorting through the plastic totes that had arrived from the warehouse. "Look... It's all arrived."

"Amazing!" Chloe said, placing down her Maison Marais bag (which had now become her favourite), before heading over to take a closer look.

Carmen had set up a rail and had a box of hangers close-by, hanging each item as she unpacked it. A pink sequin mini-skirt from The Glitterati immediately caught Chloe's eye, as well as a pink marabou feather coat and a gold lamé dress which was connected at the midriff with a large gold metal ring—both from the same brand.

"Don't you think this is all a bit, well... Young, for me?" Chloe said, but what she really meant was slutty.

"That's the idea, dummy! Listen, the evening shoot is fun-disco-minx Chloe—while the day looks will be more serious and fashion," Carmen said, totally unswayed by her doubts.

"Morning ladies!" Veronica said, popping her head in. They had now gotten used to her morning visits. "I need to see you in my office at ten."

"Sure," Chloe said, slightly worried by her serious tone. "What do you think that's about?"

"She probably just wants to catch up about the shoot or something," Carmen said, totally unnerved and immersed in getting the looks hung up.

"No, she can see for herself how it's all going," Chloe said, waving at the mountain of totes.

"Well, I guess we'll find out at ten… Have you had any ideas?" Carmen said, gesturing towards the 'Chloe' bag which had taken pride of place on her desk.

Chloe sat down and powered up her computer, ready for another tirade of daily emails that awaited her—usually from Morgana. As she waited for it to boot, she stared at the bag, she hadn't given it a moment's thought, but watching Carmen hang a mint green velvet dress in the background gave her a sudden burst of inspiration. "That's it! Bring that dress over here for a minute."

Carmen did as she was told, wondering what on Earth this cheap 'clubbing' dress had to do with designing a luxurious Maison Marais bag.

Chloe took it from her and draped it over one side of the bag, before taking a picture on her phone. "Jean wants something that says, 'New York,' right? Well, there's nothing more symbolic than the Statue Of Liberty, is there? Did you request more accessories for the shoot?"

Carmen dashed back over to the stack of totes and ran her finger down the packing list on the side of each one until she found the one that contained accessories. Chloe helped her lift and move the boxes that were piled on top of each other, until they reached the one they wanted, before cutting the security loop tag off to open the flaps. She dug around, selecting a necklace with three strands of faux-pearls and a pair of cherry shaped enamel earrings, while Carmen watched her in the moment. "To make it more luxurious, the logo can be embellished with pearls," Chloe said, placing a row around the 'MM' buckle, before taking another snap on her phone.

"I see," Carmen said, squinting to envision it. "And what about those cherry earrings?"

"Well, not exactly a cherry," Chloe began, as she hooked one around the chain like a charm. "But an apple—The Big Apple!" Energised with motivation, Chloe emailed the pictures from her phone to her computer right away to forward onto Jean-Paul, before she opened up any other email in her inbox.

From: Chloe Ravens
To: Jean-Paul Baptiste

Subject: New York Exclusive Chloe Bag

Dear Jean-Paul,

Wow—I am honoured that you have chosen me to collaborate with you on this project! Please see attached an idea I have for the Fifth Avenue exclusive bag.

I was thinking it should be a luxurious but fun evening bag made from 'Statue Of Liberty' green velvet—perhaps embroidered with the 'MM' monogram in single stitching? The buckle embellished with pearls and a 'Big Apple' bag charm (excuse the cherry earring, but you get the gist).

Looking forward to hearing what you think!

Chloe x

StacksOfStyle.com
New York, NY

Ten o'clock had come around fast and it was time to find out what bombshell Veronica wanted to drop on them now. Walking into the adjoining boardroom to her office, Chloe and Carmen were surprised to see a packed room, with what appeared to be the entire tech team. They knew that because the tech guys only wore band Tees and board shorts with flip-flops—no matter what the weather or season. Bill, and of course, Morgana was also present.

"Come in guys," Veronica said, motioning with her hand for them to hurry along. "Okay, thank you all for making this last-minute meeting, I know you're all busy with the campaign, but I have instructed the tech team to start phase two of the StacksOfStyle site build!"

'*What?*' Chloe thought to herself, looking to Carmen in shock. What the hell did this mean? Veronica could see they were baffled by the expression on both of their faces.

"Let me explain… Now that The 'Raven' capsule is nearly ready to launch, and with the P.S.L deal a done thing, we need to prepare the next step of our plan—to launch Stacks as a fully functional website." Chloe couldn't help but drop her jaw, letting out a squeal, before clasping her hands over her mouth. This was actually happening! Carmen grabbed her arm, shaking her with excitement. "This is where the real work starts! I have asked tech to start building the framework for the new site, using the product pages they have built for the 'pop-up' on your current site as a skeleton to feature more designers. As I have proposed, we will ask five designers to produce exclusive products for the launch— have you selected the ones you want to work with from the list?"

"Yes, we have," Carmen said, looking to Chloe for agreement—even though she was the president of StackOfStyle and would have to make even more difficult decisions than this in the years to come on her own.

"Great," Bill said, taking over. "I will approach those brands and ask them to design five products each—no more than that— we don't want to go too heavy on stock just yet. They will be just exclusive colours or variations of their most popular items, for example."

"And then, of course, we will have the Pandora Simmons collection that you have already selected, arriving early next year and we will look to re-stock the 'Raven' capsule once we have discovered how well that performs next week," Veronica said.

"Next week!" Chloe blurted.

"Well, yes… With the campaign as good as in the can, and the collection coming into the warehouse any day now, we should be ready to launch by then. Tech is ready to plug in your 'pop-up' extension into Stacks and the product pages for DivaFeet are completed already… Now, after we have launched the 'Raven' capsule—and it's been a major sell out—I will need you to fully focus on building the new site with these guys… That means closing down the current blog, halting social media posts, and cracking on with this project—you won't have time to do everything. Plus, I want you to save your editorial voice for the relaunch, that's the unique selling point of StacksOfStyle, after all."

"And we'll need to approve the designs these brands come up with so that they are produced in time for launch—which we have pencilled for late February," Bill said.

Chloe counted in her head, that was just under four months away! 'Is it even possible to build an e-commerce website in such little time,' she wondered?

"And obviously this is a secret project… Morgana will release an official press statement once we have everything in place, but regardless, we are pressing ahead with P.S.L sold exclusively on Stacks—as well as the 'Raven' line—not to mention the Pandora Simmons collaboration too!"

Chloe was struggling to keep up with it all, but she was glad to see Carmen jotting down notes. First, they had the 'Raven' capsule launching, then they had to get Pandora's designs made (ready for her show, and then for retail), and then there was all this work on StacksOfStyle to do—not to mention the Maison Marais collaboration. But she didn't dare bring that up right now, Morgana would only come up with some dumb idea to tie that into their website relaunch somehow—which Veronica would jump right on.

"So, who have you decided to go with?" Bill said, eager to know who would be the first brands stocked on S.O.S, other than 'Raven' and P.S.L.

Chloe had picked Bombster: a hip bomber jacket label that only made decorative and embroidered slogan jackets, Misty Jones: who made social media-worthy eye-wear, Aristotle: a small label focusing on everyday basics, Creative Corps: designer inspired sports-wear, and The Glitterati: which made sense, since she was now wearing it in the campaign.

"Perfect! Okay, so here's where we go from here… Bill, you can start talks with these brands, tech will begin site build phase two, and we will all meet again next Tuesday to touch base," Veronica said, signalling that she was now done with the meeting and had her own work to get on with. As did Chloe and Carmen, but they were glued to their seats, hugging each other as everyone else left.

"Exciting times ahead right?" Veronica said, perching on the tabletop. "I have big expectations from you guys, but I know we can do this together… And I have a lot of money riding on it now. But here's the thing, DivaFeet's customers are crying for something new—we have reached maximum selling potential—and with StacksOfStyle, we can offer a more upmarket, designer offering to our customers who have grown up with us. Fast fashion will always be around, but now is the time for a more curated eye, and I want us to be at the forefront of that."

Veronica's pep-talk was exactly what Chloe needed to hear, it gave her the strength to suck it up and get back to their make-shift glass office, and get to work on putting the looks together for the evening's shoot on the town—even if that meant dressing like a hooker and selling herself as the face of the 'Raven' line.

Something that she was now fully on board with, now that Veronica had put all her power behind StacksOfStyle.com.

20

Chloe had done exactly what Gray and Zoe asked for. She had washed her hair that morning and tied it back, turning up to work sans-make-up, and in return, they kept to their word too. Arriving at the DivaFeet offices, dead on six p.m.—complete with cases full of make-up and hair equipment.

"Gray, Zoe! So nice to see you!" Carmen said, air-kissing them on each side of their faces. "Chloe's upstairs waiting for you guys."

The working day had been a mad rush getting everything prepared for this evening, as well as meeting with Derek and the production team once more to go through the shoot schedule. It was decided that they would try and set out in time to catch the light of both dusk and darkness. That gave them little time to get hair and make-up sorted, but Zoe planned to build up on make-up as the night went on, and no doubt Gray would amp up the hair too.

Carmen guided them from the reception up to their office upstairs, where Chloe was waiting with a freshly cleaned face, prepped with serum and moisturiser, ready to be worked on with her hair finally let loose. "So this the StackOfStyle office right here," Carmen said, leading them to their start-up hub. "It's not usually this messy!"

"Hey, guys!" Chloe said, getting up to greet them, having seen them pass along outside the glass walls (she had been nervously waiting for them).

As the afternoon went on, she grew more and more anxious, hoping that she wouldn't mess it up or be awkward on location in the city with people staring at her—wondering who she was to warrant a photo-shoot. But this was New York and everything went down in this city, she had nothing to stress about apart from getting her 'schmize' on.

"Wow, guys! You really have made it since last time we saw you," Gray said, wheeling his case in, setting it down to give her a hug.

"Tell me about it… You have no idea," Chloe said, letting him go to kiss Zoe.

"So what's going on with Gianni?" Zoe said with gossip-hungry eyes.

Chloe rolled her eyes up to the ceiling, but she had become accustomed to it by now and it was a question that she was asking once again. What *was* going on with her and Gianni? Would he still be interested in her, even if they did see each other again soon? Or would the Maison Marais store opening be too far down the line—would he have moved on by then?

"Well, Chloe here spent a few days in Milan and then Paris with him," Carmen shared excitedly. "And what's more, she met Jean-Paul Baptiste and they hit it off! He's asked her to design an exclusive bag for the Maison Marais store re-opening on Fifth Avenue."

"Amazing! And I see things are ramping up here too," Zoe said, unlocking her case to start unpacking her brushes and product kit.

"Thank you so much for agreeing to this at such short notice… Shall we get started?" Chloe said, wary of time.

"Yes, we should! We don't have much time before we gotta leave," Carmen added. "However, you should know that we have just secured a deal with Pandora Simmons London to exclusively stock their brand, and with that comes access to couture gowns!"

Carmen pulled out Pandy's sketch and showed them the idea for Gabi's dress, which started the conversation about styling her for the awards season. Gray and Zoe liked what she was presenting, but the decision wasn't theirs to make (it was Gabi who needed to be convinced), but with them onboard it had set the wheels in motion at least. Carmen placed a copy of the sketch in an envelope and gave it to Zoe to show her. She spent the most time around Gabi as her make-up artist—but for now, they had another deadline to meet.

Gray got to work first, brushing through her hair before taking a curling brush and a hairdryer to her locks, bringing it back to life. While he did that, Zoe smeared base foundation all over her face and patted it with a sponge, ready for him to finish so she could get in and apply the rest.

"Let me show you some of the looks," Carmen said to her, so she could see what colours she had to work with. Like Chloe, the purple sequin mini-skirt instantly spoke to her, inspiring her use a matching glitter on her eyelid—along with a popping pink lipstick to match the marabou feather coat.

"Right, this is as good as we are going to get it I think," Gray said, stepping back after blow-drying, brushing, curling and hair spraying—resulting in a big and vampy sixties style bouffant.

"Oh good, you're nearly ready," Derek said, poking his head around the office door. "We are looking to set out in about ten? Is that enough time?"

They all looked at each other; Chloe was far from ready!

"Sure, shall we meet you downstairs?" Carmen said, taking control of the planning so Chloe wouldn't stress about it.

"Sounds great! See you downstairs… Looking great so far!" Derek rushed off to load his car with the lighting equipment he needed and made double sure all of his battery packs were charged and ready to go.

Meanwhile, Zoe had expertly started to apply eye shadow, blanking out all the chatter around her so she wouldn't feel rushed. She was an expert and knew how to keep calm whilst having a steady hand. Years of applying make-up to Gabi's face on location, at fashion and movie sets, taught her how to hold her nerve—this was nothing new. Plus, the pair of them were doing an unpaid favour, however, Chloe turned out would be good enough. Plus, they were industry professionals, they could do their work blindfolded and it would still look amazing.

After she had applied a bronze contour, Zoe finished off the eye make-up with a heavy pile of powder under her eyes, before blending a black smokey colour on her lower lid—and purple glitter on the upper lid—sweeping off the excess powder that had dropped down without making a mark. All that was left to do now was a quick black liner and wingtip, and then the pink lips with a sparkly gloss over the top. The rest could be touched up on location.

Carmen had started to yank the garments for the first outfit off their hangers, ready to help Chloe get into—starting with the sequin mini-skirt look. As soon as Zoe had finished Chloe's lip, she started undressing, not bothered by others in the room or the glass walls since most of the office had gone home already. Carmen helped her pull on a neon yellow spandex crop top, followed by the sequin mini and lastly, the pink feather coat which was to be finished off with the black leather knee-high boots. A chunky gold necklace, large gold hoop earrings and a matching gold chain belt styled the look, along with stacks of bangled on both arms.

"Okay, guys... Let's move it, let's go!" Carmen yelled, grabbing the laundry bags she had pre-packed with the other looks and 'Raven' samples. Zoe and Gray quickly packed the essentials into their work bags, ready to touch up where needed on-the-go. As they left the office, Chloe caught a glimpse of her reflection in the glass walls as she walked along the office. Some employees, staying late to catch up on their work, stopped what they were doing on their computers to have a look.

Downstairs, Derek's team were ready with light stands, flashboards, and bags of camera equipment to assist. "Wow! You look great," Derek said, already sensing that this shoot was going to be an easy one for him. "Why don't we start here... Just stand in front of the front desk and pose, maybe place your bag on the counter or something?"

Chloe did what she was told, but having an audience had already started to get to her and she felt rather stupid dressed up like a drag queen. She stood awkwardly in front of the reception desk, which had the DivaFeet logo on the wall behind it—along with the newly added 'StacksOfStyle.com' underneath it. The photographer took a few shots before asking her to loosen up a little—to which she rolled and shrugged her shoulders. 'Uh... Lighten up!' she said to herself, before having a 'fuck it' moment.

They didn't have a lot of time to capture the shots they needed, and she certainly didn't have time to be shy. Pushing herself up on the reception countertop, she sat sit crossed legged with her hand planted either side, showing off the boots. This *was* a shoot to show off the collection after all.

"Now we're talking!" Derek encouraged, which led her to lay along the desk, resting on one elbow supporting her head with a sultry look. "Okay, I think we got this now… So, let's head downtown and shoot the neon backdrop scenes."

But they didn't have to wait long before shooting outside took place, making use of an empty street, Derek made Chloe pose by the huge industrial bins of the Garment District—showcasing the boots and bag as well as character shots of her. Now Chloe had broken the seal, she ran ahead a few steps and took a twirl making the feather jacket flutter in the breeze.

"Great, give us more action," Derek said, briefly looking back on what they had just captured. To which she laughed, blew kisses, and spun around before it was time to get in the cars and head to the first location.

Derek and his team jumped in the car with the equipment, while the others jumped in another to take them down to Times Square—where neon was aplenty. As soon as they had reached there, the evening had started to set already and Zoe quickly applied more glitter to Chloe's lids and dusted her face with powder once more. Gray primped her hair and gave it a good spray to keep it in shape. Derek and the rest of the crew met them in front of one of the last remaining peep show theatres (which wasn't exactly where Chloe wanted to be hanging around, dressed like a showgirl herself).

"Let's get some attitude shots here real quick before we get moved on by the owners," Derek directed.

With no time to be shy now, Chloe did exactly that. Pulling a sultry face, tilting her head back and holding out the bag so it could be clearly seen. Derek called for some close-up shots, before asking her to change her pose to a stronger stance—leaning against the brightly lit windows. The photographer made sure to capture the bag and boots separately, as well as some background shots so they could easily PhotoShop product images over the top back in the office.

"Okay, let's keep moving on guys!" Following his command, they moved along to Father Duffy Square, which was packed with tourists, as usual, causing Chloe to get a lot of attention from the crowd. But the onlookers didn't make her embarrassed like she had expected to feel, instead, they gave her the confidence to be the supermodel that Veronica wanted her to be.

Standing on the illuminated red steps, Chloe struck a pose—making sure the boots were the centre stage of the image yet again. She followed it by sitting down, with her knees bent inwards and the bag set down in front of her—giving plenty of shoulder—before laying back on the stairs with one leg trawling down the staircase. Flaunting herself in public in front of a camera crew made an audience swarm around her—all vying to see who she was and what was happening.

"I think we've got enough… Shall we change outfit and do the same?" Derek said, looking back on the shots on the camera.

"Good idea," Carmen said, looking around for a place to change. "Looks like it's gonna have to be McDonald's!"

It wasn't exactly shoot location glamour, but the restaurant toilets were the only option unless she wanted to get dressed out in the open and probably get arrested in the process. However, Chloe took it all in her stride and followed Carmen to get dressed into the revealing gold lamé dress, with gold evening sandals and the clutch bag to match from the capsule.

"I got an idea," Carmen said, heading over to the counter, pushing her way to the front.

"Now's not the time to get a snack!" Chloe yelled, over the herds of people pushing her out of the way to join the line.

"Props!" Carmen said, when she finally returned with a bag of food and a milkshake.

Heading back out to the steps, crowds of people stared at her once more—dressed even more appropriate for the sex shops she was stood outside only moments ago. Scantily clad in October, the thought of Veronica not approving the images crossed Chloe's mind. But she didn't have time to worry about it now; it was too late for second thoughts. Chloe took to the steps once again, posing this way and that.

"Here… Now take a bite out, or something," Carmen shouted to her, unravelling the wrapper on a double cheeseburger to Derek's amusement.

"Great idea—love it!" the photographer called, ready with his camera to get the shot.

Chloe posed with the burger in her hand, pretending to take a bite seductively before actually taking a bite (she had to admit it, she was rather hungry and there was no denying that it tasted like heaven). Ready with another pair of pumps, Carmen jumped in and helped Chloe unbuckle the sandals to swap them over. Derek directed more shots on the steps before suggesting they moved on and did some walking shots, down Seventh Avenue—making sure to get the bustling background in.

"Right ladies… I think we got what we need," Derek said, calling a 'wrap' on the shoot. Chloe felt quite dismayed that it was all over already, she was starting to enjoy being the centre of attention, but if Veronica approved these shots, then she could be assured that even more attention would come her way.

*

The following day in the office was not like any other, it was time to now shoot the day looks. Swapping Fifth Avenue for her desk was a welcome break from emails and meetings—and having shot the most fun part of the campaign the night before—it had got her in the mood (although the looks were more subdued this time). Carmen had picked out soft pastel pieces, casual denim jeans, and smart blazers. And as Gray and Zoe couldn't take another day of free work, Chloe had to do her own make-up and hair, which wasn't too difficult considering 'natural' make-up was needed. Although, washing the hairspray and combing out Gray's back-combing had been quite a feat in itself.

The light of day didn't call for the whole crew and lights either, and with just Carmen and Derek, passers-by just assumed they were taking casual snaps—which wasn't out of the ordinary. Back at the office, they took themselves up to the rooftop of DivaFeet's office to grab some last-minute skyline images, making the most of the clear day before heading back inside to catch up on work before the weekend.

Dressing back into her day clothes, Chloe finally turned on her computer to check if she had any last-minute meeting requests from Morgana (she loved to stick in a meeting right when every-one was getting ready to enjoy the weekend). And in true style, there was indeed a 'catch up' invitation, pending her acceptance. "Eurgh!" Chloe moaned.

"What now?" Carmen said, just returning from the mailroom with a stack of envelopes.

"Morgana! Wants to catch up with us at five–thirty… I swear this woman has no life!"

"Well, at least we have a team behind us that are on it," Carmen offered in consolation, sifting through the mail. "Ooh, this one's for you," she said, flinging a black envelope across the room at Chloe's desk before ripping open her own mail. Chloe extended her arm to slide the envelope across the desk towards her, but left it—it was probably just junk. Carmen on the other hand excitedly ripped her way through a large plastic covered slab. "Oh my God!" she screamed.

It was December's issue of Vanguard Fashion magazine. Chloe stopped what she was doing and ran over to her desk, watching Carmen flick through it to find her feature over her shoulder. Turning page after page, passing a series of decadent adverts, she finally landed on the article.

<u>RISE LIKE A RAVEN</u>
Feature by Dina Volkes

Who is Chloe Ravens? That was the question on everyone's lips at New York Fashion Week this summer, but it wasn't until Milan Fashion

Week that I found out just who this new face on the scene, really is. The Four Seasons in Milan is always brimming with the crème de la crème of fashion (no matter what time of year), so the fact that Miss Ravens stayed here during her visit suggests that she has already made a name for herself in fashion.

Her suite is none other than the penthouse, usually booked by Gianni Palazzo himself, which brings us to the other question on our lips. Gianni Palazzo is known for his romances with models, actresses, and some of the world's most famous women—and it seems Chloe is very much in his sights.

'We haven't known each other long... But Gianni is a creative pioneer and when we met, I like to think that our creative souls instantly understood each other,' she says on the topic, dressed in Palazzo couture. She has definitely caught the eye of the fashion emperor, but don't underestimate her as being the typical fashionista. Founder of StacksOfStyle.com, Chloe has a capsule collection launching this year called 'Raven, by Chloe Ravens,' exclusively revealed here.

Chloe Ravens is also the women behind many famous dresses this season, notably Gabriela Gracia's recent red carpet gowns (also vintage Palazzo), making Chloe and Gianni quite the power couple already. 'Raven, by Chloe Ravens' collection is the first step on a journey that will see StacksOfStyle grow it into an e-commerce site—not just a fashion blog. 'I want my followers to read an article and be able to click and shop the looks... I see StacksOfStyle as the future of online shopping for designer pieces,' she goes on to say.

My time with Chloe is short and brief, but I am left with the sense that she is determined and quite relatable to the many women out there—in our current revolution of female empowerment—who also want to start their own businesses. Expect the raven to rise, but with Gianni by your side, is there any possibility of failure to fly? With Palazzo's star continuing to rise on its own accord, with the newly formed Palazzo Group venture and Maison Marais now under their belt, we think not.

'Raven, by Chloe Ravens' will be available to purchase online at www.DivaFeet.com this winter.

Chloe snatched the magazine from Carmen, reading it for herself once again, taking in the photograph that accompanied it. Pictured next to the article, Chloe sat on the sofa wearing the famous lace dress that she had now sold for charity.

"This is amazing! *You* look amazing!" Carmen shrilled.

"I'm just relieved she had something nice to say about me, I could swear during the interview she was trying to come for me,"

"I told you... She was just pressing your buttons to get to the real information, and she's included the collection—which is exactly what we wanted!"

Chloe was indeed pleased they had featured the 'Raven' capsule, complete with their own model images on the opposing page—taken in the aviary at the Bronx zoo (which explained the state the samples arrived back in). Although her portrait had most likely undergone some 'treatment' from their photographic designers, she was grateful that her own picture had come out rather stunning—because *everyone* would surely see it.

"You have to take this to Veronica immediately," Carmen said, looking at the article over Chloe's shoulder. "You should probably tell her about the Maison Marais collaboration too."

That was another thing, she did need to tell Veronica about her latest news; besides, it would only instil more confidence in her—and possibly even more financial investment.

**

They had only been back in London for forty–eight hours, but work on the next collection had already begun. Dom and Pandy had worked all night gathering clippings and for the collection, sketching out ideas for garments they had talked about on the plane journey home. With the prospect of dressing Gabriela Gracia at The Golden Globes, they would be mad not to feature a similar dress in the collection too, in case her dress was a hit.

There was no doubt that leopard print would make an appearance again, and as this was a fall/winter collection, they started off the looks with a leopard print overcoat with matching boots. The same boots as the 'Raven' line knee-high's, which would be easy for them to produce—that was one design for the collaboration down.

Tailoring was another focus for the collection, with masculine, oversized blazers paired with culotte style pants—similar to those in the summer collection but in heavy winter wool. As soon as Pandy was happy with a design, she passed it over to Jonty to start drafting a pattern—or cutting from an existing pattern that could be tweaked—before passing the pieces to Heather and JoJo to mock up a calico toile.

Meanwhile, Dom made sure all the orders they had taken were confirmed with the factories, now that they were sure they would be able to pay the cost of production. The most important order to be produced was, of course, S.O.S's—making sure that Chloe would be one of the very first vendor's to receive the line (and more importantly the zero–one–five dress). Now that they too had financial support, a weight had been lifted and even Pandora seemed happier and at ease—banging out sketch after sketch without having to be forced.

The studio had come alive, with Pandy blasting out her favourite tunes to motivate her own whimsical energy. Dom made a note to try and use some of the music in the final show—it was only fitting since they had influenced Pandy's sketches. The collection had started to take a seventies turn, with a peacock patterned cape and wide lapels on the suit jackets. Not to mention the use of chain-mail and faux-fur on dresses, outerwear, and bags—in a 'barbaric' sort of way.

The usually chatty and loud Pandora had been silenced, immersed in her work, designing—untroubled by whether this was going to be a success or not. With her wonderful team behind her (and with confidence installed in her from overseas), she was free to design the clothes she had always wanted to design. Dom's commercial eye also helped her to see where money could be made, making sure that there were enough options for buyers to envision in their stores. But it was also vital that the newly successful zero–one–five dress also had a revamp—something Pandy left Dom to come up with himself. And the answer was simple: instead of a revealing bust line, he added full sleeves, half-sleeves, and introduced two-piece corset tops and skirts—splitting the original dress pattern in two and expanding the line in one go.

***

"Derek's shown some of the images already, and I have to say, they look amazing!" Morgana gushed, as Chloe and Carmen sat down in a booth with her at the end of the day.

'Really? Well, I haven't even seen them myself yet,' Chloe thought to herself. But then again, she wasn't as eager as Morgana was to have her fingers in all the pies; she preferred to let people get on with their work as experts in their field—rather than be a meddling nuisance over their shoulder.

"Veronica's asked to see some proofs over the weekend, so Derek's working hard on getting them ready… She also wants to release a press statement early next week, alongside one of the images—which is what I wanted to talk to you about."

'Okay, maybe this meeting *was* necessary,' Chloe thought, perking up.

"Carmen, can you reach out to all the contacts who have photographed the samples and let them know they can push their articles if they haven't already… As for marketing, we are working on the social media content for both your Instagram account and DivaFeet's."

"Sounds like you're on top of it all—as always, Morgana," Chloe said, wanting to get out of this meeting, so she could go and see Veronica herself before she left. She still had to show her the Vanguard article and tell her about designing the limited edition bag with Maison Marais.

"Well, Vangaurd have already published Chloe's article," Carmen let slip, passing Morgana the magazine.

"Amazing! Has Veronica seen this?"

"Not yet… I'm going to see her after this in fact; I want to show her myself," Chloe said, yanking the magazine back out of her hands before she could run off with it and pass this off as her own doing.

That brought the meeting to an abrupt close, and Chloe didn't have to go far before she caught Veronica walking through the office to leave for the weekend. "Oh, Veronica… Before you leave, I have something very special to show you," Chloe said, hiding the copy of Vanguard behind her back.

"Some campaign shots?" Veronica said, heaving her bag strap over her shoulder with her phone in the other hand.

"No… Something better I'd say," she said, finally spreading the magazine open to reveal her article.

"Oh my… I completely forgot!" Veronica said, flipping to the magazine's cover to check that it was indeed Vanguard. "Can I take this with me? I need to head out, I'm leaving town for the weekend, but I'll see you bright and early on Monday morning… We have a big week ahead; I trust Morgana has told you the official press release will go out?"

"She did… But there's something else," Chloe said, biting her lip.

Veronica shook her head, what else could there be other than this amazing achievement of being featured in *the* fashion Bible?

"Well, remember I was introduced to Jean-Paul Baptiste?"

"Of course, you've been carrying that bag ever since he sent it to you… Rubbing my nose in it, might I add!"

"Well, soon you will have your very own I'm sure—but not just any bag… Jean has asked me to design a limited edition version for the Fifth Avenue store re-opening!"

"*What!*" Veronica shouted, causing the few employees that were still working at their desks to look over to see what the fuss was all about. "Seriously, I don't know how you do it, but keep on doing it! I take it you're back in touch with Gianni then?"

Chloe smiled awkwardly, it seemed all anyone was interested in was her getting it back on with Gianni, and she knew it made sense. But it just felt like Veronica wanted her to step things up with him for a publicity stunt before it was all lost. Then again, that wasn't such a bad idea with more at stake than ever. Although, deep in the back of Chloe's mind, she wanted more than just a business fling with him.

Realising that she was making huge steps in becoming a fashion mogul herself, she was slowly coming to terms with the fact that maybe—just maybe—she was turning into the kind of woman Graziana would approve of in the end. Maybe now *was* the right time to see him again?

****

The weekend was well spent relaxing, cleaning up the apartment, and taking time to soak up everything that had been happening—whilst soaking in the bathtub. But like most weekends, it was all over way too soon. Monday morning was bright and crisp, which called for dressing more appropriately for the cold weather that was now starting to turn—the seasons had changed as much as Chloe's life. Making her way into work, much earlier than usual at veronica's request—even before Carmen had arrived with coffee—Chloe started up her computer.

But as she was about to sit down and get stuck into her emails, the black envelope she had forgotten about in the haze of excitement caused by the arrival of Vanguard's December issue, was still waiting to be opened. Turning it over to carefully open the seal, the silver raised lettering on the back made her rip it without care—pulling out a sheet of thick card, printed in matching silver lettering.

MAISON MARAIS

F/W COLLECTION RUNWAY SHOW
PLACE DU TROCADÉRO
PARIS
JANVIER 2nd

It was for real. Jean-Paul wanted her to be a part of Maison Marais' success, and now he wanted her at the fashion show in Paris. And there it was in black and white (well, black and silver), her ticket to see Gianni again. Although there would be a six-month gap since they last saw each other, Chloe hoped that distance really did make the heart grow fonder. And by then, she would have so much more to be proud of, she would be a different woman from the last time he saw her.

"Morning! Good weekend?" Carmen said, walking into the office. "What you got there?"

"Morning—it's an invitation to the Maison Marais show in January," Chloe said, shaking her head in amazement, passing it over for Carmen to see with her own eyes.

"Well, I better be your plus one! That's all I'm saying."

"Carmen, you're the president of this company, if anyone is coming it's you!" Chloe said reassuringly.

"Well, you're not the only one with good news," Carmen said leaning over Chloe's desk, fanning herself with the show invite.

"Oh yeah? Who did you sleep with this weekend?"

"Excuse me… A lady never tells! No, it's much more exciting than any man could ever be, darling… Zoe called—Gabi loves the dress! She wants to try it for a fitting, so you better tell Dom to get sewing that gown, pronto… I'll forward you her measurements."

"Wow, that is great news!" Chloe said, immediately opening an email to Dom and Pandy.

"And that's not the only thing we have to be excited about… Come, we better get to this meeting before we embarrass ourselves by being the last ones there, again."

And for once, this was one meeting Chloe was happy to attend, almost skipping to the boardroom. Over the weekend, Veronica had emailed key departments to attend an early morning meeting, extremely pleased with the campaign shots Derek had worked non-stop on since the shoot.

Taking their seats in the meeting room, along with Derek himself, Bill, Morgana, and the press team, they waited eagerly for Veronica to arrive. "Hey, you two," Derek said, coming over to where Carmen and Chloe were sat. "I think you'll love how the shots turned out," he said, taking out his phone to give them a sneak peek. "This is the one Veronica wants to use in the press release."

Chloe and Carmen leaned in to look at his screen and were amazed at the results. Edited, retouched and rejigged in full colour was Chloe, dressed in her sequin mini-skirt and feather coat—leaning against the sex shop window with its neon lights reflecting in the background. But, instead of 'SEX! SEX! SEX!' Derek had super-imposed a neon sign for 'Raven.' Chloe looked at Carmen with her jaw dropped—she looked like an actual model and she couldn't believe it.

"Good morning everyone," Veronica said, prompting Derek to take his seat and for everyone else to stop chatting. "Thank you all for coming in so early… Today, I want the official press release to go out for the 'Raven' collection… Derek and his team have done a wonderful job on the campaign and I've approved the images to be used across all channels including advertising. The communication will not only detail the release date for the collection, but it will also unveil our plans for the new shop-able site, StacksOfStyle!"

The room erupted in applause, including Chloe and Carmen who clapped the loudest.

"Also, we'll finally reveal that Stacks is exclusively stocking Pandora Simmons London, and detail our investment in the British fashion brand of the future—as well as the upcoming accessories collaboration project… Bill has also been working hard on this project over the past few days, and has secured buying agreements from Bombster, Misty Jones, Aristotle, Creative Corps, and The Glitterati—who will all make small exclusive pieces for the relaunch next year! While all that is exciting, in the meantime we need to finalise all of our assets—ready for the 'Raven, by Chloe Ravens' line to sell, sell, sell!"

Veronica had successfully energised the room to get to work on releasing the press statement and getting everything in motion, ready for the capsule collection release.

Chloe and Carmen had spent all day with the tech team, testing pages, approving site banners and the 'pop-up' page that would override the existing S.O.S website. Knowing that there was no going back, now that the press release had gone out, had made everyone work harder than before on piecing together the final elements.

The bustle of a busy Monday had made it speed along—right up until the end of the day—with more emails than ever dropping into Chloe's inbox. But the attention didn't stop at just emails, waiting for her downstairs in reception was the most elegant, yet over the top, bouquet of flowers. Fifty stems of powder pink roses, surrounded by lily of the valley and unnecessary amounts of foliage, greeted her at the front desk with a simple notecard inserted in the middle.

Congratulations,
G x

Taking in the gentle smell of a sweet rose, Chloe didn't need to think too hard to know who these had come from. Carrying the flowers back up to her desk, craning her neck around the enormous bouquet to make sure of her footing, she placed them in the centre of her desk for all to see.

"Oh, wow! Someone has an admirer," Carmen said, returning from the bathroom. "Something you're not telling me?"

"Nothing you don't know already—they're from Gianni… Well, I'm sure Joli arranged them to be sent over, but still…"

"So he's seen the press release then," Carmen said, reading the notecard.

And that made Chloe think even more about him, he clearly still had his eye on her even though they hadn't been in touch—which was a good thing. Even the ringing from her desk phone didn't jolt her out of thinking about what the future could bring, and how their next meeting might play out. Carmen saved the call, realising that Chloe wasn't going to answer it. "Good afternoon, StacksOfStyle… Oh hi, how are you? Oh right, I see… Well, we didn't think you'd be interested… No, not at all—tell Hilary we sincerely apologise for this oversight and we'd love to accept the offer… I'll put you in touch with our buying team."

Listening to Carmen on the phone (probably accepting more work) had finally brought Chloe's rose-scented daydream to an end. "What's all that about?" she asked, as soon as the phone was placed back down.

"That was Hilary Van Furstein's assistant… Apparently, Gianni isn't the only one to see the press release—and she's pissed!" Carmen said, with a smile.

Chloe wondered why on Earth pissing off the legendary New York fashion designer was a reason to smile about.

"She's pissed that we didn't ask her to be one of our launching designers!" Carmen shrilled. "She said, after everything she had done to support us, she expects us to stock H.V.F as one of the first luxury brands to feature on S.O.S."

Chloe was astounded, securing an account with an esteemed label was not easy. She was surprised that she would even *want* to be sold on their website in the first place.

"Turns out they designed a summer collection for SAKS… Bikinis, tote bags, and wrap dresses—but they didn't take it… So it looks like it ours now," Carmen said, already on her way out to rush over to Bill's desk to tell him the good news.

"I'll get the press team to send an updated version of the statement!" Chloe shouted after her, which Carmen turned back to give her the thumbs up.

Although it was early days, StacksOfStyle had already acquired seven designer brands, as well as a blessing from Gianni. But something told Chloe that even more brands would want to jump on the bandwagon, once they saw the successful launch of the 'Raven' line on DivaFeet. She could just feel it in her bones that the tide was now turning in her favour. Now, people *wanted* to work with her—no more needing to prove herself. People were finally listening and recognising her talents.

21

By the time October had been and gone, Chloe couldn't turn a corner in the city without seeing herself sprawled out on the Times Square steps—in that tight gold dress—with 'Raven, by Chloe Ravens' in electric pink neon script next to it. She only had to open her apartment blinds to see herself staring back, eating a cheeseburger seductively.

And finally, the day had come, the one which felt like it *would* never come, was now here. The collection had been delivered and unpacked in the warehouse, both DivaFeet and the StacksOfStyle homepage were ready to go live with dedicated editorial, campaign images, and banners on every web page. Even a special tab in the navigation bar of DivaFeet.com had been created to land shoppers directly on the collection. The whole team had arrived early to prepare for the launch of 'Raven, by Chloe Ravens,' everyone who had worked on the project had gathered in the boardroom, ready for tech to push the campaign. With champagne ready to be popped and monochrome 'Raven' printed balloons positioned all over the office, today was going to be a very special day in Chloe's career.

"Okay everyone," Veronica commanded. "In exactly *FIVE* minutes, all of your hard work will be finally out there for the public to shop and enjoy, and we will see amazing results—I'm sure of it... Chloe, Carmen—would you like to say a few words before we begin the countdown?"

Dressed and groomed extra smartly, ready for all eyes to be on her for the entire day, Chloe pushed a strand of hair behind her ear, before clearing her throat to make a quick, off-the-cuff speech.

"Thank you... Carmen and I would just like to thank everyone in this amazing team for helping us make our dreams a reality. Just a few months ago, I was working on the shop floor at Palazzo, in what felt like a dead-end job. But it was there that I met Carmen, and since then my life has never been the same... Carmen, you have taught me everything you know and without you, this could never be possible... I know that together we will make milestones that we would never reach alone."

Carmen, fanned herself, feeling tears welling in her eyes at the gratitude and kindness coming from her friend—and now business partner.

"And without you Veronica, without your belief in me, this collection would not have been possible... So thank you!" Chloe continued, causing Veronica to also get emotional.

With nothing else left to say, Chloe started to applaud, whilst Veronica checked her wristwatch and signalled to the tech team— it was time. Stationed nearby to click the 'Live' button, one of the tech guys had set up a laptop—connected to the boardroom's large screen so that everyone could see the homepage. "Okay, everyone..." she said, hushing them by flapping her hands. "Let the countdown begin!"

And in chorus, everyone, including Morgana, Bill, Sam, Lily, and even Derek counted down: *"FIVE, FOUR, THREE, TWO, ONE!"*

Click!

Onscreen, DivaFeet's homepage froze as the refresh wheel spun around in circles. For a moment, Chloe worried that it had crashed the site altogether, but after a few seconds, the screen flashed white—before finally returning. DivaFeet's homepage was now updated with the image of Chloe in front of a neon-signed sex shop—only it was 'Raven' that was for sale!

The tech guy minimised the screen and typed into the address bar of a new browser, immediately bringing up the 'pop-up' over-lay that had taken over the site—now clicking through to DivaFeet. Another round of applause began, resulting in Veronica popping open a bottle of champagne and pouring a glass for everyone in the room.

"Well, kiddos, here we are..." she said, handing Chloe and Carmen a glass. "Here's to making money!"

They both said cheers to that by clinking their glasses together—taking a morning swig of fizz to steady their nerves—now the real truth was about to be told. Veronica demanded the boardroom screen be switched to the internal ordering system so they could watch the orders pour in

It had only been five minutes since the collection had gone live, and no orders had come through yet. Chloe's stomach knotted, if this collection flopped then she could be in trouble. Veronica had pledged serious money behind the new e-commerce S.O.S site with a budget for buying stock, as well as getting behind P.S.L. But Morgana (of all people) cut the tension with a loud, whooping cheer—the first sale had come in; Veronica immediately clicked on the order number to see what had been purchased. It was the collection's 'hero' item from the collection—the knee-high leather boots. Clicking back out onto the main ordering page, two, three, five—ten orders had come in, one after the other.

"We've sold-out of the knee-high boots already!" the tech guy announced.

"*What?*" Chloe shrieked, looking at Carmen, puzzled.

"Quick! List them as 'Coming Soon!' I don't want anything to say: 'Sold Out!'" Veronica commanded.

"I'll put in a re-order right away," Bill said, rushing back to his desk.

"Okay, now the evening purse and sandals are starting to sell through," Morgana said, now on her own laptop, checking out the action for herself.

Chloe whipped out her phone and checked the S.O.S website to see what was left onsite, but she had trouble logging on. "The S.O.S micro-site has crashed!" she yelled, about to have a meltdown. How could her website crash on such an important day?

"Great!" Veronica said, fist punching the air.

"Great?" Chloe said. What was *great* about this situation?

"Honey, that's what we want! That means demand is high and people are logging on bright and early to snap up your designs! And on your website too!" Of course, it was good news. StacksOfStyle was only a little blog that wasn't made to handle hundreds—thousands even—of clicks per minute. Of course, it would inevitably crash. What was more important was that DivaFeet remained stable—that was the true cash cow in this operation. The S.O.S overlay was just a marketing tool.

Some of the team had returned to their desks, ready to get to work from their own stations—working on site traffic and backing up the servers with more power to fall back on. Veronica called the warehouse manager to make sure every order for the 'Raven' collection was prioritised for shipping immediately. Chloe and Carmen also went back to their desks in their glass office, jogging down the office hall to get there real quick.

"Can you believe this is actually happening?"

"No *actually*… I can't!" Chloe said, shocked that pieces were already selling out so fast.

They both remained glued to the DivaFeet website all morning, constantly checking product pages to see if items would add to bag, checking the internal sales system—watching the inventory deplete with every minute—with more and more orders coming through. They clicked through every order to check exactly what had been purchased, with some customers checking out with the complete collection.

Buyers from all over America, Europe—even Australia and Dubai—were logging on to place their orders before they could be disappointed. Some orders contained multiples of the same item, which Veronica instructed Chloe and Carmen to get onto customer care to cancel so that everyone had a fair chance in ordering the pieces they really wanted.

After all, these were clearly placed by scalper's who were only buying the collection to resell for a quick buck, causing *real* fashionistas to lose out. This was turning out to be a crash course in online sales. Addicted, they watched the ordering system refresh with new orders, right up until everything had sold-out (with exception of the gold raven shaped keyring which still had plenty of units left in-stock). Everything else now had '*Coming Soon*' badges where the '*Add To Bag*' function was moments ago so that shoppers who had missed out still felt like there was hope.

"Wow!" Carmen said, exasperated as she opened another bottle of champagne to celebrate. "Veronica will be freaking out! I bet you, even she didn't think it was going to be *this* successful!"

Within moments of everything selling out, Bill had sent an email to the entire 'Raven' team to let them know that Veronica had given him the go-ahead for a complete re-stock on the collection. If Veronica needed proof that she had placed her bets on the right horse, then she now had it in the form of winnings—and she wanted more.

*

The Thanksgiving holiday had given everyone a well-deserved break from the demands of building a new website, planning out future editorials, and stressful product launches. With the S.O.S site now closed down (so that they could focus on producing the e-commerce site), attention was now on dressing Gabi for the Golden Globes—and with no sign of a dress from Pandora yet—things were getting tight.

The final sales reports for the 'Raven' capsule collection had also finally come in (now that the twenty–eight day returns policy had ended for most customers). But it was obvious from how quickly it sold-out, that the 'Raven' capsule had indeed been a success and it was time to move on to the next project—which was set to make even more money. Chloe handed Sam and Lily a swatch of pastel colours and samples of embellishments, simply recreating the existing collection in a new format with a few extra designs added from the DivaFeet archive. A sort of hybrid collection, inspired by the Palazzo and Maison Marais collections she had seen in Paris and Milan.

Meanwhile, across the Atlantic, Dom and Pandora were also working hard on their fall/winter collection. With just a few months to go until Fashion Week, they had started to finalise samples cut from the patterns Jonty had drafted from Pandy's sketches. Heather and JoJo got to work on making them, while Dom and Pandy looked at the shoes and accessories once more.

Keeping it as simple as possible, Pandora designed three bags: an envelope style clutch, a round-shaped handbag with metal chains, and a leather shoulder bag. And using the 'Raven' line designs as templates, they created four shoe designs to piece the collection together.

Together, Dom and Pandy decided to make the popular knee-high boots in their signature leopard print, the gold sandal to be reincarnated with a huge feather on the back that went all the way up to the calf, and the pumps to be made in black patent leather—also in a striking red leather to match Pandy's hair and lipstick. With the 'Raven X P.S.L' collection in the bag, all they needed to do now was to send their designs over to Chloe so she could help get Sam and Lily on the case for production—in time for both the show and for launching the collection.

With Heather and JoJo busy sewing runway samples in the background, Dom and Pandy could now finally get down to making Gabriela's red carpet dress. They had managed to source bolts of feather-light leopard print chiffon from Soho's Broadwick Street that was chic enough for an awards night, but Pandy wanted it to sparkle. Before they could start cutting the pattern pieces, Dom and Pandy stayed up for four nights in a row—stoning every inch of the fabric in ombré Swarovski crystals. Placing each one by hand, the tiny stones had completely ruined their hands, but it would be all worth it in the end.

In the meantime, Jonty redrafted the pattern for the gown to match Pandy's sketch—complete with a mermaid skirt and long train. He even ran up a calico toile to see if Gabi really was that curvaceous and petite. The bustier insert was the one section of the dress that could be made straight away, so Jonty got the black silk pieces cut out, ready to be passed to Heather for boning and stitching.

Pandora, however, wanted to sew the dress herself, ensuring that every seam was perfect and lined properly. That way, she would know that the finished garment would be perfect and fit for Gabi. Under Dom's watchful eye, he helped her stitch the dress on her industrial machine, helping to pass the metres of fabric through the station's worktop. They stopped frequently to pin it on the dress-form and assess their work—ensuring that the fabric was handled very carefully and that there was no need to unpick and stitch again. This was not a job to be rushed, even if they did have plenty of work left to do on the runway collection.

**

"Here you go ladies, congratulations!" Veronica said, passing over a statement to Chloe and Carmen. It was a breakdown of sales for the 'Raven, by Chloe Ravens' collection, which had grossed $195,000. Reading the report, and after deducting production costs (and of course, Veronica's sixty percent), they had pocketed a $50,000 pay-check between them. But they had promised Veronica, that this time profits would go back into producing the next collection, building up their own source of finance to bankroll the project. "Now, I know we're winding down for the Holidays and all, but don't forget we have a lot of work to do… The next 'Raven' collection for one, then we need to produce the samples for the P.S.L show—and for retail—as well as launching Stacks early next year," Veronica listed. "How's the tech-build going?"

"They have everything under control and on schedule… It's just a matter of mirroring the pages already created and used for the 'Raven' capsule and syncing it to the DivaFeet back-end ordering system," Chloe said matter of factly, appearing to be on top of things. "And as for the P.S.L samples, Dom's sent over the designs for the collection which I've passed to our design team to get working on sample production… We can edit the retail collection after the show has happened and we can assess the reaction to it."

"Great! And what about stock for Stacks… How's that all coming along?"

"We have a meeting with Bill this afternoon to catch up on that… Hilary Van Furstein is ready to ship whenever since they've already produced it and we're simply buying it from them… But that leads me on to the next question we'll be faced with when we come back in the New Year," Chloe said.

343

"Oh? And what's that?"

"Well, as you know I've designed the Maison Marais bag for the store re-opening and Jean-Paul has invited us both to Paris Fashion Week... We were wondering if we would be able to use some of the investment for travel budget?"

"And we hope to go to London too... For the Pandora Simmons show—not to mention, visit our American brands to buy their next season too. We have to work ahead on the following season to ensure S.O.S has enough new product offering past the coming summer season... And then there's the small matter of finalising our salaries," Carmen continued.

"I see..." Veronica said, realising that this was going to end up in another payout. "Yes, I suppose you do need to get yourselves out there and start finding new brands. And of course, you have to be at the Maison Marais show... *And* the Pandora Simmons show—to hype up the collaboration project. Just make sure everything is covered while you're gone—you'll need to be on video call every day with the team here... And don't overspend on fancy hotels!"

"Of course... Happy Holidays!" Chloe said with a smile, excited that the coming year would bring the opportunity to travel without the need to be whisked off in style by Gianni Palazzo. She would most likely see him again at the Maison Marais show, all the same—but this time it was by her own success and hard work.

Office life towards the end of the year meant rushing from meeting to meeting, coming up with last-minute solutions for the website, and making sure things were on track with the various teams invested in the project. Leaving Veronica's office, they rushed to meet Bill over in the booth's to put out another fire—before everyone switched off for the Holiday. "Have you seen the results for the collection?" Carmen said, as they walked nearer towards the booth, where he was sat ready and waiting.

"I sure have! I've been checking in on Sam and Lily about the next collection too—some fantastic ideas there... We're also expecting re-stock on the first collection to hit in late January too," Bill said, laying out printed emails in front of him.

"Sounds great… And what's the latest with the relaunch brands?" Chloe said, sitting down to join him, pushing her hair behind her ears to get stuck into this discussion.

"I've received all the ideas back from our chosen brands, which I have right here," he said, sliding through the pieces of paper on the table.

"I love this!" Carmen said, picking up the line drawing for a bomber jacket with a detailed back panel.

"Me too! So, Bombster has designed their signature jacket for us in black velvet, but with 'Raven' on the back in this fantastic, hot pink embroidery… As well as this one, in white with the 'Raven' emblem on the chest," he said, passing Chloe the drawings for that design too.

"Fantastic! I love them… In fact, I have to have one for Paris? You think they can make me one by then?"

"Oh, you're going to Paris Fashion Week?"

"We sure are!" Carmen said, hunching her shoulders excitedly with a grin.

"Jean-Paul's invited us to the show, and since I've designed the Fifth Avenue store re-opening bag, it's sort of a PR thing I guess," Chloe said, looking through the other Bombster designs. "I'm good with all of these here—Can we leave it up to you to decide on units?"

"Sure, I think this will be one of the major brands to launch with, and especially if you wear the jacket to Paris—I'll work on that and get back to you regarding cost… So, Misty Jones have reproduced their signature cat-eye, round and square frames for us, with a special heart-shaped frame with a gold raven on the arm—that's the exclusive style of course."

Bill once again shuffled through his papers to find the styles for approval, before moving on to Aristotle's proposal which consisted of their most-loved basic blouses, T-shirts, jeans and work pants. Creative Corps had created chic and tailored track tops and matching sweatpants in exclusive colours, while The Glitterati provided them with the party-wear. Sequin dresses (inspired by the skirt she wore in the 'Raven' campaign), metallic pleated skirts and a T-shirt with 'Raven' emblazoned on the chest in a silver glitter print.

After discussing their most favourite pieces, and where the bulk of the money should be placed behind, they called an end to the meeting. Carmen had received an email from the mailroom during the meeting and was eager to stop by and see if Gabi's dress had finally arrived. Dom had sent them an email with the tracking and they had waited days for it to arrive—worried that it had gotten lost somewhere. If Gabi was to wear the dress to The Golden Globes, then they had to act quick.

Now working nine-to-five with no free time meant that Carmen couldn't fly out to see Gabi in L.A and personally fit it for her like she usually would. And with time ticking away, she was hoping Gabi hadn't given up and chosen another option already. Everyone wanted to dress Gabriela Gracia and would be chucking dresses at her no doubt, but Carmen was relieved to find a huge cardboard wardrobe box waiting for her in the mailroom with her name scribbled on the side in black Sharpie.

Getting the post guy to help her cart it back to her desk on a trolley, Chloe was also relieved to see that it was most likely to be the elusive dress—only seen in sketch form so far.

"It's here?" she said, rushing over to help them offload it.

"What else can it be?" Carmen said, already scoring the top with a pair of scissors.

Chloe helped her rip open the packing tape, scoring the partition of the hanging wardrobe box, before finally getting a peek at what was inside. A rose-pink garment bag with 'Pandora Simmons London' printed in gold revealed itself, and they both let out a huge puff of relief.

"Thank *fuck* for that!" Carmen said, looking at Chloe while taking it off the plastic bar.

Chloe helped her to carefully pull out the bottom half, before opening the glass office door (the highest point she could find to clip the hanger on to). Standing by with her breath held, Chloe waited for Carmen to unzip the bag, which she did ever so slowly—nervously even. What if the dress was a complete disaster?

Taking the zip all the way down, Carmen looked at Chloe first before peeling the garment bag open, revealing a glimmer of crystal sparkle that reflected off the office tube lights. "Oh my…" Chloe gasped, clasping her hands together as Carmen swept the train out of the bag to see the dress in its entirety.

The dress was stunning, sexy and different—exactly what Gabi liked—and with metres of delicate leopard chiffon that spilt out onto the floor, it was a showstopper! "She's going to *adore* it!" Carmen said softly, inspecting the dress up close. "I've got to get this sent to L.A right away!"

"Do you really think she'll love it?" Chloe asked, knowing that without Carmen being there to convince her, she might not choose to wear it on the red carpet.

"It sucks that I can't fly out to see her… She's been working with this other stylist, Leon Patrick—a complete prick! But if he has any taste…" Carmen said, taking a quick snap of it on her phone, before zipping it back up and placing it inside the box— ready to be sealed up and sent to California.

"Has she mentioned anything about the Oscars?" Chloe said, heading over to her desk drawer to find packing tape.

"She knows I'm busy working on S.O.S, so she hasn't been in touch that much lately," Carmen said, holding the box flaps closed together—waiting for Chloe with the tape.

Chloe could hear she sounded down about losing her high profile client to work with her on StacksOfStyle, but this gig was worth more than dressing a celebrity… And hopefully, in time, it *would* pay off. Ripping strips off the roll with an irritating screeching noise, Chloe made sure the box was well and truly taped, but as she did, she had one of her brainwaves.

"You know, I have an idea… When I was in Paris, Jean-Paul was jealous that we dressed Gabi in Palazzo for the retrospective and he said that he hoped we would dress her in Maison Marais one day… What if that day just so happened to be the Oscars?"

"Well, of course… That would be amazing!" Carmen said, wide-eyed at Chloe's idea to get working with Gabi once more. "But do you think he actually would, or was it all talk?"

"Sure, why not? Gabi is a megastar! Besides, I designed something for him, now he needs to design something for us," Chloe said, sitting back down at her computer, already copying Gabi's measurements into a new email.

"*Yes!* Yes, he *fucking* does! You get to work on that, while I get this baby back down to the mailroom," Carmen said, heaving the dress box back on to the trolley.

***

With the dress off to L.A, the capsule now sold-out and waiting to be restocked—and work on the new S.O.S website underway—the end of the year was speeding along into the Holidays in record timing. Noticing that the office had started thinning out as workers made their way back to their families and friends for the season's celebrations, Chloe began to take down her office decorations and pack up too. There was only so much that could be done with half the workforce in the office anyway.

"Ready to go back home?" Carmen said, still tapping away at her keyboard—wondering where Chloe thought she was going so soon.

"Ready as I'll ever be," Chloe smirked sarcastically, knowing that Carmen wasn't actually asking. She hadn't been back to Boston for Christmas in quite a while, but this was the first one without Dom (whom she usually spent it with)—otherwise, she'd be spending in New York alone. This year, she had a good reason to go home—she had advanced her career and had lots to talk about. And for the first time in years, had bought them wonderful gifts that weren't courtesy of Palazzo's fifty-percent staff discount (which were never truly appreciated anyway). "How about you?" Chloe said, shutting down her computer.

"The usual… An Italian, New York Christmas. Which means I'll be pounds heavier when I see you next."

"Is that a polite way to tell *me* not to eat too much?" Chloe said, giving her a raised eye. Carmen never had an issue when it came down to keeping trim and slender.

"You're welcome to spend it with us if you're thinking of changing your mind… But you have to come to mass at the Catholic church on Christmas morning—that's the rule!"

"*Pur-lease!* So I can combust into flames the moment I step over the threshold? No thank you… I'm actually looking forward to seeing everyone," Chloe said, giving Carmen a hug to end their year of friendship with.

Those would be her famous last words.

****

"Aunt Chloe, Aunt Chloe—what did you bring me?" cried Dylan, the minute her mom opened the door to her on Christmas Eve.

"You're home! I can't believe you're home for the Holidays!" her mom screamed, rushing to the door. "Bob! Chloe's here!"

Already the noise level was way too much—even for a New Yorker!

"Honey! Welcome home, darling," her dad said, coming to greet her at the door; taking Dylan's hand before he ran outside, like a puppy.

"Come in, come in—everyone is here! How have you been?"

"Tired… Glad to be home mom," Chloe said, leaving her New York head at the door—reminding herself to simply enjoy being with her family (although her work laptop weighted her bag, like usual—just in case).

"So, you do remember us!" her older sister said with a hint of sarcasm—or was it jealousy? Brenda was a mother to two boys, Dylan (a hectic three-year-old) and a nine-year-old iPad addict—Michael. The only thing they had in common was blonde, frizzy hair—although Chloe's had been coiffed and tamed while Brenda's was more like a Bob Ross do. "I've just made some seriously strong egg-nog… You look like you could do with some," Brenda said, over a screaming Dylan in the background. He was on a sugar high, having pinched all of grandma's chocolate decorations off the tree.

'Oh right, she's not a bitch; she's just a mother—and drunk,' Chloe reminded herself.

"Haven't we got anything else?" she said, setting her case and bag against the wall in the hallway—not quite wanting to risk a lethal concoction just yet.

"You're just in time for dinner... I've got fish-pie in the oven!" her mom said, darting off to the kitchen to check it wasn't being cremated.

"Come... I've got a hip flask of vodka in my nappy bag—or mom's got wine in the cooler," Brenda said, heading to the kitchen; desperate for a drinking partner.

"Dylan's still wearing nappies?" Chloe said, more shocked at the need to still carry around a nappy bag, than her sister being wasted.

"Chloe... You should see the amount of shit *that* kid produces. Hell yeah, he's still wearing nappies!"

"Wait—I bought champagne!" Chloe said, taking the bottle out of her bag.

"Ooh... If I were you, I woulda drank that on the way here," Brenda said, taking it from her to read the label.

"Where's David?" Chloe said, peeping her head into the living room; watching her dad help Dylan reach one of the highest hung chocolates on the tree—noticing Brenda's husband was missing.

"He's at home with *his* mother! He wanted us to go to *his* parents this year, but there was no way in I was gonna spend Christmas in Oregon with that bitch! Especially after mom said you were coming home... I want to hear all about your glamorous life! Don't think I haven't read what they've been printing about you in those glossy magazines missy... Dad—no more chocolates... Stick Peppa *fucking* Pig on or something," Brenda said, muttering the latter.

"Is everything... Fine?" Chloe said, wondering if her sister's marriage was on the rocks.

"Ugh! You don't get to quiz me, Chloe... This is the one time I get to ask you all the questions while I drink, okay? So, tell me... Are you still screwing that Palazzo daddy?"

Their mom nearly dropped the fish pie on the kitchen floor, luckily managing to save it by sliding the hot ovenware dish back on the wire rack before shutting the oven door for another fifteen minutes.

Chloe shook her head. Wow. Brenda *was* drunk!

"Sure you don't wanna try my egg-nog?"

"Nooo, thank you! I'll stick to a nice glass of white wine," Chloe said, heading to the cooler to select a sauvignon blanc.

"Bren, darling… How about a nice glass of water?" her mom said, already drafting a glass from the kitchen tap. "That's got more liqueur, than anything!"

Popping the cork and fetching a glass from the cabinet, Chloe noted her front-page article from the New York News—the one with her and Gianni—as well as her Vanguard magazine clipping pinned to the cork-board by the fridge. 'So they *have* been following what I've been up to,' Chloe thought with a smile.

"You might wanna get an injunction out on her," Brenda said, tilting her egg-nog towards their mother. "*She's obsessed with you!*" she said, frying her vocal cords.

"I'm just so proud of you!" their mom said, holding Chloe's face. "Alice, from the pharmacy, said she saw you on TV!"

"Alice must be blind, mother! Chloe's been on every billboard in this state for the past two months, selling handbags and hamburgers… In case you haven't noticed that too."

Chloe laughed, if there was one thing she did miss, it was Brenda's blunt humour. Their mother pursed her lips and poured herself a glass of wine. If she was going to put up with this much sass, then she needed to be merry herself at the very least.

"Well, things are going really well for me finally," she said, like she had to defend her choice to leave home and almost cut them off for the most parts of the years she had been in New York. It wasn't her fault she chose to chase a career while Brenda chose to marry and have a family (another subject that was bound to come up over dinner).

"So, are you rich now?" Brenda said, sitting at the kitchen island.

"Comfortable… I'm earning more than what I ever did on the shop floor at Palazzo, that's for sure!"

"Gianni seems like a nice chap!" her mother said, trying to make sweet conversation, nudging towards relationships (and no doubt the question of marriage and kids).

"He's a multi-millionaire… He could be a total bastard and I'd still encourage you to go there! So, what *is* going on here… All we know is what we've read in the gossip columns," Brenda said with a saucy smile, naturally wanting to know all the details.

"Well, we're just friends I guess," Chloe started, before seeing Brenda's forehead rise, as if to say: 'Whatever.' "I mean, he's helped me raise my profile and we've been on a few dates."

"In Milan, Paris… Where next?" Brenda said, tilting her head back to drain the last of her egg-nog, before taking a gulp of water as per mother's suggestion.

"Well, next year I'm going back to Paris and then London for work… And then I'll be back in New York working on the website relaunch," Chloe said, trying not to sound like she was boasting.

"Will you go on more dates with him do you think?" Mom said, also wanting to know more.

"Who cares?" Brenda said. All she wanted to know was if the sex was good; romance was dead for Brenda.

"*Brendaaaa!*" Dad called from the living room. "You better come in here!"

"See, this is what happens when you have kids, Chloe… Go to Paris I say, don't listen to mom… Now, I'm gonna leave you to go clean up chocolate flavoured sick, no doubt—do not reveal anything without me!"

Chloe laughed, sipping her wine as she watching her mother get up and check the oven once again. "You know… It will cook quicker if you leave the door shut, right?" she joked, getting up to take the plates out of the cupboard.

"I just want you to be happy," her mother said, out of the blue.

"I… I am happy, mom," Chloe shrugged, taking out enough cutlery for everyone—jangling it together intentionally to cut the awkwardness out of the air with a sound.

"You just work so hard, and I know you're determined and successful—but life isn't just about work."

"No, apparently it's about husbands that abandon you at Christmas while you clean up a three-year-old's puke—wasted!" Chloe said as if her sister's alternative was something to aspire to. "I'm building a career—a business—and for the first time I'm doing something for me."

"As long as you're happy, I'm fine with it... Seriously!" her mother said, taking a step back from the conversation and taking the fish pie into the dining room—which had been decorated like Santa's grotto.

Something told Chloe that coming home for Christmas was going to be nothing more than dodging bullets about getting married (or finding a man, at least), but dinner had gone much better than she had anticipated. Her father was more interested in the business side of fashion and was impressed with his daughters business mind—crunching the numbers with her at the table. It was like Veronica had suddenly crashed dinner for an impromptu sales meeting.

"*Shit!* You *are* rich!" Brenda said, finding out how much her 'Raven' deal was worth (not to mention the sale of shares to Veronica for StacksOfStyle).

"Shi-yo-rish!" Dylan copied with a cheeky smile.

"Don't say mommy's *special* words... Dad, stop laughing—you're encouraging him," Brenda said, pulling Dylan's chair closer to the table so that the pile of mashed up fish pie already on the floor, didn't grow.

"Not yet I'm not... It's all tied up in investment—which is why I have no time for men!" Chloe said, shooting her mom a loving look, telling her to back off subtly.

"You're still young and when you're rich, you don't need a man Chloe... Just freeze your eggs and do it alone I say... Say, can I help choose the father from the catalogue? I've always wanted to go to L.A... Isn't that where they design the best babies?" Brenda said, getting up from the table as if designing babies and fashion were the same thing.

Chloe just rolled her eyes and helped her mom start to clear the table. After scrapping the plates and loading the dishwasher, Chloe went to shut the backyard door which was sending a chill through the kitchen (her mother had opened it to get the smell of fish out of the house). As she went to close the door, she noticed Brenda, sitting outside on the concrete steps. "Smoking now, are we?" Chloe laughed.

"*Shhh!*"

"Oh, come on! You're not in high school Bren… Mom can't tell you off now."

"You want one?" Brenda said, offering her the packet.

"Na—actually…" Chloe started, before pausing. After being home for less than four hours, she actually *did* want one.

"Here, light it off mine… I don't have a lighter; I used the stove—I don't smoke usually."

"So why now?" Chloe said, taking her half-smoked butt to light hers with.

"Oh, you know… De-stressing without David moaning at me for swearing in front of the kids. Men have it so easy, Chloe… You know, I envy you," Brenda said, taking a long drag.

"Well, according to mom *you're* the one to envy!"

"Don't listen to her… She's just a greedy grandma who wants more—but she's not the one who hasn't slept for nine years!"

"Are things bad at home?" Chloe managed to say, after a moment of awkward silence.

"Not terrible, just—just boring… Whoever tells you married life is bliss, is lying! It's hard work—which is why you should continue to work hard on your own shit… At least you're getting paid at the end of the day!"

Chloe laughed, puffing out smoke into the cold winter air. Sat with her sister, smoking like schoolgirls behind their mother's back, she realised that she wasn't just working hard for herself—she was doing it for them too. When she laid down to sleep at night, it wasn't counting money bags that sent her to sleep. Or imagining all the designer handbags and clothes she would be able to afford to fill her walk-in wardrobe with.

What she dreamt about was a huge house, where all of her family lived a good, healthy life together… Although that was a sheer fantasy—she wasn't crazy enough to *actually* live with them all under one roof! But the sentiment was still the same. She wanted them to know she had made 'it,' because their life was equally as fabulous as hers. Stubbing out her cigarette on the concrete step, Chloe got up and dusted herself down. "Come on… Let me show you how we make cocktails in New York," Chloe said, holding her hand out to haul Brenda up.

Christmas at home wasn't about the glamorous life she was trying to keep up within the city, it was about spending time with her sister and reminding herself of her motivation to work hard. And just or a moment, she wondered if Gianni was spending Christmas with Graziana in Milan and if it was filled with as many a-funny-moment as hers had been so far?

Something told her that it probably wasn't, instead of surrounded by famous faces and fashion industry know-it-alls—who could never replace family. In her head, she wished him a Merry Christmas, as well as wishing that she would indeed see him again in Paris. If a wish was ever going to come true, surely Christmas was the time to ask for it?

22

The rest of the Holidays were spent with family, eating, drinking, arguing and counting down the days until she returned to New York. Thank goodness she had brought her laptop, providing some normality through work (usually after everyone had played with their gifts, stuffed themselves silly, or passed out on hot whiskey). By the time New Year's Eve came around, it wasn't only the new calendar year Chloe was counting down to; she was eager to get back to the office and make all the projects in her mind a reality.

Being back at home for Christmas wasn't all bad though. Brenda had given her little sister an idea—she needed another billboard campaign to capture everyone's attention. If mother and Alice from the pharmacy were keeping tabs on her, then surely the key demographic they were targeting were taking note too? But this time it needed to be more mysterious, instead of flaunting herself so openly.

The house style for the new-look S.O.S site was simply white, with a black sans-serif logo—and Chloe wanted to use that branding to define their image. She wanted magazines to simply feature a white page, with 'StackOfStyle.com, Get Ready For A Clicking!' (which she had already emailed over to Morgana, and received feedback on within twenty–four hours).

Finally returning back to an empty office, on the third day of the new year, Chloe enjoyed the silence by getting on top of her work emails—without meddling Morgana or Veronica demanding updates every hour. Then she had to check out flights to London and Paris, and adequate hotels that Veronica would sign off for Paris and London Fashion Week. In addition, she also received an invite to the Hilary Van Furstein show and to view the collection in the showroom—Chloe's diary was already filling up for the first trimester of the year. But before she could jet off to London, she had to make sure the to-do list was at least in motion. The progress on the build for StacksOfStyle needed to be ramped up, ready for testing.

The marketing campaign for launch day still needed to be discussed, and stock had to arrive at the warehouse in time—and then be processed. With the rest of the office returning to work the following week, Chloe had managed to get caught up and back in the swing of getting up for work (much to the annoyance of everyone else, who were only just starting day one).

"*Happy New Year!*" Carmen declared, sauntering into the office—looking more tired than refreshed and renewed.

"You too!" Chloe said, getting up from her desk to give her a hug. "How was your time off?"

"Great, we had a lot of fun! How was yours, more important-ly?"

"Yeah… Nice, if hanging out with two kids, a drunk sister, and a nosey mother is your thing… No—it was great actually. But I won't lie, there were times I was biting my nails to get back to New York."

"Is *this* your first day back?" Carmen said, already draining a coffee, noticing that she was rather laid back for her first day back at school.

"No, I came back last week… Just to catch up on stuff and get things planned. Oh, I submitted travel for London and Paris—check your email when you have a minute."

"Wow! You really are a ball-breaker, you know that? I've only just got through the door—can I take my coat off at least?" Carmen laughed, although she really meant it.

"We actually have a *shit* tonne of work to do!" Chloe snapped back.

'Here she goes again,' Carmen thought, Chloe was back to her usual-uptight-self. Worrying about *all* the work they had to complete, rather than enjoying building a business together. "And whenever have we *not* got shit done? We are the 'get shit done crew,' remember?"

"I know, but I'm freaking out—stock will start delivering to the warehouse next month and we have no site to sell it on."

"Yet!" Carmen said, finally logging onto her computer. "Tech will have something to show us for testing in the coming weeks... Anyway, you *are* coming to mine to watch the Golden Globes tonight?"

"Oh my God," Chloe said, completely forgetting that tonight was an important night, and for Dom and Pandy too. "Of course... Did she receive the dress? Have you heard from Gray and Zoe? Do you think she's gonna wear the dress?"

Carmen gave her an eye as if to say: 'Calm down, bitch—it's too early.'

"Stop stressing... Gabi has the dress, but I haven't heard from them yet—I've already emailed Dom to let him know that it's out of our hands right now. I guess, the only way we'll find out, is to watch it! Now, my turn—have *you* heard anything from Jean-Paul about the Oscars?"

'*Fuck!*' Chloe winced, jotting down yet another task she needed to chase up.

"Well, get hold of Claudette—today!" Carmen said, seeing the answer on Chloe's panicked face.

"On it!" Chloe said, grabbing her phone and heading out of the office to make the call. Claudette's phone, however, just kept ringing and going to voicemail (which was en Français), and with no solid confirmation that Maison Marais *would* dress Gabi for the Oscars, all they could do was keep on working through their workload—and pray that Gabi wore Pandora's leopard fantasy to The Golden Globes!

*

It seemed that Leon Patrick did have taste, after all. Gabi did sparkle in leopard on the red carpet of The Golden Globes and had proudly flaunted that it was made by Pandora Simmons. The next day, her picture was splashed across tabloids, gossip columns, and had even made the news as she accepted the award for Best

Performance by an Actress in a Motion Picture, for her film: 'Beat The Odds.' And now she was tipped to win an Oscar for her debut role as a poverty-stricken dancer from Brooklyn-turned Broadway star. Even the soundtrack featured her own songs—also receiving a nomination. And with one gong safely under Gabi's belt, Chloe eventually received a reply from Claudette.

Maison Marais had agreed to dress Gabi for the Oscar's and was flying one of their designers out to L.A with options for her to choose from and have fitted in time. Veronica was equally as thrilled with Gabi's win, the world now knew Pandora Simmons' name, and soon the label would be available to buy on S.O.S, which she hoped would result in sales. It was also a win for Chloe and Carmen; it also meant Veronica's confidence in them had grown even more—happily sending them off to Fashion Week with a generous budget to grow the business.

New York Fashion Week had made the already busy city, busier—and the same could be said for Chloe and Carmen's schedule. But this season was going to be different—exciting even. Since they had announced their retail plans for S.O.S, they had been swamped with show invites from well-known designers, such as Hilary Van Furstein—one of New York's most globally successful designers, and Lisa Lennard—nineties girl-group member, now turned fashionista.

Although this time around, all the fun parties and late nights out had to be reigned in. This time they had to be up early and out for showroom appointments at potential brands to stock on-site—making a good first impression. And turning up late, with a hangover, was not how they wanted to represent StacksOfStyle.

With the news that they were launching their own website, even smaller brands were throwing themselves at them—desperate to be added to their list of designers. But with no revenue coming in from the new website just yet, Chloe and Carmen had to be savvy and take this chance to build brand relationships first, rather than promise huge orders and buying agreements. They had responsibilities with the up-and-coming designers they had already agreed to take on, not to mention a Hilary Van Furstein capsule, which had been their largest expense—but also their most illustrious signing so far. "What's next?" Carmen said, climbing back into their car after they met with Misty Jones and Creative Corps, downtown in Manhattan.

"Next stop is Bombster," Chloe said, loud enough so that the driver could hear where to take them to next.

This year, Bombster's temporary showroom was located under a converted railway arch in Brooklyn. To get there, they passed over Williamsburg Bridge, which filled Chloe with nostalgia. This was her neighbourhood not so long ago, and it was also where StacksOfStyle had been born. Since then, both her life and the website had upgraded somewhat, but this part of town still felt like home—she knew it too well to feel a stranger.

Even though Bombster was a small label, they had made waves on the celebrity scene with their handmade remakes of classic varsity and baseball jackets—embroidered with clever slogans and crystal-encrusted details. Walking into the white-painted brick-walled showroom, Chloe and Carmen were immediately greeted by the designer herself, Melba Lowry.

Melba was in her twenties with beautiful brown hair that complemented her youthful, glowing skin, and wearing one of her own baseball jackets with ripped blue jeans and sneakers. "Chloe?" she said, approaching her with a handshake.

"Yes, hi… This is Carmen," Chloe said, taking Melba's hand and going in for an air kiss.

"I've been dying to meet you guys," Melba said. "I can't thank you enough for having Bombster on site—I'm so excited."

"And so are we," Carmen said, looking at the models who were walking around, pausing in front of anyone who seemed remotely interested in what they were wearing. A tall black girl with an afro stood in front of her, wearing a red sequinned bomber with a black and gold lurex ribbed trim.

"Please, come this way… I have the samples for the launch collection ready for you," Melba said, walking them over to a rail at the back. "These are all the designs that you guys approved and are currently in production—obviously they have been made by hand, so not indicative of the final product," she said, excusing the rushed quality.

Chloe and Carmen were excited to see the designs made into reality, trying them on and taking snaps on their phones to show Bill back at the office. Chloe instantly went for the black style that had 'Raven' crystallised on the back. "So, when can we get delivery?" she said, keeping the jacket on and snapping the back of it in the mirror.

"End of February, I'd say… Unless you want to make changes, then I'd have to speak to the factory and implement those, which will set us back."

"All looks great to me," Carmen added, as she tried on a white jacket with a gold raven motif on the front—not wanting to hold up production unnecessarily.

"Oh, that reminds me… Bill mentioned you wanted to wear this jacket at London Fashion Week? By all means, take the sample with you," Melba said, watching Chloe admire it. "And this one looks great on you Carmen… You should wear it right away too."

"Now, that's an idea… I don't suppose you could personalise it with my name on the back as well?"

"Of course, leave it with me and I'll have it done and sent over to you by the end of the week," Melba said, knowing that this was her busiest week of the year—but it was nothing that her interns couldn't handle.

"Great! Let's take a look at the new collection shall we?" Carmen said, moving on to the other rails lined around the edge of the room. They noted down the style and fabric numbers of all the designs that had caught their eye—along with their cost price—ready to crunch numbers with Bill back in the office.

"I'll need the order finalised by the end of the week… Of course, I can extend it by a few days for you, but we'll need to make sure we have enough fabric in stock to make your order," Melba said, showing them out, now that they were ready to leave for their next appointment.

"Got it," Chloe said, carrying her bomber jacket in a white paper bag. "We'll be in touch very soon!"

"Love the collection, darling," Carmen said, kissing her good-bye.

The next stop was back over the bridge at Aristotle's, where the same conversation and meeting would pretty much happen—viewing the samples of their launch collection and ensuring they had enough stock on order, ready for the fall season. The following day went by quickly, visiting The Glitterati, as well as a few other new brands that had invited them to walk through their collections.

But the main event of New York Fashion Week was, of course, Hilary's show at Pier 57—where she notoriously always showed. Although Chloe and Carmen were pleased to be going as guests this time, not involved with styling and curating the show like last season. And by gosh, did they swerve a bullet! This year, Hilary had the place flooded deep with autumn tone leaves and fake trees—transporting them to Central Park. "It would have been cheaper to just have shown in the *actual* park!" Chloe muttered, sat in her front-row seat dressed in one of Hilary's classic wrap dresses, paired with her very own black leather 'Raven' boots.

"Hilary gets what Hilary wants, remember?" Carmen managed to say before the music and lights went down, signalling the start of the show.

Fleetwood Mac begun to play as the first model walked out, dressed in a denim Western shirt and matching flared jeans with a woven leather band across her forehead. The Seventies and the Canadian tuxedo were back in fashion it seemed. Khaki green wrap dresses in both short and longer lengths were also included, as well as trench coats and knee-high boots—which Chloe could have sworn Hilary had lifted from her line—but then again, it was quite the compliment. Their showroom appointment wasn't until they got back from Paris, so instead of attending some vapid Fashion Week party after the show, they fought the crowd of fashionistas outside photographing themselves to get back to the car—and back to the office.

"All set for London?" Veronica said, passing their office at the end of the day.

"Getting there," Chloe said, looking up from her computer.

"Glad to see you're working late and not getting drunk at some party," Veronica said, happy that they were taking this business seriously. "Anyway, I'm out of here to do exactly just that with Karen! See you when you're back from Paris? Au revoir!"

Which reminded her—she was yet to pack for the trip. Sure, it was annoying but it wouldn't be such a chore; she was finally getting to travel to Europe for work and the possibility of seeing Gianni again was growing nearer and nearer. But all the romance of what *could* happen in Paris had been quickly squashed by the need to get as much work done before they left. Especially as the samples for the Pandora Simmons show, which had been rush manufactured, still needed to get sent over to London.

In-person, the P.S.L designs looked daring, electric, and different to anything she had seen lately, giving Chloe another reason to start packing when she got home—she couldn't wait to see them coming down the runway in London.

**

"I say we cut this look and replace it with the sheepskin coat," Dom said, watching a model walk down the centre of their East London studio.

With the show looming, a run-through was underway—although this time things had been more considered and planned. Which was wise, as they had to make this collection as much of a success as the last—even more so. The backing of an investor (not to mention the press from Gabriela Gracia at The Golden Globes) now came with a higher expectation on Pandora Simmons London. And while Veronica's investment plan had helped make things easier for them to focus on creating, it didn't alleviate Pandy's 'artistic' paranoia. All week she second-guessed the entire collection and with the spring/summer collection now starting to hit the stores, Pandora felt the pressure to perform.

As well as helping her to nail the fall/winter collection, Dom also had to ensure their suppliers were delivering the spring collection on time; he was the one that needed to freak out—not her. But Dom had learnt the cycle of Pandora's creative ways, and knowing he would have to hold her hand along the way, he hired two interns to help him—allowing him to focus his attention on Pandy. He too had a reputation to keep up with now, and he couldn't allow himself to be spread thinly; making sure Pandy kept it together to deliver a great collection was his top priority. Much like last time, all-night shifts were spent perfecting the fit, the order of looks, and the styling of the show—which was so important now that the label had the industry's attention.

Financial backing also meant that for the first time, Pandora could afford to put on an independent show and headline the London Fashion Week calendar under her own name—and this show was going to be a theatrical production! Dom and Pandy had drafted in another ex-collegiate (a set designer who was well experienced in fashion show spectacles and had worked with some of 'the greats') to ensure that the clothes weren't the only thing people would be talking about.

And soon enough, they would find out if they had done enough to be the talk of Fashion Week once again—because the evening of the show had quickly arrived. Chloe and Carmen had landed in London with just enough time to check into their hotel in Shoreditch, get ready, and then head straight back out for the show—due to start at eight p.m. "Do you know exactly where we're going?" Carmen said, fussing over her black leather dress (which Dom had sent over for her to wear) as they made their way down to the foyer—shrugging her personalised bomber jacket over her shoulders at the same time.

"It's cool... We're not late and we're not too far from the location—I think," Chloe said, checking the show invite which was a folded up piece of notebook paper, sealed with Pandy's very own lipstick mark—like a love letter.

Not entirely sure herself, she typed the address into Uber. Typically, there were no drivers available to pick them up, and the surcharge was enormously high for the ten-minute-max drive to the location.

"Hi, can you please help us get a car to take us here," Chloe said, sticking the invitation under the nose of the woman behind the front desk.

"Madam, you *do* realise The Archway is just around the corner?" the receptionist said, irked by Chloe's 'American' brashness.

"And Madam, you *do* realise I will have trouble simply walking down the steps of your entrance in these heels, and in *this* tight dress?" Carmen snorted.

Chloe looked down at her own feet, she too wouldn't last long walking in her black heels, and her outfit wasn't fit for walking the streets of East London either. Dom had also sent a dress over to the Ace hotel for her to wear (a purple and green tartan version of the zero–one–five). She had also dressed down her look with the personalised 'Raven' satin bomber, draped around her shoulders.

"I'll see if I can call a car for you," the receptionist relented with a bitchy grin.

"Come on… Let's grab a glass of champagne while we wait," Chloe said, strutting towards the bar next to the hotel's lobby.

Stood at the bar, downing (rather than sipping) their drinks, Chloe kept watch in case the receptionist signalled that their driver had arrived—but there was no sign of a car waiting outside for them.

"*Fuck*," Chloe blurted, checking the time on her phone. "Come on, we're gonna have to walk."

"*What?* No…" Carmen started, but before she could finish, Chloe was already heading down the entrance steps onto the street.

"Have a wonderful evening ladies!" the receptionist said, delighted to be proving them right. However, it turned out that she *was* right—walking was indeed quicker than waiting for a car (even in towering heels).

The Archway was neatly tucked under a railway bridge, a hole in the wall that could be easily missed—but not tonight. Black velvet ropes lined the narrow pavement—forcing people to walk out into the road. The entrance was flanked by two heavy-set security guards to stop non-invited hopefuls from entering, while the interns checked for invites and names against the official guest-list. Once past the security checks, Chloe and Carmen walked into a 1940s train station ticket hall, clad in original tiles and exposed brick walls, with shots of tequila being poured out in place of edible pre-show canapés.

But behind the scenes was where the real action of any fashion show happened, and this one was no different. "Why isn't she *fucking* dressed yet?" Pandy shouted, pointing to a model, still walking about topless, in panties.

Pandy's temper wasn't the only thing that was hotting up; the atmosphere was sweltering with hairstylists blowing and teasing hair into huge beehive nests, while make-up artists tried to keep make-up matte and slip-free from the rising heat. "Calm down will you?" Dom shouted back, pulling in a dress—safety pinning it with large kilt pins to secure it at the back.

"Is Carly here yet?" Pandy said, pushing her way through the crowd of backstage crew and models that were dressed and ready, just to reach him. "It should be more like this!" Taking charge, she re-pinned the dress so that the hem appeared raised on one side before her phone buzzed again in her bra. "Carly? Where the *fuck* are you?"

"I'm nearly there, I'm nearly there—I'm fifteen minutes away!" Carly shouted back, stuck in traffic on the Old Street roundabout.

"You!" Pandy shouted, calling over to the model still walking around in next-to-nothing as she ate a chocolate-dipped strawberry. "Finish your dinner and get dressed into look one—*Now!*"

"But that's Carly's look!" Dom said, rubbing his face with failure at keeping her calm.

"Not now it ain't… Carly's *fucking* cancelled!"

The model she had just pinned up to the hilt smirked with glee at overhearing that the latest sensation, Carly Wattmore, had been fired on the spot in front of everyone. Since launching her career at London Fashion Week last, not only had she walked for Palazzo and Maison Marais, but she had also developed an ego and a persona on the party circuit—which was even too big for the designer that had discovered her it seemed.

"Right… I'm ready to go as soon as she is," Pandy said, knocking back her fourth shot of tequila, referring to Carly's replacement.

And it was about time. Outside the guests had been sat in their seats for at least thirty minutes. Reclaimed church pews were covered in webs of ivy, lining the length of a slippery black latex-like runway, smothered in a veil of dry ice—flanked with white pillar candles all the way down the catwalk. It was like a scene straight out of 'Phantom Of The Opera,' Chloe thought.

"Wow, this looks—"

"Like a fire hazard?" Carmen said, raising an eyebrow—finishing Chloe's sentence.

"I was gonna say… *Expensive.*"

"Well, it's a good job Veronica's not here… She'd be counting her cash and supplying them with an invoice afterwards."

Naturally, their seats were in the front row, right at the top end of the runway, opposite Lou Banks—Chloe gave him a wave from across the black lake chasm between them. As usual, the editor of British Vanguard was sat next to him with Naomi on his other side, who looked rather peeved at having to wait for the show to start. But the rigged lights hanging above their heads suddenly snapped to black—causing the audience to cheer with relief. And out of nowhere, two massive flame cannons blasted out shards of fire at the top of the runway, underneath a large train station clock which now said nine p.m—a whole hour after the show was due to start!

"*Fucking hell!*" Chloe flustered, checking her eyebrows were intact—hoping there were no lip-readers in the house.

Luckily, the harsh beats of electronica covered up her swearing, as the flames settled down with the piercing synths of the music (if they fired on for any longer, then they would have turned the hanging clock above into a melting Dali-esque sculpture). With the audience's attention now fully captured, a heady kick-drum beat took over and the first model stepped out wearing a purple tartan frock-coat, plumped out with tulle petticoat layers underneath (the same fabric as Chloe's dress).

Peacock feathers sprouted from the model's oversized, back-combed beehive as she sauntered down the runway with smudged red lipstick (an avant-garde portrayal of Pandora's signature lip colour). Carly's last-minute replacement relished in owning the opening number, with one hand in her pocket and the other swinging a ball-shaped leather handbag, sporting a menacing look as the audience watched—fixated on her dramatic entrance.

The looks grew darker and darker as the models passed each other, up and down the runway. Horns, feathers, models carrying ram skulls in place of handbags, all appeared down the catwalk as the show romped on and the music changed into a fast electronic remix. Backstage, Jonty helped models change into their second look with Heather and JoJo making stylistic adjustments, before heading back in line to make their exit once more—this time in edgy evening wear.

"Pandy… I'm here! I'm so sorry!" huffed Carly, over the loud holler of backstage madness.

Pandora and Dom were styling and dressing the model in the final dress, which Pandora finished before addressing her. "You're too late! We've started without ya love!"

"Pandy, I'm sorry—I was stuck."

"I don't care! You will never walk for me ever again, you hear? You're fired!"

Pandora returned to the line of models waiting to walk, like planes waiting for taking off down the runway, leaving Carly to stomp out of the venue (probably to head back into town for a drinking session). The air backstage had turned frosty and staunch, but Pandora wasn't going to be pushed over by some 'sensation' that she had propelled into stardom. Back on the runway, the final looks of the show were a constant stream of models in variations of the zero–one–five dress: long, short, sleeved, halter-neck, tartan, lurex, latex, and leather. The very last dress, however, was a statement piece to symbolise the entire show.

A captivating ball gown made from sheets of silver that tiered down to the floor in layers, with a cast-metal breast plated top half. In place of a handbag, the model carried a sword and a shield, embossed with 'Pandora Simmons London' around the edges and with Pandy's profile engraved in the centre—like Boudicca. Dry iced swept the catwalk once more—slowly making the final model disappear as she walked off—ready for the rest of them to pour out in succession. Dressed in key looks from the show, the models walked the length of the catwalk once more to thundering applause.

"Get out there!" Dom urged, dragging Pandy to the edge of the runway as the last model was about to return in her armoured dress.

Pandora quickly blotted her face with a hand towel—held out by one of the make-up artists—and tucked her denim shirt into the waist of her black leather skirt, before heading out onto the runway in her clompy platform heels. She briskly walked halfway down the catwalk, put her hands to together in thanks and took a quick bow, before turning and jogging back up the runway to escape the attention.

The house lights returned in a full flash, much to the shock of the audience, while the production crew quickly snuffed out all of the candles before someone could get burnt, or worse—the place burnt down altogether! "*Wow!* What a show!" Chloe said, looking at Carmen; bewildered by what she had just witnessed.

Carmen was completely blown away—speechless. "I... I need a moment to process."

"Chloe, darling!" Lou shouted, making his way through the burnt-out candles which were now melted to the floor in pools of wax.

"Lou! So nice to see you again!" she greeted, air-kissing him. "This is Carmen, the president of StacksOfStyle."

Carmen took his hand and leant in for a similar air kiss.

"We missed you at the Maison Marais show last season," Lou said, holding his hand up to acknowledge Vanguard's editor, who was now leaving with Naomi.

"I know... Work came up, I had to fly back to New York, but we'll see you this time around!" Chloe said, not wanting to get into the real reason why she was exiled.

"I can't wait!" Lou said, holding Chloe's hands. "I heard all about your new website! Genius idea—loved the capsule collection by the way!"

He had lied, he hadn't seen a single piece from the 'Raven' collection, but he had heard of its sell-out success in the media and more the to point, the announcement that P.S.L were to sell and collaborate with her on an accessories line. "What did you think of the show?" he said. "Any idea on what you'll be buying for next season?"

"We absolutely loved it!" Chloe said, feeling her phone vibrate in her bomber jacket pocket.

"I never expected such a dramatic show," Carmen added, giving Chloe the chance to check her phone without seeming rude.

The missed call was from Dom.

"Listen, are you coming backstage to see the guys?" Chloe said, her phone ringing once more—this time she had to accept it. "Excuse me—Dom? Yes... We're still here... Okay, two minutes... We're coming now with Lou."

Heading behind the set design, still smoking from the snuffed out candles, into the tight backstage area (that was now a mini after-party with champagne flowing), they were greeted with photographers taking pictures of Pandora taking pictures with some of her models.

"Chloe!" Dom called out, with champagne in hand. "You made it!"

"Of course we made it... We work together now, remember?" Chloe said, giving him a heartfelt hug and a kiss on the cheek.

"Congratulations, darling," Carmen said, taking her turn to kiss him.

"We meet again young man," Lou said, leaning in after Carmen.

"Lou, I can't thank you enough for the kind words you wrote about our last show."

"And I can't wait to write more words of praise for this collection," he chuckled with a jolly smile. "Where's Pandora? I'd love to have a few words with you all since you're in partnership now."

"Of course, let me get her," Dom said, squeezing past models, make-up artists, and hangers-on to reach her before she got too smashed. She had already enjoyed copious amounts of champagne on top of knocks of tequila she had sunk to suppress her nerves.

"Love your jackets ladies," Lou said, noticing they had their names on the backs.

"These ol' things?" Chloe joked, giving him another flash of the back. "These are from Bombster, both jackets will be available to buy on StacksOfStyle later this year."

Lou took out his phone, ready to record the latest fashion news to include in his write-up. "And what else can we expect for the launch?"

"We have a selection of designers, all creating exclusive pieces for us—including Hilary Van Furstein," Carmen added, stepping up to her role of president.

"Wow! What a fantastic label to have on board… Who else can we expect?"

"Well, we want to keep some things a surprise, but we hope to discover more brands to welcome onsite during Fashion Week," Carmen said, aware that he was recording.

"Guys!" Pandy yelled, chucking her arms in the air and shutting her eyes in euphoria. Dom was right, she was smashed, but happily smashed; she was ecstatic that the show had gone well, despite Carly Wattmore not appearing.

"Pandora, darling… The collection was divine, this show is a sign that London still has talent… But tell me about your venture with StacksOfStyle," Lou said, holding his phone out to capture her voice over the background din—although, he didn't need to. Pandy's voice could be heard from a mile off—especially when drunk.

"Well, these girls have become really good friends and I can't thank them enough for their support and belief in me… All the shoes and accessories in this collection have been made with their help, and later this year, they'll be available to buy online from StacksOfStyle," Pandy said, rather concisely—considering she had put a few drinks away.

And that was a good point... They were so distracted by the scale of the show and the theatrical presentation, that Chloe and Carmen didn't even notice the shoes they had helped them to produce (and the fact the dry-ice masked them somewhat).

"As well as stocking the ready-to-wear online for the U.S market, we'll also be the first to launch the P.S.L footwear and accessories collection, in collaboration with our 'Raven' line," Chloe quickly added, remembering she was here to do some plugging ahead of all these projects actually releasing into the wild.

"And will you also be making an appearance at the Palazzo show next week?" Lou said, with his cheeky smile.

Chloe knew exactly what he was alluding to; it seemed no matter how hard she tried, her dalliance with Gianni would never go away. No matter how hard she worked, it seemed she would always be known as 'Gianni's girl.'

"We're gonna stay here in London; we have business to discuss with Dom and Pandora, and also select our order for the collection... But, as I said earlier, you will indeed see us at the Maison Marais show in Paris—where I expect to see Gianni *and* Jean-Paul," Chloe said with a smirk, knowing that she had to keep the speculation alive to remain relevant in high-fashion circles.

While the rest of the fashion industry moved on to Milan to see what the Italians had up their sleeves, Chloe and Carmen stayed put in London with Pandy and Dom. Instead of watching shows and drinking Italian coffee and wine, they set up temporary desks at the studio to catch up with the team back in New York to make sure projects were moving along nicely without them in the office.

And while Gianni did cross Chloe's mind, knowing that this time last Fashion Week she was by his side (and in his bed), Gianni had more important things on his mind... Although they were somewhat influenced by her.

Even though the Palazzo show was only a few days away, Gianni had other important business matters to attend to first. Chloe's recent online success, selling her Palazzo wardrobe for charity and gathering designers to launch her very own site after a successful capsule collection, had not escaped his attention. In fact, it made him question his own online business, and Graziana knew just the person who could help them turn it around.

"Tell me, Don... How can we better the Palazzo e-commerce operation?" Gianni said, sipping a lunchtime whiskey in his Milan office.

"Well, online businesses need a lot of attention—a lot of expertise in tech and logistics... Not to mention global warehouses and excellent customer service teams—but this is what MiBellaModa does best. Currently we have our own team running the website and shipping orders, but we outsource most of the tech side, which can be an expense," Graziana cut in. "But we know we can do more, sell more, and that's why we have come to you."

"And that's exactly where I can help... I can take all of those over-heads away, while you focus on simply designing fabulous fashion."

The online luxury giant, MiBellaModa.com, was founded and owned by fellow Italian, Don Carlo. He was fashion's 'super-geek' who had created a website for designers to off-load their past collections—whilst still offering a 'luxury' service. He had also quite cleverly sold warehouse space around the globe direct to labels, servicing their very own websites and looking after the logistics and customer service for them—and now he wanted one of Italy's most famous luxury exports under his control.

"You will still have input over the front-end of the website—creating homepage articles and promotions—while my team will look after everything else… From the ordering process, down to delivery—even after-sales," Don continued, his beady eyes magnified through his black round-frame spectacles. "Just think, you won't even need your distribution centres to hold inventory for the website any longer—freeing up space… Those workers can focus on handling your own boutique's stock, and shipping to the many distributors you have globally. Not only will you save money, but you will be saving manpower *and* have a luxury e-commerce platform to match your magnificent in-store experience. Online is the way forward, Gianni—everyone knows that. Don't be one of the brands that get left behind… There is big money to be made in this game, if you know the rules—luckily for you—I'm an expert."

And Gianni did know that online was big business. He and Graziana knew how much old stock they shifted onto M.B.M each season, and if anyone could make Palazzo's online business model work, it was Don Carlo. Gianni swigged back the last of the whiskey in his cut-crystal short glass, clinking the ice against his teeth and wiping his lips after. Don's offer was attractive, especially now he had even more overheads to think of with Maison Marais—and they too would need an online platform that was cost-effective and 'with the times.' "Okay… Well, let's do this—let's come up with a plan and get this going as soon as possible… Then we'll discuss Maison Marais' online store if all goes well with migrating Palazzo onto your platform."

"*Fantastic!* It has long been my dream of mine to work with this prestigious Italian fashion house," Don said, clapping his hands together, leaping out of his chair to hold his hand out to shake on it. "It will be a pleasure to work together."

"Great! Well, I trust you and Graziana will take care of the particulars and get the ball rolling," Gianni said, getting up to shake his hand. "Say, have you heard of Chloe Ravens, Don?"

"Your *friend* from New York?"

"Yes, she's a *friend*," Gianni laughed under his breath. He too couldn't shake off his association with her. "You should check her out, she's doing very well with her online collection and now she's launching a new multi-brand website."

"*Ha!* I mean, it's more of a blog really… Everyone's a fashion blogger these days," Graziana scowled as she stood up. She was the same height as Don Carlo—in heels—and he also spoke the same language her in business. If you didn't prove yourself in terms of financial gain, then you were nothing to him.

"I wish her every success, but when it comes to online luxury fashion, she will be *no* competitor to MiBellaModa… Welcome to the family, Gianni."

*

Once again, the Palazzo show had been the highlight of Milan Fashion Week, and Graziana did her part—playing up to the press. Making her entrance wearing a low-cut, black leather catsuit with gold zippers down the side and a series of gold buckled belts, wrapped around her tiny waist—complete with a gold choker that spelt out '*P-A-L-A-Z-Z-O.*'

As usual, the show was held at the Palazzo showroom, this time with a black 'wet-look,' mirrored runway and gold confetti raining down—simulating the change of season. The first section of the show started off rather softly, continuing on from their dreamy pastel summer collection with a palette of creams and beiges, browns and khakis. As the models trickled down the slick runway, the looks turned darker with black leather ensembles and gold-tone accessories—finished off with a series of slippery black and luxuriously gold chainmail fabric evening gowns.

But it was the short black leather dress, modelled by Carly Wattmore, which was the most iconic look from the entire collection. Similar to Graziana's catsuit, it was low-cut and quite raunchy, worn with a 'bondage-style' biker cap adorned with '*P-A-L-A-Z-Z-O*' in gold letters. She quite literally dominated the catwalk, swishing a black leather whip with a gold handle, and towering black spike-heeled boots—strapped up with gold belt buckles around her ankles.

This time, Carly had learnt her lesson and turned up professionally on time and sober—although she wouldn't dare anger

Gianni and Graziana—her self-righteous attitude remained. She knew she would be the face of Fashion Week yet again, she didn't need Pandora Simmons to keep that title. Carly had walked for every major designer in Milan this season and now she was set to do the same in Paris.

Gianni had flown her to Paris in his private jet along with Graziana onboard, which had been captured by the press as they made their way to Charle de Gaulle airport from Milan. Carly was booked to walk for the Maison Marais show, and Gianni was of course here to view the collection in support of Jean-Paul. At least, that's what he told himself. He knew that Jean-Paul had taken a liking to Chloe and had invited her to the show; was he only going to Paris to see her again, or was it simply a business affair? Either way, Carly's company was just a distraction from the stresses of work, even if Graziana *did* like her over Chloe. Being seen with Carly only boosted his profile in the media, keeping him fresh and on-trend in an industry that was so easy to become irrelevant.

Even though Gianni looked great for a man in his forties, he was constantly surrounded by young, beautiful women—but that wasn't enough for Graziana. The woman who would get to settle down with her brother had to match his status, and Carly didn't depend on him to build herself a reputation—she had already made a name on her own.

Place du Trocadéro had been under construction all week, with an army of construction workers building the set for the Maison Marais show. Bleacher stands had been erected for the who's-who of fashion to watch the show from the sidelines of the square-shaped marbled floor space—the famous Eiffel Tower centre-frame in the background. Pandora wasn't the only designer this season intending to be remembered, although her show couldn't quite compete with the Eiffel Tower.

And as for Jean-Paul, there was no competition. With his spring/summer collection being snapped up by fashionistas wanting to be dressed in the latest 'it' brand, he was hoping to keep the momentum going by consciously designing a collection that was pretty much the same as the first. He was perfecting the new brand image of Maison Marais and drilling it into editors and buyers that this was the style that Maison Marais would now be known for: gaunt models with pale skin, wearing designs that could have quite easily been rescued from thrift stores.

That was in fact how he sought inspiration for his collections: scouring vintage stores and markets for original pieces to pick apart and remake with a more contemporary edge, using luxurious fabrics. The eighties had been decadent enough the first time around, but now they were luxurious and chic—redrafted with his know-how in tailoring and dress-making. His silhouette was slim and cigarette-like, clients had even complained that the spring/summer collection was cut too small (having to go several sizes up to be able to squeeze into them)—no vanity sizing here.

But that was the power of having Jean-Paul design for Maison Marais, his loyal followers wanted to wear his clothes that much, that they were prepared to go from a size zero to a size six. They would simply cut out the label to save themselves from embarrassment—some would even re-stitch a label in with a smaller size. And that was exactly why Gianni had installed him as creative director for the French fashion house.

Chloe and Carmen had left London on the day of the Maison Marais show, setting off from Kings Cross on the Eurostar to check into their hotel, nearby to the Louvre. They had the day to check-in and head out to a few showrooms to meets brands and check out their collections, before getting ready for the show in the evening. Chloe had brought her Maison Marais polka dot dress with her, along with her bag to finally wear at the show. Even though it was from the current collection, at least she would be able to wear it in the surroundings it had been intended for originally.

Their seats weren't in the front row this time, but they still had a great view of the runway, lit up with twinkling palm trees along the opposite side—with the Eiffel Tower in blackness at the top of the catwalk.

"Wow, this is so… extra!" Chloe said, wearing her bomber jacket once again over her Maison Marais dress. The winter in Paris had been harsh and she wished she had brought a heavier coat, but she still wanted everyone to see she was wearing Maison Marais at the same time.

"Well, it's Jean-Paul... What did you expect?" Carmen said, wrapped up in a more appropriate black wool coat that was belted and svelte, matched with the black 'Raven' capsule boots she had saved back from the press sample cupboard.

"Can you see him?" Chloe said.

Carmen knew who she was talking about, it was all she could talk about on the Eurostar. She jerked her head upwards and over the rows in front of them, getting a look at the frow. "Nope... He's not here yet."

"He's probably backstage somewhere... Jean-Paul must be nervous as hell right now."

"He's used to it... Where's the after-party at again? That's where you *will* see him if you have any chance," Carmen said.

"Hotel Costes... That's Jean-Paul's hangout," Chloe said, checking her phone to see that it was now exactly eight p.m. "Isn't it meant to start now?"

"You know these things always run late... Even the Eiffel Tower illuminations will wait for Maison Marais."

And that's exactly what the latticed wrought-iron landmark did—eventually glittering in lights at eight–fifteen—when the drumbeat of the show's music finally began to pulsate. Everyone sat up and looked forward, finding the first model to step out, wearing a simple black pantsuit and blazer combo, marching down the runway with hands in her pockets.

Model after model walked down the long Trocadéro runway in all-black silhouettes, from black shearling-lined safari jackets to sequin mini dresses of various iterations. Polka dots made another appearance, as did power shoulders and prom-style puffball dresses in jewel tones, followed by black lurex fitted gowns with silver glitter accents that sparkled under the lights of the palm trees lining the stretch. Just before it could start to drizzle with rain, the show came to a close with the full line-up of models taking their final walk down the catwalk. The rows of seats in the stand suddenly illuminated as guests captured the final walk-out of the show on their phones. And as soon as Carly Wattmore (the last model on the runway) was about to turn right—off into blackness—guests had already begun climbing out of their seats. Either rushing off to another evening show, or to attend the after-party. And that was where Carmen and Chloe were destined for, also getting up to get out of the vicinity and into a car. And that in itself, in any city during Fashion Week, was a sport!

"You look perfect," Carmen said, side glancing at Chloe, who was reapplying her lipstick in a hand mirror in the back of their car.

"Just making sure... There *will* be paparazzi if Gianni and Graziana are there already," Chloe said.

"I thought you were playing it cool, anyway? So what if you do see him? Are you gonna tell him *all* about his evil sister?" Carmen taunted.

Chloe sighed, she had a point. "I *am* cool... Really! I'm more interested in our business relationship... But it's just that *'what if'* in the back of my mind... I mean, there's definitely something there between us."

"Well, in that case, you have nothing to lose... If he asks you why you left last time, just tell him," Carmen urged, using her hands to gesture how bored she was of this subject now. "Look, I get that he's a great contact to have and you have to keep him sweet... But you *can* do that without sleeping with him you know?"

"What do you think I've been doing? Secretly jetting off to bed him behind your back? It's been months since we last spoke... He's probably *dying* to ask why I stood him up, if anything."

Carmen rolled her eyes, she still didn't understand where the need to be accepted by Gianni Palazzo came from. They were making their own name for themselves—they *had* made their own name—but Chloe was still stuck in her old ways; still controlled by the corporate world of Palazzo. Carmen thought the whole point of building your own business was to get away from all that, not to court it... But here they were, in Paris, and about to find out if Gianni still did give a damn.

Hotel Costes did indeed have reporters and photographers outside waiting to snap the celebrity guests that were arriving for the 'invite-only' Maison Marais party. But it had been months since the paparazzi last cared to chase Chloe Ravens down, and without Gianni on her arm, she and Carmen managed to enter with just a few shots being taken as they walked up the steps—past the gold draped curtained entrance. Out back, the terrace had been cleared for people to congregate, with tables and chairs around the outside and a champagne bar. Most of the models from the show had shown up, including Carly Wattmore, but Chloe noticed she was without Gianni.

"Chloe! You're here!" Claudette said, turning around to escape a conversation—only to bump into another.

"Yes, of course... This is my friend, Carmen," Chloe said, air-kissing her before Carmen did the same.

"Listen, I'll be right back... I'll let Jean-Paul know you're here!" Claudette said, rushing off; clearly busy at work and not partying.

Meanwhile, Carmen managed to grab two glasses of champagne from a passing waiter. "When in Paris," she said, handing Chloe a glass.

It was exactly what Chloe needed to steady her nerves (almost downing it in one), and as she drained the glass of its last drops, she could hear Graziana's voice behind her.

"Ciao, amore... Lovely to see you... Yes—amazing show, wasn't it?"

"*Fuck*," Chloe muttered under breath, searching for the waiter to swap her glass for a full one.

Carmen looked over her shoulder to see who she was cursing at. "Oh... *Her!*"

But it was too late for Chloe to dodge her now and *way* too early to make a French exit—Graziana was heading their way. Making her way through an adoring crowd of fashion folk and Maison Marais models, she eventually passed Chloe, double-taking as she did. Yes, it *was* Chloe Ravens—her *fucking* name emblazoned on the back of her bomber jacket gave it away.

"Oh… *You're* here," Graziana said, sucking her cheeks in even more.

"Hi, Graziana," Chloe managed with a fake smile. "Nice to see you again." But before Graziana could even hear the latter, she was off with a swish of her platinum hair that almost whipped Chloe in the face.

"Jeez… I can see what you mean now—she *is* a bitch!" Carmen snorted. "Come, let's hit the bar, darling."

And the bar was exactly where the party was at. Propped up against it were Jean-Paul and Gianni, they had gone straight there after taking pictures at the entrance to escape the attention from the rest of the party guests. But it was too late for Chloe to turn back around and vanish now—Carmen had already caught the attention of the bartender and ordered two gin cocktails and Jean-Paul had already spotted her. Chloe fussed with her hair, waiting behind Carmen for their drinks to be served, trying to look as though she hadn't seen Gianni and Jean-Paul at the bar.

"Chloe!" Jean-Paul bellowed over the music and chatter of the bar. "Cherie! You're here!"

Gianni slowly looked up as he swigged on his whiskey on the rocks. Looking handsome as ever, dressed in a light grey sharkskin suit with a white shirt unbuttoned underneath—enough to see a spurt of chest hair and his gold chain hang low down into the crease of his chest. His hair was still jaw length and dark slicked back and tucked behind his ears. Chloe could smell the tobacco— with a dash of vanilla—cologne pouring off him. She breathed it in, like an intoxicating form of oxygen infiltrating her, making her come alive inside—she forgot the power just the smell of him had over her. "Of course! We wouldn't miss this for the world!" she said, as Jean-Paul gave her a hug, swaying her side to side on her teetering heels.

"You look amazing in this dress! Gianni—look who's here!" Jean said, turning her around to face him with his arm wrapped around her waist.

Chloe slowly lifted her head to meet his gaze, her stomach tensed as her heart felt like it was about to lurch up into her throat and get lodged there—making her unable to speak. Now was not the time to puke… Not on his beautiful suit, anyway. '*Fuck*,' she thought to herself, as she met his steely blue eyes that still sparkled with youth, even though the creases around them had deepened since the last time she remembered looking at them, close-up.

"Chloe," he began, unsure of what to say. "It's been a while."

"Too long, if you ask me!" Jean said with a laugh. "And, thanks to her, *I* have Gabriela Gracia dressed for the Oscar's… Not you!" he teased, poking his tongue out.

"Is that so?" Gianni smiled. "Well, serves me right I guess… I should have seen that one coming."

"When Claudette told me you wanted us to dress Gabi, I was thrilled… But I was too busy with the show to travel to L.A… Anyway, we sent some amazing gowns with one of my designers—she informs me that Gabi has chosen *the* best dress!"

"Are you coming over to Jean's tomorrow?" Gianni said, playing it cool, taking another gulp of amber. "He's having an Oscar's viewing party."

"Did someone say party?" Carmen said, returning to Chloe with drinks.

"Oh, Gianni… You remember my friend, Carmen?"

"Sure," he said, unsure where he had seen her familiar face before.

Carmen put him out of his misery. "Yes, we met at the retrospective party… Thanks to you, *I* finally get discount at your store!"

"That's right… How could I forget," Gianni said, leaning in to kiss her cheek.

"Carmen's the president of StacksOfStyle," Chloe said, presenting her to Jean-Paul.

"Oh, yes! Congratulations are in order… When will the website launch?" Jean said, letting go of Chloe's waist in exchange for his champagne glass, holding it up to toast before taking a mouthful.

"Early spring," Carmen said, raising her glass too.

"Congratulations, Chloe," Gianni said, softly touching her arm. A shudder of electricity shot through her entire body, right down to her inner organs and back up through the epidermis of her skin, where his hand had just left off. For a moment (which felt like minutes longer than it was), she locked onto his eyes and gazed aimlessly—feeling the desire to be with him all over again. Looking on, Carmen rolled her eyes—trying not to shake her head with too much sarcasm—as she sipped her cocktail.

"You *must* come tomorrow… I'll send you my address," Jean said, bringing the conversation back to his viewing party, unable to help himself—playing the match-maker.

"We'd love to," Carmen snapped before Chloe could come up with some lame excuse and sabotage herself even more.

"Gianni! Giiianni!"

Graziana's grating voice calling out had made the entire bar look around at her—she had Carly on her arm. But her tanned face dropped when she saw who was standing with him, sipping cocktails; she didn't hesitate to squeeze in to separate them—dropping Carly off at Gianni's side like some sort of delivery. Leaning over the bar, she clicked her fingers for the bartender's attention.

"You remember Chloe?" Gianni said, awkwardly.

"Nice to meet you," Carly said as she draped herself off his shoulder, causing a dimple in the pad of his suit jacket which annoyed Chloe.

'We've met before, bitch,' Chloe wanted to say. She hated people that were so up their own asses that everyone else didn't matter, but she managed to contain herself.

"In fact, you know my friends, Pandora and Dom?" Chloe said with a grin. It was all she needed to say to wipe the smile off Carly's face.

"That was an amazing show! London Fashion Week is back on the map because of her! How on Earth did she manage to pull that off?" Jean said.

"I agree, it was a spectacle," Gianni said, realising there was a connection here. "Did that have something to do with you too?"

Chloe shrugged. Although she couldn't exactly take the credit for the collection itself, it had become possible because of her savvy business mind, introducing Pandora to Veronica.

"We share the same investor… And we're the exclusive stockist for Pandora Simmons in the U.S," Carmen proudly stated, even if Chloe was too shy to speak up.

"That's it… You're all part of the same group," Gianni said, raising an eyebrow at Chloe, still fixated on her—even though Carmen was doing the talking. And this was the real reason he was enamoured by her. Yes, she was beautiful, different, *real*, but she was also very intuitive and clever. He liked that about her. He also liked that she wasn't over-confident about her achievements, where others would lap up the attention at what she had created in such a small space of time. "I'm in the process of relaunching our online business too… Maybe you can give me a few pointers?"

"Oh, she doesn't have time for that!" Graziana interrupted, leaning back off the bar with her martini in hand to hijack the conversation once more—spilling her drink on Chloe's shoes (which appeared to be on purpose). "Chloe here has her own little online *shop* to deal with… What is it again? Oh, yes… Your eBay store—where you sell all your old clothes."

"*That* was for charity," Carmen said sharply. "StacksOfStyle is the new online destination for fashion… Stores are dead now."

Graziana planted her drink down on the bar so she could crease with laughter. "Oh, I'm sorry… Who are you? The latest comedienne? You *are* very funny… Anyway boys, come out to the terrace, people are waiting to congratulate you."

Taking her drink, Graziana grabbed her brother's arm to whisk him away—far away from Chloe.

"See you tomorrow?" Gianni managed to say before he was gone.

"Come, come out to the terrace ladies," Jean said, doing what he was told; following Graziana.

"I'd rather go home and wash my make-up off," Chloe said, leaning into Carmen, finishing her drink in one.

"I couldn't agree more… A nightcap at the hotel is in order!"

**

The next morning, they did actually have to be up early for more showroom appointments, which Carmen had forgotten all about thanks to a few rounds of cocktails back at their hotel. But Chloe had printed out a military-style schedule, ensuring there was no way she would forget their appointments.

The Syndicate was an American label designed by the Wilson twins (child actresses that had now turned their hand to producing extortionate high-fashion), and Chloe was determined to secure the buying rights for the following season—adding them to the digital racks of S.O.S. Their cavernous showroom housed their minimal collection, consisting of mainly black and grey tones, with no colours or prints to be seen. But it was very highly executed in terms of quality, considering it *was* made by the Wilson twins—now stick-thin slaves to the fashion industry.

After securing an agreement with their showroom director, they chose a selection of dresses, winter coats and tailored suit separates to consider—once they had time to go through their budget for fall/winter with Bill back in the New York office. Lisa Lennard was another label that held their showroom appointments in Paris (despite showing in New York), and another 'celebrity' line that Veronica would be pleased with them securing for S.O.S. Lisa was an ex-girl group member of the nineties phenomenon that was, The Vibe Girls.

Her designs were colourful, with copper, green, and beige—all the usual fall hues. Svelte dresses styled with oversized outer-coats, wide-legged pants with fitted double-breasted blazers, and frou-frou frilly shirts with large cuffs made up her latest collection, which Chloe and Carmen sifted through to narrow down into an offering for site launch.

Afterwards, they stopped off for lunch at Café Charlot, nearby Lisa's showroom in the Marais. Carmen was just pleased that their work was now over with and she could relax and enjoy Paris.

"I'll have the chicken salad… She'll have steak and frites," Carmen said, handing the menu back to the waiter.

"Make that two salads, s'il vous plaît," Chloe quickly corrected, shooting Carmen a look.

"What's the matter? Appetite's gone after last night's encounter?"

"You could say that… See what I mean now? That Graziana is something else…"

"She's a *cunt*—I get it, Chloe," Carmen said, surprising Chloe with her language in public. "What? They all speak French, they don't understand," waving her hand at the other lunchtime diners.

"There's no way I could survive that… Even if Gianni and I—"

"Would you just listen to yourself? Look, he likes you—you like him… Either suck it up or forget about it!"

Chloe chewed her lip, she knew this was tiring for Carmen to listen to (especially when they were working to build a business together), but she couldn't drop it. "I'm sorry… It's just so, frustrating… And no matter what I do, she will never approve o me."

"Darling, if anyone doesn't approve—it's *you!* Look at you… You're hot, intelligent, and an all-round *fucking* awesome person. Can you own that for a minute? Last night, the two most important people there adored you, and here you are doubting yourself as we sit here in Paris! Mother-fucking *Paris*, Chloe! We were just stylists a few months back—now we are entrepreneurs! If that doesn't make you worthy, then quite frankly, nothing will."

Chloe sighed, she knew she was right but she still couldn't hide her past from Gianni. She had to tell him before it came from Graziana (or worse, from Regina), making her out to look like some sort of catfish.

"Just tell him… I bet you he won't even give a shit! Tell him tonight at Jean-Paul's party… If you won't, I will!" Carmen said, placing her napkin on her lap. "Has he sent you his address yet?"

"I have it here," Chloe said, opening up an email on her phone from Claudette. "He lives on the other side of the river."

"Cool… We get to see how these designers live!" Carmen said, lightning up a Vogue cigarette.

"Are you smoking now?" Chloe said, wafting the smoke away from her face.

"Only when in Paris, darling."

"It says, from Midnight to sunrise… We're gonna be tired on the plane home."

"That's what plane journeys are for… Plus, if you get your way, we'll be flying back to New York on Gianni's private jet," Carmen laughed, taking a drag of her skinny cigarette.

"Very funny!" Chloe scolded. "But maybe, you're right… I should just tell him. This is all nonsense. If I remove the lies, then Graziana has nothing on me—and Regina for that matter… What if she's there tonight?"

"Who, Regina? Then I'll be *fucking* amazed!"

"No—Graziana!"

"Then it will be even better… Tell him *all* about your Palazzo past right there in front of her, and shut her up once and for all."

For the rest of the afternoon, they relaxed at their hotel and got ready for Jean's party, carefully selecting outfits—not quite knowing who was going to be there, or what to expect. Chloe chose a simple pair of black jeans with a white sweater and her 'Raven' bomber once again, while Carmen wore a black roll-neck sweater-dress with her knee-high boots worn over the top of black wool tights.

Taking a car over to the other side of the river, they passed the Louvre as they made their way over the Ponts des Arts bridge, carrying on past the Musee d'Orsay—through to the backstreets. Jean-Paul's beige coloured brick townhouse looked authentically Parisienne, yet very modern with its own driveway and mini courtyard—which the driver pulled into to drop them off. It was at least four storeys high, and the grey slated rooftop looked as though it had a loft conversion.

"Bonsoir!" Claudette said, opening the front door to greet them in the courtyard. "Follow me, the party is just starting!"

"And it's only just Midnight, Cinderella… So don't think you can slink off early this time," Carmen muttered as they walked in behind her.

The hall was creamy white, with black and white marble flooring and a single staircase that had an ornate bannister. They both looked up to the high ceiling that was decorated with beautiful

Empire style plasterwork and cornice detailing around the edge. Claudette led them up the stairs to the first floor, with parquet wood flooring in a honey colour and large windows that were draped with white linens.

"Look who I found outside," Claudette said, entering a rather large dining room that appeared to be the entire first-floor level, designed for the sole purpose of entertainment.

"More gorgeous ladies," Jean-Paul said, getting up from his seat at the candle-lit table. "Come and join us… This is two of my wonderful designers; Marie and Juliette… Gianni—who you already know of course—and my sister, Celine."

Chloe and Carmen went around the table, introducing themselves to Jean's guests until Chloe reached Gianni—he got up to give her a kiss on the cheek. "Nice to see you, two nights in a row," he said, sitting back down causally.

Chloe couldn't help but feel excited at the sensation of his lips and rugged stubble rubbing against her soft cheek in comparison, while her heart palpitated at the just sight of him. He was dressed down in a pair of beige corduroys, a white T-shirt, and a burgundy shawl cardigan—casual and sexy, in a masculine way.

"Sit—sit! We're having some… What do you call it? Er, finger food!" Jean said, handing them both a small plate to help themselves, before emptying a bottle of white wine into their glasses. "Claudette, be a dear and get some more wine from the fridge."

"What have you two been up to today?" Gianni said, wine in hand—leaning back in his chair.

Chloe sensed he was already loosened by the French wine as she sat down next to him. "We met with a few designers, The Syndicate and Lisa Lennard."

"*Pah!*" Marie scoffed, almost dribbling wine down her chin. Chloe noted she looked particularly 'French,' with short platinum bobbed hair, red lipstick and black winged eyeliner. Her navy and white striped top didn't help either. "I'm sorry… The Wilson Twins and Lisa Lennard are *not* designers!"

"Well, whatever they are, they'll be great to have onsite," Carmen said, taking a gulp of wine.

"J-P was telling us all about your new website," Juliette said, the much friendlier of the two. Chloe nodded politely, still working out the vibe of the guests, happy to let Carmen do the talking.

"I love online shopping," Celine said, leaning on her elbows on the table with her long brown hair flowing over her shoulders. "Who has the time to go to a boutique these days?"

"Well, congratulations on your new signings," Gianni said, clinking his glass against Chloe's—his arm now resting on the back of her chair. "Online is definitely a huge business… As I was saying last night, Palazzo Group has just signed with MiBellaModa… I've been meaning to pick your brains about that, actually."

"I'm sure you're in good hands," Chloe said, not wanting to talk about work or discuss anything that would lead onto Graziana for that matter.

"So… Do we know which dress Gabi is wearing?" Carmen said, scooping up a small wedge of deep-fried brie, before spooning cranberry sauce next to it on her plate.

"Marie has just flown back from L.A… Only she knows—I don't want to know," Jean-Paul said, flapping his hands dramatically. "Ah, wine… Top up, top-up!"

Claudette unscrewed the cork and filled everyone's glass, including her own—tonight she was off-duty for once. Although her phone was always nearby, glowing in the candle-light with emails popping through—non-stop. After she had topped everyone up (and briefly checked her phone), she dashed to the other end of the room to switch on the TV, ready for 'Live' from the red carpet.

"So, where are you guys from?" Celine asked, intrigued by the new additions to their soirée.

"We're both from New York—well, Boston… Carmen has Italian heritage, but we both live and work in New York."

"I love New York! Will you be there for the new store opening?"

"I thought you said you didn't have time for shops!" Jean snapped playfully at his sister. "In fact, Chloe here has designed the special edition bag for the opening—of course, she'll be there… We'll all be there, darling."

"And I'll be in New York quite a bit this spring," Gianni dropped, tucking a strand of hair behind his ear.

Chloe's eyes grew with excitement at this revelation—but what did it mean? She couldn't quite process her reality right now, it was like she was living in a dream and completely missed the gravity of his words. The candle-lit late-night setting of their Midnight feast made it all seem even more surreal.

Here she was, sat around a table with two of the world's most famous fashion designers—drinking wine. It was most likely the wine that was making her giddy, but she couldn't help feeling even more attracted to Gianni, now she was up close and personal with him. She shuddered at the anticipation of his next move, his arm still on the back of her chair—wanting him to swap the chair back for her shoulders at least. She wanted to feel his warm touch, badly.

"How come?" Carmen dug further, sensing that Chloe was too 'absent' to ask.

"Well, the store opening for one, but the Palazzo retrospective exhibition opens at the Met in May—you guys should be at the gala, by the way."

"Great, we'll be there!" Carmen said, wide-eyed at Chloe who was now gazing at Gianni. "Won't we, Chloe?"

"Excellent!" Jean clapped, standing up. "We get to see each other much more this year! Now... Everybody grab a plate, get your drinks! Let's go to the sofa's and get ready for the moment we have all been waiting for!"

Carmen filled her plate with pastry parcels and French bread (which she had told herself she would only have a bite of, but couldn't resist more), while Chloe carried herself and her wine over to the sofa area, closely followed by Gianni so he could purposely sit next to her.

Everyone took their seats and comfortably sat back, with just the glow of the TV and a few dim lamps. Chloe sat down on one of the sofas; Gianni plonked himself down next to her, almost wedging her in between him and the arm-rest. His thigh touched hers, and she made no effort to move away from him; she could feel the electricity between them transmit—even when fully clothed and in the company of others. "No Graziana tonight?" she managed to say, rather sheepishly.

"She's flown back to Italy… She gets bored easily at Fashion Week."

'Thank *fuck* for that,' Chloe said to herself.

"Why… You miss her?"

Chloe looked at him with a raised eyebrow. She was starting to warm up to him now they were all relaxed, merry, and cosy on the sofa together. On the other sofa, Carmen seemed to be hitting it off with Jean-Paul, Marie, and Juliette—which gave them time to be alone as they waited for the red carpet coverage to start.

"I know she can be a handful at times."

"At times?" Chloe said, sitting up to look at him square in the face.

"Well, I'm used to her… I can handle her… Why, are you bothered by her?" Gianni said, turning to face her.

Carmen looked over, mid-flow of telling her audience about how she had met Chloe on the shop floor at Palazzo—only to see the two of them face-to-face, looking like they were about to kiss.

"Wait… *You* worked at Palazzo?" Jean-Paul laughed out loud.

Chloe could feel the blood rise up to her face—she could murder Carmen right now! And Carmen knew she was in for trouble later, but if she didn't bring it up, then Chloe would have just dodged it and be stuck in the same place—worrying about her secret persona being discovered. Anyway, it was more 'natural' for Carmen to drop it into the conversation, it gave Chloe a hook without needing to fish for it—Carmen glared at her to take the bait. "Err, well… I did, but not for long," she admitted, trying her best to not look Gianni in the eye as she said it.

"Yeah—right! Five years! You get less for robbery back in New York!" Carmen dropped in, which ruffled a few laughs.

"My dear, working at Palazzo for that long… What crime did you commit?" Jean added, laughing hysterically at his own joke.

Chloe, meanwhile, wanted to die! She wanted the floor to disconnect and open up for her to slip through the cracks and back into a taxi—magicking herself back to the hotel. "Why didn't you tell me? " Gianni laughed, before seeing her embarrassment blush in her reddened cheeks. "Wait a minute… Is this why you left me in Paris?" he said, sitting up even more—almost climbing onto the back cushions.

"Well, anyway… Chloe left and started to work for me, styling Gabi," Carmen continued, sensing she needed another nudge.

"Why didn't you say something?" Gianni said, touching her knee.

"What was I supposed to say? 'Oh hi, I used to work for you.' What with all the camera's flashing and everyone calling for a picture, it wasn't exactly on my mind at the time."

"Whenever… We spent two nights together!"

"It just didn't *feel* right… Besides, let's just say I didn't exactly resign on the best of terms," Chloe said, looking down into her glass.

"Oh really? Now you *definitely* have to tell me what went on!" Gianni laughed, placing his arm behind her head.

"Where do I start… Let's just say, Regina and I did *not* get on."

"I see," Gianni said, cutting his eye. "She can be a tough one, I guess."

"A tough one? She's a total bitch," Chloe said, there was no point holding back now. "Anyway… That's all in the past."

"Seriously, I don't care… You should have just said."

Chloe looked to the ceiling, wondering how she was going to come clean about Graziana if she was now being honest and open with him—or if she should even bother saying anything at all. Surely it was no secret that they weren't exactly best friends?

"It's not that I wanted to lie to you, or leave you there… I just didn't think it was relevant, especially because…" Chloe paused, carefully selecting her words. "Because… I didn't know what *this* was," she said, motioning her hands back and forth between them.

"We were having fun, no?" Gianni said, moving his hand to stroke a strand of her hair away from her face—her head jittered as he touched her ear. "Did I do something wrong? You wouldn't even answer my calls."

"No! No, you did everything right… It was all me."

"Oh, you're gonna pull the *'it's not you, it's me'* card?" Gianni shrugged, massaging her ear lobe between his fingertips. Chloe felt like dynamite was exploding inside of her, which made it even harder for her to concentrate on what she was saying. But maybe that was his plan, to weaken her defences and force the truth out.

"Look, Gianni, I like you a lot but I'm from a different place," she began, not quite sure how to explain how Graziana had ordered her to stay away. And she definitely wasn't going to mention that Regina had threatened to ruin her—as well as telling her to stay away from him too. "Anyway, I thought you and Carly were a *thing* now?"

"What? *No!* Don't believe everything you read in the press," Gianni huffed, sweeping back hair away from his face—annoyed at being implicated with the young model, not by choice.

"Okay, you two… Quiet now," Jean shouted, turning up the volume—totally unbothered that she used to be a boutique girl. Most people in fashion started there anyway—it was no big deal.

Rachel Rodriguez, the pop sensation who had driven herself to rehab and back into the limelight, had stepped onto the red carpet outside the Dolby theatre—this time on her own. She had publicly ended her relationship with her model boyfriend, Hunter, outside an In-N-Out Burger parking lot. All the famous faces, nominees, and superstars of Hollywood were now starting to arrive in their designer gowns as Marie and Carmen had found common ground with their bitchy commentary—amusing Jean-Paul in the process. Raucous laugher filled the room as a 'Real Housewife' turned up with her director husband in a terribly revealing dress, for a woman of her age.

By now, Gianni had muscled his way even closer to Chloe, with his arm comfortably resting across the back of her neck and on her shoulder. All she had to do was tilt her head slightly to the left and her head would be resting on his chest—but she resisted. She had to get up and leave the room to re-sync herself. "Claudette? Where's the bathroom?" she said getting up, re-adjusting her outfit.

"Down the hall, second right," she directed, with no intention of showing her where to go. She was sat down on the floor with a cushion, a bowl of popcorn, and a bottle of wine all to herself.

Chloe found the bathroom and locked the door. Turning on the tap, she stared at herself in the large gold framed mirror, hardly believing where she was and that her truth finally out. There was nothing she could do about it now and it certainly hadn't put Gianni off her it seemed. If she had come clean about Regina and Graziana, then maybe that would have been different, but she didn't have time to dwell on it—the locked door jolted. "Just one-second," Chloe called flushing the loo and rinsing her hands one last time. 'I'm gonna kill you,' she muttered to herself, opening the door. "Did you have to—" she started, flinging the door open—only to find Gianni on the other side, and not Carmen as she had expected.

"I had to come and kiss you!" He bolted forward, grabbing her by her waist, edging her into the bathroom as he landed his lips on hers—kicking the door shut behind him. She let him take her, she let him put his tongue inside her mouth as he backed her onto the sink. His rough stubble and his passionate, hard kiss scratched against her face—but she didn't care—she wanted him.

"*Guys!* Hurry up!" they heard Jean-Paul yell.

Gianni pulled away, wiping her lips with his thumb before returning to the rest of the party—trying to act as casual as possible.

"Seriously, guys?" Jean-Paul teased, grabbing a fist of popcorn from Claudette's bowl to throw at Gianni; knowing he had slipped off to see Chloe in private. Carmen and Marie (now best of friends) giggled like schoolgirls, huddled up together under a blanket.

Gabriela Gracia had finally arrived on the red carpet to flashes and reporters holding out their microphones for her. She was sporting a new shoulder-length hairstyle that was blown straight, with one side pinned back to reveal drop diamond earrings. Her dress, a silver sequinned, one-shouldered design shone like a mirrorball in the L.A Sunshine. The long gown was slit high to reveal her famous legs, and on her feet, both Chloe and Carmen were stunned to see she was wearing the pair of silver sandals from the

'Raven' line that they had gifted to her. On a high and having fun with their new friends, they stayed up late, waiting to watch Gabi accept her Oscar for Best Actress, as well as Best Original Song for 'My Time To Shine,' which she performed a teary rendition of, live. Jean-Paul was thrilled, he even cried—while Gianni moved his hand to hold Chloe's during a romantic moment. And as she listened to Gabi sing, she wondered if this was her time to shine as well.

By now, everyone had started to get sleepy, and Chloe had relented by letting her head rest on Gianni's chest. "Will you stay with me?" he said.

It was now nearly five in the morning—it was time to go. Claudette had passed out on the sofa, sprawled across Juliette and Marie, who were also bleary-eyed. "I can't, we have to catch a flight back to New York in just a few hours—and I still have to pack!" Chloe realised, but not regretting she had spent the night with him instead.

"Sure… Well, I'll see you in New York anyway," he said, giving her a hug as she got up to leave before taking her by the chin and kissing her one last time—this time, in front of everyone.

Jean-Paul had called them a car, and gave both her and Carmen a parting hug, echoing Gianni. "See you in New York!"

Chloe and Carmen said their goodbyes to Marie, Juliette, and Celine (careful not to wake Claudette), and made their way downstairs to get into the waiting car in the cold morning light. Sat in the back of the car, they drove off back to their hotel, feeling like they had stayed out all night at a dirty club, or something. Exhausted, they both flopped their heads back on the head-rests, fully aware that they had the task of packing up and catching a flight ahead of them.

Carmen rolled her head over to look at Chloe, she had her eyes shut but she knew she wasn't sleeping—she was blissfully taking in Gianni's parting kiss, this time leaving with his number safely stored in her phone. "See bitch… I told you he wouldn't give a shit," Carmen smiled.

24

They didn't remember much of the plane journey back to New York—they had both taken sleeping pills to induce them into a much-needed sleep. But waking up, having touched down at JFK airport had been a bit of a shocker—at least they didn't have to go straight back to the office!

However, it did feel good to be back in New York, and Chloe felt good about getting closure—as well as a new opening—with Gianni. A weight had been lifted off her shoulders somewhat; finally, he knew her truth, and now she could focus on important work—getting S.O.S launch-ready and back online. A lot had changed while they were away, the advertising strategy had begun.

'Get Ready For A Clicking—StacksOfStyle.Com—Coming Soon,' printed in simple black text against a white background could be found on billboards and bus stops all around the city. And spotting them through the car window on the way back home from the airport, gave Chloe all the motivation she needed to get back to work the next day.

"Hey… You're back!" Veronica said, noticing Chloe and Carmen at their desks. "Now, I've never doubted you, girls… But Gabi, wearing our 'Raven' shoes has sent our customer care lines through the roof! You shoulda told me, I would have placed a re-order in advance!"

"Well, believe it or not… Even *we* didn't know she'd be wearing them," Carmen said.

"Well, anyway—I've demanded them to be fast-tracked and re-ordered! And, have you seen your photo's from London and Paris all over the Internet, wearing those bombers? We've already had tonnes of requests for them too—make sure you talk to Bill about quantities for those!"

"Did you see Pandora's show?" Chloe said, sure she would be pleased with them too.

"Don't get me started! The best quarter of a mil' I've ever spent! So, how *was* Fashion Week?"

"Great! We managed to get some amazing brands for next season too... The Syndicate, Lisa Lennard... Not to mention an amazing selection from P.S.L," Chloe reeled off. "Actually, we need to sit down with you and Bill to discuss budget."

"Yes, of course... Also, I've arranged for you to spend a few days at our warehouse in New Jersey. I want you to show the packing team how you want Stacks' orders to be packed, train our customer care line in the tone of voice—that sort of thing. We have lots to do, and little time to do it in before we launch."

"Sounds great," Chloe chirped, happy to finally get her teeth sunk into the juicy parts.

Veronica was about to head out of their glass box to get back to her own desk before she remembered one more important thing to ask. "Did you see Gianni?"

Chloe stopped what she was doing, briefly looked at Carmen before smiling back at Veronica. Of course, she wanted to know, and she would be even more delighted if she found out all there was to know from Paris—but some things were best left kept quiet. "I did... We both saw him at the Maison Marais after-party and at Jean-Paul's Oscar's party." Chloe teased.

"Oh, you never said anything about an Oscar's party?" Veronica salivated, leaning against the doorway with her arms folded for more titbits.

"It was a last-minute invite from Jean-Paul," Carmen added, chewing her lip; trying to keep herself from laughing. 'Boy, if only she really knew... She'd be pumping millions more into this operation,' she thought.

"Fantastic... See—didn't I tell you that Gianni would be a good contact for you to keep?"

"Yes, well... Gianni and Jean-Paul will both be here in New York very soon. There's a lot going on: the store opening, the retrospective exhibition, Palazzo are renovating their own online store with MiBellaModa… So there will be plenty of press opportunities to get the launch of S.O.S out there," Chloe said, bringing it back to business and not at all about her personal relationship with Gianni.

"Excellent work guys… I'll schedule that meeting with Bill and I, but we have a big gathering later this afternoon with tech to view the website—testing has been very successful while you've been away and we have lots to show you!"

And this meeting was the big one. Everyone from tech, editorial, art and design, buying and merchandising—even the photo studio—had gathered in the boardroom to go through the final stages of the website before they launch. The editorial team presented the new homepage, with an all-singing-all-dancing feature on their exclusive collections, style tips and trends, as well as 'what to wear' guides for the upcoming summer season.

The art and design team went on to unveil the brand new packaging that orders would be shipped in. White boxes, stacked inside each other like Russian dolls—from large to small gift boxes—were presented and passed around the room. Holding one in her hands, Chloe's face lit up with excitement. They were exactly how she and Carmen had explained how they wanted them to be. White, canvas-grained boxes with 'StacksOfStyle' printed in the black sans-serif logo in the centre. Tone-on-tone white tissue paper had been specially made with 'StacksOfStyle' printed in diagonal rows for wrapping and stuffing the boxes, along with swing tags that would be attached to every item sold—carefully stating their returns policy. Afterwards, buying and merchandising shared their exciting developments—including the product lines that had already been delivered to the warehouse.

Then, the photo studio chipped in to confirm all of the inventory they had already styled and shot for the site's product pages, along with their plan to upload new items every Friday—slowly drip-feeding new arrivals to keep customers clicking each week. But it was the tech team that had the biggest reveal of them all, uncovering the new-look site banner and how to navigate around the new-look website.

"So, onscreen is the site we've been working on," Bob said, standing there in his band tee and board shorts—completed with flip-flops—in winter. "So far, there are no reported bugs, but we still need to test a few areas to stabilise it for public use—but all of that is on course for completion. Thankfully, our current DivaFeet systems are used to handling high traffic, so S.O.S should perform the same way—since we replicated the front and back-end systems—just presented in a new format."

Before he lost everyone in tech speak, Bob swiftly moved on with a set-by-step guide. On the boardroom TV, a chic, white background web page loaded up with the black 'StacksOfStyle' banner at the top. A navigation bar ran underneath it with click-through options for *What's New, Designers, Clothing, Accessories, Shoes,* and the *S.O.S Fashion Guide.* In the main body of the homepage was their first editorial feature, showcasing new products and designers exclusive to S.O.S. Covering each section, Bob demonstrated how to simply add products to the shopping bag, as well as account registration and how to check-out—all features were exactly the same as DivaFeet.

"So, are we on track to launch at the end of this month?" Veronica said, wanting to see the dollars roll in from all the hard work required to pull this off—as well as see the money she had ploughed into it again.

"Well, as soon as the warehouse has been briefed on operations, we're pretty much ready to go," Morgana said, jumping in at the chance to have her moment. "Our marketing campaign has been successful—we've had DivaFeet's phone lines inundated with requests for a 'Raven' re-stock—as well as the bomber jackets you guys wore at Fashion Week. I say we're on course to launch in two weeks... We can update our editorial and online advertising to feature the launch date too."

Chloe and Carmen looked at each other—this was it. They were more than thrilled with everyone's hard work to date and just as excited as Veronica to start seeing the cash flow in. And Chloe was eager to stay one step ahead of Palazzo's own online relaunch—something she had learnt at her time working for them.

Staying one step ahead of Regina Hall had been her goal for most of her career, and now she had something to prove—not only to her—but to Graziana too. She could be successful on her own; she didn't need to depend upon Palazzo or Gianni.

"Well, that settles it… Girls, work with our copywriters to finalise the customer service communications and make that visit to the warehouse! I'm happy to launch when everything is in place… Morgana, prepare the press release!"

*

After a week of sitting down with each department, signing off on all areas of the website, Chloe and Carmen took a little trip up to Mahwah. The warehouse in New Jersey was situated off a highway, nearby to other industrial estates. From the outside, the white-tiled square building looked like any other corporation owned facility, but the inside was a different story. The main entrance was set back in a huge car lot, with FedEx lorries driving in and out, collecting the mass of orders that DivaFeet shipped out daily. Meanwhile, the reception looked exactly like the one back at the DivaFeet headquarters in New York—complete with a fashionista receptionist behind the front desk.

"Good morning! Welcome to DivaFeet's distribution centre ladies… You must be Chloe and Carmen?" the girl behind the desk said, instantly sensing that these two well-styled women were the visitors she had been expecting from head office.

"Yes, good morning," Chloe said, surprised to see that the warehouse looked so 'on brand' and not the dusty oversized garage she had expected.

"So Doreen, our facility manager, will be with you shortly… She's going to give you the grand tour. You'll need these passes to gain entry, but before we can sign you into the main centre, I'm gonna have to ask you to hand those over," she said, looking down at Carmen's pumps and Chloe's equally as high stilettos.

"Hahahaha! Nice try… Beauties, aren't they?" Carmen laughed, slamming her hand down on the counter.

"No, seriously… You need to change into a pair of those boots over there," the young girl said, pointing over to a cage of work boots with her pen.

The wire rack of boots looked like a second-hand military surplus store. Black dishevelled boots with frayed laces and steel-capped toes stared back at them—reeking of sweat. They hardly matched Carmen's black seventies style dress and fur gilet combo—or Chloe's vintage monochrome Chanel jacket for that matter.

"Health and safety before fashion, I'm afraid… You should find all sizes there; you can take a clear plastic bag to carry your personal belongings in, or you can use one of the lockers."

"I can't believe I'm about to put my feet in these things… God knows who's worn these before us!" Carmen said, taking off her black shades in disbelief; swapping her Choo's for practicality.

"If this is gonna be a regular thing, then we're gonna have to bring our own," Chloe agreed.

"Good morning! I see you're ready to enter the mothership!" a sturdy woman greeted.

It was the facility manager, Doreen, wearing a hi-vis vest and sporting a cropped hairstyle (probably due to health and safety too). She held out her hand to greet them, almost taking their arms off like an orangutan with her shovel-like hand.

"Make sure those laces are nice and tight, ladies… I don't want any trips, slips, or busted knee-caps… You'd be surprised how many of my workers try and sue me… Here, I got you both a little present." Doreen headed back over to the front desk and came back with a box containing two white construction hats—another outfit killer. "Ms Meyer said you were a tough crowd to please—so I had them personalised for you!"

Chloe and Carmen glanced at each other in horror; Veronica definitely didn't tell them about this, if she had then they wouldn't have visited so freely. Doreen proudly handed over their hats, which she had personally decorated with black stick-on initials on each one. The first thing Carmen noticed, wasn't how hideous they were, but that her 'C' was wonky. Not that a perfectly centred letter would help her right now in the style stakes anyway.

"Okay, looking good… Now I can show you where the magic happens," Doreen winked, slapping on her well-worn hard hat in one swoop. You could tell she was genuinely excited every time she entered the warehouse; she was like a mole, ready to take you down to her burrow.

The stylish reception area was, in fact, nothing but a mirage. Through the double doors, a cement walled corridor awaited them with security standing at a set of stadium turnstiles on the other end. Chloe and Carmen followed Doreen, with their clear plastic bags guarding their designer shoes, safely in hand.

"Hi Glenn, these guys are from head office… Just scan your lanyards on this reader here and turn the gate," Doreen demonstrated, passing through herself. On the other side, a series of staff lockers lined the walls, with some workers getting stashing their belongings before they started their shift. No personal items, phones, food or drink was allowed past this point—aggressive signage plastered made sure this law was enforced. "I designed those," Doreen proudly admitted as Chloe read it.

Outside the locker room, another large outside yard awaited them with cages of shippers being hauled out by staff to awaiting delivery trucks. In front of them, a massive hanger with a row of numbered corrugated iron shutters stared back at them. It was more like a military base than a stock room.

"That's the main building… Unit one is for deliveries: all stock comes in and is counted and put away into location. Unit two is outbound. See those guys pulling those cages? Each one contains around five–hundred orders or so, all going to those trucks over there to our customers. Unit three is inbound: returns and exchanges… We don't talk about that section much, it's as backed up as a constipated pregnant lady. Unit four is the entrance to the customer care office, five is the staff canteen, and six is our storage unit—we keep packaging and important supplies there… Step this way, I'll show you inside the plant… Just keep within the yellow pedestrian lines, and you won't get run over."

Chloe looked in awe at the scale of the large building as she followed Doreen into unit one. Inside, workers decked out in yellow vests, hard hats, and work-boots slaved away on but-ter-smooth concrete floors—marked out with yellow hazard lines. At this point, Carmen was just grateful they weren't asked to wear a yellow vest as well. Doreen pulled herself up a set of iron stairs, up onto a gangway where she waited for Chloe and Carmen to carefully take each step and catch up. Now they understood why heels were not permitted.

"So, this here is the viewing platform—that's my office right there," she said, pointing over to a cubicle that was covered in scratched, plastic windows. "I can see everyone from my station, and this platform here runs right through to unit three—so I can check no one's slacking in my team... So, where we're standing right now is inbound. This is where we have been receiving your stock and processing it all into locations within the warehouse—ready to be picked."

Chloe and Carmen watched on as staff unloaded palettes with boxes containing goods—ready to be opened up, tagged, and sort-ed. They walked further down the platform, eventually standing in front of the outbound unit, where more palettes of boxes were being sorted into cages—this time packed up and ready to be shipped out. Another hundred metres down the gangway, even more boxes were being loaded in! This time, banks of workers were opening them up and scanning their contents—processing returns and issuing refunds—before chucking the items into skip trolleys behind them for handlers to place back into stock.

"See the rows of huge shelving units in the back? Those are the stock locations where our robots pick the orders, before dropping them into totes. Eventually, they pass down that slide and onto the conveyer belt, to our packers—over there," she said, pointing.

They both stood still, staring on in amazement—this really was a mothership—like nothing they could ever imagine or seen before. The vast scale of the floor to ceiling shelves, at least ten storeys high, with narrow alleys that only electronic carts could fit down to select stock—had completely shut them up. Suddenly, sacrificing their heels seemed like a small offering in return for the major scale operation Veronica had given back to them. They stood there, leaning against the railing as Doreen explained how the carts scaled the mainframe, looking for the item that had been ordered onsite—until it reached the location that contained the piece—dropping into a plastic tote like a gigantic vending machine on steroids. Once the robot carrying the tote had completed collecting its order, the most magical thing happened—it was dropped down one of the several spiral slides that piped the totes down to the packing lanes.

"Come, let's go see where those totes end up," Doreen said, leading them back down the stairwell on the opposite side, taking them further into the warehouse.

Keeping to the yellow hazard lines, they walked deeper into the warehouse, towards the conveyor belt, which shuffled black plastic tote boxes along in a queue—ready to be picked up by a packer and boxed up to its final destination.

"All of these boxes here have now picked their orders, and now they're passing along this line to end up with these guys over here," Doreen said, walking over to a line of packers. "Guys, I know y'all super busy, but this is Carmen and Chloe from head office. These are the ladies behind our new website, StacksOfStyle."

The packers stopped for a brief moment, gave a quick wave, and carried on packing up their order before their service level time was up—which they were assessed on when pay raises came around. Doreen let them walk around and witness what went into packing a customer's order. Chloe stood behind one woman who took a T-shirt out of the tote in front of her, expertly folded it and wrapped it up in tissue before placing into an outer carton—repeating the process until the whole order was complete. "Wanna help?" the woman said, turning to Chloe.

"Sure!" she accepted, wondering if this was a good idea.

"Tape this box up, using only one scratch of tape to seal it," she said, handing her a tape gun.

Chloe's hands shook under the pressure at the simple task—which she had done so often before—but it wasn't as easy at it looked with a time target on her head. The packer then handed over the packing labels, which Chloe slapped on top of the box—

managing to screw it up, placing it at an angle. "Okay, a little bit too much tape on that one and it's not perfectly centred—but it'll do... Now you can press this button here," the packer said, pointing to a red buzzer under her workstation which sent the box along down the conveyer belt to be dropped off into a skip. In a matter of seconds, a new tote had arrived in front of them as she accepted a new order on her computer monitor above head.

"I'll leave you to this one," Chloe smiled, patting the woman on her shoulder; she had been humbled, simply with packing tape and a shipping label.

"Isn't this amazing?" Carmen said, walking back over to Chloe after sending off her taped up box down the line (which she had packed perfectly).

"I had no idea that *this* is what's behind DivaFeet!"

"Okay, you two, time for a quick break and then we have a meeting with the customer care manager. This is where you can change back into your glam shoes and I'll take those hats off you, for now."

Doreen walked them back out towards the yard and back into unit five—the staff canteen. Even that was a huge scale operation, with a menu that changed daily and catered for by an onsite kitchen. Rows of white benches sat thousands of staff as they took their well-earned breaks. On the menu today was pizza, sausages and mash potato, macaroni cheese, and a selection of salads and sandwiches. Carmen picked up a tuna salad, while Chloe enjoyed a slice of pizza with a side salad. "I could get used to this," she said, excited to tuck into her free meal.

"I dunno... You would get bored after a week or two," Carmen said, fussing at her salad with her fork while hordes of workers started to fill the canteen—joining the food line.

"Isn't this place amazing? Can you believe it? *This* is where S.O.S will ship thousands of orders!"

"Well, that's the goal," Carmen said, giving up on eating to put her pumps back on.

"If anyone is capable of packing that volume of orders every day, it's these guys—we just gotta make sure we do our part."

"In that case, eat up and get your shoes back on!"

Chloe did what she was told, enjoying her pizza slice, before removing her feet from the sweaty boots in exchange for her heels once more. Once their lunch hour was up, they carried their boots in their plastic bags and walked back out into the yard to find the customer care office. A crowd of workers on a cigarette break stared back at them, they weren't used to a fashion show in Mahwah.

At least the customer care unit was like being back in civilisation—decorated just like the New York office—with white walls, glass meeting rooms, and banks of desks where agents sat with headsets glued to their heads. Phone lines buzzed as agents helped customers place orders over the phone—reeling off script they had now perfected—and the sound of fingers tapping furiously on keyboards made them feel back in their comfort zone. Just like the New York HQ, this office also had a boardroom where Chloe and Carmen headed to meet back up with Doreen. "Good lunch?"

"Meh," Carmen grunted.

"Oh it was lovely, thanks," Chloe beamed over Carmen's ungratefulness.

"Sorry I'm late," a young woman said as she entered the room, sliding the glass door shut.

"This is Maisey, our customer care manager."

Maisey was obviously a local New Jersey gal, with big blow-dried hair, wearing a pencil skirt with a low cut top—revealing an ample bosom. Her platform shoes were more suited to a night on the pole than a day shift at the office—but she seemed bubbly and sweet.

"Oh, that's okay—we haven't started yet. So Chloe and Carmen here have just had the grand tour."

"Pretty awesome, *riiight?*" Maisey said, making her way to the front to take a seat next to Doreen. "I've worked here for eight years now, and it amazes me every day."

"Let's make a start," Doreen said, motioning for them to take a seat. "Here are your beautiful packing boxes, which I have asked a packer to mock-up for us."

Doreen placed five white S.O.S boxes on top of the table with a thud. Extra small for small accessories, small for single items, medium for shoeboxes, large for garments that required a single fold strategy, and extra large for orders containing almost anything and everything. "As you can see, each box has your ribbon tied with a bow—this will then be placed into an outer cardboard shipper, with a single layer of tissue on top before it's taped up."

Doreen slid the medium box to Maisey to take over. "So, once the customer receives their order, they will open the outer box to reveal this beautifully wrapped branded box—just like receiving a gift to yourself in the mail!"

Carmen snorted a laugh at Maisey's enthusiasm, which got her a nudge in the ribs from Chloe. With her salon perfect nails in hot pink lacquer, Maisey took one end of the black gross-grain ribbon and pulled it free from the box, before sliding it over to Chloe.

"See how the ribbon has been printed with 'S.O.S' in white to match your branding?" She then continued to present the box, like a hand model on a shopping channel, revealing the 'StacksOf-Style' logo printed on the lid. She lifted the lid and inside was a top layer of tissue paper which had the packing slip and returns label on top. Underneath, she revealed a sweater wrapped in a singular piece of tissue, which was further padded out with more tissue around the sides. "This is how we propose your orders to be packed, but obviously we can make any changes, as you wish."

"Do we have to use so much paper?" Carmen sniffed.

"Oh, all our products are certified from a sustainable source and totally recyclable!"

"I think it's beautiful," Chloe said, taking the box to inspect it for herself.

"So, I received the customer care copy from head office… I've created all the templates for our agents to use, along with your brand header and footer—this will ensure both tone of voice and branding are in uniform."

Everything from order confirmations, order cancellations, returns and exchange notifications—even apology emails for late deliveries—had been pre-planned. Maisey logged onto her laptop to show them how they would look in a customer's inbox. Chloe was impressed, the final pieces of her online puzzle were slotting into place, and she felt great!

Never did she imagine that her website would become an online store with a full team behind it—which they were about to meet. Maisey walked them back through the office and over to a bank of desks, where five agents had been dedicated to working solely on StacksOfStyle. "Guys, this is Chloe Ravens and Carmen Visconti—founder and president of StacksOfStyle!"

The agents stopped tapping at their keyboards to look up and say hi. Chloe and Carmen walked around their desks, shaking hands as they introduced themselves. Chloe was pleasantly surprised to find she was somewhat of a celebrity—one girl flashed her flat-soled 'Raven' shoes she had managed to snag with her discount on DivaFeet.

"These guys have been working with me to make sure all the email templates are in place. We have the S.O.S customer service email inbox all set up and ready for our customers to reach us on. The S.O.S phone line will ring through to this exact team, and when we launch, we will divert calls to the DivaFeet agents to take over the night shift—we're twenty–four hours here. Right now we're testing that the DivaFeet ordering system has synced to the front-end of the S.O.S site. These guys are placing 'test' orders and making sure we can reserve items for clients—as well as make online returns—and all the things we know we will need from the data we have on servicing the DivaFeet customer… Take a look," Maisey said, no longer sounding like the bimbo Carmen had judged her to be; now sounding very much the expert on managing an online sales team.

Chloe sat down next to one of the assistants, who started to take her through how to locate an order on the system, searching by the customer's name or email—or directly with an order number. She needed to know what the staff had to deal with for her to understand how her business would actually work. He continued to bring up an order on his screen and clicked through the options to make a return, refund, or exchange. Carmen equally found it interesting, browsing the StacksOfStyle test site—looking at what stock had been photographed and prepared for the first live product push.

The rest of the afternoon had been spent sitting with their small team, learning all the tricks of the system and how to pull sales reports with Maisey, so they could check and feedback to Veronica each week. Chloe even answered the phone to a DivaFeet customer, helping them to place an order for a pair of shoes.

The experience was an exciting rush—not like work at all— and she hoped that she could continue this sense of fun for them, no matter how big the site got in the future. She was so grateful to her team for all their hard work, for sharing her dream, that she vowed to visit them every month to work from the warehouse for a day—which Carmen (surprisingly) also agreed to.

**

StacksOfStyle wasn't the only website getting ready to launch their new service. The MiBellaModa office in Milan had been working tirelessly on migrating Palazzo's systems over to their infrastructure—ready to handle their orders. Palazzo's e-commerce team had also been busy, transferring stock over to M.B.M's warehouse, getting ready to wind down their own team so they could focus solely on stock for their own stores and licensed distributors. And the success of the project meant a lot to Don Carlo, it was more than just another major brand to add to the long list he had already procured.

The Palazzo Group was set to become a major rival to all the other fashion conglomerates, and with two of the biggest labels in the industry under Gianni's belt, Don Carlo also wanted a piece of the action. But he didn't want Gianni to simply buy MiBellaModa, he was far too ambitious to walk away from the company her had built up from scratch to become the world's luxury online fashion guru. No, he wanted to join forces with The Palazzo Group. But for now, making the Palazzo website a success and getting Graziana on his side was the first step in his plan. In time he would get his greedy little hands on Maison Marais, and along with his existing catalogue of designer websites, MiBellaModa would own the majority percentage of all luxury fashion sales placed online—globally. Anytime someone ordered a piece of designer goodness online, through their laptops, phones and tablets, it would almost certainly come from one of his controlled sites.

Meanwhile, Gianni was busy working on the next spring/summer collection with his design team, and the thought of seeing Chloe again had put him in a good mood. Even Joli had noticed he had snapped out from being a grump to being energetic—humorous even. Maybe it was down to the fact that things were going well in the business, or that he was looking forward to the Maison Marais store opening, or maybe it was the Palazzo retrospective exhibition that was about to open at The Met that had lifted his spirits? Whatever it was, it made her job a whole lot easier.

The Palazzo archive team had shipped containers of vintage pieces, including all the looks shown in the retrospective fashion show—even custom pieces designed for celebrities had been recalled. It was going to be the largest gathering of Palazzo pieces ever curated for a single exhibition, and a record number of tickets had been pre-sold in moments of them going on sale. Gianni had good reason to be in a good mood—what with Maison Marais' new direction being perceived well under Jean-Paul's leadership. And with Gabriela Gracia accepting an Oscar in a Maison Marais creation, the talk of the industry had been about Jean-Paul's re-imagining of the iconic French house.

And in London, Dom and Pandora had been just as busy. Not only had they just finished another busy showroom season for the fall/winter collection, but magazines and photographers were all clambering to get their hands on some of the most dramatic looks from the show. On top of that, sell-through for the current spring/summer collection was looking rather good.

They too were enjoying the benefits of the 'Gabriela-effect' after she wore the custom leopard dress at the Golden Globes. Now, even more boutiques and department stores wanted to open accounts with them, and Dom's new interns meant that they could cope with the demand—allowing him to focus on the design process with Pandora for their next collection, rather than chasing orders and production issues all day.

And likewise, in Paris, Jean-Paul had also turned his hand to designing the next collection with Marie and Juliette. In between gathering material for the mood-board and coming up with the basis of the collection, he had video meetings and phone calls with Regina in New York—updating him on the progress of the Fifth Avenue makeover—making sure everything was going to plan for the opening. By now, it hadn't escaped Regina's attention that Chloe Ravens had somehow managed to worm her way into Maison Marais, as twenty limited-edition 'Chloe' bags had been delivered.

Luscious mint green, plush velvet bags—quilted with the 'MM' monogram pattern—were ready for 'invite-only' guests to snap up at the Fifth Avenue re-opening. In some ways, Regina found it amusing. Chloe's career at Palazzo had ended with a bag, and now here she was, starting again with her very own design. Although, Jean-Paul had added a handle made from a series of woven gunmetal chains, along with a yellow 'flame' enamel key fob that hung over the front of the bag with a red apple charm—a nod to New York's most famous landmark.

Gianni wasn't the only one who couldn't wait to see Chloe again; Jean-Paul was also excited to see her face when she saw her design, realised in person. He also couldn't wait to party with Carmen again—she had been a riot in Paris and he was hoping she would be up for some fun in New York too. With that in mind, he asked Claudette to help him pick two dresses from the collection to send to them to wear at the store opening. Claudette chose a long black chiffon dress, with silver stars woven into the fabric for Carmen, while Jean selected a short red sequin mini-dress for Chloe.

He was inspired by Chloe's red Palazzo dress that she had worn when she was first photographed with Gianni on the red carpet (the moment that had started it all between the two), and he wanted to recreate the moment of 'lust at first sight' all over again. Even Jean could see that they had something special between them, and he wanted them to get serious about it—unlike Graziana, Jean-Paul thought Chloe was just perfect for Gianni.

Not only was she pretty, stylish, and charming, but she was intelligent and creative—and Gianni needed more than just beauty. If that was the case, then surely he would have settled by now? Beauty was all around him; what he needed was a challenge, someone he could mentor, someone he could learn from—someone he could fall in love with.

***

"How was New Jersey, girls?" Veronica chirped, poking her head into their office.

"It was amazing! I can't believe what goes on down there," Chloe said, jumping up from her desk. " Everything's been taken care of; Maisey's a superstar! Actually, we're going to work a day, every month there—aren't we Carmen?"

Carmen simply nodded.

Although she had been impressed by the whole operation, she wasn't looking forward to wearing those stale smelling work boots again.

"Well, you may be there sooner than you think... I've got great news!"

'On no—she better not be relocating us there!' Carmen worried, her heart plummeting to the depths of her bowels, like a fairground thrill.

"Morgana and I have very cleverly arranged for you two to appear on the cover of The New York Times magazine! We've pitched you as fashion's dynamic duo—and that's not all... Helena Skeibovitz is shooting it! She wants to do something fabulous, something glam—but something that reflects the website at the same time. I've suggested a high-fashion shoot at the warehouse, with all the machinery and boxes around you... Now, that's fabulous! Don't ya think?" Veronica said, with jazz hands.

412

Carmen was more than relieved, she had to give it to her this time—it was indeed a fabulous concept. And at least this, way she wouldn't have to wear those *fucking* boots again the next time she visited! Plus, Helena was one of America's greatest modern-day portrait photographers, capturing some of the most famous names in film, music, fashion—even Presidents and world leaders. The chance to be photographed by *the* Helena Skeibovitz was definitely worth the trip back to Mahwah alone.

"That's—that's incredible!" Chloe stammered, this time grateful for Morgana's hard work—even if she was overbearing at the best of times. Already, StacksOfStyle was making front-page news, and they hadn't even sold a single thing yet.

Within days, Chloe and Carmen were back down at the warehouse—this time with Zoe and Gray to help make them magazine cover ready. And yes, Carmen had gotten her wish—Doreen had allowed the entire crew to enter the warehouse without the vests, hard hats, and musty boots (but she had made them sign a waiver to cover her back). Veronica had also authorised them to shoot for an hour, between eleven and Midnight (the least busy time for receiving orders), so that they wouldn't interrupt business operations.

"This is where all the orders come from?" Zoe asked, equally as gagged by the scale of it all.

"Uh-huh," Chloe muttered, with her eyes popped open and her mouth parted as she applied liquid eyeliner on her. "I couldn't quite believe it either… I still don't actually. I never imagined that the little blog I started from my apartment in Williamsburg is now about to be a full-on fashion website that you can order from, right to your door!"

Now that all the hard work had been done, Chloe finally woke up each day, excited by her achievements—alive with anticipation for launch day. It was Carmen who was the one being stressed more so these days. As president of the business, she had been in meetings back to back, ensuring every team from tech to buying—right down to the photo studio and even Maisey in customer care—were finalising their work, ready for site launch. If anything went wrong, then she could be sure she would be blamed for it. She had gone from zero knowledge in computers other than ordering on Amazon, to understanding the basics of HTML code within months.

Earlier that day, Maisey had gift-wrapped a mountain of boxes, all complete with the black and white S.O.S ribbons in a mix of sizes. One of the packing slides and conveyor belts in the warehouse had been halted and cleared so that the boxes could be lined up along it, with space in between for Chloe and Carmen to pose with a trail of boxes behind them. Behind it, the warehouses' vast alley-ways of stock shelving towered under the fluorescent strip lighting, serving as the industrial backdrop that the New York Times wanted—all they needed now was the glam factor.

Gray had blow-dried Carmen's straight hair into a mass of big, loose curls—using hair extensions—while Chloe's blonde frizz was pumped up and back-combed out. With their hair and make-up complete, they swapped their comfy casuals for long cocktail dresses. Chloe had picked out a P.S.L dress—since that was one of the main launching designers—while Carmen opted for a long kaftan-style dress by Hilary Van Furstein.

Matched with high heels, they looked completely out of place in the industrial unit. Night workers stopped what they were doing to watch them strut into the warehouse, pounding the smooth cement floor with the click-clack of their heels (an unusual sound in such a strict health and safety zone).

"Good evening ladies… You both look fantastic," Helena said, shaking their hands lightly. "It's great to meet you!"

"And a pleasure to meet you!" Carmen gushed in the presence of the legendary female photographer.

"Okay, as you can see, this is our first location and then maybe afterwards we will do some others elsewhere… Let's do solo takes first, then we'll get both of you up there."

Helena's assistant helped Chloe up the step ladder and onto the conveyer belt, surrounded by StacksOfStyle—quite literally.

"Okay, just give us a few turns," Helena called, as she got ready to capture Chloe.

Chloe could feel eyes on her from all around the warehouse, but standing up there surrounded by her very own branded boxes, she started to feel like the Queen of the Internet that she had always wanted to become. And stood in front of Helena, she couldn't freeze now—this was her one and only chance to be photographed by a living artist.

She took a deep breath and recalled her poses from when she first met Gianni on the red carpet. With one hand on her hip, she swished the skirt of her long dress to reveal a bit of leg. Then she lifted one foot up onto the box next to her, before changing to rest one elbow on her bent knee—her hand on her face, as she stared down the camera lens. Helena gave her assistant a 'thumbs up,' signalling her to turn on the fan, which blew out Chloe's big hair, making her dress waft breezily—like a superstar on stage.

Next, it was Carmen's turn, again without, and then with the fan—her straight hair flicked behind her as she posed. She even laid down on the conveyer with her back arched and one leg bent, up in the air. Then finally, it was time for the pair to pose together. Carmen stood behind Chloe, with her arm on her shoulder as Chloe stood strong with her arms folded in front of her as they poised their heads in the air.

"Got it!" Helena called.

Gray and Zoe quickly nipped in to primp and perfect them once more, ready for more shots to be taken around the warehouse, and it ended up being rather fun. Chloe posed next to a stack of boxes, while Carmen hung off a ladder—pretending to pick an order, with her leg kicked out behind her.

Throughout the entire shoot, the warehouse staff watched on in amazement, this level of glamour had never reached Mahwah before, and they suspected it was only going to get more fabulous with Chloe and Carmen around.

25

The New York Times magazine cover story came out the following week, and Veronica was rather pleased with herself. It did exactly what she wanted it to do, broadcasting StacksOfStyle's launch to almost every New York commuter, and if people hadn't already heard of Chloe Ravens, then they certainly had now.

She hoped that by generating such high profile intrigue, it would only make people search and click on launch day, as they asked themselves: 'What is this StacksOfStyle?'. While the magazine cover displayed Chloe and Carmen up on the conveyer belt together, the accompanying article featured their solo shots, describing them as the 'Stylists To The Stars—And Now *You!*'

Needless to say, the article banged on about Chloe's dalliances with Gianni, as well as their links to DivaFeet and P.S.L—as their exclusive U.S retailer. Fashion SOS was on its way out into the world, and with launch day now here, Chloe and Carmen had very quickly transformed into the dynamic duo that Veronica had promised to make them. The DivaFeet office had been decorated in black and white balloons (this time printed with StacksOfStyle. com). White buttercream cupcakes with rice paper logo's and cartons of popcorn in black and white striped boxes had also been distributed around the office, which didn't surprise Chloe upon arrival—Veronica loved to make a show of things.

Hardly being able to sleep the night before, Chloe arrived at the office early (*way* earlier than usual) with a full face of make-up on, dressed in a simple yet chic black shift dress with a blazer over the top. She was closely followed by Carmen (who was also dressed to play the part of president), wearing a black blazer and slim black drain pipe-pants with black high-heels. They had learnt from the 'Raven' launch day and made a pact to both wear chic and simple black outfits. "Are you ready for this?" Carmen said, arriving with coffee—like she did most mornings.

"Is that an Irish coffee by any chance?" Chloe said, taking a cup out of the cardboard tray.

"Err, no… But we can make it one? I'm sure Veronica will have some booze in her office."

"She might do after today… What if this goes horribly wrong?"

"What could possibly go wrong?" Carmen said, perching on top of her desk. "We have the best tech team, buyers, creatives, oh… And *US!* I think we've got this…"

"I hope you're right… I'm just worried," Chloe said, sipping her coffee.

"It's just excited nervousness… I feel it too; don't worry. Come on, we better get to the boardroom and help set up," Carmen said, checking her watch.

StacksOfStyle was due to be pushed live at nine a.m, opening its virtual doors to online shoppers around the world. The first homepage article was by Chloe and Carmen themselves, welcoming everyone to the newest fashion hotspot. And the first selection of products to upload of course featured their five exclusive capsule collections from Bombster, Misty Jones, Aristotle, Creative Corps and The Glitterati.

And with the 'Raven, by Chloe Ravens' line now fully restocked, it was time for it to return to StacksOfStyle.com as its very own private label. Veronica was hopeful that it would sell out again off the back of Gabriela wearing the silver sandals at the Oscars' and had insisted that the collection uploaded on launch day. The boardroom started to fill out, with everyone who had worked for months on end to make this project possible making their way over. Morgana, Bill, Bob from tech, Derek from art and design, Veronica, and of course, Chloe and Carmen all sat around the large square table—watching the TV screen which had been live-linked to Doreen and Maisey at the warehouse in New Jersey.

"Okay, everyone… If I can get your attention, please! We have just fifteen minutes before we push this thing live, and I would like to say a few words… Firstly, good morning New Jersey!" Veronica waved at the webcam. "When I first met Chloe, I knew that she was one to keep an eye on. You are tenacious, determined, but you are also a very warm person that people wanna get to know, and I just knew that I wanted to help you with your idea—luckily for me, it turned out your ideas were good! But that's why we're here today… Your personality and hard work have got you this far, and with Carmen as your partner, mentor, friend—president, I cannot wait to see where you take StacksOfStyle."

Listening to Veronica, Chloe started to feel tears of joy pool in her eyes. But it was all true, her personality and hard work *had* got her to this point. Although, she couldn't have done it without Carmen *and* Veronica—especially Veronica! Her investment and existing business model had helped her turn her blog into an online shopping magazine. No more would readers have to search for that dress in the photo, wished they knew who made that perfect blazer, scoured the Internet for *that* bag… Now they could simply read, click, buy, and wear—without even leaving the comfort of their own sofa.

"Guys, get the champagne open," Veronica ordered, flapping her hands towards the ice buckets on the table. "Chloe, Carmen… Come up here, bring a glass with you."

Bob had his laptop synced to the boardroom screen with the back-end system ready to switch the website live. This was it, this was the moment that they had been working towards for almost a year. Edging her way to the front of the room, Chloe's palms started to get clammy and warm, leaving mirky fingerprints on her champagne flute, while Carmen managed to look poised and very much like the president of the company that she had been appointed to be.

"Okay… Just like last time, click this traffic light system to green—and that will publish us live online," Bob said, handing over the controls to Chloe.

"Settle down everyone," Veronica yelled, tapping a pen against her glass. "Everyone got a glass? Good! *Ten, nine,*" she started, encouraging everyone to countdown with her. *"Eight, seven, six, five, four, THREE—TWO—ONE!"*

And on *one*, Chloe did exactly what Bob had instructed her to do and clicked the 'Live' button—which blinked amber before turning solid green. He swiftly took over and entered the URL for the homepage so that it would be shared on the huge TV screen for everyone to see.

"And we're live!" Veronica saluted with her champagne glass in the air. "We *are* live, right?"

For a moment, the web page on the screen circled with the classic rotating 'wheel of doom' as it searched for the homepage online (you would think the office of an online company would have the best Internet connection). But soon enough, the new website for S.O.S fully loaded onscreen, and everyone released their bated breaths—toasting each other. Carmen turned to hug Chloe before they both clinked glasses together—this was the first day of their new career together.

"Congratulations!" Veronica said, hugging them both after they had had their moment. "Bob, how we looking?"

"All good and stable," he said, clicking around the system, pulling up graph reports that monitored visitors and activity. "So far, we have… Ten visitors."

"Amazing! Doreen, Maisey… Are you still with us?" Veronica said, making sure her satellite guests were still with them—much like a TV news reporter.

"We sure are, M'am," Doreen said, raising her mug of charred black filter coffee.

"Let's all keep an eye out for the first order," Veronica said. "Make sure it's wrapped perfectly! We'll be in touch if there's any activity on our end."

For the entire morning, Chloe, Carmen, Morgana, Veronica and Bob all worked from the boardroom—waiting for that first order to come through. And when it did, the room erupted once more.

"Oh my God! What is it? How *much* is it?" Veronica yelled as they all gathered around Bob's screen.

"It's… A pair of sunglasses for $40," Bob said. "Going to a *guy* in Pittsburgh!"

Chloe looked at Carmen—she looked back at her. It wasn't exactly what they had been expecting, but nonetheless, it was an order.

"Wait… We got another one—a bomber jacket and a T-shirt… Here in New York," Bob said, tapping away at his laptop.

Chloe high-fived Carmen, wearing those jackets around Fashion Week had paid off it seemed.

"Excellent! Chloe, get onto the warehouse and make sure they are packed immediately," Veronica said, leaving the boardroom to take a phone call.

Chloe called Maisey right away, reminding her to make sure the packer followed their strict packing guidelines. The thrill of the first two orders coming through had almost distracted them from noticing all of the others that were starting to trickle in. Misty Jones sunglasses, dresses by The Glitterati, tops and pants from Aristotle, and of course, more Bombster jackets!

By the end of the day, the 'Raven' line had also performed extremely well, but this time they had re-ordered enough to cope with demand (except for the shoes worn by Gabriela Gracia which had clean sold-out). Carmen and Chloe worked long into the evening, way after all their other teams had left—ordering pizzas and beers for those that stayed behind with them to help. Checking the sales screen for their first trading day, they were happy to reveal that they had made $25,000 in Net sales—Chloe text Veronica straight away to tell her the good news.

"If we take this much every day, it means we will sell out of our exclusive collections faster than we thought! We need to get the P.S.L collection up immediately!" Chloe said, now starting to worry that they didn't have enough stock rather than no customers.

"The editorial team are finishing the interview copy with Pandora and Dom, we'll be on course to upload the collection next Friday," Carmen reminded her, adamant that they were going to stick to their once-a-week upload schedule for new arrivals.

The rest of the week went by very much the same: checking for new orders, liaising with tech to make sure there were no bugs on any of the pages that stopped shoppers from checking out, and making sure the P.S.L collection was ready to upload at the end of it. Chloe was keen to get the collection up onsite, since it was selling well in stores across Europe, and she was certain the zero–one–five dress would be a bestseller for them.

The Hilary Van Furstein capsule could wait at least another week to upload; it was important that they didn't peak too soon, and had something in their arsenal to keep customers coming back online each week—and ordering! Bill had re-ordered more bomber jackets (which had now completely sold-out) as well as checking up with the suppliers on the progress of the second 'Raven' collection that was being produced to cope with the demand for summer styles.

Meanwhile, over at the distribution centre, phone calls had flooded their tiny customer care team, demanding to be placed on the waiting list for the famous Gabriela Gracia shoes (as they had now been dubbed by customers). Packers at the lanes on the warehouse floor were busy, perfectly wrapping orders in white boxes with black ribbons to be shipped out—on their way to their new homes and hopefully not to be returned.

Getting up early in the morning had now become exciting, as Chloe and Carmen were eager to witness every moment of their baby flourish—followed by even more later nights. But work had become addictive and prising themselves away from the office was difficult to do, it was what they had dreamt about for so many months and now it was all going to plan. In recognition, Chloe framed their New York Times magazine cover shoot and hung it up in the office—a reminder of their beginning.

But for Chloe, it had all started in her apartment in Williams-burg—shooting looks with Dom after a hard day's work on the shop floor of Palazzo. Staying up late to write articles, posting on Instagram, being late the next day for work because instead of leaving on time, she had carefully poured over her clothes and make-up—making sure she was worthy of the 'gram.'

And now she was surrounded by her own team, in her own office, selling her own collections—on her very own website! This *was* the dream, and she was *now* living it. For the very first time in months, she looked around and took it all in as she stopped to eat a sandwich at her desk—watching everyone outside the glass walls working hard to make StacksOfStyle a success.

Another thought crossed her mind… Her achievements were now out there for everyone else to see: Gianni, Graziana, Regina—*especially* Regina! 'I'd sure love to see that bitch's face now,' Chloe smirked, slurping on her iced coffee—finally feeling good enough for Gianni.

*

The office had been flooded with flowers and cards from well-wishers; Kim had sent a beautiful bouquet of flowers from her and Dionne, as did Claudette on behalf of Jean-Paul. Hilary Van Furstein sent over a bottle of champagne with a handwritten card (saying she couldn't wait for them to upload the H.V.F collection), while Dom and Pandora had sent them even more flowers. But the most interesting of them all was waiting for her at the reception desk as she came to work the next morning. "Oh, good morning… I have something for you," Bethany said, getting up to dash over to her little side office.

Tired from returning to the office (that she had only just left six hours ago) Chloe waited patiently with her eyes closed—catching a few extra winks.

"This came for you," she said, returning with a small red Cartier bag.

"For me?" Chloe said, pleasantly surprised. "No card?"

"Only the bag was delivered, maybe it's inside?"

"Sure… Thanks," Chloe said, puzzled by who would send her something from Cartier, of *all* places!

But as she made her way up to the office, red bag in hand, she knew exactly who this was from—and she didn't know how she felt about it. In some ways, what happened in Paris had been more of closure to carry on, than an opening. It had allowed her to get back to work and forget the feelings of doubt, insecurity and failure—everything she felt when she was around anything to do with Palazzo. But it was the possibilities of what her friendship with Gianni could bring that intrigued her; it was the 'what if's' that made her hang on to the idea of being in his world. What if she did give him a chance and ignore the Regina and Graziana's in her life? What if she *could* have her dream job—running StacksOf-Style—as well as having a sensational, hot (and very high-profile) romance with Gianni all at the same time?

What she did know, was that where her head was at right now—where her life was heading—was just perfect, and she didn't want anything to upset it. So much had already changed in her life, she wasn't quite ready for more big changes; for once, she simply wanted to enjoy the moment she was in.

"Morning... *Ooh*, what's all this?" Carmen said, noticing the red bag in her hand as soon as Chloe entered the office. "Treat yourself already?"

"Nope... It was left at reception for me," Chloe said, setting it down on her desk while she took off her coat to get the day started.

"Well... Aren't you going to open it?" Carmen said, dashing over to her desk—clearly more excited than Chloe was.

She was more apprehensive than anything, but sensing Carmen wasn't going to give up until she opened it, she pursed her lips and snatched the bag off her desk. Untying the red and gold ribbon from the handles—still pouting at the pressure pouring off Carmen's stare. Opening the bag, she finally pulled out a red box with gold gilded edges.

"Do you think it's diamonds?" Carmen said, with her hands on her face in delight. "Well, open the *damn* thing!"

Chloe lifted the top half of the box, revealing a gold Love bangle with white diamonds, alternated with Cartier signature screws along the width of the bracelet.

"*Fuck!* It *is* diamonds!" Carmen yelped. "This thing is worth like... $10,000!"

Chloe couldn't believe her eyes; why would Gianni send her such an expensive gift? She allowed Carmen to take over, handing her the box for her to admire while she searched for a note inside the bag. A crisp white envelope laid flat against the side of the bag—easily dismissed in the excitement of it all. Chloe scored the fold open and pulled out the notecard inside.

Congratulations!
I'll see you after work…
G x

"Oh my God!" Chloe said, feeling her face drain white.

"What? What is it?" Carmen said, now trying on the bracelet for herself.

"It's from Gianni," Chloe said, passing the note to Carmen.

"Of course it's from Gianni! Who the *hell* did you think it was from? The boogeyman, for fuck's sake?" Carmen said, too busy unlocking the bangle to take the note to read the obvious.

"I… I don't understand? Is he in New York?"

"Hasn't he messaged you?"

"Nothing, nothing since Paris—and now this… Wait, what does he mean by 'I'll see you after work'?"

"Well, that's it—he must be in town then… The Maison Marais store opening *is* in a few weeks, after all… Something tells me you'll need to pop out at lunch and grab something else to wear," Carmen said, eyeing up Chloe's basic black blazer and pantsuit business combo.

"You think he's really going to pick me up after work?" Chloe scoffed, denying that any of this was at all possible. "Anyway, I don't have time to go shopping… Or go back to the apartment for that matter!"

"Leave it with me," Carmen said, already picking up her desk phone.

True to his word, Gianni was indeed in New York. He had flown over to oversee the final stages of the Maison Marais Fifth Avenue store to ensure all of the final fittings were in place—ready for the opening night. But Chloe didn't have time to worry about his sudden arrival now. Her day was filled with emails, meetings, and compiling reports for Veronica—not to mention attending one of Morgana's lengthy marketing meetings about future campaigns that weren't even in sight yet. Even the Cartier bangle, sitting in its red box on her desk, couldn't distract her from her work. Carmen, however, was having none of it—she knew Chloe simply needed a nudge—and by the end of the day, she had the perfect solution.

"This is for you," she said, swinging a Hilary Van Furstein bag in the doorway of their office.

Chloe briefly looked up from her screen, tapping away at a spreadsheet—writing her first sales report. "What's this? Not another gift?"

"No, *silly!* I had an emergency dress biked over for this evening… You know, just in case."

"Oh, just in case I need to go home and have a hot soak and an early night? You shouldn't have…"

"Oh, no you don't," Carmen said, dumping the bag on Chloe's desk, pointing a finger in her face—her other hand on hip. "Now, you listen to me… I haven't listened to you moan and whine about this man for months, only for you to now not give a shit all of a sudden… I flew to *fucking* Paris to play gooseberry in front of you two! I've listened to you gripe about his *sister*—you care about this man and you *are* going to see him this evening and that's final! For the record, this is Gianni making an effort—a Cartier bracelet kinda effort—and I'm pretty sure he wouldn't just do that for anyone… So, on that note—I'll finish the damn report… Will you just go, please?"

Chloe wheeled her chair back, staring Carmen out as she did. She wasn't going to win the contest, and like usual, Carmen was right. She *was* the president of the company, and she *was* more than capable of compiling a sales report while she took off early for once. Reluctantly, Chloe got up and took the bag from her desk, reaching inside to pull out a short summer dress printed with a bold H.V.F floral pattern—holding it up for inspection. "Well, I haven't heard from him… So I guess I'll just be heading home," Chloe said, wondering if she had enough time to go home and get ready if he was indeed in town, or whether she would get away with a night in, all to herself.

"Whatever… Can you just forward me that report and get the hell outta here?" Carmen said for the last time. "And make sure you put that *fucking* diamond bracelet on your arm!"

Taken back by her demands, Chloe did exactly what she was told and stuffed the dress back into the paper bag before grabbing her things to go. "Cool, I'll see you in the morning?"

"Or maybe not? Take the morning off… You know—if you need to," Carmen winked.

Picking up the Cartier box from her desk, Chloe finally left the office and skipped down the mezzanine stairs to walk past the banks of desks below, towards the elevators back down to reception. As she strolled, her phone buzzed in the depths of her handbag. It didn't matter if she left early or not, the day never seemed to end, and there were always emails that needed replying to. Fumbling for her phone, a simple text message awaited her— simple yet alarming.

> Outside…
> Black Mercedes :)

"*Fuck!*" Chloe cursed under her breath, she hated it when Carmen was right (which was most of the time). Why was she so oblivious to the things that were so obvious to everyone else? Here she was, still deluding herself that she was heading home for a hot bath and a glass of wine in front of Netflix, while Gianni waited outside for her. Taking a detour, she dashed into the women's bathroom and locked herself into a cubicle. She whipped out the black and pink floral dress out of the bag and undressed.

The feeling of her bare feet on the cold bathroom floor made her feel icky. She replaced her black pantsuit with the dress, before wiping the in-soles of her black heels with a face-wipe from her make-up bag. Slipping them back on, she headed back out to the row of sinks—now she had to patch up her make-up. She didn't have the time (or the products) to do a fresh face, so she blotted her existing make-up with a paper towel and quickly buffed her cheeks with bronzer, reapplying her lipstick last. Rummaging around her handbag, she discovered a few stray hair grips, and with wetted fingertips, she swept back one side—clipping it into place—flicking the other side over her shoulder.

Looking in the mirror, she had made do with what little she had, and the dress was quite cute after all—it was amazing how a quick change could suddenly make you feel revived. Now, there was just one final touch to add—the bracelet. She opened the red leather box and took out the bracelet, quickly figuring out how the clasp worked before clamping it around her wrist—like it was some flimsy costume piece she had just ordered off DivaFeet with her staff discount.

She stuffed the empty box, along with her work clothes (saving the blazer to wrap around her shoulders), into the empty H.V.F boutique bag and grabbed her handbag off the bathroom side to finally leave the office. She tried her best not to make eye contact with anyone as she made her way back over to the elevators; eventually making it down to the ground floor without having to explain to any of her colleagues where she was going, all dressed up. Stepping out of the elevator, she dashed over to the reception desk (which was now left deserted for the evening) and chucked the H.V.F bag behind it to collect in the morning—she wasn't going to meet Gianni with her dirty laundry on her arm.

She quickly checked her face in the reflection of the glass backdrop of the reception and straightened out her dress. Checking her appearance—knowing that this was as good as it was going to get—she couldn't believe what was happening. It was crazy, but she couldn't possibly keep Gianni waiting any longer, so she took a deep breath and walked over to the office entrance—looking out of the tall glass windows to see if she could see a black Mercedes.

Pushing the door release button, she stepped outside onto the sidewalk—trying her best to act natural and leave her nerves behind. Looking left then right, she heard a car horn beep—parked further up the street (they had waited so long for her to come down that they had to circle the block a few times). Noticing his passenger approaching from behind in his mirror, the driver stepped out to open the door for her. Chloe stepped up her pace a little, making sure she didn't lose the momentum of her strut—but making her hair bounced a little at the same time. "Good evening Ma'am," the driver said, to which she nodded—confirming it was, in fact, her that they had waited over half-an-hour for.

Chloe could smell Gianni's cologne oozing out of the car, even before she had a single foot inside it. She took a deep breath of 'fresh' New York air before lowering herself, preparing for her head to swirl from his heady scent as she sat on the backseat next to him.

"Well, hello… Businesswoman of the year," Gianni said, leaning in for a peck on her lips.

She let him kiss her quickly, before setting her bag down between them and buckling up—noticing that he looked casually handsome in a black suit with a white V-neck T-shirt underneath. "Oh, I don't know about that," she said, puckering her lips from where he had just kissed her as she tried her best not to look at him. She didn't want him to see the huge grin on her face, and she didn't want to admit to herself that she was very happy to smell him—see him again. She straightened out her face by taking a breath through her nose.

"Well, it looks to me like things are going well… Very well in fact."

"Why are you here?" Chloe said, tossing her head to face him as the driver pulled out to drive off.

"Why am I here?" Gianni said, rather coquettish. "I did say I would… I thought you'd be pleased to see me?"

"I didn't mean it like that," she said, realising that she sounded like a total bitch. "I simply meant, I didn't expect you to surprise me like this," holding up her wrist to flash the Cartier bracelet at him.

"Ah, you got my gift I see… I wasn't due to arrive until next week, but I had to check on a few things ahead of the opening—and I couldn't wait to see you."

"Well, thank you… It was a bit overwhelming—the gift and your arrival! Anyway, where are you taking me?" she said, chewing her lip—trying her best not to fall for his charms so quickly.

"I thought we'd just have dinner together… I wanted to take you out and celebrate the launch of StacksOfStyle," he said, looking down at her wrist—taking her hand to bring it up to his lips. Joli had chosen well, yet again.

Shuddering at the tingling sensation of his warm, tough lips planting against her soft hand, Chloe took in another breath—her lungs topping up on his irresistible scent. She had only been in his presence for five minutes and already she was swept back into his world of luxury and lust. In the craziness of launching the website and knuckling down to work, she had forgotten how amazing it felt to be back in his good books—and how much she truly desired him.

"I saw your cover story by the way… Very chic, and very sexy! There's nothing like a strong woman owning her power!"

Chloe puffed out a laugh. How ironic, here she was completely powerless to this man and yet he thought she was powerful and strong. 'If only he knew how weak I am for him,' she thought to herself, hating how much control he had over her without even trying.

"What's so funny?" he laughed back, watching her pinch the bridge of her nose as she looked out of the window. "Seriously though… How's it all going? It's not easy running a company, right?"

"So far, so good… Veronica's on my back about sales and stuff, but that's to be expected I guess," she said, finally taking him seriously.

"And how are sales?"

"Great! Beyond our expectations… This week we're launching Pandora Simmons, so we're hoping for another great weekend… How're things with you?" she said, wanting to take the heat off her, just for a moment.

"Oh, the usual… Busy designing the next collection, shipping the archive pieces over here for the exhibition… And then there's the Palazzo website—you haven't been the only one busy online."

"Of course, you mentioned you were changing things up with MiBellaModa… And how is that all going?"

"Like you say—so far, so good… Don Carlo knows exactly what he's doing and it's taken a lot of work off our hands if I'm honest… I've just given him the go-ahead to take over Maison Marais' e-commerce too."

"Wow! You *have* been busy," Chloe said, trying to wonder what it must be like, not only directing Palazzo but Maison Marais too—and with an exhibition at the Met on the horizon too. Although, he did have Graziana to help him with the business side of things. And with this reminder, StacksOfStyle suddenly seemed like a walk in the park—Carmen was a Godsend in comparison.

Having filled most of the car ride with business talk, the driver finally pulled over in full view of Brooklyn bridge. Down Under the Manhattan Bridge Overpass was home to the trendiest restaurants, bars and hotspots—sandwiched between Brooklyn and Manhattan bridge. Gianni got out and walked around the back of the car to open the door for Chloe. She shrugged her blazer back over her shoulders and took her handbag off the seat, accepting his hand to step out.

"I bet you guys come here all the time," Gianni said, holding her hand.

"Can't say we do," Chloe said, looking up at the white letters above the entrance, spelling out 'Empire Stores.' From the outside, it looked like a regular New York red brick building, but Dumbo House was one of the most exclusive members places to be seen at. Walking through the central double doors of Empire Stores, Gianni nodded at the front desk who let them walk straight past to the bronze doored elevator—waiving the formalities of signing in because of who he was.

"I called ahead and booked a table on the terrace upstairs, there's a great view of the two bridges from up here… I think you'll like it."

And he wasn't wrong. Passing through the stylish club area, Chloe was glad she took Carmen's advice and changed into something more suitable. The interior featured a Manhattan blue ceiling and matching pillars with large floor to ceiling windows looking out onto the waterfront.

The stylish brass bar was bustling with after-work cocktail drinkers, while the terrace above was equally as busy with clusters of friendship circles meeting for an evening outdoors. A waiter led them over to their table in full view of Manhattan bridge in the evening's sky on one side—Brooklyn bridge in the near distance on the other. The marble slab table was low between two wicker garden sofas, plump with cushions—an outdoor bar under a brown wooden beamed pergola just behind them—and the East River below. Gianni ordered a bottle of champagne as Chloe took in the vista before sitting down with her legs tucked sideways in her dress. "Well, this is awesome… I can't believe Carmen hasn't brought me here already, she knows all the hot-spots in this city!"

"Well, we must come here more often… I'll sort out membership's for you guys."

"Oh, there's no need," Chloe said, noting he had just used the term '*we*.'

"There's every need… The founder and president of StacksOf-Style *must* be members. Consider it done."

Chloe felt herself blushing as she looked down, placing a napkin on her lap to distract him from her embarrassment. Maybe it was time she started splashing out a little on a lifestyle to match her title—not to mention the calibre of man she was attempting to date?

"I've been waiting to see you ever since Paris… As you know I've been very busy, but with the store opening and the exhibition coming up—I'm gonna be staying here for a while," Gianni said, leaning back into his sofa; staring at Chloe sat opposite him.

"Oh, really?" Chloe said, interested to see where the conversation was heading.

"I was hoping we could see more of each other… Now that the air has been cleared between us, that is… I'm hoping things will be easier without my sister here too," Gianni laughed, knowing she could certainly get in the way.

Chloe smirked, he wasn't wrong about that and at least she wouldn't be faced with explaining the situation between them. But even without Graziana, the sound of spending more time with

Gianni both pleased and daunted her. It was typical, now that she had a business to run and very little time to herself, he suddenly wanted to make more for her—but she wanted to find the time to spend with him. "That sounds wonderful," she said, picking up the menu before placing it back down. "You know, what happened in Paris…"

"What *happened* in Paris? Chloe, we like each other, right? There, I said it… I want to spend time with you, I want to know where this is going."

He looked into her eyes, rather seriously this time; it made her sit up. She didn't expect him to come out with it so bluntly, but she liked what she was hearing and her heart skipped with excitement. She looked out over the view; if she looked at him any longer, she would want to kiss him in full view of other members sat around them—they were already looking over and discussing the fact that he was Gianni Palazzo.

"Are you ready to order some food now?" the waiter said, returning with a bottle of champagne in an ice bucket.

******

After they had eaten, Gianni swapped seats to sit beside her and face the view together. Tipsy from the fizz, Chloe rested her head on his shoulder as the evening grew darker. Much to her surprise, it had turned out to be a rather romantic, yet chilled evening. "So, have you given any more thought about what I said earlier? About us spending time together?"

Chloe turned her head to look up at him. His sexy, stubbled face was in reach of her lips, she could still smell his cologne and the champagne was making her want to kiss him—but she didn't have to move an inch. Gianni could sense she wanted him, and that was the answer he was looking for. He leant into the short distance between them and planted a gentle kiss on her lips. Chloe closed her eyes and breathed in as she pushed her mouth against his, but he pulled away before things could get too messy in public.

"Why don't we get out of here? Back to mine?"

"Uh... I'd love to, but it's kinda getting late," Chloe said, sitting up to check the time on her phone. "Tomorrow's a big day at work... We're launching P.S.L and I have to—"

"That's okay, I understand... You're running a business now... Like I said, we can see each other any time, now that I'm here for a while... I'll take you home."

Chloe felt dumb, she had just turned down spending the night with him—a moment she had longed to have again for a long time. But he was right, she had responsibilities now and she had to remind herself that it wasn't worth giving up for any man—Gianni Palazzo included. And she had been there and done that with him all before anyway; if he was serious about her, then he would wait until the time was right—it wasn't like he was going anywhere.

The car ride back to Greenwich Village was far more cosier than before—snuggled up in the backseat holding hands. "I know I said it before, but I'm really impressed with what you've created... It's exciting times ahead for you two," Gianni said, kissing her head.

"It's an exhausting time!" Chloe said, stifling a yawn. She hadn't drunk alcohol since the site launched, and it had definitely caught up with her.

"You'll get used to it... When the money rolls in and you see the life you have created for yourself, it will all be worth it... You better not get too big for your boots and forget about me!"

"*Ha!* I hardly think that's possible," Chloe laughed, sitting up to look out of the window—seeing she was nearly home. "How can I forget the biggest designer in the fashion industry?"

"Now I know you're talking about Jean-Paul!"

"Thank you for a lovely evening—and for the gift," she said, jangling the bangle in front of him. "And the answer is yes, by the way."

"Yes, to what?"

"Now you're just making me say it out loud."

"Well, I did," Gianni teased.

"I'd love to spend time with you while you're here in New York... Satisfied now?"

He placed one arm on the back of the car seat as he cupped her face in his other hand, pulling her in for a longer kiss—a private kiss that she was now allowed to sink into—her hand resting on his chest. The feeling of his firm, warm chest through this T-shirt made her want to rip his shirt off right there in the back of his car (it did have tinted windows after all). But she stopped herself, she had been a lady all evening; it would be a shame to let it all slip at the last hurdle.

"Call me tomorrow?" she said, grabbing the door handle.

"What—no coffee?"

Chloe dipped her head and gave him a sarcastic look, before finally getting out the car. Looking up at her apartment entrance as she stepped out, she couldn't bear going inside alone—not now he was finally here in the same city. She turned around to shut the door, but looking at his handsome face—looking forlorn and sweet—she couldn't resist. "You coming up for this coffee, or what?"

Gianni's mouth curled into a cunning smile—he had gotten his way—and wasted no time to hop out of the car to follow her inside. Right now, she was glad to be living at Dom's place and not back at her old Williamsburg apartment—even though Dom's place could never match the lavish lifestyle Gianni was used to.

"Well, it's not much... But it's home for now," she said, turning the key and opening the door. She took a few steps inside before Gianni grabbed her waist, turned her around and pushed her up against the wall—raising both of her hands above her head in arrest. He waited for a beat before kissing her, looking into her eyes as he did. She could feel his breath on her face which turned her on, waiting in anticipation for him to kiss her.

He pressed himself against up her, and instead of going in for a full lip-lock, he started to caress her neck softly with wetted lips—all the way up to her ear lobe which turned her into putty. He let go of her arms so he could run his hands down the sides of her waist as she wrapped a leg around his. He was turning her wild as she ran her fingers through his hair, but she couldn't take it any longer and grabbed his face to pull him up to face her.

Finally, he kissed her deeply, his lips enveloping hers as his warm tongue slid into her mouth and locked with hers. 'So much for making him wait,' she thought to herself, unable to wait any longer; leading him over to the sofa in the lounge.

She kicked off her shoes and shrugged her jacket to the floor as he did the same—chucking his blazer onto the armchair. Resuming his position, he propped himself over her as she laid back on the sofa, caressing her leg all the way to lift her dress up, over her thighs. His touch on her body made her skin come alive with electricity, and she could feel he was just as excited to finally have her.

Chloe prompted him to lift up his T-shirt, making him stop to whip it off while she unbuckled his belt. He was now topless, with just his gold chain hanging down in between the crease of his golden chest—just a sprinkle of dark hair in the middle. Chloe forgot how wonderful his body was, manly, tanned, and toned—the right amount of definition that made him look great, both in and out of clothes.

She grabbed the back of his head, pulling him back down on top of her to kiss him, making her shudder from the sensation of his warm, naked skin as she caressed his back. He kissed her for a while more, before pausing to catch his breath. "Wait," Chloe said. "Your driver's still outside?"

"Yeah… Tommy always waits for me."

"While you make out with women?" Chloe said, puzzled by how casual he had said it.

"Well, if you came back to my place this wouldn't be a problem… Or I could always stay here if you want me to tell him to go home?

Chloe propped herself up in disbelief. "You… Stay here?"

"Why do you say it like that? Don't you want me to stay with you?"

"It's not like that… It's just, I thought you would prefer—"

"What I'd prefer, is to stay with you… I've waited long enough and I'm not sleeping alone tonight now that I have you, right here in my hands."

Chloe stared back at him, realising he was serious—but also coming to terms with the fact that she wouldn't be able to sleep if she didn't have her way too. "Okay… But I have to be at work at nine," she said, not wanting to prove Carmen right yet again by coming into work any later.

"Fine with me… I'll have Tommy return in the morning to collect us… I'll just call him to bring up my overnight bag up."

"You have an overnight bag with you?" Chloe laughed, starting to think he had orchestrated this whole evening—right down to this very moment.

"When you travel as much as I do—and own a global group like Palazzo—then you have to be ready to up and leave at any moment," he said, reaching into his jacket pocket for his phone.

While Gianni put his T-shirt back on and buckled up his pants to head downstairs to the car, Chloe got up and adjusted her dress before dashing to the bathroom. Shutting the door, she filled the sink basin with warm water and sunk a sponge into it to give herself a mini wash, before spritzing herself with perfume to freshen up as best as she could.

Heading back out, with Gianni still gone, she went to see what drink she had in the kitchen—if any. Opening the refrigerator, knowing there wasn't going to be champagne (or even wine), she took out two bottles of beer and uncapped them—taking a much-needed gulp. Gianni *fucking* Palazzo was going to spend the night at hers, this was surreal!

'Wait until I tell Dom about this,' she said to herself, before realising that the thought of them *'at it'* in his bed would most likely freak him out—which made her struggle to swallow a mouthful of beer as she laughed at the thought. "No sex in my bed!" she recalled him saying when he handed over the keys to his place, almost a year ago. Well, it was a little too late for that now and even though work was only nine hours away, this was worth being tired and hungover for. The apartment buzzer sounded, jolting her out of her thoughts. She answered it on the panel in the hallway, opened the door and raced back to the kitchen to appear natural, leaning against the side—sipping her beer.

"All set for a sleep-over," Gianni said, walking back in with his carry-on sized case in hand.

Chloe held out a beer for him to join her in the kitchen, which he accepted and clinked his bottle against hers before taking a swig—until the bubbles in the neck of the bottle calmed.

"So… Where were we?" he said, putting down the beer as he wiped his mouth.

Chloe raised an eyebrow and batted her eyes at him—he knew exactly where they had left things. Instead of making the first move, she made him wait by taking another mouthful of cold beer, before putting it down on the counter—just in time as he took her by the waist.

Hitching her up onto the kitchen counter in one effortless swoop, Gianni went in for a lager infused kiss, spreading her legs to move in closer—right there in the kitchen. If Dom didn't like the thought of her having sex in his bed, then she better not tell him about this either…

<h1 style="text-align:center">26</h1>

Day-break poured in through a crack in the bedroom curtains, which hadn't been fully drawn in the rush of passion. It was a quarter to six; Chloe always woke up in anticipation of her six a.m alarm but she didn't expect her bed to be empty just yet. Scrunching her eyes, she looked around the room, expecting to find Gianni sitting on the end of her bed, getting dressed to leave—but he wasn't.

'Has he left already?' she wondered, still coming to terms with only having four hours of sleep. She flipped the bed sheets back and swung her feet off the mattress, down onto the carpet— stretching out as she sat up. Once on her feet, she slipped on a silk robe that was hanging on the back of the door and made her way to the bathroom to see if he was having a shower; but having only just stepped out of the bedroom, the smell of cooking confirmed he was still indeed here. "What are you doing?" she said, tightening the belt on her robe as she walked into the kitchen—fussing with her hair, which was a haystack mess.

"After last night, I was starving! I found pancake mix in your cupboards… The bacon looks questionable, but if I nuke it enough in the pan, I'm sure we'll be fine."

Chloe stood and smiled, watching him scrape the edges of the batter mix in the pan. She would have expected him to have left early for whatever meeting he had in his busy schedule, but to find him making breakfast in her kitchen, she did not expect!

"I'm gonna take a shower… I'll be right back to enjoy your yummy looking pancakes," she said, blowing him a kiss before dashing off.

Under the hot water of the shower, Chloe couldn't help but smile as she lathered up her body, washing off the dried-on salty sweat from the night before. 'Maybe this thing with Gianni could work after all?' she thought to herself. The fact he was in her kitchen making breakfast was a good start. She quickly washed her hair and rinsed before brushing her teeth and gargling mouthwash. Then she had the task of applying her face creams and body lotion in record timing—wasting no time and going straight in with a pad of toner before applying serum and the rest of the potions that were the scaffolding of her daily face.

"Breakfast's ready!" Gianni called.

Pausing her beauty regime, for now, she towel-dried the dampness out of her hair, spritzed on some perfume and slipped her robe back on to head out to the kitchen. He had prepared three pancakes each with rashers of bacon. "Wow… Not the usual start to my day," she said, sitting on a stool at the kitchen worktop.

"Gotta keep your energy up after last night," he winked.

"So, what're your plans for the day?" she said, picking up her fork.

"Well, I thought I'd drop you off at the office and pop in… See Carmen and your office."

"Sorry, what?" Chloe said, almost choking on a piece of bacon.

"I want to see your office… Ya know, the place where you work? If that's okay, of course."

"Sure, why wouldn't it be?" she said, not exactly sure if it was a good idea. Introducing Gianni to the entire office was a bit like introducing him to her parents already. Plus, it would set tongues wagging—including Veronica's—and she was hoping to keep their affairs to herself for a little while longer.

"If you'd rather I didn't, that's totally fine," Gianni said, sensing apprehension.

"No, it's fine… Why wouldn't it be? It's not as if you don't know Carmen already."

"Perfect, I won't stay long anyway—I have a video call with Don Carlo—just a quick tour."

The thought of him turning up to the office with her curbed her appetite, but after managing half a plate of pancakes, she excused herself to finish getting ready and dressed while he politely cleared the dishes. Back in the bedroom, she grabbed her phone to quickly warn Carmen of what was happening—which got her an instant reply.

No way! OMG…

U stayed at his last night?
What shall I tell Veronica?

Say nothing!

I don't want her being extra, or worse…
Alerting the rest of the office…

I do NOT need an audience!

*

"Here we are!" Chloe said, with a sarcastic laugh, reaching for the car door.

"Wait," Gianni said, leaning over for a kiss before they got out into the open. His stubbly, unshaven face bristled against hers before she could pull away.

"You'll smudge my make-up," she said, gently pushing him away. Turning up to work with Gianni was enough to deal with, let alone with smeared lipstick.

She got out of the car, followed closely by Gianni—he tried to hold her hand but she shook it away to open the entrance door of DivaFeet. It was early enough to miss the morning influx of workers arriving minutes before nine, but she still didn't want to take any chances of making a scene in front of the security and front of house staff.

"Good Morning," Bethany said from behind the reception desk, standing up once she noticed who she had just walked in with.

"Morning, Bethany, I have a visitor… Mr Palazzo won't be staying long, so no need to issue a pass."

"Of course," Bethany flustered, standing up and awkwardly bowing to him—she *was* in the presence of fashion royalty after all.

Gianni smiled and waved to her as he followed Chloe over to the elevators in the office lobby. Chloe jabbed the 'call' button profusely—she just wanted to get him up to her office as quickly as possible, with as little drama on the way.

"Oh, Chloe," Bethany called over. "This bag was left behind the desk last night, I think it's your clothes from yester—"

"*Thank you!* I'll collect that later," she said, nudging Gianni into an elevator, closing the doors just as quickly as they had opened.

"Is everything okay?" Gianni smiled.

"Fine—I'm fine."

"You seem… Nervous?"

"Nervous? Why would I be nervous… This is *my* office," Chloe said, shrugging his hand off her shoulder before the doors re-opened onto the open-plan office space. "So, this is where the magic happens… These banks of desks belong to the DivaFeet team, which we currently share. Buying sits over there, that's press, then editorial, and tech over in the far corner by the boards."

Without stopping, Chloe led him along the desks and up to the mezzanine floor where the S.O.S office resided next to Veronica's—hoping they wouldn't bump into her on the way.

"And this is our office right here," she said, raising her voice to alert Carmen that their 'surprise' guest had arrived.

"Chloe—Gianni… So nice to see you again! What are you doing here?" Carmen said, trying her best to sound surprised as she got up to greet him with the obligatory air kiss.

"I told I'd be back, didn't I? I wanted to swing by and see your new office," he said, looking sound at the small glass box make-shift office that housed just their two desks.

"And what a nice surprise it is," Carmen started, only to be interrupted before she could say anything else.

"Good morning ladies… Oh, Mr Palazzo!" Veronica said, clutching her chest at the doorway—trying her best to sound (and act) surprised.

Chloe rolled her eyes. '*You told her?*' she mouthed to Carmen.

Carmen shrugged. "Bethany must have called her," she quickly whispered.

"Nice to meet you… You must be, Ms Meyer?" Gianni said, shaking her hand. "I hope you don't mind me dropping in unannounced."

"Not at all, you're welcome anytime! Has Chloe given you the tour of our office? This is only half of it, we have a distribution centre in New Jersey—which is really the heart of this operation," Veronica reeled off. "Why don't we all have coffee and breakfast in my office? I can tell you all about our business?"

"That sounds wonderful," Gianni said, looking to Chloe and Carmen for approval.

"Oh, Gianni can't stay long—he has a meeting," Chloe said, trying to save him from Veronica chewing his ear off over coffee and croissants—as much as saving herself from an awkward bombardment of questions, no doubt.

"That's not until lunchtime," he chipped in.

"Perfect! I'll just call down and order some refreshments… Come through to my office when you're ready," Veronica said, making her way back to her office.

"Sorry about that," Chloe said, putting her purse down on her desk.

"About what? She seems very sweet… And accommodating."

"Very accommodating!" Carmen said with a dry laugh. "Sorry to talk boring business matters, Gianni—I *am* happy to see you— but we have all the assets to finally push the Pandora Simmons collection live today."

Gianni, held his hands up, not wanting to get in the way of their busy day and took a seat opposite Chloe's desk to observe them at work.

"Excellent! We're already behind on uploading it," Chloe said, turning on her computer.

"I'll let the upload team know we're happy to go ahead; editorial will push the article with Pandora on the homepage to go alongside the new arrivals."

"Sounds like you have a big launch on your hands?" Gianni said, swivelling in his chair.

"You could say that… Sales have gone well, but we have a lot riding on P.S.L as Veronica owns a stake in their company now—part of the deal for having the U.S exclusive on them," Carmen filled in.

"So, let me get this straight… She's invested in your website, given you this office space, and access to her teams, and invested in a brand—just to get you exclusivity?"

"Something like that," Chloe said, briefly looking up from her inbox—only to make herself smile at what she saw staring back at her.

Here was Gianni Palazzo, sitting in their office after she had spent the night with him—in her bed! And to think that both Graziana and Regina had forbidden it, only for it to happen with not much effort on her part. Sometimes, things were just meant to happen—a lot of that kind of thing had been happening recently. No matter how hard she tried to manually shape the path of her career or love life, into the way she had always expected them to come about, they always presented themselves in a totally different way. This was just another one of those moments.

"Wow! She must really believe in you guys," he said, meeting her smile with a flirtatious wink.

"That she does!" Carmen piped up. "Come on you two… We better get this over with, before she comes looking for us—and then we'll never get rid of her."

The boardroom next to Veronica's office had been laid out with plates, coffee cups, and pastries that Bethany had quickly ordered from the café a few buildings down. "Beautiful office space you have here, Ms Meyer," Gianni said, eyeing up the boardroom's style and set-up, complete with desk mic's and large presentation screen.

"Oh please, call me Veronica… Thank you, everything we do here has style… Stacks of style, some might say!"

"Yes, I see what you mean," Gianni laughed, pouring coffee for everyone.

"Carmen was just updating me on the P.S.L collection and it looks like we can go ahead with the launch," Chloe said, trying to gain control over the conversation. The last thing she needed was for Veronica to pry into why or how she had brought him to work with her.

"You ladies do what you feel is right... I trust your judgement, but yes—that is great news since we're half-way through the summer season and we are sitting on stock."

"The interview we did with Pandora has been finished by editorial and will go live on our homepage with recommendations from the collection too," Carmen added.

"Perfect! Let's catch up at the end of the day to review sales," Veronica said, sipping her coffee. "These girls impress me every day, Gianni... They're the future of online fashion... Mark my words!"

"I agree, what they've achieved so far is very impressive... I'm actually in the process of re-working the Palazzo Group's online structure, in fact."

"Well, if you need consultants, then look no further than these two," Veronica said with fingers like pistols; sitting up and smelling another opportunity.

"That might not be such a bad idea," Gianni said, glancing at Chloe—loving how uncomfortable she was with the current situation. "But we've actually just partnered with MiBellaModa to look after our e-commerce operations. So far, things are going well. Soon we'll switch the Maison Marais site over to their systems... Our Fifth Avenue boutique is re-opening next week, and as you know, Chloe has helped Jean-Paul design a limited edition bag for the occasion."

"Of course, and maybe in the future, we can work together on a collection—just for StacksOfStyle!" Veronica added, taking another sip.

"Well, that's something to consider, for sure," Gianni politely said, trying not to commit to anything on the spot.

"These two have just come back from market and secured lots of exciting designer brands to launch onsite next season... We would love to add Palazzo and Maison Marais to our designer directory in the future... Both of your brands are leaders in the fashion industry—don't be the last to jump onboard StacksOf-Style!"

Chloe looked at Gianni with apologetic eyes, she knew this would turn into a business meeting rather than a 'quick tour' and breakfast. Gianni just smiled back; he was used to business folk trying to rope him into deals—but he had to admit that this one wasn't such a bad idea.

"Well, is that the time already?" he said, checking his watch. "I really should be letting you get to back work with your big product launch, and *I* have to get to my meeting."

"Can we get you a car?" Veronica said, standing up to see him out.

"Please, don't worry—my driver's outside... So, I'll be seeing you all at the Maison Marais store opening next week?"

"You sure will!" Veronica said, shaking his hand with a powerful arm.

Chloe laughed, Gianni looked like he was about to have his arm ripped off by an orangutang.

"Great to see you, Carmen... And I'll call you later?" he said, taking Chloe by her shoulders.

"Sure," Chloe said, turning her head to avoid kissing him in front of Veronica snd Carmen—who was waiting for that to happen. "I'll walk you out."

The rows of desks on the office floor below were now starting to fill up as staff arrived at work, but none of them seemed to care less who Chloe was escorting down the mezzanine stairs on their way back to the elevators—which suited her just fine. "So, are you all set for your meeting?"

"Don just wants to check in—you'll get to meet him at the store opening... Anyway, what're your plans for this evening?"

"After last night? Sleep, most likely," Chloe said, ushering him into the first elevator that pinged open.

"Cool, same here... I'll have Tommy come pick you up—around six–thirty?"

"Oh, I can't—"

"I'll have dinner cooked for us at mine—nothing crazy—just relax and chill... Tommy can drive you back to your place to grab the things you need first... Oh, and I almost forgot!" Gianni snapped, saving the elevator doors with his hand for Chloe to step in. "Why don't you pop over to the Maison Marais store this afternoon? Take a look before the opening? I'll let Regina know," he smirked, knowing it would get a reaction.

"Oh, *thanks* for that," Chloe sarcastically smiled with wide eyes. Regina was the last person she needed to see today. "No need... I'll call Dionne's assistant."

Before the elevator landed on the ground floor, Gianni put his arm around her and leant in for a kiss. After which, they both quickly straightend themselves up for the doors to open at reception. Gianni headed towards the main door, looking back once to wave, and after watching him climb into his car through the large wall-to-ceiling windows, Chloe turned to call the elevator again to head back upstairs.

"He's *so* handsome, isn't he?" Bethany swooned, having just watched their brief yet tender kiss; popping the D.V.F bag on top of the front desk for Chloe to finally take this time.

'So much for keeping this a secret from the rest of the office,' Chloe sighed, heading over to her with a dry smile. She grabbed the bag with pincer-like fingers, saying nothing more on the matter, making a swift turn to catch the elevator—before the doors closed on her.

**

"Ciao, Don...How are you, amore?" Graziana trilled from the luxury of her black leather chair in her Milan office. Peering down the computer's built-in camera, she flicked her hair off her shoulders and adjusting her low-cut top—making sure her appearance was acceptable for a business meeting.

"Everything's fantastic!" Don said, sitting there in his usual black roll-neck sweater and blazer, with his round-frame glasses making his eyes look even smaller on camera than what they really were—tiny black dots. "So, after our discussion earlier this week—do you think Gianni will agree to my plan?"

"I cannot say… I like your idea, and I personally think it will change the face of our industry—but it's Gianni's call at the end of the day… Just explain your vision— " she went on to say, cutting off as Gianni logged into the virtual meeting.

"Ah, Don—Grazi… Sorry, I'm late, I had a last-minute *thing* to attend," he said, not mentioning where he *really* was. It would only put Graziana in a bad mood, and she was already annoyed that he had insisted he worked from New York when he should be in Milan working on the next collection with the design team.

"No problem at all," Don said, wiping his clammy hands on his pants under his desk—out of camera view. He wasn't usually one to get nervous, but it was safe to say that if Gianni got on board with what he had up his sleeve, then it would make him a very prominent player in the business of fashion—more than what he was already. Being known as fashion's 'super-geek' had its charm, but his legacy had to mean more than just that.

"So, how are things doing?" Gianni said, sitting down at his office desk, back in his New York apartment.

"Very well indeed… How's New York?"

"Well, it's only the second day here but already it's been quite hectic," Gianni said, widening his eyes, still tired from the night before. "How's our website performing?"

"I think you'll agree that logistically, we made the right decision to power Palazzo's online operations," Don said, serious about his own achievements.

"I've sent you over the figures for last week's sales, Gianni… But it sounds like you've been too busy with other *affairs*," Graziana said, knowing exactly why he had insisted he worked from New York—and she wasn't best pleased about it.

First of all, she was the one who was meant to be in New York, finalising the Maison Marais store plans, and the Met exhibition—both were projects she had been working on for months. She had already missed out on visiting New York for the retrospective fashion show—to seal the Maison Marais deal in Paris—only to miss out once again because Gianni wanted to spend time with Chloe. And although he hadn't admitted that to her, she wasn't stupid. Thanks to *that* cover story, she had kept a close eye on Chloe and StacksOfStyle's re-launch, and noted that Gianni had 'liked' almost everything on her Instagram account.

"Er, yes… I have that information here," Gianni said, clicking around on his computer; just opening his emails now to pull up the report.

"Palazzo's website's doing very well… Order ratio is slightly down from your usual frequency, as we expected… Customers are still getting used to the new look and feel of the site," Don said, eager to excuse the dip in numbers. "However, productivity is up and cost-wise this platform will be more sustainable for the future… We have forecasted growth of almost ten percent on your last year's takings."

"Well, that's good news, at least," Gianni said, taking a sip of sparkling water—his mouth already starting to feel dehydrated.

"The *really* good news is that now we have taken over distribution, the dispatch time has improved significantly, giving your—our—customers a quicker service… Not to mention freeing up your staff and facilities to concentrate on what you do best. In time, the customer base will return and grow as we share data and clients with each other—this is only the beginning of what we can do."

"And what about Maison Marais? How is that coming along?" Gianni said, satisfied that he had heard enough to know Don had it all covered—he was the online guru after all.

"Space for stock has been created in the warehouse; we've started to receive deliveries already, transferred over from their existing warehouse… And from now on, all new stock will be received at the MiBellaModa distribution centre. Tech-wise, the back-end systems are in place; we just have some user experience aspects to test, and then we can go live with the new website."

"Yes, we have been in touch about the Maison Marais transition—it's all under control," Graziana chipped in, wanting Don to get to the real reason why they were having the video call in the first place.

"Excellent, so what are we saying? A week—two weeks 'til launch?"

"Soon, very soon, Gianni… Consider this project as 'complete,' Graziana and I will take care of things from here on and you will see your online business' running smoothly for you in the background… And on that note, I wanted to propose another project—I guess it's an offer more than a project."

"Oh yeah? What's that?" Gianni said, checking his phone for messages, hoping Chloe was missing him already and had sent him something sweet.

She had not.

"Well, with Palazzo and Maison Marais both operating on the M.B.M systems, our customer care team can now recommend, reserve, and handle orders for both of your brands in one simple phone call."

"And that's the genius part of all this!" Gianni said, raising his glass of water, taking a swig as he typed out a text message to Chloe, using only emoji's. Yes, he was *that* guy.

"But why stop there?" Don said, trying to capture his attention once more before he lost the angle of his pitch. "At the moment, you own two brands—two websites under M.B.M control… But what if, you had a stake in *all* of the designer brands we distribute?"

"Well, that would be impossible, Don—because I just can't go around snapping up shares in every fashion house there is… Palazzo and Maison Marais are quite enough as it is!"

"Agreed, that *would* be impossible… But by merging with MiBellaModa, you would own a stake in their business' too—because I own their e-commerce rights," Don said, with his cunning, lizard-like smile—his tongue quickly poking out to wet his thin lips with excitement.

Gianni finally stopped playing with his phone and sat up—abandoning his emoji message (which was for the best). "Don, it's a fabulous idea but—"

"But what, Gianni? Think about it what he is saying here," Graziana said, unable to stay out of it any longer.

"I'm proposing that we merge our businesses into one luxury group: The M.B.M-Palazzo Group—experts in both creating luxury fashion, and digital experiences to match... Together we would dominate the online luxury market, globally—and that would only grow over time. Together, we will secure more brands to join us in our vision, and we will have the monopoly on the luxury consumer—be it in brick-and-mortar or online," Don said, raising his hands to his mouth, together in prayer as he stared down the camera.

Gianni took a deep breath—it *did* sound like a fantastic venture. But as a member of the 'Palazzo' family and majority shareholder himself, he had the final say and it wasn't what he had envisioned for The Palazzo Group. If anything, he was offloading his online businesses to Don Carlo to look after and maximise—not get deeper involved in the world of e-commerce.

Something he had little knowledge of, but thanks to Chloe, he was learning more and more—and hoped the more time he spent with her, the more he would discover. But right now, Maison Marais' and Palazzo's commercial successes were his top priorities.

"I don't know Don... We've only just created The Palazzo Group. A lot of assets are tied up in that and it would be difficult to re-negotiate so soon."

"But not impossible, I'm sure there could be a way to convince the shareholders if we were standing strong as a trio—firmly believing in this joint venture," Graziana said, gesturing with her hands, frustrated that he wasn't thrilled by the idea of creating a game-changing conglomerate in the world of fashion. They would suddenly own the rights to many of the world's most desired labels in one quick deal.

Gianni paused once more as he looked down the camera. "Listen, I like the idea but I just think the timing's off... Plus, I have my eye on a project myself that I need time to explore and develop—which is also why I'm over here."

"Oh really? Anything I should know about?" Graziana said, cockily popping her head to one side. This was the first she was hearing about it; usually, it was for her to scout prospects and run them by Gianni—not the other way around.

"Remember I was telling you about Chloe Raven's website?" Gianni started, only for Graziana to dip her head and press her temples with her fingertips—fighting the urge to dig her nails into her head—she knew where this was going.

"Yes, I recall you speaking of your friend's blog," Don said, nervously jittering his leg under his table—wondering if his proposal still had a chance.

"Well, she's actually my girlfriend... It's early days," Gianni side-tracked, causing Graziana to lean back in her chair and roll her eyes on cam. "Anyway, I like what she's doing with this StacksOfStyle.com and I think there's real potential there."

"You know what they say, Gianni: 'Don't mix business with pleasure!'" Don laughed, not quite taking him seriously. Here he was talking about turning two multi-millionaire dollar businesses into one that would be worth billions—and Gianni was raving about a start-up!

"I know—I know... It's just a very interesting business model. It's essentially an online department store—not just for designer brands but for smaller labels and exclusive capsule collections... I think that's what customers want—both niche and designer pieces next to each other, in one place. It's not just an online store—they have cool editorial features too.... Today they have the Pandora Simmons collection launching alongside an interview with the designer herself... You see, it's an online magazine that you can shop! Clever, huh?"

"Very clever," Don said rather flat, not entirely sure why Gianni was more impressed with some stupid girl's website than he was with his merger plans.

To Don, StacksOfStyle sounded like a vanity project—not a money-spinner. Niche brands? Capsule collections? Editorial features? It sounded like way too many overheads to become profitable, and all Don cared about was money. Money, and his status in the industry which so far, wasn't big enough. He may have one-half of the Palazzo siblings on his side, but he still needed Gianni to help elevate his superiority in the business of fashion.

"You should really check her out… Listen, I have to go and meet Anna at the Met now—Grazi, we'll speak later?" Gianni said, leaning over his desk with his finger on the mouse, ready to exit the video call. "Ciao for now!"

Gianni's camera turned to black, leaving Don and Graziana on the call. "Well, that didn't exactly go to plan," Don said, leaning back in his chair. "So, what now?"

Graziana sat forward with her chin in her hands, thinking how else she could make her brother see sense—she too had a lot riding on him approving Don's plan. Not only would she be responsible for having brokered the Maison Marais acquisition, but she would also be credited with overseeing one of fashion's most lucrative mergers—fastening her reputation as one of the industry's most successful and formidable leaders. The business side of fashion had long been dominated by men in suits—this was her chance for them to finally take notice of her abilities. Yes, Gianni enjoyed the fame of being the face of Palazzo, but Graziana was the brains—and it was time people knew that.

"Maybe Gianni *is* right, Don," Graziana said, breathing in—making her nostrils even thinner.

"How so?" Don said, confused to hear that she was now agreeing with his decision.

"Well, didn't you hear him? Maybe you *should* check out this StacksOfStyle… If this website *really* is the cutting edge of e-commerce then you should be the one to discover it—you're the expert in online luxury fashion—not Gianni! After all, there's nothing better than a bit of stiff competition to get what you really want… Don't you think?"

Don sat up, raising his paper-thin smile into an upturned crescent, framed with deep laughter lines, like parentheses. Like him, Graziana had a cunning mind and he understood exactly what she was suggesting—and with it, he knew exactly how he was going to change her brother's mind.

***

"How's the click rate for P.S.L's landing page?" Chloe said, returning to her desk with a sandwich bag and coffees for both of them.

"Excellent, the zero–one–five dress has almost sold-out—as we expected—but the other styles from the collection are also performing quite well," Carmen said, relieved that the collection, on the whole, was being well received.

"That's amazing—I knew it would do well! Oh, you just reminded me—we need to chase the samples for the 'Raven X P.S.L' capsule… Bill needs to put the order in pretty soon if stock is to be ready and delivered in time for the coming season."

"Actually, that's something else we have to consider… Sale!"

"I was hoping you weren't going to say the 'S' word," Chloe said, sitting down at her computer after dropping Carmen's lunch off at her desk. Sale time was always hell back n the shop floor, and it was probably not going to be that much more fun online either.

"Seriously, what's the strategy here?" Carmen said, opening her bag to grab the sandwich inside. She hadn't left her desk all morning and was now famished.

"Well, I was thinking that all exclusive stock—so P.S.L and our launch collaborations—won't go into markdown… Everything else, can."

"But that's only like, ten percent of our catalogue to put on sale?" Carmen said, dropping her sandwich back down.

"If by the winter sale they haven't sold, then that's when we'll put them into markdown," Chloe said, looking rather pleased with herself as she took a bite of her turkey salad sub.

"I know that's what Veronica would want to hear… Protect our profit margins and all that, but we have to give customers what they want—and what they want is a bargain! Think about it, what would you want from us as a customer? The more customers we attract during a sales promotion, the more customers will discover us… Hopefully, they'll become addicted to receiving our nicely packed boxes in the mail and purchase full-price with us the rest of the season! Plus, we have to make room in the warehouse for the new stock which is arriving soon. I'm sure Veronica will want us to shift units and make money, rather than give us more stock space."

Chloe finished chewing the bite she had bitten off, as she mulled over Carmen's suggestion. "You're the president of this place—just make sure no key items are included in the sale, otherwise Veronica *will* lose her shit!"

"Duh! Don't worry… I'm not gonna clean the place out. I'll make a start on the sale list this afternoon so we can discuss it with Veronica and plan ahead. Anyway, plans for later? Another hot date with Gianni at his place?"

Chloe almost spat out a gulp of coffee.

That's how busy things had been—she hadn't managed to fill Carmen in on what *really* happened the night before. "What?" Carmen said, wondering what had almost made her choke. "What I have missed?"

"Well, let's just say I didn't stay at his place last night."

"Oh, which hotel is he staying at? The Four Seasons? They really should just give you a global membership."

"We didn't stay in a hotel," Chloe said, looking at Carmen with one eyebrow raised, hoping she would get the hint. She didn't, and after a beat, Chloe put her out of her misery. "He stayed at *mine!*"

"He *what?*" Carmen bellowed, loud enough for the people outside on the mezzanine landing to look into their glass fishbowl.

"I know," Chloe said, continuing to demolish her sub—there was nothing wrong with her appetite today.

"So, let me get this straight… Gianni took you out for dinner and then you ended up back at your place?"

"Pretty much," Chloe confirmed, washing down her sub with some water.

"And then he suggested that he dropped you off at work and took a look around the office? Now I get it!" Carmen said, finally taking a bite of her sandwich.

"Get what? What was there to *get?*" Chloe said, sweeping crumbs off her desk, into the wire basket.

"Why you were all cagey and nervous... You should have been parading him around the office. Instead, you couldn't wait to get rid of him."

"I just didn't want to make a scene, that's all... I'm trying to keep it casual—no statements! Although I'm sure Bethany has told everyone that we're dating already—she saw us kiss downstairs."

"So, what's the plan for this evening then?"

Chloe shook her head with a curled up smile. "Like he said, he's staying in town for a while and he wants to see where this *thing* between us going... It's my turn to stay at his apartment tonight."

"Perfect! You get to see his New York pad! I bet it's absolutely stunning... Do you know how lucky you are?" Carmen said, polishing off her sandwich.

"You're right... It *is* awesome; it just feels like the wrong timing—again!"

"Well, you know what they say... Men are like buses: they either all turn up at once, or when you're already in a taxi! Look, I know you have a lot on your plate right now with work, but you're not in this alone; you have me remember! And I know you're thinking that this is the same situation as with Brian—but it isn't!" Carmen said, getting up to perch on the end of Chloe's desk with her coffee cup in hand. "So, before you go self-sabotaging again, just look down at what's on your wrist and tell yourself you don't want this. Do you realise you are finally getting everything you have ever wanted, only to second guess it? You have not only proved Regina wrong in all of this but now you get to rub Graziana's face in it too! If this truly *isn't* what you want, then I'd be careful what you wish for in the future!"

Chloe smiled, she had heard everything she needed to hear. Standing up, she dusted herself down and grabbed her handbag, ready to leave the office once again. "Listen, Gianni wants me to pop down to Fifth Avenue to see the Maison Marais store before the grand opening... Wanna come check it out with me?"

"I'd love to but I think one of us should stay here... You know how Veronica is on upload day! She'll be asking for figures every half-hour, and we have a trade meeting at four."

"Ah! I forgot about that... I'll be back in an hour or so, just in time for the trade meeting. I'm sure Veronica won't be too mad if I'm late for the meeting—just tell her I had to go meet with our future collaboration," Chloe sarcastically winked, leaving the fort in Carmen's capable hands.

****

The hoarding was still up around the building site of Maison Marais' boutique on Fifth Avenue—situated just a few stores up on the opposite side from Palazzo (which Chloe hadn't set foot in since she had left). Black walls with the new sans-serif type-face in white screened off the work going on behind the scenes, alternated with black and white images of models dressed in Jean-Paul's latest spring/summer collection.

As she walked closer to the store, she could see that the main doorway was left open, allowing builders to come and go—carrying in tools and shop fittings to complete the renovation on time.

"Erm, hi... I'm Chloe Ravens; I'm here to see the progress of the store," she said, stopping two builders carrying a sheet of black glass inside.

"Listen, I'm just a workman... If you want entry then you gotta have a pass from the foreman."

"Can I not just speak to him now? Gianni Palazzo sent me... I can call him if that helps?"

"Like I said, if you haven't got permission, you can't come through," the builder said, carrying on through, desperate to get the heavy glass inside in one piece.

"Chloe?" a familiar voice called from deep inside.

"Kim? Thank God you're here," Chloe said, aware that she was against the clock to get back to work on time for the meeting.

"I'm great... I was rather surprised to get your email earlier, saying you were dropping by."

"Gianni suggested I popped by to have a look before the grand opening next week," Chloe said, realising she had already said too much.

"Oh, really now? Well, in that case, come on in… It's fine—she's with the team," Kim said to the builder who had just warned her about trespassing. "Watch your step… You're lucky you don't need to wear a hard hat now the building is down—everything from here on is just cosmetic."

"Oh, trust me—I'm accustomed to sporting a hard hat down at our warehouse!" Chloe laughed, and steel toe-capped boots for that matter.

She carefully stepped over the threshold and into the main entrance of the new store, it smelt like fresh paint and varnish—or some kind of strong adhesive. The main entrance was flanked with two large glass doors that had black marble slabs across them for a push bar, with a silver 'M' on either one. Open wide, they were still covered in plastic while the builders worked.

"Wow, well this is all new," she said, taking in the spacious ground floor.

The front of the store had rows of empty glass vitrines and silver mirrored shelves—presumably where bags and accessories would be displayed. Through gaps in the dust sheets, Chloe could see that the floor was covered in white marble with had swirls of black and grey veins that resembled growing vines. Builders at the back of the store were putting up more silver floating shelves and hammering together cabinet displays.

"How's everything else going under the new direction," Chloe quizzed, eager to get some gossip. The new style of shop fit wasn't a surprise, having already suspected what was to come from the refurbished showroom.

"Not bad… Although, Regina is… Well, being *Regina!*"

"Jeez… Is she here?" Chloe said, looking around; forgetting that bumping into her was a strong possibility.

"She's upstairs with Dionne, muscling in on the invitations for the opening… She doesn't trust that we can pull it off… Anyway, let me show you around! This entire ground floor will be dedicated to accessories, and shoes at the back," Kim said, pointing out where everything would be in the end.

Chloe looked back around behind her as Kim spoke, noticing that the storefront was simply two large landscape windows that had 'MAISON MARAIS' in raised silver lettering on the outside.

"The store-front's simple, yet effective," Kim said, noticing how Chloe had spotted the lack of drama or staging in the windows. "Jean-Paul doesn't want mannequins or displays, instead just a direct view into the store and the collection… And this area over here is where your limited edition bag will be displayed on the night!"

"Oh, have you seen it—is it here yet?"

"Unfortunately the stock hasn't been unpacked yet… We expect the builders to move out tomorrow, then we can get the merchandisers in—that was supposed to happen last week!"

"How many people are invited to the opening?" Chloe said, starting to think Regina was right. Filling up the vast ground floor with guests would be a hard task alone. Then, there were the ready-to-wear floors above.

"Well, this is the issue. Paris have taken care of V.I.P's, but Regina's putting pressure on us to invite clients—like *actual* clients."

"But that's impossible! This is a totally different client to what the house was used to," Chloe said, now being reminded of Regina's unrealistic expectations which hadn't changed much from when she was their leader at Palazzo.

"She's just trying to prove that she's always right… That her ways at Palazzo are the best and that Dionne's direction isn't up to the standards of The Palazzo Group."

"Are you kidding? This store *is* Dionne's!" Chloe said, careful not to speak out too loud, in case the echo of her voice in the hollow shell carried up to the floors above—even over the drilling and hammering.

"Well, are you surprised?"

"Not really, but she's already made her point—she's group director now… Has anyone taken over her old position at Palazzo yet?"

"This is the drama! I think she's trying to play chess… I have a feeling that they want to move Dionne over to Palazzo, so she can get Francesca in here as the store director," Kim said, looking to the white marble staircase in case anyone was coming down them.

"Francesca Manzetti? But she knows nothing!" Chloe blurted out, not caring who heard her this time.

"Yes, well… After what she did to you, she's due a promotion! We're seen as the 'smaller' brand of the group, and we all know she wouldn't be able to cope with running a huge store like Palazzo….She's been sniffing around here a few times with Regina, and I just know something's up."

"You need to trust your instincts! If you think something is going down, then ninety–nine percent of the time, it's because it is!" Chloe said forcefully, pointing a finger at Kim.

"The store opening is like a test for Dionne… Regina is threatening to get Myra in to take over the guest-list since we can share data now and Palazzo has a stronger client base for designer wear; she feels we don't enough high-profile clients invited… I just know they're going to use this against her… Tell her she isn't up to directing the brand into the new era and that she needs to learn more from an already established brand—or some shit like that."

"Yes, I know too well exactly the lines Regina would pull out on her to get her own way… Listen, I might be able to help you."

Kim shook her head, unable to understand how exactly she could help, watching Chloe dig down into her handbag to pull out a lavender leather Palazzo journal. Embossed with the italic '*P*,' monogram, it was the journal Melinda had given to her as a leaving gift.

"See this here?" Chloe said, holding it in front of Kim's face. "This has every client that was worth serving at Palazzo!"

"How did you—"

"Melinda gave it to me after I left Palazzo… She told me to use it wisely and that I would know when the right time to use it would come along... The truth is, it's never been the right time to use it for myself… If I contacted clients from Palazzo to invite them to shop on my website, it would be too obvious and I can't risk a data breach scandal if Regina found out—and you know that witch is hunting for a reason to screw me over still!"

Kim took the journal from Chloe and flicked through a few pages. Scores of names, addresses, email addresses, and phone numbers were neatly copied out in Melinda's handwriting that was unmistakable hers. It had all the big-name clients, every mover and shaker of New York, and every rich woman that regularly visited Melinda to spend the royalties on her wealth on the latest Palazzo collections.

"Do what you gotta do with it, just don't leave it lying around and get it back to me in twenty–four hours… I don't want it out of my sight for any longer, but I trust you with it."

Kim was shocked, not entirely sure how she was going to suddenly convince everyone that she had miraculously managed to come up with all these names last minute—but she was grateful, especially taking their tumultuous history into account. The fact that Chloe was now trusting her with this information was another example of how their friendship had grown from being opposites to now good friends.

It was funny to think that they didn't see eye-to-eye when they worked together at Palazzo, but the frustration of working under Regina Hall's regime had brought them together, and it was making them even closer once again.

"I'll have it biked over to you—first thing tomorrow morning, I promise!"

"Listen, I'd really love to stay and chat, but I *really* don't want to see Regina right now—I'll save that for the opening night! I should be getting back to the office anyway. Oh, and by the way… I'd just have this downstairs area as a cocktail and DJ area... Place the limited edition bag upstairs with the ready-to-wear," Chloe said, giving Kim a quick kiss goodbye before stepping back out onto the avenue to hail a taxi.

27

"**S**orry, I'm late… Traffic was a nightmare! Are you heading to the meeting?" Chloe said, chucking her bag down and slumping back in her chair in front of the computer—too shattered to think about any meeting.

"Don't worry yourself, darling," Carmen said, still sat at her desk tapping away on the keyboard. "Veronica cancelled the meeting… Something about a last-minute meeting with investors?"

"That's strange… Hope everything is okay? At least we can get everything tied up here before the weekend and get the hell out!" Chloe shrugged off—more grateful than concerned.

"So… Spill! How's the new store looking?"

"Minimal but stylish—very Jean-Paul… But that's not the real gossip," she said, leaning on her elbows with her face in her palms, sporting a grin.

"*Ooh*, now I wish I had come with you," Carmen said, finally taking a break from her screen.

"Regina was there—Obviously! Luckily I didn't see her, but Kim told me that she's still up to her old tricks… She reckons she wants Dionne out, and Francesca in as the store director… So, to stitch her up, she's given her the impossible task of inviting clients they've never even had to the store opening," Chloe said, throwing her hands up in the air.

"But the new look Maison Marais doesn't *have* any clients… Not yet anyway."

"Exactly! It's a set-up to make her look like an idiot so Regina can move her pawns around the board and make them play her game again… Nothing changes."

"So what's Kim gonna do about it? *Can* she do anything about it?" Carmen said, returning to her sales report, now she had heard the bulk of the story—there was nothing Kim could do.

"Well, remember Melinda gave me that journal… The one with every client from Palazzo?" Chloe said, looking rather mischievous.

"You gave it to her, didn't you? Well, I just hope you get it back and no one traces that shit back to you," Carmen said with a stern look.

"Why so serious?" Chloe snapped, expecting her to revel in her bitchy comeback.

"You just have more to lose this time around, Chloe… Losing your sales job over discount and a handbag is one thing, but now you have a company—a good one at that! A company that Regina is sure to be jealous of… If that book gets traced back to you, then you could be in trouble—that's all I'm saying on the matter."

All it took was one reckless move from Chloe, and this whole operation could be taken down by a bitter Regina—backed by Palazzo's corporate lawyers which they wouldn't be able to contend with. But this time, Carmen had a lot to lose as president of the company—any bad press would look bad on her too.

"Anyway, more importantly… Do you have any plans for your upcoming birthday?" Carmen said, changing the subject onto something more upbeat.

"Uh, I haven't had time to think about that, to be honest."

"Well, it's a big one this year! You're turning thirty—so you *have* to do something… Leave it to me."

Chloe didn't need reminding. She had been dreading it, but that was driven by the fear of failure. Now she had achieved so much in her career, that thought hadn't crossed her mind lately. Instead, the stress and work building up StacksOfStyle had taken over—not to mention her love life. But now that too had even seemed to have worked itself out, maybe it *was* time to celebrate her birthday?

"Right… Well, I've completed the sales report and figures for the P.S.L launch—I'll send them over to you and Veronica now… I'm sure she'll want to go over that on Monday, first thing—so make sure you know it inside out! I've also emailed Dom to update him on sales," Carmen said, getting ready to finish up.

"Still going to Gianni's, or do I need to talk you into that again?"

"Chill! He's sending the driver to pick me up. Just a quiet evening in, apparently," Chloe said raising an eyebrow, knowing that another late night was most likely on the cards—even if they were 'staying in.'

"Like I said earlier… Finally, you get to see the inside of the Palazzo palace! Things really are coming along with you two, aren't they? Do you think he's told Graziana yet?" Carmen said, running a quick gloss over her lip, before stashing her cosmetics pouch back into her handbag.

"I'm guessing he hasn't… If he had, I'm sure I'd have received some kind of blackmail letter or something by now—or maybe she'll just turn up at my apartment à la Regina style!"

"Does that bother you?"

"Like he said last night… We just have to take things slowly and see how this turns out. I can't keep worrying about his sister not accepting me—I've already been through that crap with Regina!"

"Yup… And that didn't work out for her, did it?" Carmen said, shutting down her computer.

"True… Anyway, get yourself out of here while you can," Chloe said, stretching her fingers before opening the sales report she had just received from Carmen in her inbox.

"You read my mind!" Carmen said, grabbing her blazer off the back of her chair. "Message me—I want to know details!"

*

Tommy, had come to collect Chloe outside the office in his tinted windowed, black Mercedes—just as Gianni had promised. Before whisking her back to Gianni's, he drove her home so she could pack an overnight bag and take a quick shower. Circling the neighbourhood while she got ready, Chloe packed all the essential items necessary, to keep up the mirage of the woman Gianni was smitten with (although, he had already seen what she looked like in the morning anyway). After reapplying her makeup and slipping into a blue gingham off-the-shoulder top with a pair of jeans and white sneakers, Chloe called Tommy to come back to fetch her.

She waited until she could see him park up from the living room window before heading back outside and climb into the backseat with her weekend bag—sitting quiet and nervously as she Tommy drove back uptown to Gianni's. She was nervous, not because she was spending the weekend with him (she had overcome that by now), but because she was spending time in his domain. Not at The Four Seasons—and definitely not at *her* apartment.

She could only ever imagine the surroundings he lived in before—the luxury, the style—but now she was about to see it in real life. And that was rather intimidating, especially after he had seen where she lived—a humble comparison no doubt. No matter how much he admitted that he liked her, she just couldn't forget that she was from a completely different world than him.

She was still a 'working' girl—which proved Graziana right in some ways. Even though Gianni was technically a 'working' man himself, he was a fashion legend—why would someone like him be interested in her? She still couldn't fathom why, and it was times like this—sat on her own in a chauffeur-driven car—that her current reality made her want to pinch herself. Because of Gianni, she had made friends with big names in fashion, secured her own fashion line and was now the owner of an online business. Even though most women would have thrown themselves at him—just to have a single night of hot sex—she was always aware of who she truly was inside.

And yes, it would have been easy for her to have jumped at him and had a fun time getting what she could from what many would see as a 'golden' opportunity—but her ambition was so much more than a rich guy with benefits. And that was exactly why he was so intrigued by her. She wasn't like any of the other women he had been with—sexy super-models and young starlet celebrities.

She certainly didn't need Regina, or Graziana, to remind her of that; she was fully aware that she was incredibly lucky, and she still didn't know why he had picked her—out of everyone he *could* have. The night they had first met, she had just put down to luck—fate even. And it was this 'fate' that was being served that kept on bringing her back to him, it was no use trying to fight it any longer.

With that thought in mind, she took a deep breath and relaxed into the leather seat, gazing out of the window to see where Tommy had delivered her. The car pulled over, midway down Park Avenue, outside a typical towering apartment block—adorned with a bottle green canopy leading out onto the sidewalk. Gold lettering on the side of it told her she was at The Grand Towers apartments. "Okay, Miss Ravens," Tommy said, pulling up the handbrake. "Ask for the penthouse on floor thirteen… Unlucky for some, right?" he said with a chuckle, looking at her in the mirror.

She looked like a deer caught in headlights.

Getting out of the car, he walked to the curb-side and opened the door for Chloe to step out. "Need a hand with your bag?"

"Oh no…It's just a holdall, Chloe said as she looked up at the light grey stone building that towered up into the sky, and certainly was as grand as it claimed to be.

"I'm gonna spin the car into the garage before I get a ticket… Samuel at the front desk will show you the way."

Chloe walked towards the entrance, under the green canopy, and was greeted by a doorman in livery—just like The Ritz. Suddenly she felt under-dressed as her sneaker soles squeaked on the polished marble and brass geometric floor. Her stylistic eye couldn't help but think it resembled the pattern of a Goyard bag.

"Good evening, how may I help you?" the concierge behind the front desk said, not recognising who she was. He knew everyone who lived at The Grand Towers—and their regular visitors— be it friends and family (or escorts).

"Hi, you must be Samuel—Tommy told me to go straight up to the thirteenth floor?" she said.

"Ah! And you must be Miss Ravens! Mr Palazzo is awaiting your arrival... Let me show you the way," he said, walking around from behind his desk, reaching out to take Chloe's bag. This time she accepted the offer as she followed him across the lobby, towards the elevators. White marble slabs covered the walls, surrounding a row of four polished brass elevator doors—mirrored by another set of four on the opposite side.

"This last one on the right-hand side, is Gianni's personal elevator—it will take you straight up to the thirteenth floor and back down—it's very quick!" he said, pressing the call button, which made the doors instantly slide open—he held them for her while she stepped inside.

The elevator walls were covered in a mahogany crocodile skin (which Chloe assumed was real) with a large coffee tinted mirror on the back wall, surrounded by a brown leather support bar. She quickly smoothed out her lipstick, pursing her lips with a quick grimace in the mirror to cheek her teeth as she ran her tongue over them—all while Samuel wasn't looking.

"I told you it was quick, didn't I?" he said, turning around, just in the nick of time, not to catch her.

The doors pinged open to face what looked like a David Hockney painting in the hallway—reminding her exactly where she was—it probably *was* a David Hockney. Stepping out of the elevator, her feet sunk into the plush lavender-grey carpet which made her want to slip off her shoes, after the day she had had. A few steps ahead, Samuel had buzzed the apartment door before she could catch up (having lagged behind to see if she could find a signature on the painting).

"Good evening, Mr Palazzo... Your visitor is here!" he said, handing over Chloe's bag.

"Thanks, Sam... Chloe—come on in!" Gianni said, giving her a hug and a kiss on the cheek at the entrance.

He was wearing a thick, beige cardigan (cashmere, of course) that made Chloe want to sink into him like a teddy bear—she could smell his usual oud-wood scent pour off him like steam. Underneath, a white V-neck T-shirt gave a glimpse of his tanned skin and a flicker of his gold chain pendant. As she parted from him, she looked downwards, noticing his slippers that had 'G and P' embroidered on either foot.

"Can I get you a drink?" he said, walking backwards into the open-plan apartment, revealing itself to Chloe, as if an Austrian curtain had lifted before her.

She was mesmerised at the light and space of the layout. This was no apartment—it was a mansion on stilts. Presented with the kitchen and living room before her, she noticed it was decorated just like his outfit—white and beige. Clean and crisp, neutral not gaudy—the total opposite of what she was expecting. At first glance, she estimated the floor space to be triple the size of her entire place (which she felt so foolish about inviting him back to now), even though she knew it would be more. The high ceiling alone made her wonder if there was a fourteenth floor at all?

"How was work?" he said, letting her look around—he could see she was floored by the large windows that lined one side of the apartment, the avenue just a thin strip below.

"Oh, fine… The usual," she stammered, looking back at him; unable to say anything more—realising it was rather rude of her to be sizing up the size of his place in front of him.

"A drink?" he pressed.

"Oh, sure… Yes, please."

She shook her head at how typically awe-struck she was behaving, walking back over to perch at the island which separated the kitchen from the lounge. A large cream marble slab sat on top of a gold mirrored base, surrounded by cream leather stools on a matching gold stand and foot bar. She noticed the backs of the stools were stitched with the 'P,' circular logo in gold thread—it was hard to miss. But at the same time, not everything was monogrammed or stamped with the company moniker—which she had expected.

Gianni opened up one of the white cupboard doors which turned out to be the wine cooler. The only thing that was obviously on display was the stainless oven and hob (clearly never used); everything else was concealed behind white doors.

"So, why just fine?" he said, bringing over a glass of white wine with three ice-cubes in (now he knew how she liked to drink her wine, which had impressed her). "How did the Pandora Simmons launch go?"

"Well, that went amazingly well," Chloe said, remembering that today had actually been successful, and now she had a glass of wine in front of her, she could relax. "We had a strong first day of sales... And I popped over to the Maison Marais store, as promised!"

"Oh yeah? How was it—what do you think?" Gianni said, leaning against the island with his arms folded—wine glass in hand—which made his biceps bulge.

"It looked beautiful... Exactly what I had in mind! I saw my friend Kim, Dionne's assistant—I used to work with her at Palazzo... They're busy putting all the finishing touches in place."

"Great—glad to hear it! Was Regina there?"

"Yes, although I didn't see her... I didn't stay long. I just popped my head in as I had to rush back for a sales meeting," she said, taking a sip of wine. It was probably the best wine she had ever tasted, sweet yet crisp from the coldness of the extra ice cubes. She could see herself getting absolutely smashed on this stuff—which was most likely his plan.

"Come... Bring your wine, let me show you around," Gianni said, getting off his elbows to walk around the island. "This is obviously the kitchen... Which I never use—in case you were wondering..."

"I was... I thought you said we were having a quiet night in—dinner?" she said, at the lack of sight or smell of cooking.

"I'll just call room service—we have that here."

"Of course you do," Chloe said, tossing her eyes—did she actually expect him to cook?

"To be honest... I prefer to stay in hotels when I travel. This place was my father's. I've had designers come in and redecorate since, but it just never really *clicked* with me."

'Well, it certainly *clicks* with me!' Chloe thought, following him into the lounge which had two large L-shaped sofas opposing each other—like Tetris blocks yet to align—with an oval glass coffee table in-between them. A rounded wall to the right side of the lounge housed a carousel staircase, leading to another floor above. The back wall of the lounge had a faux electric fireplace encased with glass and white bookshelves which flanked either side, filled with art, photography, and fashion books—as well as some older looking books. No doubt first editions by famous authors that his father had bought.

"This is obviously the lounge… oh, downstair's bathroom's over here by the way," Gianni said, pointing to a door in the wall next to the staircase, before carrying on past it. "And through here is my dining and entertainment room."

Chloe felt like she had already walked across half of the building's floor space. He obviously owned the entire thirteenth floor—and there was still an 'upstairs' to see.

"And this is where I spend a lot of my time… When I do stay here."

Gianni opened the door, revealing a home cinema room with cream leather recliner seats—it that even had beige 'P,' monogram curtains framing the huge TV screen. Chloe expected there to be some monogram, and here it was. At the back of the room was a bar area and retro arcade games lined against the wall. She could see why he spent a lot of time in here; she could see herself cosying up on a recliner watching her favourite film. And Gianni could see she was gobsmacked, her face was a naive picture which he found very endearing—reminding him that he was extremely lucky to have this life of luxury.

"Come on, you… There's more!" he said, taking her hand to guide her out and up the staircase. The fourteenth floor was just as impressive—even if it was only half of the space because he had knocked the lounge up into it for extra light. The master bedroom, large bathroom, gym and terrace and guest room (complete with a walk-in closet) all awaited her. And just as Gianni expected, she was stunned to silence.

"I didn't expect it to be so… *Huge!*"

"I could make a rude joke here," he laughed.

Chloe walked out on to the wooden decked terrace, passing a beautiful set of table and chairs large enough to host a dinner party, and leaned over the black iron railings—looking down on the avenue. Gianni walked over and grabbed her by her waist from behind, resting his chin on her shoulder. "Do you like it?"

Chloe turned around in his hold to face him and placed her arms around his neck, a waft of his cologne emerged like a soft press from a powder puff, as her arms rested on his plush cardigan. "Like it? I *love* it! I don't understand why you don't like staying here?"

"It just feels empty… But I'm glad you like it, means you'll stay more often," Gianni said, about to plant a kiss on her lips—but she cocked her head to one side which made him pause.

"What's through there?" she said, noticing the wall of sliding glass doors behind him.

"That's my office and a gym—which I also never use. The master bedroom is on the other side… I'll show you," he said, sliding the doors back to step back inside through his office.

A beautiful (and very tidy) walnut desk displayed his desktop computer—it had a leather top, perfect for sketching on. Chloe picked up one of his drawings that was left out, a simple pencil sketch of a long and very revealing dress that was slit right up to the thigh in true Palazzo fashion.

"Still working on the summer collection… Just a few ideas I had," he said, which had sounded rather like an apology.

"You still sketch?" she said, pleasantly surprised. "It's amazing… I thought you just had a design team that did all this for you."

"Well, I do, but they work on the rough ideas I give them first, then I simply approve the final pieces—everything else is done by in-house designers and merchandisers," he said, starting to sound like he was giving an interview. "Anyway, we *are* going to have dinner, and we can even have it out on the terrace if you like?"

And he wasn't lying, The Grand Towers really did have room service for the residents. A whole menu, in fact, cooked by the kitchen down in the basement and brought up to the floors above via a bell-boy and trolley. Gianni laid out the table on the terrace, while Chloe relaxed next to a log burner as she watched the Sun go down—wine in hand—with Gianni's super-soft cardigan around her shoulders. It was nice to see him do 'normal' things like lay the table. It was refreshing that he didn't have servants on hand to do everything for him (even if he did have a duo-floor penthouse apartment on Park Avenue—with full room service and private elevator).

They ordered steak and fries with green beans, and New York-style macaroni cheese to share—Chloe understood now why he didn't bother cooking. After feasting, they moved over to the outdoor rattan sofa and cosied up under a blanket next to the log burner with another bottle of wine. Gianni even made the effort to light the lanterns that edged the terrace—and for the first time in a long time—as she stared out over the skyline, Chloe was finally able to breathe.

"Right, I need the bathroom," she said, whipping back the blanket to get up.

"Oh, use the bathroom next to the guest room—across the way there... Or there's one in the master."

Heading back inside, Chloe looked for the bathroom which was directly opposite the terrace doors and easy enough to find (even after a two bottle's of wine). She drew back the door without a second thought and stepped inside, flicking on the light switch on the side—only to be amazed yet again. In case she had forgotten, a bathroom the size of her lounge reminded her just where she was. It was classic in style: black and white floor tiles, a white bathroom suite and mirrored cabinets above 'his and hers' basins, and a toilet and bidet beside each other with gold fixtures. The shower was more of a wet room and the bathtub... Well, that was more of a hot tub for four! It immediately made her want to run a bath and get in, switch on the bubbles and relax. But she did what she came to do, washed her hands (as she noted the Aesop hand wash and moisturiser) and went to head back outside.

"Oh my gosh... Your bathroom is the size of my entire apartment—and that tub!"

"Yeah... I also never use it," Gianni laughed awkwardly, starting to feel a little uncomfortable that he had *all* of this without need. Especially after seeing her place, which was still a great apartment—but it was no luxury apartment on Park Avenue.

"You know—because I only have a shower—whenever there's an opportunity to have a bath, I grab it!" Chloe said, resuming her place cosily under his armpit—under the blanket.

"Well, be my guest... You know, you can stay here whenever you want?"

"Don't tell me that... You'll never get rid of me," Chloe snorted.

"Sounds great to me," Gianni said without hesitation, causing her to look up at him. "Seriously... Stay here with me while I'm in town, and when I need to travel for business, you can have Tommy to yourself—drive you to the office."

"You're serious, aren't you?" Chloe said, now sitting up, hardly believing he was offering his beautiful apartment for her to enjoy.

"Of course I am... And I was serious about using the bathtub as well!"

Gianni got up and disappeared for a few minutes, only to come back in a white terry-cloth robe with gold cord trimming, and his initials embroidered on the chest.

"Are you gonna join me or what?" he said from the terrace doorway.

"Wow... You weren't kidding!" Chloe laughed, getting up to follow him to the bathroom.

Leaving the door open, he began to lift up her top, which she peeled off for him as he started on the top button of her jeans. Pulling her closer, he kissed her. His cool, wet lips from the cold wine soothed her warm mouth like a slice of cucumber on the eyes—she closed them in ecstasy. He leant away—now she had gotten the message to strip—and slipped off his robe before hopping into the foaming bathtub.

Whilst undressing, Chloe didn't take her eyes off him—getting a good look at his toned, tanned body. He too watched her with a devilish smile on his face, as she climbed in and sat opposite him. The hot water and foam, which smelt of sage, covered her breasts as she sunk herself under—it sure was as divine as she had imagined.

"Now for the fun part," Gianni said, leaning over the side to push a button which started the bubble jets.

He reached across for her hands and pulled her over to his side of the tub, pulling her up to sit on his lap—quite enjoying him man-handling her. She wrapped his arms around his neck and kissed him passionately, unable to deny him—or herself—any longer.

**

Waking up in a bed much bigger than her own, her body felt like it was buzzing from pure relaxation—and sex. Chloe rolled over on the crisp sheets, only to find Gianni had got up already. She propped herself up and looked around—the sixty-inch TV screen on the wall outside the closet was on the news channel with the sound down low. She recalled how she had gasped at the sight of the master suite after getting out of the hot tub (it wasn't exactly comfortable to have sex in), only to break the moment and look around his closet—while he waited patiently for her to join him in bed.

"Morning," Gianni said, coming out of the en-suite bathroom with just a towel wrapped around him as he swabbed his ears with a Q-tip. "Hungry?"

He flung the menu over to her like a frisbee which landed close to her on the bed covers. As she picked it up, her phone vibrated on the bedside table. No doubt it was Carmen, messaging her for the latest news on how her weekend had started at Casa Palazzo—but she was greeted by a text from Kim instead.

"*Shit!*" Chloe groaned as she read the message. She had completely forgotten that she had asked Kim to drop the address book back to her first thing in the morning—and here was Kim, keeping her word.

"What's up? Gianni said, slipping on soft charcoal grey sweat-pants.

"Oh, nothing important… I told Kim I'd be at my place this morning—she wanted to drop something she borrowed from me before she forgot… It's no problem— I'll see her on Monday."

"Just get her to stop by here if you like?"

"Oh, no… It's Kim from Maison Marais… I'm pretty sure you don't want your staff calling round here," Chloe said, already tapping out a reply to rearrange.

"I'm heading out to the gym… You girls can have breakfast out on the terrace, or something."

"Really? You have a gym next door…"

"I told you… I don't use it—not enough equipment," he said, climbing on the bed to kiss her. "Just be ready by noon, Jean-Paul and the girls are coming over with some dresses for you to try."

"Jean-Paul's in town?" Chloe said, re-wording her reply back to Kim with the address of The Grand Towers. Now she realised why he had invited her over for the weekend, part business-part pleasure.

'Talk about multi-tasking,' she thought to herself; although she wasn't ungrateful. Not only was she having a weekend with Gianni all in his own home, but she was about to spend it with Jean-Paul too—and get more free clothes. Something told her, that now she and Gianni *were* an item, she would be getting a lot more free clothes coming her way.

"The store opening *is* this week babe… And we need to choose a look for you," Gianni said, zipping up his matching grey hoodie and slipping on a pair of box-fresh, white Palazzo running sneakers. "See if Carmen's around, we can pick a dress for her too and do lunch afterwards."

With Gianni gone for the morning, Chloe slumped back against the pillows but before the temptation to fall back to sleep set in, she got up and grabbed the phone next to the bed—pressing the direct dial button for services. "Hi, good Morning… Yes, can I please order some coffee, the French pastries and the fruit platter, please? Thank you."

Leaping out of bed, she skipped to the en-suite bathroom to shower. Only this time, she was expecting to be presented with a beautiful and stylish bathroom, so the impact of a waterfall shower complete with gold taps and Palazzo embroidered bath towels, wasn't much of a surprise. The shower was divine! If she could, she would have spent all morning in there under the hot water—but she had visitors coming. She got out of the shower and wrapped herself in one of Gianni's personalised terry-cloth robes with gold 'GP' embroidery, heading back to her phone on the bedside table. She quickly typed a message to Carmen.

> What are you up to?
> Fancy popping over to G's place?

> J-P's in town—they wanna talk looks
> for the store opening next week...

> Come for brunch at The Grand Towers,
> Park Av... Floor 13 xxx

Placing her phone back down, she quickly called down to Samuel to let him know she was expecting guests, before drying her hair and getting dressed back into her jeans with a simple white crew-neck T-shirt. She then tackled her make-up—consisting only of the emergency products she had packed in her overnight bag. But a buzz at the door downstairs forced her to stop fussing over her face to go answer it.

"Good morning, M'am," a grey-suited waiter said, with a trolley full of pastries, coffee and fruit

"Thank you—could you bring it through to the kitchen?" she said, holding the door open for him to wheel it through and start setting it up on the kitchen island. Heading back up the spiral staircase to the bedroom, she could hear her phone buzzing against the bedside table once more—it was Carmen. "Hey... Get my message?"

"Of course I did—I'm on my way!"

"Cool, Kim's heading over too—I totally forgot she was bringing the book back to me this morning. Anyway, come straight up to floor thirteen when you get here, okay?" Ending the call, Chloe had to race back downstairs as the door buzzed, yet again.

She grabbed Gianni's beige cashmere cardigan and slipped her arms into it as she made her way down. It drowned her a little but it still looked stylish in a baggy, boyfriend way. As she got to the last step, the waiter had already answered the door and Chloe could see Kim at the entrance—waiting with trepidation.

"Hey, Kim… Come on in!" Chloe said, smiling at the waiter to let her in. "I'm so sorry to call you all the way over here; I totally forgot I was staying."

"Oh, no bother," Kim said, looking around with wide eyes—the same wide-eyed look Chloe gave when she had first set foot inside.

Now she knew how star-struck she had looked to Gianni—it was quite embarrassing now she could see it for herself. She also noticed that Kim looked so much better put-together these days. Gone was the Palazzo puppet from their time together on the shop floor, in her well kept brown suit with her black hair neatly tied back into a ponytail.

As the assistant to the store director of the new Maison Marais, she had permission to dress how she wanted—for how long, was another question entirely. Wearing a black leather motorcycle jacket, a pair of skinny grey jeans with a red and black checked flannel shirt wrapped around her waist, and a pair of black leather ankle boots with a classic 'MM' monogram handbag slung over her shoulder—Kim looked rather rock and roll for someone who used to be so uptight.

"Is that a Hockney I saw outside?" Kim said, her thumb directing over her shoulder.

"I'm pretty sure there's a Warhol in the dining room too," Chloe said. "Are you hungry? I ordered brunch… Since I put you out coming all the way over here on your Saturday, it was the least I could do."

"As I said, no bother at all… It was *you* that did me the favour," she said, lifting the flap of her purse to hand Chloe the lilac 'P,' embossed folio.

Chloe was glad to see it again, although she wasn't sure if Gianni's place was the safest to have it in her possession—there was another knock at the door.

"Is that him?" Kim said, suddenly realising the implication and the reality that she may get to meet the man himself in his own home (although the fact that her friend was sleeping with him didn't seem to bother her in the slightest).

"Oh, no… He's at the gym. That'll be Carmen, we have some work stuff to catch up on so I invited her over too."

The waiter opened the door once more and as Chloe predicted, Carmen had arrived looking perfectly groomed as always, with a fresh head of blow-dried brunette hair.

"Glad you could make it… Kim just got here too!"

"Your message was quite the surprise… I was getting my hair done when I got your text. I thought this was meant to be a romantic weekend—alone!" Carmen said, taking off her thin black oval-shaped sunglasses to kiss Kim on either side of her face.

"Okay ladies, grab a plate and some coffee—and I'll give you the tour on our way up to the terrace"

After loading up a plate each with croissants, melon and fresh berries, they carried their cups of coffee through the apartment—careful not to spill or drop anything on the cream rugs in the living area. Kim confirmed that the painting hanging in the dining room was, in fact, a genuine dollar sign silkscreen by Warhol.

"Wait until you see this then," Chloe said, opening up the double doors to the cinema room.

Carmen looked at her with pursed lips. Chloe could read her mind—what she really wanted to ask was, whether he had proposed to her yet?

"It's another life, right?" Chloe shrugged, closing the doors to lead them upstairs.

"So, have you moved in already?" Carmen said, giving her the eye, noticing she was already wearing Gianni's clothes.

"Well, funny you should say that… Not quite *living* here, Just staying for the weekend—but he said I'm welcome to stay anytime."

"So things really are serious between you two then?" Kim said, not really believing her before.

"Like I said, we're just having fun and seeing where things go... Come, let's sit outside."

"Are you kidding me?" Carmen squealed, walking over to the edge to look down at the street below, cupping her coffee in her hands.

"I know, look behind you... That's his office, and through there he has a huge master suite, and a closet the size of my whole apartment... Oh, and that's the home gym, but apparently, it's not good enough—so he goes to a private club around the block," Chloe sarcastically scoffed, taking a sip of much-needed coffee.

"If only Regina could see you now," Kim said, sitting down at the table next to her, as Carmen cupped her hands over her eyes to peer through the glass doors to spy the office.

"If only she could see *us* right now, don't you mean? She would never believe it; we used to fights like cats on the shop floor and now we're having brunch together."

"Yeah... On Gianni Palazzo's terrace!" Carmen added.

They all laughed, it was quite funny how things had turned out between them. If you told Chloe two years ago that she would be friends with her then arch-enemy, she would have never believed you. Never mind mentioning Gianni!

"So tell me," Chloe started, slamming her hand down on the table to change the subject. "How did you get on with the guest-list in the end?"

"Thanks to you, everything is under control. Regina's planning on getting Myra involved on Monday... You know, making a point that now Maison Marais is a part of the Palazzo Group that we should all share resources—like Myra is the PR guru of events or something," Kim explained once more for Carmen's benefit.

Carmen laughed, she of all people knew that Myra was far from the event planning guru Regina was making her out to be—she had learnt that her days working with her at Bullet magazine. Palazzo events usually just consisted of Myra's friends and wannabe influencers that only came to drink the free alcohol and bag the gift vouchers in the goody-bags—ditching the rest of the contents in the dumpster on the street outside the venue. That was Myra's idea of a successful event.

"Well, now she's going to absolutely freak out when she discovers we have the client guest-list done and dusted... And not only that, but we have all the major clients in this fucking town!" Kim laughed, raising her white china coffee cup that was gilded in gold around the edge with a gold 'P,' handle.

Surprised, Chloe clinked her cup against Kim's. Hearing her curse and seeing her dress like a badass was all a bit too progressive all at once. But it was nice to see that she was breaking away from being the do-gooder—and being herself. That's what working under Regina did to you, Chloe understood that because the same evolution had happened to her.

"But how will you make it look like someone literally hasn't handed you the Palazzo database?" Carmen said, with concern in her tone.

"Don't worry—no one will ever know it came from you," Kim said, touching Chloe's arm before turning to Carmen. "I took my work laptop home with me and stayed up all night last night... The thing is, we had all the clients already on the Maison Marais system—we just didn't know which ones were the ready-to-wear buyers, because all they had ever purchased from us in the past was the same monogram luggage! Thanks to Melinda's little book, I was able to search each client on our system and fill in the missing details—like it was always there, all along... Then I made a list of the top clients we should invite to the opening event and emailed them over to Dionne with the Maison Marais customer numbers from our database so she can prove to Regina they're our clients."

Chloe raised an eyebrow, that was a genius idea and one she had never thought of herself. 'Maybe I could use a similar strategy somehow for S.O.S?' she wondered.

"Anyway, I guess I'd better be off," Kim said, checking her watch as she finished her coffee.

"Oh, you don't have to leave right away," Chloe said, noticing she hadn't eaten a thing.

"I promised Dionne I'd meet her at the store… The builders have finally moved out so the merch team can get the stock in and we can dress the store. No doubt Regina will be there too, and I'd hate to leave Dionne on her own to deal with her," Kim said, picking up a croissant to take on-the-go

"I'll show you out," Chloe said, rising from her slump in her chair.

"No need… Stay put and enjoy the view ladies—I'll see you guys next week at the store opening."

"And I'll take this," Carmen said, sliding the lilac leather folio across the table and into her tote bag underneath it. "We can't have Gianni finding this now, can we?"

Once again, Chloe felt like she had been told off by the teacher, but Carmen was right on cue—energetic footsteps raced up the stairs. Gianni had returned from his gym session.

28

So much for a quiet, romantic weekend… The apartment suddenly had a party-like atmosphere, it was surprising to Chloe how this mammoth apartment could shrink so quickly. Jean-Paul had arrived with his assistant, Claudette, Marie and Juliette, with several garment bags—which they flung over one of the large sofas in the living room. "Darling, it's so good to see you again!" Jean-Paul said, grabbing Chloe, happy to find her in the company of Gianni in his very own home.

Carmen greeted Marie and Juliette like old friends reunited once more. Marie began unzipping the garment bags to show Carmen the dress they had in mind for her to wear at the store opening, while Gianni opened up a bottle of chilled champagne to welcome his guests.

"So ladies, the sooner we get you dressed for the big event, the sooner we can go out and have some fun tonight—huh?" Jean-Paul said, clapping his hands.

"Oh, it won't take long for these guys to pick a dress, I'm sure," Gianni laughed, handing out champagne in cut-crystal glasses that were etched with the italic 'P,' monogram.

"Oh, Marie—I *love* it!" Carmen gasped, holding her hands up to her mouth in prayer, as Marie held up a black chiffon dress embellished with tiny silver stars that looked like shimmering crystals from afar. It was long and floaty—almost seventies in style—like something that Stevie Nicks would have worn.

"And for you Chloe… I think you will look stunning in red," Jean-Paul announced, revealing a short dress made from matte red sequins with padded power shoulders.

"Yes, but I thought you would look much better in this one!" Juliette said, unzipping a bag to reveal a silver metallic mini-dress, with a wrap-over front and long sleeves. It caught Chloe's eye immediately, it said: 'Disco.' Together with Carmen dressed in black—and herself in silver—they would compliment the new store concept perfectly.

"*Oof!* Decisions," Chloe feigned, knowing which one she preferred. "The red dress is wonderful… But I have to agree with Juliette on this one."

Chloe turned to Carmen for her opinion, who had already slipped on her gown for Marie to start pinning to her svelte figure—she pointed to the silver dress.

"Okay, you win!" Jean-Paul huffed, throwing his arms up. "Keep both… You can wear the other one to the Palazzo exhibition gala."

"You can forget about that!" Gianni said, lounging on the empty sofa. "It may be *all* about you for now, but the gala is strictly Palazzo—she's wearing one of our dresses to that!"

Chloe looked at Gianni and smiled, it was both wonderful and terrifying to hear two of the most well-known designers volley over whose dress she was going to wear. Looking at him, she saw the same look as when she first came face-to-face with him a year ago on the red carpet—wearing *his* red dress!

"Actually… I know someone who would look just as fabulous in this dress," Chloe said, smoothing over the sequins with an idea in mind.

"Do what you like mon Cherie, but please… Go and get this dress on so I can pin it—then we can have some fun! I haven't come all this way to stay in this apartment like Rapunzel in her tower! You girls, promised us girls, a good time—remember?"

*

The weekend felt like a dream, filled with great company, good food and plenty of alcohol and laughs. Not to mention, Gianni's beautiful apartment which was starting to quickly feel like home. But a chauffeur-driven car to take her to the office helped Monday morning from being filled with the dread of going back to work. Quite the opposite—as she sat in the back of Tommy's

Mercedes, Chloe was excited for the week ahead. Excited for the store opening and excited to get back to work on her business. Hanging around Gianni and Jean-Paul over the weekend had inspired her to keep on working on StacksOfStyle and to create a global brand—just like they were. After all, if she was going to be a match for Graziana as well as her brother, then she had to think big. "Morning Carmen!" she beamed, walking into the office with a Maison Marais garment bag folded over her arm—her handbag on the other.

"Hey, you! So much for a quiet weekend, huh? I have to admit, I was hungover *all* day yesterday—Jean-Paul is an animal!" Carmen groaned, already sipping strong black coffee.

"I know… I think they were just all excited to be here and wanted to party… Gianni doesn't help though does he? Those two are double-trouble when they get together…"

"But a lot of fun! What else did you get up to?" Carmen said, cutting a suggestive look with her eyes as she sat on the edge of Chloe's desk—bracing herself for the details.

"Well… Yesterday we couldn't move, so we stayed in bed most of the day—watching movies on his huge TV at the end of the bed."

"Just 'watching' movies?"

Chloe looked back at her—a look was enough to answer that question.

"Oh, you already have your dress fitted?" Carmen said, gesturing to the garment bag Chloe had hung up on the cupboard behind her. "Perks of screwing the designer's best friend, I guess…"

"No, I haven't *actually*! It's the red dress—if you must know," Chloe said, turning on her computer to get started on answering emails.

"Changed your mind?"

"Nope… I'm gonna send this one over to Kim. I think she'll look stunning in it—and she deserves to look just as fantastic as us! *Aaand* it will *fuck* Regina off… She'll be wondering all night where and how she got this dress… Until she sees us that is—and Jean-Paul—all having a fabulous time together under her nose!"

"You need to get out more…" Carmen said, returning to her desk.

"You know me… I'll do anything to piss on that woman's parade."

"Oh, somehow I think co-designing the exclusive event bag—and having it named after you—will do the trick… I wouldn't worry about that!"

Chloe smirked, Carmen was once again, right—she knew her too well. "Anyway, don't we have a sales meeting first thing?"

"We do indeed… I'm just running over the weekend sales for P.S.L and then we can head there together. No doubt, Veronica will grill us right away on that!"

The boardroom had been filled with every department involved with S.O.S—Bill from buying, Morgana from marketing, Sam and Lily from design—but no Veronica.

"Unfortunately, Veronica has an important meeting to attend this morning, but we shall proceed," Bill started, looking around the table.

"Yes, we have a lot to go over," Morgana predictably butted in—taking over the meeting. "The article we pushed live with Pandora Simmons has really helped the launch of P.S.L—as well as us having U.S exclusivity on the collection of course."

"I'm just looking over the figures you sent and they are awesome—as we expected," Bill said, turning away from Morgana's fluff to face Carmen—hoping to get the facts out of her.

"Amazing results… Maisey has emailed me over the weekend to say that the zero–one–five dress is fully sold-out in all sizes and colours—they now have a waiting list."

"How soon can we re-stock?" Bill said, glancing over the figures with wide eyes.

"Well, this is the issue… This first season's buy was just something I took a chance on, so the final order was very minimal in terms of units… P.S.L is still a very young company and everything is manufactured to order, so to turn around a new order on old fabrics will take them some time—if at all possible. Especially as they're now working on getting the fall collection out to vendors.

The good news is that we'll receive the new season styles of this dress pretty soon—and we have ordered more stock this time," Chloe said, proudly knowing her stuff.

"Great! Maybe we should revise that order—for units on the dress alone—and place a re-order while we still can? On that note, how is the re-stock of the Raven line performing?" Bill said, now turning to Sam and Lily.

"The Raven line is still selling well; the re-stock of the first collection allowed us to fill in some of the missed sales from the first delivery—but not all of the lines are completely sold-out. The second collection is also selling very well; we produced more units on the back of the popularity of the first capsule, so it hasn't been an instant sell-out—but we've shifted much more in terms of units," Sam continued, taking ownership over the Raven line which had become hers and Lily's responsibility.

"We also have the samples back for the P.S.L collaboration, which we need signing off as soon as possible to make production," Lily added.

"Perfect—let's set something up for later this afternoon to take a look and then you can send those to London for approval… Does anyone have anything else to add?" Bill said, seeming eager to rush off himself.

"Yes, I do—summer sale," Carmen said, which made everyone sit up. "We haven't had the chance to run this by Veronica yet—we were hoping to in this session—but I've made a list of items to mark down for our very first summer sale."

Faces around the table started to look at each other, all wondering why she was proposing a sale so soon when the site was performing rather well—stock was already flying out the door. "Do you think we are established enough to offer discount items?" Morgana said, worrying about all the hard work her team had done to position S.O.S as a premium website.

"Just think about this… In a couple of months, every retailer will go on seasonal sale and we will lose customers to those competitors—and we may never get them back once they rediscover other sites that offer them a bargain. Promos can also attract new customers, and for a new business like ours, that's exactly what we need. If we want to play the game alongside well-established retailers, then we need to mimic what they're doing."

"That's a fair point," Bill said, grateful that Carmen was thinking like a businesswoman who understood how to sell—not just make things look pretty. "So what's the plan?"

"We're expecting deliveries of new season to arrive any day now, and we have more brands this time too—but with limited stock space. It'll cost the business more to take warehouse space from DivaFeet—so we need to make room. By clearing lines sooner, it proves that our stock *is* hot and that we sell-out fast!" Carmen said, nodding to Morgana to acknowledge that her efforts and expertise had been considered. "This will prompt customers to order right away in the future, rather than add to their wishlist's for later. The best way to achieve this, and please our customers, is to give them a sale! Now, I'm not saying we shift everything at bargain-basement prices... We just need to sell left-over lines from the launch collaborations, and anything from the first Raven capsule. We can continue to meet during the sale period and add more lines, if necessary."

Chloe was impressed. Carmen was developing an authoritative voice with every team meeting she attended, but as she was delivering her strategy, Chloe's attention diverted to what was going on outside the glass walls of the boardroom.

"Wonderful! Okay, I think we're done here for this morning... I will see you guys with Sam and Lily later to go over the samples," Bill said, forcing Chloe to mentally come back into the room. Chairs flew back on their wheels as the team disbanded to get back to the mountain of Monday morning tasks the meeting had already taken them away from.

"Did you see Veronica pass by?" Chloe said, walking back into their glass box with Carmen. "Who was that guy she was showing around the office?"

"I didn't see," Carmen shrugged.

"Weird... Why would she miss another sales meeting, but still be in the office giving a guided tour of the place?"

"Probably one of the board members of DivaFeet or something, or a client that she's trying to woo and get onsite—we have a lot to get on with in the meantime… We need to schedule a call with Dom and Pandora to talk about extending our order, we need to approve the 'P.S.L X Raven' samples, and then we need to go over this potential sale list at some point—not to mention look at what stock is uploading this Friday and write the homepage article."

But it was no good, Chloe's mind was elsewhere. Something in her gut was telling her that something was going on—but she didn't know what. And the feeling of suspicion followed her the next day, and the day after—knowing Veronica was still nowhere to be seen. Usually, she was popping in and out of their office, asking them for figures or pestering them about what was coming next—what their plans were for the following season.

It was especially odd that she hadn't checked in on them after a huge brand launch (one that she was invested in too). Rather than obsess about it like Chloe, Carmen rather enjoyed her distance. It meant she could finally get a lot more done and sign off on things without the need to seek Veronica's approval because she simply wasn't there to ask. Without any cause or evidence, Chloe had no other option than to get on with the work that was constantly passing her desk from Carmen.

Her evenings with Gianni had become a welcome distraction from the busy, stressful days. She had stayed at The Grand Towers every night since the weekend—she even had Tommy collect more of her things to make her stay more comfortable. And staying at Gianni's certainly had its perks: sex, luxury, a chauffeur to work, and of course, designer dresses on tap!

"Morning," Chloe said, the next day—hand-delivering a Maison Marais garment bag at Carmen's desk.

Excited, Carmen grabbed the bag straight away and unzipped it to inspect her black and silver star-studded dress inside. "Tonight's the night!" she shrieked.

"For what?" Chloe said, rather flat—not sharing the same enthusiasm. They had only been talking about the Maison Marais opening for months, but the busy week at work had taken the excitement out of it for her. All she wanted to do was go home and soak in Gianni's huge bathtub. Plus, she had done so well to dodge Regina thus far, could she really be bothered to come face-to-face with her again in public and pretend to be civil? The very thought of it exhausted her alone.

"Tonight is *the* night I get to wear this stunning thing!" Carmen said, holding up the dress against her body, swishing it side-to-side, adoringly.

Chloe rolled her eyes, she could be so predictable sometimes, but she had to admit it, she was secretly looking forward to wearing hers too.

"Zoe and Gray confirmed they will drop in this evening too... I think they want us to introduce them to Jean-Paul and get their foot in the door for his shows or something," Carmen continued to rattle on.

'Where does she get her energy from?' Chloe thought, rubbing her temples—waiting for her inbox to load on her computer screen.

"And I've invited Karen!"

"VERONICA!" Chloe blurted out, shocked to finally see her back in the office, standing at their doorway. "Where have you been?"

"Sorry girls, I had some loose ends to tie up with the board before we submit our taxes and sign off on budget for this year... Speaking of which, we need to get together and go over your budget and forecast your requirements for spend."

Carmen's face dropped, couldn't she just enjoy one day without more work landing on her lap? She didn't even take notice of the weather forecast, let alone come up with a budget and spend proposal for what they might potentially need. Chloe, on the other hand, was relieved to see the task-master she knew was back— there *was* nothing to worry about.

"Now we have our feet planted and some cash coming in, we really need to focus on your spend vs profit."

"Of course, I'll get started by updating our sales reports," Carmen said, hanging the dress up on the bookshelf behind her to sit back down at her computer. Everything had been so ad-hoc so far in terms of budget, but now it seemed things were getting more serious.

"Excellent! Make a start on getting your finances up to date and think about what you want to do this coming year... What brands do you want to add to your list, do you want to do any events? That type of thing... We can meet on Friday to go over your plan and try to cost it all up... Is that what you're wearing tonight?" Veronica said, nudging her head towards the dress as she was about to leave.

"Sure is," Carmen grinned. "Designed and picked out by Jean-Paul himself!"

"I can't wait to see you ladies there... Oh, by the way—Karen wants to buy the exclusive bag. Can you hook her up?" Veronica said, firing her fingers at Chloe like a pair of guns.

"I'll call Kim... There's only twenty bags available, so I'll have to pull some strings."

"Appreciate it," Veronica winked, exiting as quickly as she had appeared.

"*No discount this time though!*" Chloe yelled, texting Kim at the same time, which got a snigger from Carmen.

**

They allowed themselves to leave work an hour earlier than usual so they had time to go home and get ready. It was funny how much more work they could get done, knowing they had fewer hours to fit it all in. Everything was taken care of, the samples had been packed and sent over to Dom and Pandy, and Carmen had drafted her sale list. Making her way back to Park Avenue, Chloe was in better spirits about getting dressed up to go out. She had forgotten that she would be arriving not only in a custom Maison Marais dress but with Gianni on her arm—and that *was* a good reason to see Regina once again.

"Hey Sam, good day?" she said, walking up to the front desk of The Grand Towers.

Samuel looked up from his desk computer and smiled—he was starting to get used to having Chloe and her laid-back personality around. She made a welcome change from the usual stuffiness of the apartment's elite residents. "A superb day, so far... And this came for you."

Turning to reach into the stylish sixties style cupboard behind him, he placed a large black Maison Marais boutique bag on the reception desk in front of her with black, branded, streamer ribbons dangling from the rope handles. It also had a note sticking out the top with '*Chloe*' scrawled in cursive.

"Well, this is a nice surprise to come home to," Chloe said, taking the black cord handles—grimacing at having called this place home so soon. "Is Gianni back?"

"I believe Mr Palazzo was working from home today... I haven't seen him leave," Samuel said, looking back at his desktop.

"Cool—thanks, Sam." Chloe headed over to the elevators, opening the note while she waited for the doors of the private car to open.

Thank you so much for the gorgeous red dress... But Regina's making us all wear black tonight :(

Please don't be offended if you see me in some boring blazer suit! Jean-Paul's been in-store all week—he's asked me to send you these for tonight...

See you soon,
Kim x

By now, the elevator had landed on the thirteenth floor as Chloe folded the note and poked it back through the bag's opening. It was a good job Gianni had given her a spare key—she was excited to get inside and see what Jean-Paul had sent her. Inside, the apartment was still. Gianni wasn't in the kitchen or sat in the living room, and he wasn't resting in his favourite spot in the cinema either. Chloe assumed he was getting showered and ready to leave for the event himself, so she leapt her way up the spiral staircase.

As she reached the top, she could hear Gianni speaking on the phone in Italian. She stopped and poked her head in the office doorway to let him know she was back from work. And there he was—nodding and looking very serious as he looked up to give her a quick flash of his white teeth. He winked and held up his index finger to say: 'One minute.' Chloe blew him a kiss and carried on through to the master suite, leaving him to finish the call in peace.

Dumping her handbag down on the bed—she shrugged off her jacket and set the black boutique bag on the chaise at the foot of it, to finally look inside. Untying the black ribbons holding together the handles of the luxuriously thick paper bag, she threw the notecard out once more—along with layers of black tissue. Eventually, she pulled out a black shoebox with 'MAISON MA-RAIS' stamped in white lettering on the lid. She whipped off the lid and rifled through more layers of tissue before the right foot peeped through.

A flash of silver-coated leather, with a sparkling crystallised star buckle on a pointed toe, dazzled back at her (stars where a theme from the collection). The left foot was covered with black tissue and a dust-bag laid over it—but that wasn't all that was inside the shopping bag. She reached back in to grab the large soft-cloth dust-bag—instantly knowing what it was inside. Her heart began to race; she had waited a long time to finally hold it in her hands.

The plush feeling of something soft-yet-substantial, the subtle chime of chains rattling together as she lifted it out of the bag—it was her very own 'Chloe' bag! The turquoise green velvet felt magnificently plush in her hand—like no other material she had ever felt before. Her fingers gently pressed into the pile of the beautifully stitched 'MM' quilt design that was stitched all over the bag.

Five, thin gunmetal chains were wrapped into one to make a single thick, snake-like rope, while the 'MM' logo clasp on the front was embellished with halved faux pearls. Unaware that she was holding her breath, she flipped the clasp to look inside. The lining was sublime, lined in mint green lambskin, with two compartments and a handy zip section in-between them. On the back of the bag's lining, stitched onto a concealed zip compartment, a gold label was stamped with:

MAISON MARAIS

X

CHLOE RAVENS

FIFTH AVENUE EXCLUSIVE

01/20

Not only was she the proud co-designer of a Maison Marais bag, but she had the very first bag of the limited run; the most sought after number out of the entire edition. The addition of the enamel apple and flame charms dangling off the side made her smile—it gave the bag some 'Jean-Paul' tongue-in-cheek humour.

The unexpected delivery had been a wonderful surprise after a hectic day at the office, and it suddenly gave her the extra oomph she needed to get up and get into the shower—ready to go to this damn party. The hot, steamy water pouring out of the waterfall shower head covered Chloe's body, soothing her as she grabbed the soap to lather on her skin. The luxurious bathroom decor and toiletries made her feel as though she was in a hotel or a luxury spa.

At this rate, she could easily slip into bed afterwards, but Gianni made sure she was alert—breaking her daydream as he crashed into the bathroom in a hurry. "Sorry about that—phone call with Milan," he said, slipping off his boxers, watching Chloe's body glisten under the water as it trickled off her. He cleared his throat. "How was work?"

"Fine—the usual," she said, washing her face—careful not to get her clipped up hair too wet. "Veronica finally made an appearance… She's been busy with meetings and giving tours around the office to strange men—she's coming tonight."

"Strange men, you say?" Gianni crooned, stepping in to join her, giving her a peck on the lips. His neat but coarse body hair bristled against her as he took her waist to pull her closer into him—it got softer as it dampened. But something got harder as he tried to kiss her neck, his hands wandering down her back and over her buttocks. Chloe wrapped herself around him to switch positions, allowing him to immerse himself under the shower-head.

"I wish we could just stay in tonight," she said, soaping up his chest as he wetted his hair under the shower. "I'm tired of this week already, and I can see you need to *de-stress*."

Gianni rinsed his hair and opened his eyes as he manoeuvred his groin closer to hers. "We don't have to rush—they can't wait for us."

"Who said I wanted to rush?" Chloe grinned; biting her lip as she slid her hand down his chest towards his groin—coming to a stop just as she reached... Reaching back around to slap him on his ass instead.

"Oh, come on! I've had a long and stressful day!"

"Haven't we all?" she teased, getting out of the shower to dry off.

"You can't leave me like this," he moaned, gesturing his hands downwards.

"Even more reason to get ready, go to this *fucking* party, and come back home," she said, wrapping a robe around her—letting it slip off her shoulders... All the way down, so that her butt-crack was on display as she looked back at him—suggetsively biting a finger.

If there was one thing she had successfully learnt by now, it was always to leave them on their toes and wanting more... It applied to everyone and everything: Regina, Graziana, Veronica, customers—and most definitely, men!

29

Shiny and new, the black and silver mirrored block structure made it stand out like a shining beacon amongst the stores that had already stood for some time—losing their lustre as the years weathered them away. It was more suited to Rodeo Drive than Fifth Avenue (which was next on the renovation list). Black velvet ropes with silver stands looped around the corner of the store, holding back paparazzi and journalists waiting for Gianni and Jean-Paul to arrive.

Making sure everything was in place and ready for a successful event, Kim had been busy all week—but this evening was really just the start of her career at Maison Marais. The visual merchandising had peeled back the very last of the plastic that covered the glass cabinets and cleaned every surface to make sure it gleaned immaculately under the spotlights. The cocktail bar had now been set-up at the back of the ground floor, near the wall of accessories and shoes—just how Chloe had suggested it. Upstairs in the women's department, the same DJ that remixed Jean-Paul's show music had been flown in from Paris and was busy setting up his decks.

Dresses, blouses, pants, and skirts all hung neatly on silver rails that dropped down from the ceiling with white marble slabs running underneath them, where shoes were neatly displayed, sparsely in pairs. The third floor was, of course, the men's floor—smaller in size compared to the women's but just as intimidating. The same silver rails showcased the collection, only this time shoes, boots, and sneakers sat upon black marble.

Only now, had the contractors finished patching up the last of the greyish marks on the brilliant white painted walls, suffered from scuffs and scrapes of the move. Even the stock room in the basement had been laid out in orderly fashion, ready for trading the very next morning with a whole new sales team—who were about to be briefed by Dionne (overshadowed by Regina, of course). "Okay, everyone… Gather round," she ordered.

The newly hired staff—along with the original staff—answered her call. The new uniform was modern, much sexier than the conservative one before it. The ladies were fitted in a black blazer with structured shoulder pads—a simple white shirt underneath it—with black slim-fit jeans. Pointed black leather high-heels (with the thinnest of heels), certain to give them all back-ache by the end of the week, standing on marble flooring for eight hours a day. Still, they looked great.

Equally, the men were given similar attire. A black blazer and a white shirt with black jeans topped off with Cuban heeled motor-cycle style harness boots. Dionne took her place next to Regina to dress her team, while Kim stood on the sidelines—dressed in a similar black uniform, as requested. Myra had even managed to leave her desk of Palazzo's press office across the avenue to elbow her way in on proceedings (obviously narked that her expertise wasn't needed to prove her worth in the end). If only she really knew, just how Kim had managed to get all the top spending clients in the city…

"Tonight is a very special night in Maison Marais' history. Thanks to the Palazzo Group, we will take this brand into the next generation and beyond—and this evening marks the first step in bringing Parisian chic back to New York. This evening we will not only be joined by our wonderful creative director, Monsieur Jean-Paul Baptiste but also with Mr Palazzo. With that said, Dionne will inspect everyone's uniform's before our guests arrive, and I'd like to remind you that no alcohol or food is to be consumed—anyone found in breach of this will be dealt with. Also, I'm sure I don't need to say it, but at no point are you allowed to speak to, or approach, Monsieur Baptiste and Mr Palazzo—unless you are spoken to first."

Kim rolled her eyes. Regina's speech was the exact same drivel she used to preach at Palazzo events. Now she was group director, she spreading her stupid rules over to Maison Marais like the plague. From what she had heard from Chloe, Jean-Paul and Gianni weren't the types to be annoyed, should one *dare* smile or greet them.

Regina carried on with her list of 'dont's' which included: no selfies or autograph requests, no mobile phones, in fact, no small-talk between each other on the shop floor—and definitely, no breaks to be taken, sneakily in the back of house. "Do you have anything else to add?" she said, passing her hand to Dionne like she was just some hanger-on and not the store director.

"Yes," she said, looking around at her team with pride. "Just remember to smile, have fun, and enjoy tonight… What will hopefully be the start—or restart for those here with me previously—to a long and prosperous career at Maison Marais."

The team gave Dionne a soft, round of applause. It was more in line with what they expected to hear, rather than being told off like school kids. Regina gave her a side-glance—as if she had just undone the ruleset with one sentence. Still, she was the 'big boss' and they needed to respect that—especially if they wanted to last past this evening. Sensing there was nothing else left to say, Kim dashed upstairs to signal to the DJ that he could start his set, before rushing carefully back down the marble stairs——like they were made of ice.

Now, the team were hurrying to their stations to wait nervously like mannequins, statically positioned for the rest of the evening. Kim expertly dodged them in her high-heels as she made her way to the front of the store to let the security guards know they were now ready to receive guests. And just as she had done so, electronic beats started to pulse—reverberating around the marble box of a store. Next on her to-do list, was to make sure the army of handsome waiters (all of which waited for a living while waiting for their 'big modelling' break) were on standby to serve the five-star catering that was being prepared downstairs—in what would eventually become the staff kitchen and lounge.

By the time Chloe and Gianni had pulled up outside the new-look Maison Marais, the party inside was well in motion. Most of the celebs invited by the Paris press office were in attendance, while Myra's New York-based C-listers (A.K.A, her friends) were draining the free bar and wolfing down the canapés. Fashion fans had also started to congregate outside, hopeful to grab a selfie with a celebrity or two. Even Jean-Paul had arrived with Marie and Juliette and was happily greeting and chatting away to the clients Kim had secured in the eleventh hour.

Carmen had also turned up in her dazzling black and silver dress—she had caught the attention of the photographers outside and was entertaining their calls to pose. Veronica and Karen made sure they were one of the first ones there, so Karen could get her hands on the limited edition handbag. The dashing waiters circulated the combination of guests on the floor with their champagne and canapé trays. Both free alcohol and boyish good looks enticing guests into having a good time.

Back outside, the paparazzi immediately turned their focus away from trying to snap guests through the store-front glass windows, now on to Gianni—whose head had appeared from the blacked-out Mercedes. Cameras began to click and flash as he opened the car door for Chloe to step out on to the curb of Fifth Avenue. "Miss Ravens—Mr Palazzo... Look this way!" they called, all shouting for their attention as Gianni linked arms with her to walk inside together.

He quickly waved to the fashionistas who had waited, all holding their cell phones up to snap the moment for their Instagram's. The store security team had anticipated their arrival and guided them past the velvet ropes, onto the large, flat black marble step of the store. The big glass double doors were already held open for them to enter, but just as Chloe was about to walk inside, Gianni softly wrapped his arms around her waist and prompted her to turn for the cameras once more. "Always give them a little bit of what they want, to keep them off your back..." he muttered under his breath through a grin.

The flashes from the camera's brought her back to the night she first met him at New York Fashion Week. If it wasn't for them, she may never have found herself in the position she was in today, still posing for them next to Gianni—this time as his girlfriend and not some random acquaintance. With the paparazzi satisfied—for now—they finally walked into the party.

"Chloe! You look stunning," Kim greeted, going in for a kiss on the cheek.

"Thank you… I was expecting to say the same for you too, but I got your note with these babies," Chloe said, turning her shoulder and pointing her toes; showing off her bag and shoes. "Oh Gianni, have you met Kim? I told you all about her—we worked together at Palazzo."

"Of course I do," Gianni said, which is what he would have said, even if he hadn't remembered. Still, he shook her hand and leaned in for the standard 'fashion' kiss on either side of her face.

"Good evening Mr Palazzo… Chloe," Regina stepped in, having noticed they had arrived from the commotion outside. She was bolstered with Myra by her side, always hanging on, like a Kleenex on her shoe.

Chloe fought hard not to roll her eyes at the pair. Instead, she simply smiled back, a quick closed-mouth smile that unwittingly still made a dagger of a look. Gianni politely air-kissed Regina, completely ignoring Myra—failing to recognise her as Palazzo's press officer altogether.

"Regina, good to see things have wrapped up nicely… Well done!" Gianni said, looking around the ground floor entrance.

Chloe wasn't sure how much small-talk she could stand with Regina, but it could have been worse: Graziana could have turned up as well! But she wouldn't have to endure much longer, as a familiar face approached. Dressed in a slim-fit black suit with a collared white shirt, much like the rest of the staff, Dionne Blanc bravely joined them. "Dionne!" Chloe cried out, shooing Regina aside so she could make a fuss of her. Reshuffling to allow Dionne into the circle had pushed Myra completely out of it, making her look like the spare part—and not the other way around.

"Chloe, you look *A-mazing!*" Dionne said, giving her a hug.

"Gianni, this is Dionne—your fabulous store director! She has been for many years now, and knows everything about this company," Chloe said, making sure she got good words in about her before Regina could belittle her in some way. "Kim told me how hard you have both worked... Getting all the old clients back in-store?"

"Ah, it was all Kim really—I don't know how she did it, but she pulled it together," Dionne said, professionally shaking Gianni's hand.

"You need to take more credit! The store looks amazing... Such a shame you weren't allowed to dress up for the party too—I'm sure Jean-Paul would have up with something wonderful for you. In fact, I sent Kim a beautiful dress to wear for this evening—but I now understand you have to comply with uniform standards." Chloe said, taking the chance to get another dig at Regina in, while she had them all in her court.

"What are you on about?" Gianni said, confused by the random direction of her rant.

"Oh, you didn't hear? Apparently, *someone* told these guys they had to wear the staff uniform tonight... Which is a shame, because I sent over the red dress that Jean-Paul wanted me to wear? I didn't want it to go to waste, and it's such a stunning dress," Chloe said, laying it on as thickly as she could.

Regina pursed her lips and stared back at Chloe with piercing eyes, she knew full well that she had obviously had a bitch-fest with Kim, before this evening. Which was surprising; Kim was once Regina's protégé.

"Well, that certainly didn't come from me! Staff yes, but I expect the store director and the assistant to represent the brand... This is the *new* Maison Marais—whatever went on before is out the door. Anyway, *is* Jean-Paul here yet?"

"Yes, he is, Mr Palazzo... Allow me to take you to him," Regina said, cutting her eye at Chloe and biting her tongue. Tonight was not the night for old grudges to resurface, especially not now Chloe was officially dating Gianni—she had won *that* battle.

Regina led the way, through the ground floor towards the back of the store, where the cocktail bar was set up—which happened to be where Jean-Paul had set up camp. As the others walked on ahead, Chloe grabbed Kim's elbow and pulled her in close so she could speak directly in her ear over the loud, pulsating music. "Just call him Gianni, G, Gi-Gi, G-Dog—whatever you want! None of this Mr Palazzo crap! Listen, is Carmen here too?"

"Oh yeah, she's with Jean-Paul too," Kim said, weaving her way through, dodging glass counters filled with leather goods as she followed the entourage.

You couldn't miss Jean-Paul, he was wearing a black, glittery tuxedo jacket which sparkled from a distance. He dressed the camp cocktail number with a pair of black faded jeans and stacked Chelsea boots. "Gianni! You're finally here!" he shouted, putting down his martini glass to give him a hug; catching a glimpse of Chloe over his shoulder. "Okay, okay, Chloe—you win! You are an absolute vision! C'est parfait!"

"But it's all your vision though!" Chloe said, before giving him a kiss—then greeting Marie, Juliette, and Carmen in canon.

"Don't listen to him—he said the same to me," Carmen winked, taking a sip of champagne.

Regina watched on, swallowing another gulp of annoyance. Not only had Carmen and Chloe made something of a name for themselves (and rocked up looking like Maison Marais Models), but Chloe had clearly made an impression with Jean-Paul. She was no longer the silly girl from the shop floor that wanted to be something—she *was* something. For the first time, Regina admitted to herself that she should have promoted her to press office assistant after all. Maybe then, all of this wouldn't have happened and Myra would have her tucked away somewhere behind a desk. But even then, Chloe would have found a way to succeed—it was like she was being guided somehow. But no matter how hard Regina tried—or threatened her—she just couldn't keep her down. The sound of Chloe rattling on with her newfound friends jarred Regina out of her thoughts and back into the party.

"This here is Kim—a very good friend of mine… I sent her the red dress you had in mind for me. In fact, Gianni and I were just saying that she should have worn it this evening…"

Now it was Regina fighting not to roll her eyes this time, wishing Chloe would shut up about this bloody red dress!

"But of course you should, my dear… That dress was made for a beautiful woman like yourself!" Jean-Paul said, lifting Kim's hand in the air for her to twirl.

"*See!*" Chloe said to Kim with a look that said: 'F*uck* Regina!' She was in a higher position now; she was screwing *her* boss and that had extra benefits—bitchy revenge on Regina was just one of them.

"Well, it's upstairs in the office," Kim said.

"Go on then, get it on!" Carmen nudged.

Kim laughed. Chloe had some nerve doing this in front of everyone, but it would certainly make for a moment to remember. She wanted to be known in high-fashion circles—she too wanted to be remembered. Chloe was right, *fuck* Regina! This was Dionne's store and there was no room for the old rules—Gianni himself had said so.

"Mr Palazzo," Regina interrupted, changing the subject from the whole dress code debacle. "Don Carlo has also arrived and is upstairs with guests on the women's floor."

"Fabulous! Let's pop up and see him… Chloe, I especially want you to meet Don. I've told him all about you and I want you two to hit heads together—two online brains are better than one, and I'm sure he'll be a great contact for you."

"Uh, better take one of these with then," Jean-Paul said sarcastically, handing Chloe a champagne glass from a passing waiter.

Upstairs on the women's floor, Chloe was amazed to see that it was clear where the party was at. It was dimly lit compared to the bright, white lights of downstairs and she recognised a few famous faces in the crowd—Carly Wattmore was one of them. She was nestled in amongst other famous models, who had walked the Maison Marais show with her in Paris.

Dipping her head, Carly acknowledged Chloe and Gianni—raising her glass. She would speak to them later once the buzz around them had died down. Plus, Carly wasn't one to pander, she was just as important as they were—they should be coming over to speak to her. Once the socialite about town herself, Carmen also spotted people she knew—Gray and Zoe. Drifting off from the entourage, she took them downstairs to meet Juliette and Marie to help them network—leaving Chloe to do the professional spiel solo.

They found Don Carlo entertaining a group of guests, to which Regina politely interrupted by touching him on his shoulder. Like usual, he was wearing his own uniform: a slim-fit black suit, with a black roll-neck sweater underneath and his black round-frame spectacles. "Ciao, Gianni… Great to see you!" Don said, reaching out to shake his hand— his Italian accent standing out amongst a bunch of New Yorkers.

"Always a pleasure… This is my girlfriend, Chloe Ravens. Remember I told you about her website, StacksOfStyle?"

"Of course—how could I forget? It's a pleasure to meet you finally," Don said, taking Chloe's hand. "In fact, I've been talking to some of your biggest fans."

Sensing someone approach from behind, he turned around and opened up the circle.

"Chloe! You look fabulous, darling!"

"Karen! You made it !" she said, leaping forward for a kiss and brief hug. Veronica was stood with her, and although they hadn't seen much of each other lately, Chloe just gave her a smile.

"Gianni, this is Karen—one of my oldest and *biggest* clients and Palazzo… Veronica, you already know of course. Don—Veronica is my business partner, as I'm sure you have already discovered?"

Veronica downed the contents of her champagne glass—seemingly to dodge the conversation. But looking at Don and Veronica standing next to each other gave Chloe a sudden flash-back.

A snapshot—a memory.

It was almost as though she had met him before, but she knew she hadn't… Maybe she had simply seen Don's face in the media, or heard so much from Gianni about him, that it felt like she already knew him? Whatever it was, Chloe put it down to a bad case of déjà vu and tucked a strand of hair behind her ear, resuming her act of the chatty socialite she was expected to be. "I see you've made a purchase already!" she said, looking at the black boutique bag sealed with black stickers by Karen's feet.

"You know me and designer bags," she guffawed. "When Veronica said *you* designed the bag… Well, I just had to have it *even* more! Thanks for putting me on the list!" She whispered the latter.

Over Karen's shoulder, Chloe spotted something that made her feel rather smug. Emerging from the back of house, Kim appeared—wearing the red sequin dress which dripped off her figure, like wet blood. Before making her way back through the guests, she tugged and shifted the dress on her body—checking her appearance in one of the black glass walls.

The shoulder-line was strong with shoulder pads—yet feminine. The waist nipped in close to slender the frame, and the length was perfectly short on her—it was almost made for her and not Chloe. As she walked closer to them, the slashed front showed off Kim's porcelain skin and small chest—just like she was fresh off the runway. "Oh wow!" Chloe clapped, turning to Jean-Paul to get his approval. "See… I knew it would look better on her than me!"

"Magnifique! I love it, you are gorgeous darling," Jean-Paul quipped, circling Kim to make sure the zip at the back was done all the way up. "I think we could go a bit smaller, you need to show off your figure!"

"Watch it!" Chloe teased with gritted teeth. The dress *was* intended for her originally. Was he implying she was bigger than Kim?

"Actually, I need to borrow you and Chloe if that's possible?" Kim said, almost apologetically. "The photographer wants to take a few snaps with you guys by the exclusive bag display downstairs before they are all purchased."

"Certainly, come on, Gianni—you should be included in this too," Jean-Paul said, linking arms with Kim to make a start downstairs.

"Excuse us for one moment," Gianni said, too pleased for a reason to escape a deeper conversation with Don.

Back downstairs, at the front of the store, a whole wall was dedicated to Chloe's bag design. All twenty of the limited edition bags had been sold via a guest-list that had been determined by the press office back in Paris (ensuring the A-list guests got the bulk), leaving Dionne and Kim with the tricky task of deciding who got the remaining few.

Alas, ten bags dotted around on the mirror shelf served as a backdrop for press shots—before their new owners were allowed to take them home. Stood in front of the wall of bags, Chloe sandwiched herself between Jean-Paul and Gianni, while she held her own bag with both hands in front of her. The photographer took a few shots before Jean-Paul made his way back over to the cocktail bar to refill his glass. Gianni returned upstairs to entertain Don—he couldn't ignore him all evening after he had flown in from Milan.

"Actually, Chloe… We have a bit of an issue with the bags," Kim said, pulling her to one side. "We've sold all twenty bags— well nineteen—excluding yours."

"Amazing! What's the problem?" Chloe said, thrilled that her very own design had sold-out—even if you did have to sell a kidney to be selected to purchase one in the first place. The point was, the lucky few *wanted* them.

"Well, Mrs Ruthenstock wants one, and we have none left."

"Mrs Ruthenstock!" Chloe shouted, simmering down after realising she was amongst guests. "Is she here? How?"

"She was in your client book and on our database, so I sent her an invitation… I thought you'd want to see her."

"Of course," Chloe said. A lightbulb had switched on in her head; she had given Kim the client book which had *every* good customer from Palazzo, and Mrs Ruthenstock was *the* best.

"She's upstairs… But what will we say?" Kim urged, not wanting to alienate such a good client when the store hadn't even opened to the public yet.

Chloe remembered how she used to smash her target at Palazzo, thanks to Mrs Ruthenstock. And how could she forget how she had inherited boxes of designer clothes thanks to her? That boost in her wardrobe not only kickstarted her content for StacksOfStyle, but it ultimately got her working with Gabriela Gracia in the end too—all of that seemed like a lifetime away now. "Come, take me to the packing room," she said, knowing exactly what to do.

It had also been a long time since she and Kim were stood out back together in the pack and wrap room at Palazzo; being surrounded by stacks of black boutique bags and reams of tissue paper in a confined space had brought back all kinds of memories. Chloe started to empty the contents of her handbag and grabbed a small Maison Marais bag off the shelf—dumping her belongings into it.

"Wait—hold up! You're not giving her your own personal bag, are you?"

"Erm, gentle reminder… My boyfriend is Gianni Palazzo, and one of his best friends is Jean-Paul. Trust me, Mrs Ruthenstock will be your best customer if you look after her… Likewise, if you piss her off, you'll never see her again! Pass me a black box and a dust-bag."

"But don't you want to keep it in your archive?" Kim said, stunned that Chloe was willing to give her exclusive bag away. It wasn't every day a girl who started on the shop floor got to design an exclusive bag with Maison Marais.

"After this evening, I won't be seen dead with this bag again… No doubt Jean-Paul will send me the latest bag next season any-way," Chloe said, taking the box off Kim so she could line the inside with black tissue paper.

Argument settled, Kim found the right sized dust-bag and placed the handbag carefully inside it while Chloe made sure the tissue paper was perfectly measured to the width of the box. Laying the bag down inside it, as carefully as a newborn, Kim helped her pack the box into a boutique bag before sealing it up with black stickers.

Mission complete, they headed back up to the women's floor—Regina had spotted them scurrying around together like they were up to no good. She kept an eye on them as Kim led the way over to the sofa area by the fitting rooms. After browsing the collection on the rails, Mrs Ruthenstock had taken up residence on a modern black leather sofa, sipping champagne. Seeing her sitting there, flicking through the look-book, more memories came flooding back to Chloe. It was like she had never left the shop floor, and in some ways, she missed those days. "Hello, Mrs Ruthenstock?" Chloe said, curling her name higher at the end—as if she didn't believe it was actually her.

"Chloe! How lovely to see you," Mrs Ruthenstock said, getting up to kiss her. "I thought I'd never see you again after you left Palazzo... I went in one day and some stupid girl said both you *and* Dom had left! That store has gone downhill since you left."

Chloe dipped her head, blushing at the suggestion that Palazzo had suffered without her—it was quite the compliment. She was also spoilt for choice when it came down to trying to figure out who this 'stupid girl' was. "I know... I apologise for leaving like that, but things just happened," she politely skirted; this was not the time or person to have a blow-by-blow bitch-fest with about what went on behind the scenes at Palazzo. That was more Karen's 'thing,' than it was Mrs Ruthenstock's.

"Well, it certainly has... Kim tells me you have your own business now, and that you designed the event bag for this evening?"

"Yes, a lot has happened in a year... And speaking of the bag, we have a little gift from the both of us—it's the very first bag of the entire edition!" Chloe proudly presented, as Kim placed the bag down next to Mrs Ruthenstock on the sofa.

"Really? Oh my—I don't know what to say!"

"The pleasure is ours, Mrs Ruthenstock. You were my number one client at Palazzo, so it's only fitting you have the number one bag... And here's my card. This is my website—it's not all designer brands, but there may be a few things in the future that may catch your eye. In fact, Dom's moved back to London now and is working with Pandora Simmons on her label, which we exclusively stock for the U.S market—you should check it out."

"So, this is where you've been hiding!" Gianni said, creeping up behind Chloe, taking her hand and kissing the back of it.

"Gianni, I have someone very special for you to meet..."

Mrs Ruthenstock's face dropped, she was just as shocked as Chloe was to discover Gianni Palazzo—the most famous designer in the world—was clearly very familiar with her. Chloe introduced her to the man behind her favourite brand and even posed for a photograph (even the 'older generation' loved a celebrity snap, it seemed). Much to Chloe's satisfaction, Mrs Ruthenstock obliged Gianni in listing all the ways in which Palazzo, Fifth Avenue, had gone 'downhill.'

"Well, It's been wonderful to meet you Mrs Ruthenstock, but we have dinner plans," Gianni said. This was the first Chloe had heard of it, but she was happy to leave the party. "Thank you for all the constructive feedback about our Fifth Avenue store—I'm sure I'll be paying a visit while I am here."

"Keep in touch… Let's do lunch!" Chloe said, touching Mrs Ruthenstock's arm lightly before linking arms with Gianni to be escorted away. "Are we really leaving now, or were you just tired of hearing some home truths?"

"I'm not that much of a vain bastard, am I? Actually, don't answer that! The longer we stay here, the more Jean-Paul will get wasted… I think it's best we head off to dinner now, and *you* haven't had a proper chance to speak to Don yet—you should sit next to him at dinner."

Gianni was right to call time on the party—Jean-Paul was becoming very flirty with the waiters. Plus, they had done what they came to do—the store opening had been a success. Although she was exhausted after a long day, Chloe was indeed hungry. But what she was really looking forward to, was kicking off her shoes back at Gianni's apartment and not have to entertain anyone, except him, of course.

"Okay, you guys ready?" Gianni said, returning to Jean-Paul and the others. "Don, need a ride?"

"I see you've been shopping too!" Jean-Paul merrily pointed to her replacement 'handbag' dangling from her wrist.

Chloe just smiled and shrugged; she didn't have the heart or the energy to explain to him where her handbag had gone. Plus, she had to save what little enthusiasm she had left to impress Don Carlo, but she still preferred neither option. "I'll just go and find Carmen—she'll need a ride too… See you downstairs," she said, escaping once more. She couldn't quite pin-point why, but something about him just seemed, off. The fact that she had to now endure dinner, sat next to him, was another reason to want to go straight home.

Downstairs, Carmen was propped up against the bar, enjoying the free booze with Gray and Zoe, but now was the time for her to act as the president of StacksOfStyle—and sober up. "Chloe! I was just saying that we *have* to plan your thirtieth birthday!" she said, sipping on her bottomless champagne glass. Her birthday was the last thing that was on her mind right now, even the thought of having to plan something for it was a drain. Right now, she needed to focus on getting through this evening.

"To be honest, I think Gianni and I will just have a quiet dinner or somethin. And talking of dinner, we're about to head off," Chloe said, pulling Carmen to one side. "Listen, I need you to sit next to Don Carlo at dinner—make sure you have your wits about you… Gianni wants us to talk business with him—this is where you come in."

"Sure, what's the big problem?" Why she had gotten so serious all of a sudden?

"I don't know if it's because I'm tired or if I'm coming down with something, but I have a bad feeling… I can't explain it; I just need you to get me through this dinner—okay?"

"Sure thing—I'll see you there."

"No, now… You're catching a ride with us!" Chloe urged, taking her glass out of her hand and putting it down on the bar.

"Oh, okay—I wasn't going to finish that anyway," Carmen glared at Grey and Zoe with wide eyes. It was strange to see Chloe in such a panic.

Tonight was meant to be a fun evening that celebrated her collaboration with the Maison, as much as the store opening itself. Why was she being so uptight? But knowing Chloe, this was probably just one of her stress-attack episodes, where she started to lose grip and simply needed her wing-woman. With this realisation, Carmen said her goodbyes and followed Chloe out to the car. Having Carmen in the car on the way to dinner was a good plan—it was also a good thing she had had plenty to drink at the party. Her tongue was nicely loosened, dominating the conversation in the backseat. "So how long have you been working together?" Don said, sandwiched in the middle of them.

Gianni had insisted he sat up front with Tommy in the passenger seat as Don was skinnier, and he would fit more comfortably than he would. Although, Chloe knew this was just a ploy to get them acquainted before dinner.

"About two years now… I was working as a freelance stylist and Chloe used to help me with projects, but it was at the same time we met that Chloe started S.O.S."

"And now you're the president?" Don said, surprised that she had the credentials for such a position.

His inflexion made Chloe question her own situation. Most days, she felt like she had no business owning a company herself. "She's been with me since day one… She knows everything about StacksOfStyle—more than me I'd say," Chloe defended.

"Believe me, I knew very little when I started MiBellaModa… I was just a computer genius with an idea. Everyone said: 'Don, you know nothing about fashion—what makes you think you can be successful?' But I knew how to build the tech, and as they say—build it and they will come! Which is exactly what I did."

"And that's exactly what we're doing!" Carmen snapped, clutching her chest in faux-delight at having found common ground. "Consumers want to shop luxury fashion online—you've proved that yourself. But, they also want to digest fashion editorial and style advice online—all in one go… Which is what S.O.S does! We're an online magazine that you can shop from the palm of your hand! You don't even need a computer these days—just a phone and free WiFi. The future of online shopping is definitely mobile—on-the-go! Faster, with smaller, digestible articles… No one has time for reading lengthy articles anymore—which is why print is dying."

Don smiled and nodded, he was impressed with Carmen's babble—he was also an advocate of mobile technology. The tech-geek believed in its future so much, that he proved a point by only working on a mobile device or a tablet. With an innovative vision like that, he had assessed that this drunk woman *was* indeed president material. Even Chloe was impressed, but she was also still cringing at how Don had labelled himself a 'genius' to think about it any further.

"Now, now Carmen… Don't go giving all your ideas away'!" Gianni said, turning his head. "Save some for dinner at least!"

Don and Gianni both laughed; Chloe rolled her eyes. Was she really the only one that just wanted to go home to bed and cut the bullshit? But what Gianni had just said raised an alarm in her head, maybe Carmen *was* saying too much?

How much could they trust this Don Carlo, and why exactly did Gianni want them to butt heads together? Maybe she was just being paranoid, but all she could do was trust her gut instinct—and her gut said that he was a snake.

*

Only selected guests were invited to the small, private Maison Marais dinner. Thankfully, that did not include Regina, or Myra—Chloe had enough on her plate as it was. The only saviour was that she had made Carmen sit next to Don at the table, while she sat next to her—with Gianni on her other side. Jean-Paul sat opposite them with Marie and Juliette, with other guests dotted around the table in random places, which included the face of the label—Carly Wattmore.

Even though the restaurant was dimly lit, Carly's disdain for Chloe was still visible. Most likely reeling with jealousy that she had ended up with Gianni, and not her. The width of the table between them made it easy for her not to engage with Carly throughout the dinner—only too pleased that coffee was now being poured and that she would be soon back in the car, on their way home. She was also rather pleased with Carmen—she had done a stellar job with impressing Don.

And it seemed Gianni also got what he wanted out of the evening—to show off his girlfriend's successful online fashion business. Don wasn't the only one who could make online fashion work—it was a sort of threat in some ways… Not to get too demanding and just stick to the job at hand, because there was younger, fresher talent out there that could succeed him. "Well, I really must be making a move," he said, checking his watch—which Carmen noticed was a gold Patek Philippe, Nautilus.

"No, stay!" Gianni said, relaxing back in his chair, with one arm on the backrest of Chloe's. "We haven't had a sip of my favourite cognac yet."

"I'd love to, but I'm flying back to Milan in the morning... We'll be in touch I'm sure—and we should also stay in touch." He handed Carmen his business card. "I can help you secure more accounts... Any brand I have onsite can be yours too—just name it."

"See! Didn't I tell you he was a good contact?" Gianni whispered to Chloe.

She hated to admit it, but maybe she was just being paranoid after all. Maybe Don Carlo *was* a good contact to have? The sound of having any designer brand they wanted at their fingertips was exciting, and just what they needed. But it also didn't change the way she felt about him—she couldn't help it or figure out why. It was just how she felt about him; she was relieved to have survived the evening and had done what Gianni had asked of her. She politely stood up and shook Don's hand as he departed. His wimpish hold on her hand certified her right to be wary of him. A firm handshake was reassuring—his left a slimy feeling.

"So, Carmen... Where's the party at?" Jean-Paul mischievously grinned, sitting next to her in Don's space.

"You *are* the party J-P!" Carmen laughed, turning to include Chloe.

"Chloe, zut alors! Are you *actually* drinking coffee? Garçon!" he whistled, calling over the waiter. "We need cocktails, *not* coffee! Get her an espresso martini—does the same thing but with alcohol, my dear." And an espresso martini *did* do the trick—a kick of caffeine with a hit of alcohol was what she really needed. The trouble was, that one martini turned into another, and what had been a quiet dinner had now transformed into an after-party of some sorts in the bar.

"Hey, Gianni," Carmen said, grabbing his arm for attention. "You and I have to get together at some point and discuss this one's birthday—the big three-oh!"

"Of course we do," Gianni said, thankful that she had mentioned it because he would have never have known otherwise.

"I told you already, I don't want any party—will you stop?" Chloe chimed in after overhearing.

Carmen hadn't exactly managed to be discrete about it, after indulging in the cocktail list.

"Of course we have to celebrate, baby," Gianni said, pulling her in close for a kiss on the cheek.

"This one has been banging on about being a *nobody* before she hit her thirties, and now look at her! You have more to celebrate than just your age, and I'm older than you!" Carmen said, smacking her lips from the sugar-coated rim of her Pornstar.

"I agree," Gianni said, regarding Chloe and brushing hair behind her ear. "We have lots to celebrate… We'll have a party at our place!"

Chloe smacked his chest, forgetting how hard it actually was, but also revelled in the fact he had said: 'Our place.'

"Just a small party," Gianni compromised. "Just us, Veronica and some of your colleagues… Jean, will you come to Chloe's birthday party?"

"What's this? Another party?" he said, breaking away from Carly who was chewing his ear off about the first Maison Marais fragrance campaign that was she was to be the face of. "For Chloe, anything! When is it, my dear?"

"The twenty–eighth, of this month!" Carmen jumped in, not giving Chloe the chance to lie about it, as well as saving Gianni from answering (she knew he had zero idea).

"Ah, unfortunately I have to finish the next collection in Paris, but I'll be sure to send you something very special, my dear," Jean said, kissing Chloe's hand. "We can celebrate now, of course! Monsieur, one more round, sil vous plaît!"

Jean-Paul had not only commanded another round of cocktails but a burst of 'Happy Birthday' from the entire bar too, which made Chloe go the shade of the dress she had given Kim to wear this evening (luckily, she hadn't chosen it for herself). Now past Midnight, and satisfied that it was time to go home, Gianni and Chloe said goodnight to the others—leaving Carmen with Jean-Paul and the gang at the bar.

"I thought this moment would never come," Chloe said, clicking her seatbelt.

"That was fun, wasn't it? Jean-Paul is a character… I'm gonna have to keep an eye on that one," Gianni said, this time in the backseat with his hand resting on Chloe's knee.

"Tiring more like… But fun too, I guess." She smiled at him, not wanting to sound too ungrateful, before pecking his thick lips with hers.

The fresh, cool air that breezed through the gap in the lowered window—mixed with the alcohol in her system—made her feel even drunker than she had realised. 'Damn, those espresso martini's are lethal,' she thought to herself. They had been so deliciously drinkable that the actual alcohol content of martini and vodka was disguised by rich coffee—and that *was* lethal for a coffee addict (of which, she was). Back at The Grand Towers, Chloe wasted no time in kicking off her silver shoes with delight. They looked incredible but felt like torture after six hours. Gianni also untied his shoes and carried them upstairs to the bedroom, unbuttoning his shirt and belt buckle on the way. "What happened to your purse?" he said, watching her place the little black Maison Marais bag down on the chaise at the end of the bed.

"I gave it to Mrs Ruthenstock," Chloe said, slipping out of her dress.

"You gave it away, to that crazy old bat?"

"*That* crazy old bat is one of your biggest clients! She's probably single-handedly paying the bills on this apartment—that you've only just decided to live in… Just so you can stay in a hotel up the street, whenever you're in town," Chloe said, cutting a sultry eye as she walked over to the en-suite.

"I love it when you're drunk!" Gianni growled, pulling down his pants in one go.

Cock-eyed, stood in front of the bathroom mirror—trying to maintain her balance—the face that reflected back was more deranged than sultry temptress. Slutty heiress, more like… Either way, Gianni loved her playfulness and cheeky confidence, and he liked making her pay for it too—it turned him on.

"Would now be a good time to take you up on the offer you made earlier?" he said, nibbling at her neck as she attempted to take off her eye make-up.

"Well, that depends if you're going to do what I say and not go overboard with this birthday party thing," she warned, throwing the cotton pad into the sink—turning in his hold to face him.

"Why are you so against celebrating your birthday? Don't you want the whole champagne, star-studded, A-list party?"

"*Seriously?* I couldn't think of anything worse… If you got me about a year ago, I'd say yes," Chloe said, recalling her nights out with Dom—whom she hadn't thought of so much recently. That's what working hard did—it made you forget about your friends and social life. "What I'd really like, is a lovely, relaxing, quiet night—in bed!"

"Oh yeah?" Gianni said, scooping her up from behind her legs—forcing her to wrap her arms around his neck with a yelp. "Be careful what you wish for!"

He had intended it to be more of a romantic sweep, than the clumsy fireman's lift it had turned out to be, but it did the job—schlepping her back into the bedroom—flicking off the light switch on the way. Dumping her back down on the bed, he climbed on top of her, raising her hands above her head before kissing her long and hard. This was one wish he could easily grant.

30

Stirring awake, she couldn't figure out how she had got to bed—or if they had sex. Although, it was likely more than anything (they were both naked, and the bedsheets felt crumpled and clammy against her back). One thing she *did* know was that she hadn't brushed her teeth—her breath smacked like some sort of liquorice-laced-coffee-based cough syrup. She didn't have to look in the mirror to know that her stale, metallic saliva had turned her tongue into a blackened graveyard.

The blackout curtains had made the bedroom a perfect sheet of darkness, but Chloe could still feel the room spin— as though the bed was stationary, but the walls around it spun in a tumbling rotunda. If this was a theme park ride, she would definitely want to get off. 'Damn those cocktails,' she cursed, rubbing her temples. The caffeine in her system was having another surge and had woken her up.

Sitting up, she gasped in urgent need for water, but not having the energy to make it downstairs to the kitchen (even though the idea of lashings of cold water from the fridge dispenser was enticing), she dragged her dehydrated carcass to the en-suite. Trying not to stumble or wake Gianni, Chloe swiped the light switch and filled the glass next to the sink with lukewarm water.

Downing it immediately, she drafted another—this time it was cooler. She downed that one too, filling it once more afterwards. Grabbing her white terry-cloth robe off the back of the bathroom door for comfort, she wrapped the belt around her waist and made her way back to bed—all without making Gianni stir. Not even the clink of her glass hitting the bedside table as she put it down had roused him—he was a knock-out. Laying back down, she shut her eyes (the room was less 'spinny' now she had hydrated herself), but there was no way she was going to go back to sleep. Not with this much alcohol and caffeine in her system! Espresso martini's had not only perked her up at the party, but they had also successfully fucked up her sleep.

She checked her phone which was now fully charged next to the bed and saw it was only four a.m. Instead of forcing her eyes shut, she stared into the void, taking deep breaths as she recalled how she had got into this state in the first place. It was, of course, Jean-Paul's fault. It was always Jean-Paul's fault—he had filled the space of 'trouble-maker' that Dom had left behind. But there was something else preventing her from falling back to sleep. There it was again, the tense feeling in her gut… Like something was wrong, or something very bad was about to happen—a premonition? Or was she just about to chuck up? Laying there, staring into the black abyss—that was the ceiling—she tried to decipher this feeling.

Yes, she was stressed at work—but that was nothing unusual… And yes, she was tired from juggling this new life with Gianni—but this was something far more strange than a simple case of relationship anxiety (she knew what the felt like). But then, as if someone had tipped a bucket of ice-cold water over her in bed, she bolted upright. 'Oh, God' she thought, bringing her hands up to her mouth in a sudden wave of realisation.

"What is it?" Gianni moaned. She had finally jerked him awake. "Are you okay?"

"I'm fine… I just couldn't sleep… But now, I know!"

"Know what?" Gianni mumbled into his pillow.

"Where I remember Don Carlo from…"

"Yeah… Like, he is a big fashion mogul," Gianni said, rolling over to face her—wondering why she was choosing the break of dawn to only just figure out his importance.

"No, I don't mean it like that…"

"Chloe, it's the middle of the night…"

"I've seen him before," she said, ignoring him. "Yes, it *was* him! That explains Veronica and all…"

"What are you on about?' Gianni said, propping himself up on his elbows to regard her. "Are you sleep talking?"

"Don Carlo! Don't you get it? I've seen him before... Just last week he visited the office... Veronica was showing him around—giving him a tour of the office."

"*What?* No... I'm sure you're mistaking him for someone else." Gianni shook his head, settling back down into his pillow—this was insane.

"I'm telling you... It was him! I know what I saw—I'm not crazy.... She cancelled a meeting and missed an important trade meeting—finally resurfacing out of the blue... With *this* guy."

"*Really?* Ask yourself this... What would Don Carlo be doing walking around your office with Veronica for Christ's sake! And she's barking up the wrong tree—he's married with a young daughter!" Gianni scolded, the very idea was completely farfetched and this entire conversation was simply disturbing his slumber.

"I have no idea," she said, sinking back down to rest her head on her pillow. The softness felt beautifully inviting as if she would now finally fall asleep—having solved the mystery on her mind. "You're right... What would Don Carlo want with DivaFeet?" she muttered, rolling over—closing her eyes.

But her words had more power to them than she could ever know, and for Gianni, the penny had finally dropped. Chloe really was smarter, intuitive even, than he gave her credit for. Now, it was he who was wide-eyed awake and unable to sleep. Because he knew *exactly* why Don Carlo would want DivaFeet.

*

The alarm clock didn't sound, nor was it set in the first place, but Chloe didn't need one—she had Gianni making enough noise to rouse her. "Uh... What time is it?" she managed, without opening an eyelid. She feared that the room would still be spinning, and it was far too early to get up—no matter what the time was.

"It's seven–thirty," Gianni said, lacing up his shoes on the chaise at the end of the bed. "What time do you have to get up?"

"Not yet, put it that way."

Slowly, she began to open one eye, then the other one—dabbing the gooey mixture of sleep and make-up residue from the corners of her eyes with a little finger. She sat up. By some sort of miracle, her head wasn't pounding as expected, but the taste in her mouth was something else. If it didn't motivate her to get her up and brush her teeth, then nothing would. "I think we agreed we would come into the office at ten—that's our usual protocol," she yawned.

From the comfort of the bed, Chloe watched Gianni check his appearance in the bathroom mirror. 'How does he manage to look so good, even after a night out?' she wondered. She scanned his clean-cut outfit as he slipped on the matching jacket to the pants he was wearing, over a white polo shirt that showed off his biceps. If her breath wasn't absolutely reeking, she would have dragged him back to bed. Then again, she didn't have the stomach or the energy for that.

"More to the point… Why are *you* up?" she said, wondering why a man with a home office and a global workforce had to be dressed and out so early.

"I have a breakfast meeting in town," he said sharply.

Chloe felt his crankiness, waking him up in the middle of the night to share her discovery hadn't been the best idea. After spritzing cologne, he made his way over to her to soften his delivery with a kiss, but she bowed her head so he could plant his lips on her forehead instead of on her dry, stale mouth.

"I'll see you later tonight—don't sleep in!"

"I won't," she said, once he was far away enough.

But there was no chance of that, her breath was so foul, she simply had to floss and brush her teeth as a matter of urgency. Afterwards, she made her way downstairs to brew some green tea (the thought of going anywhere near coffee made her want to heave). Heading back upstairs with her mug of tea, and ignoring the temptation to crawl back into bed, she went into the bathroom and turned on the shower. Placing her mug down on the vanity, by the 'his and hers' sinks, she stared into the mirror—listening to the water running in the background—waiting for it to get hot while she sipped tea and felt sorry for herself. But as if this morning couldn't get any worse, she realised that Gianni's early morning meeting meant that Tommy would have driven him to it—she would have to hail a taxi to the office. On the other hand, she must be doing something right, when not having a chauffeur was the worst of her problems.

"Hey… You cheated!" Carmen said, walking into the office fifteen minutes after ten to find Chloe sat at her desk tapping away at the keyboard. The fact she was wearing her spectacles signalled she was struggling already (she never wore her reading glasses). "I thought we said *after* ten?"

"Blame Gianni… He got up early for a meeting and woke me up in the process. I haven't been here long."

"Looks like Veronica is having a lie-in too," Carmen said, setting her handbag down on the stack of art and design books, on the coffee table next to her desk. "I just popped by to drop off the first draft of our year ahead budget… And she's not here yet."

"Hmmm…. Either that or she's having another secret meeting," Chloe huffed.

"What's that supposed to mean?" Carmen said, hearing bitchiness rather than jovial sarcasm.

Chloe perked up, she was dying to tell her. "Last night, I finally remembered where we've seen Don Carlo before…"

Carmen looked up at her. 'Not this again,' she thought to herself but intrigued to hear what crazy theory Chloe had conjured up—even if it just made good gossip before she had to actually crack on with work. "Oh, really? Where from?"

"Right here in this very office," Chloe said, swivelling her chair to face Carmen.

"Wait… I'm still drunk—start again."

"Veronica's been having a lot of time out of the office recently—she's missed two big meetings with us—and when she eventually reappeared, she had a mysterious man on her arm… That *man* was Don Carlo!"

"Hold up… So, you're saying that Veronica was showing *Don* around the office the other day?"

"Not *you* as well… When I told Gianni, he thought I had lost it too, but I know that scrawny face and those piggy little eyes… I looked him right in the face! It's him, I knew it was him the moment we met at the party… Also, Veronica was acting rather shifty last night, didn't you notice?"

"So, what if it *was* him, *Nancy Drew?*" Carmen laughed, getting up to head back out for coffee—as well as away from this mind-fuck of a theory. "Why would it be any *our* business anyway?"

"I'm not sure," Chloe said, wondering why this wasn't reso-nating with anyone else on a more worrying scale. "I just have a *feeling*… I can't explain it."

"Maybe Veronica has been tapping him up for us to access more brands? He's been doing this far longer than we have, and I for one think he can help us… Think about it, name any designer: Gucci, Prada, Saint Laurent, McQueen! We need those brands onboard and if anyone can help, it's him."

"Okay, so all of this is just some coincidence?"

"Yeah… And a *fucking* good one if you ask me! Veronica's just as clever in business as Don Carlo is… She knows he works with Gianni on the Palazzo Group websites, and Don owns the biggest multi-brand online designer website—of which we are trying to be a competitor.

"Maybe she was getting a foot in the door before we met him last night? She knew he was going to be there last night, Gianni told us so…. If you're still paranoid, why don't you go ask her!" Carmen said, walking out to get that much-needed cup of coffee.

"Well, I would—but she's not here… Remember?" Chloe quipped with a sarcastic smirk.

**

"Well, this is a surprise," Veronica said, sitting down at the table complete with folded napkins, silver cutlery and shining cut crystal glasses. "When I got your email at six this morning, I wondered what on Earth this was all about? And then I thought, why not—even if it is just for a free brunch at The Four Seasons."

520

"Thank you for coming at such short notice," Gianni said, getting up to greet her, waiting for her to sit back down.

Veronica ordered from the waiter who was pouring water for them. "Can I get a cappuccino?"

"Make that two," Gianni said, waiting for him to leave before he began. "I know it's a rather impromptu request to meet… But something Chloe said last night got me thinking, and I thought it was best that I to talk to you about it."

Taken by surprise, Veronica sat up. "Oh, really? And what would that be?"

"This is gonna sound crazy, but just hear me out… Chloe said she had seen Don Carlo around the office, with you—is that true?"

"That girl really doesn't miss a trick, does she? You know, you should remember that if you ever think of pulling a fast one on that girl—she will sniff you out before she's even found the scent trail!"

"So it *is* true?" Gianni said, leaning in, placing his chin on the knuckles of his clasped hands.

"Look, I was just as surprised as you are now to hear from him," Veronica said, taking a sip of water. Her mouth was already awkwardly drying up. She felt as though she was being questioned by the police.

"Wait, *he* contacted *you*?" His face was now in the palm of his hands.

"Nothing has been agreed just yet—"

"*Agreed?*" Gianni blurted out, his tanned face now reddened with anger and disbelief.

"Hang on… Let me explain," Veronica said, pausing to smile at the returning waiter with their cappuccino's.

"Can I get you anything else, M'am—Sir?"

"I think we are good for now," Gianni said, nodding for him to leave, pronto. "You were saying…"

"Okay, listen to me now," she took a sip of coffee first, slurping through the foam. "Things have changed a lot recently… This thing with Chloe's business has escalated very quickly and she really *has* something special here—*you* know that!

"What she needs is to expand and capitalise on the success, and I don't think I can help her more than what I have already… I have limited funds to invest further—especially now that I have *two* new businesses—what with P.S.L too… And on top of all that, I don't have the energy to give both Pandora and Chloe the real guidance they both need and deserve—"

"Sure, I can understand that, but what is Don offering?" Gianni stressed, eager to find out the details.

"He's offering me a life-line—a get out of jail card… He wants to buy DivaFeet as an entity, including StacksOfStyle and Pandora Simmons. I for one, think it's a perfect match—think about it…

"He has access to all of the brands the girls need and he knows about e-commerce. And I can be assured that my business, the business that made all of this possible, will continue with its legacy in the process… As a businessman yourself, you know that's quite important to me."

"So, what you're saying is that you're selling *everything* to him?"

"Yes, and for a great amount of money too… My investors agree we have reached the best possible position for a buyer, and the price is right."

"How much?" Gianni said quietly, leaning in closer.

"Well, we haven't disclosed the deal just yet," Veronica stalled.

"How much!" Gianni stressed, looking at her with his piercing blue eyes. Void of any charm or seduction, now serious.

"A hundred–million—"

"*ONE–HUNDRED–MILLION DOLLARS?*" Gianni repeated out loud, wide-eyed. Sweeping back the hair off his forehead, he could feel beads of sweat forming.

"I know this may come as a shock to you *Mr Palazzo*, but DivaFeet turns over fifty–million a year alone… You think designer gear is only where the money's at? Think again!

"And yes, I'm rather surprised too—especially because Chloe and Pandora's businesses are so young—but they have potential. And that is what he sees in them, and that is why I don't think any of this couldn't have gone any better."

Gianni downed his coffee and a glass of water as he listened, but now it was his turn to do the talking. "Fair enough, I can understand your decision—and listening to what you're saying, I think it's within your best interests to sell. But there are some things you should know about Don Carlo first."

Now it was Veronica who was sweating, what did Gianni know that she didn't?

"As you know, Don looks after the online fulfilment for both Palazzo and Maison Marais. However, it was me that told him about StacksOfStyle; I told him how Chloe was on to something… At the time he couldn't care less—which is why this is alarming to me now. Don wants to merge MiBellaModa and the Palazzo Group into one—owning a large percentage of the online luxury space. While that does sound appealing, I turned it down because I'm focusing on re-positioning Palazzo and Maison Marais—that's why I've delegated the online side of things to him…. But as you said yourself, Don is a very clever man and he gets what he wants. Buying your business is just a way for him to get to me; he knew I wanted to invest in StacksOfStyle at some point."

"Well, when I suggested we should 'work together,' I simply meant a collaboration of some sort—or maybe talk you into allowing Palazzo to be stocked on Stacks even… I had no idea—"

"And that's my point, he's very cunning; he doesn't care how, or who he hurts... By owning Stacks, he knows that I'll want to protect Chloe from any damage—or possibly being forced to exit—getting what he really wants in the process: one of the biggest mergers in fashion!"

Veronica sat back with a deep sigh, she felt terrible—foolish even—but she wasn't to know Gianni was being played. And even so, why would she care? She was just about to cash out her entire business with a huge percentage on a deal worth one–hundred–million dollars.

But she *did* care about Chloe and Carmen, and she cared about Chloe's relationship with Gianni—she had even pushed her to him. And here he was, trying to protect her. It was more than what she was doing; she was about to sell out on her.

"Even so, Gianni… The deal is as good as done with my board. And if what you're saying is true, aren't you just falling into Don's trap? The only way my board will reconsider is if we get a higher offer—but then that could totally backfire and end up in a bidding war… Which would be great for me—but not for you," Veronica smiled, bringing her warm personality back. "I think you're talking to the wrong person… I think you need to talk to Chloe."

"Well, when were *you* planning on telling her about this?"

"When the deal was a sure thing and things were ready to be signed off… If you won't speak to her, then you definitely need to speak to Don—before the legal pack is completed and we come to the final agreement."

Veronica was right, Gianni needed to speak to him immediately if he was going to try and stall the discussions—or stop them altogether. That meant urgently flying back to Milan.

"Okay, send me over everything… The figures, the proposal—absolutely everything," Gianni said, signalling to the waiter for the bill.

"How can I do that? Everything is tracked by email—if this gets out that we've even had this discussion… It's insider trading, Gianni!"

"Just get back to the office, print copies of everything and courier it to me by three… Not a word of this to Chloe! I'll tell I have to go to Milan to work on the collection, but not a word about this conversation to her—or Carmen!"

***

Back in the StacksOfStyle office, it was business as usual. Carmen was grilling Morgana once more for marketing ideas to squeeze into their budget forecast (since she still had time to refine it), while Chloe went over the order for the 'Raven X P.S.L' capsule with Bill—ignoring her ringing phone on the tabletop, until it was impossible to ignore.

"I'm sorry, Bill… I have to take this call—it's Gianni. Sounds like you have everything under control anyway," she said, getting up to exit the meeting room while she saved the call. "Hey, you… What's up?"

"All good, how's your head?" Gianni said, now sat in the backseat of the Mercedes. What she didn't know was that he was actually outside, having just dropped Veronica off so she could get him the necessary paperwork.

"Not bad, all things considered… Although, I'm still unable to drink coffee," Chloe said, drafting water out of the cooler with her phone nestled between her ear and her shoulder.

"Uh, yeah… I can imagine. Listen, something's come up last minute with the collection. I have to fly back to Milan; the design team need me there."

"Oh, I see… Of course, then you must go," Chloe said, making her way back to her desk. "How long do you think you'll be gone for?"

"I'm not sure, a week? Maybe two—max! I'll be back for your birthday—I promise."

"Oh, don't worry about that… You know I'm not fussed with celebrating anyway." Finally sitting back down at her desk, Chloe realised this was the first time Gianni was leaving New York since he had come back to be with her.

"The good news is that you and Carmen will have Tommy all to yourselves to drive about town… Do something fun while I'm gone, have a few nights out, get Carmen to stay over—make use of that Soho House membership I got you!"

'Yeah, right!' Chloe thought. This was the perfect opportunity to sleep, sleep, and sleep some more. That alone was incentive enough not to miss him too much while he was gone. "Don't worry about me," she reassured him, watching Carmen walk through the office—bumping into Veronica, who had only just made it to work.

"Veronica! This is a late start, even for you!" Carmen said, nodding her head in approval at her big boss who had a night out and only just got to work.

"Rough start… I'm sure you know what I mean," Veronica said, carrying on towards her office.

"Actually, do you have five? Chloe and I have some questions, and I have the first draft of our budget as you—"

"It'll have to wait I'm afraid," Veronica snapped, surprising Carmen with her lack of interest. "Sorry—I'm behind on stuff and I've a lot to get done today."

"Sure, no worries... Let me know if there's anything I can do to help," Carmen said. It was the first time ever that she had seen her this stressed. Laying off, she made her way back to the S.O.S office. "I'd stay clear of Veronica if you I were you," she said upon entering. "Maybe *don't* ask her *that* question today."

"What question?" Chloe said, already forgetting this morning's conversation.

"You know... Your conspiracy theory?"

"Oh, right... *That!*" Chloe said, tapping on her phone before chucking it on the desk.

"She's super stressed about something, maybe your idea has merit after all... Everything okay, Chloe?" Carmen said, noticing she wasn't mentally in the room either.

"Huh? Yeah... Gianni just called to say he's flying back to Milan for work."

"Like, now," Carmen said, starting to freak out herself. "He said he would be in touch about your birthday celebrations, and now he's escaping to Milan on me?"

"The man has a travel case packed and waiting in the back of his car, twenty–four–seven... And a private jet! He's heading to the airport this afternoon. To be fair, he has been here for the longest time without travelling—considering he owns a company based in Italy and all that," Chloe said, reminding Carmen he had bigger priorities than her birthday.

"Well, he better be back in time for your birthday... That's all I'm saying!"

"He said he'd be back by then," Chloe said under her breath, gathering her things together. "Not that I'm at all bothered— lunch?"

"Ooh—yes! I'm starving... Maybe this is all just a big decoy," Carmen wondered, grabbing her purse.

"For what?" Chloe said, holding the glass door open, waiting for Carmen to finish glossing her lips and put on her jacket.

"Well, I had to remind him about your birthday… Maybe the reminder has prompted him to do something *special* for you."

"Or… Maybe he's just gotta fly back to Milan because he has a collection to design, edit, and style before Fashion Week… Oh, and run a global business at the same time," Chloe said, rolling her eyes as they finally left for lunch.

"How did things go with Bill? The studio has shot the 'Raven X P.S.L' samples already, oh and Morgana has a copy of our budget—I've asked her to scope in more events and advertising," Carmen listed, pulling out her phone as it bleeped and vibrated in her jacket pocket.

"I'm sure Morgana will do some 'blue-sky-thinking' with her team… You know how she *loves* to play the 'cheesy marketeer,'" Chloe laughed, as Carmen zoned out to read the texts she had just received.

Urgent business…
Flying back to Milan.

What U said about Chloe's
birthday… Can U sort it?

I'll be back in time.
Use the apartment, spend whatever
U need & bill it to my office…

Fly Dom, Pandora over.
I'll be back in time. G

"Are you *even* listening to me?" Chloe nudged with her elbow, calling the elevator by stabbing the button with her finger.

"Sorry, work stuff… I'll put it away now."

But walking into the elevator, Carmen couldn't help but think that maybe she was the one with the correct theory? What if Gianni was really going back to Milan to organise something romantic—something huge—for Chloe's birthday?

"Why are you looking at me like that?" Chloe said, wondering why Carmen was looking like she was about to scream.

"It's nothing," Carmen said, forcing herself to zip her mouth shut—but she just couldn't help herself. "Okay, hear me out—what if Gianni wants to propose… And he's just flying back to Milan to get you a big fat ring?"

"And get the approval of Graziana you mean? That's the only reason he would need to fly back to Milan… They do have rings here in New York too, you know?"

"But what if?" Carmen said, tugging on Chloe's arm—wishing she would just get excited for one minute.

"Okay… Now, who's the one with the wild conspiracy theory?" Chloe scoffed, holding the elevator doors open for Carmen to step out—desperate for a high-calorie lunch.

By now, Chloe was famished—almost shaking with hypoglycaemia—and all of Carmen's nonsense was making her head spin once more. But not as much as it would, if she knew the *real* reason why Gianni had to leave New York for Milan.

31

Reading through the paperwork on the plane back to Milan, Gianni discovered that Chloe had managed to keep hold of thirty–five percent shares—which he thought was rather generous of Veronica. However, Veronica did own the majority (which would be Don's, if the deal went through), and he was even more surprised to learn that Carmen also had her hand in the pot.

Don's proposal also provided compelling reading, stating that Chloe and Carmen would be locked into a five-year deal—ensuring that S.O.S would continue with both of them at the helm. If they disagreed, they could be forced to sell their shares, and if they didn't want to sell, then they would be forced to sign the contract with MiBellaModa. Don basically had them by the throat—and Gianni by the balls. He needed to think very carefully about how he was going to put a stop to all this and keep Chloe out of it as much as possible. Saving StacksOfStyle was the best birthday present he could ever give her. Since Graziana was the brains of the business (the one who dealt with contracts—*and* Don Carlo), Gianni had Joli deliver the documents to her assistant, the moment he was back in the city.

He allowed himself an early night and a late start in getting back to Palazzo's white-tiled Mecca the next day. He had a lot to catch up on, what with this year's Met Gala looming—centred around the Palazzo retrospective exhibition—and finalising the spring/summer show collection.

"Did you see the email from Anna about the gala?" Joli said, waking him from his mental list-making as he sat at his desk—twirling a gold pen between his fingers as he decided where to make a start. "She wants to know *who* will be wearing what exactly… The design team have sorted most of the looks already, but there's a few 'question-ables.'" The editor of American Vanguard had settled on an angle for the Palazzo gala. 'Retrospective' was *so* last summer. Instead, the theme was 'Palazzo: Past, Present, and Future.'

"Like, *who* and what?" he copied, downing his espresso, chucking the tiny cardboard cup into the wastebasket.

"Gabriela Gracia," Joli started, already with Anna's email at her fingertips.

"Hmmm, well she's already done the whole 'past' thing…. Present—but make it custom, of course." Simply meaning, make an entirely new dress—not in the current collection at all—but a nod to the present-day style.

"Okay, next…. Naomi?"

"Oh, definitely past! Icon for an icon."

"And, Carly Wattmore?"

"Oh, *nooo!* She's the face of Maison Marais now—tell Anna she's off the list."

"Sure," Joli winced, taking note of Gianni's savage decision. It wasn't long ago she was down-playing media speculation that they were seeing each other—now he had dropped her entirely. "Okay, last one…"

"Oh, really? I was enjoying this game," Gianni said, getting up to make his way over to the bustling atelier. "Let me guess? Graziana? No—I'm sure she was the first one to pick… I bet she's even designed it herself!"

"Chloe," she said flatly, following him out of the office—with little time for games. Her boss was back for the first time in months and she had a lot to get done and very little time to do it.

"Hmmm…. Let's give her, future," Gianni said. Chloe didn't need a vintage look, or a present one—she had done that at the spring/summer show. What she needed was the future—a new future—and a hopeful one at that. "Can I see some designs for the gala?" he called out as they entered the atelier.

Amazed to see him back in the design studio, two of his senior designers quickly got their sketches ready to show on their tab- lets, while a junior gathered an arm full of fabric samples. Gianni perused the designs, not particularly impressed by any of them—moving onto the fabric samples that were laid out. "I like the look of this," he said, taking hold of a wet-look beige PVC rectangle that was embossed with the 'P,' logo all over it. He tapped his index finger against his lips, browsing the digital sketches once more. One of the designs was a halter-neck jumpsuit with a large gold 'P,' bucked belt at the waist—trim and svelte—matching the purpose of the PVC material. "Okay, let's work on this design—but it needs to be completely embellished with clear stones and crystals... Almost as if water is dripping off this fabric."

The two designers looked at each other as if to say: *'Really? Entirely stoned and embellished—in under two months?'*

"With a marabou feather stole... Make sure the shoes are nude and crystallised to match," he casually added, like it was nothing. "Good work! That's Chloe's look out of the way. Joli—share the themes for Gabi and Naomi as we discussed... I'll leave you guys to sort all that out with Anna in copy. Okay, I'm gonna need to see a quick walk-through of the collection, in say... Fifteen?" he said with a clap of his hands, effecting fabrics to be swooshed off tables, toiles to be peeled off mannequins, and roller-rails to scuttle around him in readiness.

"*Giiiannni!* You're here!" a voice crooned. A familiar voice not only to him but to the entire atelier, who was not fazed by her presence these days. Graziana was becoming more of a prominent figure in the house since Gianni had left for New York.

"In the flesh," he said, lightly kissing his sister on both cheeks—mindful not to spoil her make-up.

Joli knew it was time to excuse herself, helping the rest of the team get the presentation together while giving them space to talk—she knew the paperwork he had her deliver late last night was important to him—and so did Marco. He refused to budge, standing just a few feet behind Graziana, like her shadow.

"So, did you take a look at what I sent over—what do you think?" he said, arms folded—ready for her honest verdict.

"I did... And I think it's a very good deal—they should accept."

Gianni rolled his eyes, he didn't expect her to have the same reaction as him—she wasn't exactly Chloe's biggest fan. "But you knew I had my eye on it first! Don't you think this is all just a bit… Calculating?"

"So what? He beat you to it… Life's a *bitch* Gianni!"

"Isn't that the truth!" he said, pressing his eyes with his thumb and forefinger, before straightening up to her. "Look, you know it's more than that… Chloe will never trust me again if I allow this to happen—she'll think I had something to do with it and I've been keeping this from her."

"But you did—you have, Gianni," Graziana laughed, it wasn't rocket science—it just part of her genius plan. A plan to get what she wanted: Chloe out of their lives once and for all, and of course, to negotiate the merger.

"Not intentionally! Jeez, Grazi… Look, have you spoken to legal about this? There must be another way…"

Graziana drew in a deep breath, flicking her head back to look up at her brother. She had always looked up to him, but here he was—asking for her help. "In fact, I have…. And there *is* another way—and you know what that involves."

He knew exactly what she was alluding to, but there was no way he would be blackmailed into signing a merger with MiBella-Moda. "Set up a meeting… I want to talk to him first—informally."

"These things are never informal, you know that," she warned, there was no point in fighting this—unless he was willing to drop it. He stared her down, fully serious. "Fine, I'll call his office… But I think we should speak to the board—I'll gather the troops. Come, Marco…"

Gianni took a deep breath, watching Graziana marched off, giving orders to Marco as he trailed behind her. Meanwhile, the design team had gathered the collection ready for his walk-through. Clashing citrus tones of lime, bright orange and acid yellow mixed with pastel lilac, powder pink and baby blue. Just a single glance at the collection-in-progress was very telling; it was clear to see who was really leading the label now—Graziana.

*

When the morning of the meeting finally arrived, the weather was suitably grey and wet. They had been advised, both by the legal team and the board. Much to Graziana's delight, they were rather impressed with Don Carlo's proposal—which prompted Gianni to wear a double-breasted grey suit with a white shirt and a red italic 'P,' patterned tie for the occasion.

Joli had been wary of his terse manner all week, and the design team hadn't escaped his wrath either. Frustrated with his sister's visible input on the collection, he had slashed many of the looks—demanding they re-designed a huge chunk of the show. He couldn't take it out on them, he had uprooted and left for New York—they naturally looked to her for leadership. But the cool, calm, and collected Gianni Palazzo was no more.

Apart from Graziana and Marco travelling in the same car—despite owning a fleet of fully furnished Palazzo cars—Joli also noted the power suit (usually reserved for important business meetings). Gone were his sneakers, casual shirts and jeans, with a casual blazer, simply thrown over. She didn't need to ask to know this visit was a serious affair.

She also knew that the highlighted papers Gianni was rifling through were about the acquisition of DivaFeet and—more importantly—StacksOfStyle. She had quickly fingered through them herself, before dropping them off at Graziana's house. Still, nothing had been mentioned to her about it all week. Joli knew her place: discretion was paramount. It wasn't to ask questions, simply just to provide solutions to those that proved troublesome. Marco's place, on the other hand, was to look good, do what he was told, and keep his eyes and ears open. "Is there anything I can take care of?" she offered, not wanting to disturb him at the same time.

"Just take minutes of the meeting," he said, not looking up from his papers. "I'm sure he's assistant will be there too, but I'll need you to type up the notes and email us the transcript this afternoon."

"Sure thing," Joli said, prepping a few pages in her notebook in advance, with ten-minute slots running down the margin—enough for a whole hour's meeting. She didn't say anything else for the rest of the journey, allowing him to prepare. Graziana, on the other hand, seemed rather cool and relaxed, perfecting her lipstick whenever the driver stopped in traffic—Marco loyally held up the mirror with the steadiest hand he could manage.

MiBellaModa's head office was situated just outside central Milan, via Morimondo—a twenty-minute drive from the Palazzo store on Montenapoleone. Their driver pulled into the gated entrance of the business park housing other offices and showrooms for luxury designers and sportswear labels alike, which finally prompted Graziana to put her compact away in her purse.

Stepping out of the car, collectively they walked towards the large white building—the Palazzo Mafia had arrived. An engraved silver plaque by the entrance gleaned bright with 'MiBellaModa S.P.A,' confirming they had arrived at the right place. Gianni held the door open for the others to walk inside, greeted by a reception area with quilted white leather sofas and a black lacquered slab for a front desk. The receptionist behind it knew exactly who Gianni and Graziana were, and quickly buzzed Don's assistant to let her know they were here. "Buongiorno," she said in her velvety accent, walking around the desk in a white shirt and black skirt combo, with red high-heels and matching lipstick to complete the dramatic (and rather dated) look.

'How very on-brand,' Joli thought, as they followed her through the main office to Don's boardroom.

Deeper inside, the office had been furnished rather like a Fellini film—but modern at the same time. White Wainscoted walls and metal pylon pillars dominated throughout, with dark brown wooden flooring and dramatic red velvet curtains, draped around meeting booths for privacy. The white walls and dark flooring carried on down the whole length of the building; banks of white desks with sections of round tables for teams to hold break-off meetings dotted around. But it was Don Carlo's office that took centre stage.

Placed at the very back, up a wide set of dark wood-stained stairs (that were used for seating office-wide presentations), the usual display of clear glass panel walls defended his day-to-day business. It spanned the entire width of the office floor, but unlike any other typical glass office, it was framed with red velvet curtains—complete with a proscenium arch style trim above—held back by gold tasselled ropes. It was *literally* a stage.

Joli thought it looked tacky—nothing compared to the chic setting of the Palazzo HQ—but Don Carlo considered himself to be quite the entertainer. He had rather foolishly self-titled himself as the showman of retail (or 'e-tail,' as he liked to call it)—a joke which was often referenced behind his back by peers in the industry. "Ciao, Ragazzi!" Don declared, emerging from the curtains with his arms out—as if this was his show.

"Good Morning, Don," Gianni said, slowly walking up the stairs—not wanting to seem out of breath already. "Thank you for fitting us in so last minute."

"My absolute pleasure… I had no idea you would be in Milan."

'Me neither,' Gianni thought.

At the top of the stairs, Gianni shook hands with him—a brief and awkward exchange. Graziana took her time, finally reaching the top to greet Don more amicably with two kisses. Stepping into his office, his assistant continued to unhook the gold ropes and draw the curtains—it was a case of what happened backstage, now stayed there.

"And how is Chloe?" Don said as they took their seats around the meeting room table.

Gianni couldn't help but succumb to the theatrics of it all, looking around at Don's decor choices. At the other end of the room was a simple white desk, with no computer or laptop, just a large Swiss ball for a chair—which was more suited to a yoga class than a chic office (but then again, a *chic* office this was not). Catching himself, he smiled and came back to the conversation.

"She's doing fine… Great, actually—you saw her just the other day at the event," he said, wary of saying anything else about her.

The last time he did that, Don stabbed him in the back and used the information for his personal gain.

"Excellent! Well, where to start? The Palazzo website is performing well, and the transition of the Maison Marais site to our systems went perfectly," Don said, pushing some figures across the table, handed from his assistant—who stared down at Joli, as if this was a 'best assistant' contest.

Joli ignored her and did exactly what she was told to do, jotting down short-hand notes for typing up later. Marco, on the other hand, didn't even bother to compete and just sat with one leg crossed over at the other, leaning back nonchalantly in his chair—scrolling through his phone.

"That's fantastic," Gianni muttered, wondering how he was going to begin the real reason for their visit. Of course, Don Carlo was no idiot—he knew exactly why they were here. And like Veronica had said, Gianni had played into his hands too easily— there was no point in holding back now. "Listen, I'm gonna just come out and say this straight up, businessman-to-businessman… Friend-to-friend."

"Of course, you know you can tell me anything, Gianni… Especially if it concerns our businesses," Don said, relaxing back into his chair to cross his legs, intertwining his fingers together.

"It's about Chloe, StacksOfStyle to be exact."

"Oh, *really?*" Don leered, peering over his black round-frame spectacles that sat on the end of his sharp nose.

"I know about your proposal to buy DivaFeet and all associated assets," Gianni said, coming out with it.

"I see," Don hissed, uncrossing his legs to lean in closer.

"You know this puts me in a very awkward position, not only because it means that you'll be acquiring my girlfriend's business, but you could potentially take her out of it too… You knew I had sights on her business and you went behind my back—"

"No, no… It wasn't like that at all. You, yourself suggested that I should take a look at her website—and I did. It just so happened that I liked what I saw… And as you know, I'm looking to expand M.B.M, and you rejected those plans. So I thought, why not invest in a start-up instead? And what better to invest, than in a recommendation of yours?" Don said quite cleverly, knowing full-well that he had Gianni exactly where he wanted him.

"I told you months back that StacksOfStyle could be very lucrative. You already know how valuable e-commerce is to the fashion industry—you *are* the industry leader, after all. But I need to protect her and her business, Don, not just for my personal interest. Look around, this is just one of many offices where you have people working for you—you don't even need a computer at your own desk! Why do you need to destroy a little start-up website, just to prove a point to me?" Gianni scoffed, extending his arm out to Don's baron desk.

"I understand where you are coming from, but I can assure you, it is not at all like how you say."

"Even so, you knew of my plans to invest in her and you crossed me," Gianni snapped, now starting to lose his cool.

"Gianni, this is strictly business… That's all. DivaFeet needs a buyer, and I'm willing to make an offer—which I assume you know about?"

"I can assure you we know very little about the discussions with yourself and DivaFeet," Graziana said, bringing the conversation back to a more professional tone; she had let Gianni rage on enough and she had an act to keep up. "However, we do know about the details of Ms Raven's assets, since Gianni is personally involved… And we know that together with her business partner, they own forty percent of the business—leaving MiBellaModa to take-over the remaining sixty–five."

"Yes, this is indeed the case," Don said, catching her eye.

Gianni took a deep breath and sat back in his chair. For Joli, this was quite the revelation—but nothing about this job fazed her now. She could write a book about the dramas she had survived during her tenure at Palazzo. "Look, Don, all I'm saying is, what would you want with DivaFeet? I mean, come on… It's just a fast-fashion business—"

"And a very successful one—did you know their turnover was $50,000,000 a year?"

"I can imagine," Gianni said, reaching for the water, wishing it was the brown stuff with a few chunks of ice. "But the thing is, I need that business—maybe not DivaFeet—but StacksOfStyle."

"And hear me on this once again, Gianni… You don't get to pick and choose what you want in business—you know that. When an opportunity presents itself, you either take it or you leave it… Now in terms of buying DivaFeet, Veronica was adamant that the sale includes all assets associated with the group—that includes all subsidiaries and properties. Since our merger plan didn't go through, I had been waiting for something else to come along—and *poof!*" Don sounded, clapping his hands together as if he were making magic. "Here it is!"

But what he had done *was*, in fact, a very clever trick. He had tricked Gianni right under his nose and not only that, but he had claimed possession of Chloe in a way that Gianni couldn't protect her from. This was no longer about money, it was about power.

"I know the merger *is* what all of this is really about… I said, not now—not no, indefinitely."

"What I'm hearing is that you didn't want to merge with MiBellaModa to create the most powerful group in our industry, but you are fully prepared to splurge a hundred–million dollars on—as you have just put it—a fast-fashion company? Not exactly fitting with the rest of your portfolio for one, and secondly, what do you know about e-commerce?

"Okay, let's say you did acquire DivaFeet and StacksOfStyle—both online businesses—how are *you* going to manage them? Because, the last time I checked, Gianni—I was taking care of the fulfilment for your very own brands! You have no warehouse space, no back-end infrastructure, no shipping or distribution networks to handle *two* established online businesses—because you handed all that over to me to focus on your retail stores, remember? They don't call me the 'geek-of-chic' for nothing," he laughed coldly.

And there it was, the hammer blow to Gianni's head—the guillotine blade to his neck—the grip around his balls had just got tighter. Don had hit him where it hurt the most, and there was no coming back from it. It was true, the day Gianni signed the agreement with Don Carlo, the Palazzo Group had no e-commerce systems left in-house—and there was no backing out of that deal now. With that in mind, there was no way that The Palazzo Group board would agree to solely invest in DivaFeet—Don knew that and so did Gianni. But Don did know that their board members *would* agree to merge The Palazzo Group with MiBellaModa—because that was a clever move. It was very much a PR stunt as it was as a profitable one.

Not only would they own their signature brands, but together they would control the websites of many other designer websites that M.B.M had in its portfolio—designer labels that didn't need to be owned by the newly formed group directly. And it would take decades for another fashion group to catch up with the technology and warehousing potential of M.B.M—not to mention the mammoth investment required to fund it.

Gianni sat back in his chair with his hands behind his head. Joli looked up at him, having scribbled everything down, as neatly as possible—understanding exactly what this spelt out for Chloe. It was very much the dagger to her heart, she had trusted Gianni and here he was talking about her like she was just another lucrative deal. Joli wondered if this was the moment Gianni would finally cave in? That's if he wanted to save StacksOfStyle from Don's corner-cutting, squeezing every profit out of it for himself, like a wet rag.

"You know what—you're right. I wish you all the best," Gianni said, standing up. It appeared that he didn't care enough to save StacksOfStyle after all.

Don snapped his head to Graziana—she was just as shocked. She had promised Gianni's approval on the merger, that he didn't need to worry about putting a hundred–million dollars where his mouth was for nothing—for they were about to share that burden together as a giant. But Gianni wasn't about to give up that easily, he knew Don wasn't the kind of man to squander millions, just to spite him. It was time he stopped playing into his hands; Don didn't really want DivaFeet or StacksOfStyle—he wanted The Palazzo Group.

"Look, Gianni... Sit down," Don stuttered, rubbing his forehead. "I can see you're in a bit of a predicament here, and as you said: we *are* friends—in and out of business... I have another suggestion: instead of merging our businesses together, why not create a new one? To test the waters, if you like?"

Gianni sat back down and looked at Joli, prompting her to also take all of this down. He wanted it on record, there was no way he was getting shafted again. "Go on," he said, Joli's pen now poised on paper.

"How about a joint venture? Proving to both our board members that merging *is* eventually the right thing to do... For example, we'll both put fifty percent into a new body—each of us owning a fair split... I'll let you mentor StackOfStyle, and I will take care of the rest."

Gianni heard him loud and clear; now he had Don where *he* wanted him—he was desperate not to throw a hundred–million dollars down the drain. By suggesting that they funded a new entity together, at least he would be splitting the cost—but what was the *real* price Gianni would have to pay?

"All I want in return is an agreement from you both... After five years, we will revisit the merger deal—unless you run the website down to the ground of course," Don joked. "But we both know that's not going to happen, so I'm safe there."

'Clever,' Gianni thought to himself, but at least it was a more affordable option. An expensive one albeit, but one that satisfied everyone involved—for the time being. It was a temporary solution, but Gianni was sure he could turn StacksOfStyle into a profitable brand that his board would want to keep—to compete with MiBellaModa. Once Gianni proved that the Palazzo family's prowess was far more fierce—and when Don Carlo had gotten tired and bored of it all—he would simply sell his half of StacksOfStyle back to him... Or even better, sell MiBellaModa entirely to The Palazzo Group. "And who would run this joint venture?" Gianni said, leaning on the table. Joli scribbled furiously while Graziana watched on in disbelief as the two men volleyed back and forth—a tennis match she was no longer the umpire of.

"Like I said, you will take care of StacksOfStyle and I will look after DivaFeet and Pandora Simmons… It would all still run from the same office as it does now—we'd have to find a new CEO of course, with Veronica gone. We'll simply just be the new guardians of the businesses… We will change what needs to be changed, but we will also support them—let the leaders own the day to day running. But once the five years are up, I want to be able to propose a full merger deal between all our assets into one."

Gianni sat back, taking a deep breath as he smoothed his hair back off his forehead. Would this all be worth it? All he knew was that he had to do it for Chloe's sake and for that reason, it *was*. He was used to women coming and going, but he knew Chloe was different—he wanted her to stay and that meant doing everything he could to fight for her. She wasn't like the others and despite Graziana's opinion, she *was* a match mentally—as well as physically. She was driven, driven to succeed and not leech of his fortune, and that was very attractive to him (and again, unlike the rest).

"Right then," Gianni said, standing up to button his blazer—prompting Joli to gather her things and do the same. "We better call Veronica and get her team over here to discuss our new offer… Of course, we also have to explain this new option to our board."

"Good," Don said, standing up, holding out his hand.

Gianni took it and shook firmly, but he may as well had his toes crossed at the same time because even after five years, he didn't see Palazzo merging with MiBellaModa. Palazzo was *the* only group in his vision, and Gianni wanted to build it up to be the leading financier of luxury fashion houses—he didn't need someone else to help him do that… But he needed StacksOfStyle—he needed Chloe. "So, what are we calling this 'new guardian' *thing?*" Gianni said, letting go of Don's slippery hand.

"Exactly that… The New Guardians!"

Gianni gave him a look from the side of his eyes, before flicking his head once in agreement. "Fine… We'll be in touch."

Joli gathered her things and got up to leave with him, as did Marco—only to pause at the top of the stairs for his boss who had stayed behind. With a serious stare—the skin on her neck taught and her jaw firm—she both hands planted on the table and leant over to Don. *"What do you think you're doing?"* she muttered, now that Gianni and Joli had disappeared through the red velvet curtains and had a chance to make a few steps ahead. "This wasn't what we agreed!"

"Yes, but this also isn't what *you* promised *me*... It's called improvisation," Don said, with his thin-lipped lizard-like excuse of a smile.

"Just remember, you wouldn't even have this chance if it wasn't for me," she leered, snatching her purse and sliding on her dark sunglasses with a flick of her blonde locks——emerging moments later from the red curtains, like a backstage groupie.

32

Carmen had been rather busy, not just with work meetings about new season stock about to hit the warehouse (and needed to be scheduled for shooting and uploading), she also had Chloe's birthday party arrangements to finalise. But she had it under control, and with the help of Samuel, Gianni's apartment was to be the scene of the crime.

Even Dom and Pandora's flights had been booked (and charged back to Gianni's office). Full catering and champagne cocktails had been selected, surprise birthday invites had been sent out to Grey, Zoe, Veronica and Karen, as well as a few other colleagues from the S.O.S team. Meanwhile, Chloe was none-the-wiser and Carmen was loving every minute of it.

"*Urgh!*" A low growl came from Chloe's desk, as her face sunk into her hands.

"What's up?" Carmen said, looking up from her screen—she had been browsing birthday cakes. Had someone let the cat out of the bag about the party?

"Joli just sent me over a sketch of the Met Gala look Gianni's designed for me."

"*Ooh!* Let's see…"

Chloe swivelled the computer around for Carmen to see the beige latex-like catsuit. "I'm waiting for your super-hero name suggestions already."

"Well, it *is* the Met Gala… You can't just turn up in a dress off the rack—and you are kinda turning up with the most important guest," Carmen said, scrunching her face.

"I guess… I just don't know if I can pull *that* off."

"Oh please! Bitch, you say this now, but you will be lapping up the attention when you're on the steps posing… More importantly, *what* am I wearing?"

"Not a clue, Joli hasn't sent me anything else… I'll ask."

"Has he mentioned when he'll be back at all?" Carmen said, fishing for details so she could pass all of this party planning back onto him.

"Just a text message here and there; I don't like to disturb him when he's working… To be honest, it's been quite nice being able to come to work, then go home and relax after."

Carmen had to admit, she did seem much more chilled recently. Her life was so high-octane since Gianni had returned as if setting up the website and running the business wasn't enough stress to handle—she had adopted his way of life and expectations. Which made her wonder if Gianni was to propose, would she be able to cope with the fame and attention it would bring?

So far the attention was manageable, just a few paparazzi at fashion shows and events. However, if they got married, she would be the media's prey—globally! Which gave Carmen another idea: if Gianni was going to propose, then the cake should double-up as an engagement *and* a birthday cake! "I gotta make a call real quick," Carmen buzzed, calling the bakery already.

But before she could head outside, Veronica lightly rapped her fingernails against their glass door. "Can I interrupt you ladies, for a moment?"

Chloe and Carmen both looked up in unison.

"Sure, how's everything going—you wanna go over the budget?" Carmen said, hanging up the call.

"Actually… I wanted to come and let you know that I've been called away for a business trip—it's nothing to worry about," she said, anticipating what was about to come by their faces.

"Oh, right," Carmen said, folding her arms—annoyed she wasn't getting the direction from her boss that she needed and expected. "So what about the budget? And what about our weekly trade meetings?"

"Look, I know I haven't been here for you girls these past few weeks, but you have everything under control… I mean, I have never had business grow and make this much money in such a short amount of time! I have every confidence in you. I'm going to be travelling from this evening, I may even pass through London and check in on Dominic and Pandora—but I'll be in touch and of course, you can email me if you need anything."

"Wait a minute, you may *pass* through London? Where exactly are you going?" Chloe said, standing up to fold her arms in confrontation—standing strong with Carmen.

"Just a meeting with the investors, they want to meet me for a summit in Paris… Before the end of the financial year," Veronica lied. "It happens every year, this year it turns out to be in Paris… So, you see, it would be silly not to check in on Pandora and Dom on the way back."

"And how long will you be gone for? At least let me give you my first draft of the budget," Carmen said, rifling through some papers on her desk—she had it printed out and ready go for days now.

"Sure, I'll take a look at it while I'm away and get back to you," Veronica said, taking the papers from her to placate her before turning to leave. It didn't matter how much Carmen had forecasted, Veronica might as well add a bunch of zero's on the end because, after this trip, none of this was going to be her decision.

"I told you something was going down, didn't I?" Chloe said, letting Veronica go with no further questioning. "I'm calling Dom… Maybe he knows something we don't—if not, then I'd better warn him she's coming."

Suddenly, Carmen's urgent phone call to the bakery wasn't a priority any more. Instead, she sank back down at her desk. 'Maybe she's right,' she thought. Things were far getting too strange these days for something *not* to be happening.

*

Another week had sped by for Carmen, thanks to the combination of work and finalising the finishing touches to Chloe's surprise birthday party. So far, everyone had managed to keep it a secret, but it was the secret that Veronica wasn't telling that was on her mind. And she too was keeping the fact that she was growing more suspicious about this whole thing from Chloe. The last thing she needed was for Chloe to get hysterical on her when they had very little information on what was really happening.

Dom had thrown cold water over the fact she had visited them in London—budget talk apparently. Which was funny, because Carmen was still waiting for Veronica to get back to her regarding their budget. But with both Dom and Pandora coming to New York, she decided she would pick their brains in person at Chloe's party. But with less than twenty–four hours to go (and Gianni still M.I.A), Carmen wasn't sure if he was even going to turn up.

"Morning!" Chloe chimed, walking to her desk as she bull-dozed such thoughts out of Carmen's head. "Any sign of Veronica?"

"Not yet… There's still time though," Carmen said, a bit too enthusiastically.

"For what?"

"Well, let's just see if she makes a miraculous appearance, shall we?" Carmen said, biting her tongue. She hadn't arranged this surprise birthday party for it to be revealed by her own admission. "Talking of miracles, any news from Gianni? It *is* your birthday tomorrow? The big *three-oh!*"

"Don't remind me," she puffed, swatting her hands in the air. "He called last night… He says he'll be back by tomorrow, but I'm not sure what time—or what he has planned. I hope he hasn't gone to any trouble… I can see why he loves that cinema room so much! I've pretty much finished Netflix now."

"And that is why me and you are at least going for a drink tomorrow—before you go back home to whatever he has up his sleeve," Carmen said, getting up to sit on Chloe's desk.

"Sure, a few drinks won't hurt I guess—and I doubt Gianni *will* be home anyway."

"Perfect!" Carmen smiled, having just arranged the perfect distraction to allow her surprise guests time to arrive at The Grand Towers. "Oh, I forgot… Tomorrow I'll be down at the warehouse in the morning—I'll be back in time for the afternoon though."

"Oh, I'll come with you… It's been a while since we went."

"Oh, no need… I'm leaving super early in the morning—and it's your birthday! I'll see you back here by lunchtime, we'll go somewhere nice—with wine!" Carmen said, quickly squashing any ideas Chloe had about tagging along.

But she didn't need to try too hard, the biggest distraction had just walked into the office.

"Ladies!" Veronica beamed, looking rather pleased with herself.

"Oh my God, Veronica!" Carmen yelped like she had just witnessed the second coming.

"How was Paris—how was London?" Chloe said, getting up from her desk, equally as surprised to see her.

"Both were fabulous, thank you… I know you must have a lot of questions, but I have back-to-back meetings all day. Let me get what I need to do out of the way and I'll fill you in on everything at the end of the week," she said, already heading out of the office to avoid dodging their questions.

"Oh… Hold up," Carmen said, chasing after her outside on the mezzanine. She wasn't going to let her slip away that easily. "What about the budget?"

"Oh, didn't I get back to you on that already?" Veronica grinned, scratching her head. "Everything's on hold for now… I'll explain at the end of the week… It makes sense to have a meeting with Dom and Pandora when they get here—I have an announcement to make."

"What kind of announcement—is everything okay?" Carmen said, turning back around, making sure Chloe was at her desk and out of earshot.

"Of course it is… Why wouldn't it be?" Veronica said, doing a good enough job to sound convincing. Carmen looked at her, she had nothing to say to that; she wasn't going to accuse her without any evidence. Plus, she didn't have a clue as to what this announcement could be, she'd just have to wait.

"Don't forget tomorrow is Chloe's birthday," Carmen said, letting it drop—for now. "Do you think you can pop some champagne and arrange a team breakfast in the morning? I told her I'll be at the warehouse, but I'll really be at Gianni's place setting up… Speaking of, I haven't heard from him at all—he better turn up!"

"Oh, he will!" Veronica said, almost too knowingly.

"Yeah, well he better—for his sake!" Carmen said, checking her phone yet again as she walked back into the S.O.S office.

"What did she say?" Chloe said, furiously tapping out an email.

"Oh, she's planned a champagne breakfast for you tomorrow… So you better turn up here nice and early!" Carmen said, getting her off her back about going to Mahwah once and for all.

She couldn't exactly tell her that the budget was now on hold and that Veronica wanted to have a meeting with everyone—that would both worry and ruin the surprise of their arrival. But what Veronica had revealed, was that Chloe's intuition was right— something was definitely happening behind the scenes. 'But wouldn't she have gone to Milan—not Paris—if he was involved?' she wondered, hoping that Gianni would make it back in time. If anyone could give her an insight into Don Carlo's moves, it was him.

The next morning, Chloe's birthday, it was sunny and bright— another reason to get up early. As well as the fact she had to be at work for this 'surprise' breakfast that Carmen had already warned her about, who had also gotten up early—to stalk the entrance of The Grand Towers from across the street. She waited outside with big black sunglasses on (a lame attempt of a disguise), waiting for Tommy to drive Chloe to work so she could get into the apartment to set up for this evening.

Within an hour of Chloe leaving for work, the kitchen had been taken over by the caterers while the living room was being transformed into a mini dance floor, complete with a mirror ball and disco lights. Then, there was the cake. Carmen's idea of having two cake toppers made now seemed a bit silly of her. One simply said: '*Happy Birthday!*' while the other read '*Congratulations!*'—just in case Gianni had returned with a ring in a box. But something was telling her that the usual birthday wish would suffice on this occasion.

"*Wow!* You really did go to town!" Gianni said, making a surprise entrance himself.

"*Gianni!*" Carmen screamed, both shocked and relieved to see him—causing the party planners to stop and look at the fashion genius in their presence. "I didn't think you were ever gonna get here!"

"I know, sorry for not being in touch more—had a hectic couple of weeks, to say the least… What's all this?" he said, noticing the two sugar-craft cake toppers on the kitchen island.

"Oh, the bakers sent the wrong topper, so I had to arrange the right one last minute!" Carmen lied. "Unless…"

"Unless what?" Gianni said, dodging the catering staff to get to his own fridge and pour some ice-cold water.

"You did get her a birthday present, right?"

"Of course… I had Joli pick out some things for me and send them here already," he said, rather pleased with himself.

"Some things eh? What kind of *things?* Any small box-shaped ones, for example?"

"You mean jewellery? Of course, only the best for Chloe… Joli found a beautiful 18 karat diamond watch—"

"*Never-mind!*" Carmen interrupted, chucking the 'Congratulations!' topper in the trash. "Look, things have been happening while you've been gone and I need answers."

"Oh yeah, what kind of things?" Gianni said, downing his water.

"Well, first of all, you rush back to Milan, then Veronica has a mysterious meeting in Paris with her investors— then she puts our budget on hold… Something's going down and I think Don Carlo has something to do with it—Chloe doesn't trust him and neither do I.

"She reckons she saw him in the office with Veronica and I have to admit, it's starting to add up a little… Veronica's holding a meeting with everyone tomorrow—she has an announcement— and if that involves us somehow, then you need to tell me right now!"

"And how would I know?" Gianni said, chugging water.

"Oh let's see... Well for one, you're business partners with Don—so you two talk, right? Secondly, I've realised how convenient this all is... I mean you leave for Milan, then a week later Veronica elopes to Paris—only to return with an announcement that requires everyone to be present for. Then—if that wasn't enough—you both suddenly show up, just in time for Chloe's birthday!" Carmen said, cocking her head and cutting an eye, reminding him she wasn't stupid.

"*Fuck!*" Gianni sighed, rubbing his face with his hands. "How much does she know?"

"So something *is* going on!" Carmen fumed, striking the marble island with her fist.

"Look, this came as a surprise to me as well, but you cannot say a word to Chloe—not until after tonight at least... Plus, I need to be the one to tell her, I need to explain."

"Tell her what? What's to explain?" Carmen shouted. "If it's something to do with our company then I have a right to know as well, I am a shareholder!"

"Come... Let's talk in private," Gianni said, pulling her away from the party planners to have a proper conversation, alone in his office. After all, he needed Carmen on his side if he was going to rescue StacksOfStyle, and her shares did play a part in making Chloe see sense.

**

Now she understood everything: why Chloe had been right to be suspicious of Don, why Gianni and Veronica had sudden business trips, and why she had stopped over at London to speak with Dom and Pandy. But she had promised to not breathe a single word of it to Chloe, which was going to be difficult because it was both exciting and important for her to know—before the bombshell landed on her lap.

It was such a delicate issue, Carmen didn't want Chloe to ever find out that she had known before her. It needed to be dealt with carefully; both Gianni and Carmen were set to lose her if she found out indirectly. Although she was mad at Gianni for putting her in this position, she trusted he had her best interests at heart. On top of that, she also had to lie about working at the warehouse and being offline—having ignored Chloe's messages and emails all morning.

Then she would have to endure lunch and drinks after work without saying a word when she really just wanted to sit her down and explain everything. She was her friend, her business partner and mentor. Not telling her felt like a betrayal, but she understood Gianni's need to be the one to do so. After all, he had put his neck on the line and his cash on the table for them.

"How were Maisey and Mahwah?" Chloe said, welcoming Carmen back into the office.

"Oh, fine… Same as usual," Carmen said, totally ignoring the huge 'three–zero' shaped silver foil balloons floating behind Chloe—and the fact it was her birthday, after what she had learned this morning. "Oh, shoot—*Happy Birthday!* I'm such a crap friend."

"No, you're not… I know you're up to something," Chloe said with a suspicious eye, leaning forward on her elbows—her chin resting on the backs of her hands.

"What did we get you?" Carmen said, ignoring her suspicion, shuffling artefacts around on her desk in a bid to appear busy and unfazed.

"*Oh, come on!* I'm not that dumb…"

"I'm sorry, what?"

"I spoke to Maisey… You could have at least told her to cover for you," Chloe laughed, shaking her head at her amateur error.

"Oh right—silly me," Carmen huffed, pleased that she hadn't intuitively detected what was really going on. "How about an early lunch? I could *really* do with a drink."

"Okay… But only if you tell me what stupid birthday celebration you have up your sleeve," Chloe said, excessively slinging her new Gucci bag on her shoulder, answering Carmen's previous question.

"Fine… It was meant to be a surprise!" Carmen said, completely missing the hint. Which wasn't like her when it came to new clothes, shoes, men or bags—sparking Chloe's suspicion even more.

"Oh... So there *is* something you're hiding? Seriously, I told you not to bother throwing a party."

"It's nothing... I was sworn not to tell you, damn it! It's just a little gathering—nothing outrageous! Come on, let's grab lunch and I'll tell all!" Carmen said, desperate to change the subject—and for a drink to steady her. She walked on ahead towards the elevator—leading the way for Chloe to follow.

"So, that's why you've been in and out of the office all week... Going to this meeting and that—you sneaky little Devil!" Chloe said, entering the elevator with her. Did she really think she could hide it from her?

"Well, don't sound so surprised... I *do* work as well don't ya know?" Carmen said, reminding herself that spoiling the surprise was nothing compared to what was actually happening behind her back.

***

It turned out to be more of a liquid lunch for Carmen, taking large gulps of pinot grigio, while Chloe hadn't drunk a single drop. "You not drinking?" Carmen said, hardly touching her caesar salad.

"Ugh... I haven't felt too good all morning... That champagne breakfast Veronica threw for me, didn't exactly set me up for the day," Chloe said, picking at her salad, hardly eating as well.

"Well, you better get prepared for the cocktail bar I have waiting back at the apartment!"

"*What?*" Chloe said, giving her a piercing, wide-eyed look.

"And a chocolate fountain, a light-up disco dance floor, and full-on catering—complete with lobster rolls."

Right now, the thought of anything fishy made Chloe's Stomach churn. She tried her best not to look ungrateful; she really did just want to go home and take a long soak before sinking into bed—even better if Gianni wasn't there too.

"Great! So what's the plan… We go for a few drinks after work and then what?"

"I thought you didn't wanna *do* anything for your birthday? Why now do you wanna know every little detail?" Carmen said, shoving a salad leaf into her mouth to stop her from saying anything more.

"Well, now it's kinda funny… You guys thought the joke was on me, but now it's really on everyone else—because I'm secretly in-the-know!"

'Oh, trust me, bitch—you know nothing!' Carmen thought to herself, washing the unwanted mouthful of food down with another large gulp of wine.

She wasn't sure if it was the wine loosening her tongue or the guilt she felt, but looking at Chloe's face from across the table, she wanted to come clean about everything. Sure, there really was a surprise party, but there was another huge surprise that was even harder to keep.

"Look, I have to tell you something," she started, dabbing the corners of her mouth with her napkin. "Gianni made me promise not to say anything but—"

The vibrating of her phone on the table stopped her from going any further, in case it was information that would prevent her from making a terrible mistake.

"He's back! I knew it… He's so predictable sometimes," Chloe said, rolling her eyes, waving off Carmen's burden. "I mean, he flies back to Milan and has you sort all of this out, and then he swans back once it's all done—typical!"

"There really is no keeping secrets from you, is there?" Carmen said, reading the message on her phone. It was Dom, letting her know they had landed safe and were now heading back to his apartment where they were staying. She really needed to speak to them, but first, she had to figure out what she was going to do with Chloe.

"So, what's the plan? We go for drinks after work and then he'll text me to say he's back, and then I go running home—only to find everyone there waiting for me, hiding under a table?"

"Okay, seriously... You should be a clairvoyant," Carmen teased, putting her phone away. Looking back up, she decided not to tell her that Dom and Pandy were in town—that was at least one surprise she could keep. She grabbed Chloe's hand from across the table and smiled thinly. "Happy Birthday, Chloe!"

"Thanks, for everything... Not just for organising the party for me," she said, gripping Carmen's hand in return.

Feeling another sharp pang of guilt jabbing at her heart, Carmen did her best not to wince, she had to keep her trust in Gianni. If she told Chloe everything now, not only would she risk the deal from materialising—saving both Palazzo and StacksOfStyle from the clutches of Don Carlo—but also put Chloe and Gianni's relationship at risk.

It was best she stuck to the plan, play her part in all of this as agreed, and then damage control afterwards. She was learning a lot about that since becoming president it seemed. But after all this worrying, there was the possibility that Chloe would take this well. After all the secret moves behind her back, she could equally be over the Moon about the possibility of going global—in their first business year too.

But Carmen knew her better than that. She was determined, hard-working, strong, stubborn, and very proud. Second chances were hard to come by and things (especially work) were taken very seriously—and personally. Chloe put everything into her work. Whether it was on the shop floor at Palazzo, working for Carmen as a backstage assistant at some fashion show, or running her own company—Chloe was all or nothing. And for this reason, Carmen kept to Gianni's plan—even if it did make her feel like a complete Judas.

For the rest of the afternoon, Carmen did all she could to avoid Chloe, in case the situation got the better of her. Plus, she was mad at Veronica for putting them in this situation in the first place, and she was going to do what Chloe wanted to do week's ago—get some answers!

Grabbing her laptop, notebook, phone—and anything else that made her look like she was attending an ordinary meeting with Morgana—she made her way to Veronica's office instead. Looking through the glass, she could see she was on a call, but it didn't stop her from entering.

"Yes, well that *is* all in the agreement—" Veronica stopped, looking up to see Carmen standing there. She could tell by the look on her face that she wasn't going to take no for an answer this time. "Let me take another look at things and call you back—I have to go right now."

Veronica placed the phone back down on the receiver, shaking her hair out—putting on a smile.

"What's up? How can I help?"

Carmen placed her things on Veronica's desk, planting both hands down on the desk to lean into her and whisper. "Gianni's back, and he's told me *everything!*"

Veronica's eyes widened as her fake smile drooped into a frown. "Sit down," she said, looking through the glass walls to see if anyone else was lurking around outside. "What do you know *exactly*?"

"*Everything!*" Carmen said, mouthing every syllable. "The sale, the reason why you've been so elusive these past weeks—the fact that you've sold up on us…"

"I know this looks bad—"

"I know exactly how it looks, and exactly what it *really* is," Carmen warned, making sure there was no room for bullshit this time.

"Does *she* know?"

"No, but she really should—and ideally before this 'announcement›, you have planned tomorrow… Gianni wants to tell her, it's not fair that she walks into the lion's den, while we all know… And she isn't as dumb as you think! She's been sniffing you out for weeks. I was the one telling her she was being paranoid, but this… This is a lot for her to take—don't you think?"

"But you can see that this *is* for the best—for her *and* Gianni—right?" Veronica said, taking a deep breath.

"Of course! That's why I've agreed to back the deal, but I still think this is all just a bit… Off!"

"I'm sorry… You weren't meant to find out either—I'll kill Gianni for telling you! You were meant to find out tomorrow, just like everyone else… But, I'm glad you're on board with it… This means a lot for you girls; Don and Gianni will take StacksOfStyle global."

"So what now?" Carmen said, pulling up a chair.

"Well, this means that this place… Stacks, P.S.L—the whole lot—will be theirs," Veronica said, almost tearfully, before coming back to the reason why she had made the decision. "It's time for me to move on… I created DivaFeet, even dabbled in funding ventures… But I'm afraid I've got a bit out of my depth, it's time I cashed in and escaped to a desert island."

"I'm not convinced Chloe's gonna take it *just* as well," Carmen said, unable to argue with Veronica. "I mean, it looks like Gianni has cheated her and now we're talking about playing with her feelings—work is one thing—but this is too much… And on top of that, I'm guessing Dom and Pandora have also agreed to the take-over? Which means all of her friends—including me—are keeping something *huge* from her! Don't you see? We are all set to lose here…"

"I know," Veronica sighed, also unable to argue with Carmen. "And that wasn't my intention—this all happened rather fast for me too… Gianni was never meant to be caught in the middle, but then, of course, I found out that Don was only procuring the sale so he could have 'one-up' on him… And as for yourself, Dom and Pandora, I feel awful—I really do! But we have a lot riding on Chloe agreeing to this, since she owns a fair chunk of shares and both of your tenures forms a part of the agreement—that's why it's best if we just leave this up to Gianni. He can talk her round and see that this is the best solution for everyone involved."

"I hope you're right," Carmen said rubbing her forehead, still not believing what was happening.

"Look, that's business for you… And this is what happens when you're in demand—people want you! I would have never found such a prestige buyer if it wasn't for you guys," Veronica said, grabbing her arm from across the table.

"Oh, so all of this is our fault?" Carmen said, tugging her arm away, pretending she needed to push her hair behind her ear, rather than appear angered.

"Not fault—credit! You are about to have *millions* invested in your business, far more than what I could ever give—which is why I haven't signed off any poxy budgets! That'll go through the roof too! The things you will be able to do, the brands you will have access to—this is just the beginning."

"And what if Chloe doesn't agree to it?"

"Unfortunately, it's not really for Chloe to decide... Sure, we need her approval since she owns a large stake, but what's she gonna do? Find another buyer? It will come as a shock, I'm sure... But it's for the best. Now, let's just let her enjoy her birthday and hope Gianni can soften the blow... This time tomorrow we'll all be celebrating and drinking champagne—trust me!"

"Yeah, sure... Where have I heard that one before!" Carmen blinked.

****

"Where have you been all afternoon?" Chloe said, wiping off her lipstick to start anew as Carmen re-appeared. "What you organising now?" Her desk was strewn with Chanel compacts and Tom Ford lipsticks, all emptied from the toiletry bag she kept in her desk drawer for emergencies like this. There was no way she was going to be taken by surprise without a full face of make-up on—especially after a long day at work. She wasn't looking—as well as feeling—too hot either (her face was a pasty shade of grey). She was glad Carmen had spoiled the surprise, otherwise, she would have turned up looking like an extra from 'Thriller.'

"Oh, just a bit of this and that," Carmen shrugged when really she had been trying to speak to Dom and Pandy in private with no luck. She left several voice messages instead, urging him to call her. "What are *you* up to?"

"What does it look like? Seriously... If you let me turn up looking like this, I would have killed you!"

Carmen drew a deep breath. If she would have killed her for not telling her about the party, then it wasn't worth thinking about how she was going to react—once she learned the *real* surprise that was waiting for her. "Come on, let's get outta here," she said, ready for yet another stiff drink.

Unlike Chloe, Carmen got the best out of her Soho House membership and was a regular at Dumbo House—where she had managed to lure Chloe to. Leaving the office earlier than usual, Chloe had Tommy drive them—making the most of having a chauffeur now Gianni was back.

"Two margarita's," Carmen ordered. "Make them *extra* strong."

"Actually, make mine non-alcoholic," Chloe said to the waiter, sitting down on the pale blue velvet sofas by the large windows, with Brooklyn Bridge on full display.

"You still feeling unwell?"

"I'm sure I'll be fine… I just feel a bit queasy still—not quite ready for drinking just yet."

"Okay, whatever… Make her's a soft-tail—bring me two… I'll need them back-to-back!" Carmen said, letting the waiter go. "Are you sure you're feeling okay?"

"Like I said, just didn't start the day too great… But I'm sure I'll perk up later, once I see everyone back at the apartment!" she grinned. "Anyway, why are you so stressed? You can relax—the secret's out now—I know!"

Carmen's face dropped, what did she suddenly know? "Know what?"

"About the party…" Chloe said, looking at her. "Unless… There's something else I should know about?"

"Not what I know of… One surprise at a time, please," Carmen lied, looking around for the waiter. "Where're these damn drinks?"

But Chloe also knew her well, and instead of pushing her to come out with it, she waited for the drinks to finally arrive—until Carmen's lips had left the glass from her very first sip. The pressure would only make her drink more. "Okay… Something's going on and I need to know," Chloe said, leaning forward in her chair, her hands placed between her legs.

"*What?* Nothing's going on," Carmen said, predictably taking a longer sip to avoid filling the space with words she regretted later—her hand nervously shaking the cocktail glass.

"You've been chasing drinks since lunchtime... Carmen, I know you! Tell me what the hell is going on—and don't tell me it's just this stupid party!"

Carmen put her glass down, slowly looking up to meet Chloe's stare, even though she told herself not to. But she was first and foremost her friend, asking her for the truth and she deserved that much—deep down she knew it was the right thing to do. It would look terrible on her if she didn't say something. She took another large gulp, almost downing the first drink.

"Okay, you're right... But you have to promise me one thing," Carmen said, safe-guarding her from the imminent fallout.

"Of course... Look, whatever this is, just tell me; you're scaring me and it's making me feel worse!" Chloe said, begging to be put out of her misery.

"It's Don Carlo..."

Chloe's face dropped. Carmen blinked long and hard, carefully selecting her next words in her head. "You were right to be suspicious."

"*What?* What do you mean?"

"You were right all along, Chloe... I'm so sorry I didn't believe you, but Don has been courting Veronica to buy out DivaFeet."

"Are you sure?" Chloe said, not quite hearing what Carmen was saying.

"*Do you know what this means?*" Carmen said, reaching for cocktail number two.

Chloe stared into space, over Carmen's shoulder. Carmen saw she understood, but there was a hint of naiveté about her expression—like this was all just some misunderstanding.

"That means StacksOfStyle and P.S.L too, damn it!" she finally said, calling the waiter over for another round. "I only found out myself today—"

"But surely Veronica would have said something if this was true... How *did* you find out?" Chloe said, reaching for Carmen's drink—taking a much-needed mouthful

"Veronica told me," she started.

"Oh, well—that's just great! So, she tells you, but not me? Am I a *fucking* nobody?"

"Not at all," Carmen said, letting Chloe keep the drink. She was about to need it even more. "Gianni told me, I forced him to—"

"*Gianni told you?*" Now she was even more confused. None of this was making sense and Carmen had to admit, she wasn't exactly doing a good job explaining this rather complicated situation—she wondered if maybe she should have left it to him after all.

"Hey, don't shoot the messenger... You're just gonna have to listen and let me explain everything."

Chloe sat back on the sofa, her arms stretching out over the back as she crossed her legs. "Take it from the top."

"Don put in an offer to buy DivaFeet... So, Gianni flew back to Milan to speak to him about it—make him back down... He felt that if anyone should be investing in us, then it should have been him."

"Wait a minute... Gianni flew back for work," Chloe corrected. "That's what he told me."

"Yes, but technically this *was* work... Don wanted to merge MiBellaModa and Palazzo to create a super-power. Gianni declined and so Don Carlo set his sights on DivaFeet—well S.O.S to be more precise... He knew that if he got his hands on our business first, then Gianni would step in to try and save us... And that's what he's done—he's saved us, Chloe!"

She couldn't believe what she was hearing. This was the biggest pile of bullshit she had ever heard, but it was so farfetched, she knew it had to be true. Her face returned to pale once again, her stomach lurched up into her throat—she knew she had to get up—pushing the table into Carmen's ribs to escape. "*Chloe!*" Carmen called, whipping the napkin off her lap to chase after her.

It was by luck that she found the bathroom in time. Racing into a cubicle, Chloe pulled up the seat and hurled what little there was in her stomach into the can, with the door still open. That was the last of her worries. Carmen locked them both into the cubicle, holding Chloe's hair back until she finished retching on her knees. Her stomach convulsed, making her propel forwards— but nothing more came out. "Breathe… I know this is a lot to take in—I'm sorry for not saying anything sooner."

Chloe leant against the wall, still on the black and white tiled floor. "Let's get out of here," she groaned.

"Sure, wait here… I'll settle the bill and call Tommy."

Left alone in the cubicle, Chloe's head swirled with confusion as anger now started to creep in. How could Carmen keep this from her—how could Veronica lie like this? If the two people she trusted the most had kept something of this magnitude from her, then what else was Gianni lying about? Did he give Carmen all of the details, or was he holding back more than what he had led her to believe? Could she ever trust this man after this?

Returning to the bathroom, Carmen found her staring into the basin by the communal sinks, her hair covering her washed-out face. She hated herself for being selfish and telling her like this; she expected weight to be lifted off her shoulders, but what she really felt was pain. Pain for destroying her friend in public to save her own skin—she had to get her home. After waiting for Tommy to come back around the block, Carmen helped her into the back of the car.

"Good evening ladies!" Tommy grinned. "To The Grand Towers?" His smile soon turned serious, seeing she was visibly shaken and had obviously been crying.

"*No!*" Chloe urged, taking a breath. "Back to my place, please—Greenwich Village."

Carmen rolled her eyes; bang went another surprise. But that was the last of her worries. Having only just told Chloe, she hadn't managed to speak to Dom and Pandora—they were now the ones about to get a surprise! She quickly messaged them to let them know they were on their way.

"Have you told Gianni… That I know?" she whimpered, her head pressed up against the cold, black-tinted glass.

"No… I haven't said anything—and I won't!" she said, putting her phone away—realising that anything she said now would sound fake.

"Good… I need you to tell me everything," she said softly, trying to stop herself from having an anxiety attack. She tried her best to take slow, deep and long breaths—but even the air was making her feel sick. They didn't talk for the rest of the journey, Carmen was happy to keep her mouth shut for once—she had said too much already.

Outside Dom's Greenwich Village apartment, Carmen buzzed the entrance while Chloe asked Tommy to stay nearby—aware that her arrival would be anticipated at The Grand Towers. "I have a key," Chloe said, reaching into her bag; confused as to why she was ringing the buzzer—who did she expect to answer?

"You're in for another surprise," Carmen said with an apologetic side glance.

And that she was. Waiting outside the apartment door was her friends from London, Dom and Pandora.

"What the—" Chloe said, slapping her own forehead before realising their presence was nothing out of the ordinary, compared to all the shit that was going on. Shit that was getting weirder and weirder by the minute, that it was now starting to seem normal. Dom and Pandora hugged her, giving Carmen a scolding eye at the same time.

"I tried to call you," Carmen mouthed.

"I'll put the kettle on," Pandora said, heading back inside to make green tea, escaping the intensity in the air.

"What're you guys doing here?" Chloe said, letting go of Dom.

"Surprise!" he mocked with a comedy grin, knowing there was very little to laugh about.

"You think I wasn't going to invite them over for your thirtieth?" Carmen said as they settled inside, trying her best to make some good out of a bad situation.

"What a *fucking* day this is turning out to be," Chloe said, slumping down on the sofa. All these years, she had been dreading her thirtieth birthday for all the wrong reasons—it was a birthday she was *never* going to forget, that's for sure!

"What exactly does she know?" Dom murmured to Carmen.

"Everything," she said out loud—there was no point hiding from her now.

"So, let me get this straight… You all knew about this?"

"Not exactly," Dom said, quick to save him and Pandora from looking like they had been in on this all along. "We only found out when Veronica came to visit us in London—but we were told she was going to tell you both, and sworn to secrecy."

"And as you know, I've only just found out today," Carmen jutted in.

"Let's go over this again," Chloe said, looking at them stood in front of her. "Don pursued Veronica to buy her out because Gianni rejected a merger? How exactly does that include us?"

Dom cast his hand over to Carmen—this was for her to deal with.

"Don Carlo used StacksOfStyle to get to Palazzo. He knew Gianni would want to protect us—*you!* That's why Don offered to buy DivaFeet—he knew that would instantly grab Gianni's attention and make him think twice about the merger… But Gianni's found a way to save us *and* Palazzo from Don Carlo… Well, for now at least."

"But why didn't Gianni say anything to me?" Chloe said, still confused. She was the one who had warned him about Don Carlo after all.

"I know it's hard to take, but this is business—it has nothing to do with your relationship," Dom added—sensing where she was going with this.

"It has *everything* to do with our relationship! How can I ever trust him again?"

"Look, I'm not taking sides here, but you have to see it from his perspective," Carmen said, now rubbing her back as Chloe laid on her side—her head buried into a cushion as she quietly started to sob.

"He didn't know what was going to happen, how this was going to play out—and he probably didn't want to scare you," Dom offered, knowing that anything he said now didn't really matter.

"Instead, he just treated me like some object he could buy!" Chloe cried, now sitting up, sniffing back tears.

"Not buy—guard!" Carmen said, looking to Dom for encouragement that she was saying the right things this time. "He's talked Don into starting a new venture with him, one that will take-over DivaFeet and the responsibility shared between them. The plan is that Don will oversee DivaFeet and P.S.L, while Gianni will look after S.O.S."

"*Fucking* great! So, basically, my boyfriend is now my boss?"

"Well, technically your boyfriend was your boss before…And that didn't stop you," Carmen smiled, trying to lighten the mood.

"Not funny… I had left Palazzo already," Chloe reminded them, rubbing her face, not caring about her make-up now. "So, when *was* I going to be told?"

"Tomorrow… Veronica's holding a meeting tomorrow since we're all here," Carmen said, throwing her hands up to include everyone in the room.

"I know this is super fucked up—I get it—but it's for the best," Pandora said, bringing over green tea in random mugs.

Chloe looked up sharply as if to say: '*Really bitch?*'

"Of course it is!" Dom said, reading her expression. "This means we'll have *millions* invested in our businesses and with Gianni's help, you can take StacksOfStyle world-wide… And as for *our* shares… They'll be worth a fuck-tonne now—think about it!"

"But, what if I'm happy with how things are already?"

"Chloe, listen to me," Carmen said, taking Chloe's chin in her hand—forcing her to look at her. "What we've created—what *you* have created—is far bigger than what it is right now. That's why we have these guys fighting over us… Isn't this what we've always wanted? No more struggling to get to the top, no more proving ourselves; we have proved ourselves, we *are* at the top! Don't you get it? *Fuck* Regina, *fuck* Gianni, *fuck* Don! We've made a name for ourselves, just as big as theirs—and we've only just begun!"

Indeed, she could see where Carmen was coming from, and it *was* what she had always wanted: to prove to people that she was more than what they had limited her to. Here was her chance to show the world and to prove that she was right about her talents all along. "It just hurts to find out this way… Like, I'm nothing in all of this," she said, starting to breathe normally now.

"But that's why you're the last one to know! You mean *everything* to Veronica, to Gianni, to us! That's why we've tried to protect you until the very last minute… *It just didn't work out the way we thought it would*," Carmen said, the latter through gritted teeth. "Everyone knows you're special, Chloe… Everyone cares about you—and you know what? I wish people felt that way about me too."

Gazing into Carmen's eyes, she could see the well of emotion that was forming in her eyes. She looked up at Dom and Pandy, who were now also teary-eyed. Deep inside she knew these people were her *real* friends, that they would never do anything to intentionally hurt her—and she couldn't stay mad at Carmen. The fact she had warned her before seeing Gianni, meant she really cared about her.

"So what now?"

"Well, I guess we just have to wait until tomorrow and find out how this is all going to play out… But you do understand you can't fight this, right?" Dom said, not wanting to carry on with any more pretence. Chloe knew exactly what this meant. Her shares were worth little against the financial might of two fashion moguls, and Veronica who owned the majority of her business clearly wanted to cash out on the maximum profit possible. She couldn't be mad at her either; she would have done the same.

"*Shit!*" Carmen said, checking her phone. A barrage of missed calls and text messages lit up her phone.

"What now?" Chloe said, blowing into her green tea, hoping it would quell the knots in her stomach that still lingered.

"It's Gianni… Everyone—except us—is at the apartment now and waiting for your arrival."

"Well, 'everyone' can *fucking* wait," Chloe said, taking another sip, with no intention to rush anywhere, anytime soon.

Carmen smiled, she should have known Chloe would kick into a sudden spell of diva-like confidence. Maybe telling her *was* the best thing she could have done? She had prepared her for what was about to come, giving her armour to confront the upcoming battle. Chloe she was beginning to see that breaking free from Veronica's financial limitations could now propel her into greater things.

Far greater than what Regina or Graziana could ever have imagined possible for her—and that provided her with some sort of satisfaction, and Carmen was right about it. They had just levelled up, far higher than the likes of Myra or Regina, who once put them down. Chloe Ravens was set to be the CEO and co-founder of a global business that no one saw coming, and with Carmen by her side, they would conquer the world—and the Internet.

"Right then," Chloe declared, slapping her lap to get up off the sofa. "There's no way we're turning up looking like hell…

"Tell Gianni, we'll be there when we get there… You two better run on ahead and keep up the farce," she said, nodding to Dom and Pandy. "I'll take a shower and get my face ready while *you* pick a couple of outfits for us to wear," she said, pointing to Carmen. "There's some oldies-but-goodies still in the closet… Look at us, all together—just like old times!"

33

"What's taking them so long?" Veronica said, starting to worry.

"I've just messaged Carmen, they're still having cocktails… They'll be here soon," Gianni said, nervously downing a short.

"I've got a bad feeling about this—where's Dom and Pandora?"

"I'm sure they'll be here any minute too."

He poured another drink. Dom and Pandora were the last on his mind.

"What if they've told her?"

"Then they'd have done me a huge favour, that's for sure!" Gianni said, raising his glass and throwing back his head. The sting from the alcohol hitting the pit of his stomach made Gianni draw a sharp breath as he slammed his glass down on the marble kitchen top—nearly making it smash.

Veronica laid off him, she knew he didn't mean it and she didn't want to stress him out more than what he was already. Everyone else was oblivious, still 'in' on the surprise party at least. Bill, Morgana, Lily, and Sam were all revelling in the lavish surroundings of Gianni Palazzo's New York apartment—spoilt with champagne cocktails on tap, served with five-star canapés and lobster rolls.

The chocolate fountain had everything you could wish to dip into its velvety Swiss volcano, frothing over four tiers—from pretzel sticks to build-your-own fresh fruit skewers. Carmen had indeed done a fantastic job, but he sound of the doorbell halted their enjoyment as they paused and looked to Gianni for direction. He waved his hands for them to simmer down and hush as he edged towards the door.

Gianni peered through the spyglass.

"It's fine guys... It's just Dom and Pandora," he announced opening the door for them.

"You haven't seen the girls, have you?" Veronica panicked, walking towards them.

"No—why would we?" Dom said, almost too quickly.

"Well, don't just stand there," Pandora said, inviting herself in, linking arms with Veronica. "You gonna offer me a drink or what?"

"Have *you* heard from them?" Gianni whispered, tugging on Dom's arm.

"Like I said, why would we have?"

"Just checking," Gianni said with a quick flash of a smile, guiding Dom inside. "Listen, do me a favour, will you? Keep Veronica distracted for me... She's doing my head in."

Feeling responsible for her, like some sort of mother figure, Dom and Pandy did just that as they joined the rest of the party anticipating Chloe's arrival—unsure of how they were going to keep up the act all night. But he didn't have to worry about making small-talk with her, Bill and Morgana had made a beeline for him while Pandy showed off the custom made dress she had designed especially for the occasion.

For Gianni, the chatter was all in-one-ear-out-the-other. Seeing all of these people in his apartment, he started to wonder if throwing a party was such a good idea after all. Now he understood Chloe's simple wish to relax at home together—alone. Just as he was about to escape and have a moment of peace in the bathroom, his phone vibrated in the back pocket of his tight Palazzo jeans. It was a text from Carmen.

"Okay, everybody! It's them this time... Turn the lights out, they're pulling up outside! See, I told you everything was fine," he said, passing Veronica as they all gathered on the make-shift dance floor in the middle of his apartment—confetti canons at the ready.

It felt like they had been waiting for ages until the key to rattled in the lock and the handle turned, but finally, Chloe appeared—prompting cheers and explosions of confetti spoiling the place with gold foil tickets. The DJ started to blast Stevie Wonder's 'Happy Birthday' while his dance floor lit-up and Chloe gave an Oscar-worthy performance at the doorway (like Eva Perón on her balcony), dressed in a black Dolce & Gabbana silk bustier dress—and a full face of make-up. It was clear for everyone to see, she hadn't turned up straight from the office looking like this; this was *no* surprise at all.

"Oh my gosh... You guys!" she feigned, walking in with her hands clapped on her face. "I wasn't expecting this!"

Gianni walked up to her with a glass of champagne. She skipped into his arms to embrace him before taking it from him. "You look amazing!" he whispered into her ear.

"Haven't you got something to say to me?" she whispered back, softly kissing his neck to make him weak.

Gianni glared over her shoulder at Carmen (who was also dressed up, early for the Met Gala) in a navy Valentino gown—something told him the jig was up.

"Well? Aren't you gonna wish me a happy birthday?" Chloe finally said with a half-lidded smirk, enjoying the power of knowledge.

"Of course... Happy birthday, baby," he said enjoying having her in his arms, in case this would be the very last time.

"*Oh my God! Dom—Pandora! What are you doing here?*" she exclaimed, releasing herself from him, greeting her guests in the middle of the disco dance floor.

Gianni took a deep breath, before taking two steps closer to Carmen. "You told her, didn't you?"

"She knew long before you even did, kiddo," Carmen rebuffed, brushing past him to grab a bottle of Dom Pérignon from the ice bucket in the kitchen—and a single glass.

The light-up dance floor had been a hit with Sam and Lily, who were clearly out of their skulls on free booze. Carmen had ordered Chloe's favourites eighties tunes to be played all night long—the new wave sounds she and Dom used to get drunk to in New York City's gay bars, before a shift at Palazzo the very next day.

Meanwhile, Morgana tapped her feet and looked on, sat on one of the L-shaped sofas with Bill—boring him intermittently with work chat. Dom had somehow found his way stuck in the middle of them, looking for a polite exit, but enjoying being excluded from an even more awkward circle at the same time. It consisted of Veronica, Pandora, Gianni and Chloe, over by the kitchen—Carmen was nowhere to be seen.

"I'm *dying* for a fag," Pandy said, merrily swayed from her peach champagne cocktail—she too was celebrating. StacksOf-Style wasn't the only one gaining major investment, now they could finally open a London boutique of their own (and no doubt a website under Don's expertise).

"Come, I'll take you up to the terrace," Chloe said, taking her hand—rescuing Dominic en route, who was still held hostage.

Now it was just Gianni and Veronica, alone at the kitchen island again. "You know she knows, right?" he said, leaning against the marble top, picking at the buffet.

"No *shit*! She certainly doesn't dress like that for the office."

"So, what do we do now?"

"Well, I suggest you end this party by Midnight… I'm sure she's just putting on a brave face right now, and you do have some explaining to do—"

"*Hey!* So do you, remember?"

"True… But if you didn't get yourself involved in all this mess, then I would have been left to explain it all myself."

"Yes, but Don was *never* going to buy your company… He was just using—do we *really* need to go over this again?"

"You're right, none of that matters now… What's done, is done. Anyway, you wanted to tell her yourself, what's changed?"

"Nothing," Gianni said, swigging ice-cold cognac from a cut-crystal short, etched with the '*P*,' monogram all around. Chloe had changed, she had suddenly become aloof towards him and he feared she would stay that way.

"Good, that's settled," Veronica swallowed, realising that now was a good time to leave—avoiding an awkward 'goodnight' exchange—knowing it would be far from, once everyone had left.

Meanwhile, up on the terrace, Pandy instantly rushed over to the railing—looking down on the avenue below. "Gorgeous apartment!"

"Wow! How you've cleaned up," Dom said proudly, with the take-over announcement set to cement their names as trailblazers in the industry—along with the likes of Palazzo itself.

"Haven't we all?" Pandy mouthed as she tried to spark the cigarette in her mouth.

"Pass me one of those would ya," a voice said from a lounger in the corner, complete with a personal supply of champagne.

It was Carmen—holding out her fingers in a 'V' sign.

"So this is where you're hiding… I didn't know you smoked? Dom said, joining her on the lounger.

"Only when in Paris," Chloe mocked. "Pass me one too."

Dom shook his head in disbelief, things were changing—things had changed.

"*What?* Can't a girl enjoy herself on her birthday?" She leaned into Pandora to light her lady-like, Vogue slim. "Anyway, smoking this is no much worse than breathing in the city air."

He couldn't exactly argue her point. She had also changed, or her attitude at least. Gone was the hurt and hard-done-by damsel in distress; now, she was fierce, confident, and sassy—she had Dom to thank for that rubbing off on her over the years. The terrace was silent as they all drew on their cigarettes—except Dom.

"So, this evening didn't turn out so bad," he said, filling the void, more so than meaning it. Three faces, smoking like a row of London chimneys, shot daggers at him: right-left and centre.

"If you mean the party… You did a great job, Carmen," Chloe said, offering a wry smile in thanks. Carmen took it as a sign of forgiveness and gave her a rueful smile in return. "So, what are we going to do about tomorrow?"

Dom, Pandy, and Carmen looked at each other in canon, before returning to face her. "Well, like I said earlier… You accept this *is* going ahead, right?" Dom said.

"I meant about *us*, knowing," Chloe said, dragging on her cigarette. "Are we gonna keep it up or is it pretty obvious by now?"

"I think Gianni and Veronica knew the minute we turned up looking like this," Carmen laughed, also taking a drag.

"Well, let's make a pact," Chloe said, picking up her champagne glass from the tiled floor. "From now on, no more secrets."

"No more secrets," Dom said, raising his glass.

"Agreed," Pandy said, following suit.

Carmen, swung her legs over the lounger to retrieve the bottle of Dom by her feet. "I'll drink to that!" she said, taking a swig from the bottle.

"Happy birthday, Chloe!" Pandy said, raising her glass once more.

"Yes, happy birthday!" Dom said, getting up to lean against the railings with her, putting his arm around her shoulders. "You always did say you wanted to be a 'somebody' before you turned thirty… And here it is—you got your wish, babe!"

She had heard that before… Many times, in fact. Turning around, forcing his arm to let loose, she dashed the smouldering butt over the railings—not caring who's scalp it landed on below. Breathing in the cool air, looking at the evening sky on Gianni's Park Avenue terrace, she realised that things certainly could be worse.

Life, wasn't at all bad, but it didn't mean Gianni was off the hook. For now, there was eighties music to be danced to and a sense of dignity to uphold… Until the guest left, at least.

*

Much to her relief, after they had sung 'Happy Birthday' to her and she had blown out the candles on the cake, most of them got the hint: time to take a piece of cake and go home. "Thanks for coming!" Chloe said, ushering Sam and Lily over to the door as they staggered, arm-in-arm. "Tommy will drive you girls home safely, okay? He's waiting outside."

She said the latter to make them leave quicker.

"We're off too, Chloe… See you tomorrow," Pandy said, giving her a hug, and then squeezing her arm for encouragement, before darting over to the kitchen to select a piece of cake wrapped up in paper towel.

"Get some sleep... And don't be too hard on the old man! He's just set us up for life!" Dom said in her ear as he kissed her cheek goodnight.

By now, everyone had left including the waiters and caterers who would return in the morning for the clear-up operation. Shutting the door, Chloe turned back to the only people left—Carmen and Gianni. They were sat in the living room on the sofas, ignoring each other, with the disco lights still flashing pink and orange—then blue and red.

"Well, thanks for a lovely evening," Chloe said, walking towards the stairs, her foot already on the first step. "I'm off to bed."

"*Wait!*" Gianni stopped. "Don't you wanna talk about this?"

"What's there to talk about," she said, backing down from the step. "I'm sure I'll hear all about it tomorrow, as you planned?"

"Don't be like that... I didn't plan for it to be like *this!*"

"*No!* You had a choice and you made it... You know what, I can't even be mad at the situation—but I can be mad at you! Dominic and Carmen have explained what this deal means for us all—I get it and I thank you... What I don't understand is why you—my boyfriend—would keep this from me?"

"What else can I say? I'm sorry—"

"On that note—I'm out," Carmen said, getting up onto her unsteady feet. There was no place left for her tonight. "I'll see you both in the morning... Call me if you need anything."

Carmen said her 'goodnight,' swaying side-to-side as she held Chloe close. Tomorrow was a new dawn on their careers and their friendship. This was just another moment that made them stronger—together.

Chloe now had to face Gianni alone. Not only did she want answers from him, but she wanted to know what this meant for *them*. He remained sat down, staring into his cognac, weary of what was about to come. He took deep breaths, so deep she could hear him expel through his nostrils in frustration. Looking at him, he seemed down on his luck—he knew he had let her down.

Walking over to him, seeing his handsome yet sullen face up close, she couldn't help but feel sorry—when all she wanted to do was slap him. Standing over him with her hands on her waist, she matched him with a deep breath. Knowing she was weak for him, and no matter what he had done, she still had feelings for him. She said nothing, but he felt her stare—he had to look at her sooner or later.

"I'm so sorry, Chloe… I fell into a trap and I had to do the right thing, not just for Palazzo, but for *you*!" he said, putting his glass down to take hold of her delicate hands.

"But did you why keep it from me?"

"Why?" he said, standing up to face her, still holding her hands. "Don't you see? I *love* you!"

And with few words, he had won her back. She had just heard Gianni Palazzo say the words, that every woman who had come before her had wanted to hear from him—but never did. What made *her* so special, she wondered? She wasn't a stunning actress or a svelte supermodel, neither was she from a wealthy family. But what she did have was guts, integrity, promise, and loyalty to her friends—she possessed everything he had ever wanted in a woman, yet only found in Chloe.

Staring into his watery-blue eyes, she placed her hands behind his neck, stroking tufts of wavy brown, slicked-back hair. And as their breaths caught each other, she couldn't help but give into him—kissing his thick lips, passionately. He laid her down on the sofa; she began unbuttoning his shirt as his mouth caressed hers—ending her birthday in a way that she never imagined. It had indeed been bitter-sweet, and she was unsure whether tomorrow it would all turn sour. But for now, at least, she felt like she was in safe hands—her future was in safe hands; Gianni's hands.

**

The alarm clock rudely went off, waking him up at six a.m sharp. He stretched an arm out to reach Chloe, across the king-size bed. "Time to get up," he moaned, still tired.

Instead of finding her laying there, his fingers stumbled on a warm spot on the Egyptian cotton sheets—where she had once laid for the past four hours. Gianni rubbed his eyes, grabbing his phone off 'charge' to double-check the time. Already his email inbox was full, but then again, it never really got cleared. It was a constant stream of unread messages, twenty–four–seven, and today was no different. But it wasn't an ordinary day—it was *the* day.

The day he had been dreading for some time had come, but thanks to Carmen breaking her silence, she had made it some-what bearable and rather exciting at the same time. It appeared as though Chloe was starting to come around to the idea of him joint-owning S.O.S. They just had to get through today's meeting and have her agree to the take-over—which could be easier said than done. But he thought he had done a good job at convincing her, post-coital—he was rather proud of it. Leaping out of bed, he could hear coughing coming from another room. He checked the en-suite bathroom, but the sound was further away. "Chloe?" he called softly, tracking the coughing to the bathroom in the hall-way—the door was ajar. "Chloe, are you all right?"

"I'm fine," she spitted, wiping her mouth—waving him to go away.

"You're not fine," he said, ignoring her, crouching on the bathroom floor to rub her back. "You're sick."

"I just too much to drink last night, that's all," she groaned.

"I'll call Veronica and tell her we're running behind," he said, kissing her head.

"Really… I'll be fine!" Calling Veronica was the last thing on her mind—Veronica could fucking wait for once.

He could see by the look on her face, *what* was really making her sick—stress. She was shaking from nerves, not sickness. He held her tight and rubbed the goose pimples forming on her arms, trying to bring the warmth of life back to her skin.

"I know you're nervous, but you have nothing to worry about," he said, still cradling her. "We have no option other than to make this a success—together… It's the only way to save StacksOfStyle from Don Carlo and halt Palazzo merging with MiBellaModa. Together we're stronger! And The Palazzo Group is worth *more* than MiBellaModa… What with Maison Marais performing better than ever. Together, we will build up StacksOfStyle and the board will see that we have *three* key businesses. Don will never catch up with us and in the end, we'll be in the position to take full control."

She looked back at him, pulling the flusher and closing the lid. He had this all thought out, she just hoped he was right. Seeing she was now steady, Gianni got up and turned on the shower— switching the water to run warm. "Take your time to get ready," he said, helping her up off the floor, holding her once more, kissing her neck. "I'll see you downstairs when you're ready to go."

Leaving her alone in the bathroom, he headed back to the bedroom to shower in the en-suite, this was just an important day for him as it was for her. He laid out a grey suit on the bed, along with a white shirt and baby blue tie. Next, he picked out a pair of Cartier cufflinks and one of his favourite time-pieces (a gold Hublot fusion on a brown crocodile skin strap)—which reminded him, Chloe never opened her present.

After he had showered and made sure he was looking sharp, he waited downstairs in the kitchen for Chloe to appear, pouring himself coffee as the morning news played on the TV in the background. The apartment was a mess from the evening before, he could only hope that the party planners would be able to restore it all before they came back home—otherwise, they would be staying at The Four Seasons. Which didn't sound like a bad idea to him.

Waiting for her downstairs, he had downed two cups of machine-brewed coffee and was now pacing the apartment, trying to clear up what he could—lining up empty glasses and beer bottles on the kitchen island. But she too was making sure she was ready for battle. Sitting in front of the vanity in the guest bedroom, she took her time to style her hair, and her make-up was nothing but perfection.

Her lips were painted bold red and her eyes were smokey and daring, even for daytime, but she wanted to look like she meant business. Because if she felt it, then she could be it—this was a time to stand strong and not agree to things that she would regret later. This was a chance to rebalance and realign StacksOfStyle, forming the basis of its future success.

It was now approaching eight o'clock and the meeting was scheduled for nine (although Gianni did warn Veronica they would be thirty minutes late). As he made another trip to the island with empties clawed in all fingers of both hands, he heard footsteps from above and doors closing. "Can I get you anything? Coffee?" he called up to her, racing back to put the glasses down on the kitchen side with a clash, fetching her gift that he had been waiting patiently to present her with.

Her shoes 'click-clacked' down the stairs, telling him she had made quite the effort—which he hadn't doubted. He waited at the foot of the stairs until she eventually appeared on the spiral case, wearing a black Palazzo jacket and matching skirt, her black leather Maison Marais bag on her shoulder. The jacket was edged with gold chains down the front opening and along the bottom, with large italic 'P,' gold buttons. The skirt had a matching gold chain belt, clipped together with another 'P,' clasp—some length left dangling down the side. A simple white vest top and a pair of black leather high-heels completed her modern power-suit.

Watching her descend, Chloe reminded him of someone. She looked powerful, strong, determined, and beautiful—someone not to be toyed with. Until it finally hit him—she reminded him of his *sister!* She was more like Graziana than they would both care to admit, and he knew that *like* his sister, she was about to become a huge player in the business of fashion. "Wow, you look… Stunning! Serious, but stunning," he said, as she reached the bottom. "Here… You never opened this."

"What is it?" she said, putting her bag down on the sofa, taking the square-shaped box wrapped up in gold paper.

"Open it and see."

She pulled the black ribbon with ease, passing it to Gianni so she could start peeling back the paper. Sliding her nail under one edge, she managed to rip open one side, causing a flash of red to appear—like blood. Instantly she knew it was another Cartier box—he had learnt well from the last gift. She gave him a half-lidded smile; she rather liked receiving red boxes.

"Joli helped me pick," he admitted, as she was prising it open.

"*OH, WOW!*" Chloe gasped, her eyes widened with surprise.

She had expected another bracelet, or maybe a pair of earrings at least—not a diamond watch. Although, the Panthère manchette was more of a statement piece than it was a watch, and it matched perfectly well with what she was wearing. Technically it was a cuff with a tiny watch-face, so Chloe told herself it was just another bangle. It also said to everyone that she had money, this deal wasn't about money—it was about business.

"Here, let me help you put it on," Gianni said, taking the box from her. He took the watch cushion out and unhooked the tiny latch, placing it around Chloe's waiting wrist before clamping it safely shut.

"Wow… It's amazing!" Chloe said, admiring it on her arm.

"Amazing, for an *amazing* woman," he said, holding her hips, going in for a peck—careful not to smudge her lipstick. "You didn't open your other presents—I moved them to the cinema room."

"That can wait," she said, wiping his bottom lip with her finger, smoothing away any rouge that had left hers. Opening birthday presents was the last thing on her mind right now.

"Ready to go?" He took her hand and together they left the apartment and headed downstairs, out to the waiting car. Even though she understood the upcoming events of this morning were inevitable, she couldn't help but feel like she was walking to her own crucifixion, and nausea started to stir within her. Looking down at her watch in the backseat of the car, with Gianni holding her other hand all the way there, she couldn't help but feel like a luxurious possession herself.

All this fighting over StacksOfStyle, like she was an object to be won, were in some ways symbolised in the watch—even though Gianni had simply intended it to be an heirloom to remember her thirtieth by. But to Chloe it represented more than that, it was a reminder of the day that changed her life forever—whether that was for good or bad remained to be discovered.

34

For the first time—that Carmen could remember—the pale grey curtains of Veronica's office had been drawn, concealing the boardroom from the rest of the office. Inside, invitees had a place around the table, reserved for them with a strategically placed name card. Hierarchy existed even around the boardroom table.

The more central you were, the more important; those in the outer seats were bound to be asked to answer any knocks at the door. DivaFeet's head of departments (including Bill and Morgana amongst others) patiently waited with Dom, Pandora and of course, Carmen.

She was nervously squirming in her seat, waiting for Chloe and Gianni to arrive, not knowing what was said between them after she had left last night. Would Chloe even turn up? Had Gianni managed to ease her worries? Had they split up in the heat of the argument? So many questions were about to be answered, including her own future with StacksOfStyle.

Don Carlo, on the other hand, looked rather smug, sitting directly next to Veronica like he had already taken the throne—the other chair next to her was vacant.

"They won't be long," Veronica said, the room silent and still in waiting.

Carmen clock-watched, jittering her leg under the table, counting down the minutes into the seconds, right up until it finally landed at nine o'clock, until finally the glass doors rattled as they drew open.

"Morning everyone," Chloe said with little enthusiasm as she entered, cutting the silence like leftover birthday cake.

Carmen sighed, despite Chloe's downtrodden manner, she had managed to pull together a look that was far from defeated.

Dating Gianni Palazzo helped in that department, of course, who soon followed her. Carmen half-smiled at Chloe, as she made her way over to where her name card was—predictably, next to Carmen.

"You look fantastic!" Carmen said quietly, now that her entrance gave the rest of the room permission to talk freely.

"Thanks... But I feel like shit."

"Uh, me too, girl!"

But Chloe's shittiness wasn't quite the same as the hangover Carmen was certain to be nursing. Taking her seat, Chloe placed her handbag under the table before tucking herself in nearer—flicking her hair off her shoulders.

"Wow!" Carmen said, snatching Chloe's wrist. "Where did you get this?"

"*Birthday gift*," Chloe said quickly with a shy smile.

She should have known that the maven for anything new and expensive would notice the thick golden shackle on her arm—it started to feel like one too.

Sensing Chloe wanted her to stop talking, she let go of her wrist; now wasn't the time for showing off. Plus, she wasn't sure she would have much to gloat about, after this meeting. After doing the rounds of the table, nobly shaking everyone's hand, Gianni took his seat next to Don Carlo, but the spot next to Veronica was still empty.

"I'm sure she'll be here any minute," Gianni laughed awkwardly, unbuttoning his blazer as he sat down.

They didn't have to wait long to find out '*she*' was in fact, the Queen of Sheba herself.

"Good morning, everyone!" Graziana trilled, whipping back the curtains—this time making an appearance as star-guest.

"*Fucking great!*" Chloe whispered, leaning in to Carmen. "I should have guessed."

Carmen elbowed her, although she wasn't ecstatic to see her either, this was not the time for bitchy exchanges or a power-tussle over Gianni for that matter. Dressed in a black pant-suit, proudly showing off her tanned cleavage with a low-cut top underneath,

Graziana threw off her shades—plunking her black crocodile skin handbag down on the table. Causing a reshuffle of chairs, she confidently filled the void next to Veronica, repositioning her handbag slightly. The shiny brass '*P*,' buckle reflected off the LED lights above, making Chloe squint as it shone in her face from across the way. It was almost too good a move, not to have been done on purpose.

"Great, shall we begin?" Don said, not wearing his regular uniform for this occasion. This time, a black roll-neck sweater had been substituted for a white collared shirt under—you guessed it—a black blazer.

"Yes, I think everyone's here now," Veronica nervously started. "Well, thank you all for attending. As you may now know, this is a historic day—not only for DivaFeet and its invested companies—but for Mr Carlo and Mr Palazzo's new partnership."

Veronica looked around, trying to speak directly in the eyes of her attendee's until she stumbled upon Chloe's. She quickly moved on, unable to look her in the eye—realising the words that were rolling out of her mouth seemed a tad hypocritical.

"After speaking with you all, I think you now know what this is all about…"

"*Pah!*" Chloe couldn't help herself from puffing. Still, it didn't ruffle Veronica from continuing—she wanted this over with, as much as Chloe did.

"In a new venture—backed by MiBellaModa and The Palazzo Group—The New Guardians will take over DivaFeet and its shares in associated companies."

Chloe immediately noticed the lack of surprise coming from Bill and Morgana. Obviously, Veronica had briefed them beforehand, which she thought was rather rich—apparently, she *had* been the last person to be told.

"If I may explain our partnership a little bit further?" Don interrupted. "MiBellaModa has unrivalled experience in e-commerce, as well as holding online distribution rights to many of the most desirable labels… While Palazzo is, of course, one of the world's most desired luxury brands, with decades of artisanship and creativity behind its heritage. Therefore, it is with both of our expertise, infrastructure, and technology that DivaFeet will benefit best—while StacksOfStyle will naturally have instant access to an extensive catalogue of designer brands. As for Pandora Simmons London… With our combined resources, you will instantly be able to scale up into the luxury market, positioning you alongside prestigious brands, like MiBellaModa, Maison Marais, and Palazzo."

Chloe shook her head, not because what Don said sounded ridiculous (in fact it sounded rather fantastic), but because it was a stretch to list MiBellaModa that high up on the list, next to the likes of Palazzo and Maison Marais.

"Which brings me on to explain how this joint venture will work… I will oversee DivaFeet, improving its inventory systems, expanding stock accessibility to our facilities in many countries—taking the brand global. Gianni will set the course for StacksOfStyle—since they will be focusing on the luxury market—ensuring that the detail and standard are in-line with the rest of the Palazzo Group."

"And what about us?" Pandora said, her accent sticking out, like the din of a cymbal.

"Primarily, I will be working with yourself and Dominic… Together we will create your online store using MiBellaModa's technology and service teams. However, over time it makes sense for your production to move to Italy—utilising the craftsmanship of The Palazzo Group. Something Gianni, Graziana, and I will be able to advise you on. We will, of course, be having separate discussions, tailoring the roadmap for the next five years."

Pandora's face lit up with excitement. Don sure sounded like he knew what he was doing, and she liked the little soundbite he had fed them so far. Production in Italy, their very own website, three of the most prominent figures in fashion acting as their mentors—what was there *not* to like? Dominic grabbed her hand under the table, equally feeling victorious. He had helped her get to this stage; if it wasn't for him, she would still be giving away her designs to the drag queens of East London for free.

"As Don says, I will look after StacksOfStyle, which will see a major investment in your buying budget—amongst other things," Gianni piped up, a bid to build up excitement for Chloe and Carmen. "You will gain access to a vast array of designer brands, as well as lifting some of the workload from yourselves as you expand your own team—moulding the business into the shape you want it to be."

Carmen tried her best not to overreact with joy and remain professional, mindful that this was a difficult matter for Chloe. She quietly regarded her, trying to spark some kind of reaction, but Chloe seemed far removed from what was happening in the room. She had completely zoned out, trying her best to stay calm and just simply get through it. Feeling her stomach knot, she didn't dare make a single move. Instead, she just focused on the art of not throwing up on the table in front of her new investors; reaching out for a glass of water, taking a cautious sip.

"*Sounds amazing*," she finally managed, low and quick.

Don watched her, sensing her discomfort. He could smell blood like a hungry shark and he was going to attack while she was bleeding. "Whilst we have agreed to the take-over in principle, a final decision will take months for both sides to finalise the hand-over—allowing a six-month 'cooling' period to perfect nuances and for any indifferences to be contested... This means that P.S.L and S.O.S share-holders will retain their current share value. However, if you did want to raise more equity, then now is a good time to have that discussion."

"I'm afraid my share isn't up for sale," Chloe spitted, making sure she was clear on that.

"And that's totally fine," Gianni eased, knowing that Don was successfully hitting her nerves.

"Great! So, it seems everyone *will* agree to the plans we have set out," Graziana said, tired of the heavy petting; she had imagined this would be ironed out already. "Let's just go through the most important details, shall we? Do keep in mind that if all is agreed, The New Guardians will officially take ownership from September this year."

"But it'll be too late to invest for our next market season by then... All of these *amazing* designers that you propose we now stock won't come cheaply—how will we afford all this?" Chloe jutted in, seizing a loop-hole to stall the discussion.

"Of course, we will unlock an emergency budget, enabling you to do this in time," Gianni said cooly; annoyingly answering with sensibility.

"And what if we *don't* agree?" she snapped.

"Er, why don't we take a deeper look at the information pack?" Veronica said, simmering the tension; trying to save Chloe from saying something she later regretted, Now was not the time to get in an emotional state. Everyone reached out for the spiral-bound packs that were laid out in front of them—it was at least four–hundred pages thick.

"The first section outlines the overall sale of DivaFeet," Graziana said confidently. She knew the terms inside out, she was the one who had devised them. "To summarise, DivaFeet have come to an agreement to sell its assets, including investment shares in subsidiaries—your businesses. This is where you come in..."

"This is where *she* needs *us*, more like," Chloe muttered to Carmen; her hands now resting on her fragile stomach under the table.

Wrapped up in her speech, Graziana didn't even notice her comment. "Fifty percent of Pandora Simmons London will be transferred over, to what is referred to as T.N.G, outlined in section two. For the saleable shares to retain their value, it's requested that you both stay in your positions for a minimum of five years—regardless of whether you sell your shares or not—since you are the designer of the brand on which its success depends upon... Oh, and the buy-back scheme previously offered will be nulled under the new terms."

Both Dom and Pandy nodded. They understood what this meant for them, and by their lack of protest, it was clear to Chloe that they were ready to agree, fuss-free. Why would they? Her dowfall, was their set-up.

"Excellent! Salaries will be negotiated separately," Graziana quipped, now casting her gaze to Chloe and Carmen. "Section three concerns StacksOfStyle. Sixty–five percent ownership, in both the website and the 'Raven' line, will be assigned to T.N.G. You are also both required to serve a minimum of five years. However, if you do wish to sell your remaining shares, T.N.G would be willing to discuss further options—freeing you from any further contractual agreement with the group."

"What!" Chloe snapped her head at Veronica, then to Gianni, fully aware that this was beginning to sound a lot like they were trying to push her out.

"Obviously, like P.S.L, we would prefer you to stay in your positions to continue the excellent work. This *is* a chance to renegotiate your individual contracts," Veronica said, looking into Chloe's eyes—trying her best to throw her a subtle life-line.

They at least had room to manoeuvre in negotiating their own terms of employment with their new 'guardians.' This was the easy part, all she had to do was stop talking, stop questioning, and start accepting—this *was* happening.

"And if we don't agree to sign to your five-year term?" Chloe said, flicking through the pages, trying to find the answer to her own question in black and white.

"Well," Veronica stuttered. "You could, of course, suggest an alternative buyer, but I doubt—"

"We doubt you will be able to find a buyer that begins to compare with the business stability and success that has been combined into T.N.G, or even one willing to offer a bid as high as ours," Don cut in.

"So, what you're saying, is that I don't have a choice—I either sell or I stay?"

Don didn't flinch. His stone-like face, pale and unbreakable expression remained.

"This isn't just about money, it's about safeguarding the future success of DivaFeet—and also *your* business. It would be regrettable to take S.O.S forward without you, but it wouldn't be impossible. If you really feel like this was the time to exit, then you can rest assured that StacksOfStyle will continue on to greatness under *our* control," he finished.

"Are you gonna say something?" Chloe said, turning to Carmen, her eyes wide with disbelief. She was being threatened and everyone was sat silent.

Gianni could see she was starting to break under the pressure and arrogance of Don Carlo. It was quite the art form to negotiate with him—even for an experienced broker—he was formidable. He had even fallen for his persuasive tactics.

"That really is a testament to all of *your* hard work," Gianni started, spitting out words without thinking, clambering to find them on the spot.

He just needed to step in and save Chloe from making a huge mistake.

"Without the strong foundation DivaFeet has provided you with, S.O.S would not exist in the way it does today… Equally, your creativity and vision have led to the success of another strong female-led company. Which is why it's so desirable to us," Gianni soothed, massaging Chloe's battered ego—rounding up Veronica and Carmen as troops on his side.

"Yes, but now it's time for the big boys to step in," Don winked sleazily, completely bulldozing Gianni's attempt of female empowerment.

Suddenly, with a rattling crash, Chloe drew back her chair and lurched up out of her seat. In a disorientated flash, she made her way past the other chairs to get to the door, covering her mouth as she flipped back the curtains in one quick matador move. Rapidly, she slid back the glass door, causing it to ricochet on the neighbouring glass pane as she fled down the mezzanine stairs.

It's loud reverb caused the entire office below to look up at the boardroom, knowing that Gianni and Graziana Palazzo were up there—together with Don Carlo and some other important figures. The rumour mill was already in full production, down in the desk banks.

"I'll go," Carmen said, gently squeezing Gianni's shoulder as he made his way to follow her.

Walking briskly to catch up, she watched as Chloe dashed into the toilets. Not wanting to cause the office to erupt in speculation, she slowed her pace, reaching the ladies bathroom. When she entered, she could hear Chloe puking on the other side of a locked cubicle. This was becoming rather familiar scene, but she had done it before—she could do it again. Carmen gave Chloe a moment, heading outside to draft water from the cooler into a cardboard cup before returning with it.

"Chloe… It's me—let me in… I have water," she said, pressed up against the door. All she could hear was Chloe spitting into the bowl before it roared with a flush. "Look, I know this is a lot to take in, but I really think this is going to be good for us… Think about it, we are finally going to be in control of a multi-million dollar company and its success will be up to us—not Gianni and definitely not Don, or Graziana! They're just enabling us financially to achieve our dreams… And much quicker than if we stuck with Veronica, and she knows it—which is why she's selling. She's not just cashing-in, Chloe… Sure, she's making a mint, but she does care about who she leaves us with."

Carmen waited for a beat, listening to the shuffling from inside until the sound drew closer to the door. The latch finally flicked open. Chloe looked beyond pale—she was green.

"Here," Carmen said, passing the water.

Chloe took the cup and walked over to the sink. She gargled and spat before taking a sip, leaning over the sink with both hands on the counter—staring at the mess in the mirror, her hair tossed and shaggy.

"It's just the way in which all of this has unfolded," Chloe started. "It would be different if we *wanted* this, sought the deal ourselves… Instead, we are being bought like a pair of shoes on our website or something—and Graziana is just fucking loving every minute… I just can't stomach her."

"I completely understand," Carmen said, leaning against the wall next to her, arms folded. "But it *was* our decision to let Veronica in on this whole thing, and now it's her decision to—"

"Yeah, I get it… We don't have a say!"

"It's not that simple… I know Don and Graziana are rubbing you up the wrong way, but what he said is true… What are we going to do? Find another buyer who will invest millions into a new start-up? You know that's impossible… Not to mention, how tiring and draining that will be on you. You can't handle the stress as it is, and we now have a pretty good deal on the table… You heard Gianni, he'll let us recruit our own team and we'll probably have our own office, instead of sharing a glass box in this dump! That's why I'm not letting you make this mistake—I've already agreed to back the deal with my five percent."

"*Stop!*" Chloe said, softly caressing her stomach in circles.

"Seriously! I've supported you and I always will, but do you think I don't want my shares to grow and be worth something more too? I'm willing to stick around for five years more to make that happen…"

Listening to Carmen was making her head spin, hearing how she had already sided with them.

But looking at Chloe, standing there—vulnerable and downtrodden—it had dawned on Carmen. "Chloe, don't take this the wrong way… But are you… *Pregnant?*"

She could hardly believe she was asking such a thing in such circumstance, but stranger things had happened lately, and this was the most natural thing that could possibly happen right now.

"*What?* No!"

"Are you sure? Think back…*Could* it be possible?"

"God… He's only just come back from Milan; not since the night of the Maison Marais party—we were *so* drunk—I don't even remember!"

'That sounds about right,' Carmen thought to herself, rolling her eyes. "Chloe, listen to me," she said, delicately taking hold of her shoulders. "If you *are* pregnant, then this is even more reason not to fight this… The future will be hard, but it will be even harder if we screw this up now… You know as much as I do that Don is only competing because he wants in on Palazzo, and that is good news for us! Yes, he's playing Gianni—but we are the *winners* in this mess."

Suddenly the tables had turned. Instead of Gianni selling out on her, she realised that what Carmen was saying was true—*they* were selling out on *him*. He was risking his company to support StacksOfStyle and they had nothing to lose. No wonder Graziana was weary of her all this time, she had unwittingly cashed-in on the Palazzo family name—without even realising it. Carmen could see Chloe's eyes glaze over as she made her way through the fog in her head. She was near the clearing now.

"Look, if we make this a success, then we can turn it all around and have more power and influence than we do now—and even more so if you *are* pregnant with Gianni's kid… Nobody's gonna fuck with you then!"

Chloe couldn't help but laugh as she smoothed her nose and mouth with prayer-like hands. Yet again, Carmen was right. Don had just invested millions into a start-up that wasn't worth a fraction of what they were buying it for—escalating their business by fast-tracking them to where they want to be.

And Carmen was right on another note: if Chloe *was* pregnant, then she needed to secure her future. Over time their share value would no doubt inflate, meaning that if she did feel like throwing the towel in after the five years were up, then she too could simply 'do a Veronica.'

"Come on, let's just get this over with and get the hell out of here," Carmen said, teasing Chloe's hair down her back with her fingertips—doing her best to calm it down as much as she had calmed her. "Like Veronica said, we'll have a chance to put our terms across when we negotiate our personal packages."

Chloe looked up at her and smiled. In fact, there were two things that she now needed to do: get this meeting over with, and get a pregnancy test… But first, she had to fix her face.

*

The following week's had been somewhat easier to handle, knowing that her life was about to change in more ways than one— and not only at work. The buy-out had been agreed by all parties, and with their legal team, Chloe and Carmen had managed to keep Bill as head buyer, and Morgana as their marketing director. As much as she annoyed Chloe, she needed workaholics on her side—and Morgana was very much like Regina in that respect. Promoting the likes of Regina rang through her mind when making the choice; she would struggle to find someone like her to do the job of two people on one salary.

As for the rest of the team, Chloe had Gianni wrapped around her little finger and suggested Dionne replaced Veronica as the CEO of DivaFeet. That way, Dionne got a promotion and well away from Regina, and Chloe had someone she trusted working alongside her. Don and Gianni were equally as thrilled with her hire, they couldn't care less who did the job, as long as the job got done.

But the most important hire for StacksOfStyle had been for the position of press officer. The news that Gianni and Don had created The New Guardians to 'develop the future of fashion' had been released, and Carmen needed urgent help keeping up with the demand for statements. And Chloe knew exactly the person to do the job, also saving her from Regina—Kim.

In a way, it was also a way of helping Regina as much as herself, for Kim and Dionne were road-blocks in her way of creating her army of people at Maison Marais—just like she had done at Palazzo. Now Chloe was responsible for creating her own army, she finally understood the importance of having people onboard that supported you—but Chloe wanted talent, not incompetence.

"Is it possible for your feet to swell, after just two months?" Chloe said, taking off one of her pumps to rub her foot under the desk.

"Don't ask me," Carmen huffed. "Are you still up for visiting this office space this afternoon?"

"Of course I am," Chloe said, putting her shoe back on, as quickly as she had taken it off. "I wouldn't miss this for the world!"

"It's okay if you can't make it… I don't want to rush you around town."

"It's only Fifth Avenue… In a taxi!"

"I'm just aware that we have a very busy period coming up, what with the Met Gala—and the summer sale."

"Stop fussing… I'm *pregnant*—not dying!"

The thought of having to get dressed up to act the part of 'the perfect other half' with Gianni at the Met Gala hadn't excited her much lately. Not only would the press hassle them about being a couple, but they would ask questions about them working together, as well as dating—which was all rather banal—but necessary to keep the press training chugging.

And if that wasn't enough, she had to try and keep the fact she was pregnant under wraps. Only Carmen (and of course, Gianni) knew, and she wanted to keep it that way for now. The only saving grace was that the beige, wet-look jumpsuit had been given to Gabriela Gracia to wear, in exchange for a demure navy gown. But the dress-code wasn't the only reason Chloe dreaded the evening of the gala.

Not only would she have to face a grilling on the red carpet, but she would also have to sit with Graziana and Don at the top table, alongside Anna from Vanguard magazine. All eyes would be on them for the entire evening. But this time it would be easier for her to ignore the politics of fashion, now she had learnt how to play by the 'big boy's' rules, as Don had said. Because now, she had something far more important that none of them could control—her own legacy—her own flesh and blood.

For that reason, Chloe was committed in making StacksOfStyle a phenomenal success, because that too was her baby. She had long been a mother before she would eventually be one without even knowing it, and when the time came for her to physically step into that role, she hoped it would only give her more knowledge, and more empathy.

With Carmen by her side, everything she had ever learnt from Regina, Veronica, Gianni, and Don, would now shape the way she led her team. She had not only learnt from her own mistakes but from theirs too, and she was hell-bent on not repeating them. And with all of that fresh in her mind, it was time for Chloe and Carmen to visit the office location up for rent.

Fifth Avenue was always where they belonged and it was now time for them to return, this time to a new home—the home of StacksOfStyle.com.